LYING UNDER THE APPLE TREE

Alice Munro was born in 1931 and is the author of twelve collections of stories, most recently *Dear Life*, and a novel, *Lives of Girls and Women*. She has received many awards and prizes, including three of Canada's Governor General's Literary Awards and two Giller Prizes, the REA Award for the Short Story, the Lannan Literary Award, the WHSmith Book Award in the UK, the National Book Critics Circle Award in the US, was shortlisted for the Booker Prize for *The Beggar Maid*, has been awarded the Man Booker International Prize 2009 for her overall contribution to fiction on the world stage and in 2013 won the Nobel Prize in Literature. Her stories have appeared in the *New Yorker, Atlantic Monthly, Paris Review* and other publications, and her collections have been translated into thirteen languages.

She lives with her husband in Clinton, Ontario, near Lake Huron in Canada.

ALICE MUNRO

Lying Under the Apple Tree

New Selected Stories

VINTAGE BOOKS
London

Published by Vintage 2014

2 4 6 8 10 9 7 5 3 1

First published in Great Britain by Chatto & Windus in 2011

Vintage
Random House, 20 Vauxhall Bridge Road,
London SW1V 2SA

www.vintage-books.co.uk

Addresses for companies within The Random House Group Limited
can be found at: www.randomhouse.co.uk/offices.htm

The Random House Group Limited Reg. No. 954009

A CIP catalogue record for this book
is available from the British Library

ISBN: 9780099593775

The Random House Group Limited supports the Forest Stewardship
Council® (FSC®), the leading international forest-certification
organisation. Our books carrying the FSC label are printed on FSC®-
certified paper. FSC is the only forest-certification scheme supported
by the leading environmental organisations, including Greenpeace.
Our paper procurement policy can be found at:
www.randomhouse.co.uk/environment

MIX
Paper from
responsible sources
FSC® C016897

Printed and bound by CPI Group (UK) Ltd, Croydon, CR0 4YY

Contents

THE LOVE OF A GOOD WOMAN (1998)

The Love of a Good Woman   3
The Children Stay   56
My Mother's Dream   79

HATESHIP, FRIENDSHIP, COURTSHIP, LOVESHIP, MARRIAGE (2001)

Hateship, Friendship, Courtship, Loveship, Marriage   115
Family Furnishings   153
The Bear Came Over the Mountain   178

RUNAWAY (2004)

Chance   217
Soon   244
Silence   272

THE VIEW FROM CASTLE ROCK (2006)

The View from Castle Rock   297
Lying Under the Apple Tree   338
Hired Girl   358

TOO MUCH HAPPINESS (2009)

Dimensions   379
Deep-Holes   402
Free Radicals   419

The Love of a Good Woman

The Love of a Good Woman

FOR THE last couple of decades, there has been a museum in Walley, dedicated to preserving photos and butter churns and horse harnesses and an old dentist's chair and a cumbersome apple peeler and such curiosities as the pretty little porcelain-and-glass insulators that were used on telegraph poles.

Also there is a red box, which has the letters D. M. WILLENS, OPTOMETRIST printed on it, and a note beside it, saying, "This box of optometrist's instruments though not very old has considerable local significance, since it belonged to Mr. D. M. Willens, who drowned in the Peregrine River, 1951. It escaped the catastrophe and was found, presumably by the anonymous donor, who dispatched it to be a feature of our collection."

The ophthalmoscope could make you think of a snowman. The top part, that is—the part that's fastened onto the hollow handle. A large disk, with a smaller disk on top. In the large disk a hole to look through, as the various lenses are moved. The handle is heavy because the batteries are still inside. If you took the batteries out and put in the rod that is provided, with a disk on either end, you could plug in an electric cord. But it might have been necessary to use the instrument in places where there wasn't any electricity.

The retinoscope looks more complicated. Underneath the round forehead clamp is something like an elf's head, with a round flat face and a pointed metal cap. This is tilted at a forty-five-degree angle to a slim column, and out of the top of the column a tiny light is supposed to shine. The flat face is made of glass and is a dark sort of mirror.

Everything is black, but that is only paint. In some places where the optometrist's hand must have rubbed most often, the paint has disappeared and you can see a patch of shiny silver metal.

I. JUTLAND

THIS PLACE was called Jutland. There had been a mill once, and some kind of small settlement, but that had all gone by the end of the last century, and the place had never amounted to much at any time. Many people believed that it had been named in honor of the famous sea battle fought during the First World War, but actually everything had been in ruins years before that battle ever took place.

The three boys who came out here on a Saturday morning early in the spring of 1951 believed, as most children did, that the name came from the old wooden planks that jutted out of the earth of the riverbank and from the other straight thick boards that stood up in the nearby water, making an uneven palisade. (These were in fact the remains of a dam, built before the days of cement.) The planks and a heap of foundation stones and a lilac bush and some huge apple trees deformed by black knot and the shallow ditch of the millrace that filled up with nettles every summer were the only other signs of what had been here before.

There was a road, or a track, coming back from the township road, but it had never been gravelled, and appeared on the maps only as a dotted line, a road allowance. It was used quite a bit in the summer by people driving to the river to swim or at night by couples looking for a place to park. The turnaround spot came before you got to the ditch, but the whole area was so overrun by nettles, and cow parsnip, and woody wild hemlock in a wet year, that cars would sometimes have to back out all the way to the proper road.

The car tracks to the water's edge on that spring morning were easy to spot but were not taken notice of by these boys, who were thinking only about swimming. At least, they would call it swimming; they would go back to town and say that they had been swimming at Jutland before the snow was off the ground.

It was colder here upstream than on the river flats close to the town. There was not a leaf out yet on the riverbank trees—the only green you saw was from patches of leeks on the ground and marsh marigolds fresh as spinach, spread along any little stream that gullied its way down to the river. And on the opposite bank under some cedars they saw what they were especially looking for—a long, low, stubborn snowbank, gray as stones.

Not off the ground.

So they would jump into the water and feel the cold hit them like ice daggers. Ice daggers shooting up behind their eyes and jabbing the tops of their skulls from the inside. Then they would move their arms and legs a few times and haul themselves out, quaking and letting their teeth rattle; they would push their numb limbs into their clothes and feel the painful recapture of their bodies by their startled blood and the relief of making their brag true.

The tracks that they didn't notice came right through the ditch—in which there was nothing growing now, there was only the flat dead straw-colored grass of the year before. Through the ditch and into the river without trying to turn around. The boys tramped over them. But by this time they were close enough to the water to have had their attention caught by something more extraordinary than car tracks.

There was a pale-blue shine to the water that was not a reflection of sky. It was a whole car, down in the pond on a slant, the front wheels and the nose of it poking into the mud on the bottom, and the bump of the trunk nearly breaking the surface. Light blue was in those days an unusual color for a car, and its bulgy shape was unusual, too. They knew it right away. The little English car, the Austin, the only one of its kind surely in the whole county. It belonged to Mr. Willens, the optometrist. He looked like a cartoon character when he drove it, because he was a short but thick man, with heavy shoulders and a large head. He always seemed to be crammed into his little car as if it was a bursting suit of clothes.

The car had a panel in its roof, which Mr. Willens opened in warm weather. It was open now. They could not see very well what was inside. The color of the car made its shape plain in the water, but the water was really not very clear, and it obscured what was not so bright. The boys squatted down on the bank, then lay on their stomachs and pushed their heads out like turtles, trying to see. There was something dark and furry, something like a big animal tail, pushed up through the hole in the roof and moving idly in the water. This was shortly seen to be an arm, covered by the sleeve of a dark jacket of some heavy and hairy material. It seemed that inside the car a man's body—it had to be the body of Mr. Willens— had got into a peculiar position. The force of the water—for even in the millpond there was a good deal of force in the water at this time of year— must have somehow lifted him from the seat and pushed him about, so that one shoulder was up near the car roof and one arm had got free. His head must have been shoved down against the driver's door and window. One front wheel was stuck deeper in the river bottom than the other, which meant that the car was on a slant from side to side as well as back to front. The window in fact must have been open and the head sticking out for the body to be lodged in that position. But they could not get to see that. They could picture Mr. Willens's face as they knew it—a big square face, which often wore a theatrical sort of frown but was never seriously intimidating. His thin crinkly hair was reddish or brassy on top, and combed diagonally over his forehead. His eyebrows were darker than his hair, thick and fuzzy like caterpillars stuck above his eyes. This was a face already grotesque to them, in the way that many adult faces were, and they were not afraid to see it drowned. But all they got to see was that arm and his pale hand. They could see the hand quite plain once they got used to looking through the water. It rode there tremulously and irresolutely, like a feather, though it looked as solid as dough. And as ordinary, once you got used to its being there at all. The fingernails were all like neat little faces, with their intelligent everyday look of greeting, their sensible disowning of their circumstances.

"Son of a gun," these boys said. With gathering energy and a tone of deepening respect, even of gratitude. "*Son of a gun.*"

IT WAS their first time out this year. They had come across the bridge over the Peregrine River, the single-lane double-span bridge known locally as Hell's Gate or the Death Trap—though the danger had really more to do with the sharp turn the road took at the south end of it than with the bridge itself.

There was a regular walkway for pedestrians, but they didn't use it. They never remembered using it. Perhaps years ago, when they were so young as to be held by the hand. But that time had vanished for them; they refused to recognize it even if they were shown the evidence in snapshots or forced to listen to it in family conversation.

They walked now along the iron shelf that ran on the opposite side of the bridge from the walkway. It was about eight inches wide and a foot or so above the bridge floor. The Peregrine River was rushing the winter load of ice and snow, now melted, out into Lake Huron. It was barely back within its banks after the yearly flood that turned the flats into a lake and tore out the young trees and bashed any boat or hut within its reach. With the runoff from the fields muddying the water and the pale sunlight on its surface, the water looked like butterscotch pudding on the boil. But if you fell into it, it would freeze your blood and fling you out into the lake, if it didn't brain you against the buttresses first.

Cars honked at them—a warning or a reproof—but they paid no attention. They proceeded single file, as self-possessed as sleepwalkers. Then, at the north end of the bridge, they cut down to the flats, locating the paths they remembered from the year before. The flood had been so recent that these paths were not easy to follow. You had to kick your way through beaten-down brush and jump from one hummock of mud-plastered grass to another. Sometimes they jumped carelessly and landed in mud or pools of leftover floodwater, and once their feet were wet they gave up caring where they landed. They squelched through the mud and splashed in the pools so that the water came in over the tops of their rubber boots. The wind was warm; it was pulling the clouds apart into threads of old wool, and the gulls and crows were quarrelling and diving over the river. Buzzards were circling over them, on the high lookout; the robins had just returned, and the red-winged blackbirds were darting in pairs, striking bright on your eyes as if they had been dipped in paint.

"Should've brought a twenty-two."

"Should've brought a twelve-gauge."

They were too old to raise sticks and make shooting noises. They spoke with casual regret, as if guns were readily available to them.

They climbed up the north banks to a place where there was bare sand. Turtles were supposed to lay their eggs in this sand. It was too early yet for that to happen, and in fact the story of turtle eggs dated from years back—none of these boys had ever seen any. But they kicked and stomped the sand, just in case. Then they looked around for the place where last year one of them, in company with another boy, had found a cow's hipbone, carried off by the flood from some slaughter pile. The river could be counted on every year to sweep off and deposit elsewhere a good number of surprising or cumbersome or bizarre or homely objects. Rolls of wire, an intact set of steps, a bent shovel, a corn kettle. The hipbone had been found caught on the branch of a sumac—which seemed proper, because all those smooth branches were like cow horns or deer antlers, some with rusty cone tips.

They crashed around for some time—Cece Ferns showed them the exact branch—but they found nothing.

It was Cece Ferns and Ralph Diller who had made that find, and when asked where it was at present Cece Ferns said, "Ralph took it." The two boys who were with him now—Jimmy Box and Bud Salter—knew why that would have to be. Cece could never take anything home unless it was of a size to be easily concealed from his father.

They talked of more useful finds that might be made or had been made in past years. Fence rails could be used to build a raft, pieces of stray lumber could be collected for a planned shack or boat. Real luck would be to get hold of some loose muskrat traps. Then you could go into business. You could pick up enough lumber for stretching boards and steal the knives for skinning. They spoke of taking over an empty shed they knew of, in the blind alley behind what used to be the livery barn. There was a padlock on it, but you could probably get in through the window, taking the boards off it at night and replacing them at daybreak. You could take a flashlight to work by. No—a lantern. You could skin the muskrats and stretch the pelts and sell them for a lot of money.

This project became so real to them that they started to worry about leaving valuable pelts in the shed all day. One of them would have to stand watch while the others went out on the traplines. (Nobody mentioned school.)

This was the way they talked when they got clear of town. They talked as if they were free—or almost free—agents, as if they didn't go to school or live with families or suffer any of the indignities put on them because of their age. Also, as if the countryside and other people's establishments would provide them with all they needed for their undertakings and adventures, with only the smallest risk and effort on their part.

Another change in their conversation out here was that they practically gave up using names. They didn't use each other's real names much anyway—not even family nicknames such as Bud. But at school nearly everyone had another name, some of these having to do with the way people looked or talked, like Goggle or Jabber, and some, like Sore-arse and Chickenfucker, having to do with incidents real or fabulous in the lives of those named, or in the lives—such names were handed down for decades—of their brothers, fathers, or uncles. These were the names they let go of when they were out in the bush or on the river flats. If they had to get one another's attention, all they said was "Hey." Even the use of names that were outrageous and obscene and that grown-ups supposedly never heard would have spoiled a sense they had at these times, of taking each other's looks, habits, family, and personal history entirely for granted.

And yet they hardly thought of each other as friends. They would never have designated someone as a best friend or a next-best friend, or joggled people around in these positions, the way girls did. Any one of at least a dozen boys could have been substituted for any one of these three, and accepted by the others in exactly the same way. Most members of that company were between nine and twelve years old, too old to be bound by yards and neighborhoods but too young to have jobs—even jobs sweeping the sidewalk in front of stores or delivering groceries by bicycle. Most of them lived in the north end of town, which meant that they would be expected to get a job of that sort as soon as they were old enough, and that none of them would ever be sent away to Appleby or to Upper Canada College. And none of them lived in a shack or had a relative in jail. Just the same, there were notable differences as to how they lived at home and what was expected of them in life. But these differences dropped away as soon as they were out of sight of the county jail and the grain elevator and the church steeples and out of range of the chimes of the courthouse clock.

ON THEIR way back they walked fast. Sometimes they trotted but did not run. Jumping, dallying, splashing, were all abandoned, and the noises they'd made on their way out, the hoots and howls, were put aside as well. Any windfall of the flood was taken note of but passed by. In fact they made their way as adults would do, at a fairly steady speed and by the most reasonable route, with the weight on them of where they had to go and what had to be done next. They had something close in front of them, a picture in front of their eyes that came between them and the world, which was the thing most adults seemed to have. The pond, the car, the arm, the hand. They had some idea that when they got to a certain spot they would start to shout. They would come into town yelling and waving their news around them and everybody would be stock-still, taking it in.

They crossed the bridge the same way as always, on the shelf. But they had no sense of risk or courage or nonchalance. They might as well have taken the walkway.

Instead of following the sharp-turning road from which you could reach both the harbor and the square, they climbed straight up the bank on a path that came out near the railway sheds. The clock played its quarter-after chimes. A quarter after twelve.

THIS WAS the time when people were walking home for dinner. People from offices had the afternoon off. But people who worked in stores were getting only their customary hour—the stores stayed open till ten or eleven o'clock on Saturday night.

Most people were going home to a hot, filling meal. Pork chops, or sausages, or boiled beef, or cottage roll. Potatoes for certain, mashed or fried; winter-stored root vegetables or cabbage or creamed onions. (A few housewives, richer or more feckless, might have opened a tin of peas or butter beans.) Bread, muffins, preserves, pie. Even those people who didn't have a home to go to, or who for some reason didn't want to go there, would be sitting down to much the same sort of food at the Duke of Cumberland, or the Merchants' Hotel, or for less money behind the foggy windows of Shervill's Dairy Bar.

Those walking home were mostly men. The women were already there—they were there all the time. But some women of middle age who worked in stores or offices for a reason that was not their fault—dead husbands or sick husbands or never any husband at all—were friends of

9

the boys' mothers, and they called out greetings even across the street (it was worst for Bud Salter, whom they called Buddy) in a certain amused or sprightly way that brought to mind all they knew of family matters, or distant infancies.

Men didn't bother greeting boys by name, even if they knew them well. They called them "boys" or "young fellows" or, occasionally, "sirs."

"Good day to you, sirs."

"You boys going straight home now?"

"What monkey business you young fellows been up to this morning?"

All these greetings had a degree of jocularity, but there were differences. The men who said "young fellows" were better disposed—or wished to seem better disposed—than the ones who said "boys." "Boys" could be the signal that a telling off was to follow, for offenses that could be either vague or specific. "Young fellows" indicated that the speaker had once been young himself. "Sirs" was outright mockery and disparagement but didn't open the way to any scolding, because the person who said that could not be bothered.

When answering, the boys didn't look up past any lady's purse or any man's Adam's apple. They said "Hullo" clearly, because there might be some kind of trouble if you didn't, and in answer to queries they said "Yessir" and "Nosir" and "Nothing much." Even on this day, such voices speaking to them caused some alarm and confusion, and they replied with the usual reticence.

At a certain corner they had to separate. Cece Ferns, always the most anxious about getting home, pulled away first. He said, "See you after dinner."

Bud Salter said, "Yeah. We got to go downtown then."

This meant, as they all understood, "downtown to the Police Office." It seemed that without needing to consult each other they had taken up a new plan of operation, a soberer way of telling their news. But it wasn't clearly said that they wouldn't be telling anything at home. There wasn't any good reason why Bud Salter or Jimmy Box couldn't have done that. Cece Ferns never told anything at home.

CECE FERNS was an only child. His parents were older than most boys' parents, or perhaps they only seemed older, because of the disabling life they lived together. When he got away from the other boys, Cece started to trot, as he usually did for the last block home. This was not because he was eager to get there or because he thought he could make anything better when he did. It may have been to make the time pass quickly, because the last block had to be full of apprehension.

His mother was in the kitchen. Good. She was out of bed though still in her wrapper. His father wasn't there, and that was good, too. His father worked at the grain elevator and got Saturday afternoon off, and if he wasn't home by now it was likely that he had gone straight to the Cumberland. That meant it would be late in the day before they had to deal with him.

Cece's father's name was Cece Ferns, too. It was a well-known and generally an affectionately known name in Walley, and somebody telling a story even thirty or forty years later would take it for granted that everybody would know it was the father who was being talked about, not the son. If a person relatively new in town said, "That doesn't sound like Cece," he would be told that nobody meant *that* Cece.

"Not him, we're talking about his old man."

They talked about the time Cece Ferns went to the hospital—or was taken there—with pneumonia, or some other desperate thing, and the nurses wrapped him in wet towels or sheets to get the fever down. The fever sweated out of him, and all the towels and sheets turned brown. It was the nicotine in him. The nurses had never seen anything like it. Cece was delighted. He claimed to have been smoking tobacco and drinking alcohol since he was ten years old.

And the time he went to church. It was hard to imagine why, but it was the Baptist church, and his wife was a Baptist, so perhaps he went to please her, though that was even harder to imagine. They were serving Communion the Sunday he went, and in the Baptist church the bread is bread but the wine is grape juice. "What's this?" cried Cece Ferns aloud. "If this is the blood of the Lamb then he must've been pretty damn anemic."

Preparations for the noon meal were under way in the Fernses' kitchen. A loaf of sliced bread was sitting on the table and a can of diced beets had been opened. A few slices of bologna had been fried—before the eggs, though they should have been done after—and were being kept slightly warm on top of the stove. And now Cece's mother had started the eggs. She was bending over the stove with the egg lifter in one hand and the other hand pressed to her stomach, cradling a pain.

Cece took the egg lifter out of her hand and turned down the electric heat, which was way too high. He had to hold the pan off the burner while the burner cooled down, in order to keep the egg whites from getting too tough or burning at the edges. He hadn't been in time to wipe out the old grease and plop a bit of fresh lard in the pan. His mother never wiped out the old grease, just let it sit from one meal to the next and put in a bit of lard when she had to.

When the heat was more to his liking, he put the pan down and coaxed the lacy edges of the eggs into tidy circles. He found a clean spoon and dribbled a little hot fat over the yolks to set them. He and his mother liked their eggs cooked this way, but his mother often couldn't manage it right. His father liked his eggs turned over and flattened out like pancakes, cooked hard as shoe leather and blackened with pepper. Cece could cook them the way he wanted, too.

None of the other boys knew how practiced he was in the kitchen—just as none of them knew about the hiding place he had made outside the house in the blind corner past the dining-room window, behind the Japanese barberry.

His mother sat in the chair by the window while he was finishing up the eggs. She kept an eye on the street. There was still a chance that his father would come home for something to eat. He might not be drunk yet. But the way he behaved didn't always depend on how drunk he was. If he came into the kitchen now he might tell Cece to make him some eggs, too. Then he might ask him where his apron was and say that he would make some fellow a dandy wife. That would be how he'd behave if he was in a good mood. In another sort of mood he would start off by staring at Cece in a certain way—that is, with an exaggerated, absurdly threatening expression—and telling him he better watch out.

"Smart bugger, aren't you? Well, all I got to say to you is better watch out."

Then if Cece looked back at him, or maybe if he didn't look back, or if he dropped the egg lifter or set it down with a clatter—or even if he was sliding around being extra cautious about not dropping anything and not making a noise—his father was apt to start showing his teeth and snarling like a dog. It would have been ridiculous—it was ridiculous—except that he meant business. A minute later the food and the dishes might be on the floor, and the chairs or the table overturned, and he might be chasing Cece around the room yelling how he was going to get him this time, flatten his face on the hot burner, how would he like that? You would be certain he'd gone crazy. But if at this moment a knock came at the door—if a friend of his arrived, say, to pick him up—his face would reassemble itself in no time and he would open the door and call out the friend's name in a loud bantering voice.

"I'll be with you in two shakes. I'd ask you in, but the wife's been pitching the dishes around again."

He didn't intend this to be believed. He said such things in order to turn whatever happened in his house into a joke.

Cece's mother asked him if the weather was warming up and where he had been that morning.

"Yeah," he said, and, "Out on the flats."

She said that she'd thought she could smell the wind on him.

"You know what I'm going to do right after we eat?" she said. "I'm going to take a hot-water bottle and go right back to bed and maybe I'll get my strength back and feel like doing something."

That was what she nearly always said she was going to do, but she always announced it as if it was an idea that had just occurred to her, a hopeful decision.

BUD SALTER had two older sisters who never did anything useful unless his mother made them. And they never confined their hair arranging, nail polishing, shoe cleaning, making up, or even dressing activities to their bedrooms or the bathroom. They spread their combs and curlers and face powder and nail polish and shoe polish all over the house. Also they loaded every chair back with their newly ironed dresses and blouses and spread out their drying sweaters on towels on every clear space of floor. (Then they screamed at you if you walked near them.) They stationed themselves in front of various mirrors—the mirror in the hall coat stand, the mirror in the dining-room buffet, and the mirror beside the kitchen door with the shelf underneath always loaded with safety pins, bobby pins, pennies, buttons, bits of pencils. Sometimes one of them would stand in front of a mirror for twenty minutes or so, checking herself from various angles, inspecting her teeth and pulling her hair back then shaking it forward. Then she would walk away apparently satisfied or at least finished—but only as far as the next room, the next mirror, where she would begin all over again just as if she had been delivered a new head.

Right now his older sister, the one who was supposed to be good-looking, was taking the pins out of her hair in front of the kitchen mirror. Her head was covered with shiny curls like snails. His other sister, on orders from his mother, was mashing the potatoes. His five-year-old brother was sitting in place at the table, banging his knife and fork up and down and yelling, "Want some service. Want some service."

He got that from their father, who did it for a joke.

Bud passed by his brother's chair and said quietly, "Look. She's putting lumps in the mashed potatoes again."

He had his brother convinced that lumps were something you added, like raisins to rice pudding, from a supply in the cupboard.

His brother stopped chanting and began complaining.

"I won't eat none if she puts in lumps. Mama, I won't eat none if she puts lumps."

"Oh, don't be silly," Bud's mother said. She was frying apple slices and onion rings with the pork chops. "Quit whining like a baby."

"It was Bud got him started," the older sister said. "Bud went and told him she was putting lumps in. Bud always tells him that and he doesn't know any better."

"Bud ought to get his face smashed," said Doris, the sister who was mashing the potatoes. She didn't always say such things idly—she had once left a claw scar down the side of Bud's cheek.

Bud went over to the dresser, where there was a rhubarb pie cooling. He took a fork and began carefully, secretly prying at it, letting out delicious steam, a delicate smell of cinnamon. He was trying to open one of the vents in the top of it so that he could get a taste of the filling. His brother saw what he was doing but was too scared to say anything. His brother was spoiled and was defended by his sisters all the time—Bud was the only person in the house he respected.

"Want some service," he repeated, speaking now in a thoughtful undertone.

Doris came over to the dresser to get the bowl for the mashed potatoes. Bud made an incautious movement, and part of the top crust caved in.

"So now he's wrecking the pie," Doris said. "Mama—he's wrecking your pie."

"Shut your damn mouth," Bud said.

"Leave that pie alone," said Bud's mother with a practiced, almost serene severity. "Stop swearing. Stop tattle-telling. Grow up."

JIMMY BOX sat down to dinner at a crowded table. He and his father and his mother and his four-year-old and six-year-old sisters lived in his grandmother's house with his grandmother and his great-aunt Mary and his bachelor uncle. His father had a bicycle-repair shop in the shed behind the house, and his mother worked in Honeker's Department Store.

Jimmy's father was crippled—the result of a polio attack when he was twenty-two years old. He walked bent forward from the hips, using a cane. This didn't show so much when he was working in the shop, because such work often means being bent over anyway. When he walked along the street he did look very strange, but nobody called him names or did an imitation of him. He had once been a notable hockey player and baseball player for the town, and some of the grace and valor of the past still hung around him, putting his present state into perspective, so that it could be seen as a phase (though a final one). He helped this perception along by cracking silly jokes and taking an optimistic tone, denying the pain that showed in his sunken eyes and kept him awake many nights. And, unlike Cece Ferns's father, he didn't change his tune when he came into his own house.

But, of course, it wasn't his own house. His wife had married him after he was crippled, though she had got engaged to him before, and it seemed the natural thing to do to move in with her mother, so that the mother could look after any children who came along while the wife went on working at her job. It seemed the natural thing to the wife's mother as well, to take on another family—just as it seemed natural that her sister Mary should move in with the rest of them when her eyesight failed, and that her son Fred, who was extraordinarily shy, should continue to live at home unless he found some place he liked better. This was a family who accepted burdens of one kind or another with even less fuss than they accepted the weather. In fact, nobody in that house would have spoken of Jimmy's father's condition or Aunt Mary's eyesight as burdens or problems, any more than they would of Fred's shyness. Drawbacks and adversity were not to be noticed, not to be distinguished from their opposites.

There was a traditional belief in the family that Jimmy's grandmother was an excellent cook, and this might have been true at one time, but in recent years there had been a falling off. Economies were practiced beyond what there was any need for now. Jimmy's mother and his uncle made decent wages and his aunt Mary got a pension and the bicycle shop was fairly busy, but one egg was used instead of three and the meat loaf got an extra cup of oatmeal. There was an attempt to compensate by overdoing the Worcestershire sauce or sprinkling too much nutmeg on the custard. But nobody complained. Everybody praised. Complaints were as rare as lightning balls in that house. And everybody said "Excuse me," even the little girls said "Excuse me," when they bumped into each other. Everybody passed and pleased and thank-you'd at the table as if there was company every day. This was the way they managed, all of them crammed so tight in the house, with clothes piled on every hook, coats hung over the banister, and cots set up permanently in the dining room for Jimmy and his uncle Fred, and the buffet hidden under a load of clothing waiting to be ironed or mended. Nobody pounded on the stairsteps or shut doors hard or turned the radio up loud or said anything disagreeable.

Did this explain why Jimmy kept his mouth shut that Saturday at dinnertime? They all kept their mouths shut, all three of them. In Cece's case it was easy to understand. His father would never have stood for Cece's claiming so important a discovery. He would have called him a liar as a matter of course. And Cece's mother, judging everything by the effect it would have on his father, would have understood—correctly— that even his going to the Police Office with his story would cause disruption at home, so she would have told him to please just keep quiet. But the two other boys lived in quite reasonable homes and they could have spoken. In Jimmy's house there would have been consternation and some disapproval, but soon enough they would have admitted that it was not Jimmy's fault.

Bud's sisters would have asked if he was crazy. They might even have twisted things around to imply that it was just like him, with his unpleasant habits, to come upon a dead body. His father, however, was a sensible, patient man, used to listening to many strange rigmaroles in his job as a freight agent at the railway station. He would have made Bud's sisters shut up, and after some serious talk to make sure Bud was telling the truth and not exaggerating he would have phoned the Police Office.

It was just that their houses seemed too full. Too much was going on already. This was true in Cece's house just as much as in the others, because even in his father's absence there was the threat and memory all the time of his haywire presence.

"Did you tell?"

"Did you?"

"Me neither."

They walked downtown, not thinking about the way they were going. They turned onto Shipka Street and found themselves going past the stucco bungalow where Mr. and Mrs. Willens lived. They were right in front of it before they recognized it. It had a small bay window on either side of the front door and a top step wide enough for two chairs, not there at present but occupied on summer evenings by Mr. Willens and his wife. There was a flat-roofed addition to one side of the house, with another door opening toward the street and a separate walk leading up to it. A sign beside that door said D. M. WILLENS, OPTOMETRIST. None of the boys themselves had visited that office, but Jimmy's aunt Mary went there regularly for her eyedrops, and his grandmother got her glasses there. So did Bud Salter's mother.

The stucco was a muddy pink color and the doors and window frames were painted brown. The storm windows had not been taken off yet, as they hadn't from most of the houses in town. There was nothing special at all about the house, but the front yard was famous for its flowers. Mrs. Willens was a renowned gardener who didn't grow her flowers in long rows beside the vegetable garden, as Jimmy's grandmother and Bud's mother grew theirs. She had them in round beds and crescent beds and all over, and in circles under the trees. In a couple of weeks daffodils would fill this lawn. But at present the only thing in bloom was a forsythia bush at the corner of the house. It was nearly as high as the eaves and it sprayed yellow into the air the way a fountain shoots water.

The forsythia shook, not with the wind, and out came a stooped brown figure. It was Mrs. Willens in her old gardening clothes, a lumpy little woman in baggy slacks and a ripped jacket and a peaked cap that might have been her husband's—it slipped down too low and almost hid her eyes. She was carrying a pair of shears.

They slowed right down—it was either that or run. Maybe they thought that she wouldn't notice them, that they could turn themselves into posts. But she had seen them already; that was why she came hastening through.

"I see you're gawking at my forsythia," said Mrs. Willens. "Would you like some to take home?"

What they had been gawking at was not the forsythia but the whole scene—the house looking just as usual, the sign by the office door, the curtains letting light in. Nothing hollow or ominous, nothing that said that Mr. Willens was not inside and that his car was not in the garage behind his office but in Jutland Pond. And Mrs. Willens out working in her yard, where anybody would expect her to be—everybody in town said so—the minute the snow was melted. And calling out in her familiar tobacco-roughened voice, abrupt and challenging but not unfriendly—a voice identifiable half a block away or coming from the back of any store.

"Wait," she said. "Wait, now, I'll get you some."

She began smartly, selectively snapping off the bright-yellow branches, and when she had all she wanted she came towards them behind a screen of flowers.

"Here you are," she said. "Take these home to your mothers. It's always good to see the forsythia, it's the very first thing in the spring." She was dividing the branches among them. "Like all Gaul," she said. "All Gaul is divided into three parts. You must know about that if you take Latin."

"We aren't in high school yet," said Jimmy, whose life at home had readied him, better than the others, for talking to ladies.

"Aren't you?" she said. "Well, you've got all sorts of things to look forward to. Tell your mothers to put them in lukewarm water. Oh, I'm sure they already know that. I've given you branches that aren't all the way out yet, so they should last and last."

They said thank you—Jimmy first and the others picking it up from him. They walked toward downtown with their arms loaded. They had no intention of turning back and taking the flowers home, and they counted on her not having any good idea of where their homes were. Half a block on, they sneaked looks back to see if she was watching.

She wasn't. The big house near the sidewalk blocked the view in any case.

The forsythia gave them something to think about. The embarrassment of carrying it, the problem of getting rid of it. Otherwise, they would have to think about Mr. Willens and Mrs. Willens. How she could be busy in her yard and he could be drowned in his car. Did she know where he was or did she not? It seemed that she couldn't. Did she even know that he was gone? She had acted as if there was nothing wrong, nothing at all, and when they were standing in front of her this had seemed to be the truth. What they knew, what they had seen, seemed actually to be pushed back, to be defeated, by her not knowing it.

Two girls on bicycles came wheeling around the corner. One was Bud's sister Doris. At once these girls began to hoot and yell.

"Oh, look at the flowers," they shouted. "Where's the wedding? Look at the beautiful bridesmaids."

Bud yelled back the worst thing he could think of.

"You got blood all over your arse."

Of course she didn't, but there had been an occasion when this had really been so—she had come home from school with blood on her skirt. Everybody had seen it, and it would never be forgotten.

He was sure she would tell on him at home, but she never did. Her shame about that other time was so great that she could not refer to it even to get him in trouble.

THEY REALIZED then that they had to dump the flowers at once, so they simply threw the branches under a parked car. They brushed a few stray petals off their clothes as they turned onto the square.

Saturdays were still important then; they brought the country people into town. Cars were already parked around the square and on the side streets. Big country boys and girls and smaller children from the town and the country were heading for the movie matinee.

It was necessary to pass Honeker's in the first block. And there, in full view in one of the windows, Jimmy saw his mother. Back at work already, she was putting the hat straight on a female dummy, adjusting the veil, then fiddling with the shoulders of the dress. She was a short woman and she had to stand on tiptoe to do this properly. She had taken off her shoes to walk on the window carpet. You could see the rosy plump cushions of her heels through her stockings, and when she stretched you saw the back of her knee through the slit in her skirt. Above that was a wide but shapely behind and the line of her panties or girdle. Jimmy could hear in his mind the little grunts she would be making; also he could smell the stockings that she sometimes took off as soon as she got home, to save them from runs. Stockings and underwear, even clean female underwear, had a faint, private smell that was both appealing and disgusting.

He hoped two things. That the others hadn't noticed her (they had, but the idea of a mother dressed up every day and out in the public world of town was so strange to them that they couldn't comment, could only dismiss it) and that she would not, please not, turn around and spot him. She was capable, if she did that, of rapping on the glass and mouthing hello. At work she lost the hushed discretion, the studied gentleness, of home. Her obligingness turned from meek to pert. He used to be delighted by this other side of her, this friskiness, just as he was by Honeker's, with its extensive counters of glass and varnished wood, its big mirrors at the top of the staircase, in which he could see himself climbing up to Ladies' Wear, on the second floor.

"Here's my young mischief," his mother would say, and sometimes slip him a dime. He could never stay more than a minute; Mr. or Mrs. Honeker might be watching.

Young mischief.

Words that were once as pleasant to hear as the tinkle of dimes and nickels had now turned slyly shaming.

They were safely past.

In the next block they had to pass the Duke of Cumberland, but Cece had no worries. If his father had not come home at dinnertime, it meant he would be in there for hours yet. But the word "Cumberland" always fell across his mind heavily. From the days when he hadn't even known what it meant, he got a sense of sorrowful plummeting. A weight hitting dark water, far down.

Between the Cumberland and the Town Hall was an unpaved alley, and at the back of the Town Hall was the Police Office. They turned into this alley and soon a lot of new noise reached them, opposing the street noise. It was not from the Cumberland—the noise in there was all muffled up, the beer parlor having only small, high windows like a public toilet. It was coming from the Police Office. The door to that office was open on account of the mild weather, and even out in the alley you could smell the pipe tobacco and cigars. It wasn't just the policemen who sat in there, especially on Saturday afternoons, with the stove going in winter and the fan in summer and the door open to let in the pleasant air on an in-between day like today. Colonel Box would be there—in fact, they could already hear the wheeze he made, the long-drawn-out aftereffects of his asthmatic laughter. He was a relative of Jimmy's, but there was a coolness in the family because he did not approve of Jimmy's father's marriage. He spoke to Jimmy, when he recognized him, in a surprised, ironic tone of voice. "If he ever offers you a quarter or anything, you say you don't need it," Jimmy's mother had told him. But Colonel Box had never made such an offer.

Also, Mr. Pollock would be there, who had retired from the drugstore, and Fergus Solley, who was not a half-wit but looked like one, because he had been gassed in the First World War. All day these men and others played cards, smoked, told stories, and drank coffee at the town's expense (as Bud's father said). Anybody wanting to make a complaint or a report had to do it within sight of them and probably within earshot.

Run the gauntlet.

They came almost to a stop outside the open door. Nobody had noticed them. Colonel Box said, "I'm not dead yet," repeating the final line of some story. They began to walk past slowly with their heads down, kicking at the gravel. Round the corner of the building they picked up speed. By the entry to the men's public toilet there was a recent streak of lumpy vomit on the wall and a couple of empty bottles on the gravel. They had to walk between the refuse bins and the high watchful windows of the town clerk's office, and then they were off the gravel, back on the square.

"I got money," Cece said. This matter-of-fact announcement brought them all relief. Cece jingled change in his pocket. It was the money his mother had given him after he washed up the dishes, when he went into the front bedroom to tell her he was going out. "Help yourself to fifty cents off the dresser," she had said. Sometimes she had money, though he never saw his father give her any. And whenever she said "Help yourself" or gave him a few coins, Cece understood that she was ashamed of their life, ashamed for him and in front of him, and these were the times when he hated the sight of her (though he was glad of the money). Especially if she said that he was a good boy and he was not to think she wasn't grateful for all he did.

They took the street that led down to the harbor. At the side of Paquette's Service Station there was a booth from which Mrs. Paquette sold hot dogs, ice cream, candy, and cigarettes. She had refused to sell them cigarettes even when Jimmy said they were for his uncle Fred. But she didn't hold it against them that they'd tried. She was a fat, pretty woman, a French Canadian.

They bought some licorice whips, black and red. They meant to buy some ice cream later when they weren't so full from dinner. They went over to where there were two old car seats set up by the fence under a tree that gave shade in summer. They shared out the licorice whips.

Captain Tervitt was sitting on the other seat.

Captain Tervitt had been a real captain, for many years, on the lake boats. Now he had a job as a special constable. He stopped the cars to let the children cross the street in front of the school and kept them from sledding down the side street in winter. He blew his whistle and held up one big hand, which looked like a clown's hand, in a white glove. He was still tall and straight and broad-shouldered, though old and white-haired. Cars would do what he said, and children, too.

At night he went around checking the doors of all the stores to see that they were locked and to make sure that there was nobody inside committing a burglary. During the day he often slept in public. When the weather was bad he slept in the library and when it was good he chose some seat out-of-doors. He didn't spend much time in the Police Office, probably because he was too deaf to follow the conversation without his hearing aid in, and like many deaf people he hated his hearing aid. And he was used to being solitary, surely, staring out over the bow of the lake boats.

His eyes were closed and his head tilted back so that he could get the sun in his face. When they went over to talk to him (and the decision to do this was made without any consultation, beyond one resigned and dubious look) they had to wake him from his doze. His face took a moment to register—where and when and who. Then he took a large old-fashioned watch out of his pocket, as if he counted on children always wanting to be told the time. But they went on talking to him, with their expressions agitated and slightly shamed. They were saying, "Mr. Willens is out in Jutland Pond," and "We seen the car," and "Drownded." He had to hold up his hand and make shushing motions while the other hand went rooting around in his pants pocket and came up with his hearing aid. He nodded his head seriously, encouragingly, as if to say, Patience, patience, while he got the device settled in his ear. Then both hands up— Be still, be still—while he was testing. Finally another nod, of a brisker sort, and in a stern voice—but making a joke to some extent of his sternness—he said, "Proceed."

Cece, who was the quietest of the three—as Jimmy was the politest and Bud the mouthiest—was the one who turned everything around.

"Your fly's undone," he said.

Then they all whooped and ran away.

THEIR ELATION did not vanish right away. But it was not something that could be shared or spoken about: they had to pull apart.

Cece went home to work on his hideaway. The cardboard floor, which had been frozen through the winter, was sodden now and needed to be replaced. Jimmy climbed into the loft of the garage, where he had recently discovered a box of old Doc Savage magazines that had once belonged to his uncle Fred. Bud went home and found nobody there but his mother, who was waxing the dining-room floor. He looked at comic books for an hour or so and then he told her. He believed that his mother had no experience or authority outside their house and that she would not make up her mind about what to do until she had phoned his father. To his surprise, she immediately phoned the police. Then she phoned his father. And somebody went to round up Cece and Jimmy.

A police car drove into Jutland from the township road, and all was confirmed. A policeman and the Anglican minister went to see Mrs. Willens.

"I didn't want to bother you," Mrs. Willens was reported to have said. "I was going to give him till dark."

She told them that Mr. Willens had driven out to the country yesterday afternoon to take some drops to an old blind man. Sometimes he got held up, she said. He visited people, or the car got stuck.

Was he downhearted or anything like that? the policeman asked her.

"Oh, surely not," the minister said. "He was the bulwark of the choir."

"The word was not in his vocabulary," said Mrs. Willens.

Something was made of the boys' sitting down and eating their dinners and never saying a word. And then buying a bunch of licorice whips. A new nickname—Deadman—was found and settled on each of them. Jimmy and Bud bore it till they left town, and Cece—who married young and went to work in the elevator—saw it passed on to his two sons. By that time nobody thought of what it referred to.

The insult to Captain Tervitt remained a secret.

Each of them expected some reminder, some lofty look of injury or judgment, the next time they had to pass under his uplifted arm, crossing the street to the school. But he held up his gloved hand, his noble and clownish white hand, with his usual benevolent composure. He gave consent.

Proceed.

II. HEART FAILURE

"Glomerulonephritis," Enid wrote in her notebook. It was the first case that she had ever seen. The fact was that Mrs. Quinn's kidneys were failing, and nothing could be done about it. Her kidneys were drying up and turning into hard and useless granular lumps. Her urine at present was scanty and had a smoky look, and the smell that came out on her breath and through her skin was acrid and ominous. And there was another, fainter smell, like rotted fruit, that seemed to Enid related to the pale-lavender-brown stains appearing on her body. Her legs twitched in spasms of sudden pain and her skin was subject to a violent itching, so that Enid had to rub her with ice. She wrapped the ice in towels and pressed the packs to the spots in torment.

"How do you contract that kind of a disease anyhow?" said Mrs. Quinn's sister-in-law. Her name was Mrs. Green. Olive Green. (It had never occurred to her how that would sound, she said, until she got married and all of a sudden everybody was laughing at it.) She lived on a farm a few miles away, out on the highway, and every few days she came and took the sheets and towels and nightdresses home to wash. She did the children's washing as well, brought everything back freshly ironed and folded. She even ironed the ribbons on the nightdresses. Enid was grateful to her—she had been on jobs where she had to do the laundry herself, or, worse still, load it onto her mother, who would pay to have it done in town. Not wanting to offend but seeing which way the questions were tending, she said, "It's hard to tell."

"Because you hear one thing and another," Mrs. Green said. "You hear that sometimes a woman might take some pills. They get these pills to take for when their period is late and if they take them just like the doctor says and for a good purpose that's fine, but if they take too many and for a bad purpose their kidneys are wrecked. Am I right?"

"I've never come in contact with a case like that," Enid said.

Mrs. Green was a tall, stout woman. Like her brother Rupert, who was Mrs. Quinn's husband, she had a round, snub-nosed, agreeably wrinkled face—the kind that Enid's mother called "potato Irish." But behind Rupert's good-humored expression there was wariness and withholding. And behind Mrs. Green's there was yearning. Enid did not know for what. To the simplest conversation Mrs. Green brought a huge demand. Maybe it was just a yearning for news. News of something momentous. An event.

Of course, an event was coming, something momentous at least in this family. Mrs. Quinn was going to die, at the age of twenty-seven. (That was the age she gave herself—Enid would have put some years on it, but once an illness had progressed this far age was hard to guess.) When her kidneys stopped working altogether, her heart would give out and she would die. The doctor had said to Enid, "This'll take you into the summer, but the chances are you'll get some kind of a holiday before the hot weather's over."

"Rupert met her when he went up north," Mrs. Green said. "He went off by himself, he worked in the bush up there. She had some kind of a job in a hotel. I'm not sure what. Chambermaid job. She wasn't raised up there, though—she says she was raised in an orphanage in Montreal. She can't help that. You'd expect her to speak French, but if she does she don't let on."

Enid said, "An interesting life."

"You can say that again."

"An interesting life," said Enid. Sometimes she couldn't help it—she tried a joke where it had hardly a hope of working. She raised her eyebrows encouragingly, and Mrs. Green did smile.

But was she hurt? That was just the way Rupert would smile, in high school, warding off some possible mockery.

"He never had any kind of a girlfriend before that," said Mrs. Green.

Enid had been in the same class as Rupert, though she did not mention that to Mrs. Green. She felt some embarrassment now because he was one of the boys—in fact, the main one—that she and her girlfriends had teased and tormented. "Picked on," as they used to say. They had picked on Rupert, following him up the street calling out, "Hello, Rupert. Hello, Ru-pert," putting him into a state of agony, watching his neck go red. "Rupert's got scarlet fever," they would say. "Rupert, you should be quarantined." And they would pretend that one of them—Enid, Joan McAuliffe, Marian Denny—had a case on him. "She wants to speak to you, Rupert. Why don't you ever ask her out? You could phone her up at least. She's dying to talk to you."

They did not really expect him to respond to these pleading overtures. But what joy if he had. He would have been rejected in short order and the story broadcast all over the school. Why? Why did they treat him this way, long to humiliate him? Simply because they could.

Impossible that he would have forgotten. But he treated Enid as if she were a new acquaintance, his wife's nurse, come into his house from anywhere at all. And Enid took her cue from him.

Things had been unusually well arranged here, to spare her extra work. Rupert slept at Mrs. Green's house, and ate his meals there. The two little girls could have been there as well, but it would have meant putting them into another school—there was nearly a month to go before school was out for the summer.

Rupert came into the house in the evenings and spoke to his children.

"Are you being good girls?" he said.

"Show Daddy what you made with your blocks," said Enid. "Show Daddy your pictures in the coloring book."

The blocks, the crayons, the coloring books, were all provided by Enid. She had phoned her mother and asked her to see what things she could find in the old trunks. Her mother had done that, and brought along as well an old book of cutout dolls which she had collected from someone—Princesses Elizabeth and Margaret Rose and their many outfits. Enid hadn't been able to get the little girls to say thank you until she put all these things on a high shelf and announced that they would stay there till thank you was said. Lois and Sylvie were seven and six years old, and as wild as little barn cats.

Rupert didn't ask where the playthings came from. He told his daughters to be good girls and asked Enid if there was anything she needed from town. Once she told him that she had replaced the lightbulb in the cellarway and that he could get her some spare bulbs.

"I could have done that," he said.

"I don't have any trouble with lightbulbs," said Enid. "Or fuses or knocking in nails. My mother and I have done without a man around the house for a long time now." She meant to tease a little, to be friendly, but it didn't work.

Finally Rupert would ask about his wife, and Enid would say that her blood pressure was down slightly, or that she had eaten and kept down pàrt of an omelette for supper, or that the ice packs seemed to ease her itchy skin and she was sleeping better. And Rupert would say that if she was sleeping he'd better not go in.

Enid said, "Nonsense." To see her husband would do a woman more good than to have a little doze. She took the children up to bed then, to give man and wife a time of privacy. But Rupert never stayed more than a few minutes. And when Enid came back downstairs and went into the front room—now the sickroom—to ready the patient for the night, Mrs. Quinn would be lying back against the pillows, looking agitated but not dissatisfied.

"Doesn't hang around here very long, does he?" Mrs. Quinn would say. "Makes me laugh. Ha-ha-ha, how-are-you? Ha-ha-ha, off-we-go. Why don't we take her out and throw her on the manure pile? Why don't we just dump her out like a dead cat? That's what he's thinking. Isn't he?"

"I doubt it," said Enid, bringing the basin and towels, the rubbing alcohol and the baby powder.

"I doubt it," said Mrs. Quinn quite viciously, but she submitted readily enough to having her nightgown removed, her hair smoothed back from her face, a towel slid under her hips. Enid was used to people making a fuss about being naked, even when they were very old or very ill. Sometimes she would have to tease them or badger them into common sense. "Do you think I haven't seen any bottom parts before?" she would say. "Bottom parts, top parts, it's pretty boring after a while. You know, there's just the two ways we're made." But Mrs. Quinn was without shame, opening her legs and raising herself a bit to make the job easier. She was a little bird-boned woman, queerly shaped now, with her swollen abdomen and limbs and her breasts shrunk to tiny pouches with dried-currant nipples.

"Swole up like some kind of pig," Mrs. Quinn said. "Except for my tits, and they always were kind of useless. I never had no big udders on me, like you. Don't you get sick of the sight of me? Won't you be glad when I'm dead?"

"If I felt like that I wouldn't be here," said Enid.

"Good riddance to bad rubbish," said Mrs. Quinn. "That's what you'll all say. Good riddance to bad rubbish. I'm no use to him anymore, am I? I'm no use to any man. He goes out of here every night and he goes to pick up women, doesn't he?"

"As far as I know, he goes to his sister's house."

"As far as you know. But you don't know much."

Enid thought she knew what this meant, this spite and venom, the energy saved for ranting. Mrs. Quinn was flailing about for an enemy. Sick people grew to resent well people, and sometimes that was true of husbands and wives, or even of mothers and their children. Both husband and children in Mrs. Quinn's case. On a Saturday morning, Enid called Lois and Sylvie from their games under the porch, to come and see their mother looking pretty. Mrs. Quinn had just had her morning wash, and was in a clean nightgown, with her fine, sparse, fair hair brushed and held back by a blue ribbon. (Enid took a supply of these ribbons with her when she went to nurse a female patient—also a bottle of cologne and a cake of scented soap.) She did look pretty—or you could see at least that she had once been pretty, with her wide forehead and cheekbones (they almost punched the skin now, like china doorknobs) and her large greenish eyes and childish translucent teeth and small stubborn chin.

The children came into the room obediently if unenthusiastically.

Mrs. Quinn said, "Keep them off of my bed, they're filthy."

"They just want to see you," said Enid.

"Well, now they've seen me," said Mrs. Quinn. "Now they can go."

This behavior didn't seem to surprise or disappoint the children. They looked at Enid, and Enid said, "All right, now, your mother better have a rest," and they ran out and slammed the kitchen door.

"Can't you get them to quit doing that?" Mrs. Quinn said. "Every time they do it, it's like a brick hits me in my chest."

You would think these two daughters of hers were a pair of rowdy orphans, wished on her for an indefinite visit. But that was the way some people were, before they settled down to their dying and sometimes even up to the event itself. People of a gentler nature—it would seem—than Mrs. Quinn might say that they knew how much their brothers, sisters, husbands, wives, and children had always hated them, how much of a disappointment they had been to others and others had been to them, and how glad they knew everybody would be to see them gone. They might say this at the end of peaceful, useful lives in the midst of loving families, where there was no explanation at all for such fits. And usually the fits passed. But often, too, in the last weeks or even days of life there was mulling over of old feuds and slights or whimpering about some unjust punishment suffered seventy years earlier. Once a woman had asked Enid to bring her a willow platter from the cupboard and Enid had thought that she wanted the comfort of looking at this one pretty possession for the last time. But it turned out that she wanted to use her last, surprising strength to smash it against the bedpost.

"Now I know my sister's never going to get her hands on that," she said.

And often people remarked that their visitors were only coming to gloat and that the doctor was responsible for their sufferings. They detested the sight of Enid herself, for her sleepless strength and patient hands and the way the juices of life were so admirably balanced and flowing in her. Enid was used to that, and she was able to understand the trouble they were in, the trouble of dying and also the trouble of their lives that sometimes overshadowed that.

But with Mrs. Quinn she was at a loss.

It was not just that she couldn't supply comfort here. It was that she couldn't want to. She could not conquer her dislike of this doomed, miserable young woman. She disliked this body that she had to wash and powder and placate with ice and alcohol rubs. She understood now what people meant when they said that they hated sickness and sick bodies; she understood the women who had said to her, I don't know how you do it, I could never be a nurse, that's the one thing I could never be. She disliked this particular body, all the particular signs of its disease. The smell of it and the discoloration, the malignant-looking little nipples and the pathetic ferretlike teeth. She saw all this as the sign of a willed corruption. She was as bad as Mrs. Green, sniffing out rampant impurity. In spite of being a nurse who knew better, and in spite of its being her job—and surely her nature—to be compassionate. She didn't know why this was happening. Mrs. Quinn reminded her somewhat of girls she had known in high school—cheaply dressed, sickly looking girls with dreary futures, who still displayed a hardfaced satisfaction with themselves. They lasted only a year or two—they got pregnant, most of them got married. Enid had nursed some of them in later years, in home childbirth, and found their confidence exhausted and their bold streak turned into meekness, or even piety. She was sorry for them, even when she remembered how determined they had been to get what they had got.

Mrs. Quinn was a harder case. Mrs. Quinn might crack and crack, but there would be nothing but sullen mischief, nothing but rot inside her.

Worse even than the fact that Enid should feel this revulsion was the fact that Mrs. Quinn knew it. No patience or gentleness or cheerfulness that Enid could summon would keep Mrs. Quinn from knowing. And Mrs. Quinn made knowing it her triumph.

Good riddance to bad rubbish.

WHEN ENID was twenty years old, and had almost finished her nurse's training, her father was dying in the Walley hospital. That was when he said to her, "I don't know as I care for this career of yours. I don't want you working in a place like this."

Enid bent over him and asked what sort of place he thought he was in. "It's only the Walley hospital," she said.

"I know that," said her father, sounding as calm and reasonable as he had always done (he was an insurance and real-estate agent). "I know what I'm talking about. Promise me you won't."

"Promise you what?" said Enid.

"You won't do this kind of work," her father said. She could not get any further explanation out of him. He tightened up his mouth as if her questioning disgusted him. All he would say was "Promise."

"What is all this about?" Enid asked her mother, and her mother said, "Oh, go ahead. Go ahead and promise him. What difference is it going to make?"

Enid thought this a shocking thing to say, but made no comment. It was consistent with her mother's way of looking at a lot of things.

"I'm not going to promise anything I don't understand," she said. "I'm probably not going to promise anything anyway. But if you know what he's talking about you ought to tell me."

"It's just this idea he's got now," her mother said. "He's got an idea that nursing makes a woman coarse."

Enid said, "Coarse."

Her mother said that the part of nursing her father objected to was the familiarity nurses had with men's bodies. Her father thought—he had decided—that such familiarity would change a girl, and furthermore that it would change the way men thought about that girl. It would spoil her good chances and give her a lot of other chances that were not so good. Some men would lose interest and others would become interested in the wrong way.

"I suppose it's all mixed up with wanting you to get married," her mother said.

"Too bad if it is," said Enid.

But she ended up promising. And her mother said, "Well, I hope that makes you happy." Not "makes him happy." "Makes *you*." It seemed that her mother had known before Enid did just how tempting this promise would be. The deathbed promise, the self-denial, the wholesale sacrifice. And the more absurd the better. This was what she had given in to. And not for love of her father, either (her mother implied), but for the thrill of it. Sheer noble perversity.

"If he'd asked you to give up something you didn't care one way or the other about, you'd probably have told him nothing doing," her mother said. "If for instance he'd asked you to give up wearing lipstick. You'd still be wearing it."

Enid listened to this with a patient expression.

"Did you pray about it?" said her mother sharply.

Enid said yes.

She withdrew from nursing school; she stayed at home and kept busy. There was enough money that she did not have to work. In fact, her mother had not wanted Enid to go into nursing in the first place, claiming that it was something poor girls did, it was a way out for girls whose parents couldn't keep them or send them to college. Enid did not remind her of this inconsistency. She painted a fence, she tied up the rosebushes for winter. She learned to bake and she learned to play bridge, taking her father's place in the weekly games her mother played with Mr. and Mrs. Willens from next door. In no time at all she became—as Mr. Willens said—a scandalously good player. He took to turning up with chocolates or a pink rose for her, to make up for his own inadequacies as a partner.

She went skating in the winter evenings. She played badminton.

She had never lacked friends, and she didn't now. Most of the people who had been in the last year of high school with her were finishing college now, or were already working at a distance, as teachers or nurses or chartered accountants. But she made friends with others who had dropped out before senior year to work in banks or stores or offices, to become plumbers or milliners. The girls in this group were dropping like flies, as they said of each other—they were dropping into matrimony. Enid was an organizer of bridal showers and a help at trousseau teas. In a couple of years would come the christenings, where she could expect to be a favorite godmother. Children not related to her would grow up calling her Aunt. And she was already a sort of honorary daughter to women of her mother's age and older, the only young woman who had time for the Book Club and the Horticultural Society. So, quickly and easily, still in her youth, she was slipping into this essential, central, yet isolated role.

But in fact it had been her role all along. In high school she was always the class secretary or class social convener. She was well liked and high-spirited and well dressed and good-looking, but she was slightly set apart. She had friends who were boys but never a boyfriend. She did not seem to have made a choice this way, but she was not worried about it, either. She had been preoccupied with her ambition—to be a missionary, at one embarrassing stage, and then to be a nurse. She had never thought of nursing as just something to do until she got married. Her hope was to be good, and do good, and not necessarily in the orderly, customary, wifely way.

At New Year's she went to the dance in the Town Hall. The man who danced with her most often, and escorted her home, and pressed her hand good night, was the manager of the creamery—a man in his forties, never married, an excellent dancer, an avuncular friend to girls unlikely to find partners. No woman ever took him seriously.

"Maybe you should take a business course," her mother said. "Or why shouldn't you go to college?"

Where the men might be more appreciative, she was surely thinking.

"I'm too old," said Enid.

Her mother laughed. "That only shows how young you are," she said. She seemed relieved to discover that her daughter had a touch of folly natural to her age—that she could think twenty-one was at a vast distance from eighteen.

"I'm not going to troop in with kids out of high school," Enid said. "I mean it. What do you want to get rid of me for anyway? I'm fine here." This sulkiness or sharpness also seemed to please and reassure her mother. But after a moment she sighed, and said, "You'll be surprised how fast the years go by."

That August there were a lot of cases of measles and a few of polio at the same time. The doctor who had looked after Enid's father, and had observed her competence around the hospital, asked her if she would be willing to help out for a while, nursing people at home. She said that she would think about it.

"You mean pray?" her mother said, and Enid's face took on a stubborn, secretive expression that in another girl's case might have had to do with meeting her boyfriend.

"That promise," she said to her mother the next day. "That was about working in a hospital, wasn't it?"

Her mother said that she had understood it that way, yes.

"And with graduating and being a registered nurse?"

Yes, yes.

So if there were people who needed nursing at home, who couldn't afford to go to the hospital or did not want to go, and if Enid went into their houses to nurse them, not as a registered nurse but as what they called a practical nurse, she would hardly be breaking her promise, would she? And since most of those needing her care would be children or women having babies, or old people dying, there would not be much danger of the coarsening effect, would there?

"If the only men you get to see are men who are never going to get out of bed again, you have a point," said her mother.

But she could not keep from adding that what all this meant was that Enid had decided to give up the possibility of a decent job in a hospital in order to do miserable backbreaking work in miserable primitive houses for next to no money. Enid would find herself pumping water from contaminated wells and breaking ice in winter washbasins and battling flies in summer and using an outdoor toilet. Scrub boards and coal-oil lamps instead of washing machines and electricity. Trying to look after sick people in those conditions and cope with housework and poor weaselly children as well.

"But if that is your object in life," she said, "I can see that the worse I make it sound the more determined you get to do it. The only thing is, I'm going to ask for a couple of promises myself. Promise me you'll boil the water you drink. And you won't marry a farmer."

Enid said, "Of all the crazy ideas."

That was sixteen years ago. During the first of those years people got poorer and poorer. There were more and more of them who could not afford to go to the hospital, and the houses where Enid worked had often deteriorated almost to the state that her mother had described. Sheets and diapers had to be washed by hand in houses where the washing machine had broken down and could not be repaired, or the electricity had been turned off, or where there had never been any electricity in the first place. Enid did not work without pay, because that would not have been fair to the other women who did the same kind of nursing, and who did not have the same options as she did. But she gave most of the money back, in the form of children's shoes and winter coats and trips to the dentist and Christmas toys.

Her mother went around canvassing her friends for old baby cots, and high chairs and blankets, and worn-out sheets, which she herself ripped up and hemmed to make diapers. Everybody said how proud she must be of Enid, and she said yes, she surely was.

"But sometimes it's a devil of a lot of work," she said. "This being the mother of a saint."

THEN CAME the war, and the great shortage of doctors and nurses, and Enid was more welcome than ever. As she was for a while after the war, with so many babies being born. It was only now, with the hospitals being enlarged and many farms getting prosperous, that it looked as if her responsibilities might dwindle away to the care of those who had bizarre and hopeless afflictions, or were so irredeemably cranky that hospitals had thrown them out.

THIS SUMMER there was a great downpour of rain every few days, and then the sun came out very hot, glittering off the drenched leaves and grass. Early mornings were full of mist—they were so close, here, to the river—and even when the mist cleared off you could not see very far in any direction, because of the overflow and density of summer. The heavy trees, the bushes all bound up with wild grapevines and Virginia creeper, the crops of corn and barley and wheat and hay. Everything was ahead of itself, as people said. The hay was ready to cut in June, and Rupert had to rush to get it into the barn before a rain spoiled it.

He came into the house later and later in the evenings, having worked as long as the light lasted. One night when he came the house was in darkness, except for a candle burning on the kitchen table.

Enid hurried to unhook the screen door.

"Power out?" said Rupert.

Enid said, "Shhh." She whispered to him that she was letting the children sleep downstairs, because the upstairs rooms were so hot. She had pushed the chairs together and made beds on them with quilts and pillows. And of course she had had to turn the lights out so that they could get to sleep. She had found a candle in one of the drawers, and that was all she needed, to see to write by, in her notebook.

"They'll always remember sleeping here," she said. "You always remember the times when you were a child and you slept somewhere different."

He set down a box that contained a ceiling fan for the sickroom. He had been into Walley to buy it. He had also bought a newspaper, which he handed to Enid.

"Thought you might like to know what's going on in the world," he said.

She spread the paper out beside her notebook, on the table. There was a picture of a couple of dogs playing in a fountain.

"It says there's a heat wave," she said. "Isn't it nice to find out about it?"

Rupert was carefully lifting the fan out of its box.

"That'll be wonderful," she said. "It's cooled off in there now, but it'll be such a comfort to her tomorrow."

"I'll be over early to put it up," he said. Then he asked how his wife had been that day.

Enid said that the pains in her legs had been easing off, and the new pills the doctor had her on seemed to be letting her get some rest.

"The only thing is, she goes to sleep so soon," she said. "It makes it hard for you to get a visit."

"Better she gets the rest," Rupert said.

This whispered conversation reminded Enid of conversations in high school, when they were both in their senior year and that earlier teasing, or cruel flirtation, or whatever it was, had long been abandoned. All that last year Rupert had sat in the seat behind hers, and they had often spoken to each other briefly, always to some immediate purpose. Have you got an ink eraser? How do you spell "incriminate"? Where is the Tyrrhenian Sea? Usually it was Enid, half turning in her seat and able only to sense, not see, how close Rupert was, who started these conversations. She did want to borrow an eraser, she was in need of information, but also she wanted to be sociable. And she wanted to make amends—she felt ashamed of the way she and her friends had treated him. It would do no good to apologize—that would just embarrass him all over again. He was only at ease when he sat behind her, and knew that she could not look him in the face. If they met on the street he would look away until the last minute, then mutter the faintest greeting while she sang out "Hello, Rupert," and heard an echo of the old tormenting tones she wanted to banish.

But when he actually laid a finger on her shoulder, tapping for attention, when he bent forward, almost touching or maybe really touching—she could not tell for sure—her thick hair that was wild even in a bob, then she felt forgiven. In a way, she felt honored. Restored to seriousness and to respect.

Where, where exactly, is the Tyrrhenian Sea?

She wondered if he remembered anything at all of that now.

She separated the back and front parts of the paper. Margaret Truman was visiting England, and had curtsied to the royal family. The King's doctors were trying to cure his Buerger's disease with vitamin E.

She offered the front part to Rupert. "I'm going to look at the crossword," she said. "I like to do the crossword—it relaxes me at the end of the day."

Rupert sat down and began to read the paper, and she asked him if he would like a cup of tea. Of course he said not to bother, and she went ahead and made it anyway, understanding that this reply might as well be yes in country speech.

"It's a South American theme," she said, looking at the crossword. "Latin American theme. First across is a musical . . . *garment*. A musical garment? Garment. A lot of letters. Oh. Oh. I'm lucky tonight. Cape

Horn!

"You see how silly they are, these things," she said, and rose and poured the tea.

If he did remember, did he hold anything against her? Maybe her blithe friendliness in their senior year had been as unwelcome, as superior-seeming to him, as that early taunting?

When she first saw him in this house, she thought that he had not changed much. He had been a tall, solid, round-faced boy, and he was a tall, heavy, round-faced man. He had worn his hair cut so short, always, that it didn't make much difference that there was less of it now and that it had turned from light brown to gray-brown. A permanent sunburn had taken the place of his blushes. And whatever troubled him and showed in his face might have been just the same old trouble—the problem of occupying space in the world and having a name that people could call you by, being somebody they thought they could know.

She thought of them sitting in the senior class. A small class, by that time—in five years the unstudious, the carefree, and the indifferent had been weeded out, leaving these overgrown, grave, and docile children learning trigonometry, learning Latin. What kind of life did they think they were preparing for? What kind of people did they think they were going to be?

She could see the dark-green, softened cover of a book called *History of the Renaissance and Reformation*. It was secondhand, or tenthhand—nobody ever bought a new textbook. Inside were written all the names of the previous owners, some of whom were middle-aged housewives or merchants around the town. You could not imagine them learning these things, or underlining "Edict of Nantes" with red ink and writing "N.B." in the margin.

Edict of Nantes. The very uselessness, the exotic nature, of the things in those books and in those students' heads, in her own head then and Rupert's, made Enid feel a tenderness and wonder. It wasn't that they had meant to be something that they hadn't become. Nothing like that. Rupert couldn't have imagined anything but farming this farm. It was a good farm, and he was an only son. And she herself had ended up doing exactly what she must have wanted to do. You couldn't say that they had chosen the wrong lives or chosen against their will or not understood their choices. Just that they had not understood how time would pass and leave them not more but maybe a little less than what they used to be.

"'Bread of the Amazon,'" she said. "'Bread of the Amazon'?"

Rupert said, "Manioc?"

Enid counted. "Seven letters," she said. "Seven."

He said, "Cassava?"

"Cassava? That's a double *s*? Cassava."

Mrs. Quinn became more capricious daily about her food. Sometimes she said she wanted toast, or bananas with milk on them. One day she said peanut-butter cookies. Enid prepared all these things—the children could eat them anyway—and when they were ready Mrs. Quinn could not stand the look or the smell of them. Even Jell-O had a smell she could not stand.

Some days she hated all noise; she would not even have the fan going. Other days she wanted the radio on, she wanted the station that played requests for birthdays and anniversaries and called people up to ask them questions. If you got the answer right you won a trip to Niagara Falls, a tankful of gas, or a load of groceries or tickets to a movie.

"It's all fixed," Mrs. Quinn said. "They just pretend to call somebody up—they're in the next room and already got the answer told to them. I used to know somebody that worked for a radio, that's the truth."

On these days her pulse was rapid. She talked very fast in a light, breathless voice. "What kind of car is that your mother's got?" she said.

"It's a maroon-colored car," said Enid.

"What *make*?" said Mrs. Quinn.

Enid said she did not know, which was the truth. She had known, but she had forgotten.

"Was it new when she got it?"

"Yes," said Enid. "Yes. But that was three or four years ago."

"She lives in that big rock house next door to Willenses?"

Yes, said Enid.

"How many rooms it got? Sixteen?"

"Too many."

"Did you go to Mr. Willens's funeral when he got drownded?"

Enid said no. "I'm not much for funerals."

"I was supposed to go. I wasn't awfully sick then, I was going with Herveys up the highway, they said I could get a ride with them and then her mother and her sister wanted to go and there wasn't enough room in back. Then Clive and Olive went in the truck and I could've scrunched up in their front seat but they never thought to ask me. Do you think he drownded himself?"

Enid thought of Mr. Willens handing her a rose. His jokey gallantry that made the nerves of her teeth ache, as from too much sugar.

"I don't know. I wouldn't think so."

"Did him and Mrs. Willens get along all right?"

"As far as I know, they got along beautifully."

"Oh, is that so?" said Mrs. Quinn, trying to imitate Enid's reserved tone. "Bee-you-tif-ley."

ENID SLEPT on the couch in Mrs. Quinn's room. Mrs. Quinn's devastating itch had almost disappeared, as had her need to urinate. She slept through most of the night, though she would have spells of harsh and angry breathing. What woke Enid up and kept her awake was a trouble of her own. She had begun to have ugly dreams. These were unlike any dreams she had ever had before. She used to think that a bad dream was one of finding herself in an unfamiliar house where the rooms kept changing and there was always more work to do than she could handle, work undone that she thought she had done, innumerable distractions. And then, of course, she had what she thought of as romantic dreams, in which some man would have his arm around her or even be embracing her. It might be a stranger or a man she knew—sometimes a man whom it was quite a joke to think of in that way. These dreams made her thoughtful or a little sad but relieved in some way to know that such feelings were possible for her. They could be embarrassing, but were nothing, nothing at all compared with the dreams that she was having now. In the dreams that came to her now she would be copulating or trying to copulate (sometimes she was prevented by intruders or shifts of circumstances) with utterly forbidden and unthinkable partners. With fat squirmy babies or patients in bandages or her own mother. She would be slick with lust, hollow and groaning with it, and she would set to work with roughness and an attitude of evil pragmatism. "Yes, this will have to do," she would say to herself. "This will do if nothing better comes along." And this coldness of heart, this matter-of-fact depravity, simply drove her lust along. She woke up unrepentant, sweaty and exhausted, and lay like a carcass until her own self, her shame and disbelief, came pouring back into her. The sweat went cold on her skin. She lay there shivering in the warm night, with disgust and humiliation. She did not dare go back to sleep. She got used to the dark and the long rectangles of the net-curtained windows filled with a faint light. And the sick woman's breath grating and scolding and then almost disappearing.

If she were a Catholic, she thought, was this the sort of thing that could come out at confession? It didn't seem like the sort of thing she could even bring out in a private prayer. She didn't pray much anymore, except formally, and to bring the experiences she had just been through to the attention of God seemed absolutely useless, disrespectful. He would be insulted. She was insulted, by her own mind. Her religion was hopeful and sensible and there was no room in it for any sort of rubbishy drama, such as the invasion of the devil into her sleep. The filth in her mind was in her, and there was no point in dramatizing it and making it seem important. Surely not. It was nothing, just the mind's garbage.

In the little meadow between the house and the riverbank there were cows. She could hear them munching and jostling, feeding at night. She thought of their large gentle shapes in there with the money musk and chicory, the flowering grasses, and she thought, They have a lovely life, cows.

It ends, of course, in the slaughterhouse. The end is disaster.

For everybody, though, the same thing. Evil grabs us when we are sleeping; pain and disintegration lie in wait. Animal horrors, all worse than you can imagine beforehand. The comforts of bed and the cows' breath, the pattern of the stars at night—all that can get turned on its head in an instant. And here she was, here was Enid, working her life away pretending it wasn't so. Trying to ease people. Trying to be good. An angel of mercy, as her mother had said, with less and less irony as time went on. Patients and doctors, too, had said it.

And all the time how many thought that she was a fool? The people she spent her labors on might secretly despise her. Thinking they'd never do the same in her place. Never be fool enough. No.

Miserable offenders, came into her head. *Miserable offenders.*

Restore them that are penitent.

So she got up and went to work; as far as she was concerned, that was the best way to be penitent. She worked very quietly but steadily through the night, washing the cloudy glasses and sticky plates that were in the cupboards and establishing order where there was none before. None. Teacups had sat between the ketchup and the mustard and toilet paper on top of a pail of honey. There was no waxed paper or even newspaper laid out on the shelves. Brown sugar in the bag was as hard as rock. It was understandable that things should have gone downhill in the last few months, but it looked as if there had been no care, no organization here, ever. All the net curtains were gray with smoke and the windowpanes were greasy. The last bit of jam had been left to grow fuzz in the jar, and vile-smelling water that had held some ancient bouquet had never been dumped out of its jug. But this was a good house still, that scrubbing and painting could restore.

Though what could you do about the ugly brown paint that had been recently and sloppily applied to the front-room floor?

When she had a moment later in the day she pulled the weeds out of Rupert's mother's flower beds, dug up the burdocks and twitch grass that were smothering the valiant perennials.

She taught the children to hold their spoons properly and to say grace.

Thank you for the world so sweet,
Thank you for the food we eat. . .

She taught them to brush their teeth and after that to say their prayers.

"God bless Mama and Daddy and Enid and Aunt Olive and Uncle Clive and Princess Elizabeth and Margaret Rose." After that each added the name of the other. They had been doing it for quite a while when Sylvie said, "What does it mean?"

Enid said, "What does what mean?"

"What does it mean 'God bless'?"

ENID MADE eggnogs, not flavoring them even with vanilla, and fed them to Mrs. Quinn from a spoon. She fed her a little of the rich liquid at a time, and Mrs. Quinn was able to hold down what was given to her in small amounts. If she could not do that, Enid spooned out flat, lukewarm ginger ale.

The sunlight, or any light, was as hateful as noise to Mrs. Quinn by now. Enid had to hang thick quilts over the windows, even when the blinds were pulled down. With the fan shut off, as Mrs. Quinn demanded, the room became very hot, and sweat dripped from Enid's forehead as she bent over the bed attending to the patient. Mrs. Quinn went into fits of shivering; she could never be warm enough.

"This is dragging out," the doctor said. "It must be those milkshakes you're giving her, keeping her going."

"Eggnogs," said Enid, as if it mattered.

Mrs. Quinn was often now too tired or weak to talk. Sometimes she lay in a stupor, with her breathing so faint and her pulse so lost and wandering that a person less experienced than Enid would have taken her for dead. But at other times she rallied, wanted the radio on, then wanted it off. She knew perfectly well who she was still, and who Enid was, and she sometimes seemed to be watching Enid with a speculative or inquiring look in her eyes. Color was long gone from her face and even from her lips, but her eyes looked greener than they had in the past—a milky, cloudy green. Enid tried to answer the look that was bent on her.

"Would you like me to get a priest to talk to you?"

Mrs. Quinn looked as if she wanted to spit.

"Do I look like a Mick?" she said.

"A minister?" said Enid. She knew this was the right thing to ask, but the spirit in which she asked it was not right—it was cold and faintly malicious.

No. This was not what Mrs. Quinn wanted. She grunted with displeasure. There was some energy in her still, and Enid had the feeling that she was building it up for a purpose. "Do you want to talk to your children?" she said, making herself speak compassionately and encouragingly. "Is that what you want?"

No.

"Your husband? Your husband will be here in a little while."

Enid didn't know that for sure. Rupert arrived so late some nights, after Mrs. Quinn had taken the final pills and gone to sleep. Then he sat with Enid. He always brought her the newspaper. He asked what she wrote in her notebooks—he noticed that there were two—and she told him. One for the doctor, with a record of blood pressure and pulse and temperature, a record of what was eaten, vomited, excreted, medicines taken, some general summing up of the patient's condition. In the other notebook, for herself, she wrote many of the same things, though perhaps not so exactly, but she added details about the weather and what was happening all around. And things to remember.

"For instance, I wrote something down the other day," she said. "Something that Lois said. Lois and Sylvie came in when Mrs. Green was here and Mrs. Green was mentioning how the berry bushes were growing along the lane and stretching across the road, and Lois said, 'It's like in "Sleeping Beauty."' Because I'd read them the story. I made a note of that."

Rupert said, "I'll have to get after those berry canes and cut them back."

Enid got the impression that he was pleased by what Lois had said and by the fact that she had written it down, but it wasn't possible for him to say so.

One night he told her that he would be away for a couple of days, at a stock auction. He had asked the doctor if it was all right, and the doctor had said to go ahead.

That night he had come before the last pills were given, and Enid supposed that he was making a point of seeing his wife awake before that little time away. She told him to go right into Mrs. Quinn's room, and he did, and shut the door after him. Enid picked up the paper and thought of going upstairs to read it, but the children probably weren't asleep yet; they would find excuses for calling her in. She could go out on the porch, but there were mosquitoes at this time of day, especially after a rain like the afternoon's.

She was afraid of overhearing some intimacy or perhaps the suggestion of a fight, then having to face him when he came out. Mrs. Quinn was building up to a display—of that Enid felt sure. And before she made up her mind where to go she did overhear something. Not the recriminations or (if it was possible) the endearments, or perhaps even weeping, that she had been half expecting, but a laugh. She heard Mrs. Quinn weakly laughing, and the laughter had the mockery and satisfaction in it that Enid had heard before but also something she hadn't heard before, not in her life—something deliberately vile. She didn't move, though she should have, and she was at the table still, she was still there staring at the door of the room, when he came out a moment later. He didn't avoid her eyes—or she his. She couldn't. Yet she couldn't have said for sure that he saw her. He just looked at her and went on outside. He looked as if he had caught hold of an electric wire and begged pardon—who of?—that his body was given over to this stupid catastrophe.

The next day Mrs. Quinn's strength came flooding back, in that unnatural and deceptive way that Enid had seen once or twice in others. Mrs. Quinn wanted to sit up against the pillows. She wanted the fan turned on.

Enid said, "What a good idea."

"I could tell you something you wouldn't believe," Mrs. Quinn said.

"People tell me lots of things," said Enid.

"Sure. Lies," Mrs. Quinn said. "I bet it's all lies. You know Mr. Willens was right here in this room?"

III. MISTAKE

MRS. QUINN had been sitting in the rocker getting her eyes examined and Mr. Willens had been close up in front of her with the thing up to her eyes, and neither one of them heard Rupert come in, because he was supposed to be cutting wood down by the river. But he had sneaked back. He sneaked back through the kitchen not making any noise—he must have seen Mr. Willens's car outside before he did that—then he opened the door to this room just easy, till he saw Mr. Willens there on his knees holding the thing up to her eye and he had the other hand on her leg to keep his balance. He had grabbed her leg to keep his balance and her skirt got scrunched up and her leg showed bare, but that was all there was to it and she couldn't do a thing about it, she had to concentrate on keeping still.

So Rupert got in the room without either of them hearing him come in and then he just gave one jump and landed on Mr. Willens like a bolt of lightning and Mr. Willens couldn't get up or turn around, he was down before he knew it. Rupert banged his head up and down on the floor, Rupert banged the life out of him, and she jumped up so fast the chair went over and Mr. Willens's box where he kept his eye things got knocked over and all the things flew out of it. Rupert just walloped him, and maybe he hit the leg of the stove, she didn't know what. She thought, It's me next. But she couldn't get round them to run out of the room. And then she saw Rupert wasn't going to go for her after all. He was out of wind and he just set the chair up and sat down in it. She went to Mr. Willens then and hauled him around, as heavy as he was, to get him right side up. His eyes were not quite open, not shut either, and there was dribble coming out of his mouth. But no skin broke on his face or bruise you could see—maybe it wouldn't have come up yet. The stuff coming out of his mouth didn't even look like blood. It was pink stuff, and if you wanted to know what it looked like it looked exactly like when the froth comes up when you're boiling the strawberries to make jam. Bright pink. It was smeared over his face from when Rupert had him facedown. He made a sound, too, when she was turning him over. *Glug-glug.* That was all there was to it. *Glug-glug* and he was laid out like a stone.

Rupert jumped out of the chair so it was still rocking, and he started picking up all the things and putting each one back where it went in Mr. Willens's box. Getting everything fitted in the way it should go. Wasting the time that way. It was a special box lined with red plush and a place in it for each one of his things that he used and you had to get everything in right or the top wouldn't go down. Rupert got it so the top went on and then he just sat down in the chair again and started pounding on his knees.

On the table there was one of those good-for-nothing cloths, it was a souvenir of when Rupert's mother and father went up north to see the Dionne Quintuplets. She took it off the table and wrapped it around Mr. Willens's head to soak up the pink stuff and so they wouldn't have to keep on looking at him.

Rupert kept banging his big flat hands. She said, Rupert, we got to bury him somewhere.

Rupert just looked at her, like to say, Why?

She said they could bury him down in the cellar, which had a dirt floor.

"That's right," said Rupert. "Where are we going to bury his car?"

She said they could put it in the barn and cover it up with hay.

He said too many people came poking around the barn.

Then she thought, Put him in the river. She thought of him sitting in his car right under the water. It came to her like a picture. Rupert didn't say anything at first, so she went into the kitchen and got some water and cleaned Mr. Willens up so he wouldn't dribble on anything. The goo was not coming up in his mouth anymore. She got his keys, which were in his pocket. She could feel, through the cloth of his pants, the fat of his leg still warm.

She said to Rupert, Get moving.

He took the keys.

They hoisted Mr. Willens up, she by the feet and Rupert by the head, and he weighed a ton. He was like lead. But as she carried him one of his shoes kind of kicked her between the legs, and she thought, There you are, you're still at it, you horny old devil. Even his dead old foot giving her the nudge. Not that she ever let him do anything, but he was always ready to get a grab if he could. Like grabbing her leg up under her skirt when he had the thing to her eye and she couldn't stop him and Rupert had to come sneaking in and get the wrong idea.

Over the doorsill and through the kitchen and across the porch and down the porch steps. All clear. But it was a windy day, and, first thing, the wind blew away the cloth she had wrapped over Mr. Willens's face.

Their yard couldn't be seen from the road, that was lucky. Just the peak of the roof and the upstairs window. Mr. Willens's car couldn't be seen.

Rupert had thought up the rest of what to do. Take him to Jutland, where it was deep water and the track going all the way back and it could look like he just drove in from the road and mistook his way. Like he turned off on the Jutland road, maybe it was dark and he just drove into the water before he knew where he was at. Like he just made a mistake.

He did. Mr. Willens certainly did make a mistake.

The trouble was it meant driving out their lane and along the road to the Jutland turn. But nobody lived down there and it was a dead end after the Jutland turn, so just the half mile or so to pray you never met anybody. Then Rupert would get Mr. Willens over in the driver's seat and push the car right off down the bank into the water. Push the whole works down into the pond. It was going to be a job to do that, but Rupert at least was a strong bugger. If he hadn't been so strong they wouldn't have been in this mess in the first place.

Rupert had a little trouble getting the car started because he had never driven one like that, but he did, and got turned around and drove off down the lane with Mr. Willens kind of bumping over against him. He had put Mr. Willens's hat on his head—the hat that had been sitting on the seat of the car.

Why take his hat off before he came into the house? Not just to be polite but so he could easier get a clutch on her and kiss her. If you could call that kissing, all that pushing up against her with the box still in one hand and the other grabbing on, and sucking away at her with his dribbly old mouth. Sucking and chewing away at her lips and her tongue and pushing himself up at her and the corner of the box sticking into her and digging her behind. She was so surprised and he got such a hold she didn't know how to get out of it. Pushing and sucking and dribbling and digging into her and hurting her all at the same time. He was a dirty old brute.

She went and got the Quintuplets cloth where it had blown onto the fence. She looked hard for blood on the steps or any mess on the porch or through the kitchen, but all she found was in the front room, also some on her shoes. She scrubbed up what was on the floor and scrubbed her shoes, which she took off, and not till she had all that done did she see a smear right down her front. How did she come by that? And the same time she saw it she heard a noise that turned her to stone. She heard a car and it was a car she didn't know and it was coming down the lane.

She looked through the net curtain and sure enough. A new-looking car and dark green. Her smeared-down front and shoes off and the floor wet. She moved back where she couldn't be seen, but she couldn't think of where to hide. The car stopped and a car door opened, but the engine didn't cut off. She heard the door shut and then the car turned around and she heard the sound of it driving back up the lane. And she heard Lois and Sylvie on the porch.

It was the teacher's boyfriend's car. He picked up the teacher every Friday afternoon, and this was a Friday. So the teacher said to him, Why don't we give these ones a lift home, they're the littlest and they got the farthest to go and it looks like it's going to rain.

It did rain, too. It had started by the time Rupert got back, walking home along the riverbank. She said, A good thing, it'll muddy up your tracks where you went to push it over. He said he'd took his shoes off and worked in his sock feet. So you must have got your brains going again, she said.

Instead of trying to soak the stuff out of that souvenir cloth or the blouse she had on, she decided to burn the both of them in the stove. They made a horrible smell and the smell made her sick. That was the whole beginning of her being sick. That and the paint. After she cleaned up the floor, she could still see where she thought there was a stain, so she got the brown paint left over from when Rupert painted the steps and she painted over the whole floor. That started her throwing up, leaning over and breathing in that paint. And the pains in her back—that was the start of them, too.

After she got the floor painted she just about quit going into the front room. But one day she thought she had better put some other cloth on that table. It would make things look more normal. If she didn't, then her sister-in-law was sure to come nosing around and say, Where's that cloth Mom and Dad brought back the time they went to see the Quints? If she had a different cloth on she could say, Oh, I just felt like a change. But no cloth would look funny.

So she got a cloth Rupert's mother had embroidered with flower baskets and took it in there and she could still smell the smell. And there on the table was sitting the dark-red box with Mr. Willens's things in it and his name on it and it had been sitting there all the time. She didn't even remember putting it there or seeing Rupert put it there. She had forgot all about it.

She took that box and hid it in one place and then she hid it in another. She never told where she hid it and she wasn't going to. She would have smashed it up, but how do you smash all those things in it? Examining things. Oh, Missus, would you like me to examine your eyes for you, just sit down here and just you relax and you just shut the one eye and keep the other one wide open. Wide open, now. It was like the same game every time, and she wasn't supposed to suspect what was going on, and when he had the thing out looking in her eye he wanted her to keep her panties on, him the dirty old cuss puffing away getting his fingers slicked in and puffing away. Her not supposed to say anything till he stops and gets the looker thing packed up in his box and all and then she's supposed to say, "Oh, Mr. Willens, now, how much do I owe you for today?"

And that was the signal for him to get her down and thump her like an old billy goat. Right on the bare floor to knock her up and down and try to bash her into pieces. Dingey on him like a blowtorch.

How'd you've liked that?

Then it was in the papers. Mr. Willens found drowned.

They said his head got bunged up knocking against the steering wheel. They said he was alive when he went in the water. What a laugh.

IV. LIES

ENID STAYED awake all night—she didn't even try to sleep. She could not lie down in Mrs. Quinn's room. She sat in the kitchen for hours. It was an effort for her to move, even to make a cup of tea or go to the bathroom. Moving her body shook up the information that she was trying to arrange in her head and get used to. She had not undressed, or unrolled her hair, and when she brushed her teeth she seemed to be doing something laborious and unfamiliar. The moonlight came through the kitchen window—she was sitting in the dark—and she watched a patch of light shift through the night, on the linoleum, and disappear. She was surprised by its disappearance and then by the birds waking up, the new day starting. The night had seemed so long and then too short, because nothing had been decided.

She got up stiffly and unlocked the door and sat on the porch in the beginning light. Even that move jammed her thoughts together. She had to sort through them again and set them on two sides. What had happened—or what she had been told had happened—on one side. What to do about it on the other. What to do about it—that was what would not come clear to her.

The cows had been moved out of the little meadow between the house and the riverbank. She could open the gate if she wanted to and go in that direction. She knew that she should go back, instead, and check on Mrs. Quinn. But she found herself pulling open the gate bolt.

The cows hadn't cropped all the weeds. Sopping wet, they brushed against her stockings. The path was clear, though, under the riverbank trees, those big willows with the wild grape hanging on to them like monkeys' shaggy arms. Mist was rising so that you could hardly see the river. You had to fix your eyes, concentrate, and then a spot of water would show through, quiet as water in a pot. There must be a moving current, but she could not find it.

Then she saw a movement, and it wasn't in the water. There was a boat moving. Tied to a branch, a plain old rowboat was being lifted very slightly, lifted and let fall. Now that she had found it, she kept watching it, as if it could say something to her. And it did. It said something gentle and final. *You know. You know.*

WHEN the children woke up they found her in bountiful good spirits, freshly washed and dressed and with her hair loose. She had already made the Jell-O crammed with fruit that would be ready for them to eat at noon. And she was mixing batter for cookies that could be baked before it got too hot to use the oven.

"Is that your father's boat?" she said. "Down on the river?"

Lois said yes. "But we're not supposed to play in it." Then she said, "If you went down with us we could." They had caught on at once to the day's air of privilege, its holiday possibilities, Enid's unusual mix of languor and excitement.

"We'll see," said Enid. She wanted to make the day a special one for them, special aside from the fact—which she was already almost certain of—that it would be the day of their mother's death. She wanted them to hold something in their minds that could throw a redeeming light on whatever came later. On herself, that is, and whatever way she would affect their lives later.

That morning Mrs. Quinn's pulse had been hard to find and she had not been able, apparently, to raise her head or open her eyes. A great change from yesterday, but Enid was not surprised. She had thought that great spurt of energy, that wicked outpouring talk, would be the last. She held a spoon with water in it to Mrs. Quinn's lips, and Mrs. Quinn drew a little of the water in. She made a mewing sound—the last trace, surely, of all her complaints. Enid did not call the doctor, because he was due to visit anyway later that day, probably early in the afternoon.

She shook up soapsuds in a jar and bent a piece of wire, and then another piece, to make bubble wands. She showed the children how to make bubbles, blowing steadily and carefully until as large a shining bladder as possible trembled on the wire, then shaking it delicately free. They chased the bubbles around the yard and kept them afloat till breezes caught them and hung them in the trees or on the eaves of the porch. What kept them alive then seemed to be the cries of admiration, screams of joy, rising up from below. Enid put no restriction on the noise they could make, and when the soapsud mixture was all used up she made more.

The doctor phoned when she was giving the children their lunch—Jell-O and a plate of cookies sprinkled with colored sugar and glasses of milk into which she had stirred chocolate syrup. He said he had been held up by a child's falling out of a tree and he would probably not be out before suppertime. Enid said softly, "I think she may be going."

"Well, keep her comfortable if you can," the doctor said. "You know how as well as I do."

Enid didn't phone Mrs. Green. She knew that Rupert would not be back yet from the auction and she didn't think that Mrs. Quinn, if she ever had another moment of consciousness, would want to see or hear her sister-in-law in the room. Nor did it seem likely that she would want to see her children. And there would be nothing good about seeing her for them to remember.

She didn't bother trying to take Mrs. Quinn's blood pressure anymore, or her temperature—just sponged off her face and arms and offered the water, which was no longer noticed. She turned on the fan, whose noise Mrs. Quinn had so often objected to. The smell rising from the body seemed to be changing, losing its ammoniac sharpness. Changing into the common odor of death.

She went out and sat on the steps. She took off her shoes and stockings and stretched out her legs in the sun. The children began cautiously to pester her, asking if she would take them down to the river, if they could sit in the boat, or if they found the oars could she take them rowing. She knew enough not to go that far in the way of desertion, but she asked them, Would they like to have a swimming pool? Two swimming pools? And she brought out the two laundry tubs, set them on the grass, and filled them with water from the cistern pump. They stripped to their underpants and lolled in the water, becoming Princess Elizabeth and Princess Margaret Rose.

"What do you think," said Enid, sitting on the grass with her head back and her eyes shut, "what do you think, if a person does something very bad, do they have to be punished?"

"Yes," said Lois immediately. "They have to get a licking."

"Who did it?" said Sylvie.

"Just thinking of anybody," said Enid. "Now, what if it was a very bad thing but nobody knew they did it? Should they tell that they did and be punished?"

Sylvie said, "I would know they did it."

"You would not," said Lois. "How would you know?"

"I would've seed them."

"You would not."

"You know the reason I think they should be punished?" Enid said. "It's because of how bad they are going to feel, in themselves. Even if nobody did see them and nobody ever knew. If you do something very bad and you are not punished you feel worse, and feel far worse, than if you are."

"Lois stold a green comb," Sylvie said.

"I did not," said Lois.

"I want you to remember that," Enid said.

Lois said, "It was just laying the side the road."

Enid went into the sickroom every half hour or so to wipe Mrs. Quinn's face and hands with a damp cloth. She never spoke to her and never touched her hand, except with the cloth. She had never absented herself like this before with anybody who was dying.

When she opened the door at around half past five she knew there was nobody alive in the room. The sheet was pulled out and Mrs. Quinn's head was hanging over the side of the bed, a fact that Enid did not record or mention to anybody. She had the body straightened out and cleaned and the bed put to rights before the doctor came. The children were still playing in the yard.

"JULY 5. Rain early a.m. L. and S. playing under porch. Fan off and on, complains noise. Half cup eggnog spoon at a time. B.P. up, pulse rapid, no complaints pain. Rain didn't cool off much. R.Q. in evening. Hay finished.

"July 6. Hot day, vy. close. Try fan but no. Sponge often. R.Q. in evening. Start to cut wheat tomorrow. Everything 1 or 2 wks ahead due to heat, rain.

"July 7. Cont'd heat. Won't take eggnog. Ginger ale from spoon. Vy. weak. Heavy rain last night, wind. R.Q. not able to cut, grain lodged some places.

"July 8. No eggnog. Ginger ale. Vomiting a.m. More alert. R.Q. to go to calf auction, gone 2 days. Dr. says go ahead.

"July 9. Vy. agitated. Terrible talk.

"July 10. Patient Mrs. Rupert (Jeanette) Quinn died today approx. 5 p.m. Heart failure due to uremia. (Glomerulonephritis.)"

ENID NEVER made a practice of waiting around for the funerals of people she had nursed. It seemed to her a good idea to get out of the house as soon as she decently could. Her presence could not help being a reminder of the time just before the death, which might have been dreary and full of physical disaster, and was now going to be glossed over with ceremony and hospitality and flowers and cakes.

Also, there was usually some female relative who would be in place to take over the household completely, putting Enid suddenly in the position of unwanted guest.

Mrs. Green, in fact, arrived at the Quinns' house before the undertaker did. Rupert was not back yet. The doctor was in the kitchen drinking a cup of tea and talking to Enid about another case that she could take up now that this was finished. Enid was hedging, saying that she had thought of taking some time off. The children were upstairs. They had been told that their mother had gone to heaven, which for them had put the cap on this rare and eventful day.

Mrs. Green was shy until the doctor left. She stood at the window to see him turn his car around and drive away. Then she said, "Maybe I shouldn't say it right now, but I will. I'm glad it happened now and not later when the summer was over and they were started back to school. Now I'll have time to get them used to living at our place and used to the idea of the new school they'll be going to. Rupert, he'll have to get used to it, too."

This was the first time that Enid had realized that Mrs. Green meant to take the children to live with her, not just to stay for a while. Mrs. Green was eager to manage the move, had been looking forward to it, probably, for some time. Very likely she had the children's rooms ready and material bought to make them new clothes. She had a large house and no children of her own.

"You must be wanting to get off home yourself," she said to Enid. As long as there was another woman in the house it might look like a rival home, and it might be harder for her brother to see the necessity of moving the children out for good. "Rupert can run you in when he gets here."

Enid said that it was all right, her mother was coming out to pick her up.

"Oh, I forgot your mother," said Mrs. Green. "Her and her snappy little car."

She brightened up and began to open the cupboard doors, checking on the glasses and the teacups—were they clean for the funeral?

"Somebody's been busy," she said, quite relieved about Enid now and ready to be complimentary.

Mr. Green was waiting outside, in the truck, with the Greens' dog, General. Mrs. Green called upstairs for Lois and Sylvie, and they came running down with some clothes in brown paper bags. They ran through the kitchen and slammed the door, without taking any notice of Enid.

"That's something that's going to have to change," said Mrs. Green, meaning the door slamming. Enid could hear the children shouting their greetings to General and General barking excitedly in return.

Two DAYS later Enid was back, driving her mother's car herself. She came late in the afternoon, when the funeral would have been well over. There were no extra cars parked outside, which meant that the women who had helped in the kitchen had all gone home, taking with them the extra chairs and teacups and the large coffeepot that belonged to their church. The grass was marked with car tracks and some dropped crushed flowers.

She had to knock on the door now. She had to wait to be asked in.

She heard Rupert's heavy, steady footsteps. She spoke some greeting to him when he stood in front of her on the other side of the screen door, but she didn't look into his face. He was in his shirtsleeves, but was wearing his suit trousers. He undid the hook of the door.

"I wasn't sure anybody would be here," Enid said. "I thought you might still be at the barn."

Rupert said, "They all pitched in with the chores."

She could smell whiskey when he spoke, but he didn't sound drunk.

"I thought you were one of the women come back to collect something you forgot," he said.

Enid said, "I didn't forget anything. I was just wondering, how are the children?"

"They're fine. They're at Olive's."

It seemed uncertain whether he was going to ask her in. It was bewilderment that stopped him, not hostility. She had not prepared herself for this first awkward part of the conversation. So that she wouldn't have to look at him, she looked around at the sky.

"You can feel the evenings getting shorter," she said. "Even if it isn't a month since the longest day."

"That's true," said Rupert. Now he opened the door and stood aside and she went in. On the table was a cup without a saucer. She sat down at the opposite side of the table from where he had been sitting. She was wearing a dark-green silk-crepe dress and suede shoes to match. When she put these things on she had thought how this might be the last time that she would dress herself and the last clothes she would ever wear. She had done her hair up in a French braid and powdered her face. Her care, her vanity, seemed foolish but were necessary to her. She had been awake now three nights in a row, awake every minute, and she had not been able to eat, even to fool her mother.

"Was it specially difficult this time?" her mother had said. She hated discussion of illness or deathbeds, and the fact that she had brought herself to ask this meant that Enid's upset was obvious.

"Was it the children you'd got fond of?" she said. "The poor little monkeys."

Enid said it was just the problem of settling down after a long case, and a hopeless case of course had its own strain. She did not go out of her mother's house in the daytime, but she did go for walks at night, when she could be sure of not meeting anybody and having to talk. She had found herself walking past the walls of the county jail. She knew there was a prison yard behind those walls where hangings had once taken place. But not for years and years. They must do it in some large central prison now, when they had to do it. And it was a long time since anybody from this community had committed a sufficiently serious crime.

SITTING ACROSS the table from Rupert, facing the door of Mrs. Quinn's room, she had almost forgotten her excuse, lost track of the way things were to go. She felt her purse in her lap, the weight of her camera in it—that reminded her.

"There is one thing I'd like to ask you," she said. "I thought I might as well now, because I wouldn't get another chance."

Rupert said, "What's that?"

"I know you've got a rowboat. So I wanted to ask you to row me out to the middle of the river. And I could get a picture. I'd like to get a picture of the riverbank. It's beautiful there, the willow trees along the bank."

"All right," said Rupert, with the careful lack of surprise that country people will show, regarding the frivolity—the rudeness, even—of visitors.

That was what she was now—a visitor.

Her plan was to wait until they got out to the middle of the river, then to tell him that she could not swim. First ask him how deep he thought the water would be there—and he would surely say, after all the rain they had been having, that it might be seven or eight, or even ten, feet. Then tell him that she could not swim.

And that would not be a lie. She had grown up in Walley, on the lake, she had played on the beach every summer of her childhood, she was a strong girl and good at games, but she was frightened of the water, and no coaxing or demonstrating or shaming had ever worked with her—she had not learned to swim.

He would only have to give her a shove with one of the oars and topple her into the water and let her sink. Then leave the boat out on the water and swim to shore, change his clothes, and say that he had come in from the barn or from a walk and found the car there, and where was she? Even the camera if found would make it more plausible. She had taken the boat out to get a picture, then somehow fallen into the river.

Once he understood his advantage, she would tell him. She would ask, Is it true?

If it was not true, he would hate her for asking. If it was true—and didn't she believe all the time that it was true?—he would hate her in another, more dangerous way. Even if she said at once—and meant it, she would mean it—that she was never going to tell.

She would speak very quietly all the time, remembering how voices carry out on the water on a summer evening.

I am not going to tell, but you are. You can't live on with that kind of secret.

You cannot live in the world with such a burden. You will not be able to stand your life.

If she had got so far, and he had neither denied what she said nor pushed her into the river, Enid would know that she had won the gamble. It would take some more talking, more absolutely firm but quiet persuasion, to bring him to the point where he would start to row back to shore.

Or, lost, he would say, What will I do? and she would take him one step at a time, saying first, Row back.

The first step in a long, dreadful journey. She would tell him every step and she would stay with him for as many of them as she could. Tie up the boat now. Walk up the bank. Walk through the meadow. Open the gate. She would walk behind him or in front, whichever seemed better to him. Across the yard and up the porch and into the kitchen.

They will say goodbye and get into their separate cars and then it will be his business where he goes. And she will not phone the Police Office the next day. She will wait and they will phone her and she will go to see him in jail. Every day, or as often as they will let her, she will sit and talk to him in jail, and she will write him letters as well. If they take him to another jail she will go there; even if she is allowed to see him only once a month she will be close by. And in court—yes, every day in court, she will be sitting where he can see her.

She does not think anyone would get a death sentence for this sort of murder, which was in a way accidental, and was surely a crime of passion, but the shadow is there, to sober her when she feels that these pictures of devotion, of a bond that is like love but beyond love, are becoming indecent.

Now it has started. With her asking to be taken on the river, her excuse of the picture. Both she and Rupert are standing up, and she is facing the door of the sickroom—now again the front room—which is shut.

She says a foolish thing.

"Are the quilts taken down off the windows?"

He doesn't seem to know for a minute what she is talking about. Then he says, "The quilts. Yes. I think it was Olive took them down. In there was where we had the funeral."

"I was only thinking. The sun would fade them."

He opens the door and she comes around the table and they stand looking into the room. He says, "You can go in if you like. It's all right. Come in."

The bed is gone, of course. The furniture is pushed back against the walls. The middle of the room, where they would have set up the chairs for the funeral, is bare. So is the space in between the north windows—that must have been where they put the coffin. The table where Enid was used to setting the basin, and laying out cloths, cotton wool, spoons, medicine, is jammed into a corner and has a bouquet of delphiniums sitting on it. The tall windows still hold plenty of daylight.

"Lies" is the word that Enid can hear now, out of all the words that Mrs. Quinn said in that room. *Lies. I bet it's all lies.*

COULD A person make up something so detailed and diabolical? The answer is yes. A sick person's mind, a dying person's mind, could fill up with all kinds of trash and organize that trash in a most convincing way. Enid's own mind, when she was asleep in this room, had filled up with the most disgusting inventions, with filth. Lies of that nature could be waiting around in the corners of a person's mind, hanging like bats in the corners, waiting to take advantage of any kind of darkness. You can never say, Nobody could make that up. Look how elaborate dreams are, layer over layer in them, so that the part you can remember and put into words is just the bit you can scratch off the top.

When Enid was four or five years old she had told her mother that she had gone into her father's office and that she had seen him sitting behind his desk with a woman on his knee. All she could remember about this woman, then and now, was that she wore a hat with a great many flowers on it and a veil (a hat quite out of fashion even at that time), and that her blouse or dress was unbuttoned and there was one bare breast sticking out, the tip of it disappearing into Enid's father's mouth. She had told her mother about this in perfect certainty that she had seen it. She said, "One of her fronts was stuck in Daddy's mouth." She did not know the word for breasts, though she did know they came in pairs.

Her mother said, "Now, Enid. What are you talking about? What on earth is a front?"

"Like an ice-cream cone," Enid said.

And she saw it that way, exactly. She could see it that way still. The biscuit-colored cone with its mound of vanilla ice cream squashed against the woman's chest and the wrong end sticking into her father's mouth.

Her mother then did a very unexpected thing. She undid her own dress and took out a dull-skinned object that flopped over her hand. "Like this?" she said.

Enid said no. "An ice-cream cone," she said.

"Then that was a dream," her mother said. "Dreams are sometimes downright silly. Don't tell Daddy about it. It's too silly."

Enid did not believe her mother right away, but in a year or so she saw that such an explanation had to be right, because ice-cream cones did not ever arrange themselves in that way on ladies' chests and they were never so big. When she was older still she realized that the hat must have come from some picture.

Lies.

SHE HADN'T asked him yet, she hadn't spoken. Nothing yet committed her to asking. It was still *before.* Mr. Willens had still driven himself into Jutland Pond, on purpose or by accident. Everybody still believed that, and as far as Rupert was concerned Enid believed it, too. And as long as that was so, this room and this house and her life held a different possibility, an entirely different possibility from the one she had been living with (or glorying in—however you wanted to put it) for the last few days. The different possibility was coming closer to her, and all she needed to do was to keep quiet and let it come. Through her silence, her collaboration in a silence, what benefits could bloom. For others, and for herself.

This was what most people knew. A simple thing that it had taken her so long to understand. This was how to keep the world habitable.

She had started to weep. Not with grief but with an onslaught of relief that she had not known she was looking for. Now she looked into Rupert's face and saw that his eyes were bloodshot and the skin around them puckered and dried out, as if he had been weeping, too.

He said, "She wasn't lucky in her life."

Enid excused herself and went to get her handkerchief, which was in her purse on the table. She was embarrassed now that she had dressed herself up in readiness for such a melodramatic fate.

"I don't know what I was thinking of," she said. "I can't walk down to the river in these shoes."

Rupert shut the door of the front room.

"If you want to go we can still go," he said. "There ought to be a pair of rubber boots would fit you somewhere."

Not hers, Enid hoped. No. Hers would be too small.

Rupert opened a bin in the woodshed, just outside the kitchen door. Enid had never looked into that bin. She had thought it contained firewood, which she had certainly had no need of that summer. Rupert lifted out several single rubber boots and even snow boots, trying to find a pair.

"These look like they might do," he said. "They maybe were Mother's. Or even mine before my feet got full size."

He pulled out something that looked like a piece of a tent, then, by a broken strap, an old school satchel.

"Forgot all the stuff that was in here," he said, letting these things fall back and throwing the unusable boots on top of them. He dropped the lid and gave a private, grieved, and formal-sounding sigh.

A house like this, lived in by one family for so long a time, and neglected for the past several years, would have plenty of bins, drawers, shelves, suitcases, trunks, crawl spaces full of things that it would be up to Enid to sort out, saving and labelling some, restoring some to use, sending others by the boxload to the dump. When she got that chance she wouldn't balk at it. She would make this house into a place that had no secrets from her and where all order was as she had decreed.

He set the boots down in front of her while she was bent over unbuckling her shoes. She smelled under the whiskey the bitter breath that came after a sleepless night and a long harsh day; she smelled the deeply sweat-soaked skin of a hardworked man that no washing—at least the washing he did—could get quite fresh. No bodily smell—even the smell of semen—was unfamiliar to her, but there was something new and invasive about the smell of a body so distinctly not in her power or under her care.

That was welcome.

"See can you walk," he said.

She could walk. She walked in front of him to the gate. He bent over her shoulder to swing it open for her. She waited while he bolted it, then stood aside to let him walk ahead, because he had brought a little hatchet from the woodshed, to clear their path.

"The cows were supposed to keep the growth down," he said. "But there's things cows won't eat."

She said, "I was only down here once. Early in the morning."

The desperation of her frame of mind then had to seem childish to her now.

Rupert went along chopping at the big fleshy thistles. The sun cast a level, dusty light on the bulk of the trees ahead. The air was clear in some places, then suddenly you would enter a cloud of tiny bugs. Bugs no bigger than specks of dust that were constantly in motion yet kept themselves together in the shape of a pillar or a cloud. How did they manage to do that? And how did they choose one spot over another to do it in? It must have something to do with feeding. But they never seemed to be still enough to feed.

When she and Rupert went underneath the roof of summer leaves it was dusk, it was almost night. You had to watch that you didn't trip over roots that swelled up out of the path, or hit your head on the dangling, surprisingly tough-stemmed vines. Then a flash of water came through the black branches. The lit-up water near the opposite bank of the river, the trees over there still decked out in light. On this side—they were going down the bank now, through the willows—the water was tea-colored but clear.

And the boat waiting, riding in the shadows, just the same.

"The oars are hid," said Rupert. He went into the willows to locate them. In a moment she lost sight of him. She went closer to the water's edge, where her boots sank into the mud a little and held her. If she tried to, she could still hear Rupert's movements in the bushes. But if she concentrated on the motion of the boat, a slight and secretive motion, she could feel as if everything for a long way around had gone quiet.

The Children Stay

Thirty years ago, a family was spending a holiday together on the east coast of Vancouver Island. A young father and mother, their two small daughters, and an older couple, the husband's parents.

What perfect weather. Every morning, every morning it's like this, the first pure sunlight falling through the high branches, burning away the mist over the still water of Georgia Strait. The tide out, a great empty stretch of sand still damp but easy to walk on, like cement in its very last stage of drying. The tide is actually less far out; every morning, the pavilion of sand is shrinking, but it still seems ample enough. The changes in the tide are a matter of great interest to the grandfather, not so much to anyone else.

Pauline, the young mother, doesn't really like the beach as well as she likes the road that runs behind the cottages for a mile or so north till it stops at the bank of the little river that runs into the sea.

If it wasn't for the tide, it would be hard to remember that this is the sea. You look across the water to the mountains on the mainland, the ranges that are the western wall of the continent of North America. These humps and peaks coming clear now through the mist and glimpsed here and there through the trees, by Pauline as she pushes her daughter's stroller along the road, are also of interest to the grandfather. And to his son Brian, who is Pauline's husband. The two men are continually trying to decide which is what. Which of these shapes are actual continental mountains and which are improbable heights of the islands that ride in front of the shore? It's hard to sort things out when the array is so complicated and parts of it shift their distance in the day's changing light.

But there is a map, set up under glass, between the cottages and the beach. You can stand there looking at the map, then looking at what's in front of you, looking back at the map again, until you get things sorted out. The grandfather and Brian do this every day, usually getting into an argument—though you'd think there would not be much room for disagreement with the map right there. Brian chooses to see the map as inexact. But his father will not hear a word of criticism about any aspect of this place, which was his choice for the holiday. The map, like the accommodation and the weather, is perfect.

Brian's mother won't look at the map. She says it boggles her mind. The men laugh at her, they accept that her mind is boggled. Her husband believes that this is because she is a female. Brian believes that it's because she's his mother. Her concern is always about whether anybody is hungry yet, or thirsty, whether the children have their sun hats on and have been rubbed with protective lotion. And what is the strange bite on Caitlin's arm that doesn't look like the bite of a mosquito? She makes her husband wear a floppy cotton hat and thinks that Brian should wear one too—she reminds him of how sick he got from the sun, that summer they went to the Okanagan, when he was a child. Sometimes Brian says to her, "Oh, dry up, Mother." His tone is mostly affectionate, but his father may ask him if that's the way he thinks he can talk to his mother nowadays.

"She doesn't mind," says Brian.

"How do you know?" says his father.

"Oh for Pete's sake," says his mother.

PAULINE SLIDES out of bed as soon as she's awake every morning, slides out of reach of Brian's long, sleepily searching arms and legs. What wakes her are the first squeaks and mutters of the baby, Mara, in the children's room, then the creak of the crib as Mara—sixteen months old now, getting to the end of babyhood—pulls herself up to stand hanging on to the railing. She continues her soft amiable talk as Pauline lifts her out—Caitlin, nearly five, shifting about but not waking, in her nearby bed—and as she is carried into the kitchen to be changed, on the floor. Then she is settled into her stroller, with a biscuit and a bottle of apple juice, while Pauline gets into her sundress and sandals, goes to the bathroom, combs out her hair—all as quickly and quiedy as possible. They leave the cottage; they head past some other cottages for the bumpy unpaved road that is still mostly in deep morning shadow, the floor of a tunnel under fir and cedar trees.

The grandfather, also an early riser, sees them from the porch of his cottage, and Pauline sees him. But all that is necessary is a wave. He and

Pauline never have much to say to each other (though sometimes there's an affinity they feel, in the midst of some long-drawn-out antics of Brian's or some apologetic but insistent fuss made by the grandmother; there's an awareness of not looking at each other, lest their look should reveal a bleakness that would discredit others).

On this holiday Pauline steals time to be by herself—being with Mara is still almost the same thing as being by herself. Early morning walks, the late-morning hour when she washes and hangs out the diapers. She could have had another hour or so in the afternoons, while Mara is napping. But Brian has fixed up a shelter on the beach, and he carries the playpen down every day, so that Mara can nap there and Pauline won't have to absent herself. He says his parents may be offended if she's always sneaking off. He agrees though that she does need some time to go over her lines for the play she's going to be in, back in Victoria, this September.

Pauline is not an actress. This is an amateur production, but she is not even an amateur actress. She didn't try out for the role, though it happened that she had already read the play. *Eurydice* by Jean Anouilh. But then, Pauline has read all sorts of things.

She was asked if she would like to be in this play by a man she met at a barbecue, in June. The people at the barbecue were mostly teachers and their wives or husbands—it was held at the house of the principal of the high school where Brian teaches. The woman who taught French was a widow—she had brought her grown son who was staying for the summer with her and working as a night clerk in a downtown hotel. She told everybody that he had got a job teaching at a college in western Washington State and would be going there in the fall.

Jeffrey Toom was his name. "Without the *B*," he said, as if the staleness of the joke wounded him. It was a different name from his mother's, because she had been widowed twice, and he was the son of her first husband. About the job he said, "No guarantee it'll last, it's a one-year appointment."

What was he going to teach?

"Dram-ah," he said, drawing the word out in a mocking way.

He spoke of his present job disparagingly, as well.

"It's a pretty sordid place," he said. "Maybe you heard—a hooker was killed there last winter. And then we get the usual losers checking in to OD or bump themselves off."

People did not quite know what to make of this way of talking and drifted away from him. Except for Pauline.

"I'm thinking about putting on a play," he said. "Would you like to be in it?" He asked her if she had ever heard of a play called *Eurydice*.

Pauline said, "You mean Anouilh's?" and he was unflatteringly surprised. He immediately said he didn't know if it would ever work out. "I just thought it might be interesting to see if you could do something different here in the land of Noël Coward."

Pauline did not remember when there had been a play by Noël Coward put on in Victoria, though she supposed there had been several. She said, "We saw *The Duchess of Malfi* last winter at the college. And the little theater did *A Resounding Tinkle,* but we didn't see it."

"Yeah. Well," he said, flushing. She had thought he was older than she was, at least as old as Brian (who was thirty, though people were apt to say he didn't act it), but as soon as he started talking to her, in this offhand, dismissive way, never quite meeting her eyes, she suspected that he was younger than he'd like to appear. Now with that flush she was sure of it.

As it turned out, he was a year younger than she was. Twenty-five.

She said that she couldn't be Eurydice; she couldn't act. But Brian came over to see what the conversation was about and said at once that she must try it.

"She just needs a kick in the behind," Brian said to Jeffrey. "She's like a little mule, it's hard to get her started. No, seriously, she's too self-effacing, I tell her that all the time. She's very smart. She's actually a lot smarter than I am."

At that Jeffrey did look directly into Pauline's eyes—impertinently and searchingly—and she was the one who was flushing.

He had chosen her immediately as his Eurydice because of the way she looked. But it was not because she was beautiful. "I'd never put a beautiful girl in that part," he said. "I don't know if I'd ever put a beautiful girl on stage in anything. It's too much. It's distracting."

So what did he mean about the way she looked? He said it was her hair, which was long and dark and rather bushy (not in style at that time), and her pale skin ("Stay out of the sun this summer") and most of all her eyebrows.

"I never liked them," said Pauline, not quite sincerely. Her eyebrows were level, dark, luxuriant. They dominated her face. Like her hair, they were not in style. But if she had really disliked them, wouldn't she have plucked them?

Jeffrey seemed not to have heard her. "They give you a sulky look and that's disturbing," he said. "Also your jaw's a little heavy and that's sort of Greek. It would be better in a movie where I could get you close up. The routine thing for Eurydice would be a girl who looked ethereal. I don't want ethereal."

As she walked Mara along the road, Pauline did work at the lines. There was a speech at the end that was giving her trouble. She bumped the stroller along and repeated to herself, " 'You are terrible, you know, you are terrible like the angels. You think everybody's going forward, as brave and bright as you are—oh, don't look at me, please, darling, don't look at me—perhaps I'm not what you wish I was, but I'm here, and I'm warm, I'm kind, and I love you. I'll give you all the happiness I can. Don't look at me. Don't look. Let me live.'"

She had left something out. "'Perhaps I'm not what you wish I was, but you feel me here, don't you? I'm warm and I'm kind—'"

She had told Jeffrey that she thought the play was beautiful.

He said, "Really?" What she'd said didn't please or surprise him—he seemed to feel it was predictable, superfluous. He would never describe a play in that way. He spoke of it more as a hurdle to be got over. Also a challenge to be flung at various enemies. At the academic snots—as he called them—who had done *The Duchess of Malfi*. And at the social twits—as he called them—in the little theater. He saw himself as an outsider heaving his weight against these people, putting on his play—he called it his—in the teeth of their contempt and opposition. In the beginning Pauline thought that this must be all in his imagination and that it was more likely these people knew nothing about him. Then something would happen that could be, but might not be, a coincidence. Repairs had to be done on the church hall where the play was to be performed, making it unobtainable. There was an unexpected increase in the cost of printing advertising posters. She found herself seeing it his way. If you were going to be around him much, you almost had to see it his way—arguing was dangerous and exhausting.

"Sons of bitches," said Jeffrey between his teeth, but with some satisfaction. "I'm not surprised."

The rehearsals were held upstairs in an old building on Fisgard Street. Sunday afternoon was the only time that everybody could get there, though there were fragmentary rehearsals during the week. The retired harbor pilot who played Monsieur Henri was able to attend every rehearsal, and got to have an irritating familiarity with everybody else's lines. But the hairdresser—who had experience only with Gilbert and Sullivan but now found herself playing Eurydice's mother—could not leave her shop for long at any other time. The bus driver who played her lover had his daily employment as well, and so had the waiter who played Orphée (he was the only one of them who hoped to be a real actor). Pauline had to depend on sometimes undependable high-school baby-sitters—for the first six weeks of the summer Brian was busy teaching summer school—and Jeffrey himself had to be at his hotel job by eight o'clock in the evenings. But on Sunday afternoons they were all there. While other people swam at Thetis Lake, or thronged Beacon Hill Park to walk under the trees and feed the ducks, or drove far out of town to the

Pacific beaches, Jeffrey and his crew labored in the dusty high-ceilinged room on Fisgard Street. The windows were rounded at the top as in some plain and dignified church, and propped open in the heat with whatever objects could be found—ledger books from the 1920s belonging to the hat shop that had once operated downstairs, or pieces of wood left over from the picture frames made by the artist whose canvases were now stacked against one wall and apparently abandoned. The glass was grimy, but outside the sunlight bounced off the sidewalks, the empty gravelled parking lots, the low stuccoed buildings, with what seemed a special Sunday brightness. Hardly anybody moved through these downtown streets. Nothing was open except the occasional hole-in-the-wall coffee shop or fly-specked convenience store.

Pauline was the one who went out at the break to get soft drinks and coffee. She was the one who had the least to say about the play and the way it was going—even though she was the only one who had read it before—because she alone had never done any acting. So it seemed proper for her to volunteer. She enjoyed her short walk in the empty streets—she felt as if she had become an urban person, someone detached and solitary, who lived in the glare of an important dream. Sometimes she thought of Brian at home, working in the garden and keeping an eye on the children. Or perhaps he had taken them to Dallas Road—she recalled a promise—to sail boats on the pond. That life seemed ragged and tedious compared to what went on in the rehearsal room—the hours of effort, the concentration, the sharp exchanges, the sweating and tension. Even the taste of the coffee, its scalding bitterness, and the fact that it was chosen by nearly everybody in preference to a fresher-tasting and maybe more healthful drink out of the cooler seemed satisfying to her. And she liked the look of the shop-windows. This was not one of the dolled-up streets near the harbor—it was a street of shoe- and bicycle-repair shops, discount linen and fabric stores, of clothes and furniture that had been so long in the windows that they looked secondhand even if they weren't. On some windows sheets of golden plastic as frail and crinkled as old cellophane were stretched inside the glass to protect the merchandise from the sun. All these enterprises had been left behind just for this one day, but they had a look of being fixed in time as much as cave paintings or relics under sand.

WHEN SHE said that she had to go away for the two-week holiday Jeffrey looked thunderstruck, as if he had never imagined that things like holidays could come into her life. Then he turned grim and slightly satirical, as if this was just another blow that he might have expected.

Pauline explained that she would miss only the one Sunday—the one in the middle of the two weeks—because she and Brian were driving up the island on a Monday and coming back on a Sunday morning. She promised to get back in time for rehearsal. Privately she wondered how she would do this—it always took so much longer than you expected to pack up and get away. She wondered if she could possibly come back by herself, on the morning bus. That would probably be too much to ask for. She didn't mention it.

She couldn't ask him if it was only the play he was thinking about, only her absence from a rehearsal that caused the thundercloud. At the moment, it very likely was. When he spoke to her at rehearsals there was never any suggestion that he ever spoke to her in any other way. The only difference in his treatment of her was that perhaps he expected less of her, of her acting, than he did of the others. And that would be understandable to anybody. She was the only one chosen out of the blue, for the way she looked—the others had all shown up at the audition he had advertised on the signs put up in cafés and bookstores around town. From her he appeared to want an immobility or awkwardness that he didn't want from the rest of them. Perhaps it was because, in the latter part of the play, she was supposed to be a person who had already died.

Yet she thought they all knew, the rest of the cast all knew, what was going on, in spite of Jeffrey's offhand and abrupt and none too civil ways. They knew that after every one of them had straggled off home, he would walk across the room and bolt the staircase door. (At first Pauline had pretended to leave with the rest and had even got into her car and circled the block, but later such a trick had come to seem insulting, not just to herself and Jeffrey, but to the others whom she was sure would never betray her, bound as they all were under the temporary but potent spell of the play.)

Jeffrey crossed the room and bolted the door. Every time, this was like a new decision, which he had to make. Until it was done, she wouldn't look at him. The sound of the bolt being pushed into place, the ominous or fatalistic sound of the metal hitting metal, gave her a localized shock of capitulation. But she didn't make a move, she waited for him to come back to her with the whole story of the afternoon's labor draining out of his face, the expression of matter-of-fact and customary disappointment cleared away, replaced by the live energy she always found surprising.

"So. TELL us what this play of yours is about," Brian's father said. "Is it one of those ones where they take their clothes off on the stage?"

"Now don't tease her," said Brian's mother.

Brian and Pauline had put the children to bed and walked over to his parents' cottage for an evening drink. The sunset was behind them, behind the forests of Vancouver Island, but the mountains in front of them, all clear now and hard-cut against the sky, shone in its pink light. Some high inland mountains were capped with pink summer snow.

"Nobody takes their clothes off, Dad," said Brian in his booming schoolroom voice. "You know why? Because they haven't got any clothes on in the first place. It's the latest style. They're going to put on a bare-naked *Hamlet* next. Bare-naked *Romeo and Juliet*. Boy, that balcony scene where Romeo is climbing up the trellis and he gets stuck in the rosebushes—"

"Oh, Brian," said his mother.

"The story of Orpheus and Eurydice is that Eurydice died," Pauline said. "And Orpheus goes down to the underworld to try to get her back. And his wish is granted, but only if he promises not to look at her. Not to look back at her. She's walking behind him—"

"Twelve paces," said Brian. "As is only right."

"It's a Greek story, but it's set in modern times," said Pauline. "At least this version is. More or less modern. Orpheus is a musician travelling around with his father—they're both musicians—and Eurydice is an actress. This is in France."

"Translated?" Brian's father said.

"No," said Brian. "But don't worry, it's not in French. It was written in Transylvanian."

"It's so hard to make sense of anything," Brian's mother said with a worried laugh. "It's so hard, with Brian around."

"It's in English," Pauline said.

"And you're what's-her-name?"

She said, "I'm Eurydice."

"He get you back okay?"

"No," she said. "He looks back at me, and then I have to stay dead."

"Oh, an unhappy ending," Brian's mother said.

"You're so gorgeous?" said Brian's father skeptically. "He can't stop himself from looking back?"

"It's not that," said Pauline. But at this point she felt that something had been achieved by her father-in-law, he had done what he meant to do, which was the same thing that he nearly always meant to do, in any conversation she had with him. And that was to break through the structure of some explanation he had asked her for, and she had unwillingly but patiently given, and, with a seemingly negligent kick, knock it into rubble. He had been dangerous to her for a long time in this way, but he wasn't particularly so tonight.

But Brian did not know that. Brian was still figuring out how to come to her rescue.

"Pauline is gorgeous," Brian said.

"Yes indeed," said his mother.

"Maybe if she'd go to the hairdresser," his father said. But Pauline's long hair was such an old objection of his that it had become a family joke. Even Pauline laughed. She said, "I can't afford to till we get the veranda roof fixed." And Brian laughed boisterously, full of relief that she was able to take all this as a joke. It was what he had always told her to do.

"Just kid him back," he said. "It's the only way to handle him."

"Yeah, well, if you'd got yourselves a decent house," said his father. But this like Pauline's hair was such a familiar sore point that it couldn't rouse anybody. Brian and Pauline had bought a handsome house in bad repair on a street in Victoria where old mansions were being turned into ill-used apartment buildings. The house, the street, the messy old Garry oaks, the fact that no basement had been blasted out under the house, were all a horror to Brian's father. Brian usually agreed with him and tried to go him one further. If his father pointed at the house next door all criss-crossed with black fire escapes, and asked what kind of neighbors they had, Brian said, "Really poor people, Dad. Drug addicts." And when his father wanted to know how it was heated, he'd said, "Coal furnace. Hardly any of them left these days, you can get coal really cheap. Of course it's dirty and it kind of stinks."

So what his father said now about a decent house might be some kind of peace signal. Or could be taken so.

Brian was an only son. He was a math teacher. His father was a civil engineer and part owner of a contracting company. If he had hoped that he would have a son who was an engineer and might come into the company, there was never any mention of it. Pauline had asked Brian whether he thought the carping about their house and her hair and the books she read might be a cover for this larger disappointment, but Brian had said, "Nope. In our family we complain about just whatever we want to complain about. We ain't subtle, ma'am."

Pauline still wondered, when she heard his mother talking about how teachers ought to be the most honored people in the world and they did not get half the credit they deserved and that she didn't know how Brian managed it, day after day. Then his father might say, "That's right," or, "I sure wouldn't want to do it, I can tell you that. They couldn't pay me to do it."

"Don't worry Dad," Brian would say. "They wouldn't pay you much."

Brian in his everyday life was a much more dramatic person than Jeffrey. He dominated his classes by keeping up a parade of jokes and antics, extending the role that he had always played, Pauline believed, with his mother and father. He acted dumb, he bounced back from pretended humiliations, he traded insults. He was a bully in a good cause—a chivvying cheerful indestructible bully.

"Your boy has certainly made his mark with us," the principal said to Pauline. "He has not just survived, which is something in itself. He has made his mark."

Your boy.

Brian called his students boneheads. His tone was affectionate, fatalistic. He said that his father was the King of the Philistines, a pure and natural barbarian. And that his mother was a dishrag, good-natured and worn out. But however he dismissed such people, he could not be long without them. He took his students on camping trips. And he could not imagine a summer without this shared holiday. He was mortally afraid, every year, that Pauline would refuse to go along. Or that, having agreed to go, she was going to be miserable, take offense at something his father said, complain about how much time she had to spend with his mother, sulk because there was no way they could do anything by themselves. She might decide to spend all day in their own cottage, reading and pretending to have a sunburn.

All those things had happened, on previous holidays. But this year she was easing up. He told her he could see that, and he was grateful to her.

"I know it's an effort," he said. "It's different for me. They're my parents and I'm used to not taking them seriously."

Pauline came from a family that took things so seriously that her parents had got a divorce. Her mother was now dead. She had a distant, though cordial, relationship with her father and her two much older sisters. She said that they had nothing in common. She knew Brian could not understand how that could be a reason. She saw what comfort it gave him, this year, to see things going so well. She had thought it was laziness or cowardice that kept him from breaking the arrangement, but now she saw that it was something far more positive. He needed to have his wife and his parents and his children bound together like this, he needed to involve Pauline in his life with his parents and to bring his parents to some recognition of her—though the recognition, from his father, would always be muffled and contrary, and from his mother too profuse, too easily come by, to mean much. Also he wanted Pauline to be connected, he wanted the children to be connected, to his own childhood—he wanted these holidays to be linked to holidays of his childhood with their lucky or unlucky weather, car troubles or driving records, boating scares, bee stings, marathon Monopoly games, to all the things that he told his mother he was bored to death hearing about. He wanted pictures from this summer to be taken, and fitted into his mother's album, a continuation of all the other pictures that he groaned at the mention of.

The only time they could talk to each other was in bed, late at night. But they did talk then, more than was usual with them at home, where Brian was so tired that often he fell immediately asleep. And in ordinary daylight it was often hard to talk to him because of his jokes. She could see the joke brightening his eyes (his coloring was very like hers—dark hair and pale skin and gray eyes, but her eyes were cloudy and his were light, like clear water over stones). She could see it pulling at the corners of his mouth, as he foraged among your words to catch a pun or the start of a rhyme—anything that could take the conversation away, into absurdity. His whole body, tall and loosely joined together and still almost as skinny as a teenager's, twitched with comic propensity. Before she married him, Pauline had a friend named Gracie, a rather grumpy-looking girl, subversive about men. Brian had thought her a girl whose spirits needed a boost, and so he made even more than the usual effort. And Gracie said to Pauline, "How can you stand the nonstop show?"

"That's not the real Brian," Pauline had said. "He's different when we're alone." But looking back, she wondered how true that had ever been. Had she said it simply to defend her choice, as you did when you had made up your mind to get married?

So talking in the dark had something to do with the fact that she could not see his face. And that he knew she couldn't see his face.

But even with the window open on the unfamiliar darkness and stillness of the night, he teased a little. He had to speak of Jeffrey as Monsieur le Directeur, which made the play or the fact that it was a French play slightly ridiculous. Or perhaps it was Jeffrey himself, Jeffrey's seriousness about the play, that had to be called in question.

Pauline didn't care. It was such a pleasure and a relief to her to mention Jeffrey's name.

Most of the time she didn't mention him; she circled around that pleasure. She described all the others, instead. The hairdresser and the harbor pilot and the waiter and the old man who claimed to have once acted on the radio. He played Orphée's father and gave Jeffrey the most trouble, because he had the stubbornest notions of his own, about acting.

The middle-aged impresario Monsieur Dulac was played by a twenty-four-year-old travel agent. And Mathias, who was Eurydice's former boyfriend, presumably around her own age, was played by the manager of a shoe store, who was married and a father of children.

Brian wanted to know why Monsieur le Directeur hadn't cast these two the other way round.

"That's the way he does things," Pauline said. "What he sees in us is something only he can see."

For instance, she said, the waiter was a clumsy Orphée.

"He's only nineteen, he's so shy Jeffrey has to keep at him. He tells him not to act like he's making love to his grandmother. He has to tell him what to do. *Keep your arms around her a little longer, stroke her here a little.* I don't know how it's going to work—I just have to trust Jeffrey, that he knows what he's doing."

"'Stroke her here a little'?" said Brian. "Maybe I should come around and keep an eye on these rehearsals."

When she had started to quote Jeffrey Pauline had felt a giving-way in her womb or the bottom of her stomach, a shock that had travelled oddly upwards and hit her vocal cords. She had to cover up this quaking by growling in a way that was supposed to be an imitation (though Jeffrey never growled or ranted or carried on in any theatrical way at all).

"But there's a point about him being so innocent," she said hurriedly. "Being not so physical. Being awkward." And she began to talk about Orphée in the play, not the waiter. Orphée has a problem with love or reality. Orphée will not put up with anything less than perfection. He wants a love that is outside of ordinary life. He wants a perfect Eurydice.

"Eurydice is more realistic. She's carried on with Mathias and with Monsieur Dulac. She's been around her mother and her mother's lover. She knows what people are like. But she loves Orphée. She loves him better in a way than he loves her. She loves him better because she's not such a fool. She loves him like a human person."

"But she's slept with those other guys," Brian said.

"Well with Mr. Dulac she had to, she couldn't get out of it. She didn't want to, but probably after a while she enjoyed it, because after a certain point she couldn't help enjoying it."

So Orphée is at fault, Pauline said decidedly. He looks at Eurydice on purpose, to kill her and get rid of her because she is not perfect. Because of him she has to die a second time.

Brian, on his back and with his eyes wide open (she knew that because of the tone of his voice) said, "But doesn't he die too?"

"Yes. He chooses to."

"So then they're together?"

"Yes. Like Romeo and Juliet. *Orphée is with Eurydice at last.* That's what Monsieur Henri says. That's the last line of the play. That's the end." Pauline rolled over onto her side and touched her cheek to Brian's shoulder—not to start anything but to emphasize what she said next. "It's a beautiful play in one way, but in another it's so silly. And it isn't really like *Romeo and Juliet* because it isn't bad luck or circumstances. It's on purpose. So they don't have to go on with life and get married and have kids and buy an old house and fix it up and—"

"And have affairs," said Brian. "After all, they're French."

Then he said, "Be like my parents."

Pauline laughed. "Do they have affairs? I can imagine."

"Oh sure," said Brian. "I meant their life."

"Logically I can see killing yourself so you won't turn into your parents," Brian said. "I just don't believe anybody would do it."

"Everybody has choices," Pauline said dreamily. "Her mother and his father are both despicable in a way, but Orphée and Eurydice don't have to be like them. They're not corrupt. Just because she's slept with those men doesn't mean she's corrupt. She wasn't in love then. She hadn't met Orphée. There's one speech where he tells her that everything she's done is sticking to her, and it's disgusting. Lies she's told him. The other men. It's all sticking to her forever. And then of course Monsieur Henri plays up to that. He tells Orphée that he'll be just as bad and that one day he'll walk down the street with Eurydice and he'll look like a man with a dog he's trying to lose."

To her surprise, Brian laughed.

"No," she said. "That's what's stupid. It's not inevitable. It's not inevitable at all."

They went on speculating, and comfortably arguing, in a way that was not usual, but not altogether unfamiliar to them. They had done this before, at long intervals in their married life—talked half the night about God or fear of death or how children should be educated or whether money was important. At last they admitted to being too tired to make sense any longer, and arranged themselves in a comradely position and went to sleep.

FINALLY A rainy day. Brian and his parents were driving into Campbell River to get groceries, and gin, and to take Brian's father's car to a garage, to see about a problem that had developed on the drive up from Nanaimo. This was a very slight problem, but there was the matter of the new-car warranty's being in effect at present, so Brian's father wanted to get it seen to as soon as possible. Brian had to go along, with his car, just in case his father's car had to be left in the garage. Pauline said that she had to stay home because of Mara's nap.

She persuaded Caitlin to lie down too—allowing her to take her music box to bed with her if she played it very softly. Then Pauline spread the script on the kitchen table and drank coffee and went over the scene in which Orphée says that it's intolerable, at last, to stay in two skins, two envelopes with their own blood and oxygen sealed up in their solitude, and Eurydice tells him to be quiet.

"Don't talk. Don't think. Just let your hand wander, let it be happy on its own."

Your hand is my happiness, says Eurydice. Accept that. Accept your happiness.

Of course he says he cannot.

Caitlin called out frequently to ask what time it was. She turned up the sound of the music box. Pauline hurried to the bedroom door and hissed at her to turn it down, not to wake Mara.

"If you play it like that again I'll take it away from you. Okay?"

But Mara was already rustling around in her crib, and in the next few minutes there were sounds of soft, encouraging conversation from Caitlin, designed to get her sister wide awake. Also of the music being quickly turned up and then down. Then of Mara rattling the crib railing, pulling herself up, throwing her bottle out onto the floor, and starting the bird cries that would grow more and more desolate until they brought her mother.

"I didn't wake her," Caitlin said. "She was awake all by herself. It's not raining anymore. Can we go down to the beach?"

She was right. It wasn't raining. Pauline changed Mara, told Caitlin to get her bathing suit on and find her sand pail. She got into her own bathing suit and put her shorts over it, in case the rest of the family arrived home while she was down there. ("Dad doesn't like the way some women just go right out of their cottages in their bathing suits," Brian's mother had said to her. "I guess he and I just grew up in other times.") She picked up the script to take it along, then laid it down. She was afraid that she would get too absorbed in it and take her eyes off the children for a moment too long.

The thoughts that came to her, of Jeffrey, were not really thoughts at all—they were more like alterations in her body. This could happen when she was sitting on the beach (trying to stay in the half shade of a bush and so preserve her pallor, as Jeffrey had ordered) or when she was wringing out diapers or when she and Brian were visiting his parents. In the middle of Monopoly games, Scrabble games, card games. She went right on talking, listening, working, keeping track of the children, while some memory of her secret life disturbed her like a radiant explosion. Then a warm weight settled, reassurance filling up all her hollows. But it didn't last, this comfort leaked away, and she was like a miser whose windfall has vanished and who is convinced such luck can never strike again. Longing buckled her up and drove her to the discipline of counting days.

Sometimes she even cut the days into fractions to figure out more exactly how much time had gone.

She thought of going into Campbell River, making some excuse, so that she could get to a phone booth and call him. The cottages had no phones—the only public phone was in the hall of the lodge. But she did not have the number of the hotel where Jeffrey worked. And besides that, she could never get away to Campbell River in the evening. She was afraid that if she called him at home in the daytime his mother the French teacher might answer. He said his mother hardly ever left the house in the summer. Just once, she had taken the ferry to Vancouver for the day. Jeffrey had phoned Pauline to ask her to come over. Brian was teaching, and Caitlin was at her play group.

Pauline said, "I can't. I have Mara."

Jeffrey said, "Who? Oh. Sorry." Then "Couldn't you bring her along?"

She said no.

"Why not? Couldn't you bring some things for her to play with?"

No, said Pauline. "I couldn't," she said. "I just couldn't." It seemed too dangerous to her, to trundle her baby along on such a guilty expedition. To a house where cleaning fluids would not be bestowed on high shelves, and all pills and cough syrups and cigarettes and buttons put safely out of reach. And even if she escaped poisoning or choking, Mara might be storing up time bombs—memories of a strange house where she was strangely disregarded, of a closed door, noises on the other side of it.

"I just wanted you," Jeffrey said. "I just wanted you in my bed."

She said again, weakly, "No."

Those words of his kept coming back to her. *I wanted you in my bed.* A half-joking urgency in his voice but also a determination, a practicality, as if "in my bed" meant something more, the bed he spoke of taking on larger, less material dimensions.

Had she made a great mistake with that refusal? With that reminder of how fenced in she was, in what anybody would call her real life?

THE BEACH was nearly empty—people had got used to its being a rainy day. The sand was too heavy for Caitlin to make a castle or dig an irrigation system—projects she would only undertake with her father, anyway, because she sensed that his interest in them was wholehearted, and Pauline's was not. She wandered a bit forlornly at the edge of the water. She probably missed the presence of other children, the nameless instant friends and occasional stone-throwing water-kicking enemies, the shrieking and splashing and falling about. A boy a little bigger than she was and apparently all by himself stood knee-deep in the water farther down the beach. If these two could get together it might be all right; the whole beach experience might be retrieved. Pauline couldn't tell whether Caitlin was now making little splashy runs into the water for his benefit or whether he was watching her with interest or scorn.

Mara didn't need company, at least for now. She stumbled towards the water, felt it touch her feet and changed her mind, stopped, looked around, and spotted Pauline. "Paw. Paw," she said, in happy recognition. "Paw" was what she said for "Pauline," instead of "Mother" or "Mommy." Looking around overbalanced her—she sat down half on the sand and half in the water, made a squawk of surprise that turned to an announcement, then by some determined ungraceful maneuvers that involved putting her weight on her hands, she rose to her feet, wavering and triumphant. She had been walking for half a year, but getting around on the sand was still a challenge. Now she came back towards Pauline, making some reasonable, casual remarks in her own language.

"Sand," said Pauline, holding up a clot of it. "Look. Mara. Sand."

Mara corrected her, calling it something else—it sounded like "whap." Her thick diaper under her plastic pants and her terry-cloth playsuit gave her a fat bottom, and that, along with her plump cheeks and shoulders and her sidelong important expression, made her look like a roguish matron.

Pauline became aware of someone calling her name. It had been called two or three times, but because the voice was unfamiliar she had not recognized it. She stood up and waved. It was the woman who worked in the store at the lodge. She was leaning over the balcony and calling, "Mrs. Keating. Mrs. Keating? Telephone, Mrs. Keating."

Pauline hoisted Mara onto her hip and summoned Caitlin. She and the little boy were aware of each other now—they were both picking up stones from the bottom and flinging them out into the water. At first she didn't hear Pauline, or pretended not to.

"Store," called Pauline. "Caitlin. Store." When she was sure Caitlin would follow—it was the word "store" that had done it, the reminder of the tiny store in the lodge where you could buy ice cream and candy and cigarettes and mixer—she began the trek across the sand and up the flight of wooden steps above the sand and the salal bushes. Halfway up she stopped, said, "Mara, you weigh a ton," and shifted the baby to her other hip. Caitlin banged a stick against the railing.

"Can I have a Fudgsicle? Mother? Can I?"

"We'll see."

"Can I please have a Fudgsicle?"

"Wait."

The public phone was beside a bulletin board on the other side of the main hall and across from the door to the dining room. A bingo game had been set up in there, because of the rain.

"Hope he's still hanging on," the woman who worked in the store called out. She was unseen now behind her counter.

Pauline, still holding Mara, picked up the dangling receiver and said breathlessly, "Hello?" She was expecting to hear Brian telling her about some delay in Campbell River or asking her what it was she had wanted him to get at the drugstore. It was just the one thing—calamine lotion—so he had not written it down.

"Pauline," said Jeffrey. "It's me."

Mara was bumping and scrambling against Pauline's side, anxious to get down. Caitlin came along the hall and went into the store, leaving wet sandy footprints. Pauline said, "Just a minute, just a minute." She let Mara slide down and hurried to close the door that led to the steps. She did not remember telling Jeffrey the name of this place, though she had told him roughly where it was. She heard the woman in the store speaking to Caitlin in a sharper voice than she would use to children whose parents were beside them.

"Did you forget to put your feet under the tap?"

"I'm here," said Jeffrey. "I didn't get along well without you. I didn't get along at all."

Mara made for the dining room, as if the male voice calling out "Under the N—" was a direct invitation to her.

"Here. Where?" said Pauline.

She read the signs that were tacked up on the bulletin board beside the phone.

No Person under Fourteen Years of Age Not Accompanied by Adult Allowed in Boats or Canoes.

Fishing Derby.

Bake and Craft Sale, St. Bartholomew's Church.

Your Life Is in Your Hands. Palms and Cards Read. Reasonable and Accurate. Call Claire. "In a motel. In Campbell River."

Pauline knew where she was before she opened her eyes. Nothing surprised her. She had slept but not deeply enough to let go of anything.

She had waited for Brian in the parking area of the lodge, with the children, and had asked him for the keys. She had told him in front of his parents that there was something else she needed, from Campbell River. He asked, What was it? And did she have any money?

"Just something," she said, so he would think that it was tampons or birth control supplies, that she didn't want to mention. "Sure."

"Okay but you'll have to put some gas in," he said.

Later she had to speak to him on the phone. Jeffrey said she had to do it.

"Because he won't take it from me. He'll think I kidnapped you or something. He won't believe it."

But the strangest thing of all the things that day was that Brian did seem, immediately, to believe it. Standing where she had stood not so long before, in the public hallway of the lodge—the bingo game over now but people going past, she could hear them, people on their way out of the dining room after dinner—he said, "Oh. Oh. Oh. Okay" in a voice that would have to be quickly controlled, but that seemed to draw on a supply of fatalism or foreknowledge that went far beyond that necessity.

As if he had known all along, all along, what could happen with her.

"Okay," he said. "What about the car?"

He said something else, something impossible, and hung up, and she came out of the phone booth beside some gas pumps in Campbell River.

"That was quick," Jeffrey said. "Easier than you expected."

Pauline said, "I don't know."

"He may have known it subconsciously. People do know."

She shook her head, to tell him not to say any more, and he said, "Sorry." They walked along the street not touching or talking.

THEY'D HAD to go out to find a phone booth because there was no phone in the motel room. Now in the early morning looking around at leisure— the first real leisure or freedom she'd had since she came into that room— Pauline saw that there wasn't much of anything in it. Just a junk dresser, the bed without a headboard, an armless upholstered chair, on the window a Venetian blind with a broken slat and curtain of orange plastic that was supposed to look like net and that didn't have to be hemmed, just sliced off at the bottom. There was a noisy air conditioner —Jeffrey had turned it off in the night and left the door open on the chain, since the window was sealed. The door was shut now. He must have got up in the night and shut it.

This was all she had. Her connection with the cottage where Brian lay asleep or not asleep was broken, also her connection with the house that had been an expression of her life with Brian, of the way they wanted to live. She had no furniture anymore. She had cut herself off from all the large solid acquisitions like the washer and dryer and the oak table and the refinished wardrobe and the chandelier that was a copy of the one in a painting by Vermeer. And just as much from those things that were particularly hers—the pressed-glass tumblers that she had been collecting and the prayer rug which was of course not authentic, but beautiful. Especially from those things. Even her books, she might have lost. Even her clothes. The skirt and blouse and sandals she had put on for the trip to Campbell River might well be all she had now to her name. She would never go back to lay claim to anything. If Brian got in touch with her to ask what was to be done with things, she would tell him to do what he liked—throw everything into garbage bags and take it to the dump, if that was what he liked. (In fact she knew that he would probably pack up a trunk, which he did, sending on, scrupulously, not only her winter coat and boots but things like the waist cincher she had worn at her wedding and never since, with the prayer rug draped over the top of everything like a final statement of his generosity, either natural or calculated.)

She believed that she would never again care about what sort of rooms she lived in or what sort of clothes she put on. She would not be looking for that sort of help to give anybody an idea of who she was, what she was like. Not even to give herself an idea. What she had done would be enough, it would be the whole thing.

What she was doing would be what she had heard about and read about. It was what Anna Karenina had done and what Madame Bovary had wanted to do. It was what a teacher at Brian's school had done, with the school secretary. He had run off with her. That was what it was called. Running off with. Taking off with. It was spoken of disparagingly, humorously, enviously. It was adultery taken one step further. The people who did it had almost certainly been having an affair already, committing adultery for quite some time before they became desperate or courageous enough to take this step. Once in a long while a couple might claim their love was unconsummated and technically pure, but these people would be thought of—if anybody believed them—as being not only very serious and high-minded but almost devastatingly foolhardy, almost in a class with those who took a chance and gave up everything to go and work in some poor and dangerous country.

The others, the adulterers, were seen as irresponsible, immature, selfish, or even cruel. Also lucky. They were lucky because the sex they had been having in parked cars or the long grass or in each other's sullied marriage beds or most likely in motels like this one must surely have been splendid. Otherwise they would never have got such a yearning for each other's company at all costs or such a faith that their shared future would be altogether better and different in kind from what they had in the past.

Different in kind. That was what Pauline must believe now—that there was this major difference in lives or in marriages or unions between people. That some of them had a necessity, a fatefulness, about them that others did not have. Of course she would have said the same thing a year ago. People did say that, they seemed to believe that, and to believe that their own cases were all of the first, the special kind, even when anybody could see that they were not and that these people did not know what they were talking about. Pauline would not have known what she was talking about.

IT WAS too warm in the room. Jeffrey's body was too warm. Conviction and contentiousness seemed to radiate from it, even in sleep. His torso was thicker than Brian's; he was pudgier around the waist. More flesh on the bones, yet not so slack to the touch. Not so good-looking in general—she was sure most people would say that. And not so fastidious. Brian in bed smelled of nothing. Jeffrey's skin, every time she'd been with him, had had a baked-in, slightly oily or nutty smell. He didn't wash last night—but then, neither did she. There wasn't time. Did he even have a toothbrush with him? She didn't. But she had not known she was staying.

When she met Jeffrey here it was still in the back of her mind that she had to concoct some colossal lie to serve her when she got home. And she—they—had to hurry. When Jeffrey said to her that he had decided that they must stay together, that she would come with him to Washington State, that they would have to drop the play because things would be too difficult for them in Victoria, she had looked at him just in the blank way you'd look at somebody the moment that an earthquake started. She was ready to tell him all the reasons why this was not possible, she still thought she was going to tell him that, but her life was coming adrift in that moment. To go back would be like tying a sack over her head.

All she said was "Are you sure?"

He said, "Sure." He said sincerely, "I'll never leave you."

That did not seem the sort of thing that he would say. Then she realized he was quoting—maybe ironically—from the play. It was what Orphée says to Eurydice within a few moments of their first meeting in the station buffet.

So her life was falling forwards; she was becoming one of those people who ran away. A woman who shockingly and incomprehensibly gave everything up. For love, observers would say wryly. Meaning, for sex. None of this would happen if it wasn't for sex.

And yet what's the great difference there? It's not such a variable procedure, in spite of what you're told. Skins, motions, contact, results. Pauline isn't a woman from whom it's difficult to get results. Brian got them. Probably anybody would, who wasn't wildly inept or morally disgusting.

But nothing's the same, really. With Brian—especially with Brian, to whom she has dedicated a selfish sort of goodwill, with whom she's lived in married complicity—there can never be this stripping away, the inevitable flight, the feelings she doesn't have to strive for but only to give in to like breathing or dying. That she believes can only come when the skin is on Jeffrey, the motions made by Jeffrey, and the weight that bears down on her has Jeffrey's heart in it, also his habits, thoughts, peculiarities, his ambition and loneliness (that for all she knows may have mostly to do with his youth).

For all she knows. There's a lot she doesn't know. She hardly knows anything about what he likes to eat or what music he likes to listen to or what role his mother plays in his life (no doubt a mysterious but important one, like the role of Brian's parents). One thing she's pretty sure of—whatever preferences or prohibitions he has will be definite.

She slides out from under Jeffrey's hand and from under the top sheet which has a harsh smell of bleach, she slips down to the floor where the bedspread is lying and wraps herself quickly in that rag of greenish-yellow chenille. She doesn't want him to open his eyes and see her from behind and note the droop of her buttocks. He's seen her naked before, but generally in a more forgiving moment.

She rinses her mouth and washes herself, using the bar of soap that is about the size of two thin squares of chocolate and firm as stone. She's hard-used between the legs, swollen and stinking. Urinating takes an effort, and it seems she's constipated. Last night when they went out and got hamburgers she found she could not eat. Presumably she'll learn to do all these things again, they'll resume their natural importance in her life. At the moment it's as if she can't quite spare the attention.

She has some money in her purse. She has to go out and buy a toothbrush, toothpaste, deodorant, shampoo. Also vaginal jelly. Last night they used condoms the first two times but nothing the third time.

She didn't bring her watch and Jeffrey doesn't wear one. There's no clock in the room, of course. She thinks it's early—there's still an early look to the light in spite of the heat. The stores probably won't be open, but there'll be someplace where she can get coffee.

Jeffrey has turned onto his other side. She must have wakened him, just for a moment.

They'll have a bedroom. A kitchen, an address. He'll go to work. She'll go to the Laundromat. Maybe she'll go to work too. Selling things, waiting on tables, tutoring students. She knows French and Latin—do they teach French and Latin in American high schools? Can you get a job if you're not an American? Jeffrey isn't.

She leaves him the key. She'll have to wake him to get back in. There's nothing to write a note with, or on.

It is early. The motel is on the highway at the north end of town, beside the bridge. There's no traffic yet. She scuffs along under the cottonwood trees for quite a while before a vehicle of any kind rumbles over the bridge—though the traffic on it shook their bed regularly late into the night.

Something is coming now. A truck. But not just a truck—there's a large bleak fact coming at her. And it has not arrived out of nowhere—it's been waiting, cruelly nudging at her ever since she woke up, or even all night.

Caitlin and Mara.

Last night on the phone, after speaking in such a flat and controlled and almost agreeable voice—as if he prided himself on not being shocked, not objecting or pleading—Brian cracked open. He said with contempt and fury and no concern for whoever might hear him, "Well then—what about the kids?"

The receiver began to shake against Pauline's ear.

She said, "We'll talk—" but he did not seem to hear her.

"The children," he said, in this same shivering and vindictive voice. Changing the word "kids" to "children" was like slamming a board down on her—a heavy, formal, righteous threat.

"The children stay," Brian said. "Pauline. Did you hear me?"

"No," said Pauline. "Yes. I heard you but—"

"All right. You heard me. Remember. The children stay."

It was all he could do. To make her see what she was doing, what she was ending, and to punish her if she did so. Nobody would blame him. There might be finagling, there might be bargaining, there would certainly be humbling of herself, but there it was like a round cold stone in her gullet, like a cannonball. And it would remain there unless she changed her mind entirely. The children stay.

Their car—hers and Brian's—was still sitting in the motel parking lot. Brian would have to ask his father or his mother to drive him up here today to get it. She had the keys in her purse. There were spare keys—he would surely bring them. She unlocked the car door and threw her keys on the seat and locked the door on the inside and shut it.

Now she couldn't go back. She couldn't get into the car and drive back and say that she'd been insane. If she did that he would forgive her, but he'd never get over it and neither would she. They'd go on, though, as people did.

She walked out of the parking lot, she walked along the sidewalk, into town.

The weight of Mara on her hip, yesterday. The sight of Caitlin's footprints on the floor.

Paw. Paw.

She doesn't need the keys to get back to them, she doesn't need the car. She could beg a ride on the highway. Give in, give in, get back to them any way at all, how can she not do that?

A sack over her head.

A fluid choice, the choice of fantasy, is poured out on the ground and instantly hardens; it has taken its undeniable shape.

THIS IS acute pain. It will become chronic. Chronic means that it will be permanent but perhaps not constant. It may also mean that you won't die of it. You won't get free of it, but you won't die of it. You won't feel it every minute, but you won't spend many days without it. And you'll learn some tricks to dull it or banish it, trying not to end up destroying what you incurred this pain to get. It isn't his fault. He's still an innocent or a savage, who doesn't know there's a pain so durable in the world. Say to yourself, You lose them anyway. They grow up. For a mother there's always waiting this private slightly ridiculous desolation. They'll forget this time, in one way or another they'll disown you. Or hang around till you don't know what to do about them, the way Brian has.

And still, what pain. To carry along and get used to until it's only the past she's grieving for and not any possible present.

HER CHILDREN have grown up. They don't hate her. For going away or staying away. They don't forgive her, either. Perhaps they wouldn't have forgiven her anyway, but it would have been for something different.

Caitlin remembers a little about the summer at the lodge, Mara nothing. One day Caitlin mentions it to Pauline, calling it "that place Grandma and Grandpa stayed at."

"The place we were at when you went away," she says. "Only we didn't know till later you went away with Orphée."

Pauline says, "It wasn't Orphée."

"It wasn't Orphée? Dad used to say it was. He'd say, And then your mother ran away with Orphée.'"

"Then he was joking," says Pauline.

"I always thought it was Orphée. It was somebody else then."

"It was somebody else connected with the play. That I lived with for a while."

"Not Orphée."

"No. Never him."

My Mother's Dream

DURING THE night—or during the time she had been asleep—there had been a heavy fall of snow.

My mother looked out from a big arched window such as you find in a mansion or an old-fashioned public building. She looked down on lawns and shrubs, hedges, flower gardens, trees, all covered by snow that lay in heaps and cushions, not levelled or disturbed by wind. The white of it did not hurt your eyes as it does in sunlight. The white was the white of snow under a clear sky just before dawn. Everything was still; it was like "O Little Town of Bethlehem" except that the stars had gone out.

Yet something was wrong. There was a mistake in this scene. All the trees, all the shrubs and plants, were out in full summer leaf. The grass that showed underneath them, in spots sheltered from the snow, was fresh and green. Snow had settled overnight on the luxury of summer. A change of season unexplainable, unexpected. Also, everybody had gone away—though she couldn't think who "everybody" was—and my mother was alone in the high spacious house amongst its rather formal trees and gardens.

She thought that whatever had happened would soon be made known to her. Nobody came, however. The telephone did not ring; the latch of the garden gate was not lifted. She could not hear any traffic, and she did not even know which way the street was—or the road, if she was out in the country. She had to get out of the house, where the air was so heavy and settled.

When she got outside she remembered. She remembered that she had left a baby out there somewhere, before the snow had fallen. Quite a while before the snow had fallen. This memory, this certainty, came over her with horror. It was as if she was awakening from a dream. Within her dream she awakened from a dream, to a knowledge of her responsibility and mistake. She had left her baby out overnight, she had forgotten about it. Left it exposed somewhere as if it was a doll she tired of. And perhaps it was not last night but a week or a month ago that she had done this. For a whole season or for many seasons she had left her baby out. She had been occupied in other ways. She might even have travelled away from here and just returned, forgetting what she was returning to.

She went around looking under hedges and broad-leaved plants. She foresaw how the baby would be shrivelled up. It would be dead, shrivelled and brown, its head like a nut, and on its tiny shut-up face there would be an expression not of distress but of bereavement, an old patient grief. There would not be any accusation of her, its mother—just the look of patience and helplessness with which it waited for its rescue or its fate.

The sorrow that came to my mother was the sorrow of the baby's waiting and not knowing it waited for her, its only hope, when she had forgotten all about it. So small and new a baby that could not even turn away from the snow. She could hardly breathe for her sorrow. There would never be any room in her for anything else. No room for anything but the realization of what she had done.

What a reprieve, then, to find her baby lying in its crib. Lying on its stomach, its head turned to one side, its skin pale and sweet as snowdrops and the down on its head reddish like the dawn. Red hair like her own, on her perfectly safe and unmistakable baby. The joy to find herself forgiven.

The snow and the leafy gardens and the strange house had all withdrawn. The only remnant of the whiteness was the blanket in the crib. A baby blanket of light white wool, crumpled halfway down the baby's back. In the heat, the real summer heat, the baby was wearing only a diaper and a pair of plastic pants to keep the sheet dry. The plastic pants had a pattern of butterflies.

My mother, still thinking no doubt about the snow and the cold that usually accompanies snow, pulled the blanket up to cover the baby's bare back and shoulders, its red-downed head.

IT IS early morning when this happens in the real world. The world of July 1945. At a time when, on any other morning, it would be demanding its first feeding of the day, the baby sleeps on. The mother, though standing on her feet and with her eyes open, is still too far deep in sleep in her head to wonder about this. Baby and mother are worn out by a long battle, and the mother has forgotten even that at the moment. Some circuits are closed down; the most unrelenting quiet has settled on her brain and her baby's. The mother—my mother—makes no sense of the daylight which is increasing every moment. She doesn't understand that the sun is coming up as she stands there. No memory of the day before, or of what happened around midnight, comes up to jolt her. She pulls the blanket up over her baby's head, over its mild, satisfied, sleeping profile. She pads back to her own room and falls down on the bed and is again, at once, unconscious.

The house in which this happens is nothing like the house in the dream. It is a one-and-a-half-story white wooden house, cramped but respectable, with a porch that comes to within a few feet of the sidewalk, and a bay window in the dining room looking out on a small hedged yard. It is on a backstreet in a small town that is indistinguishable—to an outsider—from a lot of other small towns to be found ten or fifteen miles apart in the once thickly populated farmland near Lake Huron. My father and his sisters grew up in this house, and the sisters and mother were still living here when my mother joined them—and I joined them too, being large and lively inside her—after my father was killed in the final weeks of the war in Europe.

MY MOTHER—Jill—is standing beside the dining-room table in the bright late afternoon. The house is full of people who have been invited back there after the memorial service in the church. They are drinking tea or coffee and managing to hold in their fingers the dinky sandwiches, or slices of banana bread, nut loaf, pound cake. The custard tarts or raisin tarts with their crumbly pastry are supposed to be eaten with a dessert fork off one of the small china plates that were painted with violets by Jill's mother-in-law when she was a bride. Jill picks everything up with her fingers. Pastry crumbs have fallen, a raisin has fallen, and been smeared into the green velvet of her dress. It's too hot a dress for the day, and it's not a maternity dress at all but a loose sort of robe made for recitals, occasions when she plays her violin in public. The hem rides up in front, due to me. But it's the only thing she owns that is large enough and good enough for her to wear at her husband's memorial service.

What is this eating all about? People can't help but notice. "Eating for two," Ailsa says to a group of her guests, so that they won't get the better of her by anything they say or don't say about her sister-in-law.

Jill has been queasy all day, until suddenly in the church, when she was thinking how bad the organ was, she realized that she was, all of a sudden, as hungry as a wolf. All through "O Valiant Hearts" she was thinking of a fat hamburger dripping with meat juice and melted mayonnaise, and now she is trying to find what concoction of walnuts and raisins and brown sugar, what tooth-jabbing sweetness of coconut icing or soothing mouthful of banana bread or dollop of custard, will do as a substitute. Nothing will, of course, but she keeps on going. When her real hunger is satisfied her imaginary hunger is still working, and even more an irritability amounting almost to panic that makes her stuff into her mouth what she can hardly taste any longer. She couldn't describe this irritability except to say it has something to do with furriness and tightness. The barberry hedge outside the window, thick and bristling in the sunlight, the feel of the velvet dress clinging to her damp armpits, the nosegays of curls—the same color as the raisins in the tarts—bunched on her sister-in-law Ailsa's head, even the painted violets that look like scabs you could pick off the plate, all these things seem particularly horrid and oppressive to her though she knows they are quite ordinary. They seem to carry some message about her new and unexpected life.

Why unexpected? She has known for some time about me and she also knew that George Kirkham might be killed. He was in the air force, after all. (And around her in the Kirkhams' house this afternoon people are saying—though not to her, his widow, or to his sisters—that he was just the sort you always knew would be killed. They mean because he was good-looking and high-spirited and the pride of his family, the one on whom all the hopes had been pinned.) She knew this, but she went ahead with her ordinary life, lugging her violin onto the streetcar on dark winter mornings, riding to the Conservatory where she practiced hour after hour within sound of others but alone in a dingy room with the radiator racket for company, the skin of her hands blotchy at first with the cold, then parched in the dry indoor heat. She went on living in a rented room with an ill-fitting window that let in flies in summer and a windowsill sprinkle of snow in winter, and dreaming—when she wasn't sick—of sausages and meat pies and dark chunks of chocolate. At the Conservatory people treated her pregnancy tactfully, as if it was a tumor. It didn't show for a long time anyway, as first pregnancies generally don't on a big girl with a broad pelvis. Even with me turning somersaults she played in public. Majestically thickened, with her long red hair lying in a bush around her shoulders, her face broad and glowing, her expression full of somber concentration, she played a solo in her most important recital so far. The Mendelssohn Violin Concerto.

She paid some attention to the world—she knew the war was ending. She thought that George might be back soon after I was born. She knew that she wouldn't be able to go on living in her room then—she'd have to live somewhere with him. And she knew that I'd be there, but she thought of my birth as bringing something to an end rather than starting something. It would bring an end to the kicking in the permanent sore spot on one side of her belly and the ache in her genitals when she stands up and the blood rushes into them (as if she'd had a burning poultice laid there). Her nipples will no longer be large and dark and nubbly, and she won't have to wind bandages around her legs with their swollen veins before she gets out of bed every morning. She won't have to urinate every half hour or so, and her feet will shrink back into their ordinary shoes. She thinks that once I'm out I won't give her so much trouble.

After she knew that George would not be coming back she thought about keeping me for a while in that same room. She got a book about babies. She bought the basic things that I would need. There was an old woman in the building who could look after me while she practiced. She would get a war widow's pension and in six more months she would graduate from the Conservatory.

Then Ailsa came down on the train and collected her. Ailsa said, "We couldn't leave you stuck down here all by yourself. Everybody wonders why you didn't come up when George went overseas. It's time you came now."

"MY FAMILY'S crackers," George had told Jill. "Iona's a nervous wreck and Ailsa should have been a sergeant major. And my mother's senile."

He also said, "Ailsa got the brains, but she had to quit school and go and work in the Post Office when my dad died. I got the looks and there wasn't anything left for poor old Iona but the bad skin and the bad nerves."

Jill met his sisters for the first time when they came to Toronto to see George off. They hadn't been at the wedding, which had taken place two weeks before. Nobody was there but George and Jill and the minister and the minister's wife and a neighbor called in to be the second witness. I was there as well, already tucked up inside Jill, but I was not the reason for the wedding and at the time nobody knew of my existence. Afterwards George insisted that he and Jill take some poker-faced wedding pictures of themselves in one of those do-it-yourself picture booths. He was in relentless high spirits. "That'll fix them," he said, when he looked at the pictures. Jill wondered if there was anybody special he meant to fix. Ailsa? Or the pretty girls, the cute and perky girls, who had run after him, writing him sentimental letters and knitting him argyle socks? He wore the socks when he could, he pocketed the presents, and he read the letters out in bars for a joke.

Jill had not had any breakfast before the wedding, and in the midst of it she was thinking of pancakes and bacon.

THE TWO sisters were more normal-looking than she had expected. Though it was true about George getting the looks. He had a silky wave to his dark-blond hair and a gleeful glint in his eyes and a clean-cut enviable set of features. His only drawback was that he was not very tall. Just tall enough to look Jill in the eye. And to be an air force pilot.

"They don't want tall guys for pilots," he said. "I beat them out there. The beanpole bastards. Lots of guys in the movies are short. They stand on boxes for the kissing."

(At the movies, George could be boisterous. He might hiss the kissing. He didn't go in for it much in real life either. Let's get to the action, he said.)

The sisters were short, too. They were named after places in Scotland, where their parents had gone on their honeymoon before the family lost its money. Ailsa was twelve years older than George, and Iona was nine years older. In the crowd at Union Station they looked dumpy and bewildered. Both of them wore new hats and suits, as if they were the ones who had recently been married. And both were upset because Iona had left her good gloves on the train. It was true that Iona had bad skin, though it wasn't broken out at present and perhaps her acne days were over. It was lumpy with old scars and dingy under the pink powder. Her hair slipped out in droopy tendrils from under her hat and her eyes were teary, either because of Ailsa's scolding or because her brother was going away to war. Ailsa's hair was arranged in bunches of tight permanented curls, with her hat riding on top. She had shrewd pale eyes behind sparkle-rimmed glasses, and round pink cheeks, and a dimpled chin. Both she and Iona had tidy figures—high breasts and small waists and flaring hips—but on Iona this figure looked like something she had picked up by mistake and was trying to hide by stooping her shoulders and crossing her arms. Ailsa managed her curves assertively not provocatively, as if she was made of some sturdy ceramic. And both of them had George's dark-blond coloring, but without his gleam. They didn't seem to share his sense of humor either.

"Well I'm off," George said. "I'm off to die a hero on the field at Passchendaele." And Iona said, "Oh don't say that. Don't talk like that." Ailsa twitched her raspberry mouth.

"I can see the lost-and-found sign from here," she said. "But I don't know if that's just for things you lose in the station or is it for things that they find in the trains? Passchendaele was in the First World War."

"Was it? You sure? I'm too late?" said George, beating his hand on his chest.

And he was burned up a few months later in a training flight over the Irish Sea.

AILSA SMILES all the time. She says, "Well of course I am proud. I am. But I'm not the only one to lose somebody. He did what he had to do." Some people find her briskness a bit shocking. But others say, "Poor Ailsa." All that concentrating on George, and saving to send him to law school, and then he flouted her—he signed up; he went off and got himself killed. He couldn't wait.

His sisters sacrificed their own schooling. Even getting their teeth straightened—they sacrificed that. Iona did go to nursing school, but as it turned out getting her teeth fixed would have served her better. Now she and Ailsa have ended up with a hero. Everybody grants it—a hero. The younger people present think it's something to have a hero in the family. They think the importance of this moment will last, that it will stay with Ailsa and Iona forever. "O Valiant Hearts" will soar around them forever. Older people, those who remember the previous war, know that all they've ended up with is a name on the cenotaph. Because the widow, the girl feeding her face, will get the pension.

Ailsa is in a hectic mood partly because she has been up two nights in a row, cleaning. Not that the house wasn't decently clean before. Nevertheless she felt the need to wash every dish, pot, and ornament, polish the glass on every picture, pull out the fridge and scrub behind it, wash the cellar steps off, and pour bleach in the garbage can. The very lighting fixture overhead, over the dining-room table, had to be taken apart, and every piece on it dunked in soapy water, rinsed, and rubbed dry and reassembled. And because of her work at the Post Office Ailsa couldn't start this till after supper. She is the postmistress now, she could have given herself a day off, but being Ailsa she would never do that.

Now she's hot under her rouge, twitchy in her dark-blue lace-collared crepe dress. She can't stay still. She refills the serving plates and passes them around, deplores the fact that people's tea may have got cold, hurries to make a fresh pot. Mindful of her guests' comfort, asking after their rheumatism or minor ailments, smiling in the face of her tragedy, repeating over and over again that hers is a common loss, that she must not complain when so many others are in the same boat, that George would not want his friends to grieve but to be thankful that all together we have ended the war. All in a high and emphatic voice of cheerful reproof that people are used to from the Post Office. So that they are left with an uncertain feeling of perhaps having said the wrong thing, just as in the Post Office they may be made to understand that their handwriting cannot help but be a trial or their packages are done up sloppily.

Ailsa is aware that her voice is too high and that she is smiling too much and that she has poured out tea for people who said they didn't want any more. In the kitchen, while warming the teapot, she says, "I don't know what's the matter with me. I'm all wound up.

The person she says this to is Dr. Shantz, her neighbor across the backyard.

"It'll soon be over," he says. "Would you like a bromide?"

His voice undergoes a change as the door from the dining room opens. The word "bromide" comes out firm and professional.

Ailsa's voice changes too, from forlorn to valiant. She says, "Oh, no thank you. I'll just try and keep going on my own."

IONA'S JOB is supposed to be to watch over their mother, to see that she doesn't spill her tea—which she may do not out of clumsiness but forgetfulness—and that she is taken away if she starts to sniffle and cry. But in fact Mrs. Kirkham's manners are gracious most of the time and she puts people at ease more readily than Ailsa does. For a quarter of an hour at a time she understands the situation—or she seems to—and she speaks bravely and cogently about how she will always miss her son but is grateful she still has her daughters: Ailsa so efficient and reliable, a wonder as she's always been, and Iona the soul of kindness. She even remembers to speak of her new daughter-in-law but perhaps gives a hint of being out of line when she mentions what most women of her age don't mention at a social gathering, and with men listening. Looking at Jill and me, she says, "And we all have a comfort to come."

Then passing from room to room or guest to guest, she forgets entirely, she looks around her own house and says, "Why are we here? What a lot of people—what are we celebrating?" And catching on to the fact that it all has something to do with George, she says, "Is it George's wedding?" Along with her up-to-date information she has lost some of her mild discretion. "It's not your wedding, is it?" she says to Iona. "No. I didn't think so. You never had a boyfriend, did you?" A let's-face-facts, devil-take-the-hindmost note has come into her voice. When she spots Jill she laughs.

"That's not the bride, is it? Oh-oh. Now we understand."

But the truth comes back to her as suddenly as it went away.

"Is there news?" she says. "News about George?" And it's then that the weeping starts that Ailsa was afraid of.

"Get her out of the way if she starts making a spectacle," Ailsa had said.

Iona isn't able to get her mother out of the way—she has never been able to exert authority over anybody in her life—but Dr. Shantz's wife catches the old woman's arm.

"George is dead?" says Mrs. Kirkham fearfully, and Mrs. Shantz says, "Yes he is. But you know his wife is having a baby."

Mrs. Kirkham leans against her; she crumples and says softly, "Could I have my tea?"

EVERYWHERE MY mother turns in that house, it seems she sees a picture of my father. The last and official one, of him in his uniform, sits on an embroidered runner on the closed sewing machine in the bay of the dining-room window. Iona puts flowers around it, but Ailsa took them away. She said it made him look too much like a Catholic saint. Hanging above the stairs there is one of him at six years old, out on the sidewalk, with his knee in his wagon, and in the room where Jill sleeps there's one of him beside his bicycle, with his *Free Press* newspaper sack. Mrs. Kirkham's room has the one of him dressed for the grade-eight operetta, with a gold cardboard crown on his head. Being unable to carry a tune, he couldn't have a leading role, but he was of course picked for the best background role, that of the king.

The hand-tinted studio photo over the buffet shows him at the age of three, a blurred blond tot dragging a rag doll by one leg. Ailsa thought of taking that down because it might seem tear-jerking, but she left it up rather than show a bright patch on the wallpaper. And no one said anything about it but Mrs. Shantz, who paused and said what she had said sometimes before, and not tearfully but with a faintly amused appreciation.

"Ah—Christopher Robin."

People were used to not paying much attention to what Mrs. Shantz said.

In all of his pictures George looks bright as a dollar. There's always a sunny dip of hair over his brow, unless he's wearing his officer's hat or his crown. And even when he was little more than an infant he looked as if he knew himself to be a capering, calculating, charming sort of fellow. The sort who never let people alone, who whipped them up to laugh. At his own expense occasionally, but usually at other people's. Jill recalls when she looks at him how he drank but never seemed drunk and how he occupied himself getting other drunk people to confess to him their fears, prevarications, virginity, or two-timing, which he would then turn into jokes or humiliating nicknames that his victims pretended to enjoy. For he had legions of followers and friends, who maybe latched on to him out of fear—or maybe just because, as was always said of him, he livened things up. Wherever he was was the center of the room, and the air around him crackled with risk and merriment.

What was Jill to make of such a lover? She was nineteen when she met him, and nobody had ever claimed her before. She couldn't understand what attracted him, and she could see that nobody else could understand it, either. She was a puzzle to most people of her own age, but a dull puzzle. A girl whose life was given over to the study of the violin and who had no other interests.

That was not quite true. She would snuggle under her shabby quilts and imagine a lover. But he was never a shining cutup like George. She thought of some warm and bearlike fellow, or of a musician a decade older than herself and already legendary, with a fierce potency. Her notions of love were operatic, though that was not the sort of music she most admired. But George made jokes when he made love; he pranced around her room when he had finished; he made rude and infantile noises. His brisk performances brought her little of the pleasure she knew from her assaults on herself, but she was not exactly disappointed.

Dazed at the speed of things was more like it. And expecting to be happy—grateful and happy—when her mind caught up with physical and social reality. George's attentions, and her marriage—those were all like a brilliant extension of her life. Lighted rooms showing up full of a bewildering sort of splendor. Then came the bomb or the hurricane, the not unlikely stroke of disaster, and the whole extension was gone. Blown up and vanished, leaving her with the same space and options she'd had before. She had lost something, certainly. But not something she had really got hold of, or understood as more than a hypothetical layout of the future.

She has had enough to eat, now. Her legs ache from standing so long. Mrs. Shantz is beside her, saying, "Have you had a chance to meet any of George's local friends?"

She means the young people keeping to themselves in the hall doorway. A couple of nice-looking girls, a young man still wearing a naval uniform, others. Looking at them, Jill thinks clearly that no one is really sorry. Ailsa perhaps, but Ailsa has her own reasons. No one is really sorry George is dead. Not even the girl who was crying in church and looks as if she will cry some more. Now that girl can remember that she was in love with George and think that he was in love with her—in spite of all—and never be afraid of what he may do or say to prove her wrong. And none of them will have to wonder, when a group of people clustered around George has started laughing, whom they are laughing at or what George is telling them. Nobody will have to strain to keep up with him or figure out how to stay in his good graces anymore.

It doesn't occur to her that if he had lived George might have become a different person, because she doesn't think of becoming a different person herself.

She says, "No," with a lack of enthusiasm that causes Mrs. Shantz to say, "I know. It's hard meeting new people. Particularly—if I was you I would rather go and lie down."

Jill was almost sure she was going to say "go and have a drink." But there's nothing being offered here, only tea and coffee. Jill hardly drinks anyway. She can recognize the smell on someone's breath, though, and she thought she smelled it on Mrs. Shantz.

"Why don't you?" says Mrs. Shantz. "These things are a great strain. I'll tell Ailsa. Go on now."

MRS. SHANTZ is a small woman with fine gray hair, bright eyes, and a wrinkled, pointed face. Every winter she spends a month by herself in Florida. She has money. The house that she and her husband built for themselves, behind the Kirkhams' house, is long and low and blindingly white, with curved corners and expanses of glass bricks. Dr. Shantz is twenty or twenty-five years younger than she is—a thickset, fresh, and amiable-looking man with a high smooth forehead and fair curly hair. They have no children. It is believed that she has some, from a first marriage, but they don't come to visit her. In fact the story is that Dr. Shantz was her son's friend, brought home from college, and that he fell in love with his friend's mother, she fell in love with her son's friend, there was a divorce, and here they are married, living in luxurious, close-mouthed exile.

Jill did smell whiskey. Mrs. Shantz carries a flask whenever she goes to a gathering of which—as she says—she can have no reasonable hopes. Drink does not make her fall about or garble her words or pick fights or throw her arms about people. The truth may be that she's always a little bit drunk but never really drunk. She is used to letting the alcohol enter her body in a reasonable, reassuring way, so that her brain cells never get soaked or quite dried out. The only giveaway is the smell (which many people in this dry town attribute to some medicine she has to take or even to an ointment that she has to rub on her chest). That, and perhaps a deliberateness about her speech, the way she seems to clear a space around each word. She says things of course which a woman brought up around here would not say. She tells things on herself. She tells about being mistaken every once in a while for her husband's mother. She says most people go into a tailspin when they discover their mistake, they're so embarrassed. But some women—a waitress, maybe—will fasten on Mrs. Shantz quite a dirty look, as if to say, What's he doing wasted on you?

And Mrs. Shantz just says to them, "I know. It isn't fair. But life isn't fair and you might as well get used to it."

There isn't any way this afternoon that she can space her sips properly. The kitchen and even the poky pantry behind it are places where women can be coming and going at any time. She has to go upstairs to the bathroom, and that not too often. When she does that late in the afternoon, a little while after Jill has disappeared, she finds the bathroom door locked. She thinks of nipping into one of the bedrooms and is wondering which one is empty, which occupied by Jill. Then she hears Jill's voice coming from the bathroom, saying, "Just a minute," or something like that. Something quite ordinary, but the tone of voice is strained and frightened.

Mrs. Shantz takes a quick swallow right there in the hall, seizing the excuse of emergency.

"Jill? Are you all right? Can you let me in?"

Jill is on her hands and knees, trying to mop up the puddle on the bathroom floor. She has read about the water breaking—just as she has read about contractions, show, transition stage, placenta—but just the same the escape of warm fluid surprised her. She has to use toilet paper, because Ailsa took all the regular towels away and put out the smooth scraps of embroidered linen called guest towels.

She holds on to the rim of the tub to pull herself up. She unbolts the door and that's when the first pain astonishes her. She is not to have a single mild pain, or any harbingers or orchestrated first stage of labor; it's all to be an unsparing onslaught and ripping headlong delivery.

"Easy," says Mrs. Shantz, supporting her as well as she can. "Just tell me which room is yours, we'll get you lying down."

Before they even reach the bed Jill's fingers dig into Mrs. Shantz's thin arm to leave it black and blue.

"Oh, this is fast," Mrs. Shantz says. "This is a real mover and shaker for a first baby. I'm going to get my husband."

In that way I was born right in the house, about ten days early if Jill's calculations were to be relied on. Ailsa had barely time to get the company cleared out before the place was filled with Jill's noise, her disbelieving cries and the great shameless grunts that followed.

Even if a mother had been taken by surprise and had given birth at home, it was usual by that time to move her and the baby into the hospital afterwards. But there was some sort of summer flu in town, and the hospital had filled up with the worst cases, so Dr. Shantz decided that Jill and I would be better off at home. Iona after all had finished part of her nurse's training, and she could take her two-week holiday now, to look after us.

JILL REALLY knew nothing about living in a family. She had grown up in an orphanage. From the age of six to sixteen she had slept in a dormitory. Lights turned on and off at a specified time, furnace never operating before or beyond a specified date. A long oilcloth-covered table where they ate and did their homework, a factory across the street. George had liked the sound of that. It would make a girl tough, he said. It would make her self-possessed, hard and solitary. It would make her the sort who would not expect any romantic nonsense. But the place had not been run in such a heartless way as perhaps he thought, and the people who ran it had not been ungenerous. Jill was taken to a concert, with some others, when she was twelve years old, and there she decided that she must learn to play the violin. She had already fooled around with the piano at the orphanage. Somebody took enough interest to get her a secondhand, very second-rate violin, and a few lessons, and this led, finally, to a scholarship at the Conservatory. There was a recital for patrons and directors, a party with best dresses, fruit punch, speeches, and cakes. Jill had to make a little speech herself, expressing gratitude, but the truth was that she took all this pretty much for granted. She was sure that she and some violin were naturally, fatefully connected, and would have come together without human help.

In the dormitory she had friends, but they went off early to factories and offices and she forgot about them. At the high school that the orphans were sent to, a teacher had a talk with her. The words "normal" and "well rounded" came up in the talk. The teacher seemed to think that music was an escape from something or a substitute for something. For sisters and brothers and friends and dates. She suggested that Jill spread her energy around instead of concentrating on one thing. Loosen up, play volleyball, join the school orchestra if music was what she wanted.

Jill started to avoid that particular teacher, climbing the stairs or going round the block so as not to have to speak to her. Just as she stopped reading any page from which the words "well rounded" or the word "popular" leapt out at her.

At the Conservatory it was easier. There she met people quite as un–well rounded, as hard driven, as herself. She formed a few rather absentminded and competitive friendships. One of her friends had an older brother who was in the air force, and this brother happened to be a victim and worshipper of George Kirkham's. He and George dropped in on a family Sunday-night supper, at which Jill was a guest. They were on their way to get drunk somewhere else. And that was how George met Jill. My father met my mother.

THERE HAD to be somebody at home all the time, to watch Mrs. Kirkham. So Iona worked the night shift at the bakery. She decorated cakes—even the fanciest wedding cakes—and she got the first round of bread loaves in the oven at five o'clock. Her hands, which shook so badly that she could not serve anybody a teacup, were strong and clever and patient, even inspired, at any solitary job.

One morning after Ailsa had gone off to work—this was during the short time that Jill was in the house before I was born—Iona hissed from the bedroom as Jill was going by. As if there was a secret. But who was there now in the house to keep a secret from? It couldn't be Mrs. Kirkham.

Iona had to struggle to get a stuck drawer of her bureau open. "Darn," she said, and giggled. "Darn it. There."

The drawer was full of baby clothes—not plain necessary shirts and nightgowns such as Jill had bought at a shop that sold seconds, factory rejects, in Toronto, but knitted bonnets, sweaters and bootees and soakers, handmade tiny gowns. All possible pastel colors or combinations of colors—no blue or pink prejudice—with crocheted trimming and minute embroidered flowers and birds and lambs. The sort of stuff that Jill had barely known existed. She would have known, if she had done any thorough research in baby departments or peering into baby carriages, but she hadn't.

"Of course I don't know what you've got," Iona said. "You may have got so many things already, or maybe you don't like homemade, I don't know—" Her giggling was a kind of punctuation of speech and it was also an extension of her tone of apology. Everything she said, every look and gesture, seemed to be clogged up, overlaid with a sticky honey or snuffled mucus of apology, and Jill did not know how to deal with this.

"It's really nice," she said flatly.

"Oh no, I didn't know if you'd even want it. I didn't know if you'd like it at all."

"It's lovely."

"I didn't do it all, I bought some of it. I went to the church bazaar and the Hospital Auxiliary, their bazaar, I just thought it would be nice, but if you don't like it or maybe you don't need it I can just put it in the Missionary Bale."

"I do need it," Jill said. "I haven't got anything like this at all."

"Haven't you really? What I did isn't so good, but maybe what the church ladies did or the Auxiliary, maybe you'd think that was all right."

Was this what George had meant about Iona's being a nervous wreck? (According to Ailsa, her breakdown at the nursing school had been caused by her being a bit too thin-skinned and the supervisor's being a bit too hard on her.) You might think she was clamoring for reassurance, but whatever reassurance you tried seemed to be not enough, or not to get through to her. Jill felt as if Iona's words and giggles and sniffles and damp looks (no doubt she had damp hands as well) were things crawling on her—on Jill—mites trying to get under her skin.

But this was something she got used to, in time. Or Iona toned it down. Both she and Iona felt relief—it was as if a teacher had gone out of the room—when the door closed behind Ailsa in the morning. They took to having a second cup of coffee, while Mrs. Kirkham washed the dishes. She did this job very slowly—looking around for the drawer or shelf where each item should go—and with some lapses. But with rituals, too, which she never omitted, such as scattering the coffee grounds on a bush by the kitchen door.

"She thinks the coffee makes it grow," Iona whispered. "Even if she puts it on the leaves not the ground. Every day we have to take the hose and rinse it off."

Jill thought that Iona sounded like the girls who were most picked on at the orphanage. They were always eager to pick on somebody else. But once you got Iona past her strung-out apologies or barricades of humble accusations ("Of course I'm the last person they'd consult about anything down at the shop," "Of course Ailsa wouldn't listen to my opinion," "Of course George never made any secret about how he despised me") you might get her to talk about fairly interesting things. She told Jill about the house that had been their grandfather's and was now the center wing of the hospital, about the specific shady deals that had lost their father his job, and about a romance that was going on between two married people at the bakery. She also mentioned the supposed previous history of the Shantzes, and even the fact that Ailsa was soft on Dr. Shantz. The shock treatment Iona had had after her nervous breakdown seemed perhaps to have blown a hole in her discretion, and the voice that came through this hole—once the disguising rubbish had been cleared away—was baleful and sly.

And Jill might as well spend her time chatting—her fingers had got too puffy now to try to play the violin.

AND THEN I was born and everything changed, especially for Iona.

Jill had to stay in bed for a week, and even after she got up she moved like a stiff old woman and breathed warily each time she lowered herself into a chair. She was all painfully stitched together, and her stomach and breasts were bound tight as a mummy's—that was the custom then. Her milk came in plentifully; it was leaking through the binding and onto the sheets. Iona loosened the binding and tried to connect the nipple to my mouth. But I would not take it. I refused to take my mother's breast. I screamed blue murder. The big stiff breast might just as well have been a snouted beast rummaging in my face. Iona held me, she gave me a little warm boiled water, and I quieted down. I was losing weight, though. I couldn't live on water. So Iona mixed up a formula and took me out of Jill's arms where I stiffened and wailed. Iona rocked and soothed me and touched my cheek with the rubber nipple and that turned out to be what I preferred. I drank the formula greedily and kept it down. Iona's arms and the nipple that she was in charge of became my chosen home. Jill's breasts had to be bound even tighter, and she had to forgo liquids (remember, this was in the hot weather) and endure the ache until her milk dried up.

"What a monkey, what a monkey," crooned Iona. "You are a monkey, you don't want your mommy's good milk."

I soon got fatter and stronger. I could cry louder. I cried if anybody but Iona tried to hold me. I rejected Ailsa and Dr. Shantz with his thoughtfully warmed hands, but of course it was my aversion to Jill that got the most attention.

Once Jill was out of bed Iona got her sitting in the chair where she herself usually sat to feed me; she put her own blouse around Jill's shoulders and the bottle in Jill's hand.

No use, I was not fooled. I batted my cheek against the bottle and straightened my legs and hardened my abdomen into a ball. I would not accept the substitution. I cried. I would not give in.

My cries were still thin new-baby cries, but they were a disturbance in the house, and Iona was the only person who had the power to stop them. Touched or spoken to by a non-Iona, I cried. Put down to sleep, not rocked by Iona, I cried myself into exhaustion and slept for ten minutes and woke ready to go at it again. I had no good times or fussy times. I had the Iona-times and the Iona-desertion-times, which might become—oh, worse and worse—the other-people-times, mostly Jill-times.

How could Iona go back to work, then, once her two weeks were up? She couldn't. There wasn't any question of it. The bakery had to get someone else. Iona had gone from being the most negligible to being the most important person in the house; she was the one who stood between those who lived there and constant discordance, unanswerable complaint. She had to be up at all hours to keep the household in any sort of ease. Dr. Shantz was concerned; even Ailsa was concerned.

"Iona, don't wear yourself out."

And yet a wonderful change had taken place. Iona was pale but her skin glowed, as if she had finally passed out of adolescence. She could look anybody in the eye. And there was no more trembling, hardly any giggling, no sly cringing in her voice, which had grown as bossy as Ailsa's and more joyful. (Never more joyful than when she was scolding me for my attitude to Jill.)

"Iona's in seventh heaven—she just adores that baby," Ailsa told people. But in fact Iona's behavior seemed too brisk for adoration. She did not care how much noise she made, quelling mine. She tore up the stairs calling breathlessly, "I'm coming, I'm coming, hold your horses." She would walk around with me carelessly plastered to her shoulder, held with one hand, while the other hand accomplished some task connected with my maintenance. She ruled in the kitchen, commandeering the stove for the sterilizer, the table for the mixing of the formula, the sink for the baby wash. She swore cheerfully, even in Ailsa's presence, when she had misplaced or spilled something.

She knew herself to be the only person who didn't wince, who didn't feel the distant threat of annihilation, when I sent up my first signal wail. Instead, she was the one whose heart jumped into double time, who felt like dancing, just from the sense of power she had, and gratitude.

Once her bindings were off and she'd seen the flatness of her stomach, Jill took a look at her hands. The puffiness seemed to be all gone. She went downstairs and got her violin out of the closet and took off its cover. She was ready to try some scales.

This was on a Sunday afternoon. Iona had lain down for a nap, one ear always open to hear my cry. Mrs. Kirkham too was lying down. Ailsa was painting her fingernails in the kitchen. Jill began to tune the violin.

My father and my father's family had no real interest in music. They didn't quite know this. They thought that the intolerance or even hostility they felt towards a certain type of music (this showed even in the way they pronounced the word "classical") was based on a simple strength of character, an integrity and a determination not to be fooled. As if music that departed from a simple tune was trying to put something over on you, and everybody knew this, deep down, but some people—out of pretentiousness, from want of simplicity and honesty—would never admit that it was so. And out of this artificiality and spineless tolerance came the whole world of symphony orchestras, opera, and ballet, concerts that put people to sleep.

Most of the people in this town felt the same way. But because she hadn't grown up here Jill did not understand the depth of this feeling, the taken-for-granted extent of it. My father had never made a parade of it, or a virtue of it, because he didn't go in for virtues. He had liked the idea of Jill's being a musician—not because of the music but because it made her an odd choice, as did her clothes and her way of living and her wild hair. Choosing her, he showed people what he thought of them. Showed those girls who had hoped to get their hooks in him. Showed Ailsa.

Jill had closed the curtained glass doors of the living room and she tuned up quite softly. Perhaps no sound escaped. Or if Ailsa heard something in the kitchen, she might have thought it was a sound from outdoors, a radio in the neighborhood.

Now Jill began to play her scales. It was true that her fingers were no longer puffy, but they felt stiff. Her whole body felt stiff, her stance was not quite natural, she felt the instrument clamped onto her in a distrustful way. But no matter, she would get into her scales. She was sure that she had felt this way before, after she'd had flu, or when she was very tired, having overstrained herself practicing, or even for no reason at all.

I woke without a whimper of discontent. No warning, no buildup. Just a shriek, a waterfall of shrieks descended on the house, a cry unlike any cry I'd managed before. The letting loose of a new flood of unsuspected anguish, a grief that punished the world with its waves full of stones, the volley of woe sent down from the windows of the torture chamber.

Iona was up at once, alarmed for the first time at any noise made by me, crying, "What is it, what is it?"

And Ailsa, rushing around to shut the windows, was calling out, "It's the fiddle, it's the fiddle." She threw open the doors of the living room.

"Jill. Jill. This is awful. This is just awful. Don't you hear your baby?"

She had to wrench out the screen under the living-room window, so that she could get it down. She had been sitting in her kimono to do her nails, and now a boy going by on a bicycle looked in and saw her kimono open over her slip.

"My God," she said. She hardly ever lost control of herself to this extent. "Will you put that thing away."

Jill set her violin down.

Ailsa ran out into the hall and called up to Iona.

"It's Sunday. Can't you get it to stop?"

Jill walked speechlessly and deliberately out to the kitchen, and there was Mrs. Kirkham in her stocking feet, clinging to the counter.

"What's the matter with Ailsa?" she said. "What did Iona do?"

Jill went out and sat down on the back step. She looked across at the glaring, sunlit back wall of the Shantzes' white house. All around were other hot backyards and hot walls of other houses. Inside them people well known to each other by sight and by name and by history. And if you walked three blocks east from here or five blocks west, six blocks south or ten blocks north, you would come to walls of summer crops already sprung high out of the earth, fenced fields of hay and wheat and corn. The fullness of the country. Nowhere to breathe for the reek of thrusting crops and barnyards and jostling munching animals. Woodlots at a distance beckoning like pools of shade, of peace and shelter, but in reality they were boiling up with bugs.

How can I describe what music is to Jill? Forget about landscapes and visions and dialogues. It is more of a problem, I would say, that she has to work out strictly and daringly, and that she has taken on as her responsibility in life. Suppose then that the tools that serve her for working on this problem are taken away. The problem is still there in its grandeur and other people sustain it, but it is removed from her. For her, just the back step and the glaring wall and my crying. My crying is a knife to cut out of her life all that isn't useful. To me.

"Come in," says Ailsa through the screen door. "Come on in. I shouldn't have yelled at you. Come in, people will see."

By evening the whole episode could be passed off lightly. "You must've heard the caterwauling over here today," said Ailsa to the Shantzes. They had asked her over to sit on their patio, while Iona settled me to sleep.

"Baby isn't a fan of the fiddle apparently. Doesn't take after Mommy."

Even Mrs. Shantz laughed.

"An acquired taste."

Jill heard them. At least she heard the laughing, and guessed what it was about. She was lying on her bed reading *The Bridge of San Luis Rey*, which she had helped herself to from the bookcase, without understanding that she should ask Ailsa's permission. Every so often the story blanked out on her and she heard those laughing voices over in the Shantzes' yard, then the next-door patter of Iona's adoration, and she broke out in a sullen sweat. In a fairy tale she would have risen off the bed with the strength of a young giantess and gone through the house breaking furniture and necks.

WHEN I was almost six weeks old, Ailsa and Iona were supposed to take their mother on an annual overnight visit to Guelph, to stay with some cousins. Iona wanted to take me along. But Ailsa brought in Dr. Shantz to convince her that it was not a good idea to take a small baby on such a trip in hot weather. Then Iona wanted to stay at home.

"I can't drive and look after Mother both," said Ailsa.

She said that Iona was getting too wrapped up in me, and that a day and a half looking after her own baby was not going to be too much for Jill.

"Is it, Jill?"

Jill said no.

Iona tried to pretend it wasn't that she wanted to stay with me. She said that driving on a hot day made her carsick.

"You don't drive, you just have to sit there," Ailsa said. "What about me? I'm not doing it for fun. I'm doing it because they expect us."

Iona had to sit in the back, which she said made her carsickness worse. Ailsa said it wouldn't look right to put their mother there. Mrs. Kirkham said she didn't mind. Ailsa said no. Iona rolled down the window as Ailsa started the car. She fixed her eyes on the window of the upstairs room where she had put me down to sleep after my morning bath and bottle. Ailsa waved to Jill, who stood at the front door.

"Goodbye little mother," she called, in a cheerful, challenging voice that reminded Jill somehow of George. The prospect of getting away from the house and the new threat of disruption that was lodged in it seemed to have lifted Ailsa's spirits. And perhaps it also felt good to her—felt reassuring—to have Iona back in her proper place.

IT WAS about ten o'clock in the morning when they left, and the day ahead was to be the longest and the worst in Jill's experience. Not even the day of my birth, her nightmare labor, could compare to it. Before the car could have reached the next town, I woke in distress, as if I could feel Iona's being removed from me. Iona had fed me such a short time before that Jill did not think I could possibly be hungry. But she discovered that I was wet, and though she had read that babies did not need to be changed every time they were found wet and that wasn't usually what made them cry, she decided to change me. It wasn't the first time she had done this, but she had never done it easily, and in fact Iona had taken over more often than not and got the job finished. I made it as hard as I could—I flailed my arms and legs, arched my back, tried my best to turn over, and of course kept up my noise. Jill's hands shook, she had trouble driving the pins through the cloth. She pretended to be calm, she tried talking to me, trying to imitate Iona's baby talk and fond cajoling, but it was no use, such stumbling insincerity enraged me further. She picked me up once she had my diaper pinned, she tried to mold me to her chest and shoulder, but I stiffened as if her body was made of red-hot needles. She sat down, she rocked me. She stood up, she bounced me. She sang to me the sweet words of a lullaby that were filled and trembling with her exasperation, her anger, and something that could readily define itself as loathing.

We were monsters to each other. Jill and I.

At last she put me down, more gently than she would have liked to do, and I quieted, in my relief it seemed at getting away from her. She tiptoed from the room. And it wasn't long before I started up again.

So it continued. I didn't cry nonstop. I would take breaks of two or five or ten or twenty minutes. When the time came for her to offer me the bottle I accepted it, I lay in her arm stiffly and snuffled warningly as I drank. Once half the milk was down I returned to the assault. I finished the bottle eventually, almost absent-mindedly, between wails. I dropped off to sleep and she put me down. She crept down the stairs; she stood in the hall as if she had to judge a safe way to go. She was sweating from her ordeal and from the heat of the day. She moved through the precious brittle silence into the kitchen and dared to put the coffeepot on the stove.

Before the coffee was perked I sent a meat cleaver cry down on her head.

She realized that she had forgotten something. She hadn't burped me after the bottle. She went determinedly upstairs and picked me up and walked with me patting and rubbing my angry back, and in a while I burped, but I didn't stop crying and she gave up; she laid me down.

What is it about an infant's crying that makes it so powerful, able to break down the order you depend on, inside and outside of yourself? It is like a storm—insistent, theatrical, yet in a way pure and uncontrived. It is reproachful rather than supplicating—it comes out of a rage that can't be dealt with, a birthright rage free of love and pity, ready to crush your brains inside your skull.

All Jill can do is walk around. Up and down the living-room rug, round and round the dining-room table, out to the kitchen where the clock tells her how slowly, slowly time is passing. She can't stay still to take more than a sip of her coffee. When she gets hungry she can't stop to make a sandwich but eats cornflakes out of her hands, leaving a trail all over the house. Eating and drinking, doing any ordinary thing at all, seem as risky as doing such things in a little boat out in the middle of a tempest or in a house whose beams are buckling in an awful wind. You can't take your attention from the tempest or it will rip open your last defenses. You try for sanity's sake to fix on some calm detail of your surroundings, but the wind's cries—my cries—are able to inhabit a cushion or a figure in the rug or a tiny whirlpool in the window glass. I don't allow escape.

The house is shut up like a box. Some of Ailsa's sense of shame has rubbed off on Jill, or else she's been able to manufacture some shame of her own. A mother who can't appease her own baby—what is more shameful? She keeps the doors and windows shut. And she doesn't turn the portable floor fan on because in fact she's forgotten about it. She doesn't think anymore in terms of practical relief. She doesn't think that this Sunday is one of the hottest days of the summer and maybe that is what is the matter with me. An experienced or instinctive mother would surely have given me an airing instead of granting me the powers of a demon. Prickly heat would have been what came to her mind, instead of rank despair.

Sometime in the afternoon, Jill makes a stupid or just desperate decision. She doesn't walk out of the house and leave me. Stuck in the prison of my making, she thinks of a space of her own, an escape within. She gets out her violin, which she has not touched since the day of the scales, the attempt that Ailsa and Iona have turned into a family joke. Her playing can't wake me up because I'm wide awake already, and how can it make me any angrier than I am?

In a way she does me honor. No more counterfeit soothing, no more pretend lullabies or concern for tummy-ache, no petsy-wetsy whatsa-matter. Instead she will play Mendelssohn's Violin Concerto, the piece she played at her recital and must play again at her examination to get her graduating diploma.

The Mendelssohn is her choice—rather than the Beethoven Violin Concerto which she more passionately admires—because she believes the Mendelssohn will get her higher marks. She thinks she can master—has mastered—it more fully; she is confident that she can show off and impress the examiners without the least fear of catastrophe. This is not a work that will trouble her all her life, she has decided; it is not something she will struggle with and try to prove herself at forever.

She will just play it.

She tunes up, she does a few scales, she attempts to banish me from her hearing. She knows she's stiff, but this time she's prepared for that. She expects her problems to lessen as she gets into the music.

She starts to play it, she goes on playing, she goes on and on, she plays right through to the end. And her playing is terrible. It's a torment. She hangs on, she thinks this must change, she can change it, but she can't. Everything is off, she plays as badly as Jack Benny does in one of his resolute parodies. The violin is bewitched, it hates her. It gives her back a stubborn distortion of everything she intends. Nothing could be worse than this—it's worse than if she looked in the mirror and saw her reliable face caved in, sick and leering. A trick played on her that she couldn't believe, and would try to disprove by looking away and looking back, away and back, over and over again. That is how she goes on playing, trying to undo the trick. But not succeeding. She gets worse, if anything; sweat pours down her face and arms and the sides of her body, and her hand slips—there is simply no bottom to how badly she can play.

Finished. She is finished altogether. The piece that she mastered months ago and perfected since, so that nothing in it remained formid-able or even tricky, has completely defeated her. It has shown her to herself as somebody emptied out, vandalized. Robbed overnight.

She doesn't give up. She does the worst thing. In this state of desperation she starts in again; she will try the Beethoven. And of course it's no good, it's worse and worse, and she seems to be howling, heaving inside. She sets the bow and the violin down on the living-room sofa, then picks them up and shoves them underneath it, getting them out of sight because she has a picture of herself smashing and wrecking them against a chair back, in a sickening dramatic display.

I haven't given up in all this time. Naturally I wouldn't, against such competition.

Jill lies down on the hard sky-blue brocade sofa where nobody ever lies or even sits, unless there's company, and she actually falls asleep. She wakes up after who knows how long with her hot face pushed down into the brocade, its pattern marked on her cheek, her mouth drooling a little and staining the sky-blue material. My racket still or again going on rising and falling like a hammering headache. And she has got a headache, too. She gets up and pushes her way—that's what it feels like—through the hot air to the kitchen cupboard where Ailsa keeps the 222's. The thick air makes her think of sewage. And why not? While she slept I dirtied my diaper, and its ripe smell has had time to fill the house.

222's. Warm another bottle. Climb the stairs. She changes the diaper without lifting me from the crib. The sheet as well as the diaper is a mess. The 222's not working yet and her headache increases in fierceness as she bends over. Haul the mess out, wash off my scalded parts, pin on a clean diaper, and take the dirty diaper and sheet into the bathroom to be scrubbed off in the toilet. Put them in the pail of disinfectant which is already full to the brim because the usual baby wash has not been done today. Then get to me with the bottle. I quiet again enough to suck. It's a wonder I have the energy left to do that, but I do. The feeding is more than an hour late, and I have real hunger to add to—but maybe also subvert—my store of grievance. I suck away, I finish the bottle, and then worn out I go to sleep, and this time actually stay asleep.

Jill's headache dulls. Groggily she washes out my diapers and shirts and gowns and sheets. Scrubs them and rinses them and even boils the diapers to defeat the diaper rash to which I am prone. She wrings them all out by hand. She hangs them up indoors because the next day is Sunday, and Ailsa, when she returns, will not want to see anything hanging outdoors on Sunday. Jill would just as soon not have to appear outside, anyway, especially now with evening thickening and people sitting out, taking advantage of the cool. She dreads being seen by the neighbors—even being greeted by the friendly Shantzes—after what they must have listened to today.

And such a long time it takes for today to be over. For the long reach of sunlight and stretched shadows to give out and the monumental heat to stir a little, opening sweet cool cracks. Then all of a sudden the stars are out in clusters and the trees are enlarging themselves like clouds, shaking down peace. But not for long and not for Jill. Well before midnight comes a thin cry—you could not call it tentative, but thin at least, experimental, as if in spite of the day's practice I have lost the knack. Or as if I actually wonder if it's worth it. A little rest then, a false respite or giving up. But after that a thoroughgoing, an anguished, unforgiving resumption. Just when Jill had started to make more coffee, to deal with the remnants of her headache. Thinking that this time she might sit by the table and drink it.

Now she turns the burner off.

It's almost time for the last bottle of the day. If the feeding before had not been delayed, I'd be ready now. Perhaps I am ready? While it's warming, Jill thinks she'll dose herself with a couple more 222's. Then she thinks maybe that won't do; she needs something stronger. In the bathroom cupboard she finds only Pepto-Bismol, laxatives, foot powder, prescriptions she wouldn't touch. But she knows that Ailsa takes something strong for her menstrual cramps, and she goes into Ailsa's room and looks through her bureau drawers until she finds a bottle of pain pills lying, logically, on top of a pile of sanitary pads. These are prescriptions pills, too, but the label says clearly what they're for. She removes two of them and goes back to the kitchen and finds the water in the pan around the milk boiling, the milk too hot.

She holds the bottle under the tap to cool it—my cries coming down at her like the clamor of birds of prey over a gurgling river—and she looks at the pills waiting on the counter and she thinks, *Yes.* She gets out a knife and shaves a few grains off one of the pills, takes the nipple off the bottle, picks up the shaved grains on the blade of the knife, and sprinkles them— just a sprinkle of white dust—over the milk. Then she swallows one and seven-eighths or maybe one and eleven-twelfths or even one and fifteen-sixteenths of a pill herself, and takes the bottle upstairs. She lifts up my immediately rigid body and gets the nipple into my accusing mouth. The milk is still a little too warm for my liking and at first I spit it back at her. Then in a while I decide that it will do, and I swallow it all down.

IONA IS screaming. Jill wakes up to a house full of hurtful sunlight and Iona's screaming.

The plan was that Ailsa and Iona and their mother would visit with their relatives in Guelph until the late afternoon, avoiding driving during the hot part of the day. But after breakfast Iona began to make a fuss. She wanted to get home to the baby, she said she had hardly slept all night for worrying. It was embarrassing to keep on arguing with her in front of the relatives, so Ailsa gave in and they arrived home late in the morning and opened the door of the still house.

Ailsa said, "Phew. Is this what it always smells like in here, only we're so used to it we don't notice?"

Iona ducked past her and ran up the stairs.

Now she's screaming.

Dead. Dead. Murderer.

She knows nothing about the pills. So why does she scream "Murderer"? It's the blanket. She sees the blanket pulled up right over my head. Suffocation. Not poison. It has not taken her any time, not half a second, to get from "dead" to "murderer." It's an immediate flying leap. She grabs me from the crib, with the death blanket twisted round me, and holding the blanketed bundle squeezed against her body she runs screaming out of the room and into Jill's room.

Jill is struggling up, dopily, after twelve or thirteen hours of sleep.

"You've killed my baby," Iona is screaming at her.

Jill doesn't correct her—she doesn't say, *Mine.* Iona holds me out accusingly to show me to Jill, but before Jill can get any kind of a look at me I have been snatched back. Iona groans and doubles up as if she's been shot in the stomach. Still holding on to me she stumbles down the stairs, bumping into Ailsa who is on her way up. Ailsa is almost knocked off her feet; she hangs on to the banister and Iona takes no notice; she seems to be trying to squeeze the bundle of me into a new terrifying hole in the middle of her body. Words come out of her between fresh groans of recognition.

Baby. Love my. Darling. Ooh. Oh. Get the. Suffocated. Blanket. Baby. Police.

Jill has slept with no covers over her and without changing into a nightdress. She is still in yesterday's shorts and halter, and she's not sure if she's waking from a night's sleep or a nap. She isn't sure where she is or what day it is. And what did Iona say? Groping her way up out of a vat of warm wool, Jill sees rather than hears Iona's cries, and they're like red flashes, hot veins in the inside of her eyelids. She clings to the luxury of not having to understand, but then she knows she has understood. She knows it's about me.

But Jill thinks that Iona has made a mistake. Iona has got into the wrong part of the dream. That part is all over.

The baby is all right. Jill took care of the baby. She went out and found the baby and covered it up. All right.

In the downstairs hall, Iona makes an effort and shouts some words all together. "She pulled the blanket all the way over its head, she smothered it."

Ailsa comes downstairs hanging on to the banister.

"Put it down," she says. "Put it down."

Iona squeezes me and groans. Then she holds me out to Ailsa and says, "Look. Look."

Ailsa whips her head aside. "I won't," she says. "I won't look." Iona comes close to push me into her face—I am still all wrapped up in my blanket, but Ailsa doesn't know that and Iona doesn't notice or doesn't care.

Now it's Ailsa screaming. She runs to the other side of the dining-room table screaming, "Put it down. Put it down. I'm not going to look at a corpse."

Mrs. Kirkham comes in from the kitchen, saying, "Girls. Oh, girls. What's the trouble between you? I can't have this, you know."

"Look," says Iona, forgetting Ailsa and coming around the table to show me to her mother.

Ailsa gets to the hall phone and gives the operator Dr. Shantz's number.

"Oh, a baby," says Mrs. Kirkham, twitching the blanket aside.

"She smothered it," Iona says.

"Oh, no," says Mrs. Kirkham.

Ailsa is talking to Dr. Shantz on the phone, telling him in a shaky voice to get over here at once. She turns from the phone and looks at Iona, gulps to steady herself, and says, "Now you. You pipe down."

Iona gives a high-pitched defiant yelp and runs away from her, across the hall into the living room. She is still hanging on to me.

Jill has come to the top of the stairs. Ailsa spots her.

She says, "Come on down here."

She has no idea what she's going to do to Jill, or say to her, once she gets her down. She looks as if she wants to slap her. "It's no good now getting hysterical," she says.

Jill's halter is twisted partway round so that most of one breast has got loose.

"Fix yourself up," says Ailsa. "Did you sleep in your clothes? You look drunk."

Jill seems to herself to be walking still in the snowy light of her dream. But the dream has been invaded by these frantic people.

Ailsa is able to think now about some things that have to be done. Whatever has happened, there has got to be no question of such a thing as a murder. Babies do die, for no reason, in their sleep. She has heard of that. No question of the police. No autopsy—a sad quiet little funeral. The obstacle to this is Iona. Dr. Shantz can give Iona a needle now; the needle will put her to sleep. But he can't go on giving her a needle every day.

The thing is to get Iona into Morrisville. This is the Hospital for the Insane, which used to be called the Asylum and in the future will be called the Psychiatric Hospital, then the Mental Health Unit. But most people just call it Morrisville, after the village nearby.

Going to Morrisville, they say. They took her off to Morrisville. Carry on like that and you're going to end up in Morrisville.

Iona has been there before and she can go there again. Dr. Shantz can get her in and keep her in until it's judged she's ready to come out. Affected by the baby's death. Delusions. Once that is established she won't pose a threat. Nobody will pay any attention to what she says. She will have had a breakdown. In fact it looks as if that may be the truth—it looks as if she might be halfway to a breakdown already, with that yelping and running around. It might be permanent. But probably not. There's all kinds of treatment nowadays. Drugs to calm her down, and shock if it's better to blot out some memories, and an operation they do, if they have to, on people who are obstinately confused and miserable. They don't do that at Morrisville—they have to send you to the city.

For all this—which has gone through her mind in an instant—Ailsa will have to count on Dr. Shantz. Some obliging lack of curiosity on his part and a willingness to see things her way. But that should not be hard for anybody who knows what she has been through. The investment she has made in this family's respectability and the blows she's had to take, from her father's shabby career and her mother's mixed-up wits to Iona's collapse at nursing school and George's going off to get killed. Does Ailsa deserve a public scandal on top of this—a story in the papers, a trial, maybe even a sister-in-law in jail?

Dr. Shantz would not think so. And not just because he can tote up these reasons from what he has observed as a friendly neighbor. Not just because he can appreciate that people who have to do without respectability must sooner or later feel the cold.

The reasons he has for helping Ailsa are all in his voice as he comes running in the back door now, through the kitchen, calling her name.

Jill at the bottom of the stairs has just said, "The baby's all right."

And Ailsa has said, "You keep quiet until I tell you what to say."

Mrs. Kirkham stands in the doorway between the kitchen and the hall, square in Dr. Shantz's path.

"Oh, I'm glad to see you," she says. "Ailsa and Iona are all upset with each other. Iona found a baby at the door and now she says it's dead."

Dr. Shantz picks Mrs. Kirkham up and puts her aside. He says again,

"Ailsa?" and reaches out his arms, but ends up just setting his hands down hard on her shoulders.

Iona comes out of the living room empty-handed.

Jill says, "What did you do with the baby?"

"Hid it," Iona says saucily, and makes a face at her—the kind of face a terminally frightened person can make, pretending to be vicious.

"Dr. Shantz is going to give you a needle," Ailsa says. "That'll put paid to you."

Now there is an absurd scene of Iona running around, throwing herself at the front door—Ailsa jumps to block her—and then at the stairs, which is where Dr. Shantz gets hold of her and straddles her, pinning her arms and saying, "Now, now, now, Iona. Take it easy. You'll be okay in a little while." And Iona yells and whimpers and subsides. The noises she makes, and her darting about, her efforts at escape, all seem like playacting. As if—in spite of being quite literally at her wit's end—she finds the effort of standing up to Ailsa and Dr. Shantz so nearly impossible that she can only try to manage it by this sort of parody. Which makes it clear—and maybe this is what she really intends—that she is not standing up to them at all but falling apart. Falling apart as embarrassingly and inconveniently as possible with Ailsa shouting at her, "You ought to be disgusted with yourself."

Administering the needle, Dr. Shantz says, "That-a-girl Iona. There now."

Over his shoulder he says to Ailsa, "Look after your mother. Get her to sit down."

Mrs. Kirkham is wiping tears with her fingers. "I'm all right dear," she says to Ailsa. "I just wish you girls wouldn't fight. You should have told me Iona had a baby. You should have let her keep it."

Mrs. Shantz, wearing a Japanese kimono over her summer pajamas, comes into the house by the kitchen door.

"Is everybody all right?" she calls.

She sees the knife lying on the kitchen counter and thinks it prudent to pick it up and put it in a drawer. When people are making a scene the last thing you want is a knife ready to hand.

In the midst of this Jill thinks she has heard a faint cry. She has climbed clumsily over the banister to get around Iona and Dr. Shantz—she ran partway up the stairs again when Iona came running in that direction—and has lowered herself to the floor. She goes through the double doors into the living room where at first she sees no sign of me. But the faint cry comes again and she follows the sound to the sofa and looks underneath it.

That's where I am, pushed in beside the violin.

During that short trip from the hall to the living room, Jill has remembered everything, and it seems as if her breath stops and horror crowds in at her mouth, then a flash of joy sets her life going again, when just as in the dream she comes upon a live baby, not a little desiccated nutmeg-headed corpse. She holds me. I don't stiffen or kick or arch my back. I am still pretty sleepy from the sedative in my milk which knocked me out for the night and half a day and which, in a larger quantity— maybe not so much larger, at that—would have really finished me off.

IT WASN'T the blanket at all. Anybody who took a serious look at that blanket could see that it was so light and loosely woven that it could not prevent my getting all the air I needed. You could breathe through it just as easily as through a fishnet.

Exhaustion might have played a part. A whole day's howling, such a furious feat of self-expression, might have worn me out. That, and the white dust that fell on my milk, had knocked me into a deep and steadfast sleep with breathing so slight that Iona had not been able to detect it. You would think she would notice that I was not cold and you would think that all that moaning and crying out and running around would have brought me up to consciousness in a hurry. I don't know why that didn't happen. I think she didn't notice because of her panic and the state she was in even before she found me, but I don't know why I didn't cry sooner. Or maybe I did cry and in the commotion nobody heard me. Or maybe Iona did hear me and took a look at me and stuffed me under the sofa because by that time everything had been spoiled.

Then Jill heard. Jill was the one.

Iona was carried to that same sofa. Ailsa slipped off her shoes to save the brocade, and Mrs. Shantz went upstairs to get a light quilt to put over her.

"I know she doesn't need it for warmth," she said. "But I think when she wakes up she'll feel better to have a quilt over her."

Before this, of course, everybody had gathered round to take note of my being alive. Ailsa was blaming herself for not having discovered that right away. She hated to admit that she had been afraid to look at a dead baby.

"Iona's nerves must be contagious," she said. "I absolutely should have known."

She looked at Jill as if she was going to tell her to go and put a blouse on over her halter. Then she recalled how roughly she had spoken to her, and for no reason as it turned out, so she didn't say anything. She did not even try to convince her mother that Iona had not had a baby, though she said in an undertone, to Mrs. Shantz, "Well, that could start the rumor of the century."

"I'm so glad nothing terrible happened," Mrs. Kirkham said. "I thought for a minute Iona had done away with it. Ailsa, you must try not to blame your sister."

"No Momma," said Ailsa. "Let's go sit down in the kitchen."

There was one bottle of formula made up that by rights I should have demanded and drunk earlier that morning. Jill put it on to warm, holding me in the crook of her arm all the time.

She had looked at once for the knife, when she came into the kitchen, and seen in wonderment that it wasn't there. But she could make out the faintest dust on the counter—or she thought she could. She wiped it with her free hand before she turned the tap on to get the water to heat the bottle.

Mrs. Shantz busied herself making coffee. While it was perking she put the sterilizer on the stove and washed out yesterday's bottles. She was being tactful and competent, just managing to hide the fact that there was something about this whole debacle and disarray of feelings that buoyed her up.

"I guess Iona did have an obsession about the baby," she said. "Something like this was bound to happen."

Turning from the stove to address the last of these words to her husband and Ailsa, she saw that Dr. Shantz was pulling Ailsa's hands down from where she held them, on either side of her head. Too speedily and guiltily he took his own hands away. If he had not done that, it would have looked like ordinary comfort he was administering. As a doctor is certainly entitled to do.

"You know Ailsa, I think your mother ought to lie down too," said Mrs. Shantz thoughtfully and without a break. "I think I'll go and persuade her. If she can get to sleep this may all pass right out of her head. Out of Iona's too, if we're lucky."

Mrs. Kirkham had wandered out of the kitchen almost as soon as she got there. Mrs. Shantz found her in the living room looking at Iona, and fiddling with the quilt to make sure she was well covered. Mrs. Kirkham did not really want to lie down. She wanted to have things explained to her—she knew that her own explanations were somehow out of kilter. And she wanted to have people talk to her as they used to do, not in the peculiarly gentle and self-satisfied way they did now. But because of her customary politeness and her knowledge that the power she had in the household was negligible, she allowed Mrs. Shantz to take her upstairs.

Jill was reading the instructions for making baby formula. They were printed on the side of the corn syrup tin. When she heard the footsteps going up the stairs she thought that there was something she had better do while she had the chance. She carried me into the living room and laid me down on a chair.

"There now," she whispered confidentially. "You stay still."

She knelt down and nudged and gently tugged the violin out of its hiding place. She found its cover and case and got it properly stowed away. I stayed still—not yet being quite able to turn over—and I stayed quiet.

Left alone by themselves, alone in the kitchen, Dr. Shantz and Ailsa probably did not seize this chance to embrace, but only looked at each other. With their knowledge, and without promises or despair.

IONA ADMITTED that she hadn't felt for a pulse. And she never claimed that I was cold. She said I felt stiff. Then she said not stiff but heavy. So heavy, she said, she instantly thought I could not be alive. A lump, a dead weight.

I think there is something to this. I don't believe that I was dead, or that I came back from the dead, but I do think that I was at a distance, from which I might or might not have come back. I think that the outcome was not certain and that will was involved. It was up to me, I mean, to go one way or the other.

And Iona's love, which was certainly the most wholehearted love I will ever receive, didn't decide me. Her cries and her crushing me into her body didn't work, were not finally persuasive. Because it wasn't Iona I had to settle for. (Could I have known that—could I even have known that it wasn't Iona, in the end, who would do me the most good?) It was Jill. I had to settle for Jill and for what I could get from her, even if it might look like half a loaf.

To me it seems that it was only then that I became female. I know that the matter was decided long before I was born and was plain to everybody else since the beginning of my life, but I believe that it was only at the moment when I decided to come back, when I gave up the fight against my mother (which must have been a fight for something like her total surrender) and when in fact I chose survival over victory (death would have been victory), that I took on my female nature.

And to some extent Jill took on hers. Sobered and grateful, not even able to risk thinking about what she'd just escaped, she took on loving me, because the alternative to loving was disaster.

DR. SHANTZ suspected something, but he let it go. He asked Jill how I had been the day before. Fussy? She said yes, very fussy. He said that premature babies, even slightly premature babies, were susceptible to shocks and you had to be careful with them. He recommended that I always be put to sleep on my back.

Iona did not have to have shock treatment. Dr. Shantz gave her pills. He said that she had overstrained herself looking after me. The woman who had taken over her job at the bakery wanted to give it up—she did not like working nights. So Iona went back there.

THAT'S WHAT I remember best about my summer visits to my aunts, when I was six or seven years old. Being taken down to the bakery at the strange, usually forbidden hour of midnight and watching Iona put on her white hat and apron, watching her knead the great white mass of dough that shifted and bubbled like something alive. Then cutting out cookies and feeding me the leftover bits and on special occasions sculpting a wedding cake. How bright and white that big kitchen was, with night filling every window. I scraped the wedding icing from the bowl—the melting stabbing irresistible sugar.

Ailsa thought I should not be up so late, or eat so much sweet stuff. But she didn't do anything about it. She said she wondered what my mother would say—as if Jill was the person who swung the weight, not herself. Ailsa had some rules that I didn't have to observe at home—hang up that jacket, rinse that glass before you dry it, else it'll have spots—but I never saw the harsh, hounding person Jill remembered.

Nothing slighting was ever said then, about Jill's music. After all, she made our living at it. She had not been finally defeated by the Mendelssohn. She got her diploma; she graduated from the Conservatory. She cut her hair and got thin. She was able to rent a duplex near High Park in Toronto, and hire a woman to look after me part of the time, because she had her war widow's pension. And then she found a job with a radio orchestra. She was to be proud that all her working life she was employed as a musician and never had to fall back on teaching. She said that she knew that she was not a great violinist, she had no marvellous gift or destiny, but at least she could make her living doing what she wanted to do. Even after she married my stepfather, after we moved with him to Edmonton (he was a geologist), she went on playing in the symphony orchestra there. She played up until a week before each of my half sisters was born. She was lucky, she said—her husband never objected.

Iona did have a couple of further setbacks, the more serious one when I was about twelve. She was taken to Morrisville for several weeks. I think she was given insulin there—she returned fat and loquacious. I came back to visit while she was away, and Jill came with me, bringing my first little sister who had been born shortly before. I understood from the talk between my mother and Ailsa that it would not have been advisable to bring a baby into the house if Iona was there; it might have "set her off." I don't know if the episode that sent her to Morrisville had anything to do with a baby.

I felt left out of things on that visit. Both Jill and Ailsa had taken up smoking, and they would sit up late at night, drinking coffee and smoking cigarettes at the kitchen table, while they waited for the baby's one o'clock feeding. (My mother fed this baby from her breasts—I was glad to hear that no such intimate body-heated meals had been served to me.) I remember coming downstairs sulkily because I couldn't sleep, then turning talkative, full of giddy bravado, trying to break into their conversation. I understood that they were talking over things they didn't want me to hear about. They had become, unaccountably, good friends.

I grabbed for a cigarette, and my mother said, "Go on now, leave those alone. We're talking." Ailsa told me to get something to drink out of the fridge, a Coke or a ginger ale. So I did, and instead of taking it upstairs I went outside.

I sat on the back step, but the women's voices immediately went too low for me to make out any of their soft regretting or reassuring. So I went prowling around the backyard, beyond the patch of light thrown through the screen door.

The long white house with the glass-brick corners was occupied by new people now. The Shantzes had moved away, to live year-round in Florida. They sent my aunts oranges, which Ailsa said would make you forever disgusted with the kind of oranges you could buy in Canada. The new people had put in a swimming pool, which was used mostly by the two pretty teenage daughters—girls who would look right through me when they met me on the street—and by the daughters' boyfriends. Some bushes had grown up fairly high between my aunts' yard and theirs, but it was still possible for me to watch them running around the pool and pushing each other in, with great shrieks and splashes. I despised their antics because I took life seriously and had a much more lofty and tender notion of romance. But I would have liked to get their attention just the same. I would have liked for one of them to see my pale pajamas moving in the dark, and to scream out in earnest, thinking that I was a ghost.

Hateship, Friendship, Courtship,
Loveship, Marriage

Hateship, Friendship, Courtship, Loveship, Marriage

YEARS AGO, before the trains stopped running on so many of the branch lines, a woman with a high, freckled forehead and a frizz of reddish hair came into the railway station and inquired about shipping furniture.

The station agent often tried a little teasing with women, especially the plain ones who seemed to appreciate it.

"Furniture?" he said, as if nobody had ever had such an idea before. "Well. Now. What kind of furniture are we talking about?"

A dining-room table and six chairs. A full bedroom suite, a sofa, a coffee table, end tables, a floor lamp. Also a china cabinet and a buffet.

"Whoa there. You mean a houseful."

"It shouldn't count as that much," she said. "There's no kitchen things and only enough for one bedroom."

Her teeth were crowded to the front of her mouth as if they were ready for an argument.

"You'll be needing the truck," he said.

"No. I want to send it on the train. It's going out west, to Saskatchewan."

She spoke to him in a loud voice as if he was deaf or stupid, and there was something wrong with the way she pronounced her words. An accent. He thought of Dutch—the Dutch were moving in around here—but she didn't have the heft of the Dutch women or the nice pink skin or the fair hair. She might have been under forty, but what did it matter? No beauty queen, ever.

He turned all business.

"First you'll need the truck to get it to here from wherever you got it. And we better see if it's a place in Saskatchewan where the train goes through. Otherways you'd have to arrange to get it picked up, say, in Regina."

"It's Gdynia," she said. "The train goes through."

He took down a greasy-covered directory that was hanging from a nail and asked how she would spell that. She helped herself to the pencil that was also on a string and wrote on a piece of paper from her purse: *GDYNIA.*

"What kind of nationality would that be?"

She said she didn't know.

He took back the pencil to follow from line to line.

"A lot of places out there it's all Czechs or Hungarians or Ukrainians," he said. It came to him as he said this that she might be one of those. But so what, he was only stating a fact.

"Here it is, all right, it's on the line."

"Yes," she said. "I want to ship it Friday—can you do that?"

"We can ship it, but I can't promise what day it'll get there," he said. "It all depends on the priorities. Somebody going to be on the lookout for it when it comes in?"

"Yes."

"It's a mixed train Friday, two-eighteen p.m. Truck picks it up Friday morning. You live here in town?"

She nodded, writing down the address. 106 Exhibition Road.

It was only recently that the houses in town had been numbered, and he couldn't picture the place, though he knew where Exhibition Road was. If she'd said the name McCauley at that time he might have taken more of an interest, and things might have turned out differently. There were new houses out there, built since the war, though they were called "wartime houses." He supposed it must be one of those.

"Pay when you ship," he told her.

"Also, I want a ticket for myself on the same train. Friday afternoon."

"Going same place?"

"Yes."

"You can travel on the same train to Toronto, but then you have to wait for the Transcontinental, goes out ten-thirty at night. You want sleeper or coach? Sleeper you get a berth, coach you sit up in the day car."

She said she would sit up.

"Wait in Sudbury for the Montreal train, but you won't get off there, they'll just shunt you around and hitch on the Montreal cars. Then on to Port Arthur and then to Kenora. You don't get off till Regina, and there you have to get off and catch the branch-line train."

She nodded as if he should just get on and give her the ticket.

Slowing down, he said, "But I won't promise your furniture'll arrive when you do, I wouldn't think it would get in till a day or two after. It's all the priorities. Somebody coming to meet you?"

"Yes."

"Good. Because it won't likely be much of a station. Towns out there, they're not like here. They're mostly pretty rudimentary affairs."

She paid for the passenger ticket now, from a roll of bills in a cloth bag in her purse. Like an old lady. She counted her change, too. But not the way an old lady would count it—she held it in her hand and flicked her eyes over it, but you could tell she didn't miss a penny. Then she turned away rudely, without a good-bye.

"See you Friday," he called out.

She wore a long, drab coat on this warm September day, also a pair of clunky laced-up shoes, and ankle socks.

He was getting a coffee out of his thermos when she came back and rapped on the wicket.

"The furniture I'm sending," she said. "It's all good furniture, it's like new. I wouldn't want it to get scratched or banged up or in any way damaged. I don't want it to smell like livestock, either."

"Oh, well," he said. "The railway's pretty used to shipping things. And they don't use the same cars for shipping furniture they use for shipping pigs."

"I'm concerned that it gets there in just as good a shape as it leaves here."

"Well, you know, when you buy your furniture, it's in the store, right? But did you ever think how it got there? It wasn't made in the store, was it? No. It was made in some factory someplace, and it got shipped to the store, and that was done quite possibly by train. So that being the case, doesn't it stand to reason the railway knows how to look after it?"

She continued to look at him without a smile or any admission of her female foolishness.

"I hope so," she said. "I hope they do."

THE STATION agent would have said, without thinking about it, that he knew everybody in town. Which meant that he knew about half of them. And most of those he knew were the core people, the ones who really were "in town" in the sense that they had not arrived yesterday and had no plans to move on. He did not know the woman who was going to Saskatchewan because she did not go to his church or teach his children in school or work in any store or restaurant or office that he went into. Nor was she married to any of the men he knew in the Elks or the Oddfellows or the Lions Club or the Legion. A look at her left hand while she was getting the money out had told him—and he was not surprised— that she was not married to anybody. With those shoes, and ankle socks instead of stockings, and no hat or gloves in the afternoon, she might have been a farm woman. But she didn't have the hesitation they generally had, the embarrassment. She didn't have country manners—in fact, she had no manners at all. She had treated him as if he was an information machine. Besides, she had written a town address—Exhibition Road. The person she really reminded him of was a plainclothes nun he had seen on television, talking about the missionary work she did somewhere in the jungle—probably they had got out of their nuns' clothes there because it made it easier for them to clamber around. This nun had smiled once in a while to show that her religion was supposed to make people happy, but most of the time she looked out at her audience as if she believed that other people were mainly in the world for her to boss around.

ONE MORE thing Johanna meant to do she had been putting off doing. She had to go into the dress shop called Milady's and buy herself an outfit. She had never been inside that shop—when she had to buy anything, like socks, she went to Callaghans Mens Ladies and Childrens Wear. She had lots of clothes inherited from Mrs. Willets, things like this coat that would never wear out. And Sabitha—the girl she looked after, in Mr. McCauley's house—was showered with costly hand-me-downs from her cousins.

In Milady's window there were two mannequins wearing suits with quite short skirts and boxy jackets. One suit was a rusty-gold color and the other a soft deep green. Big gaudy paper maple leaves were scattered round the mannequins' feet and pasted here and there on the window. At the time of year when most people's concern was to rake up leaves and burn them, here they were the chosen thing. A sign written in flowing black script was stuck diagonally across the glass. It said: *Simple Elegance, the Mode for Fall.*

She opened the door and went inside.

Right ahead of her, a full-length mirror showed her in Mrs. Willets's high-quality but shapeless long coat, with a few inches of lumpy bare legs above the ankle socks.

They did that on purpose, of course. They set the mirror there so you - could get a proper notion of your deficiencies, right away, and then—they hoped—you would jump to the conclusion that you had to buy something to alter the picture. Such a transparent trick that it would have made her walk out, if she had not come in determined, knowing what she had to get.

Along one wall was a rack of evening dresses, all fit for belles of the ball with their net and taffeta, their dreamy colors. And beyond them, in a glass case so no profane fingers could get at them, half a dozen wedding gowns, pure white froth or vanilla satin or ivory lace, embroidered in silver beads or seed pearls. Tiny bodices, scalloped necklines, lavish skirts. Even when she was younger she could never have contemplated such extravagance, not just in the matter of money but in expectations, in the preposterous hope of transformation, and bliss.

It was two or three minutes before anybody came. Maybe they had a peephole and were eyeing her, thinking she wasn't their kind of customer and hoping she would go away.

She would not. She moved beyond the mirror's reflection—stepping from the linoleum by the door to a plushy rug—and at long last the curtain at the back of the store opened and out stepped Milady herself, dressed in a black suit with glittery buttons. High heels, thin ankles, girdle so tight her nylons rasped, gold hair skinned back from her made-up face.

"I thought I could try on the suit in the window," Johanna said in a rehearsed voice. "The green one."

"Oh, that's a lovely suit," the woman said. "The one in the window happens to be a size ten. Now you look to be—maybe a fourteen?"

She rasped ahead of Johanna back to the part of the store where the ordinary clothes, the suits and daytime dresses, were hung.

"You're in luck. Fourteen coming up."

The first thing Johanna did was look at the price tag. Easily twice what she'd expected, and she was not going to pretend otherwise.

"It's expensive enough."

"It's very fine wool." The woman monkeyed around till she found the label, then read off a description of the material that Johanna wasn't really listening to because she had caught at the hem to examine the workmanship.

"It feels as light as silk, but it wears like iron. You can see it's lined throughout, lovely silk-and-rayon lining. You won't find it bagging in the seat and going out of shape the way the cheap suits do. Look at the velvet cuffs and collar and the little velvet buttons on the sleeve."

"I see them."

"That's the kind of detail you pay for, you just do not get it otherwise. I love the velvet touch. It's only on the green one, you know—the apricot one doesn't have it, even though they're exactly the same price."

Indeed it was the velvet collar and cuffs that gave the suit, in Johanna's eyes, its subtle look of luxury and made her long to buy it. But she was not going to say so.

"I might as well go ahead and try it on."

This was what she'd come prepared for, after all. Clean underwear and fresh talcum powder under her arms.

The woman had enough sense to leave her alone in the bright cubicle. Johanna avoided the glass like poison till she'd got the skirt straight and the jacket done up.

At first she just looked at the suit. It was all right. The fit was all right—the skirt shorter than what she was used to, but then what she was used to was not the style. There was no problem with the suit. The problem was with what stuck out of it. Her neck and her face and her hair and her big hands and thick legs.

"How are you getting on? Mind if I take a peek?"

Peek all you want to, Johanna thought, it's a case of a sow's ear, as you'll soon see.

The woman tried looking from one side, then the other.

"Of course, you'll need your nylons on and your heels. How does it feel? Comfortable?"

"The suit feels fine," Johanna said. "There's nothing the matter with the suit."

The woman's face changed in the mirror. She stopped smiling. She looked disappointed and tired, but kinder.

"Sometimes that's just the way it is. You never really know until you try something on. The thing is," she said, with a new, more moderate conviction growing in her voice, "the thing is you have a fine figure, but it's a strong figure. You have large bones and what's the matter with that? Dinky little velvet-covered buttons are not for you. Don't bother with it anymore. Just take it off."

Then when Johanna had got down to her underwear there was a tap and a hand through the curtain.

"Just slip this on, for the heck of it."

A brown wool dress, lined, with a full skirt gracefully gathered, three-quarter sleeves and a plain round neckline. About as plain as you could get, except for a narrow gold belt. Not as expensive as the suit, but still the price seemed like a lot, when you considered all there was to it.

At least the skirt was a more decent length and the fabric made a noble swirl around her legs. She steeled herself and looked in the glass.

This time she didn't look as if she'd been stuck into the garment for a joke.

The woman came and stood beside her, and laughed, but with relief.

"It's the color of your eyes. You don't need to wear velvet. You've got velvet eyes."

That was the kind of soft-soaping Johanna would have felt bound to scoff at, except that at the moment it seemed to be true. Her eyes were not large, and if asked to describe their color she would have said, "I guess they're a kind of a brown." But now they looked to be a really deep brown, soft and shining.

It wasn't that she had suddenly started thinking she was pretty or anything. Just that her eyes were a nice color, if they had been a piece of cloth.

"Now, I bet you don't wear dress shoes very often," the woman said. "But if you had nylons on and just a minimum kind of pump— And I bet you don't wear jewelry, and you're quite right, you don't need to, with that belt."

To cut off the sales spiel Johanna said, "Well, I better take it off so you can wrap it up." She was sorry to lose the soft weight of the skirt and the discreet ribbon of gold around her waist. She had never in her life had this silly feeling of being enhanced by what she had put on herself.

"I just hope it's for a special occasion," the woman called out as Johanna was hastening into her now dingy-looking regular clothes.

"It'll likely be what I get married in," said Johanna.

She was surprised at that coming out of her mouth. It wasn't a major error—the woman didn't know who she was and would probably not be talking to anybody who did know. Still, she had meant to keep absolutely quiet. She must have felt she owed this person something— that they'd been through the disaster of the green suit and the discovery of the brown dress together and that was a bond. Which was nonsense. The woman was in the business of selling clothes, and she'd just succeeded in doing that.

"Oh!" the woman cried out. "Oh, that's wonderful."

Well, it might be, Johanna thought, and then again it might not. She might be marrying anybody. Some miserable farmer who wanted a workhorse around the place, or some wheezy old half-cripple looking for a nurse. This woman had no idea what kind of man she had lined up, and it wasn't any of her business anyway.

"I can tell it's a love match," the woman said, just as if she had read these disgruntled thoughts. "That's why your eyes were shining in the mirror. I've wrapped it all in tissue paper, all you have to do is take it out and hang it up and the material will fall out beautifully. Just give it a light press if you want, but you probably won't even need to do that."

Then there was the business of handing over the money. They both pretended not to look, but both did.

"It's worth it," the woman said. "You only get married the once. Well, that's not always strictly true—"

"In my case it'll be true," Johanna said. Her face was hotly flushed because marriage had not, in fact, been mentioned. Not even in the last letter. She had revealed to this woman what she was counting on, and that had perhaps been an unlucky thing to do.

"Where did you meet him?" said the woman, still in that tone of wistful gaiety. "What was your first date?"

"Through family," Johanna said truthfully. She wasn't meaning to say any more but heard herself go on. "The Western Fair. In London."

"The Western Fair," the woman said. "In London." She could have been saying "the Castle Ball."

"We had his daughter and her friend with us," said Johanna, thinking that in a way it would have been more accurate to say that he and Sabitha and Edith had her, Johanna, with them.

"Well, I can say my day has not been wasted. I've provided the dress for somebody to be a happy bride in. That's enough to justify my existence." The woman tied a narrow pink ribbon around the dress box, making a big, unnecessary bow, then gave it a wicked snip with the scissors.

"I'm here all day," she said. "And sometimes I just wonder what I think I'm doing. I ask myself, What do you think you're doing here? I put up a new display in the window and I do this and that to entice the people in, but there are days—there are *days*—when I do not see one soul come in that door. I know—people think these clothes are too expensive—but they're *good*. They're good clothes. If you want the quality you have to pay the price."

"They must come in when they want something like those," said Johanna, looking towards the evening dresses. "Where else could they go?"

"That's just it. They don't. They go to the city—that's where they go. They'll drive fifty miles, a hundred miles, never mind the gas, and tell themselves that way they get something better than I've got here. And they haven't. Not better quality, not better selection. Nothing. Just that they'd be ashamed to say they bought their wedding outfits in town. Or they'll come in and try something on and say they have to think about it. I'll be back, they say. And I think, Oh, yes, I know what that means. It means they'll try to find the same thing cheaper in London or Kitchener, and even if it isn't cheaper, they'll buy it there once they've driven all that way and got sick of looking."

"I don't know," she said. "Maybe if I was a local person it would make a difference. It's very clique-y here, I find. You're not local, are you?"

Johanna said, "No."

"Don't you find it clique-y?"

Cleeky.

"Hard for an outsider to break in, is what I mean."

"I'm used to being on my own," Johanna said.

"But you found somebody. You won't be on your own anymore and isn't that lovely? Some days I think how grand it would be, to be married and stay at home. Of course, I used to be married, and I worked anyway. Ah, well. Maybe the man in the moon will walk in here and fall in love with me and then I'll be all set!"

JOHANNA HAD to hurry—that woman's need for conversation had delayed her. She was hurrying to be back at the house, her purchase stowed away, before Sabitha got home from school.

Then she remembered that Sabitha wasn't there, having been carried off on the weekend by her mother's cousin, her Aunt Roxanne, to live like a proper rich girl in Toronto and go to a rich girl's school. But she continued to walk fast—so fast some smart aleck holding up the wall of the drugstore called out to her, "Where's the fire?" and she slowed down a bit, not to attract attention.

The dress box was awkward—how could she have known the store would have its own pink cardboard boxes, with *Milady's* written across them in purple handwriting? A dead giveaway.

She felt a fool for mentioning a wedding, when he hadn't mentioned it and she ought to remember that. So much else had been said—or written—such fondness and yearning expressed, that the actual marrying seemed just to have been overlooked. The way you might speak about getting up in the morning and not about having breakfast, though you certainly intended to have it.

Nevertheless she should have kept her mouth shut.

She saw Mr. McCauley walking in the opposite direction up the other side of the street. That was all right—even if he had met her head-on he would never have noticed the box she carried. He would have raised a finger to his hat and passed her by, presumably noticing that she was his housekeeper but possibly not. He had other things on his mind, and for all anybody knew might be looking at some town other than the one they saw. Every working day—and sometimes, forgetfully, on holidays or Sundays—he got dressed in one of his three-piece suits and his light overcoat or his heavy overcoat, and his gray fedora and his well-polished shoes, and walked from Exhibition Road uptown to the office he still maintained over what had been the harness and luggage store. It was spoken of as an Insurance Office, though it was quite a long time since he had actively sold insurance. Sometimes people climbed the stairs to see him, maybe to ask some question about their policies or more likely about lot boundaries, the history of some piece of real estate in town or farm out in the country. His office was full of maps old and new, and he liked nothing better than to lay them out and get into a discussion that expanded far beyond the question asked. Three or four times a day he emerged and walked the street, as now. During the war he had put the McLaughlin-Buick up on blocks in the barn, and walked everywhere to set an example. He still seemed to be setting an example, fifteen years later. Hands clasped behind his back, he was like a kind landlord inspecting his property or a preacher happy to observe his flock. Of course, half the people that he met had no idea who he was.

The town had changed, even in the time Johanna had been here. Trade was moving out to the highway, where there was a new discount store and a Canadian Tire and a motel with a lounge and topless dancers. Some downtown shops had tried to spruce themselves up with pink or mauve or olive paint, but already that paint was curling on the old brick and some of the interiors were empty. Milady's was almost certain to follow suit.

If Johanna was the woman in there, what would she have done? She'd never have gotten in so many elaborate evening dresses, for a start. What instead? If you made the switch to cheaper clothes you'd only be putting yourself in competition with Callaghans and the discount place, and there probably wasn't trade enough to go around. So what about going into fancy baby clothes, children's clothes, trying to pull in the grandmothers and aunts who had the money and would spend it for that kind of thing? Forget about the mothers, who would go to Callaghans, having less money and more sense.

But if it was her in charge—Johanna—she would never be able to pull in anybody. She could see what needed to be done, and how, and she could round up and supervise people to do it, but she could never charm or entice. Take it or leave it, would be her attitude. No doubt they would leave it.

It was the rare person who took to her, and she'd been aware of that for a long time. Sabitha certainly hadn't shed any tears when she said good-bye—though you could say Johanna was the nearest thing Sabitha had to a mother, since her own mother had died. Mr. McCauley would be upset when she left because she'd given good service and it would be hard to replace her, but that would be all he thought about. Both he and his granddaughter were spoiled and self-centered. As for the neighbors, they would no doubt rejoice. Johanna had had problems on both sides of the property. On one side it was the neighbors' dog digging in her garden, burying and retrieving his supply of bones, which he could better have done at home. And on the other it was the black cherry tree, which was on the McCauleys' property but bore most of its cherries on the branches hanging over into the next yard. In both cases she had raised a fuss, and won. The dog was tied up and the other neighbors left the cherries alone. If she got up on the stepladder she could reach well over into their yard, but they no longer chased the birds out of the branches and it made a difference to the crop.

Mr. McCauley would have let them pick. He would have let the dog dig. He would let himself be taken advantage of. Part of the reason was that these were new people and lived in new houses and so he preferred not to pay attention to them. At one time there had been just three or four large houses on Exhibition Road. Across from them were the fairgrounds, where the fall fair was held (officially called the Agricultural Exhibition, hence the name), and in between were orchard trees, small meadows. A dozen years ago or so that land had been sold off in regular lot sizes and houses had been put up—small houses in alternating styles, one kind with an upstairs and the other kind without. Some were already getting to look pretty shabby.

There were only a couple of houses whose occupants Mr. McCauley knew and was friendly with—the schoolteacher, Miss Hood, and her mother, and the Shultzes, who ran the Shoe Repair shop. The Shultzes' daughter, Edith, was or had been Sabitha's great friend. It was natural, with their being in the same grade at school—at least last year, once Sabitha had been held back—and living near each other. Mr. McCauley hadn't minded—maybe he had some idea that Sabitha would be removed before long to live a different sort of life in Toronto. Johanna would not have chosen Edith, though the girl was never rude, never troublesome when she came to the house. And she was not stupid. That might have been the problem—she was smart and Sabitha was not so smart. She had made Sabitha sly.

That was all over now. Now that the cousin, Roxanne—Mrs. Huber— had shown up, the Schultz girl was all part of Sabitha's childish past.

I am going to arrange to get all your furniture out to you on the train as soon as they can take it and prepaid as soon as they tell me what it will cost. I have been thinking you will need it now. I guess it will not be that much of a surprise that I thought you would not mind it if I went along to be of help to you as I hope I can be.

This was the letter she had taken to the Post Office, before she went to make arrangements at the railway station. It was the first letter she had ever sent to him directly. The others had been slipped in with the letters she made Sabitha write. And his to her had come in the same way, tidily folded and with her name, Johanna, typed on the back of the page so there would be no mistaking. That kept the people in the Post Office from catching on, and it never hurt to save a stamp. Of course, Sabitha could have reported to her grandfather, or even read what was written to Johanna, but Sabitha was no more interested in communicating with the old man than she was in letters—the writing or the receiving of them.

The furniture was stored back in the barn, which was just a town barn, not a real barn with animals and a granary. When Johanna got her first look at everything a year or so ago, she found it grimy with dust and splattered with pigeon droppings. The pieces had been piled in carelessly without anything to cover them. She had hauled what she - could carry out into the yard, leaving space in the barn to get at the big pieces she couldn't carry—the sofa and buffet and china cabinet and dining table. The bedstead she could take apart. She went at the wood with soft dustrags, then lemon oil, and when she was finished it shone like candy. Maple candy—it was bird's-eye maple wood. It looked glamorous to her, like satin bedspreads and blond hair. Glamorous and modern, a total contrast to all the dark wood and irksome carving of the furniture she cared for in the house. She thought of it as *his* furniture then, and still did when she got it out this Wednesday. She had put old quilts over the bottom layer to protect everything there from what was piled on top, and sheets over what was on top to protect that from the birds, and as a result there was only a light dust. But she wiped everything and lemon-oiled it before she put it back, protected in the same way, to wait for the truck on Friday.

Dear Mr. McCauley,
I am leaving on the train this afternoon (Friday). I realize this is without giving my notice to you, but I will waive my last pay, which would be three weeks owing this coming Monday. There is a beef stew on the stove in the double boiler that just needs warming up. Enough there for three meals or maybe could be stretched to a fourth. As soon as it is hot and you have got all you want, put the lid on and put it away in the fridge. Remember, put the lid on at once not to take chances with it getting spoiled. Regards to you and to Sabitha and will probably be in touch when I am settled. Johanna Parry.
P.S. I have shipped his furniture to Mr. Boudreau as he may need it. Remember to make sure when you reheat there is enough water in bottom part of the double boiler.

Mr. McCauley had no trouble finding out that the ticket Johanna had bought was to Gdynia, Saskatchewan. He phoned the station agent and asked. He could not think how to describe Johanna—was she old or young-looking, thin or moderately heavy, what was the color of her coat?—but that was not necessary when he mentioned the furniture.

When this call came through there were a couple of people in the station waiting for the evening train. The agent tried to keep his voice down at first, but he became excited when he heard about the stolen furniture (what Mr. McCauley actually said was "and I believe she took some furniture with her"). He swore that if he had known who she was and what she was up to he would never have let her set foot on the train. This assertion was heard and repeated and believed, nobody asking how he could have stopped a grown woman who had paid for her ticket, unless he had some proof right away that she was a thief. Most people who repeated his words believed that he could and would have stopped her— they believed in the authority of station agents and of upright-walking fine old men in three-piece suits like Mr. McCauley.

The beef stew was excellent, as Johanna's cooking always was, but Mr. McCauley found he could not swallow it. He disregarded the instruction about the lid and left the pot sitting open on the stove and did not even turn off the burner until the water in the bottom pot boiled away and he was alerted by a smell of smoking metal.

This was the smell of treachery.

He told himself to be thankful at least that Sabitha was taken care of and he did not have that to worry about. His niece—his wife's cousin, actually, Roxanne—had written to tell him that from what she had seen of Sabitha on her summer visit to Lake Simcoe the girl was going to take some handling.

"Frankly I don't think you and that woman you've hired are going to be up to it when the boys come swarming around."

She did not go so far as to ask him whether he wanted another Marcelle on his hands, but that was what she meant. She said she would get Sabitha into a good school where she could be taught manners at least.

He turned on the television for a distraction, but it was no use.

It was the furniture that galled him. It was Ken Boudreau.

The fact was that three days before—on the very day that Johanna had bought her ticket, as the station agent had now told him—Mr. McCauley had received a letter from Ken Boudreau asking him to (a) advance some money against the furniture belonging to him (Ken Boudreau) and his dead wife, Marcelle, which was stored in Mr. McCauley's barn, or (b) if he could not see his way to doing that, to sell the furniture for as much as he could get and send the money as quickly as he could to Saskatchewan. There was no mention of the loans that had already been made by father-in-law to son-in-law, all against the value of this furniture and amounting to more than it could ever be sold for. Could Ken Boudreau have forgotten all about that? Or did he simply hope—and this was more probable—that his father-in-law would have forgotten?

He was now, it seemed, the owner of a hotel. But his letter was full of diatribes against the fellow who had formerly owned it and who had misled him as to various particulars.

"If I can just get over this hurdle," he said, "then I am convinced I can still make a go of it." But what was the hurdle? A need for immediate money, but he did not say whether it was owing to the former owner, or to the bank, or to a private mortgage holder, or what. It was the same old story—a desperate, wheedling tone mixed in with some arrogance, some sense of its being what was owed him, because of the wounds inflicted on him, the shame suffered, on account of Marcelle.

With many misgivings but remembering that Ken Boudreau was after all his son-in-law and had fought in the war and been through God-knows-what trouble in his marriage, Mr. McCauley had sat down and written a letter saying that he did not have any idea how to go about getting the best price for the furniture and it would be very difficult for him to find out and that he was enclosing a check, which he would count as an outright personal loan. He wished his son-in-law to acknowledge it as such and to remember the number of similar loans made in the past—already, he believed, exceeding any value of the furniture. He was enclosing a list of dates and amounts. Apart from fifty dollars paid nearly two years ago (with a promise of regular payments to follow), he had received nothing. His son-in-law must surely understand that as a result of these unpaid and interest-free loans Mr. McCauley's income had declined, since he would otherwise have invested the money.

He had thought of adding, "I am not such a fool as you seem to think," but decided not to, since that would reveal his irritation and perhaps his weakness.

And now look. The man had jumped the gun and enlisted Johanna in his scheme—he would always be able to get around women—and got hold of the furniture as well as the check. She had paid for the shipping herself, the station agent had said. The flashy-looking modern maple stuff had been overvalued in the deals already made and they would not get much for it, especially when you counted what the railway had charged. If they had been cleverer they would simply have taken something from the house, one of the old cabinets or parlor settees too uncomfortable to sit on, made and bought in the last century. That, of course, would have been plain stealing. But what they had done was not far off.

He went to bed with his mind made up to prosecute.

He woke in the house alone, with no smell of coffee or breakfast coming from the kitchen—instead, there was a whiff of the burned pot still in the air. An autumn chill had settled in all the high-ceilinged, forlorn rooms. It had been warm last evening and on preceding evenings —the furnace had not been turned on yet, and when Mr. McCauley did turn it on the warm air was accompanied by a blast of cellar damp, of mold and earth and decay. He washed and dressed slowly, with forgetful pauses, and spread some peanut butter on a piece of bread for his breakfast. He belonged to a generation in which there were men who were said not to be able even to boil water, and he was one of them. He looked out the front windows and saw the trees on the other side of the racetrack swallowed up in the morning fog, which seemed to be advancing, not retreating as it should at this hour, across the track itself. He seemed to see in the fog the looming buildings of the old Exhibition Grounds—homely, spacious buildings, like enormous barns. They had stood for years and years unused—all through the war—and he forgot what happened to them in the end. Were they torn down, or did they fall down? He abhorred the races that took place now, the crowds and the loudspeaker and the illegal drinking and the ruinous uproar of the summer Sundays. When he thought of that he thought of his poor girl Marcelle, sitting on the verandah steps and calling out to grown schoolmates who had got out of their parked cars and were hurrying to see the races. The fuss she made, the joy she expressed at being back in town, the hugging and holding - people up, talking a mile a minute, rattling on about childhood days and how she'd missed everybody. She had said that the only thing not perfect about life was missing her husband, Ken, left out west because of his work.

She went out there in her silk pajamas, with straggly, uncombed, dyed-blond hair. Her arms and legs were thin, but her face was somewhat bloated, and what she claimed was her tan seemed a sickly brown color not from the sun. Maybe jaundice.

The child had stayed inside and watched television—Sunday cartoons that she was surely too old for.

He couldn't tell what was wrong, or be sure that anything was. Marcelle went away to London to have some female thing done and died in the hospital. When he phoned her husband to tell him, Ken Boudreau said, "What did she take?"

If Marcelle's mother had been alive still, would things have been any different? The fact was that her mother, when she was alive, had been as bewildered as he was. She had sat in the kitchen crying while their teenage daughter, locked into her room, had climbed out the window and slid down the verandah roof to be welcomed by carloads of boys.

The house was full of a feeling of callous desertion, of deceit. He and his wife had surely been kind parents, driven to the wall by Marcelle.

When she had eloped with an airman, they had hoped that she would be all right, at last. They had been generous to the two of them as to the most proper young couple. But it all fell apart. To Johanna Parry he had likewise been generous, and look how she too had gone against him.

He walked to town and went into the hotel for his breakfast. The waitress said, "You're bright and early this morning."

And while she was still pouring out his coffee he began to tell her about how his housekeeper had walked out on him without any warning or provocation, not only left her job with no notice but taken a load of furniture that had belonged to his daughter, that now was supposed to belong to his son-in-law but didn't really, having been bought with his daughter's wedding money. He told her how his daughter had married an airman, a good-looking, plausible fellow who wasn't to be trusted around the corner.

"Excuse me," the waitress said. "I'd love to chat, but I got people waiting on their breakfast. Excuse me—"

He climbed the stairs to his office, and there, spread out on his desk, were the old maps he had been studying yesterday in an effort to locate exactly the very first burying ground in the county (abandoned, he believed, in 1839). He turned on the light and sat down, but he found he - could not concentrate. After the waitress's reproof—or what he took for a reproof—he hadn't been able to eat his breakfast or enjoy his coffee. He decided to go out for a walk to calm himself down.

But instead of walking along in his usual way, greeting people and passing a few words with them, he found himself bursting into speech. The minute anybody asked him how he was this morning he began in a most uncharacteristic, even shameful way to blurt out his woes, and like the waitress, these people had business to attend to and they nodded and shuffled and made excuses to get away. The morning didn't seem to be warming up in the way foggy fall mornings usually did; his jacket wasn't warm enough, so he sought the comfort of the shops.

People who had known him the longest were the most dismayed. He had never been anything but reticent—the well-mannered gentleman, his mind on other times, his courtesy a deft apology for privilege (which was a bit of a joke, because the privilege was mostly in his recollections and not apparent to others). He should have been the last person to air wrongs or ask for sympathy—he hadn't when his wife died, or even when his daughter died—yet here he was, pulling out some letter, asking if it wasn't a shame the way this fellow had taken him for money over and over again, and even now when he'd taken pity on him once more the fellow had connived with his housekeeper to steal the furniture. Some thought it was his own furniture he was talking about—they believed the old man had been left without a bed or a chair in his house. They advised him to go to the police.

"That's no good, that's no good," he said. "How can you get blood from a stone?"

He went into the Shoe Repair shop and greeted Herman Shultz.

"Do you remember those boots you resoled for me, the ones I got in England? You resoled them four or five years ago."

The shop was like a cave, with shaded bulbs hanging down over various workplaces. It was abominably ventilated, but its manly smells— of glue and leather and shoe-blacking and fresh-cut felt soles and rotted old ones—were comfortable to Mr. McCauley. Here his neighbor Herman Shultz, a sallow, expert, spectacled workman, bent-shouldered, was occupied in all seasons—driving in iron nails and clinch nails and, with a wicked hooked knife, cutting the desired shapes out of leather. The felt was cut by something like a miniature circular saw. The buffers made a scuffing noise and the sandpaper wheel made a rasp and the emery stone on a tool's edge sang high like a mechanical insect and the sewing machine punched the leather in an earnest industrial rhythm. All the sounds and smells and precise activities of the place had been familiar to Mr. McCauley for years but never identified or reflected upon before. Now Herman, in his blackened leather apron with a boot on one hand, straightened up, smiled, nodded, and Mr. McCauley saw the man's whole life in this cave. He wished to express sympathy or admiration or something more that he didn't understand.

"Yes, I do," Herman said. "They were nice boots."

"Fine boots. You know I got them on my wedding trip. I got them in England. I can't remember now where, but it wasn't in London."

"I remember you telling me."

"You did a fine job on them. They're still doing well. Fine job, Herman. You do a good job here. You do honest work."

"That's good." Herman took a quick look at the boot on his hand. Mr. McCauley knew that the man wanted to get back to his work, but he - couldn't let him.

"I've just had an eye-opener. A shock."

"Have you?"

The old man pulled out the letter and began to read bits of it aloud, with interjections of dismal laughter.

"Bronchitis. He says he's sick with bronchitis. He doesn't know where to turn. *I don't know who to turn to.* Well he always knows who to turn to. When he's run through everything else, turn to me. *A few hundred just till I get on my feet.* Begging and pleading with me and all the time he's conniving with my housekeeper. Did you know that? She stole a load of furniture and went off out west with it. They were hand in glove. This is a man I've saved the skin of, time and time again. And never a penny back. No, no, I have to be honest and say fifty dollars. Fifty out of hundreds and hundreds. Thousands. He was in the Air Force in the war, you know. Those shortish fellows, they were often in the Air Force. Strutting around thinking they were war heroes. Well, I guess I shouldn't say that, but I think the war spoiled some of those fellows, they never could adjust to life afterwards. But that's not enough of an excuse. Is it? I can't excuse him forever because of the war."

"No you can't."

"I knew he wasn't to be trusted the first time I met him. That's the extraordinary thing. I knew it and I let him rook me all the same. There are people like that. You take pity on them just for being the crooks they are. I got him his insurance job out there, I had some connections. Of course he mucked it up. A bad egg. Some just are."

"You're right about that."

Mrs. Shultz was not in the store that day. Usually she was the one at the counter, taking in the shoes and showing them to her husband and reporting back what he said, making out the slips, and taking the payment when the restored shoes were handed back. Mr. McCauley remembered that she had had some kind of operation during the summer.

"Your wife isn't in today? Is she well?"

"She thought she'd better take it easy today. I've got my girl in."

Herman Shultz nodded towards the shelves to the right of the counter, where the finished shoes were displayed. Mr. McCauley turned his head and saw Edith, the daughter, whom he hadn't noticed when he came in. A childishly thin girl with straight black hair, who kept her back to him, rearranging the shoes. That was just the way she had seemed to slide in and out of sight when she came to his house as Sabitha's friend. You never got a good look at her face.

"You're going to help your father out now?" Mr. McCauley said. "You're through with school?"

"It's Saturday," said Edith, half turning, faintly smiling.

"So it is. Well, it's a good thing to help your father, anyway. You must take care of your parents. They've worked hard and they're good people." With a slight air of apology, as if he knew he was being sententious, Mr. McCauley said, "Honor thy father and thy mother, that thy days may be long in the—"

Edith said something not for him to hear. She said, "Shoe Repair shop."

"I'm taking up your time, I'm imposing on you," said Mr. McCauley sadly. "You have work to do."

"There's no need for you to be sarcastic," said Edith's father when the old man had gone.

HE TOLD Edith's mother all about Mr. McCauley at supper.

"He's not himself," he said. "Something's come over him."

"Maybe a little stroke," she said. Since her own operation—for gallstones—she spoke knowledgeably and with a placid satisfaction about the afflictions of other people.

Now that Sabitha had gone, vanished into another sort of life that had, it seemed, always been waiting for her, Edith had reverted to being the person she had been before Sabitha came here. "Old for her age," diligent, critical. After three weeks at high school she knew that she was going to be very good at all the new subjects—Latin, Algebra, English Literature. She believed that her cleverness was going to be recognized and acclaimed and an important future would open out for her. The past year's silliness with Sabitha was slipping out of sight.

Yet when she thought about Johanna's going off out west she felt a chill from her past, an invasive alarm. She tried to bang a lid down on that, but it wouldn't stay.

As soon as she had finished washing the dishes she went off to her room with the book they had been assigned for literature class. *David Copperfield.*

She was a child who had never received more than tepid reproofs from her parents—old parents to have a child of her age, which was said to account for her being the way she was—but she felt in perfect accord with David in his unhappy situation. She felt that she was one like him, one who might as well have been an orphan, because she would probably have to run away, go into hiding, fend for herself, when the truth became known and her past shut off her future.

IT HAD all begun with Sabitha saying, on the way to school, "We have to go by the Post Office. I have to send a letter to my dad."

They walked to and from school together every day. Sometimes they walked with their eyes closed, or backwards. Sometimes when they met people they gabbled away softly in a nonsense language, to cause confusion. Most of their good ideas were Edith's. The only idea Sabitha introduced was the writing down of a boy's name and your own, and the stroking out of all letters that were duplicated and the counting of the remainder. Then you ticked off the counted number on your fingers, saying, *Hateship, friendship, courtship, loveship, marriage,* till you got the verdict on what could happen between you and that boy.

"That's a fat letter," said Edith. She noticed everything, and she remembered everything, quickly memorizing whole pages of the textbooks in a way the other children found sinister. "Did you have a lot of things to write to your dad?" she said, surprised, because she could not credit this—or at least could not credit that Sabitha would get them on paper.

"I only wrote on one page," Sabitha said, feeling the letter.

"A-ha," said Edith. "Ah. Ha."

"Aha what?"

"I bet she put something else in. Johanna did."

The upshot of this was that they did not take the letter directly to the Post Office, but saved it and steamed it open at Edith's house after school. They could do such things at Edith's house because her mother worked all day at the Shoe Repair shop.

Dear Mr. Ken Boudreau,

I just thought I would write and send my thanks to you for the nice things you said about me in your letter to your daughter. You do not need to worry about me leaving. You say that I am a person you can trust. That is the meaning I take and as far as I know it is true. I am grateful to you for saying that, since some people feel that a person like me that they do not know the background of is Beyond the Pale. So I thought I would tell you something about myself. I was born in Glasgow, but my mother had to give me up when she got married. I was taken to the Home at the age of five. I looked for her to come back, but she didn't and I got used to it there and they weren't Bad. At the age of eleven I was brought to Canada on a Plan and lived with the Dixons, working on their Market Gardens. School was in the Plan, but I didn't see much of it. In winter I worked in the house for the Mrs. but circumstances made me think of leaving, and being big and strong for my age got taken on at a Nursing Home looking after the old people. I did not mind the work, but for better money went and worked in a Broom Factory. Mr. Willets that owned it had an old mother that came in to see how things were going, and she and I took to each other some way. The atmosphere was giving me breathing troubles so she said I should come and work for her and I did. I lived with her 12 yrs. on a lake called Mourning Dove Lake up north. There was only the two of us, but I could take care of everything outside and in, even running the motorboat and driving the car. I learned to read properly because her eyes were going bad and she liked me to read to her. She died at the age of 96. You might say what a life for a young person, but I was happy. We ate together every meal and I slept in her room the last year and a half. But after she died the family gave me one wk. to pack up. She had left me some money and I guess they did not like that. She wanted me to use it for Education but I would have to go in with kids. So when I saw the ad Mr. McCauley put in the Globe and Mail I came to see about it. I needed work to get over missing Mrs. Willets. So I guess I have bored you long enough with my History and you'll be relieved I have got up to the Present. Thank you for your good opinion and for taking me along to the Fair. I am not one for the rides or for eating the stuff but it was still certainly a pleasure to be included.

Your friend, Johanna Parry.

Edith read Johanna's words aloud, in an imploring voice and with a woebegone expression.

"I was born in Glasgow, but my mother had to give me up when she took one look at me—"

"Stop," said Sabitha. "I'm laughing so hard I'll be sick."

"How did she get her letter in with yours without you knowing?"

"She just takes it from me and puts it in an envelope and writes on the outside because she doesn't think my writing is good enough."

Edith had to put Scotch tape on the flap of the envelope to make it stick, since there wasn't enough sticky stuff left. "She's in love with him," she said.

"Oh, puke-puke," said Sabitha, holding her stomach. "She can't be. Old Johanna."

"What did he say about her, anyway?"

"Just about how I was supposed to respect her and it would be too bad if she left because we were lucky to have her and he didn't have a home for me and Grandpa couldn't raise a girl by himself and blah-blah. He said she was a lady. He said he could tell."

"So then she falls in lo-ove."

The letter remained with Edith overnight, lest Johanna discover that it hadn't been posted and was sealed with Scotch tape. They took it to the Post Office the next morning.

"Now we'll see what he writes back. Watch out," said Edith.

No LETTER came for a long time. And when it did, it was a disappointment. They steamed it open at Edith's house, but found nothing inside for Johanna.

Dear Sabitha,

Christmas finds me a bit short this year, sorry I don't have more than a two-dollar bill to send you. But I hope you are in good health and have a Merry Christmas and keep up your schoolwork. I have not been feeling so well myself, having got Bronchitis, which I seem to do every winter, but this is the first time it landed me in bed before Christmas. As you see by the address I am in a new place. The apartment was in a very noisy location and too many people dropping in hoping for a party. This is a boardinghouse, which suits me fine as I was never good at the shopping and the cooking.

Merry Christmas and love, Dad.

"Poor Johanna," said Edith. "Her heart will be bwoken."

Sabitha said, "Who cares?"

"Unless we do it," Edith said.

"What?"

"*Answer* her."

They would have to type their letter, because Johanna would notice that it was not in Sabitha's father's handwriting. But the typing was not difficult. There was a typewriter in Edith's house, on a card table in the front room. Her mother had worked in an office before she was married and she sometimes earned a little money still by writing the sort of letters that people wanted to look official. She had taught Edith the basics of typing, in the hope that Edith too might get an office job someday.

"Dear Johanna," said Sabitha, "I am sorry I cannot be in love with you because you have got those ugly spots all over your face."

"I'm going to be serious," said Edith. "So shut up."

She typed, "I was so glad to get the letter—" speaking the words of her composition aloud, pausing while she thought up more, her voice becoming increasingly solemn and tender. Sabitha sprawled on the couch, giggling. At one point she turned on the television, but Edith said, "Puleeze. How can I concentrate on my e-motions with all that shit going on?"

Edith and Sabitha used the words "shit" and "bitch" and "Jesus Christ" when they were alone together.

Dear Johanna,

I was so glad to get the letter you put in with Sabitha's and to find out about your life. It must often have been a sad and lonely one though Mrs. Willets sounds like a lucky person for you to find. You have remained industrious and uncomplaining and I must say that I admire you very much. My own life has been a checkered one and I have never exactly settled down. I do not know why I have this inner restlessness and loneliness, it just seems to be my fate. I am always meeting people and talking to people but sometimes I ask myself, Who is my friend? Then comes your letter and you write at the end of it, Your friend. So I think, Does she really mean that? And what a very nice Christmas present it would be for me if Johanna would tell me that she is my friend. Maybe you just thought it was a nice way to end a letter and you don't really know me well enough. Merry Christmas anyway.

Your friend, Ken Boudreau.

The letter went home to Johanna. The one to Sabitha had ended up being typed as well because why would one be typed and not the other? They had been sparing with the steam this time and opened the envelope very carefully so there would be no telltale Scotch tape.

"Why couldn't we type a new envelope? Wouldn't he do that if he typed the letter?" said Sabitha, thinking she was being clever.

"Because a new *envelope* wouldn't have a *postmark* on it. Dumb-dumb."

"What if she answers it?"

"We'll read it."

"Yah, what if she answers it and sends it direct to *him*?"

Edith didn't like to show she had not thought of that.

"She won't. She's sly. Anyway, you write him back right away to give her the idea she can slip it in with yours."

"I hate writing stupid letters."

"Go on. It won't kill you. Don't you want to see what she says?"

Dear Friend,

You ask me do I know you well enough to be your friend and my answer is that I think I do. I have only had one Friend in my life, Mrs. Willets who I loved and she was so good to me but she is dead. She was a lot older than me and the trouble with Older Friends is they die and leave you. She was so old she would call me sometimes by another person's name. I did not mind it though.

I will tell you a strange thing. That picture that you got the photographer at the Fair to take, of you and Sabitha and her friend Edith and me, I had it enlarged and framed and set in the living room. It is not a very good picture and he certainly charged you enough for what it is, but it is better than nothing. So the day before yesterday I was dusting around it and I imagined I could hear you say Hello to me. Hello, you said, and I looked at your face as well as you can see it in the picture and I thought, Well, I must be losing my mind. Or else it is a sign of a letter coming. I am just fooling, I don't really believe in anything like that. But yesterday there was a letter. So you see it is not asking too much of me to be your friend. I can always find a way to keep busy but a true Friend is something else again.

Your Friend, Johanna Parry.

Of course, that could not be replaced in the envelope. Sabitha's father would spot something fishy in the references to a letter he had never written. Johanna's words had to be torn into tiny pieces and flushed down the toilet at Edith's house.

WHEN THE letter came telling about the hotel it was months and months later. It was summer. And it was just by luck that Sabitha had picked that letter up, since she had been away for three weeks, staying at the cottage on Lake Simcoe that belonged to her Aunt Roxanne and her Uncle Clark.

Almost the first thing Sabitha said, coming into Edith's house, was, "Ugga-ugga. This place stinks."

"Ugga-ugga" was an expression she had picked up from her cousins.

Edith sniffed the air. "I don't smell anything."

"It's like your dad's shop, only not so bad. They must bring it home on their clothes and stuff."

Edith attended to the steaming and opening. On her way from the Post Office, Sabitha had bought two chocolate eclairs at the bakeshop. She was lying on the couch eating hers.

"Just one letter. For you," said Edith. "Poor old Johanna. Of course he never actually *got* hers."

"Read it to me," said Sabitha resignedly. "I've got sticky guck all over my hands."

Edith read it with businesslike speed, hardly pausing for the periods.

Well, Sabitha, my fortunes have taken a different turn, as you can see I am not in Brandon anymore but in a place called Gdynia. And not in the employ of my former bosses. I have had an exceptionally hard winter with my chest troubles and they, that is my bosses, thought I should be out on the road even if I was in danger of developing pneumonia so this developed into quite an argument so we all decided to say farewell. But luck is a strange thing and just about that time I came into possession of a Hotel. It is too complicated to explain the ins and outs but if your grandfather wants to know about it just tell him a man who owed me money which he could not pay let me have this hotel instead. So here I am moved from one room in a boardinghouse to a twelve-bedroom building and from not even owning the bed I slept in to owning several. It's a wonderful thing to wake up in the morning and know you are your own boss. I have some fixing up to do, actually plenty, and will get to it as soon as the weather warms up. I will need to hire somebody to help and later on I will hire a good cook to have a restaurant as well as the beverage room. That ought to go like hotcakes as there is none in this town. Hope you are well and doing your schoolwork and developing good habits.

Love, Your Dad.

Sabitha said, "Have you got some coffee?"

"Instant," said Edith. "Why?"

Sabitha said that iced coffee was what everybody had been drinking at the cottage and they were all crazy about it. She was crazy about it too. She got up and messed around in the kitchen, boiling the water and stirring up the coffee with milk and ice cubes. "What we really ought to have is vanilla ice cream," she said. "Oh, my Gad, is it ever wonderful. Don't you want your eclair?"

Oh, my Gad.

"Yes. All of it," said Edith meanly.

All these changes in Sabitha in just three weeks—during the time Edith had been working in the shop and her mother recovering at home from her operation. Sabitha's skin was an appetizing golden-brown color, and her hair was cut shorter and fluffed out around her face. Her cousins had cut it and given her a permanent. She wore a sort of playsuit, with shorts cut like a skirt and buttons down the front and frills over the shoulders in a becoming blue color. She had got plumper, and when she leaned over to pick up her glass of iced coffee, which was on the floor, she displayed a smooth, glowing cleavage.

Breasts. They must have started growing before she went away, but Edith had not noticed. Maybe they were just something you woke up with one morning. Or did not.

However they came, they seemed to indicate a completely unearned and unfair advantage.

Sabitha was full of talk about her cousins and life at the cottage. She would say, "Listen, I've got to tell you about this, it's a scream—" and then ramble on about what Aunt Roxanne said to Uncle Clark when they had the fight, how Mary Jo drove with the top down and without a license in Stan's car (who was Stan?) and took them all to a drive-in—

and what was the scream or the point of the story somehow never became clear.

But after a while other things did. The real adventures of the summer. The older girls—that included Sabitha—slept in the upstairs of the boathouse. Sometimes they had tickling fights—they would all gang up on someone and tickle her till she shrieked for mercy and agreed to pull her pajama pants down to show if she had hair. They told stories about girls at boarding school who did things with hairbrush handles, toothbrush handles. *Ugga-ugga.* Once a couple of cousins put on a show—one girl got on top of the other and pretended to be the boy and they wound their legs around each other and groaned and panted and carried on.

Uncle Clark's sister and her husband came to visit on their honeymoon, and he was seen to put his hand inside her swimsuit.

"They really loved each other, they were at it day and night," said Sabitha. She hugged a cushion to her chest. "People can't help it when they're in love like that."

One of the cousins had already done it with a boy. He was one of the summer help in the gardens of the resort down the road. He took her out in a boat and threatened to push her out until she agreed to let him do it. So it wasn't her fault.

"Couldn't she swim?" said Edith.

Sabitha pushed the cushion between her legs. "Oooh," she said. "Feels so nice."

Edith knew all about the pleasurable agonies Sabitha was feeling, but she was appalled that anybody would make them public. She herself was frightened of them. Years ago, before she knew what she was doing, she had gone to sleep with the blanket between her legs and her mother had discovered her and told her about a girl she had known who did things like that all the time and had eventually been operated on for the problem.

"They used to throw cold water on her, but it didn't cure her," her mother had said. "So she had to be cut."

Otherwise her organs would get congested and she might die.

"Stop," she said to Sabitha, but Sabitha moaned defiantly and said, "It's nothing. We all did it like this. Haven't you got a cushion?"

Edith got up and went to the kitchen and filled her empty iced-coffee glass with cold water. When she got back Sabitha was lying limp on the couch, laughing, the cushion flung on the floor.

"What did you think I was doing?" she said. "Didn't you know I was kidding?"

"I was thirsty," Edith said.

"You just drank a whole glass of iced coffee."

"I was thirsty for water."

"Can't have any fun with you." Sabitha sat up. "If you're so thirsty why don't you drink it?"

They sat in a moody silence until Sabitha said, in a conciliatory but disappointed tone, "Aren't we going to write Johanna another letter? Let's write her a lovey-dovey letter."

Edith had lost a good deal of her interest in the letters, but she was gratified to see that Sabitha had not. Some sense of having power over Sabitha returned, in spite of Lake Simcoe and the breasts. Sighing, as if reluctantly, she got up and took the cover off the typewriter.

"My darlingest Johanna—" said Sabitha.

"No. That's too sickening."

"She won't think so."

"She will so," said Edith.

She wondered whether she should tell Sabitha about the danger of congested organs. She decided not to. For one thing, that information fell into a category of warnings she had received from her mother and never known whether to wholly trust or distrust. It had not fallen as low, in credibility, as the belief that wearing foot-rubbers in the house would ruin your eyesight, but there was no telling—someday it might.

And for another thing—Sabitha would just laugh. She laughed at warnings—she would laugh even if you told her that chocolate eclairs would make her fat.

"Your last letter made me so happy—"

"Your last letter filled me with rap-ture—" said Sabitha.

"—made me so happy to think I did have a true friend in the world, which is you—"

"I could not sleep all night because I was longing to crush you in my arms—" Sabitha wrapped her arms around herself and rocked back and forth.

"*No.* Often I have felt so lonely in spite of a gregarious life and not known where to turn—"

"What does that mean—'gregarious'? She won't know what it means."

"*She* will."

That shut Sabitha up and perhaps hurt her feelings. So at the end Edith read out, "I must say good-bye and the only way I can do it is to imagine you reading this and blushing—" "Is that more what you want?"

"Reading it in bed with your nightgown on," said Sabitha, always quickly restored, "and thinking how I would crush you in my arms and I would suck your titties—"

My Dear Johanna,
Your last letter made me so happy to think I have a true friend in the

world, which is you. Often I have felt so lonely in spite of a gregarious life and not known where to turn.

Well, I have told Sabitha in my letter about my good fortune and how I am going into the hotel business. I did not tell her actually how sick I was last winter because I did not want to worry her. I do not want to worry you, either, dear Johanna, only to tell you that I thought of you so often and longed to see your dear sweet face. When I was feverish I thought that I really did see it bending over me and I heard your voice telling me I would soon be better and I felt the ministrations of your kind hands. I was in the boardinghouse and when I came to out of my fever there was a lot of teasing going on as to, who is this Johanna? But I was sad as could be to wake and find you were not there. I really wondered if you could have flown through the air and been with me, even though I knew that could not have happened. Believe me, believe me, the most beautiful movie star could not have been as welcome to me as you. I don't know if I should tell you the other things you were saying to me because they were very sweet and intimate but they might embarrass you. I hate to end this letter because it feels now as if I have my arms around you and I am talking to you quietly in the dark privacy of our room, but I must say good-bye and the only way I can do it is to imagine you reading this and blushing. It would be wonderful if you were reading it in bed with your nightgown on and thinking how I would like to crush you in my arms.

                                                    L-v-, Ken Boudreau.

Somewhat surprisingly, there was no reply to this letter. When Sabitha had written her half-page, Johanna put it in the envelope and addressed it and that was that.

WHEN JOHANNA got off the train there was nobody to meet her. She did not let herself worry about that—she had been thinking that her letter might not, after all, have got here before she did. (In fact it had, and was lying in the Post Office, uncollected, because Ken Boudreau, who had not been seriously sick last winter, really did have bronchitis now and for several days had not come in for his mail. On this day it had been joined by another envelope, containing the check from Mr. McCauley. But payment on that had already been stopped.)

What was of more concern to her was that there did not appear to be a town. The station was an enclosed shelter with benches along the walls and a wooden shutter pulled down over the window of the ticket office. There was also a freight shed—she supposed it was a freight shed—but the sliding door to it would not budge. She peered through a crack between the planks until her eyes got used to the dark in there, and she saw that it was empty, with a dirt floor. No crates of furniture there. She called out, "Anybody here? Anybody here?" several times, but she did not expect a reply.

She stood on the platform and tried to get her bearings.

About half a mile away there was a slight hill, noticeable at once because it had a crown of trees. And the sandy-looking track that she had taken, when she saw it from the train, for a back lane into a farmer's field—that must be the road. Now she saw the low shapes of buildings here and there in the trees—and a water tower, which looked from this distance like a toy, a tin soldier on long legs.

She picked up her suitcase—this would not be too difficult; she had carried it, after all, from Exhibition Road to the other railway station—and set out.

There was a wind blowing, but this was a hot day—hotter than the weather she had left in Ontario—and the wind seemed hot as well. Over her new dress she was wearing her same old coat, which would have taken up too much room in the suitcase. She looked with longing to the shade of the town ahead, but when she got there she found that the trees were either spruce, which were too tight and narrow to give much shade, or raggedy thin-leaved cottonwoods, which blew about and let the sun through anyway.

There was a discouraging lack of formality, or any sort of organization, to this place. No sidewalks, or paved streets, no imposing buildings except a big church like a brick barn. A painting over its door, showing the Holy Family with clay-colored faces and staring blue eyes. It was named for an unheard-of saint—Saint Voytech.

The houses did not show much forethought in their situation or planning. They were set at different angles to the road, or street, and most of them had mean-looking little windows stuck here and there, with snow porches like boxes round the doors. Nobody was out in the yards, and why should they be? There was nothing to tend, only clumps of brown grass and once a big burst of rhubarb, gone to seed.

The main street, if that's what it was, had a raised wooden walk on one side only, and some unconsolidated buildings, of which a grocery store (containing the Post Office) and a garage seemed to be the only ones functioning. There was one two-story building that she thought might be the hotel, but it was a bank and it was closed.

The first human being she saw—though two dogs had barked at her—was a man in front of the garage, busy loading chains into the back of his truck.

"Hotel?" he said. "You come too far."

He told her that it was down by the station, on the other side of the tracks and along a bit, it was painted blue and you couldn't miss it.

She set the suitcase down, not from discouragement but because she had to have a moment's rest.

He said he would ride her down there if she wanted to wait a minute. And though it was a new kind of thing for her to accept such an offer, she soon found herself riding in the hot, greasy cab of his truck, rocking down the dirt road that she had just walked up, with the chains making a desperate racket in the back.

"So—where'd you bring this heat wave from?" he said.

She said Ontario, in a tone that promised nothing further.

"Ontario," he said regretfully. "Well. There 'tis. Your hotel." He took one hand off the wheel. The truck gave an accompanying lurch as he waved to a two-story flat-roofed building that she hadn't missed but had seen from the train, as they came in. She had taken it then for a large and fairly derelict, perhaps abandoned, family home. Now that she had seen the houses in town, she knew that she should not have dismissed it so readily. It was covered with sheets of tin stamped to look like bricks and painted a light blue. There was the one word HOTEL, in neon tubing, no longer lit, over the doorway.

"I am a dunce," she said, and offered the man a dollar for the ride.

He laughed. "Hang on to your money. You never know when you'll need it."

Quite a decent-looking car, a Plymouth, was parked outside this hotel. It was very dirty, but how could you help that, with these roads?

There were signs on the door advertising a brand of cigarettes, and of beer. She waited till the truck had turned before she knocked—knocked because it didn't look as if the place could in any way be open for business. Then she tried the door to see if it was open, and walked into a little dusty room with a staircase, and then into a large dark room in which there was a billiard table and a bad smell of beer and an unswept floor. Off in a side room she could see the glimmer of a mirror, empty shelves, a counter. These rooms had the blinds pulled tightly down. The only light she saw was coming through two small round windows, which turned out to be set in double swinging doors. She went on through these into a kitchen. It was lighter, because of a row of high—and dirty—windows, uncovered, in the opposite wall. And here were the first signs of life—somebody had been eating at the table and had left a plate smeared with dried ketchup and a cup half full of cold black coffee.

One of the doors off the kitchen led outside—this one was locked—and one to a pantry in which there were several cans of food, one to a broom closet, and one to an enclosed stairway. She climbed the steps, bumping her suitcase along in front of her because the space was narrow. Straight ahead of her on the second floor she saw a toilet with the seat up.

The door of the bedroom at the end of the hall was open, and in there she found Ken Boudreau.

She saw his clothes before she saw him. His jacket hanging up on a corner of the door and his trousers on the doorknob, so that they trailed on the floor. She thought at once that this was no way to treat good clothes, so she went boldly into the room—leaving her suitcase in the hall—with the idea of hanging them up properly.

He was in bed, with only a sheet over him. The blanket and his shirt were lying on the floor. He was breathing restlessly as if about to wake up, so she said, "Good morning. Afternoon."

The bright sunlight was coming in the window, hitting him almost in the face. The window was closed and the air horribly stale—smelling, for one thing, of the full ashtray on the chair he used as a bed table.

He had bad habits—he smoked in bed.

He did not wake up at her voice—or he woke only part way. He began to cough.

She recognized this as a serious cough, a sick man's cough. He struggled to lift himself up, still with his eyes closed, and she went over to the bed and hoisted him. She looked for a handkerchief or a box of tissues, but she saw nothing so she reached for his shirt on the floor, which she could wash later. She wanted to get a good look at what he spat up.

When he had hacked up enough, he muttered and sank down into the bed, gasping, the charming cocky-looking face she remembered crumpled up in disgust. She knew from the feel of him that he had a fever.

The stuff that he had coughed out was greenish-yellow—no rusty streaks. She carried the shirt to the toilet sink, where rather to her surprise she found a bar of soap, and washed it out and hung it on the door hook, then thoroughly washed her hands. She had to dry them on the skirt of her new brown dress. She had put that on in another little toilet—the *Ladies* on the train—not more than a couple of hours ago. She had been wondering then if she should have got some makeup.

In a hall closet she found a roll of toilet paper and took it into his room for the next time he had to cough. She picked up the blanket and covered him well, pulled the blind down to the sill and raised the stiff window an inch or two, propping it open with the ashtray she had emptied. Then she changed, out in the hall, from the brown dress into old clothes from her suitcase. A lot of use a nice dress or any makeup in the world would be now.

She was not sure how sick he was, but she had nursed Mrs. Willets—also a heavy smoker—through several bouts of bronchitis, and she thought she could manage for a while without having to think about getting a doctor. In the same hall closet was a pile of clean, though worn and faded, towels, and she wet one of these and wiped his arms and legs, to try to get his fever down. He came half awake at this and began to cough again. She held him up and made him spit into the toilet paper, examined it once more and threw it down the toilet and washed her hands. She had a towel now to dry them on. She went downstairs and found a glass in the kitchen, also an empty, large ginger-ale bottle, which she filled with water. This she attempted to make him drink. He took a little, protested, and she let him lie down. In five minutes or so she tried again. She kept doing this until she believed he had swallowed as much as he could hold without throwing up.

Time and again he coughed and she lifted him up, held him with one arm while the other hand pounded on his back to help loosen the load in his chest. He opened his eyes several times and seemed to take in her presence without alarm or surprise—or gratitude, for that matter. She sponged him once more, being careful to cover immediately with the blanket the part that had just been cooled.

She noticed that it had begun to get dark, and she went down into the kitchen, found the light switch. The lights and the old electric stove were working. She opened and heated a can of chicken-with-rice soup, carried it upstairs and roused him. He swallowed a little from the spoon. She took advantage of his momentary wakefulness to ask if he had a bottle of aspirin. He nodded yes, then became very confused when trying to tell her where. "In the wastebasket," he said.

"No, no," she said. "You don't mean wastebasket."

"In the— in the—"

He tried to shape something with his hands. Tears came into his eyes.

"Never mind," Johanna said. "Never mind."

His fever went down anyway. He slept for an hour or more without coughing. Then he grew hot again. By that time she had found the aspirin—they were in a kitchen drawer with such things as a screwdriver and some lightbulbs and a ball of twine—and she got a couple into him. Soon he had a violent coughing fit, but she didn't think he threw them up. When he lay down she put her ear to his chest and listened to the wheezing. She had already looked for mustard to make a plaster with, but apparently there wasn't any. She went downstairs again and heated some water and brought it in a basin. She tried to make him lean over it, tenting him with towels, so that he could breathe the steam. He would cooperate only for a moment or so, but perhaps it helped—he hacked up quantities of phlegm.

His fever went down again and he slept more calmly. She dragged in an armchair she had found in one of the other rooms and she slept too, in snatches, waking and wondering where she was, then remembering and getting up and touching him—his fever seemed to be staying down—and tucking in the blanket. For her own cover she used the everlasting old tweed coat that she had Mrs. Willets to thank for.

He woke. It was full morning. "What are you doing here?" he said, in a hoarse, weak voice.

"I came yesterday," she said. "I brought your furniture. It isn't here yet, but it's on its way. You were sick when I got here and you were sick most of the night. How do you feel now?"

He said, "Better," and began to cough. She didn't have to lift him, he sat up on his own, but she went to the bed and pounded his back. When he finished, he said, "Thank you."

His skin now felt as cool as her own. And smooth—no rough moles, no fat on him. She could feel his ribs. He was like a delicate, stricken boy. He smelled like corn.

"You swallowed the phlegm," she said. "Don't do that, it's not good for you. Here's the toilet paper, you have to spit it out. You could get trouble with your kidneys, swallowing it."

"I never knew that," he said. "Could you find the coffee?"

The percolator was black on the inside. She washed it as well as she could and put the coffee on. Then she washed and tidied herself, wondering what kind of food she should give him. In the pantry there was a box of biscuit mix. At first she thought she would have to mix it with water, but she found a can of milk powder as well. When the coffee was ready she had a pan of biscuits in the oven.

As soon as he heard her busy in the kitchen, he got up to go to the toilet. He was weaker than he'd thought—he had to lean over and put one hand on the tank. Then he found some underwear on the floor of the hall closet where he kept clean clothes. He had figured out by now who this woman was. She had said she came to bring him his furniture, though he hadn't asked her or anybody to do that—hadn't asked for the furniture at all, just the money. He should know her name, but he couldn't remember it. That was why he opened her purse, which was on the floor of the hall beside her suitcase. There was a name tag sewn to the lining.

Johanna Parry, and the address of his father-in-law, on Exhibition Road.

Some other things. A cloth bag with a few bills in it. Twenty-seven dollars. Another bag with change, which he didn't bother to count. A bright blue bankbook. He opened it up automatically, without expectations of anything unusual.

A couple of weeks ago Johanna had been able to transfer the whole of her inheritance from Mrs. Willets into her bank account, adding it to the amount of money she had saved. She had explained to the bank manager that she did not know when she might need it.

The sum was not dazzling, but it was impressive. It gave her substance. In Ken Boudreau's mind, it added a sleek upholstery to the name Johanna Parry.

"Were you wearing a brown dress?" he said, when she came up with the coffee.

"Yes, I was. When I first got here."

"I thought it was a dream. It was you."

"Like in your other dream," Johanna said, her speckled forehead turning fiery. He didn't know what that was all about and hadn't the energy to inquire. Possibly a dream he'd wakened from when she was here in the night—one he couldn't now remember. He coughed again in a more reasonable way, with her handing him some toilet paper.

"Now," she said, "where are you going to set your coffee?" She pushed up the wooden chair that she had moved to get at him more easily. "There," she said. She lifted him under the arms and wedged the pillow in behind him. A dirty pillow, without a case, but she had covered it last night with a towel.

"Could you see if there's any cigarettes downstairs?"

She shook her head, but said, "I'll look. I've got biscuits in the oven."

KEN BOUDREAU was in the habit of lending money, as well as borrowing it. Much of the trouble that had come upon him—or that he had got into, to put it another way—had to do with not being able to say no to a friend. Loyalty. He had not been drummed out of the peacetime Air Force, but had resigned out of loyalty to the friend who had been hauled up for offering insults to the C.O. at a mess party. At a mess party, where everything was supposed to be a joke and no offense taken—it was not fair. And he had lost the job with the fertilizer company because he took a company truck across the American border without permission, on a Sunday, to pick up a buddy who had got into a fight and was afraid of being caught and charged.

Part and parcel of the loyalty to friends was the difficulty with bosses. He would confess that he found it hard to knuckle under. "Yes, sir," and "no, sir" were not ready words in his vocabulary. He had not been fired from the insurance company, but he had been passed over so many times that it seemed they were daring him to quit, and eventually he did.

Drink had played a part, you had to admit that. And the idea that life should be a more heroic enterprise than it ever seemed to be nowadays.

He liked to tell people he'd won the hotel in a poker game. He was not really much of a gambler, but women liked the sound of that. He didn't want to admit that he'd taken it sight unseen in payment of a debt. And even after he saw it, he told himself it could be salvaged. The idea of being his own boss did appeal to him. He did not see it as a place where - people would stay—except perhaps hunters, in the fall. He saw it as a drinking establishment and a restaurant. If he could get a good cook. But before anything much could happen money would have to be spent. Work had to be done—more than he could possibly do himself though he was not unhandy. If he could live through the winter doing what he could by himself, proving his good intentions, he thought maybe he could get a loan from the bank. But he needed a smaller loan just to get through the winter, and that was where his father-in-law came into the picture. He would rather have tried somebody else, but nobody else could so easily spare it.

He had thought it a good idea to put the request in the form of a proposal to sell the furniture, which he knew the old man would never bestir himself enough to do. He was aware, not very specifically, of loans still outstanding from the past—but he was able to think of those as sums he'd been entitled to, for supporting Marcelle during a period of bad behavior (hers, at a time when his own hadn't started) and for accepting Sabitha as his child when he had his doubts. Also, the McCauleys were the only people he knew who had money that nobody now alive had earned.

I brought your furniture.

He was unable to figure out what that could mean for him, at present. He was too tired. He wanted to sleep more than he wanted to eat when she came with the biscuits (and no cigarettes). To satisfy her he ate half of one. Then he fell dead asleep. He came only half awake when she rolled him on one side, then the other, getting the dirty sheet out from under him, then spreading the clean one and rolling him onto that, all without making him get out of bed or really wake up.

"I found a clean sheet, but it's thin as a rag," she said. "It didn't smell too good, so I hung it on the line awhile."

Later he realized that a sound he'd been hearing for a long time in a dream was really the sound of the washing machine. He wondered how that could be—the hot-water tank was defunct. She must have heated tubs of water on the stove. Later still, he heard the unmistakable sound of his own car starting up and driving away. She would have got the keys from his pants pocket.

She might be driving away in his only worthwhile possession, deserting him, and he could not even phone the police to nab her. The phone was cut off, even if he'd been able to get to it.

That was always a possibility—theft and desertion—yet he turned over on the fresh sheet, which smelled of prairie wind and grass, and went back to sleep, knowing for certain that she had only gone to buy milk and eggs and butter and bread and other supplies—even cigarettes—that were necessary for a decent life, and that she would come back and be busy downstairs and that the sound of her activity would be like a net beneath him, heaven-sent, a bounty not to be questioned.

There was a woman problem in his life right now. Two women, actually, a young one and an older one (that is, one of about his own age) who knew about each other and were ready to tear each other's hair out. All he had got from them recently was howling and complaining, punctuated with their angry assertions that they loved him.

Perhaps a solution had arrived for that, as well.

WHEN SHE was buying groceries in the store, Johanna heard a train, and driving back to the hotel, she saw a car parked at the railway station. Before she had even stopped Ken Boudreau's car she saw the furniture crates piled up on the platform. She talked to the agent—it was his car there—and he was very surprised and irritated by the arrival of all these big crates. When she had got out of him the name of a man with a truck—a clean truck, she insisted—who lived twenty miles away and sometimes did hauling, she used the station phone to call the man and half bribed, half ordered him to come right away. Then she impressed upon the agent that he must stay with the crates till the truck arrived. By suppertime the truck had come, and the man and his son had unloaded all the furniture and carried it into the main room of the hotel.

The next day she took a good look around. She was making up her mind.

The day after that she judged Ken Boudreau to be able to sit up and listen to her, and she said, "This place is a sinkhole for money. The town is on its last legs. What should be done is to take out everything that can bring in any cash and sell it. I don't mean the furniture that was shipped in, I mean things like the pool table and the kitchen range. Then we ought to sell the building to somebody who'll strip the tin off it for junk. There's always a bit to be made off stuff you'd never think had any value. Then— What was it you had in mind to do before you got hold of the hotel?"

He said that he had had some idea of going to British Columbia, to Salmon Arm, where he had a friend who had told him one time he could have a job managing orchards. But he couldn't go because the car needed new tires and work done on it before he could undertake a long trip, and he was spending all he had just to live. Then the hotel had fallen into his lap.

"Like a ton of bricks," she said. "Tires and fixing the car would be a better investment than sinking anything into this place. It would be a good idea to get out there before the snow comes. And ship the furniture by rail again, to make use of it when we get there. We have got all we need to furnish a home."

"It's maybe not all that firm of an offer."

She said, "I know. But it'll be all right."

He understood that she did know, and that it was, it would be, all right. You could say that a case like his was right up her alley.

Not that he wouldn't be grateful. He'd got to a point where gratitude wasn't a burden, where it was natural—especially when it wasn't demanded.

Thoughts of regeneration were starting. *This is the change I need.* He had said that before, but surely there was one time when it would be true. The mild winters, the smell of the evergreen forests and the ripe apples. *All we need to make a home.*

HE HAS his pride, she thought. That would have to be taken account of. It might be better never to mention the letters in which he had laid himself open to her. Before she came away, she had destroyed them. In fact she had destroyed each one as soon as she'd read it over well enough to know it by heart, and that didn't take long. One thing she surely didn't want was for them ever to fall into the hands of young Sabitha and her shifty friend. Especially the part in the last letter, about her nightgown, and being in bed. It wasn't that such things wouldn't go on, but it might be thought vulgar or sappy or asking for ridicule, to put them on paper.

She doubted they'd see much of Sabitha. But she would never thwart him, if that was what he wanted.

This wasn't really a new experience, this brisk sense of expansion and responsibility. She'd felt something the same for Mrs. Willets—another fine-looking, flighty person in need of care and management. Ken Boudreau had turned out to be a bit more that way than she was prepared for, and there were the differences you had to expect with a man, but surely there was nothing in him that she couldn't handle.

After Mrs. Willets her heart had been dry, and she had considered it might always be so. And now such a warm commotion, such busy love.

*

MR. MCCAULEY died about two years after Johanna's departure. His funeral was the last one held in the Anglican church. There was a good turnout for it. Sabitha—who came with her mother's cousin, the Toronto woman—was now self-contained and pretty and remarkably, unexpectedly slim. She wore a sophisticated black hat and did not speak to anybody unless they spoke to her first. Even then, she did not seem to remember them.

The death notice in the paper said that Mr. McCauley was survived by his granddaughter Sabitha Boudreau and his son-in-law Ken Boudreau, and Mr. Boudreau's wife Johanna, and their infant son Omar, of Salmon Arm, B.C.

Edith's mother read this out—Edith herself never looked at the local paper. Of course, the marriage was not news to either of them—or to Edith's father, who was around the corner in the front room, watching television. Word had got back. The only news was Omar.

"Her with a *baby*," Edith's mother said.

Edith was doing her Latin translation at the kitchen table. *Tu ne quaesieris, scire nefas, quem mihi, quem tibi—*

In the church she had taken the precaution of not speaking to Sabitha first, before Sabitha could not speak to her.

She was not really afraid, anymore, of being found out—though she still could not understand why they hadn't been. And in a way, it seemed only proper that the antics of her former self should not be connected with her present self—let alone with the real self that she expected would take over once she got out of this town and away from all the people who thought they knew her. It was the whole twist of consequence that dismayed her—it seemed fantastical, but dull. Also insulting, like some sort of joke or inept warning, trying to get its hooks into her. For where, on the list of things she planned to achieve in her life, was there any mention of her being responsible for the existence on earth of a person named Omar?

Ignoring her mother, she wrote, "You must not ask, it is forbidden for us to know—"

She paused, chewing her pencil, then finished off with a chill of satisfaction, "—what fate has in store for me, or for you—"

Family Furnishings

ALFRIDA. MY father called her Freddie. The two of them were first cousins and lived on adjoining farms and then for a while in the same house. One day they were out in the fields of stubble playing with my father's dog, whose name was Mack. That day the sun shone, but did not melt the ice in the furrows. They stomped on the ice and enjoyed its crackle underfoot.

How could she remember a thing like that? my father said. She made it up, he said.

"I did not," she said.

"You did so."

"I did not."

All of a sudden they heard bells pealing, whistles blowing. The town bell and the church bells were ringing. The factory whistles were blowing in the town three miles away. The world had burst its seams for joy, and Mack tore out to the road, because he was sure a parade was coming. It was the end of the First World War.

THREE TIMES a week, we could read Alfrida's name in the paper. Just her first name—Alfrida. It was printed as if written by hand, a flowing, fountain-pen signature. Round and About the Town, with Alfrida. The town mentioned was not the one close by, but the city to the south, where Alfrida lived, and which my family visited perhaps once every two or three years.

Now is the time for all you future June brides to start registering your preferences at the China Cabinet, and I must tell you that if I were a bride-to-be—which alas I am not—I might resist all the patterned dinner sets, exquisite as they are, and go for the pearly-white, the ultra-modern Rosenthal . . .

Beauty treatments may come and beauty treatments may go, but the masques they slather on you at Fantine's Salon are guaranteed—speaking of brides—to make your skin bloom like orange blossoms. And to make the bride's mom—and the bride's aunts and for all I know her grandmom—feel as if they'd just taken a dip in the Fountain of Youth . . .

You would never expect Alfrida to write in this style, from the way she talked.

She was also one of the people who wrote under the name of Flora Simpson, on the Flora Simpson Housewives' Page. Women from all over the countryside believed that they were writing their letters to the plump woman with the crimped gray hair and the forgiving smile who was pictured at the top of the page. But the truth—which I was not to tell—was that the notes that appeared at the bottom of each of their letters were produced by Alfrida and a man she called Horse Henry, who otherwise did the obituaries. The women gave themselves such names as Morning Star and Lily-of-the-Valley and Green Thumb and Little Annie Rooney and Dishmop Queen. Some names were so popular that numbers had to be assigned to them—Goldilocks 1, Goldilocks 2, Goldilocks 3.

Dear Morning Star, Alfrida or Horse Henry would write,

Eczema is a dreadful pest, especially in this hot weather we're having, and I hope the baking soda does some good. Home treatments certainly ought to be respected, but it never hurts to seek out your doctor's advice. It's splendid news to hear your hubby is up and about again. It can't have been any fun with both of you under the weather . . .

In all the small towns of that part of Ontario, housewives who belonged to the Flora Simpson Club would hold an annual summer picnic. Flora Simpson always sent her special greetings but explained that there were just too many events for her to show up at all of them and she did not like to make distinctions. Alfrida said that there had been talk of sending Horse Henry done up in a wig and pillow bosoms, or perhaps herself leering like the Witch of Babylon (not even she, at my parents' table, could quote the Bible accurately and say "Whore") with a ciggie-boo stuck to her lipstick. But, oh, she said, the paper would kill us. And anyway, it would be too mean.

She always called her cigarettes ciggie-boos. When I was fifteen or sixteen she leaned across the table and asked me, "How would you like a ciggie-boo, too?" The meal was finished, and my younger brother and sister had left the table. My father was shaking his head. He had started to roll his own.

I said thank you and let Alfrida light it and smoked for the first time in front of my parents.

They pretended that it was a great joke.

"Ah, will you look at your daughter?" said my mother to my father. She rolled her eyes and clapped her hands to her chest and spoke in an artificial, languishing voice. "I'm like to faint."

"Have to get the horsewhip out," my father said, half rising in his chair.

This moment was amazing, as if Alfrida had transformed us into new - people. Ordinarily, my mother would say that she did not like to see a woman smoke. She did not say that it was indecent, or unladylike—just that she did not like it. And when she said in a certain tone that she did not like something it seemed that she was not making a confession of irrationality but drawing on a private source of wisdom, which was unassailable and almost sacred. It was when she reached for this tone, with its accompanying expression of listening to inner voices, that I particularly hated her.

As for my father, he had beaten me, in this very room, not with a horsewhip but his belt, for running afoul of my mother's rules and wounding my mother's feelings, and for answering back. Now it seemed that such beatings could occur only in another universe.

My parents had been put in a corner by Alfrida—and also by me—but they had responded so gamely and gracefully that it was really as if all three of us—my mother and my father and myself—had been lifted to a new level of ease and aplomb. In that instant I could see them— particularly my mother—as being capable of a kind of lightheartedness that was scarcely ever on view.

All due to Alfrida.

Alfrida was always referred to as a career girl. This made her seem to be younger than my parents, though she was known to be about the same age. It was also said that she was a city person. And the city, when it was spoken of in this way, meant the one she lived and worked in. But it meant something else as well—not just a distinct configuration of build-ings and sidewalks and streetcar lines or even a crowding together of individual people. It meant something more abstract that could be repeated over and over, something like a hive of bees, stormy but organized, not useless or deluded exactly, but disturbing and sometimes dangerous. People went into such a place when they had to and were glad when they got out. Some, however, were attracted to it—as Alfrida must have been, long ago, and as I was now, puffing on my cigarette and trying to hold it in a nonchalant way, though it seemed to have grown to the size of a baseball bat between my fingers.

MY FAMILY did not have a regular social life—people did not come to the house for dinner, let alone to parties. It was a matter of class, maybe. The parents of the boy I married, about five years after this scene at the dinner table, invited people who were not related to them to dinner, and they went to afternoon parties that they spoke of, unself-consciously, as cocktail parties. It was a life such as I had read of in magazine stories, and it seemed to me to place my in-laws in a world of storybook privilege.

What our family did was put boards in the dining-room table two or three times a year to entertain my grandmother and my aunts—my father's older sisters—and their husbands. We did this at Christmas or Thanksgiving, when it was our turn, and perhaps also when a relative from another part of the province showed up on a visit. This visitor would always be a person rather like the aunts and their husbands and never the least bit like Alfrida.

My mother and I would start preparing for such dinners a couple of days ahead. We ironed the good tablecloth, which was as heavy as a bed quilt, and washed the good dishes, which had been sitting in the china cabinet collecting dust, and wiped the legs of the dining-room chairs, as well as making the jellied salads, the pies and cakes, that had to accompany the central roast turkey or baked ham and bowls of vegetables. There had to be far too much to eat, and most of the conversation at the table had to do with the food, with the company saying how good it was and being urged to have more, and saying that they couldn't, they were stuffed, and then the aunts' husbands relenting, taking more, and the aunts taking just a little more and saying that they shouldn't, they were ready to bust.

And dessert still to come.

There was hardly any idea of a general conversation, and in fact there was a feeling that conversation that passed beyond certain understood limits might be a disruption, a showing-off. My mother's understanding of the limits was not reliable, and she sometimes could not wait out the pauses or honor the aversion to follow-up. So when somebody said, "Seen Harley upstreet yesterday," she was liable to say, perhaps, "Do you think a man like Harley is a confirmed bachelor? Or he just hasn't met the right person?"

As if, when you mentioned seeing a person you were bound to have something further to say, something *interesting*.

Then there might be a silence, not because the people at the table meant to be rude but because they were flummoxed. Till my father would say with embarrassment, and oblique reproach, "He seems to get on all right by hisself."

If his relatives had not been present, he would more likely have said "himself."

And everybody went on cutting, spooning, swallowing, in the glare of the fresh tablecloth, with the bright light pouring in through the newly washed windows. These dinners were always in the middle of the day.

The people at that table were quite capable of talk. Washing and drying the dishes, in the kitchen, the aunts would talk about who had a tumor, a septic throat, a bad mess of boils. They would tell about how their own digestions, kidneys, nerves were functioning. Mention of intimate bodily matters seemed never to be so out of place, or suspect, as the mention of something read in a magazine, or an item in the news—it was improper somehow to pay attention to anything that was not close at hand. Meanwhile, resting on the porch, or during a brief walk out to look at the crops, the aunts' husbands might pass on the information that somebody was in a tight spot with the bank, or still owed money on an expensive piece of machinery, or had invested in a bull that was a disappointment on the job.

It could have been that they felt clamped down by the formality of the dining room, the presence of bread-and-butter plates and dessert spoons, when it was the custom, at other times, to put a piece of pie right onto a dinner plate that had been cleaned up with bread. (It would have been an offense, however, not to set things out in this proper way. In their own houses, on like occasions, they would put their guests through the same paces.) It may have been just that eating was one thing, and talking was something else.

When Alfrida came it was altogether another story. The good cloth would be spread and the good dishes would be out. My mother would have gone to a lot of trouble with the food and she would be nervous about the results—probably she would have abandoned the usual turkey-and-stuffing-and-mashed-potatoes menu and made something like chicken salad surrounded by mounds of molded rice with cut-up pimientos, and this would be followed by a dessert involving gelatin and egg white and whipped cream, taking a long, nerve-racking time to set because we had no refrigerator and it had to be chilled on the cellar floor. But the constraint, the pall over the table, was quite absent. Alfrida not only accepted second helpings, she asked for them. And she did this almost absentmindedly, and tossed off her compliments in the same way, as if the food, the eating of the food, was a secondary though agreeable thing, and she was really there to talk, and make other people talk, and anything you wanted to talk about—almost anything—would be fine.

She always visited in summer, and usually she wore some sort of striped, silky sundress, with a halter top that left her back bare. Her back was not pretty, being sprinkled with little dark moles, and her shoulders were bony and her chest nearly flat. My father would always remark on how much she could eat and remain thin. Or he turned truth on its head by noting that her appetite was as picky as ever, but she still hadn't been prevented from larding on the fat. (It was not considered out of place in our family to comment about fatness or skinniness or pallor or ruddiness or baldness.)

Her dark hair was done up in rolls above her face and at the sides, in the style of the time. Her skin was brownish-looking, netted with fine wrinkles, and her mouth wide, the lower lip rather thick, almost drooping, painted with a hearty lipstick that left a smear on the teacup and water tumbler. When her mouth was opened wide—as it nearly always was, talking or laughing—you could see that some of her teeth had been pulled at the back. Nobody could say that she was good-looking— any woman over twenty-five seemed to me to have pretty well passed beyond the possibility of being good-looking, anyway, to have lost the right to be so, and perhaps even the desire—but she was fervent and dashing. My father said thoughtfully that she had zing.

Alfrida talked to my father about things that were happening in the world, about politics. My father read the paper, he listened to the radio, he had opinions about these things but rarely got a chance to talk about them. The aunts' husbands had opinions too, but theirs were brief and unvaried and expressed an everlasting distrust of all public figures and particularly all foreigners, so that most of the time all that could be gotten out of them were grunts of dismissal. My grandmother was deaf— nobody could tell how much she knew or what she thought about anything, and the aunts themselves seemed fairly proud of how much they didn't know or didn't have to pay attention to. My mother had been a schoolteacher, and she could readily have pointed out all the countries of Europe on the map, but she saw everything through a personal haze, with the British Empire and the royal family looming large and everything else diminished, thrown into a jumble-heap that it was easy for her to disregard.

Alfrida's views were not really so far away from those of the uncles. Or so it appeared. But instead of grunting and letting the subject go, she gave her hooting laugh, and told stories about prime ministers and the American president and John L. Lewis and the mayor of Montreal— stories in which they all came out badly. She told stories about the royal family too, but there she made a distinction between the good ones like the king and queen and the beautiful Duchess of Kent and the dreadful ones like the Windsors and old King Eddy, who—she said—had a certain disease and had marked his wife's neck by trying to strangle her, which was why she always had to wear her pearls. This distinction coincided pretty well with one my mother made but seldom spoke about, so she did not object—though the reference to syphilis made her wince.

I smiled at it, knowingly, with a foolhardy composure.

Alfrida called the Russians funny names. Mikoyan-sky. Uncle Joe-sky. She believed that they were pulling the wool over everybody's eyes, and that the United Nations was a farce that would never work and that Japan would rise again and should have been finished off when there was the chance. She didn't trust Quebec either. Or the pope. There was a problem for her with Senator McCarthy—she would have liked to be on his side, but his being a Catholic was a stumbling block. She called the pope the poop. She relished the thought of all the crooks and scoundrels to be found in the world.

Sometimes it seemed as if she was putting on a show—a display, maybe to tease my father. To rile him up, as he himself would have said, to get his goat. But not because she disliked him or even wanted to make him uncomfortable. Quite the opposite. She might have been tormenting him as young girls torment boys at school, when arguments are a peculiar delight to both sides and insults are taken as flattery. My father argued with her, always in a mild steady voice, and yet it was clear that he had the intention of goading her on. Sometimes he would do a turnaround, and say that maybe she was right—that with her work on the newspaper, she must have sources of information that he couldn't have. You've put me straight, he would say, if I had any sense I'd be obliged to you. And she would say, Don't give me that load of baloney.

"You two," said my mother, in mock despair and perhaps in real exhaustion, and Alfrida told her to go and have a lie-down, she deserved it after this splendiferous dinner, she and I would manage the dishes. My mother was subject to a tremor in her right arm, a stiffness in her fingers, that she believed came when she got overtired.

While we worked in the kitchen Alfrida talked to me about celebrities—actors, even minor movie stars, who had made stage appearances in the city where she lived. In a lowered voice still broken by wildly disrespectful laughter she told me stories of their bad behavior, the rumors of private scandals that had never made it into the magazines. She mentioned queers, man-made bosoms, household triangles—all things that I had found hints of in my reading but felt giddy to hear about, even at third or fourth hand, in real life.

Alfrida's teeth always got my attention, so that even in these confidential recitals I sometimes lost track of what was being said. Those teeth that were left, across the front, were each of a slightly different color, no two alike. Some with a fairly strong enamel tended towards shades of dark ivory, others were opalescent, shadowed with lilac, and giving out fish-flashes of silver rims, occasionally a gleam of gold. People's teeth in those days seldom made such a solid, handsome show as they do now, unless they were false. But these teeth of Alfrida's were unusual in their individuality, clear separation, and large size. When Alfrida let out some jibe that was especially, knowingly outrageous, they seemed to leap to the fore like a palace guard, like jolly spear-fighters.

"She always did have trouble with her teeth," the aunts said. "She had that abscess, remember, the poison went all through her system."

How like them, I thought, to toss aside Alfrida's wit and style and turn her teeth into a sorry problem.

"Why doesn't she just have them all out and be done with it?" they said.

"Likely she couldn't afford it," said my grandmother, surprising - everybody as she sometimes did, by showing that she had been keeping up with the conversation all along.

And surprising me with the new, everyday sort of light this shed on Alfrida's life. I had believed that Alfrida was rich—rich at least in comparison with the rest of the family. She lived in an apartment—I had never seen it, but to me that fact conveyed at least the idea of a very civilized life—and she wore clothes that were not homemade, and her shoes were not Oxfords like the shoes of practically all the other grown-up women I knew—they were sandals made of bright strips of the new plastic. It was hard to know whether my grandmother was simply living in the past, when getting your false teeth was the solemn, crowning expense of a lifetime, or whether she really knew things about Alfrida's life that I never would have guessed.

The rest of the family was never present when Alfrida had dinner at our house. She did go to see my grandmother, who was her aunt, her mother's sister. My grandmother no longer lived at her own house but lived alternately with one or the other of the aunts, and Alfrida went to whichever house she was living in at the time, but not to the other house, to see the other aunt who was as much her cousin as my father was. And the meal she took was never with any of them. Usually she came to our house first and visited awhile, and then gathered herself up, as if reluctantly, to make the other visit. When she came back later and we sat down to eat, nothing derogatory was said outright against the aunts and their husbands, and certainly nothing disrespectful about my grandmother. In fact, it was the way that my grandmother would be spoken of by Alfrida—a sudden sobriety and concern in her voice, even a touch of fear (what about her blood pressure, had she been to the doctor lately, what did he have to say?)—that made me aware of the difference, the coolness or possibly unfriendly restraint, with which she asked after the others. Then there would be a similar restraint in my mother's reply, and an extra gravity in my father's—a caricature of gravity, you might say—that showed how they all agreed about something they could not say.

On the day when I smoked the cigarette Alfrida decided to take this a bit further, and she said solemnly, "How about Asa, then? Is he still as much of a conversation grabber as ever?"

My father shook his head sadly, as if the thought of this uncle's garrulousness must weigh us all down.

"Indeed," he said. "He is indeed."

Then I took my chance.

"Looks like the roundworms have got into the hogs," I said. "Yup."

Except for the "yup," this was just what my uncle had said, and he had said it at this very table, being overcome by an uncharacteristic need to break the silence or to pass on something important that had just come to mind. And I said it with just his stately grunts, his innocent solemnity.

Alfrida gave a great, approving laugh, showing her festive teeth. "That's it, she's got him to a *T*."

My father bent over his plate, as if to hide how he was laughing too, but of course not really hiding it, and my mother shook her head, biting her lips, smiling. I felt a keen triumph. Nothing was said to put me in my place, no reproof for what was sometimes called my sarcasm, my being smart. The word "smart" when it was used about me, in the family, might mean intelligent, and then it was used rather grudgingly—"oh, she's smart enough some ways"—or it might be used to mean pushy, attention-seeking, obnoxious. *Don't be so smart.*

Sometimes my mother said sadly, "You have a cruel tongue."

Sometimes—and this was a great deal worse—my father was disgusted with me.

"What makes you think you have the right to run down decent - people?"

This day nothing like that happened—I seemed to be as free as a visitor at the table, almost as free as Alfrida, and flourishing under the banner of my own personality.

BUT THERE was a gap about to open, and perhaps that was the last time, the very last time, that Alfrida sat at our table. Christmas cards continued to be exchanged, possibly even letters—as long as my mother could manage a pen—and we still read Alfrida's name in the paper, but I cannot recall any visits during the last couple of years I lived at home.

It may have been that Alfrida asked if she could bring her friend and had been told that she could not. If she was already living with him, that would have been one reason, and if he was the same man she had later, the fact that he was married would have been another. My parents would have been united in this. My mother had a horror of irregular sex or flaunted sex—of any sex, you might say, for the proper married kind was not acknowledged at all—and my father too judged these matters strictly at that time in his life. He might have had a special objection, also, to a man who could get a hold over Alfrida.

She would have made herself cheap in their eyes. I can imagine either one of them saying it. *She didn't need to go and make herself cheap.*

But she may not have asked at all, she may have known enough not to. During the time of those earlier, lively visits there may have been no man in her life, and then when there was one, her attention may have shifted entirely. She may have become a different person then, as she certainly was later on.

Or she may have been wary of the special atmosphere of a household where there is a sick person who will go on getting sicker and never get better. Which was the case with my mother, whose symptoms joined together, and turned a corner, and instead of a worry and an inconvenience became her whole destiny.

"The poor thing," the aunts said.

And as my mother was changed from a mother into a stricken presence around the house, these other, formerly so restricted females in the family seemed to gain some little liveliness and increased competence in the world. My grandmother got herself a hearing aid—something nobody would have suggested to her. One of the aunts' husbands—not Asa, but the one called Irvine—died, and the aunt who had been married to him learned to drive the car and got a job doing alterations in a clothing store and no longer wore a hairnet.

They called to see my mother, and saw always the same thing—that the one who had been better-looking, who had never quite let them forget she was a schoolteacher, was growing month by month more slow and stiff in the movements of her limbs and more thick and importunate in her speech, and that nothing was going to help her.

They told me to take good care of her.

"She's your mother," they reminded me.

"The poor thing."

Alfrida would not have been able to say those things, and she might not have been able to find anything to say in their place.

Her not coming to see us was all right with me. I didn't want people coming. I had no time for them, I had became a furious housekeeper— waxing the floors and ironing even the dish towels, and this was all done to keep some sort of disgrace (my mother's deterioration seemed to be a unique disgrace that infected us all) at bay. It was done to make it seem as if I lived with my parents and my brother and my sister in a normal family in an ordinary house, but the moment somebody stepped in our door and saw my mother they saw that this was not so and they pitied us. A thing I could not stand.

I won a scholarship. I didn't stay home to take care of my mother or of anything else. I went off to college. The college was in the city where Alfrida lived. After a few months she asked me to come for supper, but I - could not go, because I worked every evening of the week except on Sundays. I worked in the city library, downtown, and in the college library, both of which stayed open until nine o'clock. Some time later, during the winter, Alfrida asked me again, and this time the invitation was for a Sunday. I told her that I could not come because I was going to a concert.

"Oh—a date?" she said, and I said yes, but at the time it was not true. I would go to the free Sunday concerts in the college auditorium with another girl, or two or three other girls, for something to do and in the faint hope of meeting some boys there.

"Well you'll have to bring him around sometime," Alfrida said. "I'm dying to meet him."

Towards the end of the year I did have someone to bring, and I had actually met him at a concert. At least, he had seen me at a concert and had phoned me up and asked me to go out with him. But I would never have brought him to meet Alfrida. I would never have brought any of my new friends to meet her. My new friends were people who said, "Have you read *Look Homeward Angel*? Oh, you have to read that. Have you read *Buddenbrooks*?" They were people with whom I went to see *Forbidden Games* and *Les Enfants du Paradis* when the Film Society brought them in. The boy I went out with, and later became engaged to, had taken me to the Music Building, where you could listen to records at lunch hour. He introduced me to Gounod and because of Gounod I loved opera, and because of opera I loved Mozart.

When Alfrida left a message at my rooming house, asking me to call back, I never did. After that she didn't call again.

SHE STILL wrote for the paper—occasionally I glanced at one of her rhapsodies about Royal Doulton figurines or imported ginger biscuits or honeymoon negligees. Very likely she was still answering the letters from the Flora Simpson housewives, and still laughing at them. Now that I was living in that city I seldom looked at the paper that had once seemed to me the center of city life—and even, in a way, the center of our life at home, sixty miles away. The jokes, the compulsive insincerity, of people like Alfrida and Horse Henry now struck me as tawdry and boring.

I did not worry about running into her, even in this city that was not, after all, so very large. I never went into the shops that she mentioned in her column. I had no reason ever to walk past the newspaper building, and she lived far away from my rooming house, somewhere on the south side of town.

Nor did I think that Alfrida was the kind of person to show up at the library. The very word, "library," would probably make her turn down her big mouth in a parody of consternation, as she used to do at the books in the bookcase in our house—those books not bought in my time, some of them won as school prizes by my teenaged parents (there was my mother's maiden name, in her beautiful lost handwriting), books that seemed to me not like things bought in a store at all, but like presences in the house just as the trees outside the window were not plants but presences rooted in the ground. *The Mill on the Floss, The Call of the Wild, The Heart of Midlothian.* "Lot of hotshot reading in there," Alfrida had said. "Bet you don't crack those very often." And my father had said no, he didn't, falling in with her comradely tone of dismissal or even contempt and to some extent telling a lie, because he did look into them, once in a long while, when he had the time.

That was the kind of lie that I hoped never to have to tell again, the contempt I hoped never to have to show, about the things that really mattered to me. And in order not to have to do that, I would pretty well have to stay clear of the people I used to know.

AT THE end of my second year I was leaving college—my scholarship had covered only two years there. It didn't matter—I was planning to be a writer anyway. And I was getting married.

Alfrida had heard about this, and she got in touch with me again.

"I guess you must've been too busy to call me, or maybe nobody ever gave you my messages," she said.

I said that maybe I had been, or maybe they hadn't.

This time I agreed to visit. A visit would not commit me to anything, since I was not going to be living in this city in the future. I picked a Sunday, just after my final exams were over, when my fiancé was going to be in Ottawa for a job interview. The day was bright and sunny—it was around the beginning of May. I decided to walk. I had hardly ever been south of Dundas Street or east of Adelaide, so there were parts of the city that were entirely strange to me. The shade trees along the northern streets had just come out in leaf, and the lilacs, the ornamental crab apple trees, the beds of tulips were all in flower, the lawns like fresh carpets. But after a while I found myself walking along streets where there were no shade trees, streets where the houses were hardly an arm's reach from the sidewalk, and where such lilacs as there were—lilacs will grow anywhere —were pale, as if sun-bleached, and their fragrance did not carry. On these streets, as well as houses there were narrow apartment buildings, only two or three stories high—some with the utilitarian decoration of a rim of bricks around their doors, and some with raised windows and limp curtains falling out over their sills.

Alfrida lived in a house, not in an apartment building. She had the whole upstairs of a house. The downstairs, at least the front part of the downstairs, had been turned into a shop, which was closed, because of Sunday. It was a secondhand shop—I could see through the dirty front windows a lot of nondescript furniture with stacks of old dishes and utensils set everywhere. The only thing that caught my eye was a honey pail, exactly like the honey pail with a blue sky and a golden beehive in which I had carried my lunch to school when I was six or seven years old. I could remember reading over and over the words on its side.

All pure honey will granulate.

I had no idea then what "granulate" meant, but I liked the sound of it. It seemed ornate and delicious.

I had taken longer to get there than I had expected and I was very hot. I had not thought that Alfrida, inviting me to lunch, would present me with a meal like the Sunday dinners at home, but it was cooked meat and vegetables I smelled as I climbed the outdoor stairway.

"I thought you'd got lost," Alfrida called out above me. "I was about to get up a rescue party."

Instead of a sundress she was wearing a pink blouse with a floppy bow at the neck, tucked into a pleated brown skirt. Her hair was no longer done up in smooth rolls but cut short and frizzed around her face, its dark brown color now harshly touched with red. And her face, which I remembered as lean and summer-tanned, had got fuller and somewhat pouchy. Her makeup stood out on her skin like orange-pink paint in the noon light.

But the biggest difference was that she had gotten false teeth, of a uniform color, slightly overfilling her mouth and giving an anxious edge to her old expression of slapdash eagerness.

"Well—haven't you plumped out," she said. "You used to be so skinny."

This was true, but I did not like to hear it. Along with all the girls at the rooming house, I ate cheap food—copious meals of Kraft dinners and packages of jam-filled cookies. My fiancé, so sturdily and possessively in favor of everything about me, said that he liked full-bodied women and that I reminded him of Jane Russell. I did not mind his saying that, but usually I was affronted when people had anything to say about my appearance. Particularly when it was somebody like Alfrida—somebody who had lost all importance in my life. I believed that such people had no right to be looking at me, or forming any opinions about me, let alone stating them.

This house was narrow across the front, but long from front to back. There was a living room whose ceiling sloped at the sides and whose windows overlooked the street, a hall-like dining room with no windows at all because side bedrooms with dormers opened off it, a kitchen, a bathroom also without windows that got its daylight through a pebbled-glass pane in its door, and across the back of the house a glassed-in sunporch.

The sloping ceilings made the rooms look makeshift, as if they were only pretending to be anything but bedrooms. But they were crowded with serious furniture—dining-room table and chairs, kitchen table and chairs, living-room sofa and recliner—all meant for larger, proper rooms. Doilies on the tables, squares of embroidered white cloth protecting the backs and arms of sofa and chairs, sheer curtains across the windows and heavy flowered drapes at the sides—it was all more like the aunts' houses than I would have thought possible. And on the dining-room wall—not in the bathroom or bedroom but in the dining room—there hung a picture that was the silhouette of a girl in a hoopskirt, all constructed of pink satin ribbon.

A strip of tough linoleum was laid down on the dining-room floor, on the path from the kitchen to the living room.

Alfrida seemed to guess something of what I was thinking.

"I know I've got far too much stuff in here," she said. "But it's my parents' stuff. It's family furnishings, and I couldn't let them go."

I had never thought of her as having parents. Her mother had died long ago, and she had been brought up by my grandmother, who was her aunt.

"My dad and mother's," Alfrida said. "When Dad went off, your grandma kept it because she said it ought to be mine when I grew up, and so here it is. I couldn't turn it down, when she went to that trouble."

Now it came back to me—the part of Alfrida's life that I had forgotten about. Her father had married again. He had left the farm and got a job working for the railway. He had some other children, the family moved from one town to another, and sometimes Alfrida used to mention them, in a joking way that had something to do with how many children there had been and how close they came together and how much the family had to move around.

"Come and meet Bill," Alfrida said.

Bill was out on the sunporch. He sat, as if waiting to be summoned, on a low couch or daybed that was covered with a brown plaid blanket. The blanket was rumpled—he must have been lying on it recently—and the blinds on the windows were all pulled down to their sills. The light in the room—the hot sunlight coming through the rain-marked yellow blinds—and the rumpled rough blanket and faded, dented cushion, even the smell of the blanket, and of the masculine slippers, old scuffed slippers that had lost their shape and pattern, reminded me—just as much as the doilies and the heavy polished furniture in the inner rooms had done, and the ribbon-girl on the wall—of my aunts' houses. There, too, you could come upon a shabby male hideaway with its furtive yet insistent odors, its shamefaced but stubborn look of contradicting the female domain.

Bill stood up and shook my hand, however, as the uncles would never have done with a strange girl. Or with any girl. No specific rudeness would have held them back, just a dread of appearing ceremonious.

He was a tall man with wavy, glistening gray hair and a smooth but not young-looking face. A handsome man, with the force of his good looks somehow drained away—by indifferent health, or some bad luck, or lack of gumption. But he had still a worn courtesy, a way of bending towards a woman, that suggested the meeting would be a pleasure, for her and for himself.

Alfrida directed us into the windowless dining room where the lights were on in the middle of this bright day. I got the impression that the meal had been ready some time ago, and that my late arrival had delayed their usual schedule. Bill served the roast chicken and dressing, Alfrida the vegetables. Alfrida said to Bill, "Honey, what do you think that is beside your plate?" and then he remembered to pick up his napkin.

He had not much to say. He offered the gravy, he inquired as to whether I wanted mustard relish or salt and pepper, he followed the conversation by turning his head towards Alfrida or towards me. Every so often he made a little whistling sound between his teeth, a shivery sound that seemed meant to be genial and appreciative and that I thought at first might be a prelude to some remark. But it never was, and Alfrida never paused for it. I have since seen reformed drinkers who behaved somewhat as he did—chiming in agreeably but unable to carry things beyond that, helplessly preoccupied. I never knew whether that was true of Bill, but he did seem to carry around a history of defeat, of troubles borne and lessons learned. He had an air too of gallant accommodation towards whatever choices had gone wrong or chances hadn't panned out.

These were frozen peas and carrots, Alfrida said. Frozen vegetables were fairly new at the time.

"They beat the canned," she said. "They're practically as good as fresh."

Then Bill made a whole statement. He said they were better than fresh. The color, the flavor, everything was better than fresh. He said it was remarkable what they could do now and what would be done by way of freezing things in the future.

Alfrida leaned forward, smiling. She seemed almost to hold her breath, as if he was her child taking unsupported steps, or a first lone wobble on a bicycle.

There was a way they could inject something into a chicken, he told us, there was a new process that would have every chicken coming out the same, plump and tasty. No such thing as taking a risk on getting an inferior chicken anymore.

"Bill's field is chemistry," Alfrida said.

When I had nothing to say to this she added, "He worked for Gooderhams."

Still nothing.

"The distillers," she said. "Gooderhams Whisky."

The reason that I had nothing to say was not that I was rude or bored (or any more rude than I was naturally at that time, or more bored than I had expected to be) but that I did not understand that I should ask questions—almost any questions at all, to draw a shy male into conversation, to shake him out of his abstraction and set him up as a man of a certain authority, therefore the man of the house. I did not understand why Alfrida looked at him with such a fiercely encouraging smile. All of my experience of a woman with men, of a woman listening to her man, hoping and hoping that he will establish himself as somebody she can reasonably be proud of, was in the future. The only observation I had made of couples was of my aunts and uncles and of my mother and father, and those husbands and wives seemed to have remote and formalized connections and no obvious dependence on each other.

Bill continued eating as if he had not heard this mention of his profession and his employer, and Alfrida began to question me about my courses. She was still smiling, but her smile had changed. There was a little twitch of impatience and unpleasantness in it, as if she was just waiting for me to get to the end of my explanations so that she could say—as she did say—"You couldn't get me to read that stuff for a million dollars."

"Life's too short," she said. "You know, down at the paper we sometimes get somebody that's been through all that. Honors English. Honors Philosophy. You don't know what to do with them. They can't write worth a nickel. I've told you that, haven't I?" she said to Bill, and Bill looked up and gave her his dutiful smile.

She let this settle.

"So what do you do for fun?" she said.

A Streetcar Named Desire was being done in a theater in Toronto at that time, and I told her that I had gone down on the train with a couple of friends to see it.

Alfrida let the knife and fork clatter onto her plate.

"That filth," she cried. Her face leapt out at me, carved with disgust. Then she spoke more calmly but still with a virulent displeasure.

"You went *all the way to Toronto* to see that filth."

We had finished the dessert, and Bill picked that moment to ask if he might be excused. He asked Alfrida, then with the slightest bow he asked me. He went back to the sunporch and in a little while we could smell his pipe. Alfrida, watching him go, seemed to forget about me and the play. There was a look of such stricken tenderness on her face that when she stood up I thought she was going to follow him. But she was only going to get her cigarettes.

She held them out to me, and when I took one she said, with a deliberate effort at jollity, "I see you kept up the bad habit I got you started on." She might have remembered that I was not a child anymore and I did not have to be in her house and that there was no point in making an enemy of me. And I wasn't going to argue—I did not care what Alfrida thought about Tennessee Williams. Or what she thought about anything else.

"I guess it's your own business," Alfrida said. "You can go where you want to go." And she added, "After all—you'll pretty soon be a married woman."

By her tone, this could mean either "I have to allow that you're grown up now" or "Pretty soon you'll have to toe the line."

We got up and started to collect the dishes. Working close to each other in the small space between the kitchen table and counter and the refrigerator, we soon developed without speaking about it a certain order and harmony of scraping and stacking and putting the leftover food into smaller containers for storage and filling the sink with hot, soapy water and pouncing on any piece of cutlery that hadn't been touched and slipping it into the baize-lined drawer in the dining-room buffet. We brought the ashtray out to the kitchen and stopped every now and then to take a restorative, businesslike drag on our cigarettes. There are things women agree on or don't agree on when they work together in this way—whether it is all right to smoke, for instance, or preferable not to smoke because some migratory ash might find its way onto a clean dish, or whether every single thing that has been on the table has to be washed even if it has not been used—and it turned out that Alfrida and I agreed. Also, the thought that I could get away, once the dishes were done, made me feel more relaxed and generous. I had already said that I had to meet a friend that afternoon.

"These are pretty dishes," I said. They were creamy-colored, slightly yellowish, with a rim of blue flowers.

"Well—they were my mother's wedding dishes," Alfrida said. "That was one other good thing your grandma did for me. She packed up all my mother's dishes and put them away until the time came when I could use them. Jeanie never knew they existed. They wouldn't have lasted long, with that bunch."

Jeanie. That bunch. Her stepmother and the half brothers and sisters.

"You know about that, don't you?" Alfrida said. "You know what happened to my mother?"

Of course I knew. Alfrida's mother had died when a lamp exploded in her hands—that is, she died of burns she got when a lamp exploded in her hands—and my aunts and my mother had spoken of this regularly. Nothing could be said about Alfrida's mother or about Alfrida's father, and very little about Alfrida herself—without that death being dragged in and tacked onto it. It was the reason that Alfrida's father left the farm (always somewhat of a downward step morally if not financially). It was a reason to be desperately careful with coal oil, and a reason to be grateful for electricity, whatever the cost. And it was a dreadful thing for a child of Alfrida's age, whatever. (That is—whatever she had done with herself since.)

If it hadn't've been for the thunderstorm she wouldn't ever have been lighting a lamp in the middle of the afternoon.

She lived all that night and the next day and the next night and it would have been the best thing in the world for her if she hadn't've.

And just the year after that the Hydro came down their road, and they didn't have need of the lamps anymore.

The aunts and my mother seldom felt the same way about anything, but they shared a feeling about this story. The feeling was in their voices whenever they said Alfrida's mother's name. The story seemed to be a horrible treasure to them, something our family could claim that nobody else could, a distinction that would never be let go. To listen to them had always made me feel as if there was some obscene connivance going on, a fond fingering of whatever was grisly or disastrous. Their voices were like worms slithering around in my insides.

Men were not like this, in my experience. Men looked away from frightful happenings as soon as they could and behaved as if there was no use, once things were over with, in mentioning them or thinking about them ever again. They didn't want to stir themselves up, or stir other - people up.

So if Alfrida was going to talk about it, I thought, it was a good thing that my fiancé had not come. A good thing that he didn't have to hear about Alfrida's mother, on top of finding out about my mother and my family's relative or maybe considerable poverty. He admired opera and Laurence Olivier's *Hamlet,* but he had no time for tragedy—for the squalor of tragedy—in ordinary life. His parents were healthy and good-looking and prosperous (though he said of course that they were dull), and it seemed he had not had to know anybody who did not live in fairly sunny circumstances. Failures in life—failures of luck, of health, of finances—all struck him as lapses, and his resolute approval of me did not extend to my ramshackle background.

"They wouldn't let me in to see her, at the hospital," Alfrida said, and at least she was saying this in her normal voice, not preparing the way with any special piety, or greasy excitement. "Well, I probably wouldn't have let me in either, if I'd been in their shoes. I've no idea what she looked like. Probably all bound up like a mummy. Or if she wasn't she should have been. I wasn't there when it happened, I was at school. It got very dark and the teacher turned the lights on—we had the lights, at school—and we all had to stay till the thunderstorm was over. Then my Aunt Lily—well, your grandmother—she came to meet me and took me to her place. And I never got to see my mother again."

I thought that was all she was going to say but in a moment she continued, in a voice that had actually brightened up a bit, as if she was preparing for a laugh.

"I yelled and yelled my fool head off that I wanted to see her. I carried on and carried on, and finally when they couldn't shut me up your grandmother said to me, 'You're just better off not to see her. You would not want to see her, if you knew what she looks like now. You wouldn't want to remember her this way.'

"But you know what I said? I remember saying it. I said, But she would want to see me. *She would want to see me.*"

Then she really did laugh, or make a snorting sound that was evasive and scornful.

"I must've thought I was a pretty big cheese, mustn't I? *She would want to see me.*"

This was a part of the story I had never heard.

And the minute that I heard it, something happened. It was as if a trap had snapped shut, to hold these words in my head. I did not exactly understand what use I would have for them. I only knew how they jolted me and released me, right away, to breathe a different kind of air, available only to myself,

She would want to see me.

The story I wrote, with this in it, would not be written till years later, not until it had become quite unimportant to think about who had put the idea into my head in the first place.

I thanked Alfrida and said that I had to go. Alfrida went to call Bill to say good-bye to me, but came back to report that he had fallen asleep.

"He'll be kicking himself when he wakes up," she said. "He enjoyed meeting you."

She took off her apron and accompanied me all the way down the outside steps. At the bottom of the steps was a gravel path leading around to the sidewalk. The gravel crunched under our feet and she stumbled in her thin-soled house shoes.

She said, "Ouch! Goddarn it," and caught hold of my shoulder.

"How's your dad?" she said.

"He's all right."

"He works too hard."

I said, "He has to."

"Oh, I know. And how's your mother?"

"She's about the same."

She turned aside towards the shop window.

"Who do they think is ever going to buy this junk? Look at that honey pail. Your dad and I used to take our lunch to school in pails just like that."

"So did I," I said.

"Did you?" She squeezed me. "You tell your folks I'm thinking about them, will you do that?"

ALFRIDA DID not come to my father's funeral. I wondered if that was because she did not want to meet me. As far as I knew she had never made public what she held against me; nobody else would know about it. But my father had known. When I was home visiting him and learned that Alfrida was living not far away—in my grandmother's house, in fact, which she had finally inherited—I had suggested that we go to see her. This was in the flurry between my two marriages, when I was in an expansive mood, newly released and able to make contact with anyone I chose.

My father said, "Well, you know, Alfrida was a bit upset."

He was calling her Alfrida now. When had that started?

I could not even think, at first, what Alfrida might be upset about. My father had to remind me of the story, published several years ago, and I was surprised, even impatient and a little angry, to think of Alfrida's objecting to something that seemed now to have so little to do with her.

"It wasn't Alfrida at all," I said to my father. "I changed it, I wasn't even thinking about her. It was a character. Anybody could see that."

But as a matter of fact there was still the exploding lamp, the mother in her charnel wrappings, the staunch, bereft child.

"Well," my father said. He was in general quite pleased that I had become a writer, but there were reservations he had about what might be called my character. About the fact that I had ended my marriage for personal—that is, wanton—reasons, and the way I went around justifying myself—or perhaps, as he would have said, weaseling out of things. He would not say so—it was not his business anymore.

I asked him how he knew that Alfrida felt this way.

He said, "A letter."

A letter, though they lived not far apart. I did feel sorry to think that he had had to bear the brunt of what could be taken as my thoughtlessness, or even my wrongdoing. Also that he and Alfrida seemed now to be on such formal terms. I wondered what he was leaving out. Had he felt compelled to defend me to Alfrida, as he had to defend my writing to other people? He would do that now, though it was never easy for him. In his uneasy defense he might have said something harsh.

Through me, peculiar difficulties had developed for him.

There was a danger whenever I was on home ground. It was the danger of seeing my life through other eyes than my own. Seeing it as an ever-increasing roll of words like barbed wire, intricate, bewildering, uncomforting—set against the rich productions, the food, flowers, and knitted garments, of other women's domesticity. It became harder to say that it was worth the trouble.

Worth my trouble, maybe, but what about anyone else's?

My father had said that Alfrida was living alone now. I asked him what had become of Bill. He said that all of that was outside of his jurisdiction. But he believed there had been a bit of a rescue operation.

"Of Bill? How come? Who by?"

"Well, I believe there was a wife."

"I met him at Alfrida's once. I liked him."

"People did. Women."

*

I HAD to consider that the rupture might have had nothing to do with me. My stepmother had urged my father into a new sort of life. They went bowling and curling and regularly joined other couples for coffee and doughnuts at Tim Horton's. She had been a widow for a long time before she married him, and she had many friends from those days who became new friends for him. What had happened with him and Alfrida might have been simply one of the changes, the wearing-out of old attachments, that I understood so well in my own life but did not expect to happen in the lives of older people—particularly, as I would have said, in the lives of people at home.

My stepmother died just a little while before my father. After their short, happy marriage they were sent to separate cemeteries to lie beside their first, more troublesome, partners. Before either of those deaths Alfrida had moved back to the city. She didn't sell the house, she just went away and left it. My father wrote to me, "That's a pretty funny way of doing things."

THERE WERE a lot of people at my father's funeral, a lot of people I didn't know. A woman came across the grass in the cemetery to speak to me—I thought at first she must be a friend of my stepmother's. Then I saw that the woman was only a few years past my own age. The stocky figure and crown of gray-blond curls and floral-patterned jacket made her look older.

"I recognized you by your picture," she said. "Alfrida used to always be bragging about you."

I said, "Alfrida's not dead?"

"Oh, no," the woman said, and went on to tell me that Alfrida was in a nursing home in a town just north of Toronto.

"I moved her down there so's I could keep an eye on her."

Now it was easy to tell—even by her voice—that she was somebody of my own generation, and it came to me that she must be one of the other family, a half sister of Alfrida's, born when Alfrida was almost grown up.

She told me her name, and it was of course not the same as Alfrida's— she must have married. And I couldn't recall Alfrida's ever mentioning any of her half family by their first names.

I asked how Alfrida was, and the woman said her own eyesight was so bad that she was legally blind. And she had a serious kidney problem, which meant that she had to be on dialysis twice a week.

"Other than that—?" she said, and laughed. I thought, yes, a sister, because I could hear something of Alfrida in that reckless, tossed laugh.

"So she doesn't travel too good," she said. "Or else I would've brought her. She still gets the paper from here and I read it to her sometimes. That's where I saw about your dad."

I wondered out loud, impulsively, if I should go to visit, at the nursing home. The emotions of the funeral—all the warm and relieved and reconciled feelings opened up in me by the death of my father at a reasonable age—prompted this suggestion. It would have been hard to carry out. My husband—my second husband—and I had only two days here before we were flying to Europe on an already delayed holiday.

"I don't know if you'd get so much out of it," the woman said. "She has her good days. Then she has her bad days. You never know. Sometimes I think she's putting it on. Like, she'll sit there all day and whatever anybody says to her, she'll just say the same thing. *Fit as a fiddle and ready for love.* That's what she'll say all day long. *Fit-as-a-fiddle-and-ready-for-love.* She'll drive you crazy. Then other days she can answer all right."

Again, her voice and laugh—this time half submerged—reminded me of Alfrida, and I said, "You know I must have met you, I remember once when Alfrida's stepmother and her father dropped in, or maybe it was only her father and some of the children—"

"Oh, that's not who I am," the woman said. "You thought I was Alfrida's sister? Glory. I must be looking my age."

I started to say that I could not see her very well, and it was true. In October the afternoon sun was low, and it was coming straight into my eyes. The woman was standing against the light, so that it was hard to make out her features or her expression.

She twitched her shoulders nervously and importantly. She said, "Alfrida was my birth mom."

Mawm. Mother.

Then she told me, at not too great length, the story that she must have told often, because it was about an emphatic event in her life and an adventure she had embarked on alone. She had been adopted by a family in eastern Ontario; they were the only family she had ever known ("and I love them dearly"), and she had married and had her children, who were grown up before she got the urge to find out who her own mother was. It wasn't too easy, because of the way records used to be kept, and the secrecy ("It was kept one hundred percent secret that she had me"), but a few years ago she had tracked down Alfrida.

"Just in time too," she said. "I mean, it was time somebody came along to look after her. As much as I can."

I said, "I never knew."

"No. Those days, I don't suppose too many did. They warn you, when you start out to do this, it could be a shock when you show up. Older -

people, it's still heavy-duty. However. I don't think she minded. Earlier on, maybe she would have."

There was some sense of triumph about her, which wasn't hard to understand. If you have something to tell that will stagger someone, and you've told it, and it has done so, there has to be a balmy moment of power. In this case it was so complete that she felt a need to apologize.

"Excuse me talking all about myself and not saying how sorry I am about your dad."

I thanked her.

"You know Alfrida told me that your dad and her were walking home from school one day, this was in high school. They couldn't walk all the way together because, you know, in those days, a boy and a girl, they would just get teased something terrible. So if he got out first he'd wait just where their road went off the main road, outside of town, and if she got out first she would do the same, wait for him. And one day they were walking together and they heard all the bells starting to ring and you know what that was? It was the end of the First World War."

I said that I had heard that story too.

"Only I thought they were just children."

"Then how could they be coming home from high school, if they were just children?"

I said that I had thought they were out playing in the fields. "They had my father's dog with them. He was called Mack."

"Maybe they had the dog all right. Maybe he came to meet them. I wouldn't think she'd get mixed up on what she was telling me. She was pretty good on remembering anything involved your dad."

Now I was aware of two things. First, that my father was born in 1902, and that Alfrida was close to the same age. So it was much more likely that they were walking home from high school than that they were playing in the fields, and it was odd that I had never thought of that before. Maybe they had said they were in the fields, that is, walking home across the fields. Maybe they had never said "playing."

Also, that the feeling of apology or friendliness, the harmlessness that I had felt in this woman a little while before, was not there now.

I said, "Things get changed around."

"That's right," the woman said. "People change things around. You want to know what Alfrida said about you?"

Now. I knew it was coming now.

"What?"

"She said you were smart, but you weren't ever quite as smart as you thought you were."

I made myself keep looking into the dark face against the light.

Smart, too smart, not smart enough.

I said, "Is that all?"

"She said you were kind of a cold fish. That's her talking, not me. I haven't got anything against you."

THAT SUNDAY, after the noon dinner at Alfrida's, I set out to walk all the way back to my rooming house. If I walked both ways, I reckoned that I would have covered about ten miles, which ought to offset the effects of the meal I had eaten. I felt overfull, not just of food but of everything that I had seen and sensed in the apartment. The crowded, old-fashioned furnishings. Bill's silences. Alfrida's love, stubborn as sludge, and inappropriate, and hopeless—as far as I could see—on the grounds of age alone.

After I had walked for a while, my stomach did not feel so heavy. I made a vow not to eat anything for the next twenty-four hours. I walked north and west, north and west, on the streets of the tidily rectangular small city. On a Sunday afternoon there was hardly any traffic, except on the main thoroughfares. Sometimes my route coincided with a bus route for a few blocks. A bus might go by with only two or three people in it. People I did not know and who did not know me. What a blessing.

I had lied, I was not meeting any friends. My friends had mostly all gone home to wherever they lived. My fiancé would be away until the next day—he was visiting his parents, in Cobourg, on the way home from Ottawa. There would be nobody in the rooming house when I got there—nobody I had to bother talking to or listening to. I had nothing to do.

When I had walked for over an hour, I saw a drugstore that was open. I went in and had a cup of coffee. The coffee was reheated, black and bitter—its taste was medicinal, exactly what I needed. I was already feeling relieved, and now I began to feel happy. Such happiness, to be alone. To see the hot late-afternoon light on the sidewalk outside, the branches of a tree just out in leaf, throwing their skimpy shadows. To hear from the back of the shop the sounds of the ball game that the man who had served me was listening to on the radio. I did not think of the story I would make about Alfrida—not of that in particular—but of the work I wanted to do, which seemed more like grabbing something out of the air than constructing stories. The cries of the crowd came to me like big heartbeats, full of sorrows. Lovely formal-sounding waves, with their distant, almost inhuman assent and lamentation.

This was what I wanted, this was what I thought I had to pay attention to, this was how I wanted my life to be.

The Bear Came Over
the Mountain

FIONA LIVED in her parents' house, in the town where she and Grant went to university. It was a big, bay-windowed house that seemed to Grant both luxurious and disorderly, with rugs crooked on the floors and cup rings bitten into the table varnish. Her mother was Icelandic—a powerful woman with a froth of white hair and indignant far-left politics. The father was an important cardiologist, revered around the hospital but happily subservient at home, where he would listen to strange tirades with an absentminded smile. All kinds of people, rich or shabby-looking, delivered these tirades, and kept coming and going and arguing and conferring, sometimes in foreign accents. Fiona had her own little car and a pile of cashmere sweaters, but she wasn't in a sorority, and this activity in her house was probably the reason.

Not that she cared. Sororities were a joke to her, and so was politics, though she liked to play "The Four Insurgent Generals" on the phonograph, and sometimes also she played the "Internationale," very loud, if there was a guest she thought she could make nervous. A curly-haired, gloomy-looking foreigner was courting her—she said he was a Visigoth—and so were two or three quite respectable and uneasy young interns. She made fun of them all and of Grant as well. She would drolly repeat some of his small-town phrases. He thought maybe she was joking when she proposed to him, on a cold bright day on the beach at Port

178

Stanley. Sand was stinging their faces and the waves delivered crashing loads of gravel at their feet.

"Do you think it would be fun—" Fiona shouted. "Do you think it would be fun if we got married?"

He took her up on it, he shouted yes. He wanted never to be away from her. She had the spark of life.

JUST BEFORE they left their house Fiona noticed a mark on the kitchen floor. It came from the cheap black house shoes she had been wearing earlier in the day.

"I thought they'd quit doing that," she said in a tone of ordinary annoyance and perplexity, rubbing at the gray smear that looked as if it had been made by a greasy crayon.

She remarked that she would never have to do this again, since she wasn't taking those shoes with her.

"I guess I'll be dressed up all the time," she said. "Or semi dressed up. It'll be sort of like in a hotel."

She rinsed out the rag she'd been using and hung it on the rack inside the door under the sink. Then she put on her golden-brown fur-collared ski jacket over a white turtle-necked sweater and tailored fawn slacks. She was a tall, narrow-shouldered woman, seventy years old but still upright and trim, with long legs and long feet, delicate wrists and ankles and tiny, almost comical-looking ears. Her hair, which was light as milkweed fluff, had gone from pale blond to white somehow without Grant's noticing exactly when, and she still wore it down to her shoulders, as her mother had done. (That was the thing that had alarmed Grant's own mother, a small-town widow who worked as a doctor's receptionist. The long white hair on Fiona's mother, even more than the state of the house, had told her all she needed to know about attitudes and politics.)

Otherwise Fiona with her fine bones and small sapphire eyes was nothing like her mother. She had a slightly crooked mouth which she emphasized now with red lipstick—usually the last thing she did before she left the house. She looked just like herself on this day—direct and vague as in fact she was, sweet and ironic.

OVER A year ago Grant had started noticing so many little yellow notes stuck up all over the house. That was not entirely new. She'd always written things down—the title of a book she'd heard mentioned on the radio or the jobs she wanted to make sure she did that day. Even her morning schedule was written down—he found it mystifying and touching in its precision.

7 a.m. Yoga. 7:30–7:45 teeth face hair. 7:45–8:15 walk. 8:15 Grant and Breakfast.

The new notes were different. Taped onto the kitchen drawers—Cutlery, Dishtowels, Knives. Couldn't she have just opened the drawers and seen what was inside? He remembered a story about the German soldiers on border patrol in Czechoslovakia during the war. Some Czech had told him that each of the patrol dogs wore a sign that said *Hund*. Why? said the Czechs, and the Germans said, Because that is a *hund*.

He was going to tell Fiona that, then thought he'd better not. They always laughed at the same things, but suppose this time she didn't laugh?

Worse things were coming. She went to town and phoned him from a booth to ask him how to drive home. She went for her walk across the field into the woods and came home by the fence line—a very long way round. She said that she'd counted on fences always taking you somewhere.

It was hard to figure out. She said that about fences as if it was a joke, and she had remembered the phone number without any trouble.

"I don't think it's anything to worry about," she said. "I expect I'm just losing my mind."

He asked if she had been taking sleeping pills.

"If I have I don't remember," she said. Then she said she was sorry to sound so flippant.

"I'm sure I haven't been taking anything. Maybe I should be. Maybe vitamins."

Vitamins didn't help. She would stand in doorways trying to figure out where she was going. She forgot to turn on the burner under the vegetables or put water in the coffeemaker. She asked Grant when they'd moved to this house.

"Was it last year or the year before?"

He said that it was twelve years ago.

She said, "That's shocking."

"She's always been a bit like this," Grant said to the doctor. "Once she left her fur coat in storage and just forgot about it. That was when we were always going somewhere warm in the winters. Then she said it was unintentionally on purpose, she said it was like a sin she was leaving behind. The way some people made her feel about fur coats."

He tried without success to explain something more—to explain how Fiona's surprise and apologies about all this seemed somehow like routine courtesy, not quite concealing a private amusement. As if she'd stumbled on some adventure that she had not been expecting. Or was playing a game that she hoped he would catch on to. They had always had their games—nonsense dialects, characters they invented. Some of Fiona's made-up voices, chirping or wheedling (he couldn't tell the doctor this), had mimicked uncannily the voices of women of his that she had never met or known about.

"Yes, well," the doctor said. "It might be selective at first. We don't know, do we? Till we see the pattern of the deterioration, we really can't say."

In a while it hardly mattered what label was put on it. Fiona, who no longer went shopping alone, disappeared from the supermarket while Grant had his back turned. A policeman picked her up as she walked down the middle of the road, blocks away. He asked her name and she answered readily. Then he asked her the name of the prime minister of the country.

"If you don't know that, young man, you really shouldn't be in such a responsible job."

He laughed. But then she made the mistake of asking if he'd seen Boris and Natasha.

These were the Russian wolfhounds she had adopted some years ago as a favor to a friend, then devoted herself to for the rest of their lives. Her taking them over might have coincided with the discovery that she was not likely to have children. Something about her tubes being blocked, or twisted—Grant could not remember now. He had always avoided thinking about all that female apparatus. Or it might have been after her mother died. The dogs' long legs and silky hair, their narrow, gentle, intransigent faces made a fine match for her when she took them out for walks. And Grant himself, in those days, landing his first job at the university (his father-in-law's money welcome in spite of the political taint), might have seemed to some people to have been picked up on another of Fiona's eccentric whims, and groomed and tended and favored. Though he never understood this, fortunately, until much later.

SHE SAID to him, at suppertime on the day of the wandering-off at the supermarket, "You know what you're going to have to do with me, don't you? You're going to have to put me in that place. Shallowlake?"

Grant said, "Meadowlake. We're not at that stage yet."

"Shallowlake, Shillylake," she said, as if they were engaged in a playful competition. "Sillylake. Sillylake it is."

He held his head in his hands, his elbows on the table. He said that if they did think of it, it must be as something that need not be permanent. A kind of experimental treatment. A rest cure.

*

THERE WAS a rule that nobody could be admitted during the month of December. The holiday season had so many emotional pitfalls. So they made the twenty-minute drive in January. Before they reached the highway the country road dipped through a swampy hollow now completely frozen over. The swamp-oaks and maples threw their shadows like bars across the bright snow.

Fiona said, "Oh, remember."

Grant said, "I was thinking about that too."

"Only it was in the moonlight," she said.

She was talking about the time that they had gone out skiing at night under the full moon and over the black-striped snow, in this place that you could get into only in the depths of winter. They had heard the branches cracking in the cold.

So if she could remember that so vividly and correctly, could there - really be so much the matter with her?

It was all he could do not to turn around and drive home.

THERE WAS another rule which the supervisor explained to him. New residents were not to be visited during the first thirty days. Most people needed that time to get settled in. Before the rule had been put in place, there had been pleas and tears and tantrums, even from those who had come in willingly. Around the third or fourth day they would start lamenting and begging to be taken home. And some relatives could be susceptible to that, so you would have people being carted home who would not get on there any better than they had before. Six months later or sometimes only a few weeks later, the whole upsetting hassle would have to be gone through again.

"Whereas we find," the supervisor said, "we find that if they're left on their own they usually end up happy as clams. You have to practically lure them into a bus to take a trip to town. The same with a visit home. It's perfectly okay to take them home then, visit for an hour or two—they're the ones that'll worry about getting back in time for supper. Meadowlake's their home then. Of course, that doesn't apply to the ones on the second floor, we can't let them go. It's too difficult, and they don't know where they are anyway."

"My wife isn't going to be on the second floor," Grant said.

"No," said the supervisor thoughtfully. "I just like to make everything clear at the outset."

THEY HAD gone over to Meadowlake a few times several years ago, to visit

Mr. Farquar, the old bachelor farmer who had been their neighbor. He had lived by himself in a drafty brick house unaltered since the early years of the century, except for the addition of a refrigerator and a television set. He had paid Grant and Fiona unannounced but well-spaced visits and, as well as local matters, he liked to discuss books he had been reading—about the Crimean War or Polar explorations or the history of firearms. But after he went to Meadowlake he would talk only about the routines of the place, and they got the idea that their visits, though gratifying, were a social burden for him. And Fiona in particular hated the smell of urine and bleach that hung about, hated the perfunctory bouquets of plastic flowers in niches in the dim, low-ceilinged corridors.

Now that building was gone, though it had dated only from the fifties. Just as Mr. Farquar's house was gone, replaced by a gimcrack sort of castle that was the weekend home of some people from Toronto. The new Meadowlake was an airy, vaulted building whose air was faintly pleasantly pine-scented. Profuse and genuine greenery sprouted out of giant crocks.

Nevertheless, it was the old building that Grant would find himself picturing Fiona in during the long month he had to get through without seeing her. It was the longest month of his life, he thought—longer than the month he had spent with his mother visiting relatives in Lanark County, when he was thirteen, and longer than the month that Jacqui Adams spent on holiday with her family, near the beginning of their affair. He phoned Meadowlake every day and hoped that he would get the nurse whose name was Kristy. She seemed a little amused at his constancy, but she would give him a fuller report than any other nurse he got stuck with.

Fiona had caught a cold, but that was not unusual for newcomers.

"Like when your kids start school," Kristy said. "There's a whole bunch of new germs they're exposed to, and for a while they just catch everything."

Then the cold got better. She was off the antibiotics, and she didn't seem as confused as she had been when she came in. (This was the first time Grant had heard about either the antibiotics or the confusion.) Her appetite was pretty good, and she seemed to enjoy sitting in the sunroom. She seemed to enjoy watching television.

One of the things that had been so intolerable about the old Meadowlake had been the way the television was on everywhere, overwhelming your thoughts or conversation wherever you chose to sit down. Some of the inmates (that was what he and Fiona called them then, not residents) would raise their eyes to it, some talked back to it, but most just sat and meekly endured its assault. In the new building, as far as he could recall, the television was in a separate sitting room, or in the bedrooms. You could make a choice to watch it.

So Fiona must have made a choice. To watch what?

During the years that they had lived in this house, he and Fiona had watched quite a bit of television together. They had spied on the lives of - every beast or reptile or insect or sea creature that a camera was able to reach, and they had followed the plots of what seemed like dozens of rather similar fine nineteenth-century novels. They had slid into an infatuation with an English comedy about life in a department store and had watched so many reruns that they knew the dialogue by heart. They mourned the disappearance of actors who died in real life or went off to other jobs, then welcomed those same actors back as the characters were born again. They watched the floorwalker's hair going from black to gray and finally back to black, the cheap sets never changing. But these, too, faded; eventually the sets and the blackest hair faded as if dust from the London streets was getting in under the elevator doors, and there was a sadness about this that seemed to affect Grant and Fiona more than any of the tragedies on *Masterpiece Theatre*, so they gave up watching before the final end.

Fiona was making some friends, Kristy said. She was definitely coming out of her shell.

What shell was that? Grant wanted to ask, but checked himself, to remain in Kristy's good graces.

IF ANYBODY phoned, he let the message go onto the machine. The people they saw socially, occasionally, were not close neighbors but people who lived around the countryside, who were retired, as they were, and who often went away without notice. The first years that they had lived here Grant and Fiona had stayed through the winter. A country winter was a new experience, and they had plenty to do, fixing up the house. Then they had gotten the idea that they too should travel while they could, and they had gone to Greece, to Australia, to Costa Rica. People would think that they were away on some such trip at present.

He skied for exercise but never went as far as the swamp. He skied around and around in the field behind the house as the sun went down and left the sky pink over a countryside that seemed to be bound by waves of blue-edged ice. He counted off the times he went round the field, and then he came back to the darkening house, turning the television news on while he got his supper. They had usually prepared supper together. One of them made the drinks and the other the fire, and they talked about his work (he was writing a study of legendary Norse wolves and particularly of the great Fenris wolf who swallows up Odin at the end of the world) and about whatever Fiona was reading and what they had been thinking during their close but separate day. This was their time of liveliest intimacy, though there was also, of course, the five or ten minutes of physical sweetness just after they got into bed—something that did not often end up in sex but reassured them that sex was not over yet.

IN A dream Grant showed a letter to one of his colleagues whom he had thought of as a friend. The letter was from the roommate of a girl he had not thought of for a while. Its style was sanctimonious and hostile, threatening in a whining way—he put the writer down as a latent lesbian. The girl herself was someone he had parted from decently, and it seemed unlikely that she would want to make a fuss, let alone try to kill herself, which was what the letter was apparently, elaborately, trying to tell him.

The colleague was one of those husbands and fathers who had been among the first to throw away their neckties and leave home to spend - every night on a floor mattress with a bewitching young mistress, coming to their offices, their classes, bedraggled and smelling of dope and incense. But now he took a dim view of such shenanigans, and Grant recollected that he had in fact married one of those girls, and that she had taken to giving dinner parties and having babies, just as wives used to do.

"I wouldn't laugh," he said to Grant, who did not think he had been laughing. "And if I were you I'd try to prepare Fiona."

So Grant went off to find Fiona in Meadowlake—the old Meadowlake —and got into a lecture theater instead. Everybody was waiting there for him to teach his class. And sitting in the last, highest row was a flock of cold-eyed young women all in black robes, all in mourning, who never took their bitter stares off him and conspicuously did not write down, or care about, anything he was saying.

Fiona was in the first row, untroubled. She had transformed the lecture room into the sort of corner she was always finding at a party—some high-and-dry spot where she drank wine with mineral water, and smoked ordinary cigarettes and told funny stories about her dogs. Holding out there against the tide, with some people who were like herself, as if the dramas that were being played out in other corners, in bedrooms and on the dark verandah, were nothing but childish comedy. As if chastity was chic, and reticence a blessing.

"Oh, phooey," Fiona said. "Girls that age are always going around talking about how they'll kill themselves."

But it wasn't enough for her to say that—in fact, it rather chilled him.

He was afraid that she was wrong, that something terrible had happened, and he saw what she could not—that the black ring was thickening, drawing in, all around his windpipe, all around the top of the room.

HE HAULED himself out of the dream and set about separating what was real from what was not.

There had been a letter, and the word "RAT" had appeared in black paint on his office door, and Fiona, on being told that a girl had suffered from a bad crush on him, had said pretty much what she said in the dream. The colleague hadn't come into it, the black-robed women had never appeared in his classroom, and nobody had committed suicide. Grant hadn't been disgraced, in fact he had got off easily when you thought of what might have happened just a couple of years later. But word got around. Cold shoulders became conspicuous. They had few Christmas invitations and spent New Year's Eve alone. Grant got drunk, and without its being required of him—also, thank God, without making the error of a confession—he promised Fiona a new life.

The shame he felt then was the shame of being duped, of not having noticed the change that was going on. And not one woman had made him aware of it. There had been the change in the past when so many women so suddenly became available—or it seemed that way to him—and now this new change, when they were saying that what had happened was not what they had had in mind at all. They had collaborated because they were helpless and bewildered, and they had been injured by the whole thing, rather than delighted. Even when they had taken the initiative they had done so only because the cards were stacked against them.

Nowhere was there any acknowledgment that the life of a philanderer (if that was what Grant had to call himself—he who had not had half as many conquests or complications as the man who had reproached him in his dream) involved acts of kindness and generosity and even sacrifice. Not in the beginning, perhaps, but at least as things went on. Many times he had catered to a woman's pride, to her fragility, by offering more affection—or a rougher passion—than anything he really felt. All so that he could now find himself accused of wounding and exploiting and destroying self-esteem. And of deceiving Fiona—as of course he had deceived her—but would it have been better if he had done as others had done with their wives and left her?

He had never thought of such a thing. He had never stopped making love to Fiona in spite of disturbing demands elsewhere. He had not stayed away from her for a single night. No making up elaborate stories in order to spend a weekend in San Francisco or in a tent on Manitoulin Island.

He had gone easy on the dope and the drink and he had continued to publish papers, serve on committees, make progress in his career. He had never had any intention of throwing up work and marriage and taking to the country to practice carpentry or keep bees.

But something like that had happened after all. He took an early retirement with a reduced pension. The cardiologist had died, after some bewildered and stoical time alone in the big house, and Fiona had inherited both that property and the farmhouse where her father had grown up, in the country near Georgian Bay. She gave up her job, as a hospital coordinator of volunteer services (in that everyday world, as she said, where people actually had troubles that were not related to drugs or sex or intellectual squabbles). A new life was a new life.

Boris and Natasha had died by this time. One of them got sick and died first—Grant forgot which one—and then the other died, more or less out of sympathy.

He and Fiona worked on the house. They got cross-country skis. They were not very sociable, but they gradually made some friends. There were no more hectic flirtations. No bare female toes creeping up under a man's pants leg at a dinner party. No more loose wives.

Just in time, Grant was able to think, when the sense of injustice wore down. The feminists and perhaps the sad silly girl herself and his cowardly so-called friends had pushed him out just in time. Out of a life that was in fact getting to be more trouble than it was worth. And that might eventually have cost him Fiona.

On the morning of the day when he was to go back to Meadowlake for the first visit, Grant woke early. He was full of a solemn tingling, as in the old days on the morning of his first planned meeting with a new woman. The feeling was not precisely sexual. (Later, when the meetings had become routine, that was all it was.) There was an expectation of discovery, almost a spiritual expansion. Also timidity, humility, alarm.

He left home too early. Visitors were not allowed before two o'clock. He did not want to sit out in the parking lot, waiting, so he made himself turn the car in a wrong direction.

There had been a thaw. Plenty of snow was left, but the dazzling hard landscape of earlier winter had crumbled. These pocked heaps under a gray sky looked like refuse in the fields.

In the town near Meadowlake he found a florist's shop and bought a large bouquet. He had never presented flowers to Fiona before. Or to anyone else. He entered the building feeling like a hopeless lover or a guilty husband in a cartoon.

"Wow. Narcissus this early," Kristy said. "You must've spent a fortune." She went along the hall ahead of him and snapped on the light in a closet, or sort of kitchen, where she searched for a vase. She was a heavy young woman who looked as if she had given up in every department except her hair. That was blond and voluminous. All the puffed-up luxury of a cocktail waitress's style, or a stripper's, on top of such a workaday face and body.

"There, now," she said, and nodded him down the hall. "Name's right on the door."

So it was, on a nameplate decorated with bluebirds. He wondered whether to knock, and did, then opened the door and called her name.

She wasn't there. The closet door was closed, the bed smoothed. Nothing on the bedside table, except a box of Kleenex and a glass of water. Not a single photograph or picture of any kind, not a book or a magazine. Perhaps you had to keep those in a cupboard.

He went back to the nurses' station, or reception desk, or whatever it was. Kristy said "No?" with a surprise that he thought perfunctory.

He hesitated, holding the flowers. She said, "Okay, okay—let's set the bouquet down here." Sighing, as if he was a backward child on his first day at school, she led him along a hall, into the light of the huge sky windows in the large central space, with its cathedral ceiling. Some people were sitting along the walls, in easy chairs, others at tables in the middle of the carpeted floor. None of them looked too bad. Old—some of them incapacitated enough to need wheelchairs—but decent. There used to be some unnerving sights when he and Fiona went to visit Mr. Farquar. Whiskers on old women's chins, somebody with a bulged-out eye like a rotted plum. Dribblers, head wagglers, mad chatterers. Now it looked as if there'd been some weeding out of the worst cases. Or perhaps drugs, surgery had come into use, perhaps there were ways of treating disfigurement, as well as verbal and other kinds of incontinence—ways that hadn't existed even those few years ago.

There was, however, a very disconsolate woman sitting at the piano, picking away with one finger and never achieving a tune. Another woman, staring out from behind a coffee urn and a stack of plastic cups, looked bored to stone. But she had to be an employee—she wore a pale-green pants outfit like Kristy's.

"See?" said Kristy in a softer voice. "You just go up and say hello and try not to startle her. Remember she may not— Well. Just go ahead."

He saw Fiona in profile, sitting close up to one of the card tables, but not playing. She looked a little puffy in the face, the flab on one cheek hiding the corner of her mouth, in a way it hadn't done before. She was watching the play of the man she sat closest to. He held his cards tilted so that she could see them. When Grant got near the table she looked up. They all looked up—all the players at the table looked up, with displeasure. Then they immediately looked down at their cards, as if to ward off any intrusion.

But Fiona smiled her lopsided, abashed, sly, and charming smile and pushed back her chair and came round to him, putting her fingers to her mouth.

"Bridge," she whispered. "Deadly serious. They're quite rabid about it." She drew him towards the coffee table, chatting. "I can remember being like that for a while at college. My friends and I would cut class and sit in the common room and smoke and play like cutthroats. One's name was Phoebe, I don't remember the others."

"Phoebe Hart," Grant said. He pictured the little hollow-chested, black-eyed girl, who was probably dead by now. Wreathed in smoke, Fiona and Phoebe and those others, rapt as witches.

"You knew her too?" said Fiona, directing her smile now towards the stone-faced woman. "Can I get you anything? A cup of tea? I'm afraid the coffee isn't up to much here."

Grant never drank tea.

He could not throw his arms around her. Something about her voice and smile, familiar as they were, something about the way she seemed to be guarding the players and even the coffee woman from him—as well as him from their displeasure—made that not possible.

"I brought you some flowers," he said. "I thought they'd do to brighten up your room. I went to your room, but you weren't there."

"Well, no," she said. "I'm here."

Grant said, "You've made a new friend." He nodded towards the man she'd been sitting next to. At this moment that man looked up at Fiona and she turned, either because of what Grant had said or because she felt the look at her back.

"It's just Aubrey," she said. "The funny thing is I knew him years and years ago. He worked in the store. The hardware store where my grandpa used to shop. He and I were always kidding around and he could not get up the nerve to ask me out. Till the very last weekend and he took me to a ball game. But when it was over my grandpa showed up to drive me home. I was up visiting for the summer. Visiting my grandparents—they lived on a farm."

"Fiona. I know where your grandparents lived. It's where we live. Lived."

"Really?" she said, not paying full attention because the cardplayer was sending her his look, which was not one of supplication but command. He was a man of about Grant's age, or a little older. Thick coarse white hair fell over his forehead, and his skin was leathery but pale, yellowish-white like an old wrinkled-up kid glove. His long face was dignified and melancholy, and he had something of the beauty of a powerful, discouraged, elderly horse. But where Fiona was concerned he was not discouraged.

"I better go back," Fiona said, a blush spotting her newly fattened face. "He thinks he can't play without me sitting there. It's silly, I hardly know the game anymore. I'm afraid you'll have to excuse me."

"Will you be through soon?"

"Oh, we should be. It depends. If you go and ask that grim-looking lady nicely she'll get you some tea."

"I'm fine," Grant said.

"So I'll leave you then, you can entertain yourself? It must all seem strange to you, but you'll be surprised how soon you get used to it. You'll get to know who everybody is. Except that some of them are pretty well off in the clouds, you know—you can't expect them all to get to know who *you* are."

She slipped back into her chair and said something into Aubrey's ear. She tapped her fingers across the back of his hand.

Grant went in search of Kristy and met her in the hall. She was pushing a cart on which there were pitchers of apple juice and grape juice.

"Just one sec," she said to him, as she stuck her head through a doorway. "Apple juice in here? Grape juice? Cookies?"

He waited while she filled two plastic glasses and took them into the room. Then she came back and put two arrowroot cookies on paper plates.

"Well?" she said. "Aren't you glad to see her participating and everything?"

Grant said, "Does she even know who I am?"

HE COULD not decide. She could have been playing a joke. It would not be unlike her. She had given herself away by that little pretense at the end, talking to him as if she thought perhaps he was a new resident.

If that was what she was pretending. If it was a pretense.

But would she not have run after him and laughed at him then, once the joke was over? She would not have just gone back to the game, surely, and pretended to forget about him. That would have been too cruel.

Kristy said, "You just caught her at sort of a bad moment. Involved in the game."

"She's not even playing," he said.

"Well, but her friend's playing. Aubrey."

"So who is Aubrey?"

"That's who he is. Aubrey. Her friend. Would you like a juice?"

Grant shook his head.

"Oh, look," said Kristy. "They get these attachments. That takes over for a while. Best buddy sort of thing. It's kind of a phase."

"You mean she really might not know who I am?"

"She might not. Not today. Then tomorrow—you never know, do you? Things change back and forth all the time and there's nothing you can do about it. You'll see the way it is once you've been coming here for a while. You'll learn not to take it all so serious. Learn to take it day by day."

DAY BY day. But things really didn't change back and forth, and he didn't get used to the way they were. Fiona was the one who seemed to get used to him, but only as some persistent visitor who took a special interest in her. Or perhaps even as a nuisance who must be prevented, according to her old rules of courtesy, from realizing that he was one. She treated him with a distracted, social sort of kindness that was successful in holding him back from the most obvious, the most necessary question. He could not demand of her whether she did or did not remember him as her husband of nearly fifty years. He got the impression that she would be embarrassed by such a question—embarrassed not for herself but for him. She would have laughed in a fluttery way and mortified him with her politeness and bewilderment, and somehow she would have ended up not saying either yes or no. Or she would have said either one in a way that gave not the least satisfaction.

Kristy was the only nurse he could talk to. Some of the others treated the whole thing as a joke. One tough old stick laughed in his face. "That Aubrey and that Fiona? They've really got it bad, haven't they?"

Kristy told him that Aubrey had been the local representative of a company that sold weed killer—"and all that kind of stuff"—to farmers.

"He was a fine person," she said, and Grant did not know whether this meant that Aubrey was honest and openhanded and kind to people, or that he was well spoken and well dressed and drove a good car. Probably both.

And then when he was not very old or even retired—she said—he had suffered some unusual kind of damage.

"His wife is the one takes care of him usually. She takes care of him at home. She just put him in here on temporary care so she could get a break. Her sister wanted her to go to Florida. See, she's had a hard time, you wouldn't ever have expected a man like him— They just went on a holiday somewhere and he got something, like some bug, that gave him a terrible high fever? And it put him in a coma and left him like he is now."

He asked her about these affections between residents. Did they ever go too far? He was able now to take a tone of indulgence that he hoped would save him from any lectures.

"Depends what you mean," she said. She kept writing in her record book while deciding how to answer him. When she finished what she was writing she looked up at him with a frank smile.

"The trouble we have in here, it's funny, it's often with some of the ones that haven't been friendly with each other at all. They maybe won't even know each other, beyond knowing, like, is it a man or a woman? You'd think it'd be the old guys trying to crawl in bed with the old women, but you know half the time it's the other way round. Old women going after the old men. Could be they're not so wore out, I guess."

Then she stopped smiling, as if she was afraid she had said too much, or spoken callously.

"Don't take me wrong," she said. "I don't mean Fiona. Fiona is a lady."

Well, what about Aubrey? Grant felt like saying. But he remembered that Aubrey was in a wheelchair.

"She's a real lady," Kristy said, in a tone so decisive and reassuring that Grant was not reassured. He had in his mind a picture of Fiona, in one of her long eyelet-trimmed blue-ribboned nightgowns, teasingly lifting the covers of an old man's bed.

"Well, I sometimes wonder—" he said.

Kristy said sharply, "You wonder what?"

"I wonder whether she isn't putting on some kind of a charade."

"A what?" said Kristy.

MOST AFTERNOONS the pair could be found at the card table. Aubrey had large, thick-fingered hands. It was difficult for him to manage his cards. Fiona shuffled and dealt for him and sometimes moved quickly to straighten a card that seemed to be slipping from his grasp. Grant would watch from across the room her darting move and quick, laughing apology. He could see Aubrey's husbandly frown as a wisp of her hair touched his cheek. Aubrey preferred to ignore her as long as she stayed close.

But let her smile her greeting at Grant, let her push back her chair and get up to offer him tea—showing that she had accepted his right to be there and possibly felt a slight responsibility for him—and Aubrey's face took on its look of sombre consternation. He would let the cards slide from his fingers and fall on the floor, to spoil the game.

So that Fiona had to get busy and put things right.

If they weren't at the bridge table they might be walking along the halls,

Aubrey hanging on to the railing with one hand and clutching Fiona's arm or shoulder with the other. The nurses thought that it was a marvel, the way she had got him out of his wheelchair. Though for longer trips—to the conservatory at one end of the building or the television room at the other—the wheelchair was called for.

The television seemed to be always turned to the sports channel and Aubrey would watch any sport, but his favorite appeared to be golf. Grant didn't mind watching that with them. He sat down a few chairs away. On the large screen a small group of spectators and commentators followed the players around the peaceful green, and at appropriate moments broke into a formal sort of applause. But there was silence everywhere as the player made his swing and the ball took its lonely, appointed journey across the sky. Aubrey and Fiona and Grant and possibly others sat and held their breaths, and then Aubrey's breath broke out first, expressing satisfaction or disappointment. Fiona's chimed in on the same note a moment later.

In the conservatory there was no such silence. The pair found themselves a seat among the most lush and thick and tropical-looking plants—a bower, if you like—which Grant had just enough self-control to keep from penetrating. Mixed in with the rustle of the leaves and the sound of splashing water was Fiona's soft talk and her laughter.

Then some sort of chortle. Which of them could it be?

Perhaps neither—perhaps it came from one of the impudent flashy-looking birds who inhabited the corner cages.

Aubrey could talk, though his voice probably didn't sound the way it used to. He seemed to say something now—a couple of thick syllables. *Take care. He's here. My love.*

On the blue bottom of the fountain's pool lay some wishing coins. Grant had never seen anybody actually throwing money in. He stared at these nickels and dimes and quarters, wondering if they had been glued to the tiles—another feature of the building's encouraging decoration.

TEENAGERS AT the baseball game, sitting at the top of the bleachers out of the way of the boy's friends. A couple of inches of bare wood between them, darkness falling, quick chill of the evening late in the summer. The skittering of their hands, the shift of haunches, eyes never lifted from the field. He'll take off his jacket, if he's wearing one, to lay it around her narrow shoulders. Underneath it he can pull her closer to him, press his spread fingers into her soft arm.

Not like today when any kid would probably be into her pants on the first date.

Fiona's skinny soft arm. Teenage lust astonishing her and flashing along all the nerves of her tender new body, as the night thickens beyond the lighted dust of the game.

MEADOWLAKE WAS short on mirrors, so he did not have to catch sight of himself stalking and prowling. But every once in a while it came to him how foolish and pathetic and perhaps unhinged he must look, trailing around after Fiona and Aubrey. And having no luck in confronting her, or him. Less and less sure of what right he had to be on the scene but unable to withdraw. Even at home, while he worked at his desk or cleaned up the house or shovelled snow when necessary, some ticking metronome in his mind was fixed on Meadowlake, on his next visit. Sometimes he seemed to himself like a mulish boy conducting a hopeless courtship, sometimes like one of those wretches who follow celebrated women through the streets, convinced that one day these women will turn around and recognize their love.

He made a great effort, and cut his visits down to Wednesdays and Saturdays. Also he set himself to observing other things about the place, as if he was a sort of visitor at large, a person doing an inspection or a social study.

Saturdays had a holiday bustle and tension. Families arrived in clusters. Mothers were usually in charge, they were like cheerful but insistent sheepdogs herding the men and children. Only the smallest children were without apprehension. They noticed right away the green and white squares on the hall floors and picked one color to walk on, the other to jump over. The bolder ones might try to hitch rides on the back of wheelchairs. Some persisted in these tricks in spite of scolding, and had to be removed to the car. And how happily, then, how readily, some older child or father volunteered to do the removing, and thus opt out of the visit.

It was the women who kept the conversation afloat. Men seemed cowed by the situation, teenagers affronted. Those being visited rode in a wheelchair or stumped along with a cane, or walked stiffly, unaided, at the procession's head, proud of the turnout but somewhat blank-eyed, or desperately babbling, under the stress of it. And now surrounded by a variety of outsiders these insiders did not look like such regular people after all. Female chins might have had their bristles shaved to the roots and bad eyes might be hidden by patches or dark lenses, inappropriate utterances might be controlled by medication, but some glaze remained, a haunted rigidity—as if people were content to become memories of themselves, final photographs.

Grant understood better now how Mr. Farquar must have felt. People here—even the ones who did not participate in any activities but sat around watching the doors or looking out the windows—were living a busy life in their heads (not to mention the life of their bodies, the portentous shifts in their bowels, the stabs and twinges everywhere along the line), and that was a life that in most cases could not very well be described or alluded to in front of visitors. All they could do was wheel or somehow propel themselves about and hope to come up with something that could be displayed or talked about.

There was the conservatory to be shown off, and the big television screen. Fathers thought that was really something. Mothers said the ferns were gorgeous. Soon everybody sat down around the little tables and ate ice cream—refused only by the teenagers, who were dying of disgust. Women wiped away the dribble from shivery old chins and men looked the other way.

There must be some satisfaction in this ritual, and perhaps even the teenagers would be glad, one day, that they had come. Grant was no expert on families.

No children or grandchildren appeared to visit Aubrey, and since they could not play cards—the tables being taken over for the ice cream parties—he and Fiona stayed clear of the Saturday parade. The conservatory was far too popular then for any of their intimate conversations.

Those might be going on, of course, behind Fiona's closed door. Grant could not manage to knock, though he stood there for some time staring at the Disney birds with an intense, a truly malignant dislike.

Or they might be in Aubrey's room. But he did not know where that was. The more he explored this place, the more corridors and seating spaces and ramps he discovered, and in his wanderings he was still apt to get lost. He would take a certain picture or chair as a landmark, and the next week whatever he had chosen seemed to have been placed somewhere else. He didn't like to mention this to Kristy, lest she think he was suffering some mental dislocations of his own. He supposed this constant change and rearranging might be for the sake of the residents—to make their daily exercise more interesting.

He did not mention either that he sometimes saw a woman at a distance that he thought was Fiona, but then thought it couldn't be, because of the clothes the woman was wearing. When had Fiona ever gone in for bright flowered blouses and electric blue slacks? One Saturday he looked out a window and saw Fiona—it must be her—wheeling Aubrey along one of the paved paths now cleared of snow and ice, and she was wearing a silly woolly hat and a jacket with swirls of blue and purple, the sort of thing he had seen on local women at the supermarket.

The fact must be that they didn't bother to sort out the wardrobes of the women who were roughly the same size. And counted on the women not recognizing their own clothes anyway.

They had cut her hair, too. They had cut away her angelic halo. On a Wednesday, when everything was more normal and card games were going on again, and the women in the Crafts Room were making silk flowers or costumed dolls without anybody hanging around to pester or admire them, and when Aubrey and Fiona were again in evidence so that it was possible for Grant to have one of his brief and friendly and maddening conversations with his wife, he said to her, "Why did they chop off your hair?"

Fiona put her hands up to her head, to check.

"Why—I never missed it," she said.

He thought he should find out what went on on the second floor, where they kept the people who, as Kristy said, had really lost it. Those who walked around down here holding conversations with themselves or throwing out odd questions at a passerby ("Did I leave my sweater in the church?") had apparently lost only some of it.

Not enough to qualify.

There were stairs, but the doors at the top were locked and only the staff had the keys. You could not get into the elevator unless somebody buzzed for it to open, from behind the desk.

What did they do, after they lost it?

"Some just sit," said Kristy. "Some sit and cry. Some try to holler the house down. You don't really want to know."

Sometimes they got it back.

"You go in their rooms for a year and they don't know you from Adam. Then one day, it's oh, hi, when are we going home. All of a sudden they're absolutely back to normal again."

But not for long.

"You think, wow, back to normal. And then they're gone again." She snapped her fingers. "Like so."

In the town where he used to work there was a bookstore that he and Fiona had visited once or twice a year. He went back there by himself. He didn't feel like buying anything, but he had made a list and picked out a couple of the books on it, and then bought another book that he noticed by chance. It was about Iceland. A book of nineteenth-century water-colors made by a lady traveller to Iceland.

Fiona had never learned her mother's language and she had never shown much respect for the stories that it preserved—the stories that Grant had taught and written about, and still did write about, in his working life. She referred to their heroes as "old Njal" or "old Snorri." But in the last few years she had developed an interest in the country itself and looked at travel guides. She read about William Morris's trip, and Auden's. She didn't really plan to travel there. She said the weather was too dreadful. Also—she said—there ought to be one place you thought about and knew about and maybe longed for—but never did get to see.

WHEN GRANT first started teaching Anglo-Saxon and Nordic Literature he got the regular sort of students in his classes. But after a few years he noticed a change. Married women started going back to school. Not with the idea of qualifying for a better job or for any job but simply to give themselves something more interesting to think about than their usual housework and hobbies. To enrich their lives. And perhaps it followed naturally that the men who taught them these things would become part of the enrichment, that these men would seem to these women more mysterious and desirable than the men they still cooked for and slept with.

The studies chosen were usually Psychology or Cultural History or English Literature. Archaeology or Linguistics was picked sometimes but dropped when it turned out to be heavy going. Those who signed up for Grant's courses might have a Scandinavian background, like Fiona, or they might have learned something about Norse mythology from Wagner or historical novels. There were also a few who thought he was teaching a Celtic language and for whom everything Celtic had a mystic allure.

He spoke to such aspirants fairly roughly from his side of the desk.

"If you want to learn a pretty language, go and learn Spanish. Then you can use it if you go to Mexico."

Some took his warning and drifted away. Others seemed to be moved in a personal way by his demanding tone. They worked with a will and brought into his office, into his regulated, satisfactory life, the great surprising bloom of their mature female compliance, their tremulous hope of approval.

He chose the woman named Jacqui Adams. She was the opposite of Fiona—short, cushiony, dark-eyed, effusive. A stranger to irony. The affair lasted for a year, until her husband was transferred. When they were saying good-bye, in her car, she began to shake uncontrollably. It was as if she had hypothermia. She wrote to him a few times, but he found the tone of her letters overwrought and could not decide how to answer. He let the time for answering slip away while he became magically and unexpectedly involved with a girl who was young enough to be her daughter.

For another and more dizzying development had taken place while he was busy with Jacqui. Young girls with long hair and sandalled feet were coming into his office and all but declaring themselves ready for sex. The cautious approaches, the tender intimations of feeling required with Jacqui were out the window. A whirlwind hit him, as it did many others, wish becoming action in a way that made him wonder if there wasn't something missed. But who had time for regrets? He heard of simultaneous liaisons, savage and risky encounters. Scandals burst wide open, with high and painful drama all round but a feeling that somehow it was better so. There were reprisals—there were firings. But those fired went off to teach at smaller, more tolerant colleges or Open Learning Centers, and many wives left behind got over the shock and took up the costumes, the sexual nonchalance of the girls who had tempted their men. Academic parties, which used to be so predictable, became a minefield. An epidemic had broken out, it was spreading like the Spanish flu. Only this time - people ran after contagion, and few between sixteen and sixty seemed willing to be left out.

Fiona appeared to be quite willing, however. Her mother was dying, and her experience in the hospital led her from her routine work in the registrar's office into her new job. Grant himself did not go overboard, at least in comparison with some people around him. He never let another woman get as close to him as Jacqui had been. What he felt was mainly a gigantic increase in well-being. A tendency to pudginess that he had had since he was twelve years old disappeared. He ran up steps two at a time. He appreciated as never before a pageant of torn clouds and winter sunset seen from his office window, the charm of antique lamps glowing between his neighbors' living-room curtains, the cries of children in the park at dusk, unwilling to leave the hill where they'd been tobogganing. Come summer, he learned the names of flowers. In his classroom, after coaching by his nearly voiceless mother-in-law (her affliction was cancer of the throat), he risked reciting and then translating the majestic and gory ode, the head-ransom, the Hofuolausn, composed to honor King Eric Blood-axe by the skald whom that king had condemned to death. (And who was then, by the same king—and by the power of poetry—set free.) All applauded—even the peaceniks in the class whom he'd cheerfully taunted earlier, asking if they would like to wait in the hall. Driving home that day or maybe another he found an absurd and blasphemous quotation running around in his head.

And so he increased in wisdom and stature—
And in favor with God and man.

That embarrassed him at the time and gave him a superstitious chill. As it did yet. But so long as nobody knew, it seemed not unnatural.

HE TOOK the book with him, the next time he went to Meadowlake. It was a Wednesday. He went looking for Fiona at the card tables and did not see her.

A woman called out to him, "She's not here. She's sick." Her voice sounded self-important and excited—pleased with herself for having recognized him when he knew nothing about her. Perhaps also pleased with all she knew about Fiona, about Fiona's life here, thinking it was maybe more than he knew.

"He's not here either," she said.

Grant went to find Kristy.

"Nothing, really," she said, when he asked what was the matter with Fiona. "She's just having a day in bed today, just a bit of an upset."

Fiona was sitting straight up in the bed. He hadn't noticed, the few times that he had been in this room, that this was a hospital bed and - could be cranked up in such a way. She was wearing one of her high-necked maidenly gowns, and her face had a pallor that was not like cherry blossoms but like flour paste.

Aubrey was beside her in his wheelchair, pushed as close to the bed as it could get. Instead of the nondescript open-necked shirts he usually wore, he was wearing a jacket and a tie. His natty-looking tweed hat was resting on the bed. He looked as if he had been out on important business.

To see his lawyer? His banker? To make arrangements with the funeral director?

Whatever he'd been doing, he looked worn out by it. He too was gray in the face.

They both looked up at Grant with a stony, grief-ridden apprehension that turned to relief, if not to welcome, when they saw who he was.

Not who they thought he'd be.

They were hanging on to each other's hands and they did not let go.

The hat on the bed. The jacket and tie.

It wasn't that Aubrey had been out. It wasn't a question of where he'd been or whom he'd been to see. It was where he was going.

Grant set the book down on the bed beside Fiona's free hand.

"It's about Iceland," he said. "I thought maybe you'd like to look at it."

"Why, thank you," said Fiona. She didn't look at the book. He put her hand on it.

"Iceland," he said.

She said, "Ice-land." The first syllable managed to hold a tinkle of interest, but the second fell flat. Anyway, it was necessary for her to turn her attention back to Aubrey, who was pulling his great thick hand out of hers.

"What is it?" she said. "What is it, dear heart?"

Grant had never heard her use this flowery expression before.

"Oh, all right," she said. "Oh, here." And she pulled a handful of tissues from the box beside her bed.

Aubrey's problem was that he had begun to weep. His nose had started to run, and he was anxious not to turn into a sorry spectacle, especially in front of Grant.

"Here. Here," said Fiona. She would have tended to his nose herself and wiped his tears—and perhaps if they had been alone he would have let her do it. But with Grant there Aubrey would not permit it. He got hold of the Kleenex as well as he could and made a few awkward but lucky swipes at his face.

While he was occupied, Fiona turned to Grant.

"Do you by any chance have any influence around here?" she said in a whisper. "I've seen you talking to them—"

Aubrey made a noise of protest or weariness or disgust. Then his upper body pitched forward as if he wanted to throw himself against her. She scrambled half out of bed and caught him and held on to him. It seemed improper for Grant to help her, though of course he would have done so if he'd thought Aubrey was about to tumble to the floor.

"Hush," Fiona was saying. "Oh, honey. Hush. We'll get to see each other. We'll have to. I'll go and see you. You'll come and see me."

Aubrey made the same sound again with his face in her chest, and there was nothing Grant could decently do but get out of the room.

"I just wish his wife would hurry up and get here," Kristy said. "I wish she'd get him out of here and cut the agony short. We've got to start serving supper before long and how are we supposed to get her to swallow anything with him still hanging around?"

Grant said, "Should I stay?"

"What for? She's not sick, you know."

"To keep her company," he said.

Kristy shook her head.

"They have to get over these things on their own. They've got short memories usually. That's not always so bad."

Kristy was not hard-hearted. During the time he had known her Grant had found out some things about her life. She had four children. She did not know where her husband was but thought he might be in Alberta. Her younger boy's asthma was so bad that he would have died one night in

January if she had not got him to the emergency ward in time. He was not on any illegal drugs, but she was not so sure about his brother.

To her, Grant and Fiona and Aubrey too must seem lucky. They had got through life without too much going wrong. What they had to suffer now that they were old hardly counted.

Grant left without going back to Fiona's room. He noticed that the wind was actually warm that day and the crows were making an uproar. In the parking lot a woman wearing a tartan pants suit was getting a folded-up wheelchair out of the trunk of her car.

THE STREET he was driving down was called Black Hawks Lane. All the streets around were named for teams in the old National Hockey League. This was in an outlying section of the town near Meadowlake. He and Fiona had shopped in the town regularly but had not become familiar with any part of it except the main street.

The houses looked to have been built all around the same time, perhaps thirty or forty years ago. The streets were wide and curving and there were no sidewalks—recalling the time when it was thought unlikely that anybody would do much walking ever again. Friends of Grant's and Fiona's had moved to places something like this when they began to have their children. They were apologetic about the move at first. They called it "going out to Barbecue Acres."

Young families still lived here. There were basketball hoops over garage doors and tricycles in the driveways. But some of the houses had gone downhill from the sort of family homes they were surely meant to be. The yards were marked by car tracks, the windows were plastered with tinfoil or hung with faded flags.

Rental housing. Young male tenants—single still, or single again.

A few properties seemed to have been kept up as well as possible by the people who had moved into them when they were new—people who hadn't had the money or perhaps hadn't felt the need to move on to someplace better. Shrubs had grown to maturity, pastel vinyl siding had done away with the problem of repainting. Neat fences or hedges gave the sign that the children in the houses had all grown up and gone away, and that their parents no longer saw the point of letting the yard be a common run-through for whatever new children were loose in the neighborhood.

The house that was listed in the phone book as belonging to Aubrey and his wife was one of these. The front walk was paved with flagstones and bordered by hyacinths that stood as stiff as china flowers, alternately pink and blue.

Fiona had not got over her sorrow. She did not eat at mealtimes, though she pretended to, hiding food in her napkin. She was being given a supplementary drink twice a day—someone stayed and watched while she swallowed it down. She got out of bed and dressed herself, but all she wanted to do then was sit in her room. She wouldn't have taken any exercise at all if Kristy or one of the other nurses, and Grant during visiting hours, had not walked her up and down in the corridors or taken her outside.

In the spring sunshine she sat, weeping weakly, on a bench by the wall. She was still polite—she apologized for her tears, and never argued with a suggestion or refused to answer a question. But she wept. Weeping had left her eyes raw-edged and dim. Her cardigan—if it was hers—would be buttoned crookedly. She had not got to the stage of leaving her hair unbrushed or her nails uncleaned, but that might come soon.

Kristy said that her muscles were deteriorating, and that if she didn't improve soon they would put her on a walker.

"But you know once they get a walker they start to depend on it and they never walk much anymore, just get wherever it is they have to go."

"You'll have to work at her harder," she said to Grant. "Try and encourage her."

But Grant had no luck at that. Fiona seemed to have taken a dislike to him, though she tried to cover it up. Perhaps she was reminded, every time she saw him, of her last minutes with Aubrey, when she had asked him for help and he hadn't helped her.

He didn't see much point in mentioning their marriage, now.

She wouldn't go down the hall to where most of the same people were still playing cards. And she wouldn't go into the television room or visit the conservatory.

She said that she didn't like the big screen, it hurt her eyes. And the birds' noise was irritating and she wished they would turn the fountain off once in a while.

So far as Grant knew, she never looked at the book about Iceland, or at any of the other—surprisingly few—books that she had brought from home. There was a reading room where she would sit down to rest, choosing it probably because there was seldom anybody there, and if he took a book off the shelves she would allow him to read to her. He suspected that she did that because it made his company easier for her— she was able to shut her eyes and sink back into her own grief. Because if she let go of her grief even for a minute it would only hit her harder when she bumped into it again. And sometimes he thought she closed her eyes to hide a look of informed despair that it would not be good for him to see.

So he sat and read to her out of one of these old novels about chaste love, and lost-and-regained fortunes, that could have been the discards of some long-ago village or Sunday school library. There had been no attempt, apparently, to keep the contents of the reading room as up-to-date as most things in the rest of the building.

The covers of the books were soft, almost velvety, with designs of leaves and flowers pressed into them, so that they resembled jewelry boxes or chocolate boxes. That women—he supposed it would be women—could carry home like treasure.

THE SUPERVISOR called him into her office. She said that Fiona was not thriving as they had hoped.

"Her weight is going down even with the supplement. We're doing all we can for her."

Grant said that he realized they were.

"The thing is, I'm sure you know, we don't do any prolonged bed care on the first floor. We do it temporarily if someone isn't feeling well, but if they get too weak to move around and be responsible we have to consider upstairs."

He said he didn't think that Fiona had been in bed that often.

"No. But if she can't keep up her strength, she will be. Right now she's borderline."

He said that he had thought the second floor was for people whose minds were disturbed.

"That too," she said.

HE HADN'T remembered anything about Aubrey's wife except the tartan suit he had seen her wearing in the parking lot. The tails of the jacket had flared open as she bent into the trunk of the car. He had got the impression of a trim waist and wide buttocks.

She was not wearing the tartan suit today. Brown belted slacks and a pink sweater. He was right about the waist—the tight belt showed she made a point of it. It might have been better if she hadn't, since she bulged out considerably above and below.

She could be ten or twelve years younger than her husband. Her hair was short, curly, artificially reddened. She had blue eyes—a lighter blue than Fiona's, a flat robin's-egg or turquoise blue—slanted by a slight puffiness. And a good many wrinkles made more noticeable by a walnut-stain makeup. Or perhaps that was her Florida tan.

He said that he didn't quite know how to introduce himself.

"I used to see your husband at Meadowlake. I'm a regular visitor there myself."

"Yes," said Aubrey's wife, with an aggressive movement of her chin.

"How is your husband doing?"

The "doing" was added on at the last moment. Normally he would have said, "How is your husband?"

"He's okay," she said.

"My wife and he struck up quite a close friendship."

"I heard about that."

"So. I wanted to talk to you about something if you had a minute."

"My husband did not try to start anything with your wife, if that's what you're getting at," she said. "He did not molest her in any way. He isn't capable of it and he wouldn't anyway. From what I heard it was the other way round."

Grant said, "No. That isn't it at all. I didn't come here with any complaints about anything."

"Oh," she said. "Well, I'm sorry. I thought you did."

That was all she was going to give by way of apology. And she didn't sound sorry. She sounded disappointed and confused.

"You better come in, then," she said. "It's blowing cold in through the door. It's not as warm out today as it looks."

So it was something of a victory for him even to get inside. He hadn't realized it would be as hard as this. He had expected a different sort of wife. A flustered homebody, pleased by an unexpected visit and flattered by a confidential tone.

She took him past the entrance to the living room, saying, "We'll have to sit in the kitchen where I can hear Aubrey." Grant caught sight of two layers of front-window curtains, both blue, one sheer and one silky, a matching blue sofa and a daunting pale carpet, various bright mirrors and ornaments.

Fiona had a word for those sort of swooping curtains—she said it like a joke, though the women she'd picked it up from used it seriously. Any room that Fiona fixed up was bare and bright—she would have been astonished to see so much fancy stuff crowded into such a small space. He could not think what that word was.

From a room off the kitchen—a sort of sunroom, though the blinds were drawn against the afternoon brightness—he could hear the sounds of television.

Aubrey. The answer to Fiona's prayers sat a few feet away, watching what sounded like a ball game. His wife looked in at him. She said, "You okay?" and partly closed the door.

"You might as well have a cup of coffee," she said to Grant.

He said, "Thanks."

"My son got him on the sports channel a year ago Christmas, I don't know what we'd do without it."

On the kitchen counters there were all sorts of contrivances and appliances—coffeemaker, food processor, knife sharpener, and some things Grant didn't know the names or uses of. All looked new and expensive, as if they had just been taken out of their wrappings, or were polished daily.

He thought it might be a good idea to admire things. He admired the coffeemaker she was using and said that he and Fiona had always meant to get one. This was absolutely untrue—Fiona had been devoted to a European contraption that made only two cups at a time.

"They gave us that," she said. "Our son and his wife. They live in Kamloops. B.C. They send us more stuff than we can handle. It wouldn't hurt if they would spend the money to come and see us instead."

Grant said philosophically, "I suppose they're busy with their own lives."

"They weren't too busy to go to Hawaii last winter. You could understand it if we had somebody else in the family, closer at hand. But he's the only one."

The coffee being ready, she poured it into two brown-and-green ceramic mugs that she took from the amputated branches of a ceramic tree trunk that sat on the table.

"People do get lonely," Grant said. He thought he saw his chance now. "If they're deprived of seeing somebody they care about, they do feel sad. Fiona, for instance. My wife."

"I thought you said you went and visited her."

"I do," he said. "That's not it."

Then he took the plunge, going on to make the request he'd come to make. Could she consider taking Aubrey back to Meadowlake maybe just one day a week, for a visit? It was only a drive of a few miles, surely it wouldn't prove too difficult. Or if she'd like to take the time off—Grant hadn't thought of this before and was rather dismayed to hear himself suggest it—then he himself could take Aubrey out there, he wouldn't mind at all. He was sure he could manage it. And she could use a break.

While he talked she moved her closed lips and her hidden tongue as if she was trying to identify some dubious flavor. She brought milk for his coffee, and a plate of ginger cookies.

"Homemade," she said as she set the plate down. There was challenge rather than hospitality in her tone. She said nothing more until she had sat down, poured milk into her coffee and stirred it.

Then she said no.

"No. I can't do that. And the reason is, I'm not going to upset him."

"Would it upset him?" Grant said earnestly.

"Yes, it would. It would. That's no way to do. Bringing him home and taking him back. Bringing him home and taking him back, that's just confusing him."

"But wouldn't he understand that it was just a visit? Wouldn't he get into the pattern of it?"

"He understands everything all right." She said this as if he had offered an insult to Aubrey. "But it's still an interruption. And then I've got to get him all ready and get him into the car, and he's a big man, he's not so easy to manage as you might think. I've got to maneuver him into the car and pack his chair along and all that and what for? If I go to all that trouble I'd prefer to take him someplace that was more fun."

"But even if I agreed to do it?" Grant said, keeping his tone hopeful and reasonable. "It's true, you shouldn't have the trouble."

"You couldn't," she said flatly. "You don't know him. You couldn't handle him. He wouldn't stand for you doing for him. All that bother and what would he get out of it?"

Grant didn't think he should mention Fiona again.

"It'd make more sense to take him to the mall," she said. "Where he - could see kids and whatnot. If it didn't make him sore about his own two grandsons he never gets to see. Or now the lake boats are starting to run again, he might get a charge out of going and watching that."

She got up and fetched her cigarettes and lighter from the window above the sink.

"You smoke?" she said.

He said no thanks, though he didn't know if a cigarette was being offered.

"Did you never? Or did you quit?"

"Quit," he said.

"How long ago was that?"

He thought about it.

"Thirty years. No—more."

He had decided to quit around the time he started up with Jacqui. But he couldn't remember whether he quit first, and thought a big reward was coming to him for quitting, or thought that the time had come to quit, now that he had such a powerful diversion.

"I've quit quitting," she said, lighting up. "Just made a resolution to quit quitting, that's all."

Maybe that was the reason for the wrinkles. Somebody—a woman— had told him that women who smoked developed a special set of fine facial wrinkles. But it could have been from the sun, or just the nature of her skin—her neck was noticeably wrinkled as well. Wrinkled neck, youthfully full and up-tilted breasts. Women of her age usually had these contradictions. The bad and good points, the genetic luck or lack of it, all mixed up together. Very few kept their beauty whole, though shadowy, as Fiona had done.

And perhaps that wasn't even true. Perhaps he only thought that because he'd known Fiona when she was young. Perhaps to get that impression you had to have known a woman when she was young.

So when Aubrey looked at his wife did he see a high-school girl full of scorn and sass, with an intriguing tilt to her robin's-egg blue eyes, pursing her fruity lips around a forbidden cigarette?

"So your wife's depressed?" Aubrey's wife said. "What's your wife's name? I forget."

"It's Fiona."

"Fiona. And what's yours? I don't think I ever was told that."

Grant said, "It's Grant."

She stuck her hand out unexpectedly across the table.

"Hello, Grant. I'm Marian."

"So now we know each other's name," she said, "there's no point in not telling you straight out what I think. I don't know if he's still so stuck on seeing your—on seeing Fiona. Or not. I don't ask him and he's not telling me. Maybe just a passing fancy. But I don't feel like taking him back there in case it turns out to be more than that. I can't afford to risk it. I don't want him getting hard to handle. I don't want him upset and carrying on. I've got my hands full with him as it is. I don't have any help. It's just me here. I'm it."

"Did you ever consider—it *is* very hard for you—" Grant said—"did you ever consider his going in there for good?"

He had lowered his voice almost to a whisper, but she did not seem to feel a need to lower hers.

"No," she said. "I'm keeping him right here."

Grant said, "Well. That's very good and noble of you."

He hoped the word "noble" had not sounded sarcastic. He had not meant it to be.

"You think so?" she said. "Noble is not what I'm thinking about."

"Still. It's not easy."

"No, it isn't. But the way I am, I don't have much choice. If I put him in there I don't have the money to pay for him unless I sell the house. The house is what we own outright. Otherwise I don't have anything in the way of resources. I get the pension next year, and I'll have his pension and my pension, but even so I could not afford to keep him there and hang on to the house. And it means a lot to me, my house does."

"It's very nice," said Grant.

"Well, it's all right. I put a lot into it. Fixing it up and keeping it up."

"I'm sure you did. You do."

"I don't want to lose it."

"No."

"I'm not *going* to lose it."

"I see your point."

"The company left us high and dry," she said. "I don't know all the ins and outs of it, but basically he got shoved out. It ended up with them saying he owed them money and when I tried to find out what was what he just went on saying it's none of my business. What I think is he did something pretty stupid. But I'm not supposed to ask, so I shut up. You've been married. You are married. You know how it is. And in the middle of me finding out about this we're supposed to go on this trip with these people and can't get out of it. And on the trip he takes sick from this virus you never heard of and goes into a coma. So that pretty well gets *him* off the hook."

Grant said, "Bad luck."

"I don't mean exactly that he got sick on purpose. It just happened. He's not mad at me anymore and I'm not mad at him. It's just life."

"That's true."

"You can't beat life."

She flicked her tongue in a cat's businesslike way across her top lip, getting the cookie crumbs. "I sound like I'm quite the philosopher, don't I? They told me out there you used to be a university professor."

"Quite a while ago," Grant said.

"I'm not much of an intellectual," she said.

"I don't know how much I am, either."

"But I know when my mind's made up. And it's made up. I'm not going to let go of the house. Which means I'm keeping him here and I don't want him getting it in his head he wants to move anyplace else. It was probably a mistake putting him in there so I could get away, but I wasn't going to get another chance, so I took it. So. Now I know better."

She shook out another cigarette.

"I bet I know what you're thinking," she said. "You're thinking there's a mercenary type of a person."

"I'm not making judgments of that sort. It's your life."

"You bet it is."

He thought they should end on a more neutral note. So he asked her if her husband had worked in a hardware store in the summers, when he was going to school.

"I never heard about it," she said. "I wasn't raised here."

*

DRIVING HOME, he noticed that the swamp hollow that had been filled with snow and the formal shadows of tree trunks was now lighted up with skunk lilies. Their fresh, edible-looking leaves were the size of platters. The flowers sprang straight up like candle flames, and there were so many of them, so pure a yellow, that they set a light shooting up from the earth on this cloudy day. Fiona had told him that they generated a heat of their own as well. Rummaging around in one of her concealed pockets of information, she said that you were supposed to be able to put your hand inside the curled petal and feel the heat. She said that she had tried it, but she couldn't be sure if what she felt was heat or her imagination. The heat attracted bugs.

"Nature doesn't fool around just being decorative."

He had failed with Aubrey's wife. Marian. He had foreseen that he might fail, but he had not in the least foreseen why. He had thought that all he'd have to contend with would be a woman's natural sexual jealousy—or her resentment, the stubborn remains of sexual jealousy.

He had not had any idea of the way she might be looking at things. And yet in some depressing way the conversation had not been unfamiliar to him. That was because it reminded him of conversations he'd had with people in his own family. His uncles, his relatives, probably even his mother, had thought the way Marian thought. They had believed that when other people did not think that way it was because they were kidding themselves—they had got too airy-fairy, or stupid, on account of their easy and protected lives or their education. They had lost touch with reality. Educated people, literary people, some rich people like Grant's socialist in-laws had lost touch with reality. Due to an unmerited good fortune or an innate silliness. In Grant's case, he suspected, they pretty well believed it was both.

That was how Marian would see him, certainly. A silly person, full of boring knowledge and protected by some fluke from the truth about life. A person who didn't have to worry about holding on to his house and could go around thinking his complicated thoughts. Free to dream up the fine, generous schemes that he believed would make another person happy.

What a jerk, she would be thinking now.

Being up against a person like that made him feel hopeless, exasperated, finally almost desolate. Why? Because he couldn't be sure of holding on to himself against that person? Because he was afraid that in the end they'd be right? Fiona wouldn't feel any of that misgiving. Nobody had beat her down, narrowed her in, when she was young. She'd been amused by his upbringing, able to think its harsh notions quaint.

Just the same, they have their points, those people. (He could hear himself now arguing with somebody. Fiona?) There's some advantage to the narrow focus. Marian would probably be good in a crisis. Good at survival, able to scrounge for food and able to take the shoes off a dead body in the street.

Trying to figure out Fiona had always been frustrating. It could be like following a mirage. No—like living in a mirage. Getting close to Marian would present a different problem. It would be like biting into a litchi nut. The flesh with its oddly artificial allure, its chemical taste and perfume, shallow over the extensive seed, the stone.

HE MIGHT have married her. Think of it. He might have married some girl like that. If he'd stayed back where he belonged. She'd have been appetizing enough, with her choice breasts. Probably a flirt. The fussy way she had of shifting her buttocks on the kitchen chair, her pursed mouth, a slightly contrived air of menace—that was what was left of the more or less innocent vulgarity of a small-town flirt.

She must have had some hopes, when she picked Aubrey. His good looks, his salesman's job, his white-collar expectations. She must have believed that she would end up better off than she was now. And so it often happened with those practical people. In spite of their calculations, their survival instincts, they might not get as far as they had quite reasonably expected. No doubt it seemed unfair.

In the kitchen the first thing he saw was the light blinking on his answering machine. He thought the same thing he always thought now. Fiona.

He pressed the button before he got his coat off.

"Hello, Grant. I hope I got the right person. I just thought of something. There is a dance here in town at the Legion supposed to be for singles on Saturday night, and I am on the supper committee, which means I can bring a free guest. So I wondered whether you would happen to be interested in that? Call me back when you get a chance."

A woman's voice gave a local number. Then there was a beep, and the same voice started talking again.

"I just realized I'd forgot to say who it was. Well you probably recognized the voice. It's Marian. I'm still not so used to these machines. And I wanted to say I realize you're not a single and I don't mean it that way. I'm not either, but it doesn't hurt to get out once in a while. Anyway, now I've said all this I really hope it's you I'm talking to. It did sound like your voice. If you are interested you can call me and if you are not you don't need to bother. I just thought you might like the chance to get out. It's Marian speaking. I guess I already said that. Okay, then. Good-bye."

Her voice on the machine was different from the voice he'd heard a short time ago in her house. Just a little different in the first message, more so in the second. A tremor of nerves there, an affected nonchalance, a hurry to get through and a reluctance to let go.

Something had happened to her. But when had it happened? If it had been immediate, she had concealed it very successfully all the time he was with her. More likely it came on her gradually, maybe after he'd gone away. Not necessarily as a blow of attraction. Just the realization that he was a possibility, a man on his own. More or less on his own. A possibility that she might as well try to follow up.

But she'd had the jitters when she made the first move. She had put herself at risk. How much of herself, he could not yet tell. Generally a woman's vulnerability increased as time went on, as things progressed. All you could tell at the start was that if there was an edge of it now, there'd be more later.

It gave him a satisfaction—why deny it?—to have brought that out in her. To have roused something like a shimmer, a blurring, on the surface of her personality. To have heard in her testy, broad vowels this faint plea.

He set out the eggs and mushrooms to make himself an omelette. Then he thought he might as well pour a drink.

Anything was possible. Was that true—was anything possible? For instance, if he wanted to, would he be able to break her down, get her to the point where she might listen to him about taking Aubrey back to Fiona? And not just for visits, but for the rest of Aubrey's life. Where - could that tremor lead them? To an upset, to the end of her self-preservation? To Fiona's happiness?

It would be a challenge. A challenge and a creditable feat. Also a joke that could never be confided to anybody—to think that by his bad behavior he'd be doing good for Fiona.

But he was not really capable of thinking about it. If he did think about it, he'd have to figure out what would become of him and Marian, after he'd delivered Aubrey to Fiona. It would not work—unless he could get more satisfaction that he foresaw, finding the stone of blameless self-interest inside her robust pulp.

You never quite knew how such things would turn out. You almost knew, but you could never be sure.

She would be sitting in her house now, waiting for him to call. Or probably not sitting. Doing things to keep herself busy. She seemed to be a woman who would keep busy. Her house had certainly shown the benefits of nonstop attention. And there was Aubrey—care of him had to continue as usual. She might have given him an early supper—fitting his meals to a Meadowlake timetable in order to get him settled for the night earlier and free herself of his routine for the day. (What would she do about him when she went to the dance? Could he be left alone or would she get a sitter? Would she tell him where she was going, introduce her escort? Would her escort pay the sitter?)

She might have fed Aubrey while Grant was buying the mushrooms and driving home. She might now be preparing him for bed. But all the time she would be conscious of the phone, of the silence of the phone. Maybe she would have calculated how long it would take Grant to drive home. His address in the phone book would have given her a rough idea of where he lived. She would calculate how long, then add to that time for possible shopping for supper (figuring that a man alone would shop every day). Then a certain amount of time for him to get around to listening to his messages. And as the silence persisted she would think of other things. Other errands he might have had to do before he got home. Or perhaps a dinner out, a meeting that meant he would not get home at suppertime at all.

She would stay up late, cleaning her kitchen cupboards, watching television, arguing with herself about whether there was still a chance.

What conceit on his part. She was above all things a sensible woman. She would go to bed at her regular time thinking that he didn't look as if he'd be a decent dancer anyway. Too stiff, too professorial.

He stayed near the phone, looking at magazines, but he didn't pick it up when it rang again.

"Grant. This is Marian. I was down in the basement putting the wash in the dryer and I heard the phone and when I got upstairs whoever it was had hung up. So I just thought I ought to say I was here. If it was you and if you are even home. Because I don't have a machine obviously, so you - couldn't leave a message. So I just wanted. To let you know."

"Bye."

The time was now twenty-five after ten.

Bye.

He would say that he'd just got home. There was no point in bringing to her mind the picture of his sitting here, weighing the pros and cons.

Drapes. That would be her word for the blue curtains—drapes. And why not? He thought of the ginger cookies so perfectly round that she'd had to announce they were homemade, the ceramic coffee mugs on their ceramic tree. A plastic runner, he was sure, protecting the hall carpet. A high-gloss exactness and practicality that his mother had never achieved but would have admired—was that why he could feel this twinge of bizarre and unreliable affection? Or was it because he'd had two more drinks after the first?

The walnut-stain tan—he believed now that it was a tan—of her face and neck would most likely continue into her cleavage, which would be deep, crepey-skinned, odorous and hot. He had that to think of, as he dialled the number that he had already written down. That and the practical sensuality of her cat's tongue. Her gemstone eyes.

FIONA WAS in her room but not in bed. She was sitting by the open window, wearing a seasonable but oddly short and bright dress. Through the window came a heady, warm blast of lilacs in bloom and the spring manure spread over the fields.

She had a book open in her lap.

She said, "Look at this beautiful book I found, it's about Iceland. You wouldn't think they'd leave valuable books lying around in the rooms. The people staying here are not necessarily honest. And I think they've got the clothes mixed up. I never wear yellow."

"Fiona . . . ," he said.

"You've been gone a long time. Are we all checked out now?"

"Fiona, I've brought a surprise for you. Do you remember Aubrey?"

She stared at him for a moment, as if waves of wind had come beating into her face. Into her face, into her head, pulling everything to rags.

"Names elude me," she said harshly.

Then the look passed away as she retrieved, with an effort, some bantering grace. She set the book down carefully and stood up and lifted her arms to put them around him. Her skin or her breath gave off a faint new smell, a smell that seemed to him like that of the stems of cut flowers left too long in their water.

"I'm happy to see you," she said, and pulled his earlobes.

"You could have just driven away," she said. "Just driven away without a care in the world and forsook me. Forsooken me. Forsaken."

He kept his face against her white hair, her pink scalp, her sweetly shaped skull. He said, Not a chance.

Runaway

Chance

HALFWAY THROUGH June, in 1965, the term at Torrance House is over. Juliet has not been offered a permanent job—the teacher she replaced has recovered—and she could now be on her way home. But she is taking what she has described as a little detour. A little detour to see a friend who lives up the coast.

About a month ago, she went with another teacher—Juanita, who was the only person on the staff near her age, and her only friend—to see a revival of a movie called *Hiroshima Mon Amour*. Juanita confessed afterwards that she herself, like the woman in the picture, was in love with a married man—the father of a student. Then Juliet said that she had found herself in somewhat the same situation but had not allowed things to go on because of the tragic plight of his wife. His wife was a total invalid, more or less brain-dead. Juanita said that she wished her lover's wife was brain-dead but she was not—she was vigorous and powerful and could get Juanita fired.

And shortly after that, as if conjured by such unworthy lies or half-lies, came a letter. The envelope looked dingy, as if it had spent some time in a pocket, and it was addressed only to "Juliet (Teacher), Torrance House, 1482 Mark St., Vancouver, B.C." The headmistress gave it to Juliet, saying, "I assume this is for you. It's strange there's no surname but they've got the address right. I suppose they could look that up."

Dear Juliet, I forgot which school it was that you're teaching at but the other day I remembered, out of the blue, so it seemed to me a sign that I should write to you. I hope you are still there but the job would have to

217

be pretty awful for you to quit before the term is up and anyway you didn't strike me as a quitter.

How do you like our west coast weather? If you think you have got a lot of rain in Vancouver, then imagine twice as much, and that's what we get up here.

I often think of you sitting up looking at the ~~stairs~~ stars. You see I wrote stairs, it's late at night and time I was in bed.

Ann is about the same. When I got back from my trip I thought she had failed a good deal, but that was mostly because I was able to see all at once how she had gone downhill in the last two or three years. I had not noticed her decline when I saw her every day.

I don't think I told you that I was stopping off in Regina to see my son, who is now eleven years old. He lives there with his mother. I noticed a big change in him too.

I'm glad I finally remembered the name of the school but I am awfully afraid now that I can't remember your last name. I will seal this anyway and hope the name comes to me.

I often think of you.

I often think of you

I often think of you zzzzzz

THE BUS takes Juliet from downtown Vancouver to Horseshoe Bay and then onto a ferry. Then across a mainland peninsula and onto another ferry and onto the mainland again and so to the town where the man who wrote the letter lives. Whale Bay. And how quickly—even before Horseshoe Bay—you pass from city to wilderness. All this term she has been living amongst the lawns and gardens of Kerrisdale, with the north shore mountains coming into view like a stage curtain whenever the weather cleared. The grounds of the school were sheltered and civilized, enclosed by a stone wall, with something in bloom at every season of the year. And the grounds of the houses around it were the same. Such trim abundance—rhododendrons, holly, laurel, and wisteria. But before you get even so far as Horseshoe Bay, real forest, not park forest, closes in. And from then on—water and rocks, dark trees, hanging moss. Occasionally a trail of smoke from some damp and battered-looking little house, with a yard full of firewood, lumber and tires, cars and parts of cars, broken or usable bikes, toys, all the things that have to sit outside when people are lacking garages or basements.

The towns where the bus stops are not organized towns at all. In some places a few repetitive houses—company houses—are built close together, but most of the houses are like those in the woods, each one in its own wide cluttered yard, as if they have been built within sight of each other only accidentally. No paved streets, except the highway that goes through, no sidewalks. No big solid buildings to house Post Offices or Municipal Offices, no ornamented blocks of stores, built to be noticed. No war monuments, drinking fountains, flowery little parks. Sometimes a hotel, which looks as if it is only a pub. Sometimes a modern school or hospital—decent, but low and plain as a shed.

And at some time—noticeably on the second ferry—she begins to have stomach-turning doubts about the whole business.

I often think of you often

I think of you often

That is only the sort of thing people say to be comforting, or out of a mild desire to keep somebody on the string.

But there will have to be a hotel, or tourist cabins at least, at Whale Bay. She will go there. She has left her big suitcase at the school, to be picked up later. She has only her travelling bag slung over her shoulder, she won't be conspicuous. She will stay one night. Maybe phone him.

And say what?

That she happens to be up this way to visit a friend. Her friend Juanita, from the school, who has a summer place—where? Juanita has a cabin in the woods, she is a fearless outdoor sort of woman (quite different from the real Juanita, who is seldom out of high heels). And the cabin has turned out to be not far south of Whale Bay. The visit to the cabin and Juanita being over, Juliet has thought—she has thought—since she was nearly there already—she has thought she might as well . . .

ROCKS, TREES, water, snow. These things, constantly rearranged, made up the scene six months ago, outside the train window on a morning between Christmas and New Year's. The rocks were large, sometimes jutting out, sometimes smoothed like boulders, dark gray or quite black. The trees were mostly evergreens, pine or spruce or cedar. The spruce trees—black spruce—had what looked like little extra trees, miniatures of themselves, stuck right on top. The trees that were not evergreens were spindly and bare—they might be poplar or tamarack or alder. Some of them had spotty trunks. Snow sat in thick caps on top of the rocks and was plastered to the windward side of the trees. It lay in a soft smooth cover over the surface of many big or small frozen lakes. Water was free of ice only in an occasional fast-flowing, dark and narrow stream.

Juliet had a book open on her lap, but she was not reading. She did not take her eyes from what was going by. She was alone in a double seat and there was an empty double seat across from her. This was the space in which her bed was made up at night. The porter was busy in this sleeping car at the moment, dismantling the nighttime arrangements. In some places the dark-green, zippered shrouds still hung down to the floor. There was a smell of that cloth, like tent cloth, and maybe a slight smell of nightclothes and toilets. A blast of fresh winter air whenever anyone opened the doors at either end of the car. The last people were going to breakfast, other people coming back.

There were tracks in the snow, small animal tracks. Strings of beads, looping, vanishing.

Juliet was twenty-one years old and already the possessor of a B.A. and an M.A. in Classics. She was working on her Ph.D. thesis, but had taken time out to teach Latin at a girls' private school in Vancouver. She had no training as a teacher, but an unexpected vacancy at half-term had made the school willing to hire her. Probably no one else had answered the ad. The salary was less than any qualified teacher would be likely to accept. But Juliet was happy to be earning any money at all, after her years on mingy scholarships.

She was a tall girl, fair-skinned and fine-boned, with light-brown hair that even when sprayed did not retain a bouffant style. She had the look of an alert schoolgirl. Head held high, a neat rounded chin, wide thin-lipped mouth, snub nose, bright eyes, and a forehead that was often flushed with effort or appreciation. Her professors were delighted with her—they were grateful these days for anybody who took up ancient languages, and particularly for someone so gifted—but they were worried, as well. The problem was that she was a girl. If she got married—which might happen, as she was not bad-looking for a scholarship girl, she was not bad-looking at all—she would waste all her hard work and theirs, and if she did not get married she would probably become bleak and isolated, losing out on promotions to men (who needed them more, as they had to support families). And she would not be able to defend the oddity of her choice of Classics, to accept what people would see as its irrelevance, or dreariness, to slough that off the way a man could. Odd choices were simply easier for men, most of whom would find women glad to marry them. Not so the other way around.

When the teaching offer came they urged her to take it. Good for you. Get out into the world a bit. See some real life.

Juliet was used to this sort of advice, though disappointed to hear it coming from these men who did not look or sound as if they had knocked about in the real world very eagerly themselves. In the town where she grew up her sort of intelligence was often put in the same category as a limp or an extra thumb, and people had been quick to point out the expected accompanying drawbacks—her inability to run a sewing machine or tie up a neat parcel, or notice that her slip was showing. What would become of her, was the question.

That occurred even to her mother and father, who were proud of her. Her mother wanted her to be popular, and to that end had urged her to learn to skate and to play the piano. She did neither willingly, or well. Her father just wanted her to fit in. You have to fit in, he told her, otherwise people will make your life hell. (This ignored the fact that he, and particularly Juliet's mother, did not fit in so very well themselves, and were not miserable. Perhaps he doubted Juliet could be so lucky.)

I do, said Juliet once she got away to college. In the Classics Department I fit in. I am extremely okay.

But here came the same message, from her teachers, who had seemed to value and rejoice in her. Their joviality did not hide their concern. Get out into the world, they had said. As if where she had been till now was nowhere.

Nevertheless, on the train, she was happy.

Taiga, she thought. She did not know whether that was the right word for what she was looking at. She might have had, at some level, the idea of herself as a young woman in a Russian novel, going out into an unfamiliar, terrifying, and exhilarating landscape where the wolves would howl at night and where she would meet her fate. She did not care that this fate—in a Russian novel—would likely turn out to be dreary, or tragic, or both.

Personal fate was not the point, anyway. What drew her in—enchanted her, actually—was the very indifference, the repetition, the carelessness and contempt for harmony, to be found on the scrambled surface of the Precambrian shield.

A shadow appeared in the corner of her eye. Then a trousered leg, moving in.

"Is this seat taken?"

Of course it wasn't. What could she say?

Tasselled loafers, tan slacks, tan and brown checked jacket with pencil lines of maroon, dark-blue shirt, maroon tie with flecks of blue and gold. All brand-new and all—except for the shoes—looking slightly too large, as if the body inside had shrunk somewhat since the purchase.

He was a man perhaps in his fifties, with strands of bright golden-brown hair plastered across his scalp. (It couldn't be dyed, could it, who would dye such a scanty crop of hair?) His eyebrows darker, reddish, peaked and bushy. The skin of his face all rather lumpy, thickened like the surface of sour milk.

Was he ugly? Yes, of course. He was ugly, but so in her opinion were many, many men of around his age. She would not have said, afterwards, that he was remarkably ugly.

His eyebrows went up, his light-colored, leaky eyes widened, as if to project conviviality. He settled down opposite her. He said, "Not much to see out there."

"No." She lowered her eyes to her book.

"Ah," he said, as if things were opening up in a comfortable way. "And how far are you going?"

"Vancouver."

"Me too. All the way across the country. May as well see it all while you're at it, isn't that right?"

"Mm."

But he persisted.

"Did you get on at Toronto too?"

"Yes."

"That's my home, Toronto. I lived there all my life. Your home there too?"

"No," said Juliet, looking at her book again and trying hard to prolong the pause. But something—her upbringing, her embarrassment, God knows perhaps her pity, was too strong for her, and she dealt out the name of her hometown, then placed it for him by giving its distance from various larger towns, its position as regarded Lake Huron, Georgian Bay.

"I've got a cousin in Collingwood. That's nice country, up there. I went up to see her and her family, a couple of times. You travelling on your own? Like me?"

He kept flapping his hands one over the other.

"Yes." No more, she thinks. No more.

"This is the first time I went on a major trip anywhere. Quite a trip, all on your own."

Juliet said nothing.

"I just saw you there reading your book all by yourself and I thought, maybe she's all by herself and got a long way to go too, so maybe we could just sort of chum around together?"

At those words, *chum around*, a cold turbulence rose in Juliet. She understood that he was not trying to pick her up. One of the demoralizing things that sometimes happened was that rather awkward and lonely and unattractive men would make a bald bid for her, implying that she had to be in the same boat as they were. But he wasn't doing that. He wanted a friend, not a girlfriend. He wanted a *chum*.

Juliet knew that, to many people, she might seem to be odd and solitary—and so, in a way, she was. But she had also had the experience, for much of her life, of feeling surrounded by people who wanted to drain away her attention and her time and her soul. And usually, she let them.

Be available, be friendly (especially if you are not *popular*)—that was what you learned in a small town and also in a girls' dormitory. Be accommodating to anybody who wants to suck you dry, even if they know nothing about who you are.

She looked straight at this man and did not smile. He saw her resolve, there was a twitch of alarm in his face.

"Good book you got there? What's it about?"

She was not going to say that it was about ancient Greece and the considerable attachment that the Greeks had to the irrational. She would not be teaching Greek, but was supposed to be teaching a course called Greek Thought, so she was reading Dodd again to see what she could pick up. She said, "I do want to read. I think I'll go to the observation car."

And she got up and walked away, thinking that she shouldn't have said where she was going, it was possible that he might get up and follow her, apologizing, working up to another plea. Also, that it would be cold in the observation car, and she would wish that she had brought her sweater. Impossible to go back now to get it.

The wraparound view from the observation car, at the back of the train, seemed less satisfying to her than the view from the sleeping-car window. There was now always the intrusion of the train itself, in front of you.

Perhaps the problem was that she was cold, just as she had thought she would be. And disturbed. But not sorry. One moment more and his clammy hand would have been proffered—she thought that it would have been either clammy or dry and scaly—names would have been exchanged, she would have been locked in. It was the first victory of this sort that she had ever managed, and it was against the most pitiable, the saddest opponent. She could hear him now, chewing on the words *chum around*. Apology and insolence. Apology his habit. And insolence the result of some hope or determination breaking the surface of his loneliness, his hungry state.

It was necessary but it hadn't been easy, it hadn't been easy at all. In fact it was more of a victory, surely, to stand up to someone in such a state. It was more of a victory than if he had been slick and self-assured. But for a while she would be somewhat miserable.

There were only two other people sitting in the observation car. Two older women, each of them sitting alone. When Juliet saw a large wolf crossing the snowy, perfect surface of a small lake, she knew that they must see it too. But neither broke the silence, and that was pleasing to her. The wolf took no notice of the train, he did not hesitate or hurry. His fur was long, silvery shading into white. Did he think it made him invisible?

While she was watching the wolf, another passenger had arrived. A man, who took the seat across the aisle from hers. He too carried a book. An elderly couple followed—she small and sprightly, he large and clumsy, taking heavy disparaging breaths.

"Cold up here," he said, when they were settled.

"Do you want me to go get your jacket?"

"Don't bother."

"It's no bother."

"I'll be all right."

In a moment the woman said, "You certainly do get a view here." He did not answer, and she tried again. "You can see all round."

"What there is to see."

"Wait till we go through the mountains. That'll be something. Did you enjoy your breakfast?"

"The eggs were runny."

"I know." The woman commiserated. "I was thinking, I should just have barged into the kitchen and done them myself."

"Galley. They call it a galley."

"I thought that was on a boat."

Juliet and the man across the aisle raised their eyes from their books at the same moment, and their glances met, with a calm withholding of any expression. And in this second or two the train slowed, then stopped, and they looked elsewhere.

They had come to a little settlement in the woods. On the one side was the station, painted a dark red, and on the other a few houses painted the same color. Homes or barracks, for the railway workers. There was an announcement that there would be a stop here for ten minutes.

The station platform had been cleared of snow, and Juliet, peering ahead, saw some people getting off the train to walk about. She would have liked to do this herself, but not without a coat.

The man across the aisle got up and went down the steps without a look around. Doors opened somewhere below, bringing a stealthy stream of cold air. The elderly husband asked what they were doing here, and what was the name of this place anyway. His wife went to the front of the car to try to see the name, but she was not successful.

Juliet was reading about maenadism. The rituals took place at night, in the middle of winter, Dodd said. The women went up to the top of Mount Parnassus, and when they were, at one time, cut off by a snowstorm, a rescue party had to be sent. The would-be maenads were brought down with their clothes stiff as boards, having, in all their frenzy, accepted rescue. This seemed rather like contemporary behavior to Juliet, it somehow cast a modern light on the celebrants' carrying-on. Would the students see it so?

Not likely. They would probably be armed against any possible entertainment, any involvement, as students were. And the ones who weren't so armed wouldn't want to show it.

The call to board sounded, the fresh air was cut off, there were reluctant shunting movements. She raised her eyes to watch, and saw, some distance ahead, the engine disappearing around a curve.

And then a lurch or a shudder, a shudder that seemed to pass along the whole train. A sense, up here, of the car rocking. An abrupt stop.

Everybody sat waiting for the train to start again, and nobody spoke. Even the complaining husband was silent. Minutes passed. Doors were opening and closing. Men's voices calling, a spreading feeling of fright and agitation. In the club car, which was just below, a voice of authority— maybe the conductor's. But it was not possible to hear what he was saying.

Juliet got up and went to the front of the car, looking over the tops of all the cars ahead. She saw some figures running in the snow.

One of the lone women came up and stood beside her.

"I felt there was something going to happen," the woman said. "I felt it back there, when we were stopped. I didn't want us to start up again, I thought something was going to happen."

The other lone woman had come to stand behind them.

"It won't be anything," she said. "Maybe a branch across the tracks."

"They have that thing that goes ahead of the train," the first woman told her. "It goes on purpose to catch things like a branch across the tracks."

"Maybe it had just fallen."

Both women spoke with the same north-of-England accent and without the politeness of strangers or acquaintances. Now that Juliet got a good look at them she saw that they were probably sisters, though one had a younger, broader face. So they travelled together but sat separately. Or perhaps they'd had a row.

The conductor was mounting the stairs to the observation car. He turned, halfway up, to speak.

"Nothing serious to worry about, folks, it seems like we hit an obstacle on the track. We're sorry for the delay and we'll get going again as soon as we can, but we could be here a little while. The steward tells me there's going to be free coffee down here in a few minutes."

Juliet followed him down the stairs. She had become aware, as soon as she stood up, that there was a problem of her own which would make it necessary for her to go back to her seat and her travelling case, whether the man she snubbed was still there or not. As she made her way through the cars she met other people on the move. People were pressing against the windows on one side of the train, or they had halted between the cars, as if they expected the doors to open. Juliet had no time to ask questions, but as she slid past she heard that it might have been a bear, or an elk, or a cow. And people wondered what a cow would be doing up here in the bush, or why the bears were not all asleep now, or if some drunk had fallen asleep on the tracks.

In the dining car people were sitting at the tables, whose white cloths had all been removed. They were drinking the free coffee.

Nobody was in Juliet's seat, or in the seat across from it. She picked up her case and hurried along to the Ladies. Monthly bleeding was the bane of her life. It had even, on occasion, interfered with the writing of important three-hour examinations, because you couldn't leave the room for reinforcements.

Flushed, crampy, feeling a little dizzy and sick, she sank down on the toilet bowl, removed her soaked pad and wrapped it in toilet paper and put it in the receptacle provided. When she stood up she attached the fresh pad from her bag. She saw that the water and urine in the bowl was crimson with her blood. She put her hand on the flush button, then noticed in front of her eyes the warning not to flush the toilet while the train was standing still. That meant, of course, when the train was standing near the station, where the discharge would take place, very disagreeably, right where people could see it. Here, she might risk it.

But just as she touched the button again she heard voices close by, not in the train but outside the toilet window of pebbled glass. Maybe train workers walking past.

She could stay till the train moved, but how long would that be? And what if somebody desperately wanted in? She decided that all she could do was to put down the lid and get out.

She went back to her own seat. Across from her, a child four or five years old was slashing a crayon across the pages of a coloring book. His mother spoke to Juliet about the free coffee.

"It may be free but it looks like you have to go and get it yourself," she said. "Would you mind watching him while I go?"

"I don't want to stay with her," the child said, without looking up.

"I'll go," said Juliet. But at that moment a waiter entered the car with the coffee wagon.

"There. I shouldn't've complained so soon," the mother said. "Did you hear it was a b-o-d-y?"

Juliet shook her head.

"He didn't have a coat on even. Somebody saw him get off and walk on up ahead but they never realized what he was doing. He must've just got round the curve so the engineer couldn't see him till it was too late."

A few seats ahead, on the mother's side of the aisle, a man said, "Here they come back," and some people got up, from Juliet's side, and stooped to see. The child stood up too, pressed his face to the glass. His mother told him to sit down.

"You color. Look at the mess you made, all over the lines."

"I can't look," she said to Juliet. "I can't stand to look at anything like that."

Juliet got up and looked. She saw a small group of men tramping back towards the station. Some had taken off their coats, which were piled on top of the stretcher that a couple of them were carrying.

"You can't see anything," a man behind Juliet said to a woman who had not stood up. "They got him all covered."

Not all of the men who proceeded with their heads lowered were railway employees. Juliet recognized the man who had sat across from her up in the observation car.

After ten or fifteen minutes more, the train began to move. Around the curve there was no blood to be seen, on either side of the car. But there was a trampled area, a shovelled mound of snow. The man behind her was up again. He said, "That's where it happened, I guess," and watched for a little while to see if there was anything else, then turned around and sat down. The train, instead of speeding to make up for lost time, seemed to be going more slowly than previously. Out of respect, perhaps, or with apprehension about what might lie ahead, around the next curve. The headwaiter went through the car announcing the first seating for lunch, and the mother and child at once got up and followed him. A procession began, and Juliet heard a woman who was passing say, "Really?"

The woman talking to her said softly, "That's what she said. Full of blood. So it must have splashed in when the train went over—"

"Don't say it."

A LITTLE later, when the procession had ended and the early lunchers were eating, the man came through—the man from the observation car who had been seen outside walking in the snow.

Juliet got up and quickly pursued him. In the black cold space between the cars, just as he was pushing the heavy door in front of him, she said, "Excuse me. I have to ask you something."

This space was full of sudden noise, the clanking of heavy wheels on the rails.

"What is it?"

"Are you a doctor? Did you see the man who—"

"I'm not a doctor. There's no doctor on the train. But I have some medical experience."

"How old was he?"

The man looked at her with a steady patience and some displeasure.

"Hard to say. Not young."

"Was he wearing a blue shirt? Did he have blondish-brown-colored hair?"

He shook his head, not to answer her question but to refuse it.

"Was this somebody you knew?" he said. "You should tell the conductor if it was."

"I didn't know him."

"Excuse me, then." He pushed open the door and left her.

Of course. He thought she was full of disgusting curiosity, like many other people.

Full of blood. That was disgusting, if you liked.

She could never tell anybody about the mistake that had been made, the horrid joke of it. People would think her exceptionally crude and heartless, were she ever to speak of it. And what was at one end of the misunderstanding—the suicide's smashed body—would seem, in the telling, to be hardly more foul and frightful than her own menstrual blood.

Never tell that to anybody. (Actually she did tell it, a few years later, to a woman named Christa, a woman whose name she did not yet know.)

But she wanted very much to tell somebody something. She got out her notebook and on one of its ruled pages began to write a letter to her parents.

We have not yet reached the Manitoba border and most people have been complaining that the scenery is rather monotonous but they cannot say that the trip has been lacking in dramatic incident. This morning we stopped at some godforsaken little settlement in the northern woods, all painted Dreary Railway Red. I was sitting at the back of the train in the Observation Car, and freezing to death because they skimp on the heat up there (the idea must be that the scenic glories will distract you from your discomfort) and I was too lazy to trudge back and get my sweater. We sat around there for ten or fifteen minutes and then started up again, and I could see the engine rounding a curve up ahead, and then suddenly there was a sort of Awful Thump . . .

She and her father and her mother had always made it their business to bring entertaining stories into the house. This had required a subtle adjustment not only of the facts but of one's position in the world. Or so Juliet had found, when her world was school. She had made herself into a rather superior, invulnerable observer. And now that she was away from home all the time this stance had become habitual, almost a duty.

But as soon as she had written the words *Awful Thump*, she found herself unable to go on. Unable, in her customary language, to go on.

She tried looking out the window, but the scene, composed of the same elements, had changed. Less than a hundred miles on, it seemed as if there was a warmer climate. The lakes were fringed with ice, not covered. The black water, black rocks, under the wintry clouds, filled the air with darkness. She grew tired watching, and she picked up her Dodd, opening it just anywhere, because, after all, she had read it before. Every few pages she seemed to have had an orgy of underlining. She was drawn to these passages, but when she read them she found that what she had pounced on with such satisfaction at one time now seemed obscure and unsettling.

. . . what to the partial vision of the living appears as the act of a fiend, is perceived by the wider insight of the dead to be an aspect of cosmic justice . . .

The book slipped out of her hands, her eyes closed, and she was now walking with some children (students?) on the surface of a lake. Everywhere each of them stepped there appeared a five-sided crack, all of these beautifully even, so that the ice became like a tiled floor. The children asked her the name of these ice tiles, and she answered with confidence, *iambic pentameter.* But they laughed and with this laughter the cracks widened. She realized her mistake then and knew that only the right word would save the situation, but she could not grasp it.

She woke and saw the same man, the man she had followed and pestered between the cars, sitting across from her.

"You were sleeping." He smiled slightly at what he had said. "Obviously."

She had been sleeping with her head hanging forward, like an old woman, and there was a dribble at the corner of her mouth. Also, she knew she must get to the Ladies Toilet at once, hoping there was nothing on her skirt. She said "Excuse me" (just what he had last said to her) and took up her case and walked away with as little self-conscious haste as she could manage.

When she came back, washed and tidied and reinforced, he was still there.

He spoke at once. He said that he wanted to apologize.

"It occurred to me I was rude to you. When you asked me—"

"Yes," she said.

"You had it right," he said. "The way you described him."

This seemed less an offering, on his part, than a direct and necessary transaction. If she did not care to speak he might just get up and walk away, not particularly disappointed, having done what he'd come to do.

Shamefully, Juliet's eyes overflowed with tears. This was so unexpected that she had no time to look away.

"Okay," he said. "It's okay."

She nodded quickly, several times, sniffled wretchedly, blew her nose on the tissue she eventually found in her bag.

"It's all right," she said, and then she told him, in a straightforward way, just what had happened. How the man bent over and asked her if the seat was taken, how he sat down, how she had been looking out the window and how she couldn't do that any longer so she had tried or had pretended to read her book, how he had asked where she had got on the train, and found out where she lived, and kept trying to make headway with the conversation, till she just picked up and left him.

The only thing she did not reveal to him was the expression *chum around*. She had a notion that if she were to say that she would burst into tears all over again.

"People interrupt women," he said. "Easier than men."

"Yes. They do."

"They think women are bound to be nicer."

"But he just wanted somebody to talk to," she said, shifting sides a little. "He wanted somebody worse than I *didn't* want somebody. I realize that now. And I don't look mean. I don't look cruel. But I was."

A pause, while she once more got her sniffling and her leaky eyes under control.

He said, "Haven't you ever wanted to do that to anybody before?"

"*Yes.* But I've never done it. I never have gone so far. And why I did it this time—it was that he was so humble. And he had all new clothes on he'd probably bought for the trip. He was probably depressed and thought he'd go on a trip and it was a good way to meet people and make friends.

"Maybe if he'd just been going a little way—," she said. "But he said he was going to Vancouver and I would have been saddled with him. For days."

"Yes."

"I really might have been."

"Yes."

"So."

"Rotten luck," he said, smiling a very little. "The first time you get up the nerve to give somebody the gears he throws himself under a train."

"It could have been the last straw," she said, now feeling slightly defensive. "It could have been."

"I guess you'll just have to watch out, in future."

Juliet raised her chin and looked at him steadily.

"You mean I'm exaggerating."

Then something happened that was as sudden and unbidden as her tears. Her mouth began to twitch. Unholy laughter was rising.

"I guess it is a little extreme."

He said, "A little."

"You think I'm dramatizing?"

"That's natural."

"But you think it's a mistake," she said, with the laughter under control. "You think feeling guilty is just an indulgence?"

"What I think is—," he said. "I think that this is minor. Things will happen in your life—things will probably happen in your life—that will make this seem minor. Other things you'll be able to feel guilty about."

"Don't people always say that, though? To somebody who is younger? They say, oh, you won't think like this someday. You wait and see. As if you didn't have a right to any serious feelings. As if you weren't capable."

"Feelings," he said. "I was talking about experience."

"But you are sort of saying that guilt isn't any use. People do say that. Is it true?"

"You tell me."

They went on talking about this for a considerable time, in low voices, but so forcefully that people passing by sometimes looked astonished, or even offended, as people may when they overhear debates that seem unnecessarily abstract. Juliet realized, after a while, that though she was arguing—rather well, she thought—for the necessity of some feelings of guilt both in public and in private life, she had stopped feeling any, for the moment. You might even have said that she was enjoying herself.

He suggested that they go forward to the lounge, where they could drink coffee. Once there Juliet discovered that she was quite hungry, though the lunch hours were long over. Pretzels and peanuts were all that could be procured, and she gobbled them up in such a way that the thoughtful, slightly competitive conversation they were having before was not retrievable. So they talked instead about themselves. His name was Eric Porteous, and he lived in a place called Whale Bay, somewhere north of Vancouver, on the west coast. But he was not going there immediately, he was breaking the trip in Regina, to see some people he had not seen for a long time. He was a fisherman, he caught prawns. She asked about the medical experience he had referred to, and he said, "Oh, it's not very extensive. I did some medical study. When you're out in the bush or on the boat anything can happen. To the people you're working with. Or to yourself."

He was married, his wife's name was Ann.

Eight years ago, he said, Ann had been injured in a car accident. For several weeks she was in a coma. She came out of that, but she was still paralyzed, unable to walk or even to feed herself. She seemed to know who he was, and who the woman who looked after her was—with the help of this woman he was able to keep her at home—but her attempts to talk, and to understand what was going on around her, soon faded away.

They had been to a party. She hadn't particularly wanted to go but he had wanted to go. Then she decided to walk home by herself, not being very happy with things at the party.

It was a gang of drunks from another party who ran off the road and knocked her down. Teenagers.

Luckily, he and Ann had no children. Yes, luckily.

"You tell people about it and they feel they have to say, how terrible. What a tragedy. Et cetera."

"Can you blame them?" said Juliet, who had been about to say something of the sort herself.

No, he said. But it was just that the whole thing was a lot more complicated than that. Did Ann feel that it was a tragedy? Probably not. Did he? It was something you got used to, it was a new kind of life. That was all.

ALL OF Juliet's enjoyable experience of men had been in fantasy. One or two movie stars, the lovely tenor—not the virile heartless hero—on a certain old recording of *Don Giovanni*. Henry V, as she read about him in Shakespeare and as Laurence Olivier had played him in the movie.

This was ridiculous, pathetic, but who ever needed to know? In actual life there had been humiliation and disappointment, which she had tried to push out of her mind as quickly as possible.

There was the experience of being stranded head and shoulders above the gaggle of other unwanted girls at the high school dances, and being bored but making a rash attempt to be lively on college dates with boys she didn't much like, who did not much like her. Going out with the visiting nephew of her thesis adviser last year and being broken into—you couldn't call it rape, she too was determined—late at night on the ground in Willis Park.

On the way home he had explained that she wasn't his type. And she had felt too humiliated to retort—or even to be aware, at that moment—that he was not hers.

She had never had fantasies about a particular, real man—least of all about any of her teachers. Older men—in real life—seemed to her to be slightly unsavory.

This man was how old? He had been married for at least eight years—and perhaps two years, two or three years, more than that. Which made him probably thirty-five or thirty-six. His hair was dark and curly with some gray at the sides, his forehead wide and weathered, his shoulders strong and a little stooped. He was hardly any taller than she was. His eyes were wide set, dark, and eager but also wary. His chin was rounded, dimpled, pugnacious.

She told him about her job, the name of the school—Torrance House. ("What do you want to bet it's called Torments?") She told him that she was not a real teacher but that they were glad to get anybody who had majored in Greek and Latin at college. Hardly anybody did anymore.

"So why did you?"

"Oh, just to be different, I guess."

Then she told him what she had always known that she should never tell any man or boy, lest he lose interest immediately.

"And because I love it. I love all that stuff. I really do."

They ate dinner together—each drinking a glass of wine—and then went up to the observation car, where they sat in the dark, all by themselves. Juliet had brought her sweater this time.

"People must think there's nothing to see up here at night," he said. "But look at the stars you can see on a clear night."

Indeed the night was clear. There was no moon—at least not yet—and the stars appeared in dense thickets, both faint and bright. And like anyone who had lived and worked on boats, he was familiar with the map of the sky. She was able to locate only the Big Dipper.

"That's your start," he said. "Take the two stars on the side of the Dipper opposite the handle. Got them? Those are the pointers. Follow them up. Follow them, you'll find the polestar." And so on.

He found for her Orion, which he said was the major constellation in the Northern Hemisphere in winter. And Sirius, the Dog Star, at that time of year the brightest star in the whole northern sky.

Juliet was pleased to be instructed but also pleased when it came her turn to be the instructor. He knew the names but not the history.

She told him that Orion was blinded by Enopion but had got his sight back by looking at the sun.

"He was blinded because he was so beautiful, but Hephaestus came to his rescue. Then he was killed anyway, by Artemis, but he got changed into a constellation. It often happened when somebody really valuable got into bad trouble, they were changed into a constellation. Where is Cassiopeia?"

He directed her to a not very obvious W.

"It's supposed to be a woman sitting down."

"That was on account of beauty too," she said.

"Beauty was dangerous?"

"You bet. She was married to the king of Ethiopia and she was the mother of Andromeda. And she bragged about her beauty and for punishment she was banished to the sky. Isn't there an Andromeda, too?"

"That's a galaxy. You should be able to see it tonight. It's the most distant thing you can see with the naked eye."

Even when guiding her, telling her where to look in the sky, he never touched her. Of course not. He was married.

"Who was Andromeda?" he asked her.

"She was chained to a rock but Perseus rescued her."

WHALE BAY.

A long dock, a number of large boats, a gas station and store that has a sign in the window saying that it is also the bus stop and the Post Office.

A car parked at the side of this store has in its window a homemade taxi sign. She stands just where she stepped down from the bus. The bus pulls away. The taxi toots its horn. The driver gets out and comes towards her.

"All by yourself," he says. "Where are you headed for?"

She asks if there is a place where tourists stay. Obviously there won't be a hotel.

"I don't know if there's anybody renting rooms out this year. I could ask them inside. You don't know anybody around here?"

Nothing to do but to say Eric's name.

"Oh sure," he says with relief. "Hop in, we'll get you there in no time. But it's too bad, you pretty well missed the wake."

At first she thinks that he said *wait*. Or *weight*? She thinks of fishing competitions.

"Sad time," the driver says, now getting in behind the wheel. "Still, she wasn't ever going to get any better."

Wake. The wife. Ann.

"Never mind," he says. "I expect there'll still be some people hanging around. Of course you did miss the funeral. Yesterday. It was a monster. Couldn't get away?"

Juliet says, "No."

"I shouldn't be calling it a wake, should I? Wake is what you have before they're buried, isn't it? I don't know what you call what takes place after. You wouldn't want to call it a party, would you? I can just run you up and show you all the flowers and tributes, okay?"

Inland, off the highway, after a quarter of a mile or so of rough dirt road, is Whale Bay Union Cemetery. And close to the fence is the mound of earth altogether buried in flowers. Faded real flowers, bright artificial flowers, a little wooden cross with the name and date. Tinselly curled ribbons that have blown about all over the cemetery grass. He draws her attention to all the ruts, the mess the wheels of so many cars made yesterday.

"Half of them had never even seen her. But they knew him, so they wanted to come anyway. Everybody knows Eric."

They turn around, drive back, but not all the way back to the highway. She wants to tell the driver that she has changed her mind, she does not want to visit anybody, she wants to wait at the store to catch the bus going the other way. She can say that she really did get the day wrong, and now she is so ashamed of having missed the funeral that she does not want to show up at all.

But she cannot get started. And he will report on her, no matter what.

They are following narrow, winding back roads, past a few houses. Every time they go by a driveway without turning in, there is a feeling of reprieve.

"Well, here's a surprise," the driver says, and now they do turn in. "Where's everybody gone? Half a dozen cars when I drove past an hour ago. Even his truck's gone. Party over. Sorry—I shouldn't've said that."

"If there's nobody here," Juliet says eagerly, "I could just go back down."

"Oh, somebody's here, don't worry about that. Ailo's here. There's her bike. You ever meet Ailo? You know, she's the one took care of things?" He is out and opening her door.

As soon as Juliet steps out, a large yellow dog comes bounding and barking, and a woman calls from the porch of the house.

"Aw go on, Pet," the driver says, pocketing the fare and getting quickly back into the car.

"Shut up. Shut up, Pet. Settle down. She won't hurt you," the woman calls. "She's just a pup."

Pet's being a pup, Juliet thinks, would not make her any less likely to knock you down. And now a small reddish-brown dog arrives to join in the commotion. The woman comes down the steps, yelling, "Pet. Corky. You behave. If they think you are scared of them they will just get after you the worse."

Her *just* sounds something like *chust*.

"I'm not scared," says Juliet, jumping back when the yellow dog's nose roughly rubs her arm.

"Come on in, then. Shut up, the two of you, or I will knock your heads. Did you get the day mixed up for the funeral?"

Juliet shakes her head as if to say that she is sorry. She introduces herself.

"Well, it is too bad. I am Ailo." They shake hands.

Ailo is a tall, broad-shouldered woman with a thick but not flabby body, and yellowish-white hair loose over her shoulders. Her voice is strong and insistent, with some rich production of sounds in the throat. A German, Dutch, Scandinavian accent?

"You better sit down here in the kitchen. Everything is in a mess. I will get you some coffee."

The kitchen is bright, with a skylight in the high, sloping ceiling. Dishes and glasses and pots are piled everywhere. Pet and Corky have followed Ailo meekly into the kitchen, and have started to lap out whatever is in the roasting pan that she has set down on the floor.

Beyond the kitchen, up two broad steps, there is a shaded, cavernous sort of living room, with large cushions flung about on the floor.

Ailo pulls out a chair at the table. "Now sit down. You sit down here and have some coffee and some food."

"I'm fine without," says Juliet.

"No. There is the coffee I have just made, I will drink mine while I work. And there are so much things left over to eat."

She sets before Juliet, with the coffee, a piece of pie—bright green, covered with some shrunken meringue.

"Lime Jell-O," she says, withholding approval. "Maybe it tastes all right, though. Or there is rhubarb?"

Juliet says, "Fine."

"So much mess here. I clean up after the wake, I get it all settled. Then the funeral. Now after the funeral I have to clean up all over again."

Her voice is full of sturdy grievance. Juliet feels obliged to say, "When I finish this I can help you."

"No. I don't think so," Ailo says. "I know everything." She is moving around not swiftly but purposefully and effectively. (Such women never want your help. They can tell what you're like.) She continues drying the glasses and plates and cutlery, putting what she has dried away in cupboards and drawers. Then scraping the pots and pans—including the one she retrieves from the dogs—submerging them in fresh soapy water, scrubbing the surfaces of the table and the counters, wringing the dish-cloths as if they were chickens' necks. And speaking to Juliet, with pauses.

"You are a friend of Ann? You know her from before?"

"No."

"No. I think you don't. You are too young. So why do you want to come to her funeral?"

"I didn't," says Juliet. "I didn't know. I just came by to visit." She tries to sound as if this was a whim of hers, as if she had lots of friends and wandered about making casual visits.

With singular fine energy and defiance Ailo polishes a pot, as she chooses not to reply to this. She lets Juliet wait through several more pots before she speaks.

"You come to visit Eric. You found the right house. Eric lives here."

"You don't live here, do you?" says Juliet, as if this might change the subject.

"No. I do not live here. I live down the hill, with my hussband." The word *hussband* carries a weight, of pride and reproach.

Without asking, Ailo fills up Juliet's coffee cup, then her own. She brings a piece of pie for herself. It has a rosy layer on the bottom and a creamy layer on top.

"Rhubarb cusstart. It has to be eaten or it will go bad. I do not need it, but I eat it anyway. Maybe I get you a piece?"

"No. Thank you."

"Now. Eric has gone. He will not be back tonight. I do not think so. He has gone to Christa's place. Do you know Christa?"

Juliet tightly shakes her head.

"Here we all live so that we know the other people's situations. We know well. I do not know what it is like where you live. In Vancouver?" (Juliet nods.) "In a city. It is not the same. For Eric to be so good to look after his wife he must need help, do you see? I am one to help him."

Quite unwisely Juliet says, "But do you not get paid?"

"Certain I am paid. But it is more than a job. Also the other kind of help from a woman, he needs that. Do you understand what I am saying? Not a woman with a hussband, I do not believe in that, it is not nice, that is a way to have fights. First Eric had Sandra, then she has moved away and he has Christa. There was a little while both Christa and Sandra, but they were good friends, it was all right. But Sandra has her kids, she wants to move away to bigger schools. Christa is an artist. She makes things out of wood that you find on the beach. What is it you call that wood?"

"Driftwood," says Juliet unwillingly. She is paralyzed by disappointment, by shame.

"That is it. She takes them to places and they sell them for her. Big things. Animals and birds but not realist. Not realist?"

"Not realistic?"

"Yes. Yes. She has never had any children. I don't think she will want to be moving away. Eric has told you this? Would you like more coffee? There is still some in the pot."

"No. No thanks. No he hasn't."

"So. Now I have told you. If you have finish I will take the cup to wash."

She detours to nudge with her shoe the yellow dog lying on the other side of the refrigerator.

"You got to get up. Lazy girl. Soon we are going home."

"There is a bus goes back to Vancouver, it goes through at ten after eight," she says, busy at the sink with her back to the room. "You can come home with me and when it is time my hussband will drive you. You can eat with us. I ride my bike, I ride slow so you can keep up. It is not far."

The immediate future seems set in place so firmly that Juliet gets up without a thought, looks around for her bag. Then she sits down again, but in another chair. This new view of the kitchen seems to give her resolve.

"I think I'll stay here," she says.

"Here?"

"I don't have anything much to carry. I'll walk to the bus."

"How will you know your way? It is a mile."

"That's not far." Juliet wonders about knowing the way, but thinks that, after all, you just have to head downhill.

"He is not coming back, you know," says Ailo. "Not tonight."

"That doesn't matter."

Ailo gives a massive, perhaps disdainful, shrug.

"Get up, Pet. Up." Over her shoulder she says, "Corky stays here. Do you want her in or out?"

"I guess out."

"I will tie her up, then, so she cannot follow. She may not want to stay with a stranger."

Juliet says nothing.

"The door locks when we go out. You see? So if you go out and want to come back in, you have to press this. But when you leave you don't press. It will be locked. Do you understand?"

"Yes."

"We did not use to bother locking here, but now there are too many strangers."

AFTER THEY had been looking at the stars, the train had stopped for a while in Winnipeg. They got out and walked in a wind so cold that it was painful for them to breathe, let alone speak. When they boarded the train again they sat in the lounge and he ordered brandy.

"Warm us up and put you to sleep," he said.

He was not going to sleep. He would sit up until he got off at Regina, some time towards morning.

Most of the berths were already made up, the dark-green curtains narrowing the aisles, when he walked her back to her car. All the cars had names, and the name of hers was Miramichi.

"This is it," she whispered, in the space between the cars, his hand already pushing the door for her.

"Say good-bye here, then." He withdrew his hand, and they balanced themselves against the jolting so that he could kiss her thoroughly. When that was finished he did not let go, but held her and stroked her back, and then began to kiss her all over her face.

But she pulled away, she said urgently, "I'm a virgin."

"Yes, yes." He laughed, and kissed her neck, then released her and pushed the door open in front of her. They walked down the aisle till she located her own berth. She flattened herself against the curtain, turning, and rather expecting him to kiss her again or touch her, but he slid by almost as if they had met by accident.

How STUPID, how disastrous. Afraid, of course, that his stroking hand would go farther down and reach the knot she had made securing the pad to the belt. If she had been the sort of girl who could rely on tampons this need never have happened.

And why *virgin*? When she had gone to such unpleasant lengths, in Willis Park, to insure that such a condition would not be an impediment? She must have been thinking of what she would tell him—she would never be able to tell him that she was menstruating—in the event that he hoped to carry things further. How could he have had plans like that, anyway? How? Where? In her berth, with so little room and all the other passengers very likely still awake around them? Standing up, swaying back and forth, pressed against a door, which anybody could come along and open, in that precarious space between the cars?

So now he could tell someone how he listened all evening to this fool girl showing off what she knew about Greek mythology, and in the end— when he finally kissed her good night, to get rid of her—she started screaming that she was a virgin.

He had not seemed the sort of man to do that, to talk like that, but she could not help imagining it.

She lay awake far into the night, but had fallen asleep when the train stopped at Regina.

LEFT ALONE, Juliet could explore the house. But she does no such thing. It is twenty minutes, at least, before she can be rid of the presence of Ailo. Not that she is afraid that Ailo might come back to check up on her, or to get something she has forgotten. Ailo is not the sort of person who forgets things, even at the end of a strenuous day. And if she had thought Juliet would steal anything, she would simply have kicked her out.

She is, however, the sort of woman who lays claim to space, particularly to kitchen space. Everything within Juliet's gaze speaks of Ailo's occupation, from the potted plants (herbs?) on the windowsill to the chopping block to the polished linoleum.

And when she has managed to push Ailo back, not out of the room but perhaps back beside the old-fashioned refrigerator, Juliet comes up against Christa. Eric has a woman. Of course he has. Christa. Juliet sees a younger, a more seductive Ailo. Wide hips, strong arms, long hair—all blond with no white—breasts bobbing frankly under a loose shirt. The same aggressive—and in Christa, sexy—lack of chic. The same relishing way of chewing up and then spitting out her words.

Two other women come into her mind. Briseis and Chryseis. Those playmates of Achilles and Agamemnon. Each of them described as being "of the lovely cheeks." When the professor read that word (which she could not now remember), his forehead had gone quite pink and he seemed to be suppressing a giggle. For that moment, Juliet despised him.

So if Christa turns out to be a rougher, more northerly version of Briseis/Chryseis, will Juliet be able to start despising Eric as well?

But how will she ever know, if she walks down to the highway and gets on the bus?

The fact is that she never intended to get on that bus. So it seems. With Ailo out of the way, it is easier to discover her own intentions. She gets up at last and makes more coffee, then pours it into a mug, not one of the cups that Ailo has put out.

She is too keyed up to be hungry, but she examines the bottles on the counter, which people must have brought for the wake. Cherry brandy, peach schnapps, Tia Maria, sweet vermouth. These bottles have been opened but the contents have not proved popular. The serious drinking has been done from the empty bottles ranged by Ailo beside the door. Gin and whisky, beer and wine.

She pours Tia Maria into her coffee, and takes the bottle with her up the steps into the big living room.

This is one of the longest days of the year. But the trees around here, the big bushy evergreens and the red-limbed arbutus, shut out the light from the descending sun. The skylight keeps the kitchen bright, while the windows in the living room are nothing but long slits in the wall, and there the darkness has already begun to accumulate. The floor is not finished—old shabby rugs are laid down on squares of plywood—and the room is oddly and haphazardly furnished. Mostly with cushions, lying about on the floor, a couple of hassocks covered in leather, which has split. A huge leather chair, of the sort that leans back and has a rest for your feet. A couch covered by an authentic but ragged patchwork quilt, an ancient television set, and brick-and-plank bookshelves—on which there are no books, only stacks of old *National Geographic*s, with a few sailing magazines and issues of *Popular Mechanics*.

Ailo obviously has not got around to cleaning up this room. There are smudges of ashes where ashtrays have been upset onto the rugs. And crumbs everywhere. It occurs to Juliet that she might look for the vacuum cleaner, if there is one, but then she thinks that even if she could get it to work it is likely that some mishap would occur—the thin rugs might get scrunched up and caught in the machine, for instance. So she just sits in the leather chair, adding more Tia Maria as the level of her coffee goes down.

Nothing is much to her liking on this coast. The trees are too large and crowded together and do not have any personality of their own—they simply make a forest. The mountains are too grand and implausible and the islands that float upon the waters of the Strait of Georgia are too persistently picturesque. This house, with its big spaces and slanted ceilings and unfinished wood, is stark and self-conscious.

The dog barks from time to time, but not urgently. Maybe she wants to come in and have company. But Juliet has never had a dog—a dog in the house would be a witness, not a companion, and would only make her feel uncomfortable.

Perhaps the dog is barking at exploring deer, or a bear, or a cougar. There has been something in the Vancouver papers about a cougar—she thinks it was on this coast—mauling a child.

Who would want to live where you have to share every part of outdoor space with hostile and marauding animals?

Kallipareos. Of the lovely cheeks. Now she has it. The Homeric word is sparkling on her hook. And beyond that she is suddenly aware of all her Greek vocabulary, of everything which seems to have been put in a closet for nearly six months now. Because she was not teaching Greek, she put it away.

That is what happens. You put it away for a little while, and now and again you look in the closet for something else and you remember, and you think, *soon.* Then it becomes something that is just there, in the closet, and other things get crowded in front of it and on top of it and finally you don't think about it at all.

The thing that was your bright treasure. You don't think about it. A loss you could not contemplate at one time, and now it becomes something you can barely remember.

That is what happens.

And even if it's not put away, even if you make your living from it, every day? Juliet thinks of the older teachers at the school, how little most of them care for whatever it is that they teach. Take Juanita, who chose Spanish because it goes with her Christian name (she is Irish) and who wants to speak it well, to use it in her travels. You cannot say that Spanish is her treasure.

Few people, very few, have a treasure, and if you do you must hang on to it. You must not let yourself be waylaid, and have it taken from you.

The Tia Maria has worked in a certain way with the coffee. It makes her feel careless, but powerful. It enables her to think that Eric, after all, is not so important. He is someone she might dally with. Dally is the word. As Aphrodite did, with Anchises. And then one morning she will slip away.

She gets up and finds the bathroom, then comes back and lies down on the couch with the quilt over her—too sleepy to notice Corky's hairs on it, or Corky's smell.

When she wakes it is full morning, though only twenty past six by the kitchen clock.

She has a headache. There is a bottle of aspirin in the bathroom—she takes two, and washes herself and combs her hair and gets her toothbrush from her bag and brushes her teeth. Then she makes a fresh pot of coffee and eats a slice of homemade bread without bothering to heat or butter it. She sits at the kitchen table. Sunlight, slipping down through the trees, makes coppery splashes on the smooth trunks of the arbutus. Corky begins to bark, and barks for quite a long time before the truck turns into the yard and silences her.

Juliet hears the door of the truck close, she hears him speaking to the dog, and dread comes over her. She wants to hide somewhere (she says later, *I could have crawled under the table,* but of course she does not think of doing anything so ridiculous). It's like the moment at school before the winner of the prize is announced. Only worse, because she has no reasonable hope. And because there will never be another chance so momentous in her life.

When the door opens she cannot look up. On her knees the fingers of both hands are interwoven, clenched together.

"You're here," he says. He is laughing in triumph and admiration, as if at a most spectacular piece of impudence and daring. When he opens his arms it's as if a wind has blown into the room and made her look up.

Six months ago she did not know this man existed. Six months ago, the man who died under the train was still alive, and perhaps picking out the clothes for his trip.

"You're here."

She can tell by his voice that he is claiming her. She stands up, quite numb, and sees that he is older, heavier, more impetuous than she has remembered. He advances on her and she feels herself ransacked from top to bottom, flooded with relief, assaulted by happiness. How astonishing this is. How close to dismay.

IT TURNS out that Eric was not taken so much by surprise as he pretended. Ailo phoned him last night, to warn him about the strange girl, Juliet, and offered to check for him as to whether the girl had got on the bus. He had thought it somehow right to take the chance that she would do so—to test fate, maybe—but when Ailo phoned to say that the girl had not gone he was startled by the joy he felt. Still, he did not come home right away, and he did not tell Christa, though he knew he would have to tell her, very soon.

All this Juliet absorbs bit by bit in the weeks and months that follow. Some information arrives accidentally, and some as the result of her imprudent probing.

Her own revelation (of nonvirginity) is considered minor.

Christa is nothing like Ailo. She does not have wide hips or blond hair. She is a dark-haired, thin woman, witty and sometimes morose, who will become Juliet's great friend and mainstay during the years ahead—though she will never quite forgo a habit of sly teasing, the ironic flicker of a submerged rivalry.

Soon

TWO PROFILES face each other. One the profile of a pure white heifer, with a particularly mild and tender expression, the other that of a green-faced man who is neither young nor old. He seems to be a minor official, maybe a postman—he wears that sort of cap. His lips are pale, the whites of his eyes shining. A hand that is probably his offers up, from the lower margin of the painting, a little tree or an exuberant branch, fruited with jewels.

At the upper margin of the painting are dark clouds, and underneath them some small tottery houses and a toy church with its toy cross, perched on the curved surface of the earth. Within this curve a small man (drawn to a larger scale, however, than the buildings) walks along purposefully with a scythe on his shoulder, and a woman, drawn to the same scale, seems to wait for him. But she is hanging upside down.

There are other things as well. For instance, a girl milking a cow, within the heifer's cheek.

Juliet decided at once to buy this print for her parents' Christmas present.

"Because it reminds me of them," she said to Christa, her friend who had come down with her from Whale Bay to do some shopping. They were in the gift shop of the Vancouver Art Gallery.

Christa laughed. "The green man and the cow? They'll be flattered."

Christa never took anything seriously at first, she had to make some joke about it. Juliet wasn't bothered. Three months pregnant with the baby that would turn out to be Penelope, she was suddenly free of nausea, and for that reason, or some other, she was subject to fits of euphoria. She thought of food all the time, and hadn't even wanted to come into the gift shop, because she had spotted a lunchroom.

She loved everything in the picture, but particularly the little figures and rickety buildings at the top of it. The man with the scythe and the woman hanging upside down.

She looked for the title. *I and the Village.*

It made exquisite sense.

"Chagall. I like Chagall," said Christa. "Picasso was a bastard."

Juliet was so happy with what she had found that she could hardly pay attention.

"You know what he is supposed to have said? *Chagall is for shopgirls,*" Christa told her. "So what's wrong with shopgirls? Chagall should have said, Picasso is for people with funny faces."

"I mean, it makes me think of their life," Juliet said. "I don't know why, but it does."

She had already told Christa some things about her parents—how they lived in a curious but not unhappy isolation, though her father was a popular schoolteacher. Partly they were cut off by Sara's heart trouble, but also by their subscribing to magazines nobody around them read, listening to programs on the national radio network, which nobody around them listened to. By Sara's making her own clothes—sometimes ineptly—from *Vogue* patterns, instead of Butterick. Even by the way they preserved some impression of youth instead of thickening and slouching like the parents of Juliet's schoolfellows. Juliet had described Sam as looking like her—long neck, a slight bump to the chin, light-brown floppy hair—and Sara as a frail pale blonde, a wispy untidy beauty.

WHEN PENELOPE was thirteen months old, Juliet flew with her to Toronto, then caught the train. This was in 1969. She got off in a town twenty miles or so away from the town where she had grown up, and where Sam and Sara still lived. Apparently the train did not stop there anymore.

She was disappointed to get off at this unfamiliar station and not to see reappear, at once, the trees and sidewalks and houses she remembered—then, very soon, her own house, Sam and Sara's house, spacious but plain, no doubt with its same blistered and shabby white paint, behind its bountiful soft-maple tree.

Sam and Sara, here in this town where she'd never seen them before, were smiling but anxious, diminished.

Sara gave a curious little cry, as if something had pecked her. A couple of people on the platform turned to look.

Apparently it was only excitement.

"We're long and short, but still we match," she said.

At first Juliet did not understand what was meant. Then she figured it out—Sara was wearing a black linen skirt down to her calves and a matching jacket. The jacket's collar and cuffs were of a shiny lime-green cloth with black polka dots. A turban of the same green material covered her hair. She must have made the outfit herself, or got some dressmaker to make it for her. Its colors were unkind to her skin, which looked as if fine chalk dust had settled over it.

Juliet was wearing a black minidress.

"I was wondering what you'd think of me, black in the summertime, like I'm all in mourning," Sara said. "And here you're dressed to match. You look so smart, I'm all in favor of these short dresses."

"And long hair," said Sam. "An absolute hippy." He bent to look into the baby's face. "Hello, Penelope."

Sara said, "What a dolly."

She reached out for Penelope—though the arms that slid out of her sleeves were sticks too frail to hold any such burden. And they did not have to, because Penelope, who had tensed at the first sound of her grandmother's voice, now yelped and turned away, and hid her face in Juliet's neck.

Sara laughed. "Am I such a scarecrow?" Again her voice was ill controlled, rising to shrill peaks and falling away, drawing stares. This was new—though maybe not entirely. Juliet had an idea that people might always have looked her mother's way when she laughed or talked, but in the old days it would have been a spurt of merriment they noticed, something girlish and attractive (though not everybody would have liked that either, they would have said she was always trying to get attention).

Juliet said, "She's so tired."

Sam introduced the young woman who was standing behind them, keeping her distance as if she was taking care not to be identified as part of their group. And in fact it had not occurred to Juliet that she was.

"Juliet, this is Irene. Irene Avery."

Juliet stuck out her hand as well as she could while holding Penelope and the diaper bag, and when it became evident that Irene was not going to shake hands—or perhaps did not notice the intention—she smiled. Irene did not smile back. She stood quite still but gave the impression of wanting to bolt.

"Hello," said Juliet.

Irene said, "Pleased to meet you," in a sufficiently audible voice, but without expression.

"Irene is our good fairy," Sara said, and then Irene's face did change. She scowled a little, with sensible embarrassment.

She was not as tall as Juliet—who was tall—but she was broader in the shoulders and hips, with strong arms and a stubborn chin. She had thick, springy black hair, pulled back from her face into a stubby ponytail, thick and rather hostile black eyebrows, and the sort of skin that browns easily. Her eyes were green or blue, a light surprising color against this skin, and hard to look into, being deep set. Also because she held her head slightly lowered and twisted her face to the side. This wariness seemed hardened and deliberate.

"She does one heck of a lot of work for a fairy," Sam said, with his large strategic grin. "I'll tell the world she does."

And now of course Juliet recalled the mention in letters of some woman who had come in to help, because of Sara's strength having gone so drastically downhill. But she had thought of somebody much older. Irene was surely no older than she was herself.

The car was the same Pontiac that Sam had got secondhand maybe ten years ago. The original blue paint showed in streaks here and there but was mostly faded to gray, and the effects of winter road salt could be seen in its petticoat fringe of rust.

"The old gray mare," said Sara, almost out of breath after the short walk from the railway platform.

"She hasn't given up," said Juliet. She spoke admiringly, as seemed to be expected. She had forgotten that this was what they called the car, though it was the name she had thought up herself.

"Oh, she never gives up," said Sara, once she was settled with Irene's help in the backseat. "And we'd never give up on her."

Juliet got into the front seat, juggling Penelope, who was beginning again to whimper. The heat inside the car was shocking, even though it had been parked with the windows down in the scanty shade of the station poplars.

"Actually I'm considering—," said Sam as he backed out, "I'm considering turning her in for a truck."

"He doesn't mean it," shrieked Sara.

"For the business," Sam continued. "It'd be a lot handier. And you'd get a certain amount of advertising every time you drove down the street, just from the name on the door."

"He's teasing," Sara said. "How am I going to ride around in a vehicle that says *Fresh Vegetables*? Am I supposed to be the squash or the cabbage?"

"Better pipe down, Missus," Sam said, "or you won't have any breath left when we reach home."

After nearly thirty years of teaching in the public schools around the county—ten years in the last school—Sam had suddenly quit and decided to get into the business of selling vegetables, full-time. He had always cultivated a big vegetable garden, and raspberry canes, in the extra lot beside their house, and they had sold their surplus produce to a few people around town. But now, apparently, this was to change into his way of making a living, selling to grocery stores and perhaps eventually putting up a market stall at the front gate.

"You're serious about all this?" said Juliet quietly.

"Darn right I am."

"You're not going to miss teaching?"

"Not on your Nelly-O. I was fed up. I was fed up to the eyeballs."

It was true that after all those years, he had never been offered, in any school, the job of principal. She supposed that was what he was fed up with. He was a remarkable teacher, the one whose antics and energy everyone would remember, his Grade Six unlike any other year in his pupils' lives. Yet he had been passed over, time and again, and probably for that very reason. His methods could be seen to undercut authority. So you could imagine Authority saying that he was not the sort of man to be in charge, he'd do less harm where he was.

He liked outdoor work, he was good at talking to people, he would probably do well, selling vegetables.

But Sara would hate it.

Juliet did not like it either. If there was a side to be on, however, she would have to choose his. She was not going to define herself as a snob.

And the truth was that she saw herself—she saw herself and Sam and Sara, but particularly herself and Sam—as superior in their own way to everybody around them. So what should his peddling vegetables matter?

Sam spoke now in a quieter, conspiratorial voice.

"What's her name?"

He meant the baby's.

"Penelope. We're never going to call her Penny. Penelope."

"No, I mean—I mean her last name."

"Oh. Well, it's Henderson-Porteous I guess. Or Porteous-Henderson. But maybe that's too much of a mouthful, when she's already called Penelope? We knew that but we wanted Penelope. We'll have to settle it somehow."

"So. He's given her his name," Sam said. "Well, that's something. I mean, that's good."

Juliet was surprised for a moment, then not.

"Of course he has," she said. Pretending to be mystified and amused. "She's his."

"Oh yes. Yes. But given the circumstances."

"I forget about the circumstances," she said. "If you mean the fact that we're not married, it's hardly anything to take into account. Where we live, the people we know, it is not a thing anybody thinks about."

"Suppose not," said Sam. "Was he married to the first one?"

Juliet had told them about Eric's wife, whom he had cared for during the eight years that she had lived after her car accident.

"Ann? Yes. Well, I don't really know. But yes. I think so. Yes."

Sara called into the front seat, "Wouldn't it be nice to stop for ice cream?"

"We've got ice cream in the fridge at home," Sam called back. And added quietly, shockingly, to Juliet, "Take her into anyplace for a treat, and she'll put on a show."

The windows were still down, the warm wind blew through the car. It was full summer—a season which never arrived, as far as Juliet could see, on the west coast. The hardwood trees were humped over the far edge of the fields, making blue-black caves of shade, and the crops and the meadows in front of them, under the hard sunlight, were gold and green. Vigorous young wheat and barley and corn and beans—fairly blistering your eyes.

Sara said, "What's this conference in aid of? In the front seat? We can't hear back here for the wind."

Sam said, "Nothing interesting. Just asking Juliet if her fellow's still doing the fishing."

Eric made his living prawn fishing, and had done so for a long time. Once he had been a medical student. That had come to an end because he had performed an abortion, on a friend (not a girlfriend). All had gone well, but somehow the story got out. This was something Juliet had thought of revealing to her broad-minded parents. She had wanted, perhaps, to establish him as an educated man, not just a fisherman. But why should that matter, especially now that Sam was a vegetable man? Also, their broad-mindedness was possibly not so reliable as she had thought.

THERE WAS more to be sold than fresh vegetables and berries. Jam, bottled juice, relish, were turned out in the kitchen. The first morning of Juliet's visit, raspberry-jam making was in progress. Irene was in charge, her blouse wet with steam or sweat, sticking to her skin between the shoulder blades. Every so often she flashed a look at the television set, which had been wheeled down the back hall to the kitchen doorway, so that you had to squeeze around it to get into the room. On the screen was a children's morning program, showing a Bullwinkle cartoon. Now and then Irene gave a loud laugh at the cartoon antics, and Juliet laughed a little, to be comradely. Of this Irene took no notice.

Counter space had to be cleared so that Juliet could boil and mash an egg for Penelope's breakfast, and make some coffee and toast for herself. "Is that enough room?" Irene asked her, in a voice that was dubious, as if Juliet was an intruder whose demands could not be foreseen.

Close-up, you could see how many fine black hairs grew on Irene's forearms. Some grew on her cheeks, too, just in front of her ears.

In her sidelong way she watched everything Juliet did, watched her fiddle with the knobs on the stove (not remembering at first which burners they controlled), watched her lifting the egg out of the saucepan and peeling off the shell (which stuck, this time, and came away in little bits rather than in large easy pieces), then watched her choosing the saucer to mash it in.

"You don't want her to drop that on the floor." This was a reference to the china saucer. "Don't you got a plastic dish for her?"

"I'll watch it," Juliet said.

It turned out that Irene was a mother, too. She had a boy three years old and a daughter just under two. Their names were Trevor and Tracy. Their father had been killed last summer in an accident at the chicken barn where he worked. She herself was three years younger than Juliet—twenty-two. The information about the children and the husband came out in answer to Juliet's questions, and the age could be figured from what she said next.

When Juliet said, "Oh, I'm sorry"—speaking about the accident and feeling that she had been rude to pry, and that it was now hypocritical of her to commiserate—Irene said, "Yeah. Right in time for my twenty-first birthday," as if misfortunes were something to accumulate, like charms on a bracelet.

After Penelope had eaten all of the egg that she would accept, Juliet hoisted her onto one hip and carried her upstairs.

Halfway up she realized that she had not washed the saucer.

There was nowhere to leave the baby, who was not yet walking but could crawl very quickly. Certainly she could not be left for even five minutes in the kitchen, with the boiling water in the sterilizer and the hot jam and the chopping knives—it was too much to ask Irene to watch her. And first thing this morning she had again refused to make friends with Sara. So Juliet carried her up the enclosed stairs to the attic—having shut the door behind—and set her there on the steps to play, while she herself looked for the old playpen. Fortunately Penelope was an expert on steps.

The house was a full two stories tall, its rooms high-ceilinged but boxlike—or so they seemed to Juliet now. The roof was steeply pitched, so that you could walk around in the middle of the attic. Juliet used to do that, when she was a child. She walked around telling herself some story she had read, with certain additions or alterations. Dancing—that too—in front of an imaginary audience. The real audience consisted of broken or simply banished furniture, old trunks, an immensely heavy buffalo coat, the purple martin house (a present from long-ago students of Sam's, which had failed to attract any purple martins), the German helmet supposed to have been brought home by Sam's father from the First World War, and an unintentionally comic amateur painting of the *Empress of Ireland* sinking in the Gulf of St. Lawrence, with matchstick figures flying off in all directions.

And there, leaning against the wall, was *I and the Village.* Face out—no attempt had been made to hide it. And no dust on it to speak of, so it had not been there long.

She found the playpen, after a few moments of searching. It was a handsome heavy piece of furniture, with a wooden floor and spindle sides. And the baby carriage. Her parents had kept everything, had hoped for another child. There had been one miscarriage at least. Laughter in their bed, on Sunday mornings, had made Juliet feel as if the house had been invaded by a stealthy, even shameful, disturbance, not favorable to herself.

The baby carriage was of the kind that folded down to become a stroller. This was something Juliet had forgotten about, or hadn't known. Sweating by now, and covered with dust, she got to work to effect this transformation. This sort of job was never easy for her, she never grasped right away the manner in which things were put together, and she might have dragged the whole thing downstairs and gone out to the garden to get Sam to help her, but for the thought of Irene. Irene's flickering pale eyes, indirect but measuring looks, competent hands. Her vigilance, in which there was something that couldn't quite be called contempt. Juliet didn't know what it could be called. An attitude, indifferent but uncompromising, like a cat's.

She managed at last to get the stroller into shape. It was cumbersome, half again as big as the stroller she was used to. And filthy, of course. As she was herself by now, and Penelope, on the steps, even more so. And right beside the baby's hand was something Juliet hadn't even noticed. A nail. The sort of thing you paid no attention to, till you had a baby at the hand-to-mouth stage, and that you had then to be on the lookout for all the time.

And she hadn't been. Everything here distracted her. The heat, Irene, the things that were familiar and the things that were unfamiliar.

I and the Village.

"Oh," said Sara. "I hoped you wouldn't notice. Don't take it to heart."

The sunroom was now Sara's bedroom. Bamboo shades had been hung on all the windows, filling the small room—once part of the verandah— with a brownish-yellow light and a uniform heat. Sara, however, was wearing woolly pink pajamas. Yesterday, at the station, with her pencilled eyebrows and raspberry lipstick, her turban and suit, she had looked to Juliet like an elderly Frenchwoman (not that Juliet had seen many elderly Frenchwomen), but now, with her white hair flying out in wisps, her bright eyes anxious under nearly nonexistent brows, she looked more like an oddly aged child. She was sitting up against the pillows with the quilts pulled up to her waist. When Juliet had walked her to the bathroom, earlier, it had been revealed that in spite of the heat she was wearing both socks and slippers in bed.

A straight-backed chair had been placed by her bed, its seat being easier for her to reach than a table. On it were pills and medicines, talcum powder, moisturizing lotion, a half-drunk cup of milky tea, a glass filmed with the traces of some dark tonic, probably iron. On top of the bed were magazines—old copies of *Vogue* and the *Ladies' Home Journal.*

"I'm not," said Juliet.

"We did have it hanging up. It was in the back hall by the dining-room door. Then Daddy took it down."

"Why?"

"He didn't say anything about it to me. He didn't say that he was going to. Then came a day when it was just gone."

"Why would he take it down?"

"Oh. It would be some notion he had, you know."

"What sort of a notion?"

"Oh. I think—you know, I think it probably had to do with Irene. That it would disturb Irene."

"There wasn't anybody naked in it. Not like the Botticelli."

For indeed there was a print of *The Birth of Venus* hanging in Sam and Sara's living room. It had been the subject of nervous jokes years ago on the occasion when they had the other teachers to supper.

"No. But it was *modern.* I think it made Daddy uncomfortable. Or maybe looking at it with Irene looking at it—that made him uncom- fortable. He might be afraid it would make her feel—oh, sort of contemptuous of us. You know—that we were weird. He wouldn't like for Irene to think we were that kind of people."

Juliet said, "The kind of people who would hang that kind of picture? You mean he'd care so much what she thought of our *pictures*?"

"You know Daddy."

"He's not afraid to disagree with people. Wasn't that the trouble in his job?"

"What?" said Sara. "Oh. Yes. He can disagree. But he's careful sometimes. And Irene. Irene is—he's careful of her. She's very valuable to us, Irene."

"Did he think she'd quit her job because she thought we had a weird picture?"

"I would have left it up, dear. I value anything that comes from you. But Daddy . . ."

Juliet said nothing. From the time when she was nine or ten until she was perhaps fourteen, she and Sara had an understanding about Sam. *You know Daddy.*

That was the time of their being women together. Home permanents were tried on Juliet's stubborn fine hair, dressmaking sessions produced the outfits like nobody else's, suppers were peanut-butter-and-tomato-and-mayonnaise sandwiches on the evenings Sam stayed late for a school meeting. Stories were told and retold about Sara's old boyfriends and girlfriends, the jokes they played and the fun they had, in the days when Sara was a schoolteacher too, before her heart got too bad. Stories from the time before that, when she lay in bed with rheumatic fever and had the imaginary friends Rollo and Maxine who solved mysteries, even murders, like the characters in certain children's books. Glimpses of Sam's besotted courtship, disasters with the borrowed car, the time he showed up at Sara's door disguised as a tramp.

Sara and Juliet, making fudge and threading ribbons through the eyelet trim on their petticoats, the two of them intertwined. And then abruptly, Juliet hadn't wanted any more of it, she had wanted instead to talk to Sam late at night in the kitchen, to ask him about black holes, the Ice Age, God. She hated the way Sara undermined their talk with wide-eyed ingenuous questions, the way Sara always tried somehow to bring the subject back to herself. That was why the talks had to be late at night and there had to be the understanding neither she nor Sam ever spoke about. *Wait till we're rid of Sara.* Just for the time being, of course.

There was a reminder going along with that. *Be nice to Sara. She risked her life to have you, that's worth remembering.*

"Daddy doesn't mind disagreeing with people that are *over* him," Sara said, taking a deep breath. "But you know how he is with people that are *under* him. He'll do anything to make sure they don't feel he's any different from them, he just has to put himself down on their level—"

Juliet did know, of course. She knew the way Sam talked to the boy at the gas pumps, the way he joked in the hardware store. But she said nothing.

"He has to suck up to them," said Sara with a sudden change of tone, a wavering edge of viciousness, a weak chuckle.

JULIET CLEANED up the stroller, and Penelope, and herself, and set off on a walk into town. She had the excuse that she needed a certain brand of mild disinfectant soap with which to wash the diapers—if she used ordinary soap the baby would get a rash. But she had other reasons, irresistible though embarrassing.

This was the way she had walked to school for years of her life. Even when she was going to college, and came home on a visit, she was still the same—a girl going to school. Would she never be done going to school? Somebody asked Sam that at a time when she had just won the Intercollegiate Latin Translation Prize, and he had said, " 'Fraid not." He told this story on himself. God forbid that he should mention prizes. Leave Sara to do that—though Sara might have forgotten just what the prize was for.

And here she was, redeemed. Like any other young woman, pushing her baby. Concerned about the diaper soap. And this wasn't just her baby. Her love child. She sometimes spoke of Penelope that way, just to Eric. He took it as a joke, she said it as a joke, because of course they lived together and had done so for some time, and they intended to go on together. The fact that they were not married meant nothing to him, so far as she knew, and she often forgot about it, herself. But occasionally—and now, especially, here at home, it was the fact of her unmarried state that gave her some flush of accomplishment, a silly surge of bliss.

"So—YOU went upstreet today," Sam said. (Had he always said *upstreet*? Sara and Juliet said *uptown*.) "See anybody you knew?"

"I had to go to the drugstore," Juliet said. "So I was talking to Charlie Little."

This conversation took place in the kitchen, after eleven o'clock at night. Juliet had decided that this was the best time to make up Penelope's bottles for tomorrow.

"Little Charlie?" said Sam—who had always had this other habit she hadn't remembered, the habit of continuing to call people by their school nicknames. "Did he admire the offspring?"

"Of course."

"And well he might."

Sam was sitting at the table, drinking rye and smoking a cigarette. His drinking whisky was new. Because Sara's father had been a drunk—not a down-and-out drunk, he had continued to practice as a veterinarian, but enough of a terror around the house to make his daughter horrified by drinking—Sam had never used to so much as drink a beer, at least to Juliet's knowledge, at home.

Juliet had gone into the drugstore because that was the only place to buy the diaper soap. She hadn't expected to see Charlie, though it was his family's store. The last she had heard of him, he was going to be an engineer. She had mentioned that to him, today, maybe tactlessly, but he had been easy and jovial when he told her that it hadn't worked out. He had put on weight around the middle, and his hair had thinned, had lost some of its wave and glisten. He had greeted Juliet with enthusiasm, with flattery for herself as well as her baby, and this had confused her, so that she had felt her face and neck hot, slightly perspiring, all the time he talked to her. In high school he would have had no time for her—except for a decent greeting, since his manners were always affable, democratic. He took out the most desirable girls in the school, and was now, as he told her, married to one of them. Janey Peel. They had two children, one of them about Penelope's age, one older. That was the reason, he said, with a candor that seemed to owe something to Juliet's own situation—that was the reason he hadn't gone on to become an engineer.

So he knew how to win a smile and a gurgle from Penelope, and he chatted with Juliet as a fellow parent, somebody now on the same level. She felt idiotically flattered and pleased. But there was more to his attention than that—the quick glance at her unadorned left hand, the joke about his own marriage. And something else. He appraised her, covertly, perhaps he saw her now as a woman displaying the fruits of a boldly sexual life. Juliet, of all people. The gawk, the scholar.

"Does she look like you?" he had asked, when he squatted down to peer at Penelope.

"More like her father," said Juliet casually, but with a flood of pride, the sweat now pearling on her upper lip.

"Does she?" said Charlie, and straightened up, speaking confidentially. "I'll tell you one thing, though. I thought it was a shame—"

*

JULIET SAID to Sam, "He told me he thought it was a shame what happened with you."

"He did, did he? What did you say to that?"

"I didn't know what to say. I didn't know what he meant. But I didn't want him to know that."

"No."

She sat down at the table. "I'd like a drink but I don't like whisky."

"So you drink now, too?"

"Wine. We make our own wine. Everybody in the Bay does."

He told her a joke then, the sort of joke that he would never have told her before. It involved a couple going to a motel, and it ended up with the line "So it's like what I always tell the girls at Sunday school—you don't have to drink and smoke to have a good time."

She laughed but felt her face go hot, as with Charlie.

"Why did you quit your job?" she said. "Were you let go because of me?"

"Come on now." Sam laughed. "Don't think you're so important. I wasn't let go. I wasn't fired."

"All right then. You quit."

"I quit."

"Did it have anything at all to do with me?"

"I quit because I got goddamn sick of my neck always in that noose. I was on the point of quitting for years."

"It had nothing to do with me?"

"All right," Sam said. "I got into an argument. There were things said."

"What things?"

"You don't need to know.

"And don't worry," he said after a moment. "They didn't fire me. They couldn't have fired me. There are rules. It's like I told you—I was ready to go anyway."

"But you don't realize," said Juliet. "You don't *realize*. You don't realize just how *stupid* this is and what a disgusting place this is to live in, where people say that kind of thing, and how if I told people I know this, they wouldn't believe it. It would seem like a joke."

"Well. Unfortunately your mother and I don't live where you live. Here is where we live. Does that fellow of yours think it's a joke too? I don't want to talk any more about this tonight, I'm going to bed. I'm going to look in on Mother and then I'm going to bed."

"The passenger train—," said Juliet with continued energy, even scorn. "It does still stop here. Doesn't it? You didn't want me getting off here. *Did you?*"

On his way out of the room, her father did not answer.

*

LIGHT FROM the last streetlight in town now fell across Juliet's bed. The big soft maple tree had been cut down, replaced by a patch of Sam's rhubarb. Last night she had left the curtains closed to shade the bed, but tonight she felt that she needed the outside air. So she had to switch the pillow down to the foot of the bed, along with Penelope, who had slept like an angel with the full light in her face.

She wished she had drunk a little of the whisky. She lay stiff with frustration and anger, composing in her head a letter to Eric. *I don't know what I'm doing here, I should never have come here, I can't wait to go home.*

Home.

WHEN IT was barely light in the morning, she woke to the noise of a vacuum cleaner. Then a voice—Sam's—interrupted this noise, and she must have fallen asleep again. When she woke up later, she thought it must have been a dream. Otherwise Penelope would have woken up, and she hadn't.

The kitchen was cooler this morning, no longer full of the smell of simmering fruit. Irene was fixing little caps of gingham cloth, and labels, onto all the jars.

"I thought I heard you vacuuming," said Juliet, dredging up cheerfulness. "I must have dreamed it. It was only about five o'clock in the morning."

Irene did not answer for a moment. She was writing on a label. She wrote with great concentration, her lips caught between her teeth.

"That was her," she said when she had finished. "She woke your dad up and he had to go and make her quit."

This seemed unlikely. Yesterday Sara had left her bed only to go to the bathroom.

"He told me," said Irene. "She wakes up in the middle of the night and thinks she's going to do something and then he has to get up and make her quit."

"She must have a spurt of energy then," said Juliet.

"Yeah." Irene was getting to work on another label. When that was done, she faced Juliet.

"Wants to wake your dad up and get attention, that's it. Him dead tired and he's got to get out of bed and tend to her."

Juliet turned away. Not wanting to set Penelope down—as if the child wasn't safe here—she juggled her on one hip while she fished the egg out with a spoon, tapped and shelled and mashed it with one hand.

While she fed Penelope she was afraid to speak, lest the tone of her voice alarm the baby and set her wailing. Something communicated itself to Irene, however. She said in a more subdued voice—but with an undertone of defiance—"That's just the way they get. When they're sick like that, they can't help it. They can't think about nobody but themselves."

SARA'S EYES were closed, but she opened them immediately. "Oh, my dear ones," she said, as if laughing at herself. "My Juliet. My Penelope."

Penelope seemed to be getting used to her. At least she did not cry, this morning, or turn her face away.

"Here," said Sara, reaching for one of her magazines. "Set her down and let her work at this."

Penelope looked dubious for a moment, then grabbed a page and tore it vigorously.

"There you go," said Sara. "All babies love to tear up magazines. I remember."

On the bedside chair there was a bowl of Cream of Wheat, barely touched.

"You didn't eat your breakfast?" Juliet said. "Is that not what you wanted?"

Sara looked at the bowl as if serious consideration was called for, but couldn't be managed.

"I don't remember. No, I guess I didn't want it." She had a little fit of giggling and gasping. "Who knows? Crossed my mind—she could be poisoning me.

"I'm just kidding," she said when she recovered. "But she's very fierce. Irene. We mustn't underestimate—Irene. Did you see the hairs on her arms?"

"Like cats' hairs," said Juliet.

"Like skunks'."

"We must hope none of them get into the jam."

"Don't make me—laugh any more—"

Penelope became so absorbed in tearing up magazines that in a while Juliet was able to leave her in Sara's room and carry the Cream of Wheat out to the kitchen. Without saying anything, she began to make an eggnog. Irene was in and out, carrying boxes of jam jars to the car. On the back steps, Sam was hosing off the earth that clung to the newly dug potatoes. He had begun to sing—too softly at first for his words to be heard. Then, as Irene came up the steps, more loudly.

> *"Irene, good ni-i-ight,*
> *Irene, good night,*
> *Good night, Irene, good night, Irene,*
> *I'll see you in my dreams."*

Irene, in the kitchen, swung around and yelled, "Don't sing that song about me."

"What song about you?" said Sam, with feigned amazement. "Who's singing a song about you?"

"You were. You just were."

"Oh—that song. That song about Irene? The girl in the song? By golly—I forgot that was your name too."

He started up again, but humming, stealthily. Irene stood listening, flushed, with her chest going up and down, waiting to pounce if she should hear a word.

"Don't you sing about me. If it's got my name in it, it's about me."

Suddenly Sam burst out in full force.

> *"Last Saturday night I got married,*
> *Me and my wife settled down—"*

"Stop it. You stop it," cried Irene, wide-eyed, inflamed. "If you don't stop I'll go out there and squirt the hose on you."

SAM WAS delivering jam, that afternoon, to various grocery stores and a few gift shops which had placed orders. He invited Juliet to come along. He had gone to the hardware store and bought a brand-new baby's car seat for Penelope.

"That's one thing we don't have in the attic," he said. "When you were little, I don't know if they had them. Anyway, it wouldn't have mattered. We didn't have a car."

"It's very spiffy," said Juliet. "I hope it didn't cost a fortune."

"A mere bagatelle," said Sam, bowing her into the car.

Irene was in the field picking more raspberries. These would be for pies. Sam tooted the horn twice and waved as they set off, and Irene decided to respond, raising one arm as if batting away a fly.

"That's a dandy girl," Sam said. "I don't know how we would have survived without her. But I imagine she seems pretty rough to you."

"I hardly know her."

"No. She's scared stiff of you."

"Surely not." And trying to think of something appreciative or at least neutral to say about Irene, Juliet asked how her husband had been killed at the chicken barn.

"I don't know if he was a criminal type or just immature. Anyway, he got in with some goons who were planning a sideline in stolen chickens and of course they managed to set off the alarm and the farmer came out with a gun and whether he meant to shoot him or not he did—"

"My God."

"So Irene and her in-laws went to court but the fellow got off. Well, he would. It must have been pretty hard on her, though. Even if it doesn't seem that the husband was much of a prize."

Juliet said that of course it must have been, and asked him if Irene was somebody he had taught at school.

"No no no. She hardly got to school, as far as I can make out."

He said that her family had lived up north, somewhere near Huntsville. Yes. Somewhere near there. One day they all went into town. Father, mother, kids. And the father told them he had things to do and he would meet them in a while. He told them where. When. And they walked around with no money to spend, until it was time. And he just never showed up.

"Never intended to show up. Ditched them. So they had to go on welfare. Lived in some shack out in the country, where it was cheap. Irene's older sister, the one who was the mainstay, more than the mother, I gather—she died of a burst appendix. No way of getting her into town, snowstorm on and they didn't have a phone. Irene didn't want to go back to school then, because her sister had sort of protected her from the way the other kids would act towards them. She may seem thick-skinned now but I guess she wasn't always. Maybe even now it's more of a masquerade."

And now, he said, now Irene's mother was looking after the little boy and the little girl, but guess what, after all these years the father had shown up and was trying to get the mother to go back to him, and if that should happen Irene didn't know what she'd do, since she didn't want her kids near him.

"They're cute kids, too. The little girl has some problem with a cleft palate and she's already had one operation but she'll need another later on. She'll be all right. But that's just one more thing."

One more thing.

What was the matter with Juliet? She felt no real sympathy. She felt herself rebelling, deep down, against this wretched litany. It was too much. When the cleft palate appeared in the story what she had really wanted to do was complain. *Too much.*

She knew she was wrong, but the feeling would not budge. She was afraid to say anything more, lest out of her mouth she betray her hard heart.

She was afraid she would say to Sam, "Just what is so wonderful about all this misery, does it make her a saint?" Or she might say, most unforgivably, "I hope you don't mean to get us mixed up with people like that."

"I'm telling you," Sam said, "at the time she came to help us out I was at wits' end. Last fall, your mother was a downright catastrophe. And not exactly that she was letting everything go. No. Better if she had let everything go. Better if she'd done nothing. What she did, she'd start one job up and then she could not get on with it. Over and over. Not that this was anything absolutely new. I mean, I always had to pick up after her and look after her and help her do the housework. Me and you both— remember? She'd always been this sweet pretty girl with a bad heart and she was used to being waited on. Once in a while over the years it did occur to me she could have tried harder.

"But it got so bad," he said. "It got so I'd come home to the washing machine in the middle of the kitchen floor and wet clothes slopping all over the place. And some baking mess she'd started on and given up on, stuff charred to a crisp in the oven. I was scared she'd set herself on fire. Set the house on fire. I'd tell her and tell her, stay in bed. But she wouldn't and then she'd be all in this mess, crying. I tried a couple of girls coming in and they just couldn't handle her. So then—Irene.

"Irene," he said with a robust sigh. "I bless the day. I tell you. Bless the day."

But like all good things, he said, this must come to an end. Irene was getting married. To a forty- or fifty-year-old widower. Farmer. He was supposed to have money and for her sake Sam guessed he hoped it was true. Because the man did not have much else to recommend him.

"By Jesus he doesn't. As far as I can see he's only got one tooth in his head. Bad sign, in my opinion. Too proud or stingy to get choppers. Think of it—a grand-looking girl like her."

"When is the event?"

"In the fall sometime. In the fall."

PENELOPE HAD been sleeping all this time—she had gone to sleep in her car seat almost as soon as they started to move. The front windows were down and Juliet could smell the hay, which was freshly cut and baled— nobody made hay coils anymore. Some elm trees were still standing, marvels now, in their isolation.

They stopped in a village built all along one street in a narrow valley. Bedrock stuck out of the valley walls—the only place for many miles around where such massive rocks were to be seen. Juliet remembered coming here when there was a special park which you paid to enter. In the park there was a fountain, a teahouse where they served strawberry shortcake and ice cream—and surely other things which she could not remember. Caves in the rock were named after each of the Seven Dwarfs. Sam and Sara had sat on the ground by the fountain eating ice cream while she had rushed ahead to explore the caves. (Which were nothing much, really—quite shallow.) She had wanted them to come with her but Sam had said, "You know your mother can't climb."

"You run," Sara had said. "Come back and tell us all about it." She was dressed up. A black taffeta skirt that spread in a circle around her on the grass. Those were called ballerina skirts.

It must have been a special day.

Juliet asked Sam about this when he came out of the store. At first he could not remember. Then he did. A gyp joint, he said. He didn't know when it had disappeared.

Juliet could see no trace anywhere along the street of a fountain or a teahouse.

"A bringer of peace and order," Sam said, and it took a moment for her to recognize that he was still talking about Irene. "She'll turn her hand to anything. Cut the grass and hoe the garden. Whatever she's doing she gives it her best and she behaves as if it's a privilege to do it. That's what never ceases to amaze me."

What could the carefree occasion have been? A birthday, a wedding anniversary?

Sam spoke insistently, even solemnly, over the noise of the car's struggle up the hill.

"She restored my faith in women."

SAM CHARGED into every store after telling Juliet that he wouldn't be a minute, and came back to the car quite a while later explaining that he had not been able to get away. People wanted to talk, people had been saving up jokes to tell him. A few followed him out to see his daughter and her baby.

"So that's the girl who talks Latin," one woman said.

"Getting a bit rusty nowadays," Sam said. "Nowadays she has her hands full."

"I bet," the woman said, craning to get a look at Penelope. "But aren't they a blessing? Oh, the wee ones."

Juliet had thought she might talk to Sam about the thesis she was planning to return to—though at present that was just a dream. Such subjects used to come up naturally between them. Not with Sara. Sara would say, "Now, you must tell me what you're doing in your studies," and Juliet would sum things up, and Sara might ask her how she kept all those Greek names straight. But Sam had known what she was talking about. At college she had mentioned how her father had explained to her what *thaumaturgy* meant, when she ran across the word at the age of twelve or thirteen. She was asked if her father was a scholar.

"Sure," she said. "He teaches Grade Six."

Now she had a feeling that he would subtly try to undermine her. Or maybe not so subtly. He might use the word *airy-fairy*. Or claim to have forgotten things she could not believe he had forgotten.

But maybe he had. Rooms in his mind closed up, the windows blackened—what was in there judged by him to be too useless, too discreditable, to meet the light of day.

Juliet spoke out more harshly than she intended.

"Does she want to get married? Irene?"

This question startled Sam, coming as it did in that tone and after a considerable silence.

"I don't know," he said.

And after a moment, "I don't see how she could."

"Ask her," Juliet said. "You must want to, the way you feel about her."

They drove for a mile or two before he spoke. It was clear she had given offense.

"I don't know what you're talking about," he said.

"Happy, Grumpy, Dopey, Sleepy, Sneezy," Sara said.

"Doc," said Juliet.

"Doc. *Doc*. Happy, Sneezy, *Doc*, Grumpy, *Bashful*, Sneezy—No. Sneezy, Bashful, Doc, Grumpy—*Sleepy*, Happy, Doc, Bashful—"

Having counted on her fingers, Sara said, "Wasn't that eight?

"We went there more than once," she said. "We used to call it the Shrine of Strawberry Shortcake—oh, how I'd like to go again."

"Well, there's nothing there," Juliet said. "I couldn't even see where it was."

"I'm sure I could have. Why didn't I go with you? A summer drive. What strength does it take to ride in a car? Daddy's always saying I haven't the strength."

"You came to meet me."

"Yes I did," said Sara. "But he didn't want me to. I had to throw a fit."

She reached around to pull up the pillows behind her head, but she could not manage it, so Juliet did it for her.

"Drat," said Sara. "What a useless piece of goods I am. I think I could handle a bath, though. What if company comes?"

Juliet asked if she was expecting anybody.

"No. But what if?"

So Juliet took her into the bathroom and Penelope crawled after them. Then when the water was ready and her grandmother hoisted in, Penelope decided that the bath must be for her as well. Juliet undressed her, and the baby and the old woman were bathed together. Though Sara, naked, did not look like an old woman as much as an old girl—a girl, say, who had suffered some exotic, wasting, desiccating disease.

Penelope accepted her presence without alarm, but kept a firm hold on her own duck-shaped yellow soap.

It was in the bath that Sara finally brought herself to ask, circumspectly, about Eric.

"I'm sure he is a nice man," she said.

"Sometimes," said Juliet casually.

"He was so good to his first wife."

"Only wife," Juliet corrected her. "So far."

"But I'm sure now you have this baby—you're happy, I mean. I'm sure you're happy."

"As happy as is consistent with living in sin," Juliet said, surprising her mother by wringing out a dripping washcloth over her soaped head.

"That's what I mean," said Sara after ducking and covering her face, with a joyful shriek. Then, "Juliet?"

"Yes?"

"You know I don't mean it if I ever say mean things about Daddy. I know he loves me. He's just unhappy."

JULIET DREAMED she was a child again and in this house, though the arrangement of the rooms was somewhat different. She looked out the window of one of the unfamiliar rooms, and saw an arc of water sparkling in the air. This water came from the hose. Her father, with his back to her, was watering the garden. A figure moved in and out among the raspberry canes and was revealed, after a while, to be Irene—though a more childish Irene, supple and merry. She was dodging the water sprinkled from the hose. Hiding, reappearing, mostly successful but always caught again for an instant before she ran away. The game was supposed to be lighthearted, but Juliet, behind the window, watched it with disgust. Her father always kept his back to her, yet she believed—she somehow *saw*— that he held the hose low, in front of his body, and that it was only the nozzle of it that he turned back and forth.

The dream was suffused with a sticky horror. Not the kind of horror that jostles its shapes outside your skin, but the kind that curls through the narrowest passages of your blood.

When she woke that feeling was still with her. She found the dream shameful. Obvious, banal. A dirty indulgence of her own.

THERE WAS a knock on the front door in the middle of the afternoon. Nobody used the front door—Juliet found it a bit stiff to open.

The man who stood there wore a well-pressed yellow shirt with short sleeves, and tan pants. He was perhaps a few years older than she was, tall but rather frail-looking, slightly hollow-chested, but vigorous in his greeting, relentless in his smiling.

"I've come to see the lady of the house," he said.

Juliet left him standing there and went into the sunroom.

"There's a man at the door," she said. "He might be selling something. Should I get rid of him?"

Sara was pushing herself up. "No, no," she said breathlessly. "Tidy me a bit, can you? I heard his voice. It's Don. It's my friend Don."

Don had already entered the house and was heard outside the sunroom door.

"No fuss, Sara. It's only me. Are you decent?"

Sara, with a wild and happy look, reached for the hairbrush she could not manage, then gave up and ran her fingers through her hair. Her voice rang out gaily. "I'm as decent as I'll ever be, I'm afraid. Come in here."

The man appeared, hurried up to her, and she lifted her arms to him. "You smell of summer," she said. "What is it?" She fingered his shirt. "Ironing. Ironed cotton. My, that's nice."

"I did it myself," he said. "Sally's over at the church messing about with the flowers. Not a bad job, eh?"

"Lovely," said Sara. "But you almost didn't get in. Juliet thought you were a salesman. Juliet's my daughter. My dear daughter. I told you, didn't I? I told you she was coming. Don is my minister, Juliet. My friend and minister."

Don straightened up, grasped Juliet's hand.

"Good you're here—I'm very glad to meet you. And you weren't so far wrong, actually. I am a sort of salesman."

Juliet smiled politely at the ministerial joke.

"What church are you the minister of?"

The question made Sara laugh. "Oh dear—that gives the show away, doesn't it?"

"I'm from Trinity," said Don, with his unfazed smile. "And as for giving the show away—it's no news to me that Sara and Sam were not involved with any of the churches in the community. I just started dropping in anyway, because your mother is such a charming lady."

Juliet could not remember whether it was the Anglican or United Church that was called Trinity.

"Would you get Don a reasonable sort of chair, dear?" said Sara. "Here he is bending over me like a stork. And some sort of refreshment, Don? Would you like an eggnog? Juliet makes me the most delicious eggnogs. No. No, that's probably too heavy. You've just come in from the heat of the day. Tea? That's hot too. Ginger ale? Some kind of juice? What juice do we have, Juliet?"

Don said, "I don't need anything but a glass of water. That would be welcome."

"No tea? Really?" Sara was quite out of breath. "But I think I'd like some. You could drink half a cup, surely. Juliet?"

In the kitchen, by herself—Irene could be seen in the garden, today she was hoeing around the beans—Juliet wondered if the tea was a ruse to get her out of the room for a few private words. A few private words, perhaps even a few words of prayer? The notion sickened her.

Sam and Sara had never belonged to any church, though Sam had told someone, early in their life here, that they were Druids. Word had gone around that they belonged to a church not represented in town, and that information had moved them up a notch from having no religion at all. Juliet herself had gone to Sunday school for a while at the Anglican Church, though that was mostly because she had an Anglican friend. Sam, at school, had never rebelled at having to read the Bible and say the Lord's Prayer every morning, any more than he objected to "God Save the Queen."

"There's times for sticking your neck out and times not to," he had said. "You satisfy them this way, maybe you can get away with telling the kids a few facts about evolution."

Sara had at one time been interested in the Baha'i faith, but Juliet believed that this interest had waned.

She made enough tea for the three of them and found some digestive biscuits in the cupboard—also the brass tray which Sara had usually taken out for fancy occasions.

Don accepted a cup, and gulped down the ice water which she had remembered to bring him, but shook his head at the cookies.

"Not for me, thanks."

He seemed to say this with special emphasis. As if godliness forbade him.

He asked Juliet where she lived, what was the nature of the weather on the west coast, what work her husband did.

"He's a prawn fisherman, but he's actually not my husband," said Juliet pleasantly.

Don nodded. Ah, yes.

"Rough seas out there?"

"Sometimes."

"Whale Bay. I've never heard of it but now I'll remember it. What church do you go to in Whale Bay?"

"We don't go. We don't go to church."

"Is there not a church of your sort handy?"

Smiling, Juliet shook her head.

"There *is* no church of our sort. We don't believe in God."

Don's cup made a little clatter as he set it down in its saucer. He said he was sorry to hear that.

"Truly sorry to hear that. How long have you been of this opinion?"

"I don't know. Ever since I gave it any serious thought."

"And your mother's told me you have a child. You have a little girl, don't you?"

Juliet said yes, she had.

"And she has never been christened? You intend to bring her up a heathen?"

Juliet said that she expected Penelope would make up her own mind about that, someday.

"But we intend to bring her up without religion. Yes."

"That is sad," said Don quietly. "For yourselves, it's sad. You and your—whatever you call him—you've decided to reject God's grace. Well. You are adults. But to reject it for your child—it's like denying her nourishment."

Juliet felt her composure cracking. "But we don't *believe*," she said. "We don't believe in God's grace. It's not like denying her nourishment, it's refusing to bring her up on lies."

"Lies. What millions of people all over the world believe in, you call lies. Don't you think that's a little presumptuous of you, calling God a lie?"

"Millions of people don't believe it, they just go to church," said Juliet, her voice heating. "They just don't think. If there is a God, then God gave me a mind, and didn't he intend me to use it?

"Also," she said, trying to hold herself steady. "Also, millions of people believe something different. They believe in Buddha, for instance. So how does millions of people believing in anything make it true?"

"Christ is alive," said Don readily. "Buddha isn't."

"That's just something to say. What does it mean? I don't see any proof of either one being alive, as far as that goes."

"*You* don't. But others do. Do you know that Henry Ford—Henry Ford the second, who has everything anybody in life could desire—nevertheless he gets down on his knees and prays to God every night of his life?"

"Henry Ford?" cried Juliet. "Henry Ford? What does anything *Henry Ford* does matter to me?"

The argument was taking the course that arguments of this sort are bound to take. The minister's voice, which had started out more sorrowful than angry—though always indicating ironclad conviction—was taking on a shrill and scolding tone, while Juliet, who had begun, as she thought, in reasonable resistance—calm, shrewd, rather maddeningly polite—was now in a cold and biting rage. Both of them cast around for arguments and refutations that would be more insulting than useful.

Meanwhile Sara nibbled on a digestive biscuit, not looking up at them. Now and then she shivered, as if their words struck her, but they were beyond noticing.

What did bring their display to an end was the loud wailing of Penelope, who had wakened wet and had complained softly for a while, then complained more vigorously, and finally given way to fury. Sara heard her first, and tried to attract their attention.

"Penelope," she said faintly, then, with more effort, "Juliet. Penelope." Juliet and the minister both looked at her distractedly, and then the minister said, with a sudden drop in his voice, "Your baby."

Juliet hurried from the room. She was shaking when she picked Penelope up, she came close to stabbing her when she was pinning on the dry diaper. Penelope stopped crying, not because she was comforted but because she was alarmed by this rough attention. Her wide wet eyes, her astonished stare, broke into Juliet's preoccupation, and she tried to settle herself down, talking as gently as she could and then picking her child up, walking with her up and down the upstairs hall. Penelope was not immediately reassured, but after a few minutes the tension began to leave her body.

Juliet felt the same thing happening to her, and when she thought that a certain amount of control and quiet had returned to both of them, she carried Penelope downstairs.

The minister had come out of Sara's room and was waiting for her. In a voice that might have been contrite, but seemed in fact frightened, he said, "That's a nice baby."

Juliet said, "Thank you."

She thought that now they might properly say good-bye, but something was holding him. He continued to look at her, he did not move away. He put his hand out as if to catch hold of her shoulder, then dropped it.

"Do you know if you have—," he said, then shook his head slightly. The *have* had come out sounding like *hab*.

"Jooze," he said, and slapped his hand against his throat. He waved in the direction of the kitchen.

Juliet's first thought was that he must be drunk. His head was wagging slightly back and forth, his eyes seemed to be filmed over. Had he come here drunk, had he brought something in his pocket? Then she remembered. A girl, a pupil at the school where she had once taught for half a year. This girl, a diabetic, would suffer a kind of seizure, become thick-tongued, distraught, staggering, if she had gone too long without food.

Shifting Penelope to her hip, she took hold of his arm and steadied him along towards the kitchen. Juice. That was what they had given the girl, that was what he was talking about.

"Just a minute, just a minute, you'll be all right," she said. He held himself upright, hands pressed down on the counter, head lowered.

There was no orange juice—she remembered giving Penelope the last of it that morning, thinking she must get more. But there was a bottle of grape soda, which Sam and Irene liked to drink when they came in from work in the garden.

"Here," she said. Managing with one hand, as she was used to doing, she poured out a glassful. "Here." And as he drank she said, "I'm sorry there's no juice. But it's the sugar, isn't it? You have to get some sugar?"

He drank it down, he said, "Yeah. Sugar. Thanks." Already his voice was clearing. She remembered this too, about the girl at the school—how quick and apparently miraculous the recovery. But before he was quite recovered, or quite himself, while he was still holding his head at a slant, he met her eyes. Not on purpose, it seemed, just by chance. The look in his eyes was not grateful, or forgiving—it was not really personal, it was just the raw look of an astounded animal, hanging on to whatever it could find.

And within a few seconds the eyes, the face, became the face of the man, the minister, who set down his glass and without another word fled out of the house.

SARA WAS either asleep or pretending to be, when Juliet went to pick up the tea tray. Her sleeping state, her dozing state, and her waking state had now such delicate and shifting boundaries that it was hard to identify them. At any rate, she spoke, she said in little more than a whisper, "Juliet?"

Juliet paused in the doorway.

"You must think Don is—rather a simpleton," Sara said. "But he isn't well. He's a diabetic. It's serious."

Juliet said, "Yes."

"He needs his faith."

"Foxhole argument," said Juliet, but quietly, and perhaps Sara did not hear, for she went on talking.

"My faith isn't so simple," said Sara, her voice all shaky (and seeming to Juliet, at this moment, strategically pathetic). "I can't describe it. But it's—all I can say—it's *something*. It's a—wonderful—*something*. When it gets really bad for me—when it gets so bad I—you know what I think then? I think, all right. I think— Soon. *Soon I'll see Juliet.*"

Dreaded (Dearest) Eric,

Where to begin? I am fine and Penelope is fine. Considering. She walks confidently now around Sara's bed but is still leery of striking out with no support. The summer heat is amazing, compared with the west coast. Even when it rains. It's a good thing it does rain because Sam is going full-tilt at the market garden business. The other day I rode around with him in the ancient vehicle delivering fresh raspberries and raspberry jam (made by a sort of junior Ilse Koch person who inhabits our kitchen) and newly dug first potatoes of the season. He is quite gung-ho. Sara stays in bed and dozes or looks at outdated fashion magazines. A minister came to visit her and he and I got into a big stupid row about the existence of God or some such hot topic. The visit is going okay though . . .

This was a letter that Juliet found years later. Eric must have saved it by accident—it had no particular importance in their lives.

SHE HAD gone back to the house of her childhood once more, for Sara's funeral, some months after that letter was written. Irene was no longer around, and Juliet had no memory of asking or being told where she was. Most probably she had married. As Sam did again, in a couple of years. He married a fellow teacher, a good-natured, handsome, competent woman. They lived in her house—Sam tore down the house where he and Sara had lived, and extended the garden. When his wife retired, they bought a trailer and began to go on long winter trips. They visited Juliet twice at Whale Bay. Eric took them out in his boat. He and Sam got along well. As Sam said, like a house afire.

When she read the letter, Juliet winced, as anybody does on discovering the preserved and disconcerting voice of some past fabricated self. She wondered at the sprightly cover-up, contrasting with the pain of her memories. Then she thought that some shift must have taken place, at that time, which she had not remembered. Some shift concerning where home was. Not at Whale Bay with Eric but back where it had been before, all her life before.

Because it's what happens at home that you try to protect, as best you can, for as long as you can.

But she had not protected Sara. When Sara had said, *soon I'll see Juliet,* Juliet had found no reply. Could it not have been managed? Why should it have been so difficult? Just to say *Yes.* To Sara it would have meant so much—to herself, surely, so little. But she had turned away, she had carried the tray to the kitchen, and there she washed and dried the cups and also the glass that had held grape soda. She had put everything away.

Silence

ON THE short ferry ride from Buckley Bay to Denman Island, Juliet got out of her car and stood at the front of the boat, in the summer breeze. A woman standing there recognized her, and they began to talk. It is not unusual for people to take a second look at Juliet and wonder where they've seen her before, and, sometimes, to remember. She appears regularly on the Provincial Television channel, interviewing people who are leading singular or notable lives, and deftly directing panel discussions, on a program called *Issues of the Day*. Her hair is cut short now, as short as possible, and has taken on a very dark auburn color, matching the frames of her glasses. She often wears black pants—as she does today—and an ivory silk shirt, and sometimes a black jacket. She is what her mother would have called a striking-looking woman.

"Forgive me. People must be always bothering you."

"It's okay," Juliet says. "Except when I've just been to the dentist or something."

The woman is about Juliet's age. Long black hair streaked with gray, no makeup, long denim skirt. She lives on Denman, so Juliet asks her what she knows about the Spiritual Balance Centre.

"Because my daughter is there," Juliet says. "She's been on a retreat there or taking a course, I don't know what they call it. For six months. This is the first time I've got to see her, in six months."

"There are a couple of places like that," the woman says. "They sort of come and go. I don't mean there's anything suspect about them. Just that they're generally off in the woods, you know, and don't have much to do with the community. Well, what would be the point of a retreat if they did?"

She says that Juliet must be looking forward to seeing her daughter again, and Juliet says yes, very much.

"I'm spoiled," she says. "She's twenty years old, my daughter—she'll be twenty-one this month, actually—and we haven't been apart much."

The woman says that she has a son of twenty and a daughter of eighteen and another of fifteen, and there are days when she'd *pay* them to go on a retreat, singly or all together.

Juliet laughs. "Well. I've only the one. Of course, I won't guarantee that I won't be all for shipping her back, given a few weeks."

This is the kind of fond but exasperated mother-talk she finds it easy to slip into (Juliet is an expert at reassuring responses), but the truth is that Penelope has scarcely ever given her cause for complaint, and if she wanted to be totally honest, at this point she would say that one day without some contact with her daughter is hard to bear, let alone six months. Penelope has worked at Banff, as a summer chambermaid, and she has gone on bus trips to Mexico, a hitchhiking trip to Newfoundland. But she has always lived with Juliet, and there has never been a six-month break.

She gives me delight, Juliet could have said. Not that she is one of those song-and-dance purveyors of sunshine and cheer and looking-on-the-bright-side. I hope I've brought her up better than that. She has grace and compassion and she is as wise as if she'd been on this earth for eighty years. Her nature is reflective, not all over the map like mine. Somewhat reticent, like her father's. She is also angelically pretty, she's like my mother, blond like my mother but not so frail. Strong and noble. Molded, I should say, like a caryatid. And contrary to popular notions I am not even faintly jealous. All this time without her—and with no word from her, because Spiritual Balance does not allow letters or phone calls—all this time I've been in a sort of desert, and when her message came I was like an old patch of cracked earth getting a full drink of rain.

Hope to see you Sunday afternoon. It's time.

Time to go home, was what Juliet hoped this meant, but of course she would leave that up to Penelope.

PENELOPE HAD drawn a rudimentary map, and Juliet shortly found herself parked in front of an old church—that is, a church building seventy-five or eighty years old, covered with stucco, not as old or anything like as impressive as churches usually were in the part of Canada where Juliet had grown up. Behind it was a more recent building, with a slanting roof and windows all across its front, also a simple stage and some seating benches and what looked like a volleyball court with a sagging net. Everything was shabby, and the once-cleared patch of land was being reclaimed by juniper and poplars.

A couple of people—she could not tell whether men or women—were doing some carpentry work on the stage, and others sat on the benches in separate small groups. All wore ordinary clothes, not yellow robes or anything of that sort. For a few minutes no notice was taken of Juliet's car. Then one of the people on the benches rose and walked unhurriedly towards her. A short, middle-aged man wearing glasses.

She got out of the car and greeted him and asked for Penelope. He did not speak—perhaps there was a rule of silence—but nodded and turned away and went into the church. From which there shortly appeared, not Penelope, but a heavy, slow-moving woman with white hair, wearing jeans and a baggy sweater.

"What an honor to meet you," she said. "Do come inside. I've asked Donny to make us some tea."

She had a broad fresh face, a smile both roguish and tender, and what Juliet supposed must be called twinkling eyes. "My name is Joan," she said. Juliet had been expecting an assumed name like Serenity, or something with an Eastern flavor, nothing so plain and familiar as Joan. Later, of course, she thought of Pope Joan.

"I've got the right place, have I? I'm a stranger on Denman," she said disarmingly. "You know I've come to see Penelope?"

"Of course. Penelope." Joan prolonged the name, with a certain tone of celebration.

The inside of the church was darkened with purple cloth hung over the high windows. The pews and other church furnishings had been removed, and plain white curtains had been strung up to form private cubicles, as in a hospital ward. The cubicle into which Juliet was directed had, however, no bed, just a small table and a couple of plastic chairs, and some open shelves piled untidily with loose papers.

"I'm afraid we're still in the process of getting things fixed up in here," Joan said. "Juliet. May I call you Juliet?"

"Yes, of course."

"I'm not used to talking to a celebrity." Joan held her hands together in a prayer pose beneath her chin. "I don't know whether to be informal or not."

"I'm not much of a celebrity."

"Oh, you are. Now don't say things like that. And I'll just get it off my chest right away, how I admire you for the work you do. It's a beam in the darkness. The only television worth watching."

"Thank you," said Juliet. "I had a note from Penelope—"

"I know. But I'm sorry to have to tell you, Juliet, I'm very sorry and I don't want you to be too disappointed—Penelope is not here."

The woman says those words—*Penelope is not here*—as lightly as possible. You would think that Penelope's absence could be turned into a matter for amused contemplation, even for their mutual delight.

Juliet has to take a deep breath. For a moment she cannot speak. Dread pours through her. Foreknowledge. Then she pulls herself back to reasonable consideration of this fact. She fishes around in her bag.

"She said she hoped—"

"I know. I know," says Joan. "She did intend to be here, but the fact was, she could not—"

"Where is she? Where did she go?"

"I cannot tell you that."

"You mean you can't or you won't?"

"I can't. I don't know. But I can tell you one thing that may put your mind at rest. Wherever she has gone, whatever she has decided, it will be the right thing for her. It will be the *right* thing for her spirituality and her growth."

Juliet decides to let this pass. She gags on the word *spirituality,* which seems to take in—as she often says—everything from prayer wheels to High Mass. She never expected that Penelope, with her intelligence, would be mixed up in anything like this.

"I just thought I should know," she says, "in case she wanted me to send on any of her things."

"Her possessions?" Joan seems unable to suppress a wide smile, though she modifies it at once with an expression of tenderness. "Penelope is not very concerned right now about her *possessions.*"

Sometimes Juliet has felt, in the middle of an interview, that the person she faces has reserves of hostility that were not apparent before the cameras started rolling. A person whom Juliet has underestimated, whom she has thought rather stupid, may have strength of that sort. Playful but deadly hostility. The thing then is never to show that you are taken aback, never to display any hint of hostility in return.

"What I mean by growth is our inward growth, of course," Joan says.

"I understand," says Juliet, looking her in the eye.

"Penelope has had such a wonderful opportunity in her life to meet interesting people—goodness, she hasn't needed to meet interesting people, she's *grown up* with an interesting person, you're her *mother*—but you know, sometimes there's a dimension that is missing, grown-up children feel that they've *missed out* on something—"

"Oh yes," says Juliet. "I know that grown-up children can have all sorts of complaints."

Joan has decided to come down hard.

"The spiritual dimension—I have to say this—was it not altogether lacking in Penelope's life? I take it she did not grow up in a faith-based home."

"Religion was not a banned subject. We could talk about it."

"But perhaps it was the way you talked about it. Your intellectual way? If you know what I mean. You are so clever," she adds, kindly.

"So you say."

Juliet is aware that any control of the interview, and of herself, is faltering, and may be lost.

"Not so *I* say, Juliet. So *Penelope* says. Penelope is a dear fine girl, but she has come to us here in great hunger. Hunger for the things that were not available to her in her home. There you were, with your wonderful busy successful life—but Juliet, I must tell you that your daughter has known loneliness. She has known unhappiness."

"Don't most people feel that, one time or another? Loneliness and unhappiness?"

"It's not for me to say. Oh, Juliet. You are a woman of marvellous insights. I've often watched you on television and I've thought, how does she get right to the heart of things like that, and all the time being so nice and polite to people? I never thought I'd be sitting talking to you face-to-face. And what's more, that I'd be in a position to *help* you—"

"I think that maybe you're mistaken about that."

"You feel hurt. It's natural that you should feel hurt."

"It's also my own business."

"Ah well. Perhaps she'll get in touch with you. After all."

PENELOPE DID get in touch with Juliet, a couple of weeks later. A birthday card arrived on her own—Penelope's—birthday, the 19th of June. Her twenty-first birthday. It was the sort of card you send to an acquaintance whose tastes you cannot guess. Not a crude jokey card or a truly witty card or a sentimental card. On the front of it was a small bouquet of pansies tied by a thin purple ribbon whose tail spelled out the words *Happy Birthday*. These words were repeated inside, with the words *Wishing you a very* added in gold letters above them.

And there was no signature. Juliet thought at first that someone had sent this card to Penelope, and forgotten to sign it, and that she, Juliet, had opened it by mistake. Someone who had Penelope's name and the date of her birth on file. Her dentist, maybe, or her driving teacher. But when she checked the writing on the envelope she saw that there had been no mistake—there was her own name, indeed, written in Penelope's own handwriting.

Postmarks gave you no clue anymore. They all said *Canada Post.* Juliet had some idea that there were ways of telling at least which province a letter came from, but for that you would have to consult the Post Office, go there with the letter and very likely be called upon to prove your case, your right to the information. And somebody would be sure to recognize her.

SHE WENT to see her old friend Christa, who had lived in Whale Bay when she herself lived there, even before Penelope was born. Christa was in Kitsilano, in an assisted-living facility. She had multiple sclerosis. Her room was on the ground floor, with a small private patio, and Juliet sat with her there, looking out at a sunny bit of lawn, and the wisteria all in bloom along the fence that concealed the garbage bins.

Juliet told Christa the whole story of the trip to Denman Island. She had told nobody else, and had hoped perhaps not to have to tell anybody. Every day when she was on her way home from work she had wondered if perhaps Penelope would be waiting in the apartment. Or at least that there would be a letter. And then there had been—that unkind card—and she had torn it open with her hands shaking.

"It means something," Christa said. "It lets you know she's okay. Something will follow. It will. Be patient."

Juliet talked bitterly for a while about Mother Shipton. That was what she finally decided to call her, having toyed with and become dissatisfied with Pope Joan. What bloody chicanery, she said. What creepiness, nastiness, behind the second-rate, sweetly religious facade. It was impossible to imagine Penelope's having been taken in by her.

Christa suggested that perhaps Penelope had visited the place because she had considered writing something about it. Some sort of investigative journalism. Fieldwork. The personal angle—the long-winded personal stuff that was so popular nowadays.

Investigating for six months? said Juliet. Penelope could have figured out Mother Shipton in ten minutes.

"It's weird," admitted Christa.

"You don't know more than you're letting on, do you?" said Juliet. "I hate to even ask that. I feel so at sea. I feel stupid. That woman intended me to feel stupid, of course. Like the character who blurts out something in a play and everybody turns away because they all know something she doesn't know—"

"They don't do that kind of play anymore," Christa said. "Now nobody knows anything. No—Penelope didn't take me into her confidence any more than she did you. Why should she? She'd know I'd end up telling you."

Juliet was quiet for a moment, then she muttered sulkily, "There have been things you didn't tell me."

"Oh, for God's sake," said Christa, but without any animosity. "Not that again."

"Not that again," Juliet agreed. "I'm in a lousy mood, that's all."

"Just hold on. One of the trials of parenthood. She hasn't given you many, after all. In a year this will all be ancient history."

Juliet didn't tell her that in the end she had not been able to walk away with dignity. She had turned and cried out beseechingly, furiously.

"What did she tell you?"

And Mother Shipton was standing there watching her, as if she had expected this. A fat pitying smile had stretched her closed lips as she shook her head.

DURING THE next year Juliet would get phone calls, now and then, from people who had been friendly with Penelope. Her reply to their inquiries was always the same. Penelope had decided to take a year off. She was travelling. Her travelling agenda was by no means fixed, and Juliet had no way of contacting her, nor any address she could supply.

She did not hear from anybody who had been a close friend. This might mean that people who had been close to Penelope knew quite well where she was. Or it might be that they too were off on trips to foreign countries, had found jobs in other provinces, were embarked on new lives, too crowded or chancy at present to allow them to wonder about old friends.

(Old friends, at that stage in life, meaning somebody you had not seen for half a year.)

Whenever she came in, the first thing Juliet did was to look for the light flashing on her answering machine—the very thing she used to avoid, thinking there would be someone pestering her about her public utterances. She tried various silly tricks, to do with how many steps she took to the phone, how she picked it up, how she breathed. *Let it be her.*

Nothing worked. After a while the world seemed emptied of the people Penelope had known, the boyfriends she had dropped and the ones who had dropped her, the girls she had gossiped with and probably confided in. She had gone to a private girls' boarding school—Torrance House—rather than to a public high school, and this meant that most of her longtime friends—even those who were still her friends at college—had come from places out of town. Some from Alaska or Prince George or Peru.

There was no message at Christmas. But in June, another card, very much in the style of the first, not a word written inside. Juliet had a drink of wine before she opened it, then threw it away at once. She had spurts of weeping, once in a while of uncontrollable shaking, but she came out of these in quick fits of fury, walking around the house and slapping one fist into her palm. The fury was directed at Mother Shipton, but the image of that woman had faded, and finally Juliet had to recognize that she was really only a convenience.

All pictures of Penelope were banished to her bedroom, with sheaves of drawings and crayonings she had done before they left Whale Bay, her books, and the European one-cup coffeemaker with the plunger that she had bought as a present for Juliet with the first money she had made in her summer job at McDonald's. Also such whimsical gifts for the apartment as a tiny plastic fan to stick on the refrigerator, a wind-up toy tractor, a curtain of glass beads to hang in the bathroom window. The door of that bedroom was shut and in time could be passed without disturbance.

JULIET GAVE a great deal of thought to getting out of this apartment, giving herself the benefit of new surroundings. But she said to Christa that she could not do that, because that was the address Penelope had, and mail could be forwarded for only three months, so there would be no place then where her daughter could find her.

"She could always get to you at work," said Christa.

"Who knows how long I'll be there?" Juliet said. "She's probably in some commune where they're not allowed to communicate. With some guru who sleeps with all the women and sends them out to beg on the streets. If I'd sent her to Sunday school and taught her to say her prayers this probably wouldn't have happened. I should have. I should have. It would have been like an inoculation. I neglected her *spirituality*. Mother Shipton said so."

WHEN PENELOPE was barely thirteen years old, she had gone away on a camping trip to the Kootenay Mountains of British Columbia, with a friend from Torrance House, and the friend's family. Juliet was in favor of this. Penelope had been at Torrance House for only one year (accepted on favorable financial terms because of her mother's once having taught there), and it pleased Juliet that she had already made so firm a friend and been accepted readily by the friend's family. Also that she was going camping—something that regular children did and that Juliet, as a child, had never had the chance to do. Not that she would have wanted to, being already buried in books—but she welcomed signs that Penelope was turning out to be a more normal sort of girl than she herself had been.

Eric was apprehensive about the whole idea. He thought Penelope was too young. He didn't like her going on a holiday with people he knew so little about. And now that she went to boarding school they saw too little of her as it was—so why should that time be shortened?

Juliet had another reason—she simply wanted Penelope out of the way for the first couple of weeks of the summer holidays, because the air was not clear between herself and Eric. She wanted things resolved, and they were not resolved. She did not want to have to pretend that all was well, for the sake of the child.

Eric, on the other hand, would have liked nothing better than to see their trouble smoothed over, hidden out of the way. To Eric's way of thinking, civility would restore good feeling, the semblance of love would be enough to get by on until love itself might be rediscovered. And if there was never anything more than a semblance—well, that would have to do. Eric could manage with that.

Indeed he could, thought Juliet, despondently.

Having Penelope at home, a reason for them to behave well—for Juliet to behave well, since she was the one, in his opinion, who stirred up all the rancor—that would suit Eric very well.

So Juliet told him, and created a new source of bitterness and blame, because he missed Penelope badly.

The reason for their quarrel was an old and ordinary one. In the spring, through some trivial disclosure—and the frankness or possibly the malice of their longtime neighbor Ailo, who had a certain loyalty to Eric's dead wife and some reservations about Juliet—Juliet had discovered that Eric had slept with Christa. Christa had been for a long time her close friend, but she had been, before that, Eric's girlfriend, his *mistress* (though nobody said that anymore). He had given her up when he asked Juliet to live with him. She had known all about Christa then and she could not reasonably object to what had happened in the time before she and Eric were together. She did not. What she did object to—what she claimed had broken her heart—had happened after that. (But still a long time ago, said Eric.) It had happened when Penelope was a year old, and Juliet had taken her back to Ontario. When Juliet had gone home to visit her parents. To visit—as she always pointed out now—to visit her dying mother. When she was away, and loving and missing Eric with every shred of her being (she now believed this), Eric had simply returned to his old habits.

At first he confessed to once (drunk), but with further prodding, and some drinking in the here-and-now, he said that possibly it had been more often.

Possibly? He could not remember? So many times he could not remember?

He could remember.

CHRISTA CAME to see Juliet, to assure her that it had been nothing serious. (This was Eric's refrain, as well.) Juliet told her to go away and never come back. Christa decided that now would be a good time to go to see her brother in California.

Juliet's outrage at Christa was actually something of a formality. She did understand that a few rolls in the hay with an old girlfriend (Eric's disastrous description, his ill-judged attempt to minimize things) were nowhere near as threatening as a hot embrace with some woman newly met. Also, her outrage at Eric was so fierce and irrepressible as to leave little room for blame of anybody else.

Her contentions were that he did not love her, had never loved her, had mocked her, with Christa, behind her back. He had made her a laughingstock in front of people like Ailo (who had always hated her). That he had treated her with contempt, he regarded the love she felt (or had felt) for him with contempt, he had lived a lie with her. Sex meant nothing to him, or at any rate it did not mean what it meant (had meant) to her, he would have it off with whoever was handy.

Only the last of these contentions had the least germ of truth in it, and in her quieter states she knew that. But even that little truth was enough to pull everything down around her. It shouldn't do that, but it did. And Eric was not able—in all honesty he was not able—to see why that should be so. He was not surprised that she should object, make a fuss, even weep (though a woman like Christa would never have done that), but that she should really be damaged, that she should consider herself bereft of all that had sustained her—and for something that had happened *twelve years ago*—this he could not understand.

Sometimes he believed that she was shamming, making the most of it, and at other times he was full of real grief, that he had made her suffer. Their grief aroused them, and they made love magnificently. And each time he thought that would be the end of it, their miseries were over. Each time he was mistaken.

In bed, Juliet laughed and told him about Pepys and Mrs. Pepys, inflamed with passion under similar circumstances. (Since more or less giving up on her classical studies, she was reading widely, and nowadays everything she read seemed to have to do with adultery.) Never so often and never so hot, Pepys had said, though he recorded as well that his wife had also thought of murdering him in his sleep. Juliet laughed about this, but half an hour later, when he came to say good-bye before going out in the boat to check his prawn traps, she showed a stony face and gave him a kiss of resignation, as if he'd been going to meet a woman out in the middle of the bay and under a rainy sky.

THERE WAS more than rain. The water was hardly choppy when Eric went out, but later in the afternoon a wind came up suddenly, from the southeast, and tore up the waters of Desolation Sound and Malaspina Strait. It continued almost till dark—which did not really close down until around eleven o'clock in this last week of June. By then a sailboat from Campbell River was missing, with three adults and two children aboard. Also two fish boats—one with two men aboard and the other with only one man—Eric.

The next morning was calm and sunny—the mountains, the waters, the shores, all sleek and sparkling.

It was possible, of course, that none of these people were lost, that they had found shelter and spent the night in any of the multitude of little bays. That was more likely to be true of the fishermen than of the family in the sailboat, who were not local people but vacationers from Seattle. Boats went out at once, that morning, to search the mainland and island shores and the water.

The drowned children were found first, in their life jackets, and by the end of the day the bodies of their parents were located as well. A grandfather who had accompanied them was not found until the day after. The bodies of the men who had been fishing together never showed up, though the remnants of their boat washed up near Refuge Cove.

Eric's body was recovered on the third day. Juliet was not allowed to see it. Something had got at him, it was said (meaning some animal), after the body was washed ashore.

It was perhaps because of this—because there was no question of viewing the body and no need for an undertaker—that the idea caught hold amongst Eric's old friends and fellow fishermen of burning Eric on the beach. Juliet did not object to this. A death certificate had to be made out, so the doctor who came to Whale Bay once a week was telephoned at his office in Powell River, and he gave Ailo, who was his weekly assistant and a registered nurse, the authority to do this.

There was plenty of driftwood around, plenty of the sea-salted bark which makes a superior fire. In a couple of hours all was ready. News had spread—

somehow, even at such short notice, women began arriving with food. It was Ailo who took charge—her Scandinavian blood, her upright carriage and flowing white hair, seeming to fit her naturally for the role of Widow of the Sea. Children ran about on the logs, and were shooed away from the growing pyre, the shrouded, surprisingly meager bundle that was Eric. A coffee urn was supplied to this half-pagan ceremony by the women from one of the churches, and cartons of beer, bottles of drink of all sorts, were left discreetly, for the time being, in the trunks of cars and cabs of trucks.

The question arose of who would speak, and who would light the pyre. They asked Juliet, would she do it? And Juliet—brittle and busy, handing out mugs of coffee—said that they had it wrong, as the widow she was supposed to throw herself into the flames. She actually laughed as she said this, and those who had asked her backed off, afraid that she was getting hysterical. The man who had partnered Eric most often in the boat agreed to do the lighting, but said he was no speaker. It occurred to some that he would not have been a good choice anyway, since his wife was an Evangelical Anglican, and he might have felt obliged to say things which would have distressed Eric if he had been able to hear them. Then Ailo's husband offered—he was a little man disfigured by a fire on a boat, years ago, a grumbling socialist and atheist, and in his talk he rather lost track of Eric, except to claim him as a Brother in the Battle. He went on at surprising length, and this was ascribed, afterwards, to the suppressed life he led under the rule of Ailo. There might have been some restlessness in the crowd before his recital of grievances got stopped, some feeling that the event was turning out to be not so splendid, or solemn, or heart-rending, as might have been expected. But when the fire began to burn this feeling vanished, and there was great concentration, even, or especially, among the children, until the moment when one of the men cried, "Get the kids out of here." This was when the flames had reached the body, bringing the realization, coming rather late, that consumption of fat, of heart and kidneys and liver, might produce explosive or sizzling noises disconcerting to hear. So a good many of the children were hauled away by their mothers—some willingly, some to their own dismay. So the final act of the fire became a mostly male ceremony, and slightly scandalous, even if not, in this case, illegal.

Juliet stayed, wide-eyed, rocking on her haunches, face pressed against the heat. She was not quite there. She thought of whoever it was—Trelawny?—snatching Shelley's heart out of the flames. The heart, with its long history of significance. Strange to think how even at that time, not so long ago, one fleshly organ should be thought so precious, the site of courage and love. It was just flesh, burning. Nothing connected with Eric.

*

PENELOPE KNEW nothing of what was going on. There was a short item in the Vancouver paper—not about the burning on the beach, of course, just about the drowning—but no newspapers or radio reports reached her, deep in the Kootenay Mountains. When she got back to Vancouver she phoned home, from her friend Heather's house. Christa answered—she had got back too late for the ceremony, but was staying with Juliet, and helping as she could. Christa said that Juliet was not there—it was a lie—and asked to speak to Heather's mother. She explained what had happened, and said that she was driving Juliet to Vancouver, they would leave at once, and Juliet would tell Penelope herself when they got there.

Christa dropped Juliet at the house where Penelope was, and Juliet went inside alone. Heather's mother left her in the sunroom, where Penelope was waiting. Penelope received the news with an expression of fright, then—when Juliet rather formally put her arms around her—of something like embarrassment. Perhaps in Heather's house, in the white and green and orange sunroom, with Heather's brothers shooting baskets in the backyard, news so dire could hardly penetrate. The burning was not mentioned—in this house and neighborhood it would surely have seemed uncivilized, grotesque. In this house, also, Juliet's manner was sprightly beyond anything intended—her behavior close to that of *a good sport*.

Heather's mother entered after a tiny knock—with glasses of iced tea. Penelope gulped hers down and went to join Heather, who had been lurking in the hall.

Heather's mother then had a talk with Juliet. She apologized for intruding with practical matters but said that time was short. She and Heather's father were driving east in a few days' time to see relatives. They would be gone for a month, and had planned to take Heather with them. (The boys were going to camp.) But now Heather had decided she did not want to go, she had begged to stay here in the house, with Penelope. A fourteen-year-old and a thirteen-year-old could not really be left alone, and it had occurred to her that Juliet might like some time away, a respite, after what she had been through. After her loss and tragedy.

So Juliet shortly found herself living in a different world, in a large spotless house brightly and thoughtfully decorated, with what are called conveniences—but to her were luxuries—on every hand. This on a curving street lined with similar houses, behind trimmed bushes and showy flower beds. Even the weather, for that month, was flawless—warm, breezy, bright. Heather and Penelope went swimming, played badminton in the backyard, went to the movies, baked cookies, gorged, dieted, worked on their tans, filled the house with music whose lyrics seemed to Juliet sappy and irritating, sometimes invited girlfriends over, did not exactly invite boys but held long, taunting, aimless conversations with some who passed the house or had collected next door. By chance, Juliet heard Penelope say to one of the visiting girls, "Well, I hardly knew him, really."

She was speaking about her father.

How strange.

She had never been afraid to go out in the boat, as Juliet was, when there was a chop on the water. She had pestered him to be taken and was often successful. When following after Eric, in her businesslike orange life jacket, carrying what gear she could manage, she always wore an expression of particular seriousness and dedication. She took note of the setting of the traps and became skilful, quick, and ruthless at the deheading and bagging of the catch. At a certain stage of her childhood— say from eight to eleven—she had always said that she was going to go out fishing when she grew up, and Eric had told her there were girls doing that nowadays. Juliet had thought it was possible, since Penelope was bright but not bookish, and exuberantly physical, and brave. But Eric, out of Penelope's hearing, said that he hoped the idea would wear off, he wouldn't wish the life on anybody. He always spoke this way, about the hardship and uncertainty of the work he had chosen, but took pride, so Juliet thought, in those very things.

And now he was dismissed. By Penelope, who had recently painted her toenails purple and was sporting a false tattoo on her midriff. He who had filled her life. She dismissed him.

But Juliet felt as if she was doing the same. Of course, she was busy looking for a job and a place to live. She had already put the house in Whale Bay up for sale—she could not imagine remaining there. She had sold the truck and given away Eric's tools, and such traps as had been recovered, and the dinghy. Eric's grown son from Saskatchewan had come and taken the dog.

She had applied for a job in the reference department of the college library, and a job in the public library, and she had a feeling she would get one or the other. She looked at apartments in the Kitsilano or Dunbar or Point Grey areas. The cleanness, tidiness, and manageability of city life kept surprising her. This was how people lived where the man's work did not take place out of doors, and where various operations connected with it did not end up indoors. And where the weather might be a factor in your mood but never in your life, where such dire matters as the changing habits and availability of prawns and salmon were merely interesting, or not remarked upon at all. The life she had been leading at Whale Bay, such a short time ago, seemed haphazard, cluttered, exhausting, by comparison. And she herself was cleansed of the moods of the last months—she was brisk and competent, and better-looking.

Eric should see her now.

She thought about Eric in this way all the time. It was not that she failed to realize that Eric was dead—that did not happen for a moment. But nevertheless she kept constantly referring to him, in her mind, as if he was still the person to whom her existence mattered more than it could to anyone else. As if he was still the person in whose eyes she hoped to shine. Also the person to whom she presented arguments, information, surprises. This was such a habit with her, and took place so automatically, that the fact of his death did not seem to interfere with it.

Nor was their last quarrel entirely resolved. She held him to account, still, for his betrayal. When she flaunted herself a little now, it was against that.

The storm, the recovery of the body, the burning on the beach—that was all like a pageant she had been compelled to watch and compelled to believe in, which still had nothing to do with Eric and herself.

She got the job in the reference library, she found a two-bedroom apartment that she could just afford, Penelope went back to Torrance House as a day student. Their affairs at Whale Bay were wound up, their life there finished. Even Christa was moving out, coming to Vancouver in the spring.

On a day before that, a day in February, Juliet stood in the shelter at the campus bus stop when her afternoon's work was over. The day's rain had stopped, there was a band of clear sky in the west, red where the sun had gone down, out over the Strait of Georgia. This sign of the lengthening days, the promise of the change of season, had an effect on her that was unexpected and crushing.

She realized that Eric was dead.

As if all this time, while she was in Vancouver, he had been waiting somewhere, waiting to see if she would resume her life with him. As if being with him was an option that had stayed open. Her life since she came here had still been lived against a backdrop of Eric, without her ever quite understanding that Eric did not exist. Nothing of him existed. The memory of him in the daily and ordinary world was in retreat.

So this is grief. She feels as if a sack of cement has been poured into her and quickly hardened. She can barely move. Getting onto the bus, getting off the bus, walking half a block to her building (why is she living here?), is like climbing a cliff. And now she must hide this from Penelope.

At the supper table she began to shake, but could not loosen her fingers to drop the knife and fork. Penelope came around the table and pried her hands open. She said, "It's Dad, isn't it?"

Juliet afterwards told a few people—such as Christa—that these seemed the most utterly absolving, the most tender words, that anybody had ever said to her.

Penelope ran her cool hands up and down the insides of Juliet's arms. She phoned the library the next day to say that her mother was sick, and she took care of her for a couple of days, staying home from school until Juliet recovered. Or until, at least, the worst was over.

During those days Juliet told Penelope everything. Christa, the fight, the burning on the beach (which she had so far managed, almost miraculously, to conceal from her). Everything.

"I shouldn't burden you with all this."

Penelope said, "Yeah, well, maybe not." But added staunchly, "I forgive you. I guess I'm not a baby."

Juliet went back into the world. The sort of fit she had had in the bus stop recurred, but never so powerfully.

Through her research work in the library, she met some people from the Provincial Television channel, and took a job they offered. She had worked there for about a year when she began to do interviews. All the indiscriminate reading she'd done for years (and that Ailo had so disapproved of, in the days at Whale Bay), all the bits and pieces of information she'd picked up, her random appetite and quick assimilation, were now to come in handy. And she cultivated a self-deprecating, faintly teasing manner that usually seemed to go over well. On camera, few things fazed her. Though in fact she would go home and march back and forth, letting out whimpers or curses as she recalled some perceived glitch or fluster or, worse still, a mispronunciation.

AFTER FIVE years the birthday cards stopped coming.

"It doesn't mean anything," Christa said. "All they were for was to tell you she's alive somewhere. Now she figures you've got the message. She trusts you not to send some tracker after her. That's all."

"Did I put too much on her?"

"Oh, Jul."

"I don't mean just with Eric dying. Other men, later. I let her see too much misery. My stupid misery."

For Juliet had had two affairs during the years that Penelope was between fourteen and twenty-one, and during both of these she had managed to fall hectically in love, though she was ashamed afterwards. One of the men was much older than she, and solidly married. The other was a good deal younger, and was alarmed by her ready emotions. Later she wondered at these herself. She really had cared nothing for him, she said.

"I wouldn't think you did," said Christa, who was tired. "I don't know."

"Oh Christ. I was such a fool. I don't get like that about men anymore. Do I?"

Christa did not mention that this might be because of a lack of candidates.

"No, Jul. No."

"Actually I didn't do anything so terrible," Juliet said then, brightening up. "Why do I keep lamenting that it's my fault? She's a conundrum, that's all. I need to face that.

"A conundrum and a cold fish," she said, in a parody of resolution.

"No," said Christa.

"No," said Juliet. "No—that's not true."

After the second June had passed without any word, Juliet decided to move. For the first five years, she told Christa, she had waited for June, wondering what might come. The way things were now, she had to wonder every day. And be disappointed every day.

She moved to a high-rise building in the West End. She meant to throw away the contents of Penelope's room, but in the end she stuffed it all into garbage bags and carried it with her. She had only one bedroom now but there was storage space in the basement.

She took up jogging in Stanley Park. Now she seldom mentioned Penelope, even to Christa. She had a boyfriend—that was what you called them now—who had never heard anything about her daughter.

Christa grew thinner and moodier. Quite suddenly, one January, she died.

YOU DON'T go on forever, appearing on television. However agreeable the viewers have found your face, there comes a time when they'd prefer somebody different. Juliet was offered other jobs—researching, writing voice-over for nature shows—but she refused them cheerfully, describing herself as in need of a total change. She went back to Classical Studies—an even smaller department than it used to be—she meant to resume writing her thesis for her Ph.D. She moved out of the high-rise apartment and into a bachelor flat, to save money.

Her boyfriend had got a teaching job in China.

Her flat was in the basement of a house, but the sliding doors at the back opened out at ground level. And there she had a little brick-paved patio, a trellis with sweet peas and clematis, herbs and flowers in pots. For the first time in her life, and in a very small way, she was a gardener, as her father had been.

Sometimes people said to her—in stores, or on the campus bus— "Excuse me, but your face is so familiar," or, "Aren't you the lady that used to be on television?" But after a year or so this passed. She spent a lot of time sitting and reading, drinking coffee at sidewalk tables, and nobody noticed her. She let her hair grow out. During the years that it had been dyed red it had lost the vigor of its natural brown—it was a silvery brown now, fine and wavy. She was reminded of her mother, Sara. Sara's soft, fair, flyaway hair, going gray and then white.

She did not have room to have people to dinner anymore, and she had lost interest in recipes. She ate meals that were nourishing enough, but monotonous. Without exactly meaning to, she lost contact with most of her friends.

It was no wonder. She lived now a life as different as possible from the life of the public, vivacious, concerned, endlessly well-informed woman that she had been. She lived amongst books, reading through most of her waking hours and being compelled to deepen, to alter, whatever premise she had started with. She often missed the world news for a week at a time.

She had given up on her thesis and become interested in some writers referred to as the Greek novelists, whose work came rather late in the history of Greek literature (starting in the first century B.C.E., as she had now learned to call it, and continuing into the early Middle Ages). Aristeides, Longus, Heliodorus, Achilles Tatius. Much of their work is lost or fragmentary and is also reported to be indecent. But there is a romance written by Heliodorus, and called the *Aethiopica* (originally in a private library, retrieved at the siege of Buda), that has been known in Europe since it was printed at Basle in 1534.

In this story the queen of Ethiopia gives birth to a white baby, and is afraid she will be accused of adultery. So she gives the child—a daughter —into the care of the gymnosophists—that is, the naked philosophers, who are hermits and mystics. The girl, who is called Charicleia, is finally taken to Delphi, where she becomes one of the priestesses of Artemis. There she meets a noble Thessalian named Theagenes, who falls in love with her and, with the help of a clever Egyptian, carries her off. The Ethiopian queen, as it turns out, has never ceased to long for her daughter and has hired this very Egyptian to search for her. Mischance and adventures continue until all the main characters meet at Meroe, and Charicleia is rescued—again—just as she is about to be sacrificed by her own father.

Interesting themes were thick as flies here, and the tale had a natural continuing fascination for Juliet. Particularly the part about the gymnosophists. She tried to find out as much as she could about these people, who were usually referred to as Hindu philosophers. Was India, in this case, presumed to be adjacent to Ethiopia? No—Heliodorus came late enough to know his geography better than that. The gymnosophists would be wanderers, far spread, attracting and repelling those they lived amongst with their ironclad devotion to purity of life and thought, their contempt for possessions, even for clothing and food. A beautiful maiden reared amongst them might well be left with some perverse hankering for a bare, ecstatic life.

Juliet had made a new friend named Larry. He taught Greek, and he had let Juliet store the garbage bags in the basement of his house. He liked to imagine how they might make the *Aethiopica* into a musical. Juliet collaborated in this fantasy, even to making up the marvellously silly songs and the preposterous stage effects. But she was secretly drawn to devising a different ending, one that would involve renunciation, and a backward search, in which the girl would be sure to meet fakes and charlatans, impostors, shabby imitations of what she was really looking for. Which was reconciliation, at last, with the erring, repentant, essentially great-hearted queen of Ethiopia.

JULIET WAS almost certain that she had seen Mother Shipton here in Vancouver. She had taken some clothes that she would never wear again (her wardrobe had grown increasingly utilitarian) to a Salvation Army Thrift Store, and as she set the bag down in the receiving room she saw a fat old woman in a muumuu fixing tags onto trousers. The woman was chatting with the other workers. She had the air of a supervisor, a cheerful but vigilant overseer—or perhaps the air of a woman who would assume that role whether she had any official superiority or not.

If she was in fact Mother Shipton, she had come down in the world. But not by very much. For if she was Mother Shipton, would she not have reserves of buoyancy and self-approbation, such as to make real downfall impossible?

Reserves of advice, pernicious advice, as well.

She has come to us here in great hunger.

JULIET HAD told Larry about Penelope. She had to have one person who knew. "Should I have talked to her about a noble life?" she said. "Sacrifice? Opening your life to the needs of strangers? I never thought of it. I must have acted as if it would have been good enough if she turned out like me. Would that sicken her?"

*

LARRY WAS not a man who wanted anything from Juliet but her friendship and good humor. He was what used to be called an old-fashioned bachelor, asexual as far as she could tell (but probably she could not tell far enough), squeamish about any personal revelations, endlessly entertaining.

Two other men had appeared who wanted her as a partner. One of them she had met when he sat down at her sidewalk table. He was a recent widower. She liked him, but his loneliness was so raw and his pursuit of her so desperate that she became alarmed.

The other man was Christa's brother, whom she had met several times during Christa's life. His company suited her—in many ways he was like Christa. His marriage had ended long ago, he was not desperate—she knew, from Christa, that there had been women ready to marry him whom he had avoided. But he was too rational, his choice of her verged on being cold-blooded, there was something humiliating about it.

But why humiliating? It was not as if she loved him.

It was while she was still seeing Christa's brother—his name was Gary Lamb—that she ran into Heather, on a downtown street in Vancouver. Juliet and Gary had just come out of a theater where they had seen an early-evening movie, and they were talking about where to go for dinner. It was a warm night in summer, the light still not gone from the sky.

A woman detached herself from a group on the sidewalk. She came straight at Juliet. A thin woman, perhaps in her late thirties. Fashionable, with taffy streaks in her dark hair.

"Mrs. Porteous. Mrs. Porteous."

Juliet knew the voice, though she would never have known the face. Heather.

"This is incredible," Heather said. "I'm here for three days and I'm leaving tomorrow. My husband's at a conference. I was thinking that I don't know anybody here anymore and then I turn around and see you."

Juliet asked her where she was living now and she said Connecticut.

"And just about three weeks ago I was visiting Josh—you remember my brother Josh?—I was visiting my brother Josh and his family in Edmonton and I ran into Penelope. Just like this, on the street. No—actually it was in the mall, that humongous mall they have. She had a couple of her kids with her, she'd brought them down to get uniforms for that school they go to. The boys. We were both flabbergasted. I didn't know her right away but she recognized me. She'd flown down, of course. From that place way up north. But she says it's quite civilized, really. And she said you were still living here. But I'm with these people—they're my husband's friends—and I really haven't had time to ring you up—"

Juliet made some gesture to say that of course there would not be time and she had not expected to be rung up.

She asked how many children Heather had.

"Three. They're all monsters. I hope they grow up in a hurry. But my life's a picnic compared with Penelope's. *Five.*"

"Yes."

"I have to run now, we're going to see a movie. I don't even know anything about it, I don't even like French movies. But it was altogether great meeting you like this. My mother and dad moved to White Rock. They used to see you all the time on TV. They used to brag to their friends that you'd lived in our house. They say you're not on anymore, did you get sick of it?"

"Something like that."

"I'm coming, I'm coming." She hugged and kissed Juliet, the way everybody did now, and ran to join her companions.

So. PENELOPE did not live in Edmonton—she had *come down* to Edmonton. Flown down. That meant she must live in Whitehorse or in Yellowknife. Where else was there that she could describe as *quite civilized*? Maybe she was being ironical, mocking Heather a bit, when she said that.

She had five children and two at least were boys. They were being outfitted with school uniforms. That meant a private school. That meant money.

Heather had not known her at first. Did that mean she had aged? That she was out of shape after five pregnancies, that she had not *taken care of herself*? As Heather had. As Juliet had, to a certain extent. That she was one of those women to whom the whole idea of such a struggle seemed ridiculous, a confession of insecurity? Or just something she had no time for—far outside of her consideration.

Juliet had thought of Penelope being involved with transcendentalists, of her having become a mystic, spending her life in contemplation. Or else—rather the opposite but still radically simple and spartan—earning her living in a rough and risky way, fishing, perhaps with a husband, perhaps also with some husky little children, in the cold waters of the Inside Passage off the British Columbia coast.

Not at all. She was living the life of a prosperous, practical matron. Married to a doctor, maybe, or to one of those civil servants managing the northern parts of the country during the time when their control is being gradually, cautiously, but with some fanfare, relinquished to the native people. If she ever met Penelope again they might laugh about how wrong

Juliet had been. When they told about their separate meetings with Heather, how weird that was, they would laugh.

No. No. The fact was surely that she had already laughed too much around Penelope. Too many things had been jokes. Just as too many things—personal things, loves that were maybe just gratification—had been tragedies. She had been lacking in motherly inhibitions and propriety and self-control.

Penelope had said that she, Juliet, was still living in Vancouver. She had not told Heather anything about the breach. Surely not. If she had been told, Heather would not have spoken so easily.

How did Penelope know that she was still here, unless she checked in the phone directory? And if she did, what did that mean?

Nothing. Don't make it mean anything.

She walked to the curb to join Gary, who had tactfully moved away from the scene of the reunion.

Whitehorse, Yellowknife. It was painful indeed to know the names of those places—places she could fly to. Places where she could loiter in the streets, devise plans for catching glimpses.

But she was not so mad. She must not be so mad.

At dinner, she thought that the news she had just absorbed put her into a better situation for marrying Gary, or living with him—whatever it was he wanted. There was nothing to worry about, or hold herself in wait for, concerning Penelope. Penelope was not a phantom, she was safe, as far as anybody is safe, and she was probably as happy as anybody is happy. She had detached herself from Juliet and very likely from the memory of Juliet, and Juliet could not do better than to detach herself in turn.

But she had told Heather that Juliet was living in Vancouver. Did she say *Juliet*? Or *Mother. My mother.*

Juliet told Gary that Heather was the child of old friends. She had never spoken to him about Penelope, and he had never given any sign of knowing about Penelope's existence. It was possible that Christa had told him, and he had remained silent out of a consideration that it was none of his business. Or that Christa had told him, and he had forgotten. Or that Christa had never mentioned anything about Penelope, not even her name.

If Juliet lived with him the fact of Penelope would never surface, Penelope would not exist.

Nor did Penelope exist. The Penelope Juliet sought was gone. The woman Heather had spotted in Edmonton, the mother who had brought her sons to Edmonton to get their school uniforms, who had changed in face and body so that Heather did not recognize her, was nobody Juliet knew.

Does Juliet believe this?

If Gary saw that she was agitated he pretended not to notice. But it was probably on this evening that they both understood they would never be together. If it had been possible for them to be together she might have said to him, *My daughter went away without telling me good-bye and in fact she probably did not know then that she was going. She did not know it was for good. Then gradually, I believe, it dawned on her how much she wanted to stay away. It is just a way that she has found to manage her life.*

It's maybe the explaining to me that she can't face. Or has not time for, really. You know, we always have the idea that there is this reason or that reason and we keep trying to find out reasons. And I could tell you plenty about what I've done wrong. But I think the reason may be something not so easily dug out. Something like purity in her nature. Yes. Some fineness and strictness and purity, some rock-hard honesty in her. My father used to say of someone he disliked, that he had no use for that person. Couldn't those words mean simply what they say? Penelope does not have a use for me.

Maybe she can't stand me. It's possible.

JULIET HAS friends. Not so many now—but friends. Larry continues to visit, and to make jokes. She keeps on with her studies. The word *studies* does not seem to describe very well what she does—*investigations* would be better.

And being short of money, she works some hours a week at the coffee place where she used to spend so much time at the sidewalk tables. She finds this work a good balance for her involvement with the old Greeks— so much so that she believes she wouldn't quit even if she could afford to.

She keeps on hoping for a word from Penelope, but not in any strenuous way. She hopes as people who know better hope for undeserved blessings, spontaneous remissions, things of that sort.

The View from Castle Rock

The View from Castle Rock

THE FIRST time Andrew was ever in Edinburgh he was ten years old. With his father and some other men he climbed a slippery black street. It was raining, the city smell of smoke filled the air, and the half-doors were open, showing the firelit insides of taverns which he hoped they might enter, because he was wet through. They did not, they were bound somewhere else. Earlier on the same afternoon they had been in some such place, but it was not much more than an alcove, a hole in the wall, with planks on which bottles and glasses were set and coins laid down. He had been continually getting squeezed out of that shelter into the street and into the puddle that caught the drip from the ledge over the entryway. To keep that from happening, he had butted in low down between the cloaks and sheepskins, wedged himself amongst the drinking men and under their arms.

He was surprised at the number of people his father seemed to know in the city of Edinburgh. You would think the people in the drinking place would be strangers to him, but it was evidently not so. Amongst the arguing and excited queer-sounding voices his father's voice rose the loudest. *America*, he said, and slapped his hand on the plank for attention, the very way he would do at home. Andrew had heard that word spoken in that same tone long before he knew it was a land across the ocean. It was spoken as a challenge and an irrefutable truth but sometimes—when his father was not there—it was spoken as a taunt or a joke. His older brothers might ask each other, "Are ye awa to America?" when one of them put on his plaid to go out and do some chore such as penning the sheep. Or, "Why don't ye be off to America?" when they had got into an argument, and one of them wanted to make the other out to be a fool.

The cadences of his father's voice, in the talk that succeeded that word, were so familiar, and Andrew's eyes so bleary with the smoke, that in no time he had fallen asleep on his feet. He wakened when several pushed together out of the place and his father with them. Some one of them said, "Is this your lad here or is it some tinker squeezed in to pick our pockets?" and his father laughed and took Andrew's hand and they began their climb. One man stumbled and another man knocked into him and swore. A couple of women swiped their baskets at the party with great scorn, and made some remarks in their unfamiliar speech, of which Andrew could only make out the words "daecent bodies" and "public footpaths."

Then his father and the friends stepped aside into a much broader street, which in fact was a courtyard, paved with large blocks of stone. His father turned and paid attention to Andrew at this point.

"Do you know where you are, lad? You're in the castle yard, and this is Edinburgh Castle that has stood for ten thousand years and will stand for ten thousand more. Terrible deeds were done here. These stones have run with blood. Do you know that?" He raised his head so that they all listened to what he was telling.

"It was King Jamie asked the young Douglases to have supper with him and when they were fair sitten down he says, oh, we won't bother with their supper, take them out in the yard and chop off their heads. And so they did. Here in the yard where we stand.

"But that King Jamie died a leper," he went on with a sigh, then a groan, making them all be still to consider this fate.

Then he shook his head.

"Ah, no, it wasn't him. It was King Robert the Bruce that died a leper. He died a king but he died a leper."

Andrew could see nothing but enormous stone walls, barred gates, a redcoat soldier marching up and down. His father did not give him much time, anyway, but shoved him ahead and through an archway, saying, "Watch your heads here, lads, they was wee little men in those days. Wee little men. So is Boney the Frenchman, there's a lot of fight in your wee little men."

They were climbing uneven stone steps, some as high as Andrew's knees—he had to crawl occasionally—inside what as far as he could make out was a roofless tower. His father called out, "Are ye all with me then, are ye all in for the climb?" and some straggling voices answered him. Andrew got the impression that there was not such a crowd following as there had been on the street.

They climbed far up in the roundabout stairway and at last came out on a bare rock, a shelf, from which the land fell steeply away. The rain had ceased for the present.

"Ah, there," said Andrew's father. "Now where's all the ones was tramping on our heels to get here?"

One of the men just reaching the top step said, "There's two-three of them took off to have a look at the Meg."

"Engines of war," said Andrew's father. "All they have eyes for is engines of war. Take care they don't go and blow themselves up."

"Haven't the heart for the stairs, more like," said another man who was panting. And the first one said cheerfully, "Scairt to get all the way up here, scairt they're bound to fall off."

A third man—and that was the lot—came staggering across the shelf as if he had in mind to do that very thing.

"Where is it then?" he hollered. "Are we up on Arthur's seat?"

"Ye are not," said Andrew's father. "Look beyond you."

The sun was out now, shining on the stone heap of houses and streets below them, and the churches whose spires did not reach to this height, and some little trees and fields, then a wide silvery stretch of water. And beyond that a pale green and grayish-blue land, part in sunlight and part in shadow, a land as light as mist, sucked into the sky.

"So did I not tell you?" Andrew's father said. "America. It is only a little bit of it, though, only the shore. There is where every man is sitting in the midst of his own properties, and even the beggars is riding around in carriages."

"Well the sea does not look so wide as I thought," said the man who had stopped staggering. "It does not look as if it would take you weeks to cross it."

"It is the effect of the height we're on," said the man who stood beside Andrew's father. "The height we're on is making the width of it the less."

"It's a fortunate day for the view," said Andrew's father. "Many a day you could climb up here and see nothing but the fog."

He turned and addressed Andrew.

"So there you are my lad and you have looked over at America," he said. "God grant you one day you will see it closer up and for yourself."

ANDREW HAS been to the Castle one time since, with a group of the lads from Ettrick, who all wanted to see the great cannon, Mons Meg. But nothing seemed to be in the same place then and he could not find the route they had taken to climb up to the rock. He saw a couple of places blocked off with boards that could have been it. But he did not even try to peer through them—he had no wish to tell the others what he was looking for. Even when he was ten years old he had known that the men with his father were drunk. If he did not understand that his father was drunk—due to his father's sure-footedness and sense of purpose, his commanding behavior—he did certainly understand that something was not as it should be. He knew he was not looking at America, though it was some years before he was well enough acquainted with maps to know that he had been looking at Fife.

Still, he did not know if those men met in the tavern had been mocking his father, or if it was his father playing one of his tricks on them.

OLD JAMES the father. Andrew. Walter. Their sister Mary. Andrew's wife Agnes, and Agnes and Andrew's son James, under two years old.

In the harbor of Leith, on the 4th of June, 1818, they set foot on board a ship for the first time in their lives.

Old James makes this fact known to the ship's officer who is checking off the names.

"The first time, serra, in all my long life. We are men of the Ettrick. It is a landlocked part of the world."

The officer says a word which is unintelligible to them but plain in meaning. Move along. He has run a line through their names. They move along or are pushed along, Young James riding on Mary's hip.

"What is this?" says Old James, regarding the crowd of people on deck. "Where are we to sleep? Where have all these rabble come from? Look at the faces on them, are they the blackamoors?"

"Black Highlanders, more like," says his son Walter. This is a joke, muttered so his father cannot hear—Highlanders being one of the sorts the old man despises.

"There are too many people," his father continues. "The ship will sink."

"No," says Walter, speaking up now. "Ships do not often sink because of too many people. That's what the fellow was there for, to count the people."

Barely on board the vessel and this seventeen-year-old whelp has taken on knowing airs, he has taken to contradicting his father. Fatigue, astonishment, and the weight of the greatcoat he is wearing prevent Old James from cuffing him.

All the business of life aboard ship has already been explained to the family. In fact it has been explained by the old man himself. He was the one who knew all about provisions, accommodations, and the kind of people you would find on board. All Scotsmen and all decent folk. No Highlanders, no Irish.

But now he cries out that it is like the swarm of bees in the carcass of the lion.

"An evil lot, an evil lot. Oh, that ever we left our native land!"

"We have not left yet," says Andrew. "We are still looking at Leith. We would do best to go below and find ourselves a place."

More lamentation. The bunks are narrow, bare planks with horsehair pallets both hard and prickly.

"Better than nothing," says Andrew.

"Oh, that it was ever put in my head to bring us here, onto this floating sepulchre."

Will nobody shut him up? thinks Agnes. This is the way he will go on and on, like a preacher or a lunatic, when the fit takes him. She cannot abide it. She is in more agony herself than he is ever likely to know.

"Well, are we going to settle here or are we not?" she says.

Some people have hung up their plaids or shawls to make a half-private space for their families. She goes ahead and takes off her outer wrappings to do the same.

The child is turning somersaults in her belly. Her face is hot as a coal and her legs throb and the swollen flesh in between them—the lips the child must soon part to get out—is a scalding sack of pain. Her mother would have known what to do about that, she would have known which leaves to mash to make a soothing poultice.

At the thought of her mother such misery overcomes her that she wants to kick somebody.

Andrew folds up his plaid to make a comfortable seat for his father. The old man seats himself, groaning, and puts his hands up to his face, so that his speaking has a hollow sound.

"I will see no more. I will not harken to their screeching voices or their satanic tongues. I will not swallow a mouth of meat nor meal until I see the shores of America."

All the more for the rest of us, Agnes feels like saying.

Why does Andrew not speak plainly to his father, reminding him of whose idea it was, who was the one who harangued and borrowed and begged to get them just where they are now? Andrew will not do it, Walter will only joke, and as for Mary she can hardly get her voice out of her throat in her father's presence.

Agnes comes from a large Hawick family of weavers, who work in the mills now but worked for generations at home. And working there they learned all the arts of cutting each other down to size, of squabbling and surviving in close quarters. She is still surprised by the rigid manners, the deference and silences in her husband's family. She thought from the beginning that they were a queer sort of people and she thinks so still.

They are as poor as her own folk, but they have such a great notion of themselves. And what have they got to back this up? The old man has been a wonder in the tavern for years, and their cousin is a raggedy lying poet who had to flit to Nithsdale when nobody would trust him to tend sheep in Ettrick. They were all brought up by three witchey-women of aunts who were so scared of men that they would run and hide in the sheep pen if anybody but their own family was coming along the road.

As if it wasn't the men that should be running from them.

Walter has come back from carrying their heavier possessions down to a lower depth of the ship.

"You never saw such a mountain of boxes and trunks and sacks of meal and potatoes," he says excitedly. "A person has to climb over them to get to the water pipe. Nobody can help but spill their water on the way back and the sacks will be wet through and the stuff will be rotted."

"They should not have brought all that," says Andrew. "Did they not undertake to feed us when we paid our way?"

"Aye," says the old man. "But will it be fit for us to eat?"

"So a good thing I brought my cakes," says Walter, who is still in the mood to make a joke of anything. He taps his foot on the snug metal box filled with oat cakes that his aunts gave him as a particular present because he was the youngest and they still thought of him as the motherless one.

"You'll see how merry you'll be if we're starving," says Agnes. Walter is a pest to her, almost as much as the old man. She knows there is probably no chance of them starving, because Andrew is looking impatient, but not anxious. It takes a good deal, of course, to make Andrew anxious. He is apparently not anxious about her, since he thought first to make a comfortable seat for his father.

MARY HAS taken Young James back up to the deck. She could tell that he was alarmed down there in the half-dark. He does not have to whimper or complain—she knows his feelings by the way he digs his little knees into her.

The sails are furled tight. "Look up there, look up there," Mary says, and points to a sailor who is busy high up in the rigging. The boy on her hip makes his sound for bird. "Sailor-peep, sailor-peep," she says. She says the right word for *sailor* but his word for *bird*. She and he communicate in a half-and-half language—half her teaching and half his invention. She believes that he is one of the cleverest children ever born into the world. Being the eldest of her family, and the only girl, she has tended all of her brothers, and been proud of them all at one time, but she has never known a child like this. Nobody else has any idea of how original and independent and clever he is. Men have no interest in children so young, and Agnes his mother has no patience with him.

"Talk like folk," Agnes says to him, and if he doesn't, she may give him a clout. "What are you?" she says. "Are you a folk or an elfit?"

Mary fears Agnes's temper, but in a way she doesn't blame her. She thinks that women like Agnes—men's women, mother women—lead an appalling life. First with what the men do to them—even so good a man as Andrew—and then what the children do, coming out. She will never forget her own mother, who lay in bed out of her mind with a fever, not knowing any of them, till she died, three days after Walter was born. She had screamed at the black pot hanging over the fire, thinking it was full of devils.

Her brothers call Mary *Poor Mary*, and indeed the meagreness and timidity of many of the women in their family has caused that word to be attached to the names they were given at their christening—names that were themselves altered to something less substantial and graceful. Isabel became Poor Tibbie; Margaret, Poor Maggie; Jane, Poor Jennie. People in Ettrick said it was a fact that the looks and the height went to the men.

Mary is under five feet tall and has a little tight face with a lump of protruding chin, and a skin that is subject to fiery eruptions that take a long time to fade. When she is spoken to her mouth twitches as if the words were all mixed up with her spittle and her crooked little teeth, and the response she manages is a dribble of speech so faint and scrambled that it is hard for people not to think her dim-witted. She has great difficulty in looking anybody in the face—even the members of her own family. It is only when she gets the boy hitched on to the narrow shelf of her hip that she is capable of some coherent and decisive speech—and then it is mostly to him.

Somebody is saying something to her now. It is a person almost as small as herself—a little brown man, a sailor, with gray whiskers and not a tooth in his head. He is looking straight at her and then at Young James and back to her again—right in the middle of the pushing or loitering, bewildered or inquisitive crowd. At first she thinks it is a foreign language he is speaking, but then she makes out the word *cu*. She finds herself answering with the same word, and he laughs and waves his arms, pointing to somewhere farther back on the ship, then pointing at James and laughing again. Something she should take James to see. She has to say, "Aye. Aye," to stop him gabbling, and then to step off in that direction so that he won't be disappointed.

She wonders what part of the country or the world he could have come from, then realizes that this is the first time in her life that she has ever spoken to a stranger. And except for the difficulty of understanding what he was saying, she has managed it more easily than when having to speak to a neighbor in the Ettrick, or to her father.

She hears the bawling of the cow before she can see it. The press of people increases around her and James, forms a wall in front of her and squeezes her from behind. Then she hears the bawling in the sky and looking up sees the brown beast dangling in the air, all caged in ropes and kicking and roaring frantically. It is held by a hook on a crane, which now hauls it out of sight. People around her are hooting and clapping hands. Some child's voice cries out in the language she understands, wanting to know if the cow will be dropped into the sea. A man's voice tells him no, she will go along with them on the ship.

"Will they milk her then?"

"Aye. Keep still. They'll milk her," says the man reprovingly. And another man's voice climbs boisterously over his.

"They'll milk her till they take the hammer to her, and then ye'll have the blood pudding for yer dinner."

Now follow the hens swung through the air in crates, all squawking and fluttering in their confinement and pecking each other when they can, so that some feathers escape and float down through the air. And after them a pig trussed up like the cow, squealing with a human note in its distress and shitting wildly in midair, so that howls of both outrage and delight rise below, depending on whether they come from those who are hit or those who see others hit.

James is laughing too, he recognizes shite, and cries out his own word for it, which is *gruggin*.

Someday he may remember this. *I saw a cow and a pig fly through the air*. Then he may wonder if it was a dream. And nobody will be there— she will certainly not be there—to tell that it was not a dream, it happened on this ship. He will know that he was once on a ship because he will have been told that, but it's possible that he will never see a ship like this again in all his waking life. She has no idea where they will go when they reach the other shore, but imagines it will be some place inland, among the hills, some place like the Ettrick.

She does not think she will live long, wherever they go. She coughs in the summer as well as the winter and when she coughs her chest aches. She suffers from sties, and cramps in the stomach, and her bleeding comes rarely but may last a month when it does come. She hopes, though, that she will not die while James is still of a size to ride on her hip or still in need of her, which he will be for a while yet. She knows that the time will come when he will turn away as her brothers did, when he will become ashamed of the connection with her. That is what she tells herself will happen, but like anybody in love she cannot believe it.

ON A trip to Peebles before they left home, Walter bought himself a book to write in, but for several days he has found too much to pay attention to, and too little space or quiet on the deck, even to open it. He has a vial of ink, as well, held in a leather pouch and strapped to his chest under his shirt. That was the trick used by their cousin, Jamie Hogg the poet, when he was out in the wilds of Nithsdale, watching the sheep. When a rhyme came on Jamie he would pull a wad of paper out of his breeks' pocket and uncork the ink which the heat of his heart had kept from freezing and write it all down, no matter where he was or in what weather.

Or so he said. And Walter had thought to put this method to the test. But it might have been an easier matter amongst sheep than amongst people. Also the wind can surely blow harder over the sea even than it could blow in Nithsdale. And it is essential of course for him to get out of the sight of his own family. Andrew might mock him mildly but Agnes would do it boldly, incensed as she could be by the thought of anybody doing anything she would not want to do. Mary, of course, would never say a word, but the boy on her hip that she idolized and spoiled would be all for grabbing and destroying both pen and paper. And there was no knowing what interference might come from their father.

Now after some investigating around the deck he has found a favorable spot. The cover of his book is hard, he has no need of a table. And the ink warmed on his chest flows as willingly as blood.

We came on board on the 4th day of June and lay the 5th, 6th, 7th, and 8th in the Leith roads getting the ship to our place where we could set sail which was on the 9th. We passed the corner of Fifeshire all well nothing occurring worth mentioning till this day the 13th in the morning when we were awakened by a cry, John O'Groats house. We could see it plain and had a fine sail across the Pentland Firth having both wind and tide in our favour and it was in no way dangerous as we had heard tell. Their was a child had died, the name of Ormiston and its body was thrown overboard sewed up in a piece of canvas with a large lump of coal at its feet . . .

He pauses in his writing to think of the weighted sack falling down through the water. Darker and darker grows the water with the surface high overhead gleaming faintly like the night sky. Would the piece of coal do its job, would the sack fall straight down to the very bottom of the sea? Or would the current of the sea be strong enough to keep lifting it up and letting it fall, pushing it sideways, taking it as far as Greenland or south to the tropical waters full of rank weeds, the Sargasso Sea? Or some ferocious fish might come along and rip the sack and make a meal of the body before it had even left the upper waters and the region of light.

He has seen drawings of fish as big as horses, fish with horns as well, and scores of teeth each like a skinner's knife. Also some that are smooth and smiling, and wickedly teasing, having the breasts of women but not the other parts which the sight of the breasts conducts a man's thoughts to. All this in a book of stories and engravings that he got out of the Peebles Subscription Library.

These thoughts do not distress him. He always sets himself to think clearly and if possible to picture accurately the most disagreeable or shocking things, so as to reduce their power over him. As he pictures it now, the child is being eaten. Not swallowed whole as in the case of Jonah but chewed into bits as he himself would chew a tasty chunk from a boiled sheep. But there is the matter of a soul. The soul leaves the body at the moment of death. But from which part of the body does it leave, what has been its particular bodily location? The best guess seems to be that it emerges with the last breath, having been hidden somewhere in the chest around the place of the heart and the lungs. Though Walter has heard a joke they used to tell about an old fellow in the Ettrick, to the effect that he was so dirty that when he died his soul came out his arsehole, and was heard to do so, with a mighty explosion.

This is the sort of information that preachers might be expected to give you—not mentioning anything like an arsehole of course but explaining something of the soul's proper location and exit. But they shy away from it. Also they cannot explain—or he has never heard one explain—how the souls maintain themselves outside of bodies until the Day of Judgment and how on that day each one finds and recognizes the body that is its own and reunites with it, though it be not so much as a skeleton at that time. *Though it be dust.* There must be some who have studied enough to know how all this is accomplished. But there are also some—he has learned this recently—who have studied and read and thought till they have come to the conclusion that there are no souls at all. No one cares to speak about these people either, and indeed the thought of them is terrible. How can they live with the fear—indeed, the certainty—of Hell before them?

There was the man like that who came from by Berwick, Fat Davey he was called, because he was so fat the table had to be cut away so he could sit down to his meal. And when he died in Edinburgh, where he was some sort of scholar, the people stood in the street outside his house waiting to see if the Devil would come to claim him. A sermon had been preached on that in Ettrick, which claimed as far as Walter could understand it that the Devil did not go in for displays of that sort and only superstitious and vulgar and Popish sort of people would expect him to, but that his embrace was nevertheless far more horrible and the torments that accompanied it more subtle than any such minds could imagine.

ON THE third day aboard ship Old James got up and started to walk around. Now he is walking all the time. He stops and speaks to anybody who seems ready to listen. He tells his name, and says that he comes from Ettrick, from the valley and forest of Ettrick, where the old Kings of Scotland used to hunt.

"And on the field at Flodden," he says, "after the battle of Flodden, they said you could walk up and down among the corpses and pick out the men from the Ettrick, because they were the tallest and the strongest and the finest-looking men on the ground. I have five sons and they are all good strong lads but only two of them are with me. One of my sons is in Nova Scotia, he is the one with my own name and the last I heard of him he was in a place called Economy, but we have not had any word of him since, and I do not know whether he is alive or dead. My eldest son went off to work in the Highlands, and the son that is next to the youngest took it into his head to go off there too, and I will never see either of them again. Five sons and by the mercy of God all grew to be men, but it was not the Lord's will that I should keep them with me. Their mother died after the last of them was born. She took a fever and she never got up from her bed after she bore him. A man's life is full of sorrow. I have a daughter as well, the oldest of them all, but she is nearly a dwarf. Her mother was chased by a ram when she was carrying her. I have three old sisters all the same, all dwarfs."

His voice rises over all the hubbub of shipboard life and his sons make tracks in some other direction in dread embarrassment, whenever they hear it.

On the afternoon of the 14th a wind came from the North and the ship began to shake as if every board that was in it would fly loose from every other. The buckets overflowed from the people that were sick and vomiting and there was the contents of them slipping all over the deck. All people were ordered below but many of them crumpled up against the rail and did not care if they were washed over. None of our family was sick however and now the wind has dropped and the sun has come out and those who did not care if they died in the filth a little while ago have got up and dragged themselves to be washed where the sailors are splashing buckets of water over the decks. The women are busy too washing and rinsing and wringing out all the foul clothing. It is the worst misery and the suddenest recovery I have seen ever in my life . . .

A young girl ten or twelve years old stands watching Walter write. She is wearing a fancy dress and bonnet and has light-brown curly hair. Not so much a pretty face as a pert one.

"Are you from one of the cabins?" she says.

Walter says, "No. I am not."

"I knew you were not. There are only four of them and one is for my father and me and one is for the captain and one is for his mother and she never comes out and one is for the two ladies. You are not supposed to be on this part of the deck unless you are from one of the cabins."

"Well, I did not know that," Walter says, but does not bestir himself to move away.

"I have seen you before writing in your book."

"I haven't seen you."

"No. You were writing, so you didn't notice."

"Well," says Walter. "I'm finished with it now anyway."

"I haven't told anybody about you," she says carelessly, as if that was a matter of choice, and she might well change her mind.

AND ON that same day but an hour or so on, there comes a great cry from the port side that there is a last sight of Scotland. Walter and Andrew go over to see that, and Mary with Young James on her hip and many others. Old James and Agnes do not go—she because she objects now to moving herself anywhere, and he on account of perversity. His sons have urged him to go but he has said, "It is nothing to me. I have seen the last of the Ettrick so I have seen the last of Scotland already."

It turns out that the cry to say farewell has been premature—a gray rim of land will remain in place for hours yet. Many will grow tired of looking at it—it is just land, like any other—but some will stay at the rail until the last rag of it fades, with the daylight.

"You should go and say farewell to your native land and the last farewell to your mother and father for you will not be seeing them again," says Old James to Agnes. "And there is worse yet you will have to endure. Aye, but there is. You have the curse of Eve." He says this with the mealy relish of a preacher and Agnes calls him an old shite-bag under her breath, but she has hardly the energy even to scowl.

Old shite-bag. You and your native land.

*

WALTER WRITES at last a single sentence.

And this night in the year 1818 we lost sight of Scotland.

The words seem majestic to him. He is filled with a sense of grandeur, solemnity, and personal importance.

16th was a very windy day with the wind coming out of the S.W. the sea was running very high and the ship got her gib-boom broken on account of the violence of the wind. And this day our sister Agnes was taken into the cabin.

Sister, he has written, as if she were all the same to him as poor Mary, but that is hardly the case. Agnes is a tall well-built girl with thick dark hair and dark eyes. The flush on one of her cheeks slides into a splotch of pale brown as big as a handprint. It is a birthmark, which people say is a pity, because without it she would be handsome. Walter can hardly bear looking at it, but this is not because it is ugly. It is because he longs to touch it, to stroke it with the tips of his fingers. It looks not like ordinary skin but like the velvet on a deer. His feelings about her are so troubling that he can only speak unpleasantly to her if he speaks at all. And she pays him back with a good seasoning of contempt.

AGNES THINKS that she is in the water and the waves are heaving her up and slamming her down again. Every time the waves slap her down it is worse than the time before and she sinks farther and deeper, with the moment of relief passing before she can grab it, for the wave is already gathering its power to hit her again.

Then sometimes she knows she is in a bed, a strange bed and strangely soft, but it is all the worse for that because when she sinks down there is no resistance, no hard place where the pain has to stop. And here or on the water people keep rushing back and forth in front of her. They are all seen sideways and all transparent, talking very fast so she can't make them out, and maliciously taking no heed of her. She sees Andrew in the midst of them, and two or three of his brothers. Some of the girls she knows are there too—the friends she used to lark around with in Hawick. And they do not give a glance or a poor penny for the plight she is in now.

She shouts at them to take themselves off but not one of them pays any attention and she sees more of them coming right through the wall. She never knew before that she had so many enemies. They are grinding her and pretending they don't even know it. Their movement is grinding her to death.

Her mother bends over her and says in a drawling, cold, lackadaisical voice, "You are not trying, my girl. You must try harder." Her mother is all dressed up and talking fine, like some Edinburgh lady.

Evil stuff is poured into her mouth. She tries to spit it out, knowing it is poison.

I will just get up and get out of this, she thinks. She starts trying to pull herself loose from her body, as if it were a heap of rags all on fire.

A man's voice is heard, giving some order.

"Hold her," he says and she is split and stretched wide open to the world and the fire.

"Ah—ah—ahh," the man's voice says, panting as if he has been running in a race.

Then a cow that is so heavy, bawling heavy with milk, rears up and sits down on Agnes's stomach.

"Now. Now," says the man's voice, and he groans at the end of his strength as he tries to heave it off.

The fools. The fools, ever to have let it in.

She was not better till the 18th when she was delivered of a daughter. We having a surgeon on board nothing happened. Nothing occurred till the 22nd this was the roughest day we had till then experienced. The gib-boom was broken a second time. Nothing worth mentioning happened Agnes was mending in an ordinary way till the 29th we saw a great shoal of porpoises and the 30th (yesterday) was a very rough sea with the wind blowing from the west we went rather backwards than forwards . . .

"In the Ettrick there is what they call the highest house in Scotland," James says, "and the house that my grandfather lived in was a higher one than that. The name of the place is Phauhope, they call it Phaup, my grandfather was Will O'Phaup and fifty years ago you would have heard of him if you came from any place south of the Forth and north of the Debatable Lands."

Unless a person stops up his ears, what is to be done but listen? thinks Walter. There are people who curse to see the old man coming but there do seem to be others who are glad of any distraction.

He is telling about Will and his races, and the wagers on him, and other foolishness more than Walter can bear.

"And he married a woman named Bessie Scott and one of his sons was named Robert and that same Robert was my father. My father. And I am standing here in front of you."

"In but one leap Will could clear the river Ettrick, and the place is marked."

FOR THE first two or three days Young James has refused to be unfastened from Mary's hip. He has been bold enough, but only if he can stay there. At night he has slept in her cloak, curled up beside her, and she has wakened aching along her left side because she lay stiffly all night not to disturb him. Then in the space of one morning he is down and running about and kicking at her if she tries to hoist him up.

Everything on the ship is calling out for his attention. Even at night he tries to climb over her and run away in the dark. So she gets up aching not only from her stiff position but from lack of sleep altogether. One night she drops off and the child gets loose but most fortunately stumbles against his father's body in his bid for escape. Henceforth Andrew insists that he be tied down every night. He howls of course, and Andrew shakes him and cuffs him and then he sobs himself to sleep. Mary lies by him softly explaining how this is necessary so that he should not fall off the ship into the ocean, but he regards her at these times as his enemy and if she puts a hand to stroke his face he tries to bite it with his baby teeth. Every night he goes to sleep in a rage, but in the morning when she unties him, still half-asleep and full of his infant sweetness, he clings to her drowsily and she is suffused with love.

The truth is that she loves even his howls and his rages and his kicks and his bites. She loves his dirty and his curdled smells as well as his fresh ones. As his drowsiness leaves him his clear blue eyes, looking into hers, fill with a marvellous intelligence and an imperious will, which seem to her to come straight from Heaven. (Though her religion has always taught her that self-will comes from the opposite direction.) She loved her brothers too when they were sweet and wild and had to be kept from falling into the burn, but surely not as passionately as she loves James.

Then one day he is gone. She is in the line for the wash water and she turns around and he is not beside her. She has just been speaking a few words to the woman ahead of her, answering a question about Agnes and the infant, she has just told its name—Isabel—and in that moment he has got away. When she was saying the name, Isabel, she felt a surprising longing to hold that new, exquisitely light bundle, and as she abandons her place in line and chases about for sight of James it seems to her that he must have felt her disloyalty and vanished to punish her.

Everything in an instant is overturned. The nature of the world is altered. She runs back and forth, crying out James's name. She runs up to strangers, to sailors who laugh at her as she begs them, "Have you seen a little boy, have you seen a little boy this high, he has blue eyes?"

"I seen a fifty or sixty of them like that in the last five minutes," a man says to her. A woman trying to be kind says that he will turn up, Mary should not worry herself, he will be playing with some of the other children. Some women even look about as if they would help her to search, but of course they cannot, they have their own responsibilities.

This is what Mary plainly sees, in those moments of anguish—that the world which has turned into a horror for her is still the same ordinary world for all these other people and will remain so even if James has truly vanished, even if he has crawled through the ship's railings—she has noticed, all over, the places where this could be possible—and is swallowed in the ocean.

The most brutal and unthinkable of all events, to her, could seem to most others like a sad but not extraordinary misadventure. It would not be unthinkable to them.

Or to God. For in fact when God makes some rare and remarkably beautiful human child, is He not particularly tempted to take His creature back, as if the world did not deserve it?

But she is praying to Him, all the time. At first she only called on the Lord's name. But as her search grows more specific and in some ways more bizarre—she is ducking under clotheslines that people have contrived for privacy, she thinks nothing of interrupting folk at any business, she flings up the lids of their boxes and roots in their bedclothes, not even hearing them when they curse her—her prayers also become more complicated and audacious. She seeks for something to offer, something that could be the price of James's being restored to her. But what does she have? Nothing of her own—not health or prospects or anybody's regard. There is no piece of luck or even a hope she can offer to give up. What she has is James.

And how can she offer James for James?

This is what is knocking around in her head.

But what about her love of James? Her extreme and perhaps idolatrous, perhaps wicked love of another creature. She will give up that, she will give it up gladly, if only he isn't gone, if only he can be found. If only he isn't dead.

SHE RECALLS all this, an hour or two after somebody has noticed the boy peeping out from under an empty bucket, listening to the hubbub. And she retracted her vow at once. She grabbed him in her arms and held him hard against her and took deep groaning breaths, while he struggled to get free.

Her understanding of God is shallow and unstable and the truth is that except in a time of terror such as she has just experienced, she does not really care. She has always felt that God or even the idea of Him was more distant from her than from other people. Also she does not fear His punishments after death as she should and she does not even know why. There is a stubborn indifference in her mind that nobody knows about. In fact, everybody may think that she clings secretly to religion because so little else is available to her. They are quite wrong, and now she has James back she gives no thanks but thinks what a fool she was and how she could not give up her love of him any more than stop her heart beating.

AFTER THAT, Andrew insists that James be tied not only by night but to the post of the bunk or to their own clothesline on the deck, by day. Mary wishes him to be tethered to her but Andrew says a boy like that would kick her to pieces. Andrew has trounced him for the trick he played, but the look in James's eyes says that his tricks are not finished.

THAT CLIMB in Edinburgh, that sighting across the water, was a thing Andrew did not even mention to his own brothers—America being already a sore enough matter. The oldest brother, Robert, went off to the Highlands as soon as he was grown, leaving home without a farewell on an evening when his father was at Tibbie Shiel's. He made it plain that he was doing this in order not to have to join any expedition that their father might have in mind. Then the brother James perversely set out for America on his own, saying that at least if he did that, he could save himself hearing any more about it. And finally Will, younger than Andrew but always the most contrary and the most bitterly set against the father, Will too had run away, to join Robert. That left only Walt, who was still childish enough to be thinking of adventures—he had grown up bragging about how he was going to fight the French, so maybe now he thought he'd fight the Indians.

And then there was Andrew himself, who ever since that day on the rock has felt about his father a deep bewildered sense of responsibility, much like sorrow.

But then, Andrew feels a responsibility for everybody in his family. For his often ill-tempered young wife, whom he has again brought into a state of peril, for the brothers far away and the brother at his side, for his pitiable sister and his heedless child. This is his burden—it never occurs to him to call it love.

AGNES KEEPS asking for salt, till they begin to fear that she will fuss herself into a fever. The two women looking after her are cabin passengers, Edinburgh ladies, who took on the job out of charity.

"You be still now," they tell her. "You have no idea what a fortunate lassie you are that we had Mr. Suter on board."

They tell her that the baby was turned the wrong way inside her, and they were all afraid that Mr. Suter would have to cut her, and that might be the end of her. But he had managed to get it turned so that he could wrestle it out.

"I need salt for my milk," says Agnes, who is not going to let them put her in her place with their reproaches and Edinburgh speech. They are idiots anyway. She has to tell them how you must put a little salt in the baby's first milk, just place a few grains on your finger and squeeze a drop or two of milk onto it and let the child swallow that before you put it to the breast. Without this precaution there is a good chance that it will grow up half-witted.

"Is she even a Christian?" says the one of them to the other.

"I am as much as you," Agnes says. But to her own surprise and shame she starts to weep aloud, and the baby howls along with her, out of sympathy or out of hunger. And still she refuses to feed it.

Mr. Suter comes in to see how she is. He asks what all the grief is about, and they tell him the trouble.

"A newborn baby to get salt on its stomach—where did she get the idea?"

He says, "Give her the salt." And he stays to see her squeeze the milk on her salty finger, lay the finger to the infant's lips, and follow it with her nipple.

He asks her what the reason is and she tells him.

"And does it work every time?"

She tells him—a little surprised that he is as stupid as they are, though kinder—that it works without fail.

"So where you come from they all have their wits about them? And are all the girls strong and good-looking like you?"

She says that she would not know about that.

Sometimes visiting young men, educated and from the town, used to hang around her and her friends, complimenting them and trying to work up a conversation, and she always thought any girl was a fool who allowed it, even if the man was handsome. Mr. Suter is far from handsome—he is too thin, and his face is badly pocked, so that at first she took him for an old fellow. But he has a kind voice, and if he is teasing her a little there could be no harm in it. No man would have the nature left to deal with a woman after looking at them spread wide, their raw parts open to the air.

"Are you sore?" he says, and she believes there is a shadow on his damaged cheeks, a slight blush rising. She says that she is no worse than she has to be, and he nods, picks up her wrist, and bows over it, strongly pressing her pulse.

"Lively as a racehorse," he says, with his hands still above her, as if he did not know where to drop them next. Then he decides to push back her hair and press his fingers to her temples, as well as behind her ears.

She will recall this touch, this curious, gentle, tingling pressure, with an addled mixture of scorn and longing, for many years to come.

"Good," he says. "No touch of a fever."

He watches, for a moment, the child sucking.

"All's well with you now," he says, with a sigh. "You have a fine daughter and she can say all her life that she was born at sea."

ANDREW ARRIVES later and stands at the foot of the bed. He has never looked on her in such a bed as this (a regular bed even though bolted to the wall). He is red with shame in front of the ladies, who have brought in the basin to wash her.

"That's it, is it?" he says, with a nod—not a glance—at the bundle beside her.

She laughs in a vexed way and asks, what did he think it was? That is all it takes to knock him off his unsteady perch, puncture his pretense of being at ease. Now he stiffens up, even redder, doused with fire. It isn't just what she has said, it is the whole scene, the smell of the infant and milk and blood, most of all the basin, the cloths, the women standing by, with their proper looks that can seem to a man both admonishing and full of derision.

He can't think of another word to say, so she has to tell him, with rough mercy, to get on his way, there's work to do here.

Some of the girls used to say that when you finally gave in and lay down with a man—even granting he was not the man of your first choice—it gave you a helpless but calm and even sweet feeling. Agnes does not recall that she felt that with Andrew. All she felt was that he was an honest lad and the one that she needed in her circumstances, and that it would never occur to him to run off and leave her.

*

315

WALTER HAS continued to go to the same private place to write in his book and nobody has caught him there. Except the girl, of course. But things are even now with her. One day he arrived at the place and she was there before him, skipping with a red-tasselled rope. When she saw him she stopped, out of breath. And no sooner did she catch her breath but she began to cough, so that it was several minutes before she could speak. She sank down against the pile of canvas that concealed the spot, flushed and her eyes full of bright tears from the coughing. He simply stood and watched her, alarmed at this fit but not knowing what to do.

"Do you want me to fetch one of the ladies?"

He is on speaking terms with the Edinburgh women now, on account of Agnes. They take a kind interest in the mother and baby and Mary and Young James, and think that the old father is comical. They are also amused by Andrew and Walter, who seem to them so bashful. Walter is actually not so tongue-tied as Andrew is, but this business of humans giving birth (though he is used to it with sheep) fills him with dismay or outright disgust. Agnes has lost a great part of her sullen allure because of it. (As happened before, when she gave birth to Young James. But then, gradually, her offending powers returned. He thinks that unlikely to happen again. He has seen more of the world now, and on board this ship he has seen more of women.)

The coughing girl is shaking her curly head violently.

"I don't want them," she says, when she can gasp the words out. "I have never told anybody you come here. So you mustn't tell anybody about me."

"Well you are here by rights."

She shakes her head again and gestures for him to wait till she can speak more easily.

"I mean that you saw me skipping. My father hid my skipping rope but I found where he hid it—but he doesn't know that."

"It isn't the Sabbath," Walter says reasonably. "So what is wrong with you skipping?"

"How do I know?" she says, regaining her saucy tone. "Perhaps he thinks I am too old for it. Will you swear not to tell anyone?" She holds up her forefingers to make a cross. The gesture is innocent, he knows, but nevertheless he is shocked, knowing how some people might look at it.

But he says that he is willing to swear.

"I swear too," she says. "I won't tell anyone you come here."

After saying this quite solemnly, she makes a face.

"Though I was not going to tell about you anyway."

What a queer self-important little thing she is. She speaks only of her father, so he thinks it must be she has no brothers or sisters and—like himself—no mother. That condition has probably made her both spoiled and lonely.

FOLLOWING THIS swearing, the girl—her name is Nettie—becomes a frequent visitor when Walter intends to write in his book. She always says that she does not want to disturb him but after keeping ostentatiously quiet for about five minutes she will interrupt him with some question about his life or bit of information about hers. It is true that she is motherless and an only child and she has never even been to school. She talks most about her pets—those dead and those living at her house in Edinburgh—and a woman named Miss Anderson who used to travel with her and teach her. It seems she was glad to see the back of this woman, and surely Miss Anderson would be glad to depart, after all the tricks that were played on her—the live frog in her boot and the woolen but lifelike mouse in her bed. Also Nettie's stomping on books that were not in favor and her pretense of being struck deaf and dumb when she got sick of reciting her spelling exercises.

She has been back and forth to America three times. Her father is a wine merchant whose business takes him to Montreal.

She wants to know all about how Walter and his people live. Her questions are by country standards quite impertinent. But Walter does not really mind—in his own family he has never been in a position that allowed him to instruct or teach or tease anybody younger than himself, and in a way it gives him pleasure.

It is certainly true, though, that in his own world, nobody would ever have got away with being so pert and forward and inquisitive as this Nettie. What does Walter's family have for supper when they are at home, how do they sleep? Are there animals kept in the house? Do the sheep have names, and what are the sheepdogs' names, and can you make pets of them? Why not? What is the arrangement of the scholars in the schoolroom, what do they write on, are the teachers cruel? What do some of his words mean that she does not understand, and do all the people where he is talk like him?

"Oh, aye," says Walter. "Even His Majesty the Duke does. The Duke of Buccleugh."

She laughs and freely pounds her little fist on his shoulder.

"Now you are teasing me. I know it. I know that dukes are not called Your Majesty. They are not."

One day she arrives with paper and drawing pencils. She says she has brought them to keep her busy so she will not be a nuisance to him. She says that she will teach him to draw if he wants to learn. But his attempts make her laugh, and he deliberately does worse and worse, till she laughs so hard she has one of her coughing fits. (These don't bother him so much anymore because he has seen how she always manages to survive them.) Then she says she will do some drawings in the back of his notebook, so that he will have them to remember the voyage. She does a drawing of the sails up above and of a hen that has escaped its cage somehow and is trying to travel like a seabird over the water. She sketches from memory her dog that died, Pirate. At first she claims his name was Walter but relents and admits later that she was not telling the truth. And she makes a picture of the icebergs she has seen, higher than houses, on one of her past voyages with her father. The setting sun shone through these icebergs and made them look—she says—like castles of gold. Rose-colored and gold.

"I wish I had my paint box. Then I could show you. But I do not know where it is packed. And my painting is not very good anyway, I am better at drawing."

Everything that she has drawn, including the icebergs, has a look that is both guileless and mocking, peculiarly expressive of herself.

"THE OTHER day I was telling you about that Will O'Phaup that was my grandfather but there was more to him than I told you. I did not tell you that he was the last man in Scotland to speak to the fairies. It is certain that I have never heard of any other, in his time or later."

Walter has been trapped into hearing this story—which he has, of course, heard often before, though not by his father's telling. He is sitting around a corner where some sailors are mending the torn sails. They talk among themselves from time to time—in English, maybe, but not any English that Walt can well make out—and occasionally they seem to listen to a bit of what Old James is telling. By the sounds that are made throughout the story Walter can guess that the out-of-sight audience is made up mostly of women.

But there is one tall well-dressed man—a cabin passenger, certainly—who has paused to listen within Walter's view. There is a figure close to this man's other side, and at one moment in the tale this figure peeps around to look at Walter and he sees that it is Nettie. She seems about to laugh but she puts a finger to her lips as if warning herself—and Walter—to keep silent.

The man must of course be her father. The two of them stand there listening quietly till the tale is over.

Then the man turns and speaks directly, in a familiar yet courteous way, to Walter.

"There is no telling what happened to the fellow's sheep. I hope the fairies did not get them."

Walter is alarmed, not knowing what to say. But Nettie looks at him with calming reassurance and the slightest smile, then drops her eyes and waits beside her father as a demure little miss should.

"Are you writing down what you can make of this?" the man asks, nodding at Walter's notebook.

"I am writing a journal of the voyage," Walter says stiffly.

"Now that is interesting. That is an interesting fact because I too am keeping a journal of this voyage. I wonder if we find the same things worth writing of."

"I only write what happens," Walt says, wanting to make clear that this is a job for him and not any idle pleasure. Still he feels that some further justification is called for. "I am writing to keep track of every day so that at the end of the voyage I can send a letter home."

The man's voice is smoother and his manner gentler than any address Walter is used to. He wonders if he is being made sport of in some way. Or if Nettie's father is the sort of person who strikes up an acquaintance with you in the hope of getting hold of your money for some worthless investment.

Not that Walter's looks or dress would mark him out as any likely prospect.

"So you do not describe what you see? Only what—as you say—is *happening*?"

Walter is about to say no, and then yes. For he has just thought, if he writes that there is a rough wind, is that not describing? You do not know where you are with this kind of person.

"You are not writing about what we have just heard?"

"No."

"It might be worth it. There are people who go around now prying into every part of Scotland and writing down whatever these old country folk have to say. They think that the old songs and stories are disappearing and that they are worth recording. I don't know about that, it isn't my business. But I would not be surprised if the people who have written it all down will find that it was worth their trouble—I mean to say, there will be money in it."

Nettie speaks up unexpectedly.

"Oh, hush, Father. The old fellow is going to start again."

This is not what any daughter would say to her father in Walter's experience, but the man seems ready to laugh, looking down at her fondly.

"Just one more thing I have to ask," he says. "What do you think of this about the fairies?"

"I think it is all nonsense," says Walter.

"He *has* started again," says Nettie crossly.

And indeed, Old James's voice has been going this little while, breaking in determinedly and reproachfully on those of his audience who might have thought it was time for their own conversations.

". . . and still another time, but in the long days in the summer, out on the hills late in the day but before it was well dark . . ."

The tall man nods but looks as if he had something still to inquire of Walter. Nettie reaches up and claps her hand over his mouth.

"And I will tell you and swear my life upon it that Will could not tell a lie, him that in his young days went to church to the preacher Thomas Boston, and Thomas Boston put the fear of the Lord like a knife into every man and woman, till their dying day. No, never. He would not lie."

"So THAT was all nonsense?" says the tall man quietly, when he is sure that the story has ended. "Well I am inclined to agree. You have a modern turn of mind?"

Walter says yes, he has, and he speaks more stoutly than he did before. He has heard these stories his father is spouting, and others like them, for the whole of his life, but the odd thing is that until they came on board this ship he never heard them from his father. The father he has known up till a short while ago would, he is certain, have had no use for them.

"This is a terrible place we live in," his father used to say. "The people is all full of nonsense and bad habits and even our sheep's wool is so coarse you cannot sell it. The roads are so bad a horse cannot go more than four miles in an hour. And for ploughing here they use the spade or the old Scotch plough though there has been a better plough in other places for fifty years. Oh, aye, aye, they say when you ask them, oh aye but it's too steep hereabouts, the land is too heavy."

"To be born in the Ettrick is to be born in a backward place," he would say. "Where the people is all believing in old stories and seeing ghosts and I tell you it is a curse to be born in the Ettrick."

And very likely that would lead him on to the subject of America, where all the blessings of modern invention were put to eager use and the people could never stop improving the world around them.

But harken at him now.

"I don't believe those were fairies," Nettie says.

"So do you think they were his neighbors all the time?" says her father. "Do you think they were playing a trick on him?"

Never has Walter heard a father speak to a child so indulgently. And fond as he has grown of Nettie he cannot approve of it. It can only make her believe that there are no opinions on the face of the earth that are more worthy of being listened to than hers.

"No I do not," she says.

"What then?" says her father.

"I think they were dead people."

"What do you know about dead people?" her father asks her, finally speaking with some sternness. "Dead people won't rise up till the Day of Judgment. I don't care to hear you making light about things of that sort."

"I was not making light," says Nettie carelessly.

The sailors are scrambling loose from their sails and pointing at the sky, far to the west. They must see there something that excites them. Walter makes bold to ask, "Are they English? I cannot tell what they say."

"Some of them are English, but from parts that sound foreign to us. Some are Portuguese. I cannot make them out either but I think that they are saying they see the rotches. They all have very keen eyes."

Walter believes that he too has very keen eyes, but it takes him a moment or two before he can see these birds, the ones that must be called rotches. Flocks and flocks of seabirds flashing and rising overhead, mere bright speckles on the air.

"You must make sure to mention those in your journal," Nettie's father says. "I have seen them when I made this voyage before. They feed on fish and here is the great place for them. Soon you'll see the fishermen as well. But the rotches filling the sky are the very first sign that we must be on the Grand Banks of Newfoundland.

"You must come up and talk to us on the deck above," he says, in bidding good-bye to Walter. "I have business to think about and I am not much company for my daughter. She is forbidden to run around because she is not quite recovered from the cold she had in the winter but she is fond of sitting and talking."

"I don't believe it is the rule for me to go there," says Walter, in some confusion.

"No, no, that is no matter. My girl is lonely. She likes to read and draw but she likes company too. She could show you how to draw, if you like. That would add to your journal."

If Walter flushes it is not noticed. Nettie remains quite composed.

So THEY sit out in the open and draw and write. Or she reads aloud to him from her favorite book, which is *The Scottish Chiefs*. He already knows much about what happens in the story—who does not know about William Wallace?—but she reads smoothly and at just the proper speed and makes some things solemn and others terrifying and something else comical, so that he is as much in thrall to the book as she is herself. Even though, as she says, she has read it twelve times already.

He understands a little better now why she has all those questions to ask him. He and his folk remind her of some people in her book. Such people as there were out on the hills and valleys in the olden times. What would she think if she knew that the *old fellow,* the old tale-spinner spouting all over the boat and penning people up to listen as if they were the sheep and he was the sheepdog—if she knew that he was Walter's father?

She would be delighted, probably, more curious about Walter's family than ever. She would not look down on them, except in a way she could not help or know about.

We came on the fishing banks of Newfoundland on the 12th of July and on the 19th we saw land and it was a joyful sight to us. It was a part of Newfoundland. We sailed between Newfoundland and St. Paul's Island and having a fair wind both the 18th and the 19th we found ourselves in the river on the morning of the 20th and within sight of the mainland of North America. We were awakened at about 1 o'clock in the morning and I think every passenger was out of bed at 4 o'clock gazing at the land, it being wholly covered with wood and quite a new sight to us. It was a part of Nova Scotia and a beautiful hilly country. We saw several whales this day such creatures as I never saw in my life.

This is the day of wonders. The land is covered with trees like a head with hair and behind the ship the sun rises tipping the top trees with light. The sky is clear and shining as a china plate and the water just playfully ruffled with wind. Every wisp of fog has gone and the air is full of the resinous smell of the trees. Seabirds are flashing above the sails all golden like creatures of Heaven, but the sailors raise a few shots to keep them from the rigging.

Mary holds Young James up so that he may always remember this first sight of the continent that will forever be his home. She tells him the name of this land—Nova Scotia.

"It means New Scotland," she says.

Agnes hears her. "Then why doesn't it say so?"

Mary says, "It's Latin, I think."

Agnes snorts with impatience. The baby has been waked up early by all the hubbub and celebration, and now she is miserable, wanting to be on the breast all the time, wailing whenever Agnes tries to take her off. Young James, observing all this closely, makes an attempt to get on the other breast, and Agnes bats him off so hard that he staggers.

"Suckie-laddie," Agnes calls him. He yelps a bit, then crawls around behind her and pinches the baby's toes.

Another whack.

"You're a rotten egg, you are," his mother says. "Somebody's been spoiling you till you think you're the Laird's arse."

Agnes's roused voice always makes Mary feel as if she is about to catch a blow herself.

Old James is sitting with them on the deck, but pays no attention to this domestic unrest.

"Will you come and look at the country, Father?" says Mary uncertainly. "You can have a better view from the rail."

"I can see it well enough," Old James says. Nothing in his voice suggests that the revelations around them are pleasing to him.

"Ettrick was covered with trees in the old days," he says. "The monks had it first and after that it was the royal forest. It was the King's forest. Beech trees, oak trees, rowan trees."

"As many trees as this?" says Mary, made bolder than usual by the novel splendors of the day.

"Better trees. Older. It was famous all over Scotland. The Royal Forest of Ettrick."

"And Nova Scotia is where our brother James is," Mary continues.

"He may be or he may not. It would be easy to die here and nobody know you were dead. Wild animals could have eaten him."

"Come near this baby again and I'll skin you alive," says Agnes to Young James who is circling her and the baby, pretending that they hold no interest for him.

Agnes is thinking it would serve him right, the fellow who never even took his leave of her. But she has to hope he will show up sometime and see her married to his brother. So that he will wonder. Also he will understand that in the end he did not get the better of her.

Mary wonders how her father can talk in that way, about how wild animals could have eaten his own son. Is that how the sorrows of the years take hold on you, to turn your heart of flesh to a heart of stone, as it says in the old song? And if it is so, how carelessly and disdainfully might he talk about her, who never meant to him a fraction of what the boys did?

Somebody has brought a fiddle on to the deck and is tuning up to play. People who have been hanging onto the rail and pointing out to each other what any one of them could see on their own—likewise repeating the name that by now everyone knows, Nova Scotia—are distracted by these sounds and begin to call for dancing. They call out the names of the reels and dances they want the fiddler to play. Space is cleared and couples line up in some sort of order and after a lot of uneasy fiddle-scraping and impatient shouts of encouragement, the music comes through and gathers its authority and the dancing begins.

Dancing, at seven o'clock in the morning.

Andrew comes up from below, bearing their supply of water. He stands and watches for a little, then surprises Mary by asking, would she dance?

"Who will look after the boy?" says Agnes immediately. "I am not going to get up and chase him." She is fond of dancing, but is prevented now, not only by the nursing baby but by the soreness of the parts of her body that were so battered in the birth.

Mary is already refusing, saying she cannot go, but Andrew says, "We will put him on the tether."

"No, no," says Mary. "I've no need to dance." She believes that Andrew has taken pity on her, remembering how she used to be left on the sidelines in school games and at the dancing, though she can actually run and dance perfectly well. Andrew is the only one of her brothers capable of such consideration, but she would almost rather he behaved like the others, and left her ignored as she has always been. Pity does gall her.

Young James begins to complain loudly, having recognized the word *tether*.

"You be still," says his father. "Be still or I'll clout you."

Then Old James surprises them all by turning his attention to his grandson.

"You. Young lad. You sit by me."

"Oh, he will not sit," says Mary. "He will run off and then you cannot chase him, Father. I will stay."

"He will sit," says Old James.

"Well, settle it," says Agnes to Mary. "Go or stay."

Young James looks from one to the other, cautiously snuffling.

"Does he not know even the simplest word?" says his grandfather. "Sit. Lad. Here."

"He knows all kinds of words," says Mary. "He knows the name of the gib-boom."

Young James repeats, "Gib-boom."

"Hold your tongue and sit down," says Old James. Young James lowers himself, reluctantly, to the spot indicated.

"Now go," says Old James to Mary. And all in confusion, on the verge of tears, she is led away.

"What a suckie-laddie she's made of him," says Agnes, not exactly to her father-in-law but into the air. She speaks almost indifferently, teasing the baby's cheek with her nipple.

PEOPLE ARE dancing, not just in the figure of the reel but quite outside of it, all over the deck. They are grabbing anyone at all and twirling around. They are even grabbing some of the sailors if they can get hold of them. Men dance with women, men dance with men, women dance with women, children dance with each other or all alone and without any idea of the steps, getting in the way—but everybody is in everybody's way already and it is no matter. Some children dance in one spot, whirling around with their arms in the air till they get so dizzy they fall down. Two seconds later they are on their feet, recovered, and ready to begin the same thing all over again.

Mary has caught hands with Andrew, and is swung around by him, then passed on to others, who bend to her and fling her undersized body about. She has lost sight of Young James and cannot know if he has remained with his grandfather. She dances down at the level of the children, though she is less bold and carefree. In the thick of so many bodies she is helpless, she cannot pause—she has to stamp and wheel to the music or be knocked down.

"Now YOU listen and I will tell you," says Old James. "This old man, Will O'Phaup, my grandfather—he was my grandfather as I am yours— Will O'Phaup was sitting outside his house in the evening, resting himself, it was mild summer weather. All alone, he was.

"And there was three little lads hardly bigger than you are yourself, they came around the corner of Will's house. They told him good evening. *Good evening to you, Will O'Phaup*, they says.

"*Well good evening to you, lads, what can I do for you?*

"*Can you give us a bed for the night or a place to lay down*, they says. And *Aye*, he says, *Aye, I'm thinking three bits of lads like yourselves should not be so hard to find the room for.* And he goes into the house with them following and they says, *And by the by could you give us the key, too, the big silver key that you had of us?* Well, Will looks around, and he looks for the key, till he thinks to himself, what key was that? And turns around to ask them. *What key was that?* For he knew he never had such a thing in his life. Big key or silver key, he never had it. *What key are you talking to me about?* And turns himself round and they are not there. Goes out of the house, all round the house, looks to the road. No trace of them. Looks to the hills. No trace.

"Then Will knew it. They was no lads at all. Ah, no. They was no lads at all."

Young James has not made any sound. At his back is the thick and noisy wall of dancers, to the side his mother, with the small clawing beast that bites into her body. And in front of him is the old man with his rumbling voice, insistent but remote, and his blast of bitter breath, his sense of grievance and importance absolute as the child's own. His nature hungry, crafty, and oppressive. It is Young James's first conscious encounter with someone as perfectly self-centered as himself.

He is barely able to focus his intelligence, to show himself not quite defeated.

"Key," he says. "Key?"

AGNES, WATCHING the dancing, catches sight of Andrew, red in the face and heavy on his feet, linked arm to arm with various jovial women. They are doing the "Strip the Willow" now. There is not one girl whose looks or dancing gives Agnes any worries. Andrew never gives her any worries anyway. She sees Mary tossed around, with even a flush of color in her cheeks—though she is too shy, and too short, to look anybody in the face. She sees the nearly toothless witch of a woman who birthed a child a week after her own, dancing with her hollow-cheeked man. No sore parts for her. She must have dropped the child as slick as if it was a rat, then given it over to one or the other of her weedy-looking daughters to mind.

She sees Mr. Suter, the surgeon, out of breath, pulling away from a woman who would grab him, ducking through the dance and coming to greet her.

She wishes he would not. Now he will see who her father-in-law is, he may have to listen to the old fool's gabble. He will get a look at their drab, and now not even clean, country clothes. He will see her for what she is.

"So here you are," he says. "Here you are with your treasure."

That is not a word that Agnes has ever heard used to refer to a child. It seems as if he is talking to her in the way he might talk to a person of his own acquaintance, some sort of a lady, not as a doctor talks to a patient. Such behavior embarrasses her and she does not know how to answer.

"Your baby is well?" he says, taking a more down-to-earth tack. He is still catching his breath from the dancing, and his face, though not flushed, is covered with a fine sweat.

"Aye."

"And you yourself? You have your strength again?"

She shrugs very slightly, so as not to shake the child off the nipple.

"You have a fine color, anyway, that is a good sign."

She thinks that he sighs as he says this, and wonders if that may be because his own color, seen in the morning light, is sickly as whey.

He asks then if she will permit him to sit and talk to her for a few moments, and once more she is confused by his formality, but says he may do as he likes.

Her father-in-law gives the surgeon—and her as well—a despising glance, but Mr. Suter does not notice it, perhaps does not even understand that the old man, and the fair-haired boy who sits straight-backed and facing this old man, have anything to do with her.

"The dancing is very lively," he says. "And you are not given a chance to decide who you would dance with. You get pulled about by all and sundry." And then he asks, "What will you do in Canada West?"

It seems to her the silliest question. She shakes her head—what can she say? She will wash and sew and cook and almost certainly suckle more children. Where that will be does not much matter. It will be in a house, and not a fine one.

She knows now that this man likes her, and in what way. She remembers his fingers on her skin. What harm can happen, though, to a woman with a baby at her breast?

She feels stirred to show him a bit of friendliness.

"What will you do?" she says.

He smiles and says that he supposes he will go on doing what he has been trained to do, and that the people in America—so he has heard—are in need of doctors and surgeons just like other people in the world.

"But I do not intend to get walled up in some city. I'd like to get as far as the Mississippi River, at least. Everything beyond the Mississippi used to belong to France, you know, but now it belongs to America and it is wide open, anybody can go there, except that you may run into the Indians. I would not mind that either. Where there is fighting with the Indians, there'll be all the more need for a surgeon."

She does not know anything about this Mississippi River, but she knows that he does not look like a fighting man himself—he does not look as if he could stand up in a quarrel with the brawling lads of Hawick, let alone red Indians.

Two dancers swing so close to them as to put a wind into their faces. It is a young girl, a child really, whose skirts fly out—and who should she be dancing with but Agnes's brother-in-law, Walter. Walter makes some sort of silly bow to Agnes and the surgeon and his father, and the girl pushes him and turns him around and he laughs at her. She is all dressed up like a young lady, with bows in her hair. Her face is lit with enjoyment, her cheeks are glowing like lanterns, and she treats Walter with great familiarity, as if she had got hold of a large toy.

"That lad is your friend?" says Mr. Suter.

"No. He is my husband's brother."

The girl is laughing quite helplessly, as she and Walter—through her heedlessness—have almost knocked down another couple in the dance. She is not able to stand up for laughing, and Walter has to support her. Then it appears that she is not laughing but in a fit of coughing and every time the fit seems ready to stop she laughs and gets it started again. Walter is holding her against himself, half-carrying her to the rail.

"There is one lass that will never have a child to her breast," says Mr. Suter, his eyes flitting to the sucking child before resting again on the girl. "I doubt if she will live long enough to see much of America. Does she not have anyone to look after her? She should not have been allowed to dance."

He stands up so that he can keep the girl in view as Walter holds her by the rail.

"There, she has got stopped," he says. "No hemorrhaging. At least not this time."

Agnes does not pay attention to most people, but she can sense things about any man who is interested in her, and she can see now that he takes a satisfaction in the verdict he has passed on this young girl. And she understands that this must be because of some condition of his own— that he must be thinking that he is not so badly off, by comparison.

There is a cry at the rail, nothing to do with the girl and Walter. Another cry, and many people break off dancing, hurrying to look at the water. Mr. Suter rises and goes a few steps in that direction, following the crowd, then turns back.

"A whale," he says. "They are saying there is a whale to be seen off the side."

"You stay here," cries Agnes in an angry voice, and he turns to her in surprise. But he sees that her words are meant for Young James, who is on his feet.

"This is your lad then?" says Mr. Suter as if he has made a remarkable discovery. "May I carry him over to have a look?"

AND THAT is how Mary—happening to raise her face in the crush of passengers—beholds Young James, much amazed, being carried across the deck in the arms of a hurrying stranger, a pale and determined though slyly courteous-looking dark-haired man who is surely a foreigner. A child-stealer, or child-murderer, heading for the rail.

She gives so wild a shriek that anybody would think she was in the Devil's clutches herself, and people make way for her as they would do for a mad dog.

"Stop thief, stop thief," she is crying. "Take the boy from him. Catch him. James. James. Jump down!"

She flings herself forward and grabs the child's ankles, yanking him so that he howls in fear and outrage. The man bearing him nearly topples over but doesn't give him up. He holds on and pushes at Mary with his foot.

"Take her arms," he shouts, to those around them. He is short of breath. "She is in a fit."

Andrew has pushed his way in, among people who are still dancing and people who have stopped to watch the drama. He manages somehow to get hold of Mary and Young James and to make clear that the one is his son and the other his sister and that it is not a question of fits. Young James throws himself from his father to Mary and then begins kicking to be let down.

All is shortly explained with courtesies and apologies from Mr. Suter—through which Young James, quite recovered to himself, cries out over and over again that he must see the whale. He insists upon this just as if he knew perfectly well what a whale was.

Andrew tells him what will happen if he does not stop his racket.

"I had just stopped for a few minutes' talk with your wife, to ask her if she was well," the surgeon says. "I did not take time to bid her good-bye, so you must do it for me."

THERE ARE whales for Young James to see all day and for everybody to see who can be bothered. People grow tired of looking at them.

"Is there anybody but a fine type of rascal would sit down to talk with a woman that had her bosoms bared," says Old James, addressing the sky.

Then he quotes from the Bible regarding whales.

"There go the ships and there is that leviathan whom thou hast made to play therein. That crooked serpent, the dragon that is in the sea."

But he will not stir himself to go and have a look.

Mary remains unconvinced by the surgeon's story. Of course he would have to say to Agnes that he was taking the child to look at the whale. But that does not make it the truth. Whenever the picture of that devilish man carrying Young James flashes through her mind, and she feels in her chest the power of her own cry, she is astonished and happy. It is still her own belief that she has saved him.

NETTIE'S FATHER'S name is Mr. Carbert. Sometimes he sits and listens to Nettie read or talks to Walter. The day after all the celebration and the dancing, when many people are in a bad humor from exhaustion and some from drinking whiskey, and hardly anybody looks at the shore, he seeks Walter out to talk to him.

"Nettie is so taken with you," he says, "that she has got the idea that you must come along with us to Montreal."

He gives an apologetic laugh, and Walter laughs too.

"Then she must think that Montreal is in Canada West," says Walter.

"No, no. I am not making a joke. I looked out for you to talk to you on purpose when she was not with us. You are a fine companion for her and it makes her happy to be with you. And I can see you are an intelligent lad and a prudent one and one who would do well in my business."

"I am with my father and my brother," says Walter, so startled that his voice has a youthful yelp in it. "We are going to get land."

"Well then. You are not the only son your father has. There may not be enough good land for all of you. And you may not always want to be a farmer."

Walter says to himself, that is true.

"My daughter now, how old do you think she is?"

Walter cannot think. He shakes his head.

"She is fourteen, nearly fifteen," Nettie's father says. "You would not think so, would you? But it does not matter, that is not what I am talking about. Not about you and Nettie, anything in years to come. You understand that? There is no question of years to come. But I would like for you to come with us and let her be the child that she is and make her happy now with your company. Then I would naturally want to repay you, and there would also be work for you and if all went well you could count on advancement."

Both of them at this point notice that Nettie is coming towards them. She sticks out her tongue at Walter, so quickly that her father apparently does not notice.

"No more now. Think about it and pick your time to tell me," says her father. "But sooner rather than later would be best."

We were becalmed the 21st and 22nd but we had rather more wind the 23rd but in the afternoon were all alarmed by a squall of wind accompanied by thunder and lightening which was very terrible and we had one of our mainsails that had just been mended torn to rags again with the wind. The squall lasted about 8 or 10 minutes and the 24th we had a fair wind which set us a good way up the River, where it became more strait so that we saw land on both sides of the River. But we becalmed again till the 31st when we had a breeze only two hours . . .

Walter has not taken long to make up his mind. He knows enough to thank Mr. Carbert, but says that he has not thought of working in a city, or any indoor job. He means to work with his family until they are set up with some sort of house and land to farm and then when they do not need his help so much he thinks of being a trader to the Indians, a sort of explorer. Or a miner for gold.

"As you will," says Mr. Carbert. They walk several steps together, side by side. "I must say I had thought you were rather more serious than that. Fortunately I said nothing to Nettie."

But Nettie has not been fooled as to the subject of their talks together. She pesters her father until he has to let her know how things have gone and then she seeks out Walter.

"I will not talk to you anymore from now on," she says, in a more grown-up voice than he has ever heard from her. "It is not because I am angry but just because if I go on talking to you I will have to think all the time about how soon I'll be saying good-bye to you. But if I stop now I will have already said good-bye so it will all be over sooner."

She spends the time that is left walking sedately with her father in her finest clothes.

Walter feels sorry to see her—in these lady's cloaks and bonnets she seems lost, she looks more of a child than ever, and her show of haughtiness is touching—but there is so much for him to pay attention to that he seldom thinks of her when she is out of sight.

Years will pass before she will reappear in his mind. But when she does, he will find that she is a source of happiness, available to him till the day he dies. Sometimes he will even entertain himself with thoughts of what might have happened, had he taken up the offer. Most secretly, he will imagine a radiant recovery, Nettie's acquiring a tall and maidenly body, their life together. Such foolish thoughts as a man may have in secret.

Several boats from the land came alongside of us with fish, rum, live sheep, tobacco, etc. which they sold very high to the passengers. The 1st of August we had a slight breeze and on the morning of the 2nd we passed by the Isle of Orleans and about six in the morning we were in sight of Quebec in as good health I think as when we left Scotland. We are to sail for Montreal tomorrow in a steamboat . . .

My brother Walter in the former part of this letter has written a large journal which I intend to sum up in a small ledger. We have had a very prosperous voyage being wonderfully preserved in health. Out of three hundred passengers only 3 died, two of which being unhealthy when they left their native land and the other a child born in the ship. Our family has been as healthy on board as in their ordinary state in Scotland. We can say nothing yet about the state of the country. There is a great number of people landing here but wages is good. I can neither advise nor discourage people from coming. The land is very extensive and very thin-peopled. I think we have seen as much land as might serve all the people in Britain uncultivated and covered with wood. We will write you again as soon as settled.

When Andrew has added this paragraph, Old James is persuaded to add his signature to those of his two sons before this letter is sealed and posted to Scotland, from Quebec. He will write nothing else, saying, "What does it matter to me? It cannot be my home. It can be nothing to me but the land where I will die."

"It will be that for all of us," says Andrew. "But when the time comes we will think of it more as a home."

"Time will not be given to me to do that."

"Are you not well, Father?"

"I am well and I am not."

Young James is now paying occasional attention to the old man, sometimes stopping in front of him and looking straight into his face and saying one word to him, with a sturdy insistence, as if that could not help but lead to a conversation.

He chooses the same word every time. *Key.*

"He bothers me," Old James says. "I don't like the boldness of him. He will go on and on and not remember a thing of Scotland where he was born or the ship he travelled on, he will get to talking another language the way they do when they go to England, only it will be worse than theirs. He looks at me with the kind of a look that says he knows that me and my times is all over with."

"He will remember plenty of things," says Mary. Since the dancing on deck and the incident of Mr. Suter she has grown more forthright within the family.

"And he doesn't mean his look to be bold," she says. "It is just that he is interested in everything. He understands what you say, far more than you think. He takes everything in and he thinks about it. He may grow up to be a preacher."

Although she has such a stiff and distant regard for her religion, that is still the most distinguished thing that she can imagine a man to be.

Her eyes fill with tears of enthusiasm, but the rest of them look down at the child with sensible reservations.

Young James stands in the midst of them—bright-eyed, fair, and straight. Slightly preening, somewhat wary, unnaturally solemn, as if he has indeed felt descend on him the burden of the future.

The adults too feel the astonishment of the moment, as if they have been borne for these past six weeks not on a ship but on one great wave, which has landed them with a mighty thump among such clamor of the French tongue and cries of gulls and clanging of Papist church bells, altogether an infidel commotion.

Mary thinks that she could snatch up Young James and run away into some part of the strange city of Quebec and find work as a sewing-woman (talk on the boat has made her aware that such work is in demand) and bring him up all by herself as if she were his mother.

Andrew thinks of what it would be like to be here as a free man, without wife or father or sister or children, without a single burden on your back, what could you do then? He tells himself it is no use to think about it.

Agnes has heard women on the boat say that the officers you see in the street here are surely the best-looking men you can meet anywhere in the world, and she thinks now that this is surely true. A girl would have to watch herself with them. She has heard also that the men anyplace over here are ten or twenty times more numerous than the women. That must mean you can get what you want out of them. Marriage. Marriage to a man with enough money to let you ride in a carriage and buy paints to cover any birthmark on your face and send presents to your mother. If you were not married already and dragged down with two children.

Walter reflects that his brother is strong and Agnes is strong—she can help him on the land while Mary cares for the children. Whoever said that he should be a farmer? When they get to Montreal he will go and attach himself to the Hudson's Bay Company and they will send him to the frontier where he will find riches as well as adventure.

OLD JAMES has sensed defection, and begins to lament openly.

"How shall we sing the Lord's song in a strange land?"

BUT HE recovered himself. Here he is, a year or so later, in the New World, in the new town of York which is just about to have its name changed to Toronto. He is writing to his eldest son Robert.

. . . the people here speaks very good English there is many of our Scots words they cannot understand what we are saying and they live far more independent then King George . . . There is a Road goes Straight North from York for fifty miles and the farm Houses almost all Two Stories High. Some will have as good as 12 Cows and four or five horses for they pay no Taxes just a perfect trifell and ride in their Gigs or chire like Lords . . . there is no Presbetarian minister in this town as yet but there is a large English Chapel and Methodist Chapel . . . the English minister reads all that he Says unless it be for his Clark Craying always at the end of every Period Good Lord Deliver us and the Methodist prays as Loud as Ever He Can and the people is all doun on there knees Craying Amen so you can Scarce Hear what the Priest is Saying and I have Seen some of them Jumping up as if they would have gone to Heaven Soul and Body but there Body was a filthy Clog to them for they always fell down again altho craying O Jesus O Jesus as He had been there to pull them up threw the Loft . . . Now Robert I do not advise you to Come Hear so you may take your own will when you did not come along with us I do not Expect Ever to See you again . . . May the good will of Him that Dwelt in the Bush rest up on you . . . if I had thought that you would have deserted us I would not have comed hear it was my ame to get you all Near me made me Come to America but mans thoughts are Vanity for have Scattered you far wider but I Can not help it now . . . I shall say no more but wish that the God of Jacob be your god and may be your gide for Ever and Ever is the sincer prayer of your Loving Father till Death . . .

There is more—the whole letter passed on by Hogg's connivance and printed in *Blackwoods Magazine,* where I can look it up today.

And some considerable time after that, he writes another letter, addressed to the Editor of *The Colonial Advocate,* and published in that newspaper. By this time the family is settled in Esquesing Township, in Canada West.

. . . The Scots Bodys that lives heare is all doing Tolerably well for the things of this world but I am afraid that few of them thinks about what will Come of thear Soul when Death there Days doth End for they have found a thing they call Whiskey and a great mony of them dabbales and drinks at it till they make themselves worse than a ox or an ass . . . Now sir I could tell you bit of Stories but I am afraid you will put me in your Calonial Advocate I do not Like to be put in prent I once wrote a bit of a letter to my Son Robert in Scotland and my friend James Hogg the Poet put it in Blackwoods Magazine and had me all through North America before I knew my letter was gone Home . . . Hogg poor man has spent most of his life in conning Lies and if I read the Bible right I think it says that all Liares is to have there pairt in the Lake that Burns with Fire and Brimstone but I supose they find it a Loquarative trade for I belive that Hogg and Walter Scott has got more money for Lieing than old Boston and the Erskins got for all the Sermons ever they Wrote . . .

And I am surely one of the liars the old man talks about, in what I have written about the voyage. Except for Walter's journal, and the letters, the story is full of my invention.

The sighting of Fife from Castle Rock is related by Hogg, so it must be true.

THOSE TRAVELLERS lie buried—all but one of them—in the graveyard of Boston Church, in Esquesing, in Halton County, almost within sight, and well within sound, of Highway 401 north of Milton, which at that spot may be the busiest road in Canada.

The church—built on what was once the farm of Andrew Laidlaw—is of course named for Thomas Boston. It is built of blackened limestone blocks. The front wall rises higher than the rest of the building—rather in the style of the false fronts on old-fashioned main streets—and it has an archway on top of it, rather than a tower—for the church bell.

Old James is here. In fact he is here twice, or at least his name is, along with the name of his wife, born Helen Scott, and buried in Ettrick in the year 1800. Their names appear on the same stone that bears the names of Andrew and Agnes. But surprisingly, the same names are written on another stone that looks older than others in the graveyard—a darkened, blotchy slab such as you are more apt to see in the churchyards of the British Isles. Anyone trying to figure this out might wonder if they carried it across the ocean, with the mother's name on it, waiting for the father's to be added—if it was perhaps an awkward burden, wrapped in sacking and tied with stout cord, borne by Walter down into the hold of the ship.

But why would someone have taken the trouble to have the names also added to those on the newer column above Andrew and Agnes's grave?

It looks as if the death and burial of such a father was a matter worth recording twice over.

Nearby, close to the graves of her father and her brother Andrew and her sister-in-law Agnes, is the grave of Little Mary, married after all and buried beside Robert Murray, her husband. Women were scarce and so were prized in the new country. She and Robert did not have any children together, but after Mary's early death he married another woman and by her he had four sons who lie here, dead at the ages of two, and three, and four, and thirteen. The second wife is there too. Her stone says *Mother.* Mary's says *Wife.*

And here is the brother James who was not lost to them, who made his way from Nova Scotia to join them, first in York and then in Esquesing, farming with Andrew. He brought a wife with him, or found her in the community. Perhaps she helped with Agnes's babies before she started having her own. For Agnes had a great number of pregnancies, and raised many children. In a letter written to his brothers Robert and William in Scotland, telling of the death of their father, in 1829 (a cancer, not much pain until near the end, though *it eat away a great part of his cheek and jaw*), Andrew mentions that his wife has been feeling poorly for the past three years. This may be a roundabout way of saying that during those years she bore her sixth, seventh, and eighth child. She must have recovered her health, for she lived into her eighties.

ANDREW GAVE the land that the church is built on. Or possibly sold it. It is hard to measure devoutness against business sense. He seems to have prospered, though he spread himself less than Walter. Walter married an American girl from Montgomery County in New York State. Eighteen when she married him, thirty-three when she died after the birth of her ninth child. Walter did not marry again, but farmed successfully, educated his sons, speculated in land, and wrote letters to the government complaining about his taxes, also objecting to the township's partici-pation in a proposed railway—the interest being squandered, he says, for the benefit of capitalists in Britain.

Nevertheless it is a fact that he and Andrew supported the British governor, Sir Francis Bond Head, who was surely representing those capitalists, against the rebellion led by their fellow Scot, William Lyon Mackenzie, in 1837. They wrote to the governor a letter of assiduous flattery, in the grand servile style of their times. Some of their descendants might wish this not to be true, but there is not much to be done about the politics of our relatives, living or dead.

And Walter was able to take a trip back to Scotland, where he had himself photographed wearing a plaid and holding on to a bouquet of thistles.

On the stone commemorating Andrew and Agnes (and Old James and Helen) there appears also the name of their daughter Isabel, who like her mother Agnes died an old woman. She has a married name, but there is no further sign of her husband.

Born at Sea.

And here also is the name of Andrew and Agnes's firstborn child, Isabel's elder brother. His dates as well.

Young James was dead within a month of the family's landing at Quebec. His name is here but surely he cannot be. They had not taken up their land when he died, they had not even seen this place. He may have been buried somewhere along the way from Montreal to York or in that hectic new town itself. Perhaps in a raw temporary burying ground now paved over, perhaps without a stone in a churchyard where other bodies would someday be laid on top of his. Dead of some mishap in the busy streets of York, or of a fever, or dysentery—of any of the ailments, the accidents, that were the common destroyers of little children in his time.

Lying Under the Apple Tree

OVER ON the other side of town lived a woman named Miriam McAlpin, who kept horses. These were not horses that belonged to her—she boarded them and exercised them for their owners, who were harness-racing people. She lived in a house that had been the original farmhouse, close to the horse barns, with her old parents, who seldom came outside. Beyond the house and the barns was an oval track on which Miriam or her stable boy, or sometimes the owners themselves, could be seen now and then on the low seat of a flimsy-looking sulky, flying along and beating up the dust.

In one of the pasture fields for the horses, next to the town street, there were three apple trees, the remains of an old orchard. Two of them were small and bent and one was quite large, like a nearly grown maple. They were never pruned or sprayed and the apples were scabby, not worth stealing, but most years there was an abundant flowering, apple blossoms hanging on everywhere, so that the branches looked from a little way off to be absolutely clotted with snow.

I HAD inherited a bicycle, or at least I had the use of one left behind by our part-time hired man when he went away to work in an aircraft factory. It was a man's bike, of course, high-seated and lightweight, of some odd-looking make long discontinued.

"You're not going to ride that to school, are you?" my sister said, when I had started practice rides up and down our lane. My sister was younger than I was, but she sometimes suffered anxiety on my behalf, understanding perhaps before I did the various ways in which I could risk making a fool of myself. She was thinking not just of the look of the bike but of the fact that I was thirteen and in my first year at high school, and that this was a watershed year as far as girls riding bikes to school was concerned. All girls who wanted to establish their femininity had to quit riding them. Girls who continued to ride either lived too far out in the country to walk—and had parents who could not afford to board them in town—or were simply eccentric and unable to take account of certain unstated but far-reaching rules. We lived just beyond the town limits, so if I showed up riding a bicycle—and particularly this bicycle—it would put me in the category of such girls. Those who wore women's oxford shoes and lisle stockings and rolled their hair.

"Not to school," I said. But I did start making use of the bike, riding it out to the country along the back roads on Sunday afternoons. There was hardly a chance then of meeting anybody I knew, and sometimes I met nobody at all.

I liked to do this because I was secretly devoted to Nature. The feeling came from books, at first. It came from the girls' stories by the writer L. M. Montgomery, who often inserted some sentences describing a snowy field in moonlight or a pine forest or a still pond mirroring the evening sky. Then it had merged with another private passion I had, which was for lines of poetry. I went rampaging through my school texts to uncover them before they could be read and despised in class.

To betray either of these addictions, at home or at school, would have put me into a condition of permanent vulnerability. Which I felt that I was in already, to some extent. All someone had to say, in a certain voice, was *you would,* or *how like you,* and I felt the taunt, the chastening air, the lines drawn. But now that I had the bike, I could ride on Sunday afternoons into territory that seemed waiting for the kind of homage I ached to offer. Here were the sheets of water from the flooded creeks flashing over the land, and here were the banks of trillium under the red-budded trees. And the chokecherries, the pin cherries, in the fencerows, breaking into tender bits of bloom before there was a leaf on them.

The cherry blossoms got me thinking about the trees in Miriam McAlpin's field. I wanted to look at them when they flowered. And not just to look at them—as you could do from the street—but to get underneath those branches, to lie down on my back with my head against the trunk of the tree and to see how it rose, as if out of my own skull, rose up and lost itself in an upside-down sea of blossom. Also to see if there were bits of sky showing through, so that I could screw up my eyes to make them foreground not background, bright-blue fragments on that puffy white sea. There was a formality about this idea that I longed for. It was almost like kneeling down in church, which in our church we didn't do. I had done it once, when I was friends with Delia Cavanaugh and her mother took us to the Catholic church on a Saturday to arrange the flowers. I crossed myself and knelt in a pew and Delia said—not even whispering—"What are you doing that for? You're not supposed to do that. Just us."

I LEFT the bike lying in the grass. It was evening, I had ridden through town on back streets. There was nobody in the stable yard or around the house. I got myself over the fence. I tried to go as quickly as possible, without running, over the ground where the horses had been cropping the early grass. I ducked under the branches of the big tree and went on stooping and stumbling, sometimes hit in the face by the blossoms, till I reached the trunk and could do what I'd come to do.

I lay down flat on my back. There was a root of the tree making a hard ridge under me, so I had to shift around. And there were last year's apples, dark as chunks of dried meat, that I had to get out of the way before I could settle. Even then, when I composed myself, I was aware of my body's being in an odd and unnatural situation. And when I looked up at all the dangling pearly petals with their faint rosy smear, all the pre-arranged nosegays, I was not quite swept into the state of mind, of worship, that I had been hoping for. The sky was thinly clouded, and what I could see of it reminded me of dingy bits of china.

Not that this wasn't worth doing. At least—as I began to understand as I got to my feet and scrambled out of there—it was worth having done. It was along the lines of an acknowledgment, rather than an experience. I hurried across the field and over the fence, retrieved my bicycle, and was in fact starting to ride away when I heard a loud whistle, and my name.

"Hey. You. Yeah. You."

It was Miriam McAlpin.

"You come on over here for a minute."

I wheeled around. There in the driveway between the old house and the horse barns, Miriam was talking to two men, who must have driven up in the car parked beside the road. They were wearing white shirts, suit vests, and trousers—just the same thing any man who worked at a desk or behind a counter in those days would be wearing from the time he got dressed in the morning till he got undressed to go to bed. Next to them, Miriam in her work pants and loose checked shirt looked like a cocky twelve-year-old boy, though she was a woman of between twenty-five and thirty. Either that, or she looked like a jockey. Cropped hair, hunched shoulders, raw skin. She gave me a look that was threatening and derisive.

"I saw you," she said. "Over in our field."

I said nothing. I knew what the next question would be and I was trying to think of an answer.

"So. What were you doing there?"

"Looking for something," I said.

"Looking for something. Yeah. What?"

"A bracelet."

I had never owned a bracelet in my life.

"So. Why did you think it was in there?"

"I thought I'd lost it."

"Yeah. In there. How come?"

"Because I was in there the other day looking for morels," I floundered. "I had it on then and I thought it could have slipped off."

It was true enough that people looked for morels under old apple trees in the spring. Though I don't suppose they wore bracelets while they were at it.

"Unh-hunh," said Miriam. "Did you find any? Whatchamacallums? Morels?"

I said no.

"That's good. 'Cause they would've been mine."

She looked me up and down and said what she'd been wanting to say all along. "You're starting early, aren't you?"

One of the men was looking at the ground, but I thought he was smiling. The other looked straight at me, raising his eyebrows slightly in droll reproach. Men who knew who I was, men who knew my father, would probably not have let their looks say so much.

I understood. She thought—they all thought—that I had been under the tree, yesterday evening or some other evening, with a man or a boy.

"You go on home," Miriam said. "You and your bracelets go on home and don't ever come back monkeying around on my property in the future. Go on."

Miriam McAlpin was well known for her tendency to bawl people out. I had once heard her in the grocery store, carrying on at the top of her voice about some bruised peaches. The way she was treating me was predictable, and the suspicions she had of me seemed to rouse an unambiguous feeling in her—pure disgust—which did not surprise me.

It was the men who made me sick. The looks they gave me, of proper disapproval and sneaky appraisal. The slight dull droop and thickening of their features, as the level of sludge rose in their heads.

The stable boy had come out while this was going on. He was leading a horse belonging to one or both of the men. He halted in the yard, did not come closer. He seemed not to be looking at his boss, or the horse owners, or at me, not to take any interest in the scene. He would be used to Miriam's way of telling people off.

People's thoughts about me—not just the kind of thoughts the men or Miriam might be having, each kind rather dangerous in its own way—but any thoughts at all, seemed to me a mysterious threat, a gross impertinence. I hated even to hear a person say something relatively harmless.

"I seen you walking down the street the other day. Looked like you were off in the clouds."

Judgments and speculations all like a swarm of bugs trying to get into my mouth and eyes. I could have swatted them, I could have spat.

"Dirt," my sister whispered to me when I got home. "Dirt on the back of your blouse."

She watched me take it off in the bathroom, and scrub at it with a hard bar of soap. We didn't have running hot water except in the winter, so she offered to get me some from the kettle. She didn't ask me how the dirt had got there, she was only hoping to get rid of the evidence, keep me out of trouble.

On Saturday nights there was always a crowd on the main street. At that time there wasn't such a thing as a mall anywhere in the county, and it wasn't until several years after the war that the big shopping night would shift to Friday. The year I'm talking about is 1944, when we still had ration books and there were a lot of things you couldn't buy—like new cars and silk stockings—but the farmers came into town with some money in their pockets and the stores had brightened up after the Depression doldrums and everything stayed open till ten o'clock.

Most town people did their shopping during the week and in the daytime. Unless they worked in the stores or restaurants they stayed out of the way on Saturday evenings, playing cards with their neighbors or listening to the radio. Newly married couples, engaged couples, couples who were "going out," cuddled in the movie house or drove, if they could get the gas coupons, to one of the dance halls on the lakeshore. It was the country people who took over the street and the country men and girls on the loose who went into Neddy's Night Owl, where the platform was raised above a dirt floor and every dance cost ten cents.

I stood close to the platform with some friends of my own age. Nobody came along to pay ten cents for any of us. No wonder. We laughed loudly, we criticized the dancing, the haircuts, the clothes. We sometimes spoke of a girl as a slut, or a man as a fairy, though we did not have a precise definition of either of these words.

Neddy himself, who sold the tickets, was apt to turn to us and say, "Don't you think you girls need some fresh air?" And we would swagger off. Or else we would get bored and leave on our own initiative. We bought ice-cream cones and gave each other licks to try the different flavors, and walked along the street in a haughty style, swinging around the knots of talkers and through the swarms of children squirting water at each other from the drinking fountain. Nobody was worth our notice.

The girls who took part in this parade were not out of the top drawer— as my mother would have said, with a wistful and lightly sarcastic edge to her voice. Not one of them had a sunroom on their house or a father who wore a suit on any day but Sunday. Girls of that sort were at home now, or in each other's houses, playing Monopoly or making fudge or trying out hairstyles. My mother was sorry not to see me accepted into that crowd.

But it was all right with me. This way, I could be a ringleader and a loudmouth. If that was a disguise it was one that I managed easily. Or it might not have been a disguise, but just one of the entirely disjointed and dissimilar personalities I seemed to be made up of.

On a vacant lot at the north end of town some members of the Salvation Army had set up their post. There was a preacher and a small choir to sing the hymns and a fat boy on the drum. Also a tall boy to play the trombone, a girl playing the clarinet, some half-grown children equipped with tambourines.

Salvation Army people were even less top drawer than the girls I was with. The man who was doing the preaching was the drayman who delivered coal. No doubt he had washed himself clean, but his face still had a gray shadow. Sweat was running down it from the exertion of his preaching and it seemed as if his sweat must be gray too. Some cars would honk to drown him out as they passed. (In spite of the waste of gas, there were certain cars driven, by young men, up the street to the north end, and down the street to the south end, over and over again.) Most people walked past with uneasy but respectful faces, but some halted to watch. As we did, waiting for something to laugh at.

The instruments were raised for a hymn, and I saw that the boy who lifted the trombone was the same stable boy who had stood in the yard while Miriam McAlpin was giving me the dressing-down. He smiled at me with his eyes as he began to play, and he seemed to be smiling not to recall my humiliation but with irrepressible pleasure, as if the sight of me woke the memory of something quite different from that scene, a natural happiness.

"There is Power, Power, Power, Power, Power in the Blood," sang the choir. The tambourines were waved above the players' heads. Joy and lustiness infected the bystanders, so that most people began to sing along with a jolly irony. And we permitted ourselves to sing with the others.

Soon after that the service was at an end. The stores were closing up, and we took our separate ways home. There was a shortcut for me, a footbridge over the river. When I had nearly reached the end of it I heard heavy running, some sort of thumping, behind me. The boards shuddered under my feet. I turned sideways, backing against the railing, slightly scared but concerned not to show it. There were no lights near the footbridge and now it was quite dark.

When he got close I saw that it was the trombone player in his heavy dark uniform. The trombone case made the thumping sound, knocking against the railing.

"Okay," he said, out of breath. "It's just me. I was only trying to catch up with you."

"How did you know it was me?" I said.

"I could see a little. I knew you lived out this way. I could tell it was you by the way you walk."

"How?" I said. With most people, such presumption would have made me too angry to ask.

"I don't know. It's just the way you walk."

HIS NAME was Russell Craik. His family belonged to the Salvation Army, his father being the drayman-preacher and his mother one of the hymn-singers. Because he had worked with his father and got used to horses, he had been hired by Miriam McAlpin as soon as he left school. That was after Grade Eight. It was not at all uncommon in those years for boys to do that. Because of the war, there were lots of jobs for them to take up while they were waiting, as he was, to be old enough to go into the Army. He would be old enough in September.

If Russell Craik had wanted to take me out in the usual way, to take me to the movies or to dances, there would not have been a chance of its being allowed. My mother would have pronounced that I was too young. Probably she would have felt it was not necessary to say that he worked as a stable boy and his father delivered coal and his whole family put on Salvation Army outfits and regularly testified on the street. Those considerations would have meant something to me too, if it had come to displaying him publicly as my boyfriend. They would have meant something at least until he got into the Army and became presentable. But as it was, I didn't have to think about any of that. Russell could not take me to the movies or to a dance hall because his religion forbade him to go there himself. The arrangement that developed between us seemed easy, almost natural, to me because it was in some ways—not all—much like the casual, hardly recognized, and temporary pairing off of boys and girls of my age, not his.

We rode bicycles, for one thing. Russell did not own a car and did not have any access to one, though he could drive—he drove the horse-barn truck. He never called for me at my house and I never suggested it. We rode out of town separately on Sunday afternoons and met always at the same place, a crossroads school two or three miles out of town. All the country schools had names by which they were known, rather than by the official numbers carved above their doors. Never S.S. No. 11, or S.S. No. 5, but Lambs' School and Brewsters' School and the Red Brick School and the Stone School. The one we chose, already familiar to me, was called the School of the Flowing Well. A thin stream of water flowed continuously out of a pipe in a corner of the school yard, to justify this name.

Around that yard, which was kept mowed even in the summer holidays, there were mature maple trees that cast nearly black pools of shade. In one corner was a stone pile with long grass growing out of it, where we concealed our bikes.

The road in front of the school yard was neat and gravelled, but the side road, climbing a hill, was not much more than a lane in a field, or a dirt track. On one side of it was pasture field dotted with hawthorns and juniper, and on the other a stand of oak and pine trees, with a hollow between it and the bank of the road. In this hollow was a dump—not the official township dump, just an informal dump that the country people had made. This interested Russell, and every time we passed it we had to lean over and peer down into the hollow, to see if there was anything new in it. There never was, the dump had probably not been used for years— but quite often he could pick out something that he had not noticed before.

"See? That's the grille of a V-8."

"See under the buggy wheel? That's an old battery radio."

I had been on this road a few times by myself and had not once seen that the dump was there, but I knew about other things. I knew that when we went over the hill the oak and pine trees would be swallowed up in spruce and tamarack and cedar, and so would the bumpy pasture, and all that we would see, for a long time, would be swamp growth on either side, with glimpses of high-bush cranberries nobody could ever get to, and some formal-looking crimson flower I was not sure of the name of—I thought it was called the Devil's paintbrush. On a branch of cedar somebody had hung the skull of a small animal, and this Russell would take note of, wondering every time if it was a ferret's or a weasel's or a mink's.

It was proof anyway, he said, that somebody had been on this road before us. Probably walking, probably not in a car—the cedars grew in too close, and the plank bridge over the creek at the lowest level of the swamp was a primitive affair, springy under our feet and without railings. Beyond that the land rose slowly, and the mucky ground was left behind and finally there were farm fields on either side, glimpsed through large beech trees. Such heavy trees and so many of them that their smooth gray light seemed actually to make a change in the air, cooling it down as if you had entered some high hall or church.

And the track would end, after the usual mile and a quarter measurement of country blocks, running into another straight gravel road. We turned and walked back the same way.

There were hardly any birds to be heard in the hot middle of the day, and none to be seen, and there were not many mosquitos because the ponds in the low ground had mostly dried up. But there were dragonflies over the creek and often clouds of very small butterflies, such a pale green that you thought maybe they were just catching a reflection of the leaves.

What there was to be heard at every stage of the walk was Russell's unhurried, pleased voice. He talked about his family—there were two older sisters who were gone from home and a younger brother and two younger sisters and they were all musical, each one playing some instrument. The younger brother's name was Jackie—he was learning the trombone, to take over from Russell. The sisters at home were Mavis and Annie and the grown-up ones were Iona and Isabel. Iona was married to a man who worked on the Hydro lines, and Isabel was a chambermaid in a large hotel. Another sister, Edna, had died of polio in an iron lung after being sick for only two days at the age of twelve. She was the only one in the family to have blond hair. The brother Jackie had nearly died also, of blood poison from stepping on a board with a rusty nail. Russell himself used to have tough feet from going barefoot in the summer. He could walk on gravel or thistles or stubble and he never got any kind of wound.

He had shot up in height in Grade Eight to be nearly as tall as he was now, and he got the part of Ali Baba in the school operetta. That was because he could sing, as well as being tall.

He had learned to drive his uncle's car when his uncle came over from Port Huron. His uncle was in the plumbing business and he traded in his car for a new one every two years. He let Russell drive before he was old enough to get a license. But Miriam McAlpin would not let him drive her truck until he got one. He drove it now, with and without the horse trailer hitched on. To Elmira, to Hamilton, once to Peterborough. It was tricky driving because a horse trailer could roll over. She came with him sometimes, but she let him drive.

His voice changed when he talked of Miriam McAlpin. It became wary, half-contemptuous, half-amused. She was a Tartar, he said. But okay if you knew how to handle her. She liked horses better than she liked people. She would have been married by now if she could have married a horse.

I did not speak much about myself and I did not listen to him all that closely. His talk was like a curtain of easy rain between me and the trees, the light and shadows on the road, the clear-running creek, the butterflies, and all that part of myself that would have paid attention to these things if I had been alone. A lot of me was under cover, as it was with my friends on Saturday nights. But the change now was not so deliberate and voluntary. I was half-hypnotized, not just by the sound of his voice but by the bright breadth of his shoulders in a clean, short-sleeved shirt, by his tawny throat and thick arms. He had washed himself with Lifebuoy soap—I knew the smell of it as everybody did—but washing was as far as most men went in those days, they didn't bother about the sweat that would accumulate in the near future. So I could smell that too. And just faintly the smell of horses, bridles, barns, and hay.

When I wasn't with him I would try to remember—was he good-looking or was he not? His body was fairly lean but he had a slight fleshiness about the face, an authoritative pout to his lips, and his wide-open clear blue eyes showed something like an obstinate naïveté, an innocent self-regard. All that I might not have cared for much in another person.

"I grind my teeth at night," he said. "I never wake up, but it wakes Jackie up and is he ever mad. He gives me a kick and I turn over in my sleep and that fixes it. Because I only do it when I'm laying on my back."

"Would you kick me?" he said, and he reached across the foot or so of air that was between us, shot full of sunlight, and picked up my hand. He said that he got so hot in bed he kicked all the covers off, and that made Jackie mad as well.

I wanted to ask him if he wore just his pyjama tops or just the bottoms, or both, or nothing at all, but the last possibility made me feel too weak to open my mouth. Our fingers worked together, all on their own, until they got so sweaty that they gave up, and separated.

It was not until we got back to the school yard and were about to pick up our bikes and ride back to town—separately—that the reason for our walk, the only reason as far as I could understand it, received our whole attention. He would pull me into the shade and put his arms around me and begin to kiss me. Hidden from the road he would press me up against a tree trunk and we would kiss chastely at first and then more fervently, and wind ourselves together—still upright—with a shaky urgency. And after—how long?—five or ten minutes of this we would separate and pick up our bikes and say good-bye. My mouth would be rubbed sore and my cheeks and chin scraped by bristles that were not visible on his face. My back would hurt from being shoved against the tree and the front of my body would ache from the pressure of his. My stomach, though quite flat, had a little give to it, but I had noted that his had none. I thought that men must have a firmness and even a protuberance to their stomachs, that was not evident until you were held very tightly against them.

It seems so strange that knowing as much as I knew, I did not realize what this pressure was. I had a fairly accurate idea of a man's body, but somehow I had missed the information that there was this change in size and condition. I seem to have believed that a penis was at maximum size all the time, and in its classic shape, but in spite of this could be kept dangling down inside the leg of the pants, not hoisted up to put pressure against another body in this way. I had heard a lot of jokes, and I had seen animals coupling, but somehow, when education is informal, gaps can occur.

Now AND then he would speak about God. His tone at such times was firm and factual, as if God were a superior officer, was occasionally gracious but often inflexible and impatient, in a manly way. When the war was over and he was out of the Army ("If I'm not killed," he said cheerfully), there would still be the commands of God and *his* Army to be reckoned with.

"I'll have to do what God wants me to."

That struck me. What terrible docility it took, to be such a believer.

Or—when you considered the war and the ordinary Army—just to be a man.

The thought of his future might have come to him because we had noticed, on the trunk of a beech tree—those trees whose gray bark is ideal for messages—a carved face and a date. The year was 1909. During the time since, the tree had been growing, its trunk had been widening, so that the outlines of the face had broadened at the sides to become blotches wider than the face itself. The rest of the date had been blotched out entirely, and the numbers of the year might soon be illegible as well.

"That was before the First World War," I said. "Whoever did it might be dead now. He might've been killed in that war.

"Or he could just be dead anyway," I added hastily.

It was on that day, I believe, that we got so hot on the way back that we took off our shoes and socks and lowered ourselves from the planks to stand in the knee-high water of the creek. We splashed our arms and faces.

"You know that time I got caught coming out from under the apple tree?" I said, to my own surprise.

"Yeah."

"I told her I was looking for a bracelet, but it wasn't true. I went in there for another reason."

"Is that right?"

By now I wished I had not started this.

"I wanted to get under the big tree when it was all in bloom and look up at it from underneath."

He laughed. "That's funny," he said. "I wanted to do that too. I never did, but I thought about it."

I was surprised, and somehow not quite pleased, to find that we had had this urge in common. But surely I would not have told him if I hadn't hoped that it was something he would understand?

"Come to our place for supper," he said.

"Don't you have to ask your mother if it's all right?"

"She don't care."

My mother would have cared, if she had known. But she didn't know, because I lied and said I was going to my friend Clara's. Now that my father had to be at the Foundry by five o'clock—even on Sundays, because he was the watchman—and my mother was so often not feeling well, our suppers had become rather haphazard. If I cooked, there were things that I liked. One was sliced bread and cheese with milk and beaten eggs poured over it, baked in the oven. Another, also oven-baked, was a loaf of tinned meat coated with brown sugar. Or heaps of slices of raw potato that had been fried to a crisp. Left to themselves, my brother and sister would make a supper of something like sardines on soda crackers or peanut butter on graham wafers. Erosion of regular customs in our house seemed to make my deception easier.

Perhaps my mother, if she had known, would have found a way to say to me that once you went into certain houses as an equal and a friend—and this was true even if they were in a way perfectly respectable houses—you showed that the value you put on yourself was not very high, and after that others would value you accordingly. I would have argued with her, of course, and the more fiercely because I would have known that what she was saying was true, as far as life in that town went. I was the one, after all, who would make any excuse now not to go with my friends past the corner where Russell and his family stationed themselves on Saturday nights.

I sometimes thought ahead hopefully to the time when Russell would have put away that slightly comic dark-blue red-piped uniform and replaced it with khaki. It seemed as if much more than the uniform might be changed, that an identity itself could be peeled away and a fresh one shine out, unassailable, once he was dressed as a fighting man.

THE CRAIKS lived on a narrow diagonal street only a block long, not far from the horse barns. I had never had any reason to walk along this street before. The houses were close to the sidewalk and close to each other with no room for driveways or side yards in between. The people who owned cars had to park them partly on the sidewalk and partly on the strips of grass that served as front lawns. The Craiks' large wooden house was painted yellow—Russell had told me to look for the yellow house—but the paint was weathered and blistered.

Just as the brown paint was, that had once, ill-advisedly, covered the red brick of the house that I lived in. When it came to ready money our two families were not so far apart. Not far apart at all.

Two little girls were sitting on the front step, maybe stationed there in case I should have forgotten the house's description.

They jumped up, however, without a word, and ran into the house as if I'd been a wildcat after them. The screen door banged in my face and I was left staring down a long bare hallway. I could hear a subdued commotion in the back of the house, perhaps having to do with who should go to greet me. And then Russell himself came down the stairs, his hair dark from a recent wetting, and let me in.

"So you got here okay," he said. He backed off from touching me.

Mr. and Mrs. Craik did not wear their Salvation Army uniforms around home. I don't know why I had thought they would. The father, whose street preaching was always on the ferocious side, wrathful even when he held out the hope of mercy and salvation, and whose expression when he sat hunched on the coal wagon was always one of disgruntlement, came forward now as a scrubbed and tidy man with a shining bald head, and greeted me as if he was actually glad to see me in his house. The mother was tall, like Russell, large-boned and flat-fronted, with gray hair chopped off at the level of her ears. Russell had to tell her my name twice, through the racket she was making mashing the potatoes, before he could get her to turn around. She wiped her hand on her apron as if she had thought of shaking mine, but she did not do so. She said that she was pleased to meet me. Her voice when she sang the street-corner hymns was full and sweet, but when she spoke now it cracked with embarrassment like an adolescent boy's.

Russell's father was ready to step into the breach. He asked me if I had any experience of banty hens. I said no, and he said he had thought I might have, being brought up on a farm.

"The hens are my hobby," he said. "Come and have a look."

The two girls had reappeared and were hanging around in the hall doorway. They were about to follow their father and Russell and me out into the backyard, but their mother called to them.

"Annieanmavis! You stay here an put the plates on the table."

The banty rooster was named King George.

"That's a joke," Mr. Craik said. "On account of George is my name."

The hens were named after Mae West and Tugboat Annie and Daisy Mae and other personalities from the movies or comic strips or popular folklore. This surprised me because of the fact that movies were forbidden to this family and the movie theatre was singled out in the Saturday sermons as a place to be specially abhorred. I had thought the comic strips would be out of bounds as well. Perhaps it was all right to give such names to silly hens. Or perhaps the Craiks had not always belonged to the Salvation Army.

"How do you tell which is which?" I said. I didn't have my wits about me at all, or else I would have seen that each was distinctly marked, had its own pattern of red and brown and rust and gold feathers.

Russell's brother had turned up from somewhere. He snickered.

"Oh, you learn to," the father said. He began to identify each one for me, but the hens were getting flustered by all the attention and scattered around the yard so that he couldn't keep them straight. The rooster was bold and pecked at my shoe.

"Don't be alarmed," Russell's father said. "He's just showing off."

"Do they lay eggs?" was my next foolish-sounding question.

"Oh, they do, they do, but not so's it's a common occurrence. No. Not even enough for our own table. Oh no, they're an ornamental breed, that's what they are. Ornamental breed."

"You're going to get a clout," Russell said to his brother, behind my back.

At supper, the father gave Russell a nod to ask the Blessing, and Russell did so. Blessings here were leisurely and composed on the spot to suit the occasion, nothing like the Bless-this-food-to-our-use-and-us-to-thy-service that used to be mumbled at our table at home when we ate as a family. Russell spoke slowly and confidently and mentioned the name of everyone at the table—including me, asking that the Lord should make me welcome. The chill thought came to me that the war might not rescue him entirely, that when it was through with him he might revert to the other Army and put on the old uniform, that he might even have a gift and a hankering for public preaching.

There were no bread-and-butter plates. You put your slice of bread on the oilcloth or on the side of your big plate. And you wiped your plate clean with a piece of bread before the pie was set down on it.

The rooster appeared in the doorway but was ordered away by Mr. Craik. This caused Mavis and Annie to giggle and hold their mouths.

"Choke on your food and it'll serve you right," said Russell.

Mrs. Craik avoided saying my name—she said in a harsh whisper to Russell, "Pass her the tomatoes"—but this seemed to be the result of extreme shyness, not of ill will. Mr. Craik continued to show an unperturbed sense of social occasion, asking me how my mother's health was, and what hours my father worked at the Foundry and how he liked his job there, did he find it a change from being his own boss? His way of speaking to me was more that of a teacher or a shopkeeper or even a professional man in town, than that of the man on the coal wagon. And he seemed to take it for granted that our families were on an equal footing and had a comfortable acquaintance with each other. This was close to the truth, as far as the equal footing went, and it was also true that my father had a comfortable acquaintance with almost everybody. Nevertheless it made me feel uneasy, even a little ashamed, because I was deceiving this family and my own, I was at this table under false pretenses.

But it seemed to me then that Russell and I would have been under false pretenses at any family supper table where we had to sit as if we were concerned with nothing but the food and whatever conversation was offered. While in fact we were marking time, our urgent needs were not to be met here, and our only real concern was to get at each other's skin.

It never crossed my mind that a young couple in our situation did indeed belong right here, that we were entered on the first stage of a life that would turn us, soon enough, into the Father and the Mother. Russell's parents probably knew this, and may have been privately dismayed, but decently hopeful, or resigned. Russell was already a force in the family whom they did not control. And Russell knew it, if he was capable at the moment of thinking that far ahead. He hardly looked at me, but when he did it was a steady look, laying claim, and it hit me and resonated as if I'd been a drum.

It was late in the summer now, the evenings closed in early. The light was turned on in the kitchen when we did the dishes. The dishpan was set on the table, the water had been heated on the stove, which was just the way things were managed when I washed the dishes at home. The mother washed, the sisters and I dried. Perhaps relieved that the meal was over and that I would soon be going home, Russell's mother made a few statements.

"It always takes more dishes than you'd think it would for to make a meal."

"Don't bother with them pots, I'll set them on the stove."

"That looks like it's about it now."

This last sentence sounded like a thank-you that she didn't know how to say.

So close to me and to their mother, Mavis and Annie had not dared giggle. When we got in each other's way at the draining pan they had said softly, "Parmee."

Russell came in from helping his father put the banties to roost. He said, "I guess it's time for you to be getting home," as if getting me home was just another nightly chore, instead of our anticipated first walk in the dark together. Mutely, exquisitely anticipated, on my part, the thought of it growing all through the dish-drying routine and even transforming that into a feminine ritual mysteriously linked to what was to come.

It was not so dark as I had hoped. To get me home we would have to cross the town, east to west, and almost certainly we would be noticed.

But that was not where we were going. At the end of this short street Russell put his hand on my back—a quick, functional pressure, to head me not towards home but towards Miriam McAlpin's horse barn.

I turned around to see if anybody was spying on us.

"What if your brother or sisters followed us?"

"They wouldn't," he said. "I'd kill them."

The barn was painted red, the color plain in the half-dark. The stable doors were on the lower level in the back. On the upper barn doors, which faced the street, were painted two prancing white horses. A gangway of stone and earth was built up to these doors—this was the way the loads of hay were driven in. In one of these big upper doors there was an ordinary-sized door, fitted snugly so that you would hardly notice it, holding the hoof and part of one painted horse's back legs. It was locked, but Russell had the key.

He pulled me inside after him. And once he had closed the door behind us we were in what was at first pitch-black darkness. All around us, almost choking us, the smell of that summer's new hay. Russell led me by the hand just as confidently as if he could see. His hand was hotter than mine.

After a moment I could see something myself. Bales of hay set one on top of another like giant bricks. We were in some sort of loft, overlooking the stable. Now I could get a strong smell of horses, as well as of hay, and hear continual shuffling and munching and gentle bumping around in the stalls. Most horses would be out in the pasture all night at this time of year, but these were probably too valuable to be left outside in the dark.

Russell put my hand on the rung of a ladder, by which we could climb to the top of the hay bales.

"Want me to go first or after?" he whispered.

Why whisper? Would we disturb the horses? Or does it just always seem natural to whisper in the dark? Or when you have gone weak in the legs but aching, determined, in another part of your body.

Something happened then. I thought for a moment that it was an explosion. Lightning hitting. Or even an earthquake. It seemed to me that the whole barn shook as it filled with light. Of course I had never been anywhere near an explosion or within a mile of a place where lightning struck, never felt one tremor of an earthquake. I had heard guns going off but always out of doors and at some distance. I had never heard the blast of a shotgun indoors under a high roof.

That was what I had heard now. Miriam McAlpin had shot her gun off, shot it up into the mow, then at once turned on all the barn lights. The horses had gone wild, whinnying and tossing themselves about and kicking the sides of their stalls, but you could still hear Miriam yelling.

"I know you're there. I know you're there."

"Go home," Russell was hissing into my ear. He spun me around towards the door.

"Go on home," he said angrily, or at least with an urgency like anger. As if I'd been a dog following him, or one of his little sisters, who had no right to be here.

Perhaps he said that too in a whisper, perhaps not. With the noise that the horses and Miriam made together, it wouldn't have mattered. He gave me one strong and untender push, then turned towards the stable and hollered, "Don't shoot, it's me . . . Hey Miriam. It's me."

"I know you're there—"

"It's me. It's Russ." He had run to the front of the haymow.

"Who's up there? Russ? Is that you? *Russ*?"

There must have been a ladder going down to the stable. I heard Russell's voice descending. He sounded bold but shaky, as if he was not quite sure that Miriam would not start shooting again.

"It's just me. I come in the top way."

"I heard somebody," said Miriam disbelievingly.

"I know. It was me. I just come in to see Lou. How her leg was."

"It was you?"

"Yeah. I told you."

"You were up in the mow."

"I come in by the top door."

He sounded more in control now. He was able to ask a question of his own.

"How long you been in here?"

"I just came in now. I was in the house and suddenly it hit me, there's something wrong at the barn."

"What'd you fire off the gun for? You could've killed me."

"If anybody was in here I wanted to give them a scare."

"You could've waited. You could've yelled first. You could've killed me."

"It never crossed my mind it was you."

Then Miriam McAlpin cried out again, as if she'd just spotted a new intruder.

"I could've killed you. Oh, Russ. I never thought. I could've shot you."

"Okay. Calm down," Russell said. "You could've but you didn't."

"You could be shot now and I'd be the one that did it."

"You didn't."

"What if I had, though? Jesus. Jesus. What if I had?"

She was weeping and saying something like this over and over, but in a muffled voice, as if something was stuffed into her mouth.

Or as if she was being held, pressed against something, somebody, that could comfort and quiet her.

Russell's voice, swelling with mastery, soothing.

"Okay. Yeah. So okay, honey. Okay."

That was the last thing I heard. What a strange word to speak to Miriam McAlpin. *Honey.* The word he'd used to me, during our bouts of kissing. Commonplace enough, but then it had seemed something I could suck up, a sweet mouthful like the stuff itself. Why would he say it now, when I wasn't anywhere near him? And in just the same way. Just the same.

Into the hair, against the ear, of Miriam McAlpin.

I had been standing by the door. I had been afraid that the noise of opening it might be heard below in spite of the disturbance the horses were still making. Or else I had not really understood that my presence here was unwanted, my part was over. Now I had to get out. I didn't care if they heard. But I don't suppose they did. I pulled the door shut, then ran down the gangway and along the street. I would have gone on running, but I realized that somebody might see me and wonder what was the matter. I had to be content with walking very fast. It was hard to stop for a moment, even to cross the highway that was also the main street of town.

*

I DIDN'T see Russell again. He did become a soldier. He was not killed in the war, and I don't think he continued in the Salvation Army. The summer after all this had happened I saw his wife—a girl I had known by sight in high school. She had been a couple of years ahead of me, and had dropped out to work in the creamery. She was with Mrs. Craik and she was heavily pregnant. They were looking through a bargain bin outside Stedman's store, one afternoon. She looked disconsolate and plain— maybe that was the effect of her pregnancy, though I had thought her plain enough before. Or at least insignificant and shy. She still looked shy, though hardly insignificant. Her body seemed abject but amazing, grotesque. And a thrill of sexual envy, of longing, went through me, at the sight of her and the thought of how she had got that way. Such submission, such necessity.

At some time after he came home from the war Russell took up carpentry and through that work he became a contractor, building houses for the ever-growing subdivisions around Toronto. I know that much because he appeared at a high-school reunion, apparently quite prosperous, joking about how he didn't have any right to be there, since he had never even gone to high school. Report of this came to me from Clara, who had kept in touch.

Clara said that his wife was blond now, rather fat, wearing a bare-backed sundress. A bun of blond hair stuck up above the hole in the crown of her sunhat. Clara had not talked to them and so she was not actually sure whether this was the same wife or a new one.

It was probably not the same wife, though it may have been. Clara and I talked about how reunions occasionally reveal how those who seemed most secure have been somewhat diminished or battered by life, and those who were at the fringes, who seemed to droop and ask pardon, have blossomed. So that might have happened with the girl I had seen in front of Stedman's.

Miriam McAlpin stayed on at the horse barn until it burned down. I don't know the reason, it could have been the usual one—damp hay, spontaneous combustion. All of the horses were saved, but Miriam was hurt, and after that she lived on a disability pension.

EVERYTHING WAS normal when I got home that evening. This was the summer when my brother and sister had learned to play solitaire, and played it at every opportunity. They were sitting now at either end of the dining-room table, nine and ten years old and grave as an old couple, the cards spread out in front of them. My mother had already gone to bed. She spent many hours in bed, but she never seemed to sleep as other people did, she just dozed for short periods of the day and night, maybe got up and drank tea or sorted out a drawer. Her life had stopped being securely connected at any point with the life of the family.

She called from bed to ask if I had had a nice supper at Clara's, and what did I have for dessert?

"Cottage pudding," I said.

I thought that if I said any part of the truth, if I said "pie," I would immediately betray myself. She did not care, she only wanted a bit of conversation, but I was not able to supply it. I tucked the quilt in around her feet, as she asked me to, and went downstairs and into the living room, where I sat on the low stool in front of the bookcase and took out a book. I sat there squinting at the print in the dim light that still came in the window beside me, until I had to rise and turn on the lamp. Even then I didn't settle myself in a chair to be comfortable but continued to sit hunched on the stool, filling my mind with one sentence after another, slamming them into my head just so I would not have to think about what had happened.

I don't know which book it was that I had picked up. I had read them all before, all the novels in that bookcase. There were not many. *The Sun Is My Undoing. Gone with the Wind. The Robe. Sleep in Peace. My Son, My Son. Wuthering Heights. The Last Days of Pompeii.* The selection did not reflect any particular taste, and in fact my parents often could not say how a certain book came to be there—whether it had been bought or borrowed or whether somebody had left it behind.

It must have meant something, though, that at this turn of my life I grabbed up a book. Because it was in books that I would find, for the next few years, my lovers. They were men, not boys. They were self-possessed and sardonic, with a ferocious streak in them, reserves of gloom. Not Edgar Linton, not Ashley Wilkes. Not one of them companionable or kind.

It was not as if I had given up on passion. Passion, indeed, whole-hearted, even destructive passion, was what I was after. Demand and submission. I did not exclude a certain kind of brutality. But no confusion, no double-dealing, or sleazy sort of surprise or humiliation. I could wait, and all my due would come to me, I thought, when I was full-blown.

Hired Girl

Mrs. Montjoy was showing me how to put the pots and pans away. I had put some of them in the wrong places.

Above all things, she said, she hated a higgledy-piggledy cupboard.

"You waste more time," she said. "You waste more time looking for something because it wasn't where it was last time."

"That's the way it was with our hired girls at home," I said. "The first few days they were there they were always putting things away where we couldn't find them.

"We called our maids hired girls," I added. "That was what we called them, at home."

"Did you?" she said. A moment of silence passed. "And the colander on that hook there."

Why did I have to say what I had said? Why was it necessary to mention that we had hired girls at home?

Anybody could see why. To put myself somewhere near her level. As if that was possible. As if anything I had to say about myself or the house I came from could interest or impress her.

It was true, though, about the hired girls. In my early life there was a procession of them. There was Olive, a soft drowsy girl who didn't like me because I called her Olive Oyl. Even after I was made to apologize she didn't like me. Maybe she didn't like any of us much because she was a Bible Christian, which made her mistrustful and reserved. She used to sing as she washed the dishes and I dried. *There is a Balm in Gilead* . . . If I tried to sing with her she stopped.

Then came Jeanie, whom I liked, because she was pretty and she did my hair up in pin curls at night when she did her own. She kept a list of the boys she went out with and made peculiar signs after their names: x x x o o * *. She did not last long.

Neither did Dorothy, who hung the clothes on the line in an eccentric way—pinned up by the collar, or by one sleeve or one leg—and swept the dirt into a corner and propped the broom up to hide it.

And when I was around ten years old hired girls became a thing of the past. I don't know if it was because we became poorer or because I was considered old enough to be a steady help. Both things were true.

Now I was seventeen and able to be hired out myself, though only as summer help because I had one more year to go at high school. My sister was twelve, so she could take over at home.

Mrs. Montjoy had picked me up at the railway station in Pointe au Baril, and transported me in an outboard-motor boat to the island. It was the woman in the Pointe au Baril store who had recommended me for the job. She was an old friend of my mother's—they had taught school together. Mrs. Montjoy had asked her if she knew of a country girl, used to doing housework, who would be available for the summer, and the woman had thought that it would be the very thing for me. I thought so too—I was eager to see more of the world.

Mrs. Montjoy wore khaki shorts and a tucked-in shirt. Her short, sun-bleached hair was pushed behind her ears. She leapt aboard the boat like a boy and gave a fierce tug to the motor, and we were flung out on the choppy evening waters of Georgian Bay. For thirty or forty minutes we dodged around rocky and wooded islands with their lone cottages and boats bobbing beside the docks. Pine trees jutted out at odd angles, just as they do in the paintings.

I held on to the sides of the boat and shivered in my flimsy dress.

"Feeling a tad sick?" said Mrs. Montjoy, with the briefest possible smile. It was like the signal for a smile, when the occasion did not warrant the real thing. She had large white teeth in a long tanned face, and her natural expression seemed to be one of impatience barely held in check. She probably knew that what I was feeling was fear, not sickness, and she threw out this question so that I—and she—need not be embarrassed.

Here was a difference, already, from the world I was used to. In that world, fear was commonplace, at least for females. You could be afraid of snakes, thunderstorms, deep water, heights, the dark, the bull, and the lonely road through the swamp, and nobody thought any the worse of you. In Mrs. Montjoy's world, however, fear was shameful and always something to be conquered.

The island that was our destination had a name—Nausicaa. The name was written on a board at the end of the dock. I said it aloud, trying to show that I was at ease and quietly appreciative, and Mrs. Montjoy said with slight surprise, "Oh, yes. That was the name it already had when Daddy bought it. It's for some character in Shakespeare."

I opened up my mouth to say no, no, not Shakespeare, and to tell her that Nausicaa was the girl on the beach, playing ball with her friends, surprised by Ulysses when he woke up from his nap. I had learned by this time that most of the people I lived amongst did not welcome this kind of information, and I would probably have kept quiet even if the teacher had asked us in school, but I believed that people out in the world—the real world—would be different. Just in time I recognized the briskness of Mrs. Montjoy's tone when she said "some character in Shakespeare"—the suggestion that Nausicaa, and Shakespeare, as well as any observations of mine, were things she could reasonably do without.

The dress I was wearing for my arrival was one I had made myself, out of pink and white striped cotton. The material had been cheap, the reason being that it was not really meant for a dress but for a blouse or a nightgown, and the style I had chosen—the full-skirted, tight-waisted style of those days—was a mistake. When I walked, the cloth bunched up between my legs, and I kept having to yank it loose. Today was the first day the dress had been worn, and I still thought that the trouble might be temporary—with a firm enough yank the material might be made to hang properly. But I found when I took off my belt that the day's heat and my hot ride on the train had created a worse problem. The belt was wide and elasticized, and of a burgundy color, which had run. The waistline of the dress was circled with strawberry dye.

I made this discovery when I was getting undressed in the loft of the boathouse, which I was to share with Mrs. Montjoy's ten-year-old daughter, Mary Anne.

"What happened to your dress?" Mary Anne said. "Do you sweat a lot? That's too bad."

I said that it was an old dress anyway and that I hadn't wanted to wear anything good on the train.

Mary Anne was fair-haired and freckled, with a long face like her mother's. But she didn't have her mother's look of quick judgments marshalled at the surface, ready to leap out at you. Her expression was benign and serious, and she wore heavy glasses even when sitting up in bed. She was to tell me soon that she had had an operation to get her eyes straightened, but even so her eyesight was poor.

"I've got Daddy's eyes," she said. "I'm intelligent like him too so it's too bad I'm not a boy."

Another difference. Where I came from, it was generally held to be more suspect for boys to be smart than for girls to be, though not particularly advantageous for one or the other. Girls could go on to be teachers, and that was all right—though quite often they became old maids—but for boys to continue with school usually meant they were sissies.

All night long you could hear the water slapping against the boards of the boathouse. Morning came early. I wondered whether I was far enough north of home for the sun to actually be rising sooner. I got up and looked out. Through the front window, I saw the silky water, dark underneath but flashing back from its surface the light of the sky. The rocky shores of this little cove, the moored sailboats, the open channel beyond, the mound of another island or two, shores and channels beyond that. I thought that I would never, on my own, be able to find my way back to the mainland.

I did not yet understand that maids didn't have to find their way anywhere. They stayed put, where the work was. It was the people who made the work who could come and go.

The back window looked out on a gray rock that was like a slanting wall, with shelves and crevices on it where little pine and cedar trees and blueberry bushes had got a foothold. Down at the foot of this wall was a path—which I would take later on—through the woods, to Mrs. Montjoy's house. Here everything was still damp and almost dark, though if you craned you could see bits of the sky whitening through the trees on top of the rock. Nearly all of the trees were strict-looking, fragrant evergreens, with heavy boughs that didn't allow much growth underneath—no riot of grapevine and brambles and saplings such as I was used to in the hardwood forest. I had noticed that when I looked out from the train on the day before—how what we called the bush turned into the more authentic-looking *forest*, which had eliminated all lavishness and confusion and seasonal change. It seemed to me that this real forest belonged to rich people—it was their proper though sombre playground—and to Indians, who served the rich people as guides and exotic dependents, living out of sight and out of mind, somewhere that the train didn't go.

Nevertheless, on this morning I was really looking out, eagerly, as if this was a place where I would live and everything would become familiar to me. And everything did become familiar, at least in the places where my work was and where I was supposed to go. But a barrier was up. Perhaps *barrier* is too strong a word—there was not a warning so much as something like a shimmer in the air, an indolent reminder. *Not for you*. It wasn't a thing that had to be said. Or put on a sign.

Not for you. And though I felt it, I would not quite admit to myself that such a barrier was there. I would not admit that I ever felt humbled or lonely, or that I was a real servant. But I stopped thinking about leaving the path, exploring among the trees. If anybody saw me I would have to explain what I was doing, and *they*—Mrs. Montjoy—would not like it.

And to tell the truth, this wasn't so different from the way things were at home, where taking any impractical notice of the out-of-doors, or mooning around about Nature—even using that word, *Nature*—could get you laughed at.

MARY ANNE liked to talk when we were lying on our cots at night. She told me that her favorite book was *Kon-Tiki* and that she did not believe in God or Heaven.

"My sister is dead," she said. "And I don't believe she is floating around somewhere in a white nightie. She is just dead, she is just nothing.

"My sister was pretty," she said. "Compared to me she was, anyway. Mother wasn't ever pretty and Daddy is really ugly. Aunt Margaret used to be pretty but now she's fat, and Nana used to be pretty but now she's old. My friend Helen is pretty but my friend Susan isn't. You're pretty, but it doesn't count because you're the maid. Does it hurt your feelings for me to say that?"

I said no.

"I'm only the maid when I'm here."

It wasn't that I was the only servant on the island. The other servants were a married couple, Henry and Corrie. They did not feel diminished by their jobs—they were grateful for them. They had come to Canada from Holland a few years before and had been hired by Mr. and Mrs. Foley, who were Mrs. Montjoy's parents. It was Mr. and Mrs. Foley who owned the island, and lived in the large white bungalow, with its awnings and verandas, that crowned the highest point of land. Henry cut the grass and looked after the tennis court and repainted the lawn chairs and helped Mr. Foley with the boats and the clearing of paths and the repairs to the dock. Corrie did the housework and cooked the meals and looked after Mrs. Foley.

Mrs. Foley spent every sunny morning sitting outside on a deck chair, with her feet stretched out to get the sun and an awning attached to the chair protecting her head. Corrie came out and shifted her around as the sun moved, and took her to the bathroom, and brought her cups of tea and glasses of iced coffee. I was witness to this when I went up to the

Foleys' house from the Montjoys' house on some errand, or to put something into or remove something from the freezer. Home freezers were still rather a novelty and a luxury at this time, and there wasn't one in the Montjoys' cottage.

"You are not going to suck the ice cubes," I heard Corrie say to Mrs. Foley. Apparently Mrs. Foley paid no attention and proceeded to suck an ice cube, and Corrie said, "Bad. No. Spit out. Spit right out in Corrie's hand. Bad. You didn't do what Corrie say."

Catching up to me on the way into the house, she said, "I tell them she could choke to death. But Mr. Foley always say, give her the ice cubes, she wants a drink like everybody else. So I tell her and tell her. Do not suck ice cubes. But she won't do what I say."

Sometimes I was sent up to help Corrie polish the furniture or buff the floors. She was very exacting. She never just wiped the kitchen counters—she scoured them. Every move she made had the energy and concentration of somebody rowing a boat against the current and every word she said was flung out as if into a high wind of opposition. When she wrung out a cleaning rag she might have been wringing the neck of a chicken. I thought it might be interesting if I could get her to talk about the war, but all she would say was that everybody was very hungry and they saved the potato skins to make soup.

"No good," she said. "No good to talk about that."

She preferred the future. She and Henry were saving their money to go into business. They meant to start up a nursing home. "Lots of people like her," said Corrie, throwing her head back as she worked to indicate Mrs. Foley out on the lawn. "Soon more and more. Because they give them the medicine, that makes them not die so soon. Who will be taking care?"

One day Mrs. Foley called out to me as I crossed the lawn.

"Now, where are you off to in such a hurry?" she said. "Come and sit down by me and have a little rest."

Her white hair was tucked up under a floppy straw hat, and when she leaned forward the sun came though the holes in the straw, sprinkling the pink and pale-brown patches of her face with pimples of light. Her eyes were a color so nearly extinct I couldn't make it out and her shape was curious—a narrow flat chest and a swollen stomach under layers of loose, pale clothing. The skin of the legs she stuck out into the sunlight was shiny and discolored and covered with faint cracks.

"Pardon my not having put my stockings on," she said. "I'm afraid I'm feeling rather lazy today. But aren't you the remarkable girl. Coming all that way by yourself. Did Henry help you carry the groceries up from the dock?"

Mrs. Montjoy waved to us. She was on her way to the tennis court, to give Mary Anne her lesson. Every morning she gave Mary Anne a lesson, and at lunch they discussed what Mary Anne had done wrong.

"There's that woman who comes to play tennis," Mrs. Foley said of her daughter. "She comes every day, so I suppose it's all right. She may as well use it if she hasn't a court of her own."

Mrs. Montjoy said to me later, "Did Mrs. Foley ask you to come over and sit on the grass?"

I said yes. "She thought I was somebody who'd brought the groceries."

"I believe there was a grocery girl who used to run a boat. There hasn't been any grocery delivery in years. Mrs. Foley does get her wires crossed now and then."

"She said you were a woman who came to play tennis."

"Did she really?" Mrs. Montjoy said.

THE WORK that I had to do here was not hard for me. I knew how to bake, and iron, and clean an oven. Nobody tracked barnyard mud into this kitchen and there were no heavy men's work clothes to wrestle through the wringer. There was just the business of putting everything perfectly in place and doing quite a bit of polishing. Polish the rims of the burners of the stove after every use, polish the taps, polish the glass door to the deck till the glass disappears and people are in danger of smashing their faces against it.

The Montjoys' house was modern, with a flat roof and a deck extending over the water and a great many windows, which Mrs. Montjoy would have liked to see become as invisible as the glass door.

"But I have to be realistic," she said. "I know if you did that you'd hardly have time for anything else." She was not by any means a slave driver. Her tone with me was firm and slightly irritable, but that was the way it was with everybody. She was always on the lookout for inattention or incompetence, which she detested. *Sloppy* was a favorite word of condemnation. Others were *wishy-washy* and *unnecessary*. A lot of things that people did were unnecessary, and some of these were also wishy-washy. Other people might have used the words *arty* or *intellectual* or *permissive*. Mrs. Montjoy swept all those distinctions out of the way.

I ate my meals alone, between serving whoever was eating on the deck or in the dining room. I had almost made a horrible mistake about that. When Mrs. Montjoy caught me heading out to the deck with three plates—held in a show-off waitress-style—for the first lunch, she said, "Three plates there? Oh, yes, two out on the deck and yours in here. Right?"

I read as I ate. I had found a stack of old magazines—*Life* and *Look* and

Time and *Collier's*—at the back of the broom closet. I could tell that Mrs. Montjoy did not like the idea of my sitting reading these magazines as I ate my lunch, but I did not quite know why. Was it because it was bad manners to eat as you read, or because I had not asked permission? More likely she saw my interest in things that had nothing to do with my work as a subtle kind of impudence. Unnecessary.

All she said was, "Those old magazines must be dreadfully dusty."

I said that I always wiped them off.

Sometimes there was a guest for lunch, a woman friend who had come over from one of the nearby islands. I heard Mrs. Montjoy say ". . . have to keep your girls happy or they'll be off to the hotel, off to the port. They can get jobs there so easily. It's not the way it used to be."

The other woman said, "That's so true."

"So you just make allowances," said Mrs. Montjoy. "You do the best with them you can." It took me a moment to realize who they were talking about. Me. "Girls" meant girls like me. I wondered, then, how I was being kept happy. By being taken along on the occasional alarming boat ride when Mrs. Montjoy went to get supplies? By being allowed to wear shorts and a blouse, or even a halter, instead of a uniform with a white collar and cuffs?

And what hotel was this? What port?

"WHAT ARE you best at?" Mary Anne said. "What sports?"

After a moment's consideration, I said, "Volleyball." We had to play volleyball at school. I wasn't very good at it, but it was my best sport because it was the only one.

"Oh, I don't mean team sports," said Mary Anne. "I mean, what are you *best* at. Such as tennis. Or swimming or riding or what? My really best thing is riding, because that doesn't depend so much on your eyesight. Aunt Margaret's best used to be tennis and Nana's used to be tennis too, and Grandad's was always sailing, and Daddy's is swimming I guess and Uncle Stewart's is golf and sailing and Mother's is golf and swimming and sailing and tennis and everything, but maybe tennis a little bit the best of all. If my sister Jane hadn't died I don't know what hers would have been, but it might have been swimming because she could swim already and she was only three."

I had never been on a tennis court and the idea of going out in a sailboat or getting up on a horse terrified me. I could swim, but not very well. Golf to me was something that silly-looking men did in cartoons. The adults I knew never played any games that involved physical action. They sat down and rested when they were not working, which wasn't often. Though on winter evenings they might play cards. Euchre. Lost Heir. Not the kind of cards Mrs. Montjoy ever played.

"Everybody I know works too hard to do any sports," I said. "We don't even have a tennis court in our town and there isn't any golf course either." (Actually we had once had both these things, but there hadn't been the money to keep them up during the Depression and they had not been restored since.) "Nobody I know has a sailboat."

I did not mention that my town did have a hockey rink and a baseball park.

"Really?" said Mary Anne thoughtfully. "What do they do then?"

"*Work.* And they never have any money, all of their lives."

Then I told her that most people I knew had never seen a flush toilet unless it was in a public building and that sometimes old people (that is, people too old to work) had to stay in bed all winter in order to keep warm. Children walked barefoot until the frost came in order to save on shoe leather, and died of stomach aches that were really appendicitis because their parents had no money for a doctor. Sometimes people had eaten dandelion leaves, nothing else, for supper.

Not one of these statements—even the one about dandelion leaves—was completely a lie. I had heard of such things. The one about flush toilets perhaps came closest to the truth, but it applied to country people, not town people, and most of those it applied to would be of a generation before mine. But as I talked to Mary Anne all the isolated incidents and bizarre stories I had heard spread out in my mind, so that I could almost believe that I myself had walked with bare blue feet on cold mud—I who had benefited from cod liver oil and inoculations and been bundled up for school within an inch of my life, and had gone to bed hungry only because I refused to eat such things as junket or bread pudding or fried liver. And this false impression I was giving seemed justified, as if my exaggerations or near lies were substitutes for something I could not make clear.

How to make clear, for instance, the difference between the Montjoys' kitchen and our kitchen at home. You could not do that simply by mentioning the perfectly fresh and shining floor surfaces of one and the worn-out linoleum of the other, or the fact of soft water being pumped from a cistern into the sink contrasted with hot and cold water coming out of taps. You would have to say that you had in one case a kitchen that followed with absolute correctness a current notion of what a kitchen ought to be, and in the other a kitchen that changed occasionally with use and improvisation, but in many ways never changed at all, and belonged entirely to one family and to the years and decades of that family's life. And when I thought of that kitchen, with the combination wood and electric stove that I polished with waxed-paper bread wrappers, the dark old spice tins with their rusty rims kept from year to year in the cupboards, the barn clothes hanging by the door, it seemed as if I had to protect it from contempt—as if I had to protect a whole precious and intimate though hardly pleasant way of life from contempt. Contempt was what I imagined to be always waiting, swinging along on live wires, just under the skin and just behind the perceptions of people like the Montjoys.

"That isn't fair," said Mary Anne. "That's awful. I didn't know people could eat dandelion leaves." But then she brightened. "Why don't they go and catch some fish?"

"People who don't need the fish have come and caught them all already. Rich people. For fun."

Of course some of the people at home did catch fish when they had time, though others, including me, found the fish from our river too bony. But I thought that would keep Mary Anne quiet, especially since I knew that Mr. Montjoy went on fishing trips with his friends.

She could not stop mulling over the problem. "Couldn't they go to the Salvation Army?"

"They're too proud."

"Well I feel sorry for them," she said. "I feel really sorry for them, but I think that's stupid. What about the little babies and the children? They ought to think about them. Are the children too proud too?"

"Everybody's proud."

WHEN MR. Montjoy came to the island on weekends, there was always a great deal of noise and activity. Some of that was because there were visitors who came by boat to swim and have drinks and watch sailing races. But a lot of it was generated by Mr. Montjoy himself. He had a loud blustery voice and a thick body with a skin that would never take a tan. Every weekend he turned red from the sun, and during the week the burned skin peeled away and left him pink and muddy with freckles, ready to be burned again. When he took off his glasses you could see that one eye was quick and squinty and the other boldly blue but helpless-looking, as if caught in a trap.

His blustering was often about things that he had misplaced, or dropped, or bumped into. "Where the hell is the—?" he would say, or "You didn't happen to see the—?" So it seemed that he had also misplaced, or failed to grasp in the first place, even the name of the thing he was looking for. To console himself he might grab up a handful of peanuts or pretzels or whatever was nearby, and eat handful after handful until they were all gone. Then he would stare at the empty bowl as if that too astounded him.

One morning I heard him say, "Now where in hell is that—?" He was crashing around out on the deck.

"Your book?" said Mrs. Montjoy, in a tone of bright control. She was having her midmorning coffee.

"I thought I had it out here," he said. "I was reading it."

"The Book-of-the-Month one?" she said. "I think you left it in the living room."

She was right. I was vacuuming the living room, and a few moments before I had picked up a book pushed partway under the sofa. Its title was *Seven Gothic Tales.* The title made me want to open it, and even as I overheard the Montjoys' conversation I was reading, holding the book open in one hand and guiding the vacuum cleaner with the other. They couldn't see me from the deck.

"Nay, I speak from the heart," said Mira. "I have been trying for a long time to understand God. Now I have made friends with him. To love him truly you must love change, and you must love a joke, these being the true inclinations of his own heart."

"There it is," said Mr. Montjoy, who for a wonder had come into the room without his usual bumping and banging—or none at least that I had heard. "Good girl, you found my book. Now I remember. Last night I was reading it on the sofa."

"It was on the floor," I said. "I just picked it up."

He must have seen me reading it. He said, "It's a queer kind of book, but sometimes you want to read a book that isn't like all the others."

"I couldn't make heads or tails of it," said Mrs. Montjoy, coming in with the coffee tray. "We'll have to get out of the way here and let her get on with the vacuuming."

Mr. Montjoy went back to the mainland, and to the city, that evening. He was a bank director. That did not mean, apparently, that he worked in a bank. The day after he had gone I looked everywhere. I looked under the chairs and behind the curtains, in case he might have left that book behind. But I could not find it.

"I ALWAYS thought it would be nice to live up here all the year round, the way you people do," said Mrs. Foley. She must have cast me again as the girl who brought the groceries. Some days she said, "I know who you are now. You're the new girl helping the Dutch woman in the kitchen. But

I'm sorry, I just can't recall your name." And other days she let me walk by without giving any greeting or showing the least interest.

"We used to come up here in the winter," she said. "The bay would be frozen over and there would be a road across the ice. We used to go snowshoeing. Now that's something people don't do anymore. Do they? Snowshoeing?"

She didn't wait for me to answer. She leaned towards me. "Can you tell me something?" she said with embarrassment, speaking almost in a whisper. "Can you tell me where Jane is? I haven't seen her running around here for the longest time."

I said that I didn't know. She smiled as if I was teasing her, and reached out a hand to touch my face. I had been stooping down to listen to her, but now I straightened up, and her hand grazed my chest instead. It was a hot day and I was wearing my halter, so it happened that she touched my skin. Her hand was light and dry as a wood shaving, but the nail scraped me.

"I'm sure it's all right," she said.

After that I simply waved if she spoke to me and hurried on my way.

On a Saturday afternoon towards the end of August, the Montjoys gave a cocktail party. The party was given in honor of the friends they had staying with them that weekend—Mr. and Mrs. Hammond. A good many small silver forks and spoons had to be polished in preparation for this event, so Mrs. Montjoy decided that all the silver might as well be done at the same time. I did the polishing and she stood beside me, inspecting it.

On the day of the party, people arrived in motorboats and sailboats. Some of them went swimming, then sat around on the rocks in their bathing suits, or lay on the dock in the sun. Others came up to the house immediately and started drinking and talking in the living room or out on the deck. Some children had come with their parents, and older children by themselves, in their own boats. They were not children of Mary Anne's age—Mary Anne had been taken to stay with her friend Susan, on another island. There were a few very young ones, who came supplied with folding cribs and playpens, but most were around the same age as I was. Girls and boys fifteen or sixteen years old. They spent most of the afternoon in the water, shouting and diving and having races to the raft.

Mrs. Montjoy and I had been busy all morning, making all the different things to eat, which we now arranged on platters and offered to people. Making them had been fiddly and exasperating work. Stuffing various mixtures into mushroom caps and sticking one tiny slice of something on top of a tiny slice of something else on top of a precise fragment of toast or bread. All the shapes had to be perfect—perfect triangles, perfect rounds and squares, perfect diamonds.

Mrs. Hammond came into the kitchen several times and admired what we were doing.

"How marvellous everything looks," she said. "You notice I'm not offering to help. I'm a perfect mutt at this kind of thing."

I liked the way she said that. *I'm a perfect mutt.* I admired her husky voice, its weary good-humored tone, and the way she seemed to suggest that tiny geometrical bits of food were not so necessary, might even be a trifle silly. I wished I could be her, in a sleek black bathing suit with a tan like dark toast, shoulder-length smooth dark hair, orchid-colored lipstick.

Not that she looked happy. But her air of sullenness and complaint seemed glamorous to me, her hints of cloudy drama enviable. She and her husband were an altogether different type of rich people from Mr. and Mrs. Montjoy. They were more like the people I had read about in magazine stories and in books like *The Hucksters*—people who drank a lot and had love affairs and went to psychiatrists.

Her name was Carol and her husband's name was Ivan. I thought of them already by their first names—something I had never been tempted to do with the Montjoys.

Mrs. Montjoy had asked me to put on a dress, so I wore the pink and white striped cotton, with the smudged material at its waist tucked under the elasticized belt. Nearly everybody else was in shorts and bathing suits. I passed among them, offering food. I was not sure how to do this. Sometimes people were laughing or talking with such vigor that they didn't notice me, and I was afraid that their gestures would send the food bits flying. So I said, "Excuse me—would you like one of these?" in a raised voice that sounded very determined or even reproving. Then they looked at me with startled amusement, and I had the feeling that my interruption had become another joke.

"Enough passing for now," said Mrs. Montjoy. She gathered up some glasses and told me to wash them. "People never keep track of their own," she said. "It's easier just to wash them and bring in clean ones. And it's time to get the meatballs out of the fridge and heat them up. Could you do that? Watch the oven—it won't take long."

While I was busy in the kitchen I heard Mrs. Hammond calling, "Ivan! Ivan!" She was roaming through the back rooms of the house. But Mr. Hammond had come in through the kitchen door that led to the woods. He stood there and did not answer her. He came over to the counter and poured gin into his glass.

"Oh, Ivan, there you are," said Mrs. Hammond, coming in from the living room.

"Here I am," said Mr. Hammond.

"Me, too," she said. She shoved her glass along the counter.

He didn't pick it up. He pushed the gin towards her and spoke to me. "Are you having fun, Minnie?"

Mrs. Hammond gave a yelp of laughter. "Minnie? Where did you get the idea her name was Minnie?"

"Minnie," said Mr. Hammond. Ivan. He spoke in an artificial, dreamy voice. "Are you having fun, Minnie?"

"Oh yes," I said, in a voice that I meant to make as artificial as his. I was busy lifting the tiny Swedish meatballs from the oven and I wanted the Hammonds out of my way in case I dropped some. They would think that a big joke and probably report on me to Mrs. Montjoy, who would make me throw the dropped meatballs out and be annoyed at the waste. If I was alone when it happened I could just scoop them up off the floor.

Mr. Hammond said, "Good."

"I swam around the point," Mrs. Hammond said. "I'm working up to swimming around the entire island."

"Congratulations," Mr. Hammond said, in the same way that he had said "Good."

I wished that I hadn't sounded so chirpy and silly. I wished that I had matched his deeply skeptical and sophisticated tone.

"Well then," said Mrs. Hammond. Carol. "I'll leave you to it."

I had begun to spear the meatballs with toothpicks and arrange them on a platter. Ivan said, "Care for some help?" and tried to do the same, but his toothpicks missed and sent meatballs skittering onto the counter.

"Well," he said, but he seemed to lose track of his thoughts, so he turned away and took another drink. "Well, Minnie."

I knew something about him. I knew that the Hammonds were here for a special holiday because Mr. Hammond had lost his job. Mary Anne had told me this. "He's very depressed about it," she had said. "They won't be poor, though. Aunt Carol is rich."

He did not seem depressed to me. He seemed impatient—chiefly with Mrs. Hammond—but on the whole rather pleased with himself. He was tall and thin, he had dark hair combed straight back from his forehead, and his mustache was an ironic line above his upper lip. When he talked to me he leaned forward, as I had seen him doing earlier, when he talked to women in the living room. I had thought then that the word for him was *courtly*.

"Where do you go swimming, Minnie? Do you go swimming?"

"Yes," I said. "Down by the boathouse." I decided that his calling me Minnie was a special joke between us.

"Is that a good place?"

"Yes." It was, for me, because I liked being close to the dock. I had never, till this summer, swum in water that was over my head.

"Do you ever go in without your bathing suit on?"

I said, "No."

"You should try it."

Mrs. Montjoy came through the living-room doorway, asking if the meatballs were ready.

"This is certainly a hungry crowd," she said. "It's the swimming does it. How are you getting on, Ivan? Carol was just looking for you."

"She was here," said Mr. Hammond.

Mrs. Montjoy dropped parsley here and there among the meatballs. "Now," she said to me. "I think you've done about all you need to here. I think I can manage now. Why don't you just make yourself a sandwich and run along down to the boathouse?"

I said I wasn't hungry. Mr. Hammond had helped himself to more gin and ice cubes and had gone into the living room.

"Well. You'd better take something," Mrs. Montjoy said. "You'll be hungry later."

She meant that I was not to come back.

On my way to the boathouse I met a couple of the guests—girls of my own age, barefoot and in their wet bathing suits, breathlessly laughing. They had probably swum partway round the island and climbed out of the water at the boathouse. Now they were sneaking back to surprise somebody. They stepped aside politely, not to drip water on me, but did not stop laughing. Making way for my body without a glance at my face.

They were the sort of girls who would have squealed and made a fuss over me, if I had been a dog or a cat.

THE NOISE of the party continued to rise. I lay down on my cot without taking off my dress. I had been on the go since early morning and I was tired. But I could not relax. After a while I got up and changed into my bathing suit and went down to swim. I climbed down the ladder into the water cautiously as I always did—I thought that I would go straight to the bottom and never come up if I jumped—and swam around in the shadows. The water washing my limbs made me think of what Mr. Hammond had said and I worked the straps of my bathing suit down, finally pulling out one arm after the other so that my breasts could float free. I swam that way, with the water sweetly dividing at my nipples . . .

I thought it was not impossible that Mr. Hammond might come looking for me. I thought of him touching me. (I could not figure out exactly how he would get into the water—I did not care to think of him stripping off his clothes. Perhaps he would squat down on the deck and I would swim over to him.) His fingers stroking my bare skin like ribbons of light. The thought of being touched and desired by a man that old—forty, forty-five?—was in some way repulsive, but I knew I would get pleasure from it, rather as you might get pleasure from being caressed by an amorous tame crocodile. Mr. Hammond's—Ivan's—skin might be smooth, but age and knowledge and corruptness would be on him like invisible warts and scales.

I dared to lift myself partly out of the water, holding with one hand to the dock. I bobbed up and down and rose into the air like a mermaid. Gleaming, with nobody to see.

Now I heard steps. I heard somebody coming. I sank down into the water and held still.

For a moment I believed that it was Mr. Hammond, and that I had actually entered the world of secret signals, abrupt and wordless forays of desire. I did not cover myself but shrank against the dock, in a paralyzed moment of horror and submission.

The boathouse light was switched on, and I turned around noiselessly in the water and saw that it was old Mr. Foley, still in his party outfit of white trousers and yachting cap and blazer. He had stayed for a couple of drinks and explained to everybody that Mrs. Foley was not up to the strain of seeing so many people but sent her best wishes to all.

He was moving things around on the tool shelf. Soon he either found what he wanted or put back what he had intended to put back, and he switched off the light and left. He never knew that I was there.

I pulled up my bathing suit and got out of the water and went up the stairs. My body seemed such a weight to me that I was out of breath when I got to the top.

The sound of the cocktail party went on and on. I had to do something to hold my own against it, so I started to write a letter to Dawna, who was my best friend at that time. I described the cocktail party in lurid terms—people vomited over the deck railing and a woman passed out, falling down on the sofa in such a way that part of her dress slid off and exposed a purple-nippled old breast (I called it a bezoom). I spoke of Mr. Hammond as a letch, though I added that he was very good-looking. I said that he had fondled me in the kitchen while my hands were busy with the meatballs and that later he had followed me to the boathouse and grabbed me on the stairs. But I had kicked him where he wouldn't forget and he had retreated. *Scurried away,* I said.

"So hold your breath for the next installment," I wrote. "Entitled, 'Sordid Adventures of a Kitchen Maid.' Or 'Ravaged on the Rocks of Georgian Bay.'"

When I saw that I had written "ravaged" instead of "ravished," I thought I could let it go, because Dawna would never know the difference. But I realized that the part about Mr. Hammond was overdone, even for that sort of letter, and then the whole thing filled me with shame and a sense of my own failure and loneliness. I crumpled it up. There had not been any point in writing this letter except to assure myself that I had some contact with the world and that exciting things—sexual things— happened to me. And I hadn't. They didn't.

"MRS. FOLEY asked me where Jane was," I had said, when Mrs. Montjoy and I were doing the silver—or when she was keeping an eye on me doing the silver. "Was Jane one of the other girls who worked here in the summer?"

I thought for a moment that she might not answer, but she did.

"Jane was my other daughter," she said. "She was Mary Anne's sister. She died."

I said, "Oh. I didn't know." I said, "Oh. I'm sorry.

"Did she die of polio?" I said, because I did not have the sense, or you might say the decency, not to go on. And in those days children still died of polio, every summer.

"No," said Mrs. Montjoy. "She was killed when my husband moved the dresser in our bedroom. He was looking for something he thought he might have dropped behind it. He didn't realize she was in the way. One of the casters caught on the rug and the whole thing toppled over on her."

I knew every bit of this, of course. Mary Anne had already told me. She had told me even before Mrs. Foley asked me where Jane was and clawed at my breast.

"How awful," I said.

"Well. It was just one of those things."

My deception made me feel queasy. I dropped a fork on the floor.

Mrs. Montjoy picked it up.

"Remember to wash this again."

How strange that I did not question my right to pry, to barge in and bring this to the surface. Part of the reason must have been that in the society I came from, things like that were never buried for good, but ritualistically resurrected, and that such horrors were like a badge people wore—or, mostly, that women wore—throughout their lives.

Also it may have been because I would never quite give up when it came to demanding intimacy, or at least some kind of equality, even with a person I did not like.

Cruelty was a thing I could not recognize in myself. I thought I was blameless here, and in any dealings with this family. All because of being young, and poor, and knowing about Nausicaa.

I did not have the grace or fortitude to be a servant.

ON MY last Sunday I was alone in the boathouse, packing up my things in the suitcase I had brought—the same suitcase that had gone with my mother and father on their wedding trip and the only one we had in the house. When I pulled it out from under my cot and opened it up, it smelled of home—of the closet at the end of the upstairs hall where it usually sat, close to the mothballed winter coats and the rubber sheet once used on children's beds. But when you got it out at home it always smelled faintly of trains and coal fires and cities—of travel.

I heard steps on the path, a stumbling step into the boathouse, a rapping on the wall. It was Mr. Montjoy.

"Are you up there? Are you up there?"

His voice was boisterous, jovial, as I had heard it before when he had been drinking. As of course he had been drinking—for once again there were people visiting, celebrating the end of summer. I came to the top of the stairs. He had a hand against the wall to steady himself—a boat had gone by out in the channel and sent its waves into the boathouse.

"See here," said Mr. Montjoy, looking up at me with frowning concentration. "See here—I thought I might as well bring this down and give it to you while I thought of it.

"This book," he said.

He was holding *Seven Gothic Tales.*

"Because I saw you were looking in it that day," he said. "It seemed to me you were interested. So now I finished it and I thought I might as well pass it along to you. It occurred to me to pass it along to you. I thought, maybe you might enjoy it."

I said, "Thank you."

"I'm probably not going to read it again though I thought it was very interesting. Very unusual."

"Thank you very much."

"That's all right. I thought you might enjoy it."

"Yes," I said.

"Well then. I hope you will."

"Thank you."

"Well then," he said. "Good-bye."

I said, "Thank you. Good-bye."

Why were we saying good-bye when we were certain to see each other again before we left the island, and before I got on the train? It might have meant that this incident, of his giving me the book, was to be closed, and I was not to reveal or refer to it. Which I didn't. Or it might have been just that he was drunk and did not realize that he would see me later. Drunk or not, I see him now as pure of motive, leaning against the boathouse wall. A person who could think me worthy of this gift. Of this book.

At the moment, though, I didn't feel particularly pleased, or grateful, in spite of my repeated thank-yous. I was too startled, and in some way embarrassed. The thought of having a little corner of myself come to light, and be truly understood, stirred up alarm, just as much as being taken no notice of stirred up resentment. And Mr. Mountjoy was probably the person who interested me least, whose regard meant the least to me, of all the people I had met that summer.

He left the boathouse and I heard him stumping along the path, back to his wife and his guests. I pushed the suitcase aside and sat down on the cot. I opened the book just anywhere, as I had done the first time, and began to read.

> The walls of the room had once been painted crimson, but with time the colour had faded into a richness of hues, like a glassful of dying roses . . . Some potpourri was being burned on the tall stove, on the sides of which Neptune, with a trident, steered his team of horses through high waves . . .

I forgot Mr. Mountjoy almost immediately. In hardly any time at all I came to believe that this gift had always belonged to me.

Too Much Happiness

Dimensions

DOREE HAD to take three buses—one to Kincardine, where she waited for the one to London, where she waited again for the city bus out to the facility. She started the trip on a Sunday at nine in the morning. Because of the waiting times between buses, it took her till about two in the afternoon to travel the hundred-odd miles. All that sitting, either on the buses or in the depots, was not a thing she should have minded. Her daily work was not of the sitting-down kind.

She was a chambermaid at the Blue Spruce Inn. She scrubbed bathrooms and stripped and made beds and vacuumed rugs and wiped mirrors. She liked the work—it occupied her thoughts to a certain extent and tired her out so that she could sleep at night. She was seldom faced with a really bad mess, though some of the women she worked with could tell stories to make your hair curl. These women were older than she was, and they all thought she should try to work her way up. They told her she should get trained for a job behind the desk while she was still young and decent-looking. But she was content to do what she did. She didn't want to have to talk to people.

None of the people she worked with knew what had happened. Or, if they did, they didn't let on. Her picture had been in the paper—they'd used the picture he took of her and the three kids, the new baby, Dimitri, in her arms, and Barbara Ann and Sasha on either side, looking on. Her hair had been long and wavy and brown then, natural in curl and colour, as he liked it, and her face bashful and soft—a reflection less of the way she was than of the way he wanted to see her.

Since then, she had cut her hair short and bleached and spiked it, and she had lost a lot of weight. And she went by her second name now: Fleur. Also, the job they had found for her was in a town a good distance away from where she used to live.

This was the third time she had made the trip. The first two times he had refused to see her. If he did that again she would just quit trying. Even if he did see her, she might not come again for a while. She was not going to go overboard. As a matter of fact, she didn't really know what she was going to do.

On the first bus she was not too troubled. Just riding along and looking at the scenery. She had grown up on the coast, where there was such a thing as spring, but here winter jumped almost directly into summer. A month ago there had been snow, and now it was hot enough to go bare-armed. Dazzling patches of water lay in the fields, and the sunlight was pouring down through the naked branches.

On the second bus she began to feel jittery, and she couldn't help trying to guess which of the women around her might be bound for the same place. They were women alone, usually dressed with some care, maybe to make themselves look as if they were going to church. The older ones looked like they belonged to strict, old-fashioned churches where you had to wear a skirt and stockings and some sort of hat, while the younger ones might have been part of a livelier congregation that accepted pantsuits, bright scarves, earrings, and puffy hairdos.

Doree didn't fit into either category. In the whole year and a half she had been working she had not bought herself a single new piece of clothing. She wore her uniforms at work and her jeans everywhere else. She had got out of the way of wearing makeup because he hadn't allowed it, and now, though she could have, she didn't. Her spikes of corn-coloured hair didn't suit her bony bare face, but it didn't matter.

On the third bus she got a seat by the window and tried to keep herself calm by reading the signs—both the advertising and street signs. There was a certain trick she had picked up to keep her mind occupied. She took the letters of whatever words her eyes lit on, and she tried to see how many new words she could make out of them. "Coffee," for instance, would give you "fee," and then "foe," and "off" and "of," and "shop" would provide "hop" and "sop" and "so" and—wait a minute—"posh." Words were more than plentiful on the way out of the city, as they passed billboards, monster stores, car lots, even balloons moored on roofs to advertise sales.

DOREE HAD not told Mrs. Sands about her last two attempts, and probably wouldn't tell her about this one either. Mrs. Sands, whom she saw on

Monday afternoons, spoke of moving on, though she always said that it would take time, that things should not be hurried. She told Doree that she was doing fine, that she was gradually discovering her own strength.

"I know those words have been done to death," she said. "But they're still true."

She blushed at what she heard herself say—"death"—but did not make it worse by apologizing.

When Doree was sixteen—that was seven years ago—she'd gone to visit her mother in the hospital every day after school. Her mother was recovering from an operation on her back, which was said to be serious but not dangerous. Lloyd was an orderly. He and Doree's mother had in common the fact that they both were old hippies—though Lloyd was actually a few years the younger—and whenever he had time he'd come in and chat with her about the concerts and protest marches they'd both attended, the outrageous people they'd known, drug trips that had knocked them out, that sort of thing.

Lloyd was popular with the patients because of his jokes and his sure, strong touch. He was stocky and broad-shouldered and authoritative enough to be sometimes taken for a doctor. (Not that he was pleased by that—he held the opinion that a lot of medicine was a fraud and a lot of doctors were jerks.) He had a sensitive reddish skin and light hair and bold eyes.

He kissed Doree in the elevator and told her she was a flower in the desert. Then he laughed at himself and said, "How original can you get?"

"You're a poet and don't know it," she said, to be kind.

One night her mother died suddenly, of an embolism. Doree's mother had a lot of women friends who would have taken Doree in—and she stayed with one of them for a time—but the new friend Lloyd was the one Doree preferred. By her next birthday she was pregnant, then married. Lloyd had never been married before, though he had at least two children whose whereabouts he was not certain of. They would have been grown up by then, anyway. His philosophy of life had changed as he got older—he believed now in marriage, constancy, and no birth control. And he found the Sechelt Peninsula, where he and Doree lived, too full of people these days—old friends, old ways of life, old lovers. Soon he and Doree moved across the country to a town they picked from a name on the map: Mildmay. They didn't live in town; they rented a place in the country. Lloyd got a job in an ice-cream factory. They planted a garden. Lloyd knew a lot about gardening, just as he did about house carpentry, managing a woodstove, and keeping an old car running.

Sasha was born.

*

"Perfectly natural," Mrs. Sands said.

Doree said, "Is it?"

Doree always sat on a straight-backed chair in front of a desk, not on the sofa, which had a flowery pattern and cushions. Mrs. Sands moved her own chair to the side of the desk, so they could talk without any kind of barrier between them.

"I've sort've been expecting you would," she said. "I think it's what I might have done in your place."

Mrs. Sands would not have said that in the beginning. A year ago, even, she'd have been more cautious, knowing how Doree would have revolted, then, at the idea that anybody, any living soul, could be in her place. Now she knew that Doree would just take it as a way, even a humble way, of trying to understand.

Mrs. Sands was not like some of them. She was not brisk, not thin, not pretty. Not too old either. She was about the age that Doree's mother would have been, though she did not look as if she'd ever been a hippie. Her greying hair was cut short and she had a mole riding on one cheekbone. She wore flat shoes and loose pants and flowered tops. Even when they were of a raspberry or turquoise colour these tops did not make her look as if she really cared what she put on—it was more as if somebody had told her she needed to smarten herself up and she had obediently gone shopping for something she thought might do that. Her large, kind, impersonal sobriety drained all assaulting cheerfulness, all insult, out of those clothes.

"Well the first two times I never saw him," Doree said. "He wouldn't come out."

"But this time he did? He did come out?"

"Yes, he did. But I wouldn't hardly have known him."

"He'd aged?"

"I guess so. I guess he's lost some weight. And those clothes. Uniforms. I never saw him in anything like that."

"He looked to you like a different person?"

"No." Doree caught at her upper lip, trying to think what the difference was. He'd been so still. She had never seen him so still. He hadn't even seemed to know that he would sit down opposite her. Her first words to him had been "Aren't you going to sit down?" And he had said, "Is it all right?"

"He looked sort of vacant," she said. "I wondered if they had him on drugs?"

"Maybe something to keep him on an even keel. Mind you, I don't know. Did you have a conversation?"

Doree wondered if it could be called that. She had asked him some stupid, ordinary questions. How was he feeling? (Okay.) Did he get enough to eat? (He thought so.) Was there anyplace where he could walk if he wanted to? (Under supervision, yes. He guessed you could call it a place. He guessed you could call it walking.)

She'd said, "You have to get fresh air."

He'd said, "That's true."

She nearly asked him if he had made any friends. The way you ask your kid about school. The way, if your kids went to school, you would ask them.

"Yes, yes," Mrs. Sands said, nudging the ready box of Kleenex forward. Doree didn't need it; her eyes were dry. The trouble was in the bottom of her stomach. The heaves.

Mrs. Sands just waited, knowing enough to keep her hands off.

And, as if he'd detected what she was on the verge of saying, Lloyd had told her that there was a psychiatrist who came and talked to him every so often.

"I tell him he's wasting his time," Lloyd said. "I know as much as he does."

That was the only time he had sounded to Doree anything like himself.

All through the visit her heart had kept thumping. She'd thought she might faint or die. It costs her such an effort to look at him, to get him into her vision as this thin and grey, diffident yet cold, mechanically moving yet uncoordinated man.

She had not said any of this to Mrs. Sands. Mrs. Sands might have asked—tactfully—who she was afraid of. Herself or him?

But she wasn't *afraid*.

WHEN SASHA was one and a half, Barbara Ann was born, and, when Barbara Ann was two, they had Dimitri. They had named Sasha together, and they made a pact after that that he would name the boys and she would name the girls.

Dimitri was the first one to be colicky. Doree thought that he was maybe not getting enough milk, or that her milk was not rich enough. Or too rich? Not right, anyway. Lloyd had a lady from the La Leche League come and talk to her. Whatever you do, the lady said, you must not put him on a supplementary bottle. That would be the thin edge of the wedge, she said, and pretty soon you would have him rejecting the breast altogether.

Little did she know that Doree had been giving him a supplement already. And it seemed to be true that he preferred that—he fussed more and more at the breast. By three months he was entirely bottle-fed, and then there was no way to keep it from Lloyd. She told him that her milk had dried up, and she'd had to start supplementing. Lloyd squeezed one breast after the other with frantic determination and succeeded in getting a couple of drops of miserable-looking milk out. He called her a liar. They fought. He said that she was a whore like her mother.

All those hippies were whores, he said.

Soon they made up. But whenever Dimitri was fretful, whenever he had a cold, or was afraid of Sasha's pet rabbit, or still hung on to chairs at the age when his brother and sister had been walking unsupported, the failure to breast-feed was recalled.

THE FIRST time Doree had gone to Mrs. Sands's office, one of the other women there had given her a pamphlet. On the front of it was a gold cross and words made up of gold and purple letters. "When Your Loss Seems Unbearable . . ." Inside there was a softly coloured picture of Jesus and some finer print Doree did not read.

In her chair in front of the desk, still clutching the pamphlet, Doree began to shake. Mrs. Sands had to pry it out of her hand.

"Did somebody give you this?" Mrs. Sands said.

Doree said, "Her," and jerked her head at the closed door.

"You don't want it?"

"When you're down is when they'll try to get at you," Doree said, and then realized this was something her mother had said when some ladies with a similar message came to visit her in the hospital. "They think you'll fall on your knees and then it will be all right."

Mrs. Sands sighed.

"Well," she said, "it's certainly not that simple."

"Not even possible," Doree said.

"Maybe not."

They never spoke of Lloyd in those days. Doree never thought of him if she could help it, and then only as if he were some terrible accident of nature.

"Even if I believed in that stuff," she said, meaning what was in the pamphlet, "it would be only so that . . ." She meant to say that such belief would be convenient because she could then think of Lloyd burning in hell, or something of that sort, but she was unable to go on, because it was too stupid to talk about. And because of the familiar impediment, that was like a hammer hitting her in the belly.

LLOYD THOUGHT that their children should be educated at home. This was not for religious reasons—going against dinosaurs and cavemen and monkeys and all that—but because he wanted them to be close to their parents and to be introduced to the world carefully and gradually, rather than thrown into it all at once. "I just happen to think they are my kids," he said. "I mean, they are our kids, not the Department of Education's kids."

Doree was not sure that she could handle this, but it turned out that the Department of Education had guidelines, and lesson plans that you could get from your local school. Sasha was a bright boy who practically taught himself to read, and the other two were still too little to learn much yet. In evenings and on weekends Lloyd taught Sasha about geography and the solar system and the hibernation of animals and how a car runs, covering each subject as the questions came up. Pretty soon Sasha was ahead of the school plans, but Doree picked them up anyway and put him through the exercises right on time so that the law would be satisfied.

There was another mother in the district doing homeschooling. Her name was Maggie, and she had a minivan. Lloyd needed his car to get to work, and Doree had not learned to drive, so she was glad when Maggie offered her a ride to the school once a week to turn in the finished exercises and pick up the new ones. Of course they took all the children along. Maggie had two boys. The older one had so many allergies that she had to keep a strict eye on everything he ate—that was why she taught him at home. And then it seemed that she might as well keep the younger one there as well. He wanted to stay with his brother and he had a problem with asthma, anyway.

How grateful Doree was then, comparing her healthy three. Lloyd said it was because she'd had all her children when she was still young, while Maggie had waited until she was on the verge of the menopause. He was exaggerating how old Maggie was, but it was true that she had waited. She was an optometrist. She and her husband had been partners, and they hadn't started their family until she could leave the practice and they had a house in the country.

Maggie's hair was pepper-and-salt, cropped close to her head. She was tall, flat-chested, cheerful, and opinionated. Lloyd called her the Lezzie. Only behind her back, of course. He kidded with her on the phone but mouthed at Doree, "It's the Lezzie." That didn't really bother Doree—he called lots of women Lezzies. But she was afraid that the kidding would seem overly friendly to Maggie, an intrusion, or at least a waste of time.

"You want to speak to the ole lady? Yeah. I got her right here. Workin' at the scrub board. Yeah, I'm a real slave driver. She tell you that?"

DOREE AND Maggie got into the habit of shopping for groceries together after they'd picked up the papers at the school. Then sometimes they'd get takeout coffees at Tim Hortons and drive the children to Riverside Park. They sat on a bench while Sasha and Maggie's boys raced around or hung from the climbing contraptions, and Barbara Ann pumped on the swing and Dimitri played in the sandbox. Or they sat in the mini, if it was cold. They talked mostly about the children and things they cooked, but somehow Doree found out how Maggie had trekked around Europe before training as an optometrist, and Maggie found out how young Doree had been when she got married. Also about how easily she had become pregnant at first, and how she didn't so easily anymore, and how that made Lloyd suspicious, so that he went through her dresser drawers looking for birth-control pills—thinking she must be taking them on the sly.

"And are you?" Maggie asked.

Doree was shocked. She said she wouldn't dare.

"I mean, I'd think that was awful to do, without telling him. It's just kind of a joke when he goes looking for them."

"Oh," Maggie said.

And one time Maggie said, "Is everything all right with you? I mean in your marriage? You're happy?"

Doree said yes, without hesitation, After that she was more careful about what she said. She saw that there were things that she was used to that another person might not understand. Lloyd had a certain way of looking at things: that was just how he was. Even when she'd first met him, in the hospital, he'd been like that. The head nurse was a starchy sort of person, so he'd call her Mrs. Bitch-out-of-Hell, instead of her name, which was Mrs. Mitchell. He said it so fast that you could barely catch on. He'd thought that she picked favourites, and he wasn't one of them. Now there was someone he detested at the ice-cream factory, somebody he called Suck-Stick Louie. Doree didn't know the man's real name. But at least that proved that it wasn't only women who provoked him.

Doree was pretty sure that these people weren't as bad as Lloyd thought, but it was no use contradicting him. Perhaps men just had to have enemies, the way they had to have their jokes. And sometimes Lloyd did make the enemies into jokes, just as if he was laughing at himself. She was even allowed to laugh with him, as long as she wasn't the one who started the laughing.

She hoped he wouldn't get that way about Maggie. At times she was afraid she saw something of the sort coming. If he prevented her from riding to the school and the grocery store with Maggie it would be a big inconvenience. But worse would be the shame. She would have to make up some stupid lie to explain things. But Maggie would know—at least she would know that Doree was lying, and she would interpret that probably as meaning that Doree was in a worse situation than she really was. Maggie had her own sharp way of looking at things.

Then Doree asked herself why she should care what Maggie might think. Maggie was an outsider, not even somebody Doree felt comfortable with. It was Lloyd said that, and he was right. The truth of things between them, the bond, was not something that anybody else could understand and it was not anybody else's business. If Doree could watch her own loyalty it would be all right.

IT GOT worse, gradually. No direct forbidding, but more criticism. Lloyd coming up with the theory that Maggie's boys' allergies and asthma might be Maggie's fault. The reason was often the mother, he said. He used to see it at the hospital all the time. The overcontrolling, usually over-educated mother.

"Some of the time kids are just born with something," Doree said, unwisely. "You can't say it's the mother every time."

"Oh. Why can't I?"

"I didn't mean *you*. I didn't mean you can't. I mean, couldn't they be born with things?"

"Since when are you such a medical authority?"

"I didn't say I was."

"No. And you're not."

Bad to worse. He wanted to know what they talked about, she and Maggie.

"I don't know. Nothing really."

"That's funny. Two women riding in a car. First I heard of it. Two women talking about nothing. She is out to break us up."

"Who is? *Maggie?*"

"I've got experience of her kind of woman."

"What kind?"

"Her kind."

"Don't be silly."

"Careful. Don't call me silly."

"What would she want to do that for?"

"How am I supposed to know? She just wants to do it. You wait. You'll see. She'll get you over there bawling and whining about what a bastard I am. One of these days."

AND IN fact it turned out as he had said. At least it would certainly have looked that way, to Lloyd. She did find herself at around ten o'clock one night in Maggie's kitchen, sniffling back her tears and drinking herbal tea. Maggie's husband had said, "What the hell?" when she knocked—she heard him through the door. He hadn't known who she was. She'd said, "I'm really sorry to bother you—" while he stared at her with lifted eyebrows and a tight mouth. And then Maggie had come.

Doree had walked all the way there in the dark, first along the gravel road that she and Lloyd lived on, and then on the highway. She headed for the ditch every time a car came, and that slowed her down considerably. She did take a look at the cars that passed, thinking that one of them might be Lloyd. She didn't want him to find her, not yet, not till he was scared out of his craziness. Other times she had been able to scare him out of it herself, by weeping and howling and even banging her head on the floor, chanting, "It's not true, it's not true, it's not true" over and over. Finally he would back down. He would say, "Okay, okay. I'll believe you. Honey, be quiet. Think of the kids. I'll believe you, honest. Just stop."

But tonight she had pulled herself together just as she was about to start that performance. She had put on her coat and walked out the door, with him calling after her, "Don't do this. I warn you!"

Maggie's husband had gone to bed, not looking any better pleased about things, while Doree kept saying, "I'm sorry. I'm so sorry, barging in on you at this time of night."

"Oh, shut up," Maggie said, kind and businesslike. "Do you want a glass of wine?"

"I don't drink."

"Then you'd better not start now. I'll get you some tea. It's very soothing. Raspberry-chamomile. It's not the kids, is it?"

"No."

Maggie took her coat and handed her a wad of Kleenex for her eyes and nose. "Don't tell me anything yet. We'll soon get you settled down."

Even when she was partly settled down, Doree didn't want to blurt out the whole truth and let Maggie know that she herself was at the heart of the problem. More than that, she didn't want to have to explain Lloyd. No matter how worn out she got with him, he was still the closest person in the world to her, and she felt that everything would collapse if she were to bring herself to tell someone exactly how he was, if she were to be entirely disloyal.

She said that she and Lloyd had got into an old argument and she was so sick and tired of it that all she'd wanted was to get out. But she would get over it, she said. They would.

"Happens to every couple sometime," Maggie said.

*

THE PHONE rang then, and Maggie answered.

"Yes. She's okay. She just needed to walk something out of her system. Fine. Okay then, I'll deliver her home in the morning. No trouble. Okay. Good night."

"That was him," she said. "I guess you heard."

"How did he sound? Did he sound normal?"

Maggie laughed. "Well, I don't know how he sounds when he's normal, do I? He didn't sound drunk."

"He doesn't drink either. We don't even have coffee in the house."

"Want some toast?"

IN THE morning, early, Maggie drove her home. Maggie's husband hadn't left for work yet, and he stayed with the boys.

Maggie was in a hurry to get back, so she just said, "Bye-bye. Phone me if you need to talk," as she turned the minivan around in the yard.

It was a cold morning in early spring, snow still on the ground, but there was Lloyd sitting on the steps without a jacket on.

"Good morning," he said, in a loud, sarcastically polite voice. And she said good morning, in a voice that pretended not to notice his.

He did not move aside to let her up the steps.

"You can't go in there," he said.

She decided to take this lightly.

"Not even if I say please? Please."

He looked at her but did not answer. He smiled with his lips held together.

"Lloyd?" she said. "Lloyd?"

"You better not go in."

"I didn't tell her anything, Lloyd. I'm sorry I walked out. I just needed a breathing space, I guess."

"Better not go in."

"What's the matter with you? Where are the kids?"

He shook his head, as he did when she said something he didn't like to hear. Something mildly rude, like "holy shit."

"*Lloyd*. Where are the kids?"

He shifted just a little, so that she could pass if she liked.

Dimitri still in his crib, lying sideways. Barbara Ann on the floor beside her bed, as if she'd got out or been pulled out. Sasha by the kitchen door—he had tried to get away. He was the only one with bruises on his throat. The pillow had done for the others.

"When I phoned last night?" Lloyd said. "When I phoned, it had already happened.

"You brought it all on yourself," he said.

THE VERDICT was that he was insane, he couldn't be tried. He was criminally insane—he had to be put in a secure institution.

Doree had run out of the house and was stumbling around the yard, holding her arms tight across her stomach as if she had been sliced open and was trying to keep herself together. This was the scene that Maggie saw, when she came back. She had had a premonition, and had turned the van around in the road. Her first thought was that Doree had been hit or kicked in the stomach by her husband. She could understand nothing of the noises Doree was making. But Lloyd, who was still sitting on the steps, moved aside courteously for her, without a word, and she went into the house and found what she was now expecting to find. She phoned the police.

For some time Doree kept stuffing whatever she could grab into her mouth. After the dirt and grass it was sheets or towels or her own clothing. As if she were trying to stifle not just the howls that rose up but the scene in her head. She was given a shot of something, regularly, to quiet her down, and this worked. In fact she became very quiet, though not catatonic. She was said to be stabilized. When she got out of the hospital and the social worker brought her to this new place, Mrs. Sands took over, found her somewhere to live, found her a job, established the routine of talking with her once a week. Maggie would have come to see her, but she was the one person Doree could not stand to see. Mrs. Sands said that that feeling was natural—it was the association. She said that Maggie would understand.

Mrs. Sands said that whether or not Doree continued to visit Lloyd was up to her. "I'm not here to approve or disapprove, you know. Did it make you feel good to see him? Or bad?"

"I don't know."

Doree could not explain that it had not really seemed to be him she was seeing. It was almost like seeing a ghost. So pale. Pale, loose clothes on him, shoes that didn't make any noise—probably slippers—on his feet. She had the impression that some of his hair had fallen out. His thick and wavy, honey-coloured hair. There seemed to be no breadth to his shoulders, no hollow in his collarbone where she used to rest her head.

What he had said, afterwards, to the police—and it was quoted in the newspapers—was "I did it to save them the misery."

What misery?

"The misery of knowing that their mother had walked out on them," he said.

That was burned into Doree's brain, and maybe when she decided to try to see him it had been with the idea of making him take it back. Making him see, and admit, how things had really gone.

"You told me to stop contradicting you or get out of the house. So I got out of the house.

"I only went to Maggie's for one night. I fully intended to come back. I wasn't walking out on anybody."

She remembered perfectly how the argument had started. She had bought a tin of spaghetti that had a very slight dent in it. Because of that it had been on sale, and she had been pleased with her thriftiness. She had thought she was doing something smart. But she didn't tell him that, once he had begun questioning her about it. For some reason she'd thought it better to pretend she hadn't noticed.

Anybody would notice, he said. We could have all been poisoned. What was the matter with her? Or was that what she had in mind? Was she planning to try it out on the kids or on him?

She told him not to be crazy.

He had said it wasn't him who was crazy. Who but a crazy woman would buy poison for her family?

The children had been watching from the doorway of the front room. That was the last time she'd seen them alive.

So was that what she had been thinking—that she could make him see, finally, who it was who was crazy?

WHEN SHE realized what was in her head, she should have got off the bus. She could have got off even at the gates, with the few other women who plodded up the drive. She could have crossed the road and waited for the bus back to the city. Probably some people did that. They were going to make a visit and then decided not to. People probably did that all the time.

But maybe it was better that she had gone on, and seen him so strange and wasted. Not a person worth blaming for anything. Not a person. He was like a character in a dream.

She had dreams. In one dream she had run out of the house after finding them, and Lloyd had started to laugh in his old easy way, and then she had heard Sasha laughing behind her and it had dawned on her, wonderfully, that they were all playing a joke.

"YOU ASKED me if it made me feel good or bad when I saw him? Last time you asked me?"

"Yes, I did," Mrs. Sands said.

"I had to think about it."

"Yes."

"I decided it made me feel bad. So I haven't gone again."

It was hard to tell with Mrs. Sands, but the nod she gave seemed to show some satisfaction or approval.

So when Doree decided that she would go again, after all, she thought it was better not to mention it. And since it was hard not to mention whatever happened to her—there being so little, most of the time—she phoned and cancelled her appointment. She said that she was going on a holiday. They were getting into summer, when holidays were the usual thing. With a friend, she said.

"YOU AREN'T wearing the jacket you had on last week."

"That wasn't last week."

"Wasn't it?"

"It was three weeks ago. The weather's hot now. This is lighter, but I don't really need it. You don't need a jacket at all."

He asked about her trip, what buses she'd had to take from Mildmay.

She told him that she wasn't living there anymore. She told him where she lived, and about the three buses.

"That's quite a trek for you. Do you like living in a bigger place?"

"It's easier to get work there."

"So you work?"

She had told him last time about where she lived, the buses, where she worked.

"I clean rooms in a motel," she said. "I told you."

"Yes, yes. I forgot. I'm sorry. Do you ever think of going back to school? Night school?"

She said she did think about it but never seriously enough to do anything. She said she didn't mind the work she was doing.

Then it seemed as if they could not think of anything more to say.

He sighed. He said, "Sorry. Sorry. I guess I'm not used to conversation."

"So what do you do all the time?"

"I guess I read quite a bit. Kind of meditate. Informally."

"Oh."

"I appreciate your coming here. It means a lot to me. But don't think you have to keep it up. I mean, just when you want to. If something comes up, or if you feel like it—what I'm trying to say is, just the fact that you could come at all, that you even came once, that's a bonus for me. Do you get what I mean?"

She said yes, she thought so.

He said that he didn't want to interfere with her life.

"You're not," she said.

"Was that what you were going to say? I thought you were going to say something else."

In fact, she had almost said, What life?

No, she said, not really, nothing else.

"Good."

THREE MORE weeks and she got a phone call. It was Mrs. Sands herself on the line, not one of the women in the office.

"Oh, Doree. I thought you might not be back yet. From your holiday. So you are back?"

"Yes," Doree said, trying to think where she could say she had been.

"But you hadn't got around to arranging another appointment?"

"No. Not yet."

"That's okay. I was just checking. You are all right?"

"I'm all right."

"Fine. Fine. You know where I am if you ever need me. Ever just want to have a talk."

"Yes."

"So take care."

She hadn't mentioned Lloyd, hadn't asked if the visits had continued. Well, of course, Doree had said that they weren't going to. But Mrs. Sands was pretty good, usually, about sensing what was going on. Pretty good at holding off, too, when she understood that a question might not get her anywhere. Doree didn't know what she would have said, if asked— whether she would have backtracked and told a lie or come out with the truth. She had gone back, in fact, the very next Sunday after he more or less told her it didn't matter whether she came or not.

He had a cold. He didn't know how he got it.

Maybe he had been coming down with it, he said, the last time he saw her, and that was why he'd been so morose.

"Morose." She seldom had anything to do, nowadays, with anyone who used a word like that, and it sounded strange to her. But he had always had a habit of using such words, and of course at one time they hadn't struck her as they did now.

"Do I seem like a different person to you?" he asked.

"Well, you look different," she said cautiously. "Don't I?"

"You look beautiful," he said sadly.

Something softened in her. But she fought against it.

"Do you feel different?" he asked. "Do you feel like a different person?"
She said she didn't know. "Do you?"
He said, "Altogether."

LATER IN the week a large envelope was given to her at work. It had been addressed to her care of the motel. It contained several sheets of paper, with writing on both sides. She didn't think at first of its being from him—she somehow had the idea that people in prison were not allowed to write letters. But, of course, he was a different sort of prisoner. He was not a criminal; he was only criminally insane.

There was no date on the document and not even a "Dear Doree." It just started talking to her in such a way that she thought it had to be some sort of religious invitation:

People are looking all over for the solution. Their minds are sore (from looking). So many things jostling around and hurting them. You can see in their faces all their bruises and pains. They are troubled. They rush around. They have to shop and go to the laundromat and get their hair cut and earn a living or pick up their welfare cheques. The poor ones have to do that and the rich ones have to look hard for the best ways to spend their money. That is work too. They have to build the best houses with gold faucets for their hot and cold water. And their Audis and magical toothbrushes and all possible contraptions and then burglar alarms to protect against slaughter and all (neigh) neither rich nor poor have any peace in their souls. I was going to write "neighbour" instead of "neither," why was that? I have not got any neighbour here. Where I am at least people have got beyond a lot of confusion. They know what their possessions are and always will be and they don't even have to buy or cook their own food. Or choose it. Choices are eliminated.

All we that are here can get is what we can get out of our own minds.

At the beginning all in my head was purturbation (Sp?). There was everlasting storm, and I would knock my head against cement in the hope of getting rid of it. Stopping my agony and my life. So punishments were meted. I got hosed down and tied up and drugs introduced in my bloodstream. I am not complaining either, because I had to learn there is no profit in that. Nor is it any different from the so-called real world, in which people drink and carry on and commit crimes to eliminate their thoughts which are painful. And often they get hauled off and incarcerated but it is not long enough for them to come

*out on the other side. And what is that? It is either total insanity or
peace.*

*Peace. I arrived at peace and am still sane. I imagine reading this
now you are thinking I am going to say something about God Jesus or
at any rate Buddha as if I had arrived at a religious conversion. No. I
do not close my eyes and get lifted up by any specific Higher Power. I do
not really know what is meant by any of that. What I do is Know
Myself. Know Thyself is some kind of Commandment from somewhere,
probably the Bible so at least in that I have followed Christianity. Also,
To Thy Own Self Be True—I have attempted that it is in the Bible also.
It does not say which parts—the bad or the good—to be true to so it is
not intended as a guide to morality. Also Know Thyself does not relate
either to morality as we know it in Behaviour. But Behaviour is not
really my concern because I have been judged quite correctly as a person
who cannot be trusted to judge how he should behave and that is the
reason I am here.*

*Back to the Know part of Know Thyself. I can say perfectly soberly
that I know myself and I know the worst I am capable of and I know
that I have done it. I am judged by the World as a Monster and I have
no quarrel with that, even though I might say in passing that people
who rain down bombs or burn cities or starve and murder hundreds of
thousands of people are not generally considered Monsters but are
showered with medals and honours, only acts against small numbers
being considered shocking and evil. This being not meant as an excuse
but just observation.*

*What I Know in Myself is my own Evil. That is the secret of my
comfort. I mean I know my Worst. It may be worse than other people's
worst but in fact I do not have to think or worry about that. No excuses.
I am at peace. Am I a Monster? The World says so and if it is said so
then I agree. But then I say, the World does not have any real meaning
for me. I am my Self and have no chance to be any other Self. I could
say that I was crazy then but what does that mean? Crazy. Sane. I am
I. I could not change my I then and I cannot change it now.*

*Doree, if you have read this far, there is one special thing I want to
tell you about but cannot write it down. If you ever think of coming
back here then maybe I can tell you. Do not think I am heartless. It isn't
that I wouldn't change things if I could, but I can't.*

*I am sending this to your place of work which I remember and the
name of the town so my brain is working fine in some respects.*

She thought that they would have to discuss this piece of writing at
their next meeting and she read it over several times, but she could not

think of anything to say. What she really wanted to talk about was whatever he had said was impossible to put in writing. But when she saw him again he behaved as if he had never written to her at all. She searched for a topic and told him about a once-famous folksinger who had stayed at the motel that week. To her surprise he knew more than she did about the singer's career. It turned out that he had a television, or at least access to one, and watched some shows and, of course, the news, regularly. That gave them a bit more to talk about, until she could not help herself.

"What was the thing you couldn't tell me except in person?"

He said he wished she hadn't asked him. He didn't know if they were ready to discuss it.

Then she was afraid that it would be something she really could not handle, something unbearable, such as that he still loved her. "Love" was a word she could not stand to hear.

"Okay," she said. "Maybe we're not."

Then she said, "Still, you better tell me. If I walked out of here and was struck down by a car, then I would never know, and you would never have the chance to tell me again."

"True," he said.

"So what is it?"

"Next time. Next time. Sometimes I can't talk anymore. I want to but I just dry up, talking."

I have been thinking of you Doree ever since you left and regret I disappointed you. When you are sitting opposite me I tend to get more emotional than perhaps I show. It is not my right to go emotional in front of you, since you certainly have the right more than me and you are always very controlled. So I am going to reverse what I said before because I have come to the conclusion I can write to you after all better than I can talk.

Now where do I start.

Heaven exists.

That is one way but not right because I never believed in Heaven and Hell, etc. As far as I was concerned that was always a pile of crap. So it must sound pretty weird of me to bring up the subject now.

I will just say then: I have seen the children.

I have seen and talked to them.

There. What are you thinking at the moment? You are thinking well, now he is really round the bend. Or, it's a dream and he can't distinguish a dream, he doesn't know the difference between a dream and awake. But I want to tell you I do know the difference and what I know is, they exist. I say they exist, not they are alive, because alive

*means in our particular Dimension, and I am not saying that is where
they are. In fact I think they are not. But they do exist and it must be
that there is another Dimension or maybe innumerable Dimensions,
but what I know is that I have got across to whatever one they are in.
Possibly I got hold of this from being so much on my own and having to
think and think and with such as I have to think about. So after such
suffering and solitude there is a Grace that has seen the way to giving
me this reward. Me the very one that deserves it the least to the world's
way of thinking.*

*Well if you have kept reading this far and not torn this to pieces you
must want to know something. Such as how they are.*

*They are fine. Really happy and smart. They don't seem to have any
memory of anything bad. They are maybe a little older than they were
but that is hard to say. They seem to understand at different levels. Yes.
You can notice with Dimitri he has learned to talk which he was not
able to do. They are in a room I can partly recognize. It's like our house
but more spacious and nice. I asked them how they were being looked
after and they just laughed at me and said something like they were
able to look after themselves. I think Sasha was the one who said that.
Sometimes they talk separately or at least I can't separate their voices
but their identities are quite clear and, I must say, joyful.*

*Please don't conclude that I am crazy. That is the fear that made me
not want to tell you about this. I was crazy at one time but believe me I
have shed all my old craziness like the bear that sheds his coat. Or
maybe I should say the snake that sheds his skin. I know that if I had
not done that I would never have been given this ability to reconnect
with Sasha and Barbara Ann and Dimitri. Now I wish that you could
be granted this chance as well because if it is a matter of deserving, then
you are way ahead of me. It may be harder for you to do because you
live in the world so much more than I do but at least I can give you this
information—the Truth—and in telling you I have seen them, I hope
that it will make your heart lighter.*

Doree wondered what Mrs. Sands would say or think if she read this
letter. Mrs. Sands would be careful, of course. She would be careful not to
pass an outright verdict of craziness, but she would carefully, kindly, steer
Doree around in that direction.

Or you might say she wouldn't steer—she would just pull the
confusion away so that Doree would have to face what would seem to
have been her own conclusion all along. She would have to put the whole
dangerous nonsense—this was Mrs. Sands speaking—out of her mind.

That was why Doree was not going anywhere near her.

Doree did think that he was crazy. And in what he had written there seemed to be some trace of the old bragging. She didn't write back. Days went by. Weeks. She didn't alter her opinion, but she still held on to what he'd written, like a secret. And from time to time, when she was in the middle of spraying a bathroom mirror or tightening a sheet, a feeling came over her. For almost two years she had not taken any notice of the things that generally made people happy, such as nice weather or flowers in bloom or the smell of a bakery. She still did not have that spontaneous sense of happiness, exactly, but she had a reminder of what it was like. It had nothing to do with the weather or flowers. It was the idea that the children were in what he had called their Dimension that came sneaking up on her in this way, and for the first time brought a light feeling to her, not pain.

In all the time since what had happened, any thought of the children had been something she had to get rid of, pull out immediately like a knife in her throat. She could not think their names, and if she heard a name that sounded like one of theirs she had to pull that out too. Even children's voices, their shrieks and slapping feet as they ran to and from the motel swimming pool, had to be banished by a sort of gate that she could slam down behind her ears. What was different now was that she had a refuge she could go to as soon as such dangers rose anywhere around her.

And who had given it to her? Not Mrs. Sands—that was for sure. Not in all those hours sitting by the desk with the Kleenex discreetly handy.

Lloyd had given it to her. Lloyd that terrible person, that isolated and insane person.

Insane if you wanted to call it that. But wasn't it possible that what he said was true—that he had come out on the other side? And who was to say that the visions of a person who had done such a thing and made such a journey might not mean something?

This notion wormed its way into her head and stayed there.

Along with the thought that Lloyd, of all people, might be the person she should be with now. What other use could she be in the world—she seemed to be saying this to somebody, probably to Mrs. Sands—what was she here for if not at least to listen to him?

I didn't say "forgive," she said to Mrs. Sands in her head. I would never say that. I would never do it.

But think. Aren't I just as cut off by what happened as he is? Nobody who knew about it would want me around. All I can do is remind people of what nobody can stand to be reminded of.

Disguise wasn't possible, not really. That crown of yellow spikes was pathetic.

*

So SHE found herself travelling on the bus again, heading down the highway. She remembered those nights right after her mother had died, when she would sneak out to meet Lloyd, lying to her mother's friend, the woman she was staying with, about where she was going. She remembered the friend's name, her mother's friend's name. Laurie.

Who but Lloyd would remember the children's names now, or the colour of their eyes. Mrs. Sands, when she had to mention them, did not even call them children but "your family," putting them in one clump together.

Going to meet Lloyd in those days, lying to Laurie, she had felt no guilt, only a sense of destiny, submission. She had felt that she was put on earth for no reason other than to be with him and to try to understand him.

Well, it wasn't like that now. It was not the same.

She was sitting in the front seat across from the driver. She had a clear view through the windshield. And that was why she was the only passenger on the bus, the only person other than the driver, to see a pickup truck pull out from a side road without even slowing down, to see it rock across the empty Sunday-morning highway in front of them and plunge into the ditch. And to see something even stranger: the driver of the truck flying through the air in a manner that seemed both swift and slow, absurd and graceful. He landed in the gravel at the edge of the pavement.

The other passengers didn't know why the driver had put on the brakes and brought them to a sudden uncomfortable stop. And at first all that Doree thought was, How did he get out? The young man or boy, who must have fallen asleep at the wheel. How did he fly out of the truck and launch himself so elegantly into the air?

"Fellow right in front of us," the driver said to the passengers. He was trying to speak loudly and calmly, but there was a tremor of amazement, something like awe, in his voice. "Just plowed across the road and into the ditch. We'll be on our way again as soon as we can, and in the meantime please don't get out of the bus."

As if she had not heard that, or had some special right to be useful, Doree got out behind him. He did not reprimand her.

"Goddamn asshole," he said as they crossed the road, and there was nothing in his voice now but anger and exasperation. "Goddamn asshole kid, can you believe it?"

The boy was lying on his back, arms and legs flung out, like somebody making an angel in the snow. Only there was gravel around him, not snow. His eyes were not quite closed. He was so young, a boy who had shot up tall before he even needed to shave. Possibly without a driver's licence.

The driver was talking on his phone.

"Mile or so south of Bayfield, on Twenty-one, east side of the road."

A trickle of pink foam came out from under the boy's head, near the ear. It did not look like blood at all, but like the stuff you skim off from strawberries when you're making jam.

Doree crouched down beside him. She laid a hand on his chest. It was still. She bent her ear close. Somebody had ironed his shirt recently—it had that smell.

No breathing.

But her fingers on his smooth neck found a pulse.

She remembered something she'd been told. It was Lloyd who had told her, in case one of the children had an accident and he wasn't there. The tongue. The tongue can block the breathing, if it has fallen into the back of the throat. She laid the fingers of one hand on the boy's forehead and two fingers of the other hand under his chin. Press down on the forehead, press up the chin, to clear the airway. A slight but firm tilt.

If he still didn't breathe she would have to breathe into him.

She pinches the nostrils, takes a deep breath, seals his mouth with her lips, and breathes. Two breaths and check. Two breaths and check.

Another male voice, not the driver's. A motorist must have stopped. "You want this blanket under his head?" She shook her head slightly. She had remembered something else, about not moving the victim, so that you do not injure the spinal cord. She enveloped his mouth. She pressed his warm fresh skin. She breathed and waited. She breathed and waited again. And a faint moisture seemed to rise against her face.

The driver said something, but she could not look up. Then she felt it for sure. A breath out of the boy's mouth. She spread her hand on the skin of his chest and at first she could not tell if it was rising and falling because of her own trembling.

Yes. Yes.

It was a true breath. The airway was open. He was breathing on his own. He was breathing.

"Just lay it over him," she said to the man with the blanket. "To keep him warm."

"Is he alive?" the driver said, bending over her.

She nodded. Her fingers found the pulse again. The horrible pink stuff had not continued to flow. Maybe it was nothing important. Not from his brain.

"I can't hold the bus for you," the driver said. "We're behind schedule as it is."

The motorist said, "That's okay. I can take over."

Be quiet, be quiet, she wanted to tell them. It seemed to her that silence was necessary, that everything in the world outside the boy's body had to concentrate, help it not to lose track of its duty to breathe.

Shy but steady whiffs now, a sweet obedience in the chest. Keep on, keep on.

"You hear that? This guy says he'll stay and watch out for him," the driver said. "Ambulance is coming as fast as they can."

"Go on," Doree said. "I'll hitch a ride to town with them and catch you on your way back tonight."

He had to bend to hear her. She spoke dismissively, without raising her head, as if she were the one whose breath was precious.

"You sure?" he said.

Sure.

"You don't have to get to London?"

No.

Deep-Holes

Sᴀʟʟʏ ᴘᴀᴄᴋᴇᴅ devilled eggs—something she hated to take on a picnic, because they were so messy. Ham sandwiches, crab salad, lemon tarts— also a packing problem. Kool-Aid for the children, a half-size Mumm's for herself and Alex. She would have just a sip, because she was still nursing. She had bought plastic champagne glasses for this occasion, but when Alex spotted her handling them he got the real ones—a wedding present—out of the china cabinet. She protested, but he insisted, and took charge of them himself, the wrapping and packing.

"Dad is really a sort of bourgeois *gentilhomme*," Kent was to say to Sally some years later when he was in his teens and acing everything at school. So sure of becoming some sort of scientist that he could get away with spouting French around the house.

"Don't make fun of your father," said Sally mechanically.

"I'm not. It's just that most geologists seem so grubby."

Tʜᴇ ᴘɪᴄɴɪᴄ was in honour of Alex's publishing his first solo article in *Zeitschrift für Geomorphology*. They were going to Osler Bluff because it figured largely in the article, and because Sally and the children had never been there.

They drove a couple of miles down a rough country road—having turned off a decent unpaved country road—and there was a place for cars to park, with no cars in it at present. The sign was roughly painted on a board and needed retouching.

Cᴀᴜᴛɪᴏɴ. ᴅᴇᴇᴘ-ʜᴏʟᴇs.

Why the hyphen? Sally thought. But who cares?

The entrance to the woods looked quite ordinary and unthreatening. Sally understood, of course, that these woods were on top of a high bluff, and she expected a daunting lookout somewhere. She did not expect to find what had to be skirted almost immediately in front of them.

Deep chambers, really, some as big as a coffin, some much bigger than that, like rooms cut out of the rocks. Corridors zigzagging between them and ferns and mosses growing out of their sides. Not enough greenery, however, to make any sort of cushion over the rubble that seemed so far below. The path went meandering amongst them, over hard earth or shelves of not-quite-level rock.

"Ooee," came the call of the boys, Kent and Peter, nine and six years old, running ahead.

"No tearing around in here," called Alex. "No stupid showing off, you hear me? You understand? Answer me."

They called okay, and he proceeded, carrying the picnic basket and apparently believing that no further fatherly warning was necessary. Sally stumbled along faster than was easy for her, with the diaper bag and the baby Savanna. She couldn't slow down till she had her sons in sight, saw them trotting along taking sidelong looks into the black chambers, still making exaggerated but discreet noises of horror. She was nearly crying with exhaustion and alarm and some familiar sort of seeping rage.

The outlook did not appear until they had gone along these dirt and rock paths for what seemed to her like half a mile, and was probably a quarter-mile. Then there was a brightening, an intrusion of sky, and a halt of her husband ahead. He gave a cry of arrival and display, and the boys hooted with true astonishment. Sally, emerging from the woods, found them lined up on an outcrop above the treetops—above several levels of treetops, as it turned out—with the summer fields spread far below in a shimmer of green and yellow.

As soon as she was put down on her blanket Savanna began to cry.

"Hungry," said Sally.

Alex said, "I thought she got her lunch in the car."

"She did. But she's hungry again."

She got Savanna latched onto one side and with her free hand unfastened the picnic basket. This was not of course how Alex had planned things. But he gave a good-humoured sigh and retrieved the champagne glasses from their wrappings in his pockets, placing them on their sides on a patch of grass.

"Glug-glug I'm thirsty too," said Kent, and Peter immediately imitated him.

"Glug-glug me too glug-glug."

"Shut up," said Alex

Kent said, "Shut up, Peter."

Alex said to Sally, "What did you bring for them to drink?"

"Kool-Aid in the blue jug. And the plastic glasses in a napkin underneath."

Of course Alex believed that Kent had started that nonsense not because he was really thirsty but because he was crudely excited by the sight of Sally's breast. He thought it was high time Savanna was transferred to the bottle— she was nearly six months old. And he thought Sally was far too casual about the whole procedure, sometimes going around the kitchen doing things with one hand while the infant guzzled. With Kent sneaking peeks and Peter referring to Mommy's milk-jugs. That came from Kent, Alex said. Kent was a sneak and a trouble-maker and the possessor of a dirty mind.

"Well, I have to keep doing those things," said Sally.

"Nursing's not one of the things you have to do. You could have her on the bottle tomorrow."

"I will soon. Not quite tomorrow, but soon."

But here she is, still letting Savanna and the milk-jugs dominate the picnic.

The Kool-Aid is poured, then the champagne. Sally and Alex touch glasses, with Savanna in their way. Sally has her sip and wishes she could have more. She smiles at Alex to communicate this wish, and maybe the wish that it would be nice to be alone with him. He drinks his champagne, and as if her sip and smile had been enough to soothe him, he starts in on the picnic. She instructs him as to which sandwiches have the mustard he likes and which have the mustard she and Peter like and which are for Kent who likes no mustard at all.

While this is going on, Kent manages to slip in behind her and finish up her champagne. Peter must have seen him do this, but for some peculiar reason he does not tell on him. Sally discovers what has happened sometime later and Alex never knows about it at all, because he soon forgets there was anything left in her glass and packs it neatly away with his own, while telling the boys about dolomite. They listen, presumably, while they gobble up the sandwiches and ignore the devilled eggs and crab salad and grab the tarts.

Dolomite, Alex says. That is the thick caprock they see. Underneath it is shale, clay turned into rock, very fine, fine grained. Water works through the dolomite and when it gets to the shale it just lies there, it can't get through the thin layers, the fine grain. So the erosion—that's the destruction of the dolomite—works and works it way back to the source, eats a channel back, and the caprock develops vertical joints; do they know what vertical means?

"Up and down," says Kent lackadaisically.

"Weak vertical joints, and they get to lean out and then they leave crevasses behind them and after millions of years they break off altogether and go tumbling down the slope."

"I have to go," says Kent.

"Go where?"

"I have to go pee."

"Oh for God's sake, go."

"Me too," says Peter.

Sally clamps her mouth down on the automatic injunction to be careful. Alex looks at her and approves of the clamping down. They smile faintly at each other.

Savanna has fallen asleep, her lips slack around the nipple. With the boys out of the way, it's easier to detach her. Sally can burp her, settle her on her blanket, without worrying about an exposed breast. If Alex finds the sight distasteful—she knows he does, he dislikes the whole conjunction of sex and nourishment, his wife's breast turned into udders—he can look away, and he does.

As she buttons herself up there comes a cry, not sharp but lost, diminishing, and Alex is on his feet before she is, running along the path. Then a louder cry getting closer. It's Peter.

"Kent fell in. Kent fell in."

His father yells, "I'm coming."

Sally will always believe that she knew at once, even before she heard Peter's voice she knew what had happened. If any accident happened it would not be to her six-year-old who was brave but not inventive, not a show-off. It would be to Kent. She could see exactly how. Peeing into the hole, balancing on the rim, teasing Peter, teasing himself.

He was alive. He was lying far down in the rubble at the bottom of the crevasse, but he was moving his arms, struggling to push himself up. Struggling so feebly. One leg caught under him, the other oddly bent.

"Can you carry the baby?" she said to Peter. "Go back to the picnic and put her down and watch her. That's my good boy. My good strong boy."

Alex was getting down into the hole, scrambling down, telling Kent to stay still. Getting down in one piece was just possible. It would be getting Kent out that was hard.

Should she run to the car and see if there was a rope? Tie the rope around a tree trunk. Maybe tie it around Kent's body so she could lift him when Alex raised him up to her.

There wouldn't be a rope. Why should there be a rope?

Alex had reached him. He bent and lifted him. Kent gave a beseeching scream of pain. Alex draped him around his shoulders, head hanging down on one side and useless legs—one so oddly protruding—on the other. He rose, stumbled a couple of steps, and while still hanging on to Kent dropped onto his knees. He had decided to crawl, and was making his way—Sally could understand this now—to the rubble which partly filled the far end of the crevasse. He shouted some order to her without raising his head, and though she could not make out a single word she understood. She got up off her knees—why was she on her knees?—and pushed through some saplings to the rim where the rubble came to within perhaps three feet of the surface. Alex was crawling along with Kent dangling from him like a shot deer.

She called, "I'm here. I'm here."

Kent would have to be raised up by his father, pulled to the solid shelf of rock by his mother. He was a skinny boy who had not yet reached his first spurt of growth, but he seemed heavy as a bag of cement. Sally's arms could not do it on the first try. She shifted her position, crouching instead of lying flat on her stomach, and with the whole power of her shoulders and chest and with Alex supporting and shoving Kent's body from behind they heaved him over. Sally fell back with him in her arms and saw his eyes open, roll back in his head as he fainted again.

When Alex had clawed and heaved his way out they collected the other children and drove to the Collingwood Hospital. There seemed to be no internal injury. Both legs were broken. One break was clean, as the doctor put it; the other leg was shattered.

"Kids have to be watched every minute in there," he said to Sally, who had gone in with Kent while Alex managed the other children. "Haven't they got any warning signs up?"

With Alex, she thought, he would have spoken differently. That's the way boys are. Turn your back and they're tearing around where they shouldn't be. "Boys will be boys."

Her gratitude—to God, whom she did not believe in, and Alex, whom she did—was so immense that she resented nothing.

IT WAS necessary for Kent to spend the next half-year out of school, strung up for the first while in a rented hospital bed. Sally picked up and took back his school assignments, which he completed in no time. Then he was encouraged to go ahead with Extra Projects. One of these was Travels and Explorations—Choose Your Country.

"I want to pick what nobody else would pick," he said.

Now Sally told him something she had not told to another soul. She told him how she was attracted to remote islands. Not to the Hawaiian Islands or the Canaries or the Hebrides or the Isles of Greece, where everybody wanted to go, but to small or obscure islands nobody talked about and which were seldom if ever visited. Ascension, Tristan da Cunha, Chatham Islands, and Christmas Island and Desolation Island and the Faeroes. She and Kent began to collect every scrap of information they could find about these places, not allowing themselves to make anything up. And never telling Alex what they were doing.

"He would think we were off our heads," said Sally.

Desolation Island's main boast was of a vegetable of great antiquity, a unique cabbage. They imagined worship ceremonies for it, costumes, cabbage parades in its honour.

And before he was born, Sally told her son, she had seen on television the inhabitants of Tristan da Cunha disembarking at Heathrow Airport, having all been evacuated due to a great earthquake on their island. How strange they looked, docile and dignified, like human creatures from another century. They must have adjusted to London, more or less, but when the volcano quieted down they wanted to go home.

When Kent could go back to school things changed, of course, but he still seemed old for his age, patient with Savanna who had grown venturesome and stubborn, and with Peter who always burst into the house as if on a gale of calamity. And he was especially courteous to his father, bringing him the paper that had been rescued from Savanna and carefully refolded, pulling out his chair at dinnertime.

"Honour to the man who saved my life," he might say, or, "Home is the hero."

He said this rather dramatically though not at all sarcastically. Yet it got on Alex's nerves. Kent got on his nerves, had done so even before the deep-hole drama happened.

"Cut that out," he said, and complained privately to Sally.

"He's saying you must have loved him, because you rescued him."

"Christ, I'd have rescued anybody."

"Don't say that in front of him. Please."

When Kent got to high school things improved with his father. He chose to study science. He picked the hard sciences, not the soft earth sciences, and even this roused no opposition in Alex. The harder the better.

But after six months at university Kent disappeared. People who knew him a little—there did not seem to be anyone claiming to be a friend—said that he had talked of going to the West Coast. And a letter came, just as his parents were deciding to go to the police. He was working in a Canadian Tire store in a suburb just north of Toronto. Alex went to see him there, to order him back to his education. But Kent refused, said he was very happy with the job he had now, and was making good money, or soon would be, as he got promoted. Then Sally went to see him, without telling Alex, and found him jolly and ten pounds heavier. He said it was the beer. He had friends now.

"It's a phase," she said to Alex when she confessed the visit. "He wants to get a taste of independence."

"He can get a bellyful of it as far as I'm concerned."

Kent had not told her where he was living, but it did not matter, because when she made her next visit she was told that he had quit. She was embarrassed—she thought she caught a smirk on the face of the employee who told her that—and she did not ask where Kent had gone. She thought he would get in touch, anyway, as soon as he had settled again.

HE DID that, three years later. His letter was mailed in Needles, California, but he told them not to take the trouble to trace him there—he was only passing through. Like Blanche, he said, and Alex said, Who the hell is Blanche?

"Just a joke," said Sally. "It doesn't matter."

Kent did not say what he was working at or where he had been or whether he had formed any connections. He did not apologize for leaving them so long without any information or ask how they were, or how his brother and sister were. Instead he wrote pages about his own life. Not the practical side of his life but what he believed he should be doing—what he was doing—with it.

"It seems so ridiculous to me," he said, "that a person should be expected to lock themselves into a suit of clothes. I mean, like the suit of clothes of an engineer or a doctor or a geologist and then the skin grows over it, over the clothes, I mean, and that person can't ever get them off. When we are given a chance to explore the whole world of inner and outer reality and to live in a way that takes in the spiritual and the physical and the whole range of the beautiful and the terrible available to mankind, that is pain as well as joy and turmoil. This way of expressing myself may seem overblown to you, but one thing I have learned to give up is intellectual pridefulness—"

"HE'S ON drugs," said Alex. "You can tell a mile off. His brain's rotted with drugs."

In the middle of the night he said, "Sex."

Sally was lying beside him wide awake.

"What about sex?"

"That's what makes you get into that state he's talking about. Become a something-or-other so you can earn a living. So you can pay for your steady sex and the consequences. That's not a consideration for him."

Sally said, "My, how romantic."

"Getting down to basics is never very romantic. He's not normal, is all I'm trying to say."

Further on in the letter—or the rampage, as Alex called it—Kent had said that he had been luckier than most people in having what he called his near-death experience, which had given him an extra awareness, and for this he must be forever grateful to his father who had lifted him back into the world and his mother who had lovingly received him there.

"Perhaps in those moments I was reborn."

Alex had groaned.

"No. I won't say it."

"Don't," said Sally. "You don't mean it."

"I don't know whether I do or not."

That letter, signed with love, was the last they had heard from him.

PETER WENT into medicine, Savanna into law.

Sally became interested in geology, to her own surprise. One time, in a trusting mood after sex, she told Alex about the islands—though not about her fantasy that Kent was now living on one or another of them. She said that she had forgotten many of the details she used to know, and that she should look all these places up in the encyclopedia where she had first got her information. Alex said that everything she wanted to know could probably be found on the Internet. Surely not something so obscure, she said, and he got her out of bed and downstairs and there in no time before her eyes was Tristan da Cunha, a green plate in the South Atlantic Ocean, with information galore. She was shocked and turned away, and Alex who was disappointed in her—no wonder—asked why.

"I don't know. I feel now as if I'd lost it."

He said that this was no good, she needed something real to do. He had just retired from his teaching at this time and was planning to write a book. He needed an assistant and he could not call on the graduate students now as he could when he was still on the faculty. (She didn't know if this was true of not.) She reminded him that she knew nothing about rocks, and he said never mind that, he could use her for scale, in the photographs.

So she became the small figure in black or bright clothing, contrasting with the ribbons of Silurian or Devonian rock. Or with the gneiss formed by intense compression, folded and deformed by clashes of the American and

Pacific plates to make the present continent. Gradually she learned to use her eyes and apply new knowledge, till she could stand in an empty suburban street and realize that far beneath her shoes was a crater filled with rubble never to be seen, that never had been seen, because there were no eyes to see it at its creation or throughout the long history of its being made and filled and hidden and lost. Alex did such things the honour of knowing about them, the very best he could, and she admired him for that, although she knew enough not to say so. They were good friends in these last years, which she did not know were their last years, though maybe he did. He went into the hospital for an operation, taking his charts and photographs with him, and on the day he was supposed to come home he died.

THIS WAS in the summer, and that fall there was a dramatic fire in Toronto. Sally sat in front of her television watching the fire for a while. It was in a district that she knew, or used to know, in the days when it was inhabited by hippies with their tarot cards and beads and paper flowers the size of pumpkins. And for a while after that when the vegetarian restaurants were being transformed into expensive bistros and boutiques. Now a block of those nineteenth-century buildings was being wiped out, and the newsman was bemoaning this, speaking of the people who had lived above the shops in old-fashioned apartments and who had now lost their homes, and were being dragged out of harm's way onto the street.

Not mentioning the landlords of such buildings, thought Sally, who were probably getting away with substandard wiring as well as epidemics of cockroaches, bedbugs, not to be complained about by the deluded or fearful poor.

She sometimes felt Alex talking in her head these days, and that was surely what was happening now. She turned off the fire.

No more than ten minutes later the phone rang. It was Savanna.

"Mom. Have you got your TV on? Did you see?"

"You mean the fire? I did have it on, but I turned it off."

"No. Did you see—I'm looking for him right now—I saw him not five minutes ago. Mom, it's Kent. Now I can't find him. But I saw him."

"Is he hurt? I'm turning it on now. Was he hurt?"

"No, he was helping. He was carrying one end of a stretcher, there was a body on it, I don't know if it was dead or just hurt. But Kent. It was him. You could even see him limping. Have you got it on now?"

"Yes."

"Okay, I'll calm down. I bet he went back in the building."

"But surely they wouldn't allow—"

Deep-Holes

"He could be a doctor for all we know. Oh fuck, now they're doing that same old guy they talked to before, his family owned some business for a hundred years—let's hang up and just keep our eyes on the screen. He's sure to come in range again."

He didn't. The shots became repetitive.

Savanna phoned back.

"I'm going to get to the bottom of this. I know a guy that works on the news. I can get to see that shot again, we have to find out."

Savanna had never known her brother very well—what was all the fuss about? Did her father's death make her feel the need of family? She should marry, soon; she should have children. But she had such a stubborn streak when she set her mind on something—was it possible she would find Kent? Her father had told her when she was about ten years old that she could gnaw an idea to the bone, she ought to be a lawyer. And from then on, that was what she said she would be.

Sally was overcome by a trembling, a longing, a weariness.

It was Kent, and within a week Savanna had found out all about him. No. Change that to found out all he meant to tell her. He had been living in Toronto for years. He had often passed the building Savanna worked in and had spotted her a couple of times on the street. Once they were nearly face to face at an intersection. Of course she wouldn't have recognized him because he was wearing a kind of robe.

"A Hare Krishna?" said Sally.

"Oh, Mom, if you're a monk it doesn't mean you're a Hare Krishna. Anyway he's not that now."

"So what is he?"

"He says he lives in the present. So I said well don't we all, nowadays, and he said no, he meant in the real present."

Where they were now, he had said, and Savanna had said, "You mean in this dump?" Because it was, the coffee shop he had asked her to meet him in was a dump.

"I see it differently," he said, but then he said he had no objection to her way of seeing it, or anybody's.

"Well, that's big of you," said Savanna, but she made a joke of it and he sort of laughed.

He said that he had seen Alex's obituary in the paper and thought it was well done. He thought Alex would have liked the geological references. He had wondered if his own name would appear, included in the family, and he was rather surprised that it was there. He wondered, Had his father told them what names he wanted listed, before he died?

411

Savanna said no, he wasn't planning on dying anything like so soon. It was the rest of the family who had a conference and decided Kent's name should be there.

"Not Dad," Kent said. "Well no."

Then he asked about Sally.

Sally felt a kind of inflated balloon in her chest.

"What did you say?"

"I said you were okay, maybe at loose ends a little, you and Dad being so close and not much time yet to get used to being alone. Then he said tell her she can come to see me if she wants to and I said I would ask you."

Sally didn't reply.

"You there, Mom?"

"Did he say when or where?"

"No. I'm supposed to meet him in a week in the same place and tell him. I think he sort of enjoys calling the shots. I thought you'd agree right away."

"Of course I agree."

"You aren't alarmed at coming in by yourself?"

"Don't be silly. Was he really the man you saw in the fire?"

"He wouldn't say yes or no. But my information is yes. He's quite well known as it turns out in certain parts of town and by certain people."

SALLY RECEIVES a note. This in itself was special, since most people she knew used e-mail or the phone. She was glad it wasn't the phone. She did not trust herself to hear his voice yet. The note instructed her to leave her car in the subway parking lot at the end of the line and take the subway to a specified station where she should get off and he would meet her.

She expected to see him on the other side of the turnstile, but he was not there. Probably he meant that he would meet her outside. She climbed the steps and emerged into the sunlight and paused, with all sorts of people hurrying and pushing past her. She had a feeling of dismay and embarrassment. Dismay because of Kent's apparent absence, and embarrassment because she was feeling just what people from her part of the country often seemed to feel, though she would never say what they said. You'd think you were in the Congo or India or Vietnam, they would say. Anyplace but Ontario. Turbans and saris and dashikis were much in evidence, and Sally was all in favour of their swish and bright colours. But they weren't being worn as foreign costumes. The wearers hadn't just arrived here; they had got past the moving-in phase. She was in their way.

On the steps of an old bank building just beyond the subway entrance, several men were sitting or lounging or sleeping. This was no longer a bank, of course, though its name was cut in stone. She looked at the name rather than the men, whose slouching or reclining or passed-out postures were such a contrast to the old purpose of the building, and the hurry of the crowd coming out of the subway.

"Mom."

One of the men on the steps came toward her in no hurry, with a slight drag of one foot, and she realized that it was Kent and waited for him.

She would almost as soon have run away. But then she saw that not all the men were filthy or hopeless looking, and that some looked at her without menace or contempt and even with a friendly amusement now that she was identified as Kent's mother.

Kent didn't wear a robe. He wore grey pants that were too big for him, belted in, and a T-shirt with no message on it and a very worn jacket. His hair was cut so short you could hardly see the curl. He was quite grey, with a seamed face, some missing teeth, and a very thin body that made him look older than he was.

He did not embrace her—indeed she did not expect him to—but put his hand just lightly on her back to steer her in the direction they were supposed to go.

"Do you still smoke your pipe?" she said, sniffing the air and remembering how he had taken up pipe smoking in high school.

"Pipe? Oh. No. It's the smoke from the fire you smell. We don't notice it anymore. I'm afraid it'll get stronger, in the direction we're walking."

"Are we going to go through where it was?"

"No, no. We couldn't, even if we wanted to. They've got it all blocked off. Too dangerous. Some buildings will have to be taken down. Don't worry, it's okay where we are. A good block and a half away from the mess."

"Your apartment building?" she said, alert to the "we."

"Sort of. Yes. You'll see."

He spoke gently, readily, yet with an effort, like someone speaking, as a courtesy, in a foreign language. And he stooped a little, to make sure she heard him. The special effort, the slight labour involved in speaking to her, as if making a scrupulous translation, seemed something she was meant to notice.

The cost.

As they stepped off a curb he brushed her arm—perhaps he had stumbled a little—and he said, "Excuse me." And she thought he gave the least shiver.

AIDS. Why had that never occurred to her before?

"No," he said, though she had certainly not spoken aloud. "I'm quite well at present. I'm not HIV positive or anything like that. I contracted malaria years ago, but it's under control. I may be a bit rundown at present but nothing to worry about. We turn here, we're right in this block."

"We" again.

"I'm not psychic," he said. "I just figured out something that Savanna was trying to get at and I thought I'd put you at rest. Here we are then."

It was one of those houses whose front doors open only a few steps from the sidewalk.

"I'm celibate, actually," he said, holding open the door.

A piece of cardboard was tacked up where one of its panes should be.

The floorboards were bare and creaked underfoot. The smell was complicated, all pervasive. The street smell of smoke had got in here, of course, but it was mixed with smells of ancient cooking, burnt coffee, toilets, sickness, decay.

"Though 'celibate' might be the wrong word. That sounds as if there's something to do with willpower. I guess I should have said 'neuter.' I don't think of it as an achievement. It isn't."

He was leading her around the stairs and into the kitchen. And there a gigantic woman stood with her back to them, stirring something on the stove.

Kent said, "Hi, Marnie. This is my mom. Can you say hello to my mom?"

Sally noticed a change in his voice. A relaxation, honesty, perhaps a respect, different from the forced lightness he managed with her.

She said, "Hello, Marnie," and the woman half turned, showing a squeezed doll's face in a loaf of flesh but not focusing her eyes.

"Marnie is our cook this week," said Kent. "Smells okay, Marnie."

To his mother he said, "We'll go and sit in my sanctum, shall we?" and led the way down a couple of steps and along a back hall. It was hard to move there because of the stacks of newspapers, flyers, magazines neatly tied.

"Got to get these out of here," Kent said. "I told Steve this morning. Fire hazard. Jeez, I used to just say that. Now I know what it means."

Jeez. She had been wondering if he belonged to some plainclothes religious order, but if he did, he surely wouldn't say that, would he? Of course it could be an order of some faith other than Christian.

His room was down some further steps, actually in the cellar. There was a cot, a battered, old-fashioned desk with cubbyholes, a couple of straight-backed chairs with rungs missing.

"The chairs are perfectly safe," he said. "Nearly all our stuff is scavenged from somewhere, but I draw the line at chairs you can't sit on."

Sally seated herself with a feeling of exhaustion.

"What are you?" she said. "What is it you do? Is this one of those halfway houses or something like that?"

"No. Not even quarter-way. We take in anybody that comes."

"Even me."

"Even you," he said without smiling. "We aren't supported by anybody but ourselves. We do some recycling with stuff we pick up. Those newspapers. Bottles. We make a bit here and there. And we take turns soliciting the public."

"Asking for charity?"

"Begging," he said.

"On the street?"

"What better place for it? On the street. And we go in some pubs that we have an understanding with, though it is against the law."

"You do that too?"

"I could hardly ask them to do it if I wouldn't. That's something I had to overcome. Just about all of us have something to overcome. It can be shame. Or it can be the concept of 'mine.' When somebody drops in a ten-dollar bill or even a loonie, that's when the private ownership kicks in. Whose is it, huh? Mine or—skip a beat—ours? If the answer comes mine it usually gets spent right away and we have the person coming back smelling of booze and saying, I don't know what's the matter with me today I couldn't get a bite. Then they might start to feel bad later and confess. Or not confess, never mind. We see them disappear for days— weeks—then show up back here when the going gets too rough. And sometimes you'll see them working the street on their own, never letting on they recognize you. Never come back. And that's all right. They're our graduates, you could say. If you believe in the system."

"Kent—"

"Around here I'm Jonah."

"Jonah?"

"I just chose it. I thought of Lazarus, but it's too self-dramatizing. You can call me Kent if you like."

"I want to know what's happened in your life. I mean, not so much these people—"

"These people are my life."

"I knew you'd say that."

"Okay, it was kind of smart-arse. But this—this is what I've been doing for—seven years? Nine years. Nine years."

She persisted. "Before that?"

"What do I know? Before that? Before that. Man's days are like grass, eh? Cut down and put into the oven. Listen to me. Soon as I meet you again I start the showing off. Cut down and put in the oven—I'm not interested in that. I live each day as it happens. Really. You wouldn't understand that. I'm not in your world, you're not in mine—you know why I wanted to meet you here today?"

"No. I didn't think of it. I mean, I thought naturally maybe the time had come—"

"Naturally. When I saw about my father's death in the paper I naturally thought, Well, where is the money? I thought, Well, she can tell me."

"It went to me," said Sally, with flat disappointment but great self-control. "For the time being. The house as well, if you're interested."

"I thought likely that was it. That's okay."

"When I die, to Peter and his boys and Savanna."

"Very nice."

"He didn't know if you were alive or dead—"

"You think I'm asking for myself? You think I'm that much of an idiot to want the money for myself? But I did make a mistake thinking how I could use it. Thinking family money, sure, I can use that. That's the temptation. Now I'm glad, I'm glad I can't have it."

"I could let—"

"The thing is, though, this place is condemned—"

"I could let you borrow."

"Borrow? We don't borrow around here. We don't use the borrow system round here. Excuse me, I've got to go get hold of my mood. Are you hungry? Would you like some soup?"

"No thanks."

When he was gone she thought of running away. If she could locate a back door, a route that didn't go through the kitchen. But she could not do it, because it would mean she would never see him again. And the backyard of a house like this, built before the days of automobiles, would have no access to the street.

It was maybe half an hour before he came back. She had not worn her watch. Thinking maybe a watch was out of favour in the life he lived and being right, it seemed. Right at least about that.

He seemed a little surprised or bewildered to find her still there.

"Sorry. I had to settle some business. And then I talked to Marnie, she always calms me down."

"You wrote a letter to us?" Sally said. "It was the last we heard from you."

"Oh, don't remind me."

"No, it was a good letter. It was a good attempt to explain what you were thinking."

"Please. Don't remind me."

"You were trying to figure out your life—"

"My life, my life, my progress, what all I could discover about my stinking self. Purpose of me. My crap. My spirituality. My intellectuality. There isn't any inside stuff, Sally. You don't mind if I call you Sally? It just comes out easier. There is only outside, what you do, every moment of your life. Since I realized this I've been happy."

"You are? Happy?"

"Sure. I've let go of that stupid self stuff. I think, How can I help? And that's all the thinking that I allow myself."

"Living in the present?"

"I don't care if you think I'm banal. I don't care if you laugh at me."

"I'm not—"

"I don't care. Listen. If you think I'm after your money, fine. I am after your money. Also I am after you. Don't you want a different life? I'm not saying I love you, I don't use stupid language. Or, I want to save you. You know you can only save yourself. So what is the point? I don't usually try to get anywhere talking to people. I usually try to avoid personal relationships. I mean I do. I do avoid them."

Relationships.

"Why are you trying not to smile?" he said. "Because I said 'relationships'? That's a cant word? I don't fuss about my words."

Sally said, "I was thinking of Jesus. 'Woman, what have I to do with thee?'"

The look that leapt to his face was almost savage.

"Don't you get tired, Sally? Don't you get tired being clever? I can't go on talking this way, I'm sorry. I've got things to do."

"So have I," said Sally. It was a complete lie. "We'll be—"

"Don't say it. Don't say, 'We'll be in touch.'"

"Maybe we'll be in touch. Is that any better?"

SALLY GETS lost, then finds her way. The bank building again, the same or possibly a whole new regiment of loiterers. The subway ride, the car park, the keys, the highway, the traffic. Then the lesser highway, the early sunset, no snow yet, the bare trees, and the darkening fields.

She loves this countryside, this time of year. Must she now think herself unworthy?

The cat is glad to see her. There are a couple of messages from friends on her machine. She heats up the single serving of lasagna. She buys these separated precooked and frozen portions now. They are quite good and not too expensive when you think of no waste. She sips from a glass of wine during the seven-minute wait.

Jonah.

She is shaking with anger. What is she supposed to do, go back to the condemned house and scrub the rotten linoleum and cook up the chicken parts that were thrown out because they're past the best-before date? And be reminded every day how she falls short of Marnie or any other afflicted creature? All for the privilege of being useful in the life somebody else— Kent—has chosen.

He's sick. He's wearing himself out, maybe he's dying. He wouldn't thank her for clean sheets and fresh food. Oh no. He'd rather die on that cot under the blanket with the burned hole in it.

But a cheque, she can write some sort of cheque, not an absurd one. Not too big or too small. He'll not help himself with it, of course. He'll not stop despising her, of course.

Despising. No. Not the point. Nothing personal.

THERE IS something, anyway, in having got through the day without its being an absolute disaster. It wasn't, was it? She had said maybe. He hadn't corrected her.

AND IT was possible, too, that age could be her ally, turning her into somebody she didn't know yet. She has seen the look on the faces of certain old people—marooned on islands of their own choosing, clear sighted, content.

Free Radicals

AT FIRST people were phoning to make sure that Nita was not too depressed, not too lonely, not eating too little or drinking too much. (She had been such a diligent wine drinker that many forgot she was now forbidden to drink at all.) She held them off, without sounding nobly grief stricken or unnaturally cheerful or absent-minded or confused. She said she didn't need groceries, she was working through what she had on hand. She had enough of her prescription pills and enough stamps for her thank-you notes.

Her better friends probably suspected the truth—that she was not bothering to eat much and that she threw out any sympathy note she happened to get. She had not even written to people at a distance, to elicit such notes. Not even to Rich's former wife in Arizona or his semi-estranged brother in Nova Scotia, though they might understand, perhaps better than the people near at hand, why she had proceeded with the non-funeral as she had done.

Rich had called to her that he was going to the village, to the hardware store. It was around ten o'clock in the morning—he had started to paint the railing of the deck. That is, he was scraping it to prepare for the painting, and the old scraper had come apart in his hand.

She did not have time to wonder about his being late. He died bent over the sidewalk sign that stood out in front of the hardware store, offering a discount on lawn mowers. He had not even had time to get into the store. He was eighty-one years old and in fine health, aside from some deafness in his right ear. He had been checked over by his doctor only the week before. Nita was to learn that the recent checkup, the clean bill of health, cropped up in a surprising number of the sudden-death stories that she was now presented with. You would almost think such visits ought to be avoided, she said.

She should have spoken like this only to her close and bad-mouthing friends, Virgie and Carol, women close to her own age, which was sixty-two. Younger people found this sort of talk unseemly and evasive. At first they were ready to crowd in on Nita. They did not actually speak of the grieving process, but she was afraid that at any moment they might start.

As soon as she got on with the arrangements, of course, all but the tried and true fell away. The cheapest box, into the ground immediately, no ceremony of any kind. The undertaker suggested that this might be against the law, but she and Rich had their facts straight. They had got their information almost a year ago, when her diagnosis became final.

"How was I to know he'd steal my thunder?"

People had not expected a traditional service, but they had looked forward to some kind of contemporary affair. Celebrating the life. Playing his favourite music, holding hands all together, telling stories that praised Rich while touching humorously on his quirks and forgivable faults.

The sort of thing that Rich had said made him puke.

So it was dealt with immediately, and the stir, the widespread warmth around Nita, melted away, though some people, she supposed, would still be saying they were concerned about her. Virgie and Carol didn't say that. They said only that she was a selfish bloody bitch if she was thinking of conking out now, any sooner than necessary. They would come round, they said, and revive her with Gray Goose.

She said she wasn't, though she could see a certain logic.

Her cancer was at present in remission—whatever that really meant. It did not mean "in retreat." Not for good, anyway. Her liver is the main theatre of operations and as long as she sticks to nibbles it is not complaining. It would only depress her friends to remind them that she can't have wine. Or vodka.

The radiation last spring had done her some good after all. Here it is midsummer. She thinks she doesn't look so jaundiced now—but maybe that only means she has got used to it.

She gets out of bed early and washes herself and dresses in anything that comes to hand. But she does dress, and wash, and she brushes her teeth and combs out her hair, which has grown back decently, grey around her face and dark at the back, the way it was before. She puts on lipstick and darkens her eyebrows, which are now very scanty, and out of a lifelong respect for a narrow waist and moderate hips, she checks on the achievements she has made in that direction, though she knows the proper word for all parts of her now might be *scrawny*.

She sits in her usual ample armchair, with piles of books and unopened magazines around her. She sips cautiously from the mug of weak herb tea that is now her substitute for coffee. At one time she thought that she could not live without coffee, but it turned out that it is really the warm large mug she wants in her hands, that is the aid to thought or whatever it is she practises through the procession of hours, or of days.

This was Rich's house. He bought it when he was with his wife, Bett. It was to be nothing but a weekend place, closed up for the winter. Two tiny bedrooms, a lean-to kitchen, half a mile from the village. But soon he was working on it, learning carpentry, building a wing for two bedrooms and bathrooms, another wing for his study, turning the original house into an open-plan living room/dining room/kitchen. Bett became interested—she had said in the beginning that she could not understand why he had bought such a dump, but practical improvements always engaged her, and she bought matching carpenter's aprons. She needed something to become involved in, having finished and published the cookbook that had occupied her for several years. They had no children.

And at the same time that Bett was telling people how she had found her role in life becoming a carpenter's helper, and how it had brought her and Rich much closer then before, Rich was falling in love with Nita. She worked in the Registrar's Office of the university where he taught Medieval Literature. The first time they had made love was amid the shavings and sawn wood of what would become the central room with its arched ceiling. Nita left her sunglasses behind—not on purpose, though Bett who never left anything behind could not believe that. The usual ruckus followed, trite and painful, and ended with Bett going off to California, then Arizona, Nita quitting her job at the suggestion of the registrar, and Rich missing out on becoming dean of arts. He took early retirement, sold the city house. Nita did not inherit the smaller carpenter's apron but read her books cheerfully in the midst of disorder, made rudimentary dinners on a hot plate, went for long exploratory walks and came back with ragged bouquets of tiger lilies and wild carrot, which she stuffed into empty paint cans. Later, when she and Rich had settled down, she became somewhat embarrassed to think how readily she had played the younger woman, the happy home wrecker, the lissome, laughing, tripping ingenue. She was really a rather serious, physically awkward, self-conscious woman—hardly a girl—who could recite all the queens, not just the kings but the queens, of England, and knew the Thirty Years' War backwards, but was shy about dancing in front of people and was never going to learn, as Bett had, to get up on a stepladder.

Their house has a row of cedars of one side and a railway embankment on the other. The railway traffic has never amounted to much, and by now there might be only a couple of trains a month. Weeds were lavish between the tracks. One time, when she was on the verge of menopause, Nita had teased Rich into making love up there—not on the ties of course but on the narrow grass verge beside them, and they had climbed down inordinately pleased with themselves.

She thought carefully, every morning when she first took her seat, of the places where Rich was not. He was not in the smaller bathroom where his shaving things still were and the prescription pills for various troublesome but not serious ailments that he refused to throw out. Nor was he in the bedroom, which she had just tidied and left. Not in the larger bathroom, which he had entered only to take tub baths. Or in the kitchen that had become mostly his domain in the last year. He was of course not out on the half-scraped deck, ready to peer jokingly in the window—through which she might, in earlier days, have pretended to be starting a striptease.

Or in the study. That was where of all places his absence had to be most firmly established. At first she had found it necessary to go to the door and open it and stand there, surveying the piles of paper, moribund computer, spilling files, books lying open or face down as well as crowded on the shelves. Now she could manage just by picturing things.

One of these days she would have to enter. She thought of it as invading. She would have to invade her husband's dead mind. This was one thing that she had never considered. Rich had seemed to her such a tower of efficiency and competence, so vigorous and firm a presence, that she had always believed, quite unreasonably, in his surviving her. Then in the last year this had become not a foolish belief at all, but in both their minds, as she thought, a certainty.

She would do the cellar first. It really was a cellar, not a basement. Planks made walkways over the dirt floor, and the small high windows were hung with dirty cobwebs. Nothing was down there that she ever needed. Just Rich's half-filled paint tins, boards of various lengths that might have come in handy someday, tools that might be usable or ready to be discarded. She had opened the door and gone down the steps just once, to see that no lights had been left on, and to assure herself that the switches were there, with labels written beside them to tell her which controlled what. When she came up she bolted the door as usual, on the kitchen side. Rich used to laugh about that habit of hers, asking what she thought could get in, through the stone walls and elf-sized windows, to menace them.

Nevertheless the cellar would be easier to start on; it would be a hundred times easier than the study.

She did make up the bed and tidy her own little mess in the kitchen or bathroom, but in general the impulse to manage any wholesale sweep of housecleaning was beyond her. She could barely throw out a twisted paper clip or a fridge magnet that had lost its attraction, let alone the dish of Irish coins that she and Rich had brought home from a trip fifteen years ago. Everything seemed to have acquired its own peculiar heft and strangeness.

Carol or Virgie phoned every day, usually toward supper time, when they must have thought her solitude might be least bearable. She said she was okay, she would come out of her lair soon, she just needed this time, she was just thinking and reading. And eating okay, and sleeping.

That was true too, except for the reading. She sat in the chair surrounded by her books without opening one of them. She had always been such a reader—that was one reason Rich said she was the right woman for him, she could sit and read and let him alone—and now she couldn't stick it for even half a page.

She hadn't been just a once-through reader either. *Brothers Karamazov, Mill on the Floss, Wings of the Dove, Magic Mountain,* over and over again. She would pick one up, thinking that she would just read that special bit—and find herself unable to stop until the whole thing was redigested. She read modern fiction too. Always fiction. She hated to hear the word "escape" used about fiction. She might have argued, not just playfully, that it was real life that was the escape. But this was too important to argue about.

And now, most strangely, all that was gone. Not just with Rich's death but with her own immersion in illness. Then she had thought the change was temporary and the magic would reappear once she was off certain drugs and exhausting treatments.

Apparently not.

Sometimes she tried to explain why, to an imaginary inquisitor.

"I got too busy."

"So everybody says. Doing what?"

"Too busy paying attention."

"To what?"

"I mean thinking."

"What about?"

"Never mind."

ONE MORNING after sitting for a while she decided that it was a very hot day. She should get up and turn on the fans. Or she could, with more environmental responsibility, try opening the front and back doors and let the breeze, if there was any, blow through the screen and through the house.

She unlocked the front door first. And even before she had allowed half an inch of morning light to show itself, she was aware of a dark stripe cutting that light off.

There was a young man standing outside the screen door, which was hooked.

"Didn't mean to startle you," he said. "I was looking for a doorbell or something. I gave a little knock on the frame here, but I guess you didn't hear me."

"Sorry," she said.

"I'm supposed to look at your fuse box. If you could tell me where it is."

She stepped aside to let him in. She took a moment to remember.

"Yes. In the cellar," she said. "I'll turn the light on. You'll see it."

He shut the door behind him and bent to take off his shoes.

"That's all right," she said. "It's not as if it's raining."

"Might as well, though. I make it a habit. Could leave you dust tracks insteada mud."

She went into the kitchen, not able to sit down again until he left the house.

She opened the door for him as he came up the steps.

"Okay?" she said. "You found it okay?"

"Fine."

She was leading him toward the front door, then realized there were no steps behind her. She turned and saw him standing in the kitchen.

"You don't happen to have anything you could fix up for me to eat, do you?"

There was a change in his voice—a crack in it, a rising pitch, that made her think of a television comedian doing a rural whine. Under the kitchen skylight she saw that he wasn't so young. When she opened the door she had just been aware of a skinny body, a face dark against the morning glare. The body, as she saw it now, was certainly skinny, but more wasted than boyish, affecting a genial slouch. His face was long and rubbery, with prominent light blue eyes. A jokey look, but a persistence, as if he generally got his way.

"See, I happen to be a diabetic," he said. "I don't know if you know any diabetics, but the fact is when you get hungry you got to eat, otherwise your system all goes weird. I should have ate before I came in here, but I let myself get in a hurry. You don't mind if I sit down?"

He was already sitting down at the kitchen table.

"You got any coffee?"

"I have tea. Herbal tea, if you'd like that."

"Sure. Sure."

She measured tea into a cup, plugged in the kettle, and opened the refrigerator.

"I don't have much on hand," she said. "I have some eggs. Sometimes I scramble an egg and put ketchup on it. Would you like that? I have some English muffins I could toast."

"English, Irish, Yukoranian, I don't care."

She cracked a couple of eggs into the pan, broke up the yolks, and stirred them all together with a cooking fork, then sliced a muffin and put it into the toaster. She got a plate from the cupboard, set it down in front of him. Then a knife and fork from the cutlery drawer.

"Pretty plate," he said, holding it up as if to see his face in it. Just as she turned her attention to the eggs she heard it smash on the floor.

"Oh mercy me," he said in a new voice, a squeaky and definitely nasty voice. "Look what I gone and done now."

"It's all right," she said, knowing now that nothing was.

"Musta slipped through my fingers."

She got down another plate, set it on the counter until she was ready to put the toasted muffin halves and then eggs smeared with ketchup on top of it.

He had stooped down, meanwhile, to gather up the pieces of broken china. He held up one piece that had broken so that it had a sharp point to it. As she set his meal down on the table he scraped the point lightly down his bare forearm. Tiny beads of blood appeared, at first separate, then joining to form a string.

"It's okay," he said. "It's just a joke. I know how to do it for a joke. If I'd of wanted to be serious we wouldn't of needed no ketchup, eh?"

There were still some pieces on the floor that he had missed. She turned away, thinking to get the broom, which was in a closet near the back door. He caught her arm in a flash.

"You sit down. You sit right here while I'm eating." He lifted the bloodied arm to show it to her again. Then he made an eggburger out of the muffin and the eggs and ate it in a very few bites. He chewed with his mouth open. The kettle was boiling. "Tea bag in the cup?" he said.

"Yes. It's loose tea actually."

"Don't you move. I don't want you near that kettle, do I?"

He poured boiling water into the cup.

"Looks like hay. Is that all you got?"

"I'm sorry. Yes."

"Don't go on saying you're sorry. If it's all you got it's all you got. You never did think I come here to look at the fuse box, did you?"

"Well yes," Nita said. "I did."

"You don't now."

"No."

"You scared?"

She chose to consider this not as a taunt but as a serious question.

"I don't know. I'm more startled than scared, I guess. I don't know."

"One thing. One thing you don't need to be scared of. I'm not going to rape you."

"I hardly thought so."

"You can't never be too sure." He took a sip of the tea and made a face. "Just because you're an old lady. There's all kinds out there, they'll do it to anything. Babies or dogs and cats or old ladies. Old men. They're not fussy. Well I am. I'm not interested in getting it any way but normal and with some nice lady I like and what likes me. So rest assured."

Nita said, "I am. But thank you for telling me."

He shrugged, but seemed pleased with himself.

"That your car out front?"

"My husband's car."

"Husband? Where's he?"

"He's dead. I don't drive. I mean to sell it, but I haven't yet."

What a fool, what a fool she was to tell him that.

"Two thousand four?"

"I think so. Yes."

"For a minute I thought you were going to trick me with the husband stuff. Wouldn't of worked, though. I can smell it if a woman's on her own. I know it the minute I walk in a house. Minute she opens the door. Instinct. So it runs okay? You know the last day he drove it?"

"The seventeenth of June. The day he died."

"Got any gas in it?"

"I would think so."

"Nice if he filled it up right before. You got the keys?"

"Not on me. I know where they are."

"Okay." He pushed his chair back, hitting one of the pieces of crockery. He stood up, shook his head in some kind of surprise, sat down again.

"I'm wiped. Gotta sit a minute. I thought it'd be better when I'd ate. I was just making that up about being a diabetic."

She pushed her chair and he jumped.

"You stay where you are. I'm not that wiped I couldn't grab you. It's only I walked all night."

"I was just going to get the keys."

"You wait till I say. I walked the railway track. Never seen a train. I walked all the way to here and never seen a train."

"There's hardly ever a train."

"Yeah. Good. I went down in the ditch going round some of them half-assed little towns. Then it come daylight I was still okay except where it crossed the road and I took a run for it. Then I looked down here and seen the house and the car and I said to myself, That's it. I could have took my old man's car, but I got some brains left in my head."

She knew he wanted her to ask what had he done. She was also sure that the less she knew the better for her.

Then for the first time since he entered the house she thought of her cancer. She thought of how it freed her, put her out of danger.

"What are you smiling about?"

"I don't know. Was I smiling?"

"I guess you like listening to stories. Want me to tell you a story?"

"May be I'd rather you'd leave."

"I will leave. First I'll tell you a story."

He put his hand in a back pocket. "Here. Want to see a picture? Here."

It was a photograph of three people, taken in a living room with closed floral curtains as a backdrop. An old man—not really old, maybe in his sixties—and a woman of about the same age were sitting on a couch. A very large younger woman was sitting in a wheelchair drawn up close to one end of the couch and a little in front of it. The old man was heavy and grey-haired, with eyes narrowed and mouth slightly open, as if he might suffer some chest wheezing, but he was smiling as well as he could. The old woman was much smaller, with dark dyed hair and lipstick, wearing what used to be called a peasant blouse, with little red bows at the wrists and neck. She smiled determinedly, even a bit frantically, lips stretched over perhaps bad teeth.

But it was the younger woman who monopolized the picture. Distinct and monstrous in her bright muumuu, dark hair done up in a row of little curls along her forehead, cheeks sloping into her neck. And in spite of all that bulge of flesh an expression of some satisfaction and cunning.

"That's my mother and that's my dad. And that's my sister Madelaine. In the wheelchair.

"She was born funny. Nothing no doctor or anybody could do for her. And ate like a pig. There was bad blood between her and me since ever I remember. She was five years older than I was and she just set out to torment me. Throwing anything at me she could get her hands on and knockin me down and tryin to run over me with her fuckin wheelchair. Pardon my French."

"It must have been hard for you. And hard for your parents."

"Huh. They just rolled over and took it. They went to this church, see, and this preacher told them, she's a gift from God. They took her with them to church and she'd fuckin howl like a fuckin cat in the backyard and they'd say oh, she's tryin to make music, oh God fuckin bless her. Excuse me again.

"So I never bothered much with sticking around home, you know, I went and got my own life. That's all right, I says, I'm not hanging around for this crap. I got my own life. I got work. I nearly always got work. I never sat around on my ass drunk on government money. On my rear end, I mean. I never asked my old man for a penny. I'd get up and tar a roof in the ninety-degree heat or I'd mop the floors in some stinkin old restaurant or go grease monkey for some rotten cheatin garage. I'd do it. But I wasn't always up for taking their shit so I wasn't lasting too long. That shit people are always handing people like me and I couldn't take it. I come from a decent home. My dad worked till he got too sick, he worked on the buses. I wasn't brought up to take shit. Okay though— never mind that. What my parents always told me was, the house is yours. The house is all paid up and it's in good shape and it's yours. That's what they told me. We know you had a hard time here when you were young and if you hadn't had such a hard time you could of got an education, so we want to make it up to you how we can. So then not long ago I'm talking to my dad on the phone and he says, of course you understand the deal. So I'm what deal? He says, It's only a deal if you sign the papers you will take care of your sister as long as she lives. It's only your home if it's her home too, he says.

"Jesus. I never heard that before. I never heard that was the deal before. I always thought the deal was, when they died she'd go into a Home. And it wasn't going to be my home.

"So I told my old man that wasn't the way I understood it and he says it's all sewed up for you to sign and if you don't want to sign it you don't have to. Your aunt Rennie will be around to keep an eye on you too so when we're gone you see you stick to the arrangements.

"Yeah, my aunt Rennie. She's my mom's youngest sister and she is one prize bitch.

"Anyway he says your aunt Rennie will be keeping an eye on you and suddenly I just switched. I said, Well, I guess that's the way it is and I guess it is only fair. Okay. Okay, is it all right if I come over and eat dinner with you this Sunday.

"Sure, he says. Glad you have come to look at it the right way. You always fire off too quick, he says, at your age you ought to have some sense.

"Funny you should say that, I says to myself.

"So over I go, and Mom has cooked chicken. Nice smell when I first go into the house. Then I get the smell of Madelaine, just her same old awful smell I don't know what it is but even if Mom washes her every day it's there. But I acted very nice. I said, This is an occasion, I should take a picture. I told them I had this wonderful new camera that developed right away and they could see the picture. Right off the bat you can see yourself, what do you think of that? And I got them all sitting in the front room just the way I showed you. Mom she says, Hurry up I have to get back in my kitchen. Do it in no time, I says. So I take their picture and she says, Come on now, let's see how we look, and I say, Hang on, just be patient, it'll only take a minute. And while they're waiting to see how they look I take out my nice little gun and bin-bang-bam I shoot the works of them. Then I take another picture and I went out to the kitchen and ate up some of the chicken and didn't look at them no more. I kind of had expected Aunt Rennie to be there too but Mom had said she had some church thing. I would of shot her too just as easy. So lookie here. Before and after."

The old man's head was fallen sideways, the old woman's backwards. Their expressions were blown away. The sister had fallen forward so there was no face to be seen, just her great flowery swathed knees and dark head with its elaborate and outdated coiffure.

"I could of just sat there feelin good for a week. I felt so relaxed. But I didn't stay past dark. I made sure I was all cleaned up and I finished off the chicken and I knew I better get out. I was prepared for Aunt Rennie walkin in, but I got out of the mood I had been in and I knew I'd have to work myself up to do her. I just didn't feel like it anymore. One thing my stomach was so full, it was a big chicken. I had ate it all instead of packin it with me because I was scared the dogs would smell it and cut up a fuss when I went by the back lanes like I figured to do. I thought that chicken inside of me would do me for a week. Yet look how hungry I was when I got to you."

He looked around the kitchen. "I don't suppose you got anything to drink here, have you? That tea was awful."

"There might be some wine," she said. "I don't know, I don't drink anymore—"

"You AA?"

"No. It just doesn't agree with me."

She got up and found her legs were shaking. Of course.

"I fixed up the phone line before I come in here," he said. "Just thought you ought to know."

Would he get careless and more easygoing as he drank, or would he get meaner and wilder? How could she tell? She found the wine without having to leave the kitchen. She and Rich used to drink red wine every day in reasonable quantities because it was supposed to be good for your heart. Or bad for something that was not good for your heart. In her fright and confusion she was not able to think what that was called.

Because she was frightened. Certainly. The fact of her cancer was not going to be any help to her at the present moment, none at all. The fact that she was going to die within a year refused to cancel out the fact that she might die now.

He said, "Hey, this is the good stuff. No screw top. Haven't you got no corkscrew?"

She moved toward a drawer, but he jumped up and put her aside, not too roughly.

"Unh-unh, I get it. You stay way from this drawer. Oh my, lots of good stuff in here."

He put the knives on the seat of his chair where she would never be able to grab them and used the corkscrew. She did not fail to see what a wicked instrument it could be in his hand but there was not the least possibility that she herself would ever be able to use it.

"I'm just getting up for glasses," she said, but he said no. No glass, he said, you got any plastic?

"No."

"Cups then. I can see you."

She set down the two cups and said, "Just a very little for me."

"And me," he said, businesslike. "I gotta drive." But he filled his cup to the brim. "I don't want no cop sticken his head in to see how I am."

"Free radicals," she said.

"What's that supposed to mean?"

"It's something about red wine. It either destroys them because they're bad or builds them up because they're good, I can't remember."

She drank a sip of the wine and it didn't make her feel sick, as she had expected. He drank, still standing. She said, "Watch for those knives when you sit down."

"Don't start kidding with me."

He gathered the knives and put them back in the drawer, and sat.

"You think I'm dumb? You think I'm nervous?"

She took a big chance. She said, "I just think you haven't ever done anything like this before."

"Course I haven't. You think I'm a murderer? Yeah, I killed them but I'm not a murderer."

"There's a difference," she said.

"You bet."

"I know what it's like. I know what it's like to get rid of somebody who has injured you."

"Yeah?"

"I have done the same thing you did."

"You never." He pushed back his chair but did not stand.

"Don't believe me if you don't want to," she said. "But I did it."

"Hell you did. How'd you do it then?"

"Poison."

"What are you talkin about? You make them drink some of this fuckin tea or what?"

"It wasn't a them, it was a her. There's nothing wrong with the tea. It's supposed to prolong your life."

"Don't want my life prolonged if it means drinkin junk like that. They can find out poison in a body when it's dead anyway."

"I'm not sure that's true of vegetable poisons. Anyway nobody would think to look. She was one of those girls who had rheumatic fever as a child and coasted along on it, can't play sports or do anything much, always having to sit down and have a rest. Her dying would not be any big surprise."

"What she ever done to you?"

"She was the girl my husband was in love with. He was going to leave me and marry her. He had told me. I had done everything for him. He and I were working on this house together, he was everything I had. We had not had any children because he didn't want them. I learned carpentry and I was frightened to get up on ladders but I did it. He was my whole life. Then he was going to kick me out for this useless whiner who worked in the registrar's office. The whole life we'd worked for was to go to her. Was that fair?"

"How would a person get poison?"

"I didn't have to get it. It was right in the back garden. Here. There was a rhubarb patch from years back. There's a perfectly adequate poison in the veins of rhubarb leaves. Not the stalks. The stalks are what we eat. They're fine. But the thin little red veins in the big rhubarb leaves, they're poisonous. I knew about this, but I have to confess I didn't know exactly what it would take to be effective so what I did was more in the nature of an experiment. Various things were lucky for me. First, my husband was away at a symposium in Minneapolis. He might have taken her along, of course, but it was summer holidays and she was the junior who had to keep the office going. Another thing, though, she might not have been absolutely on her own, there might have been another person around. And moreover, she might have been suspicious of me. I had to assume that she did not know I knew, and would still think of me as a friend. She had been entertained at my house, we were friendly. I had to count on my husband's being the kind of person who delays everything and who would tell me to see how I took it but not yet tell her he had done so. So then you say, Why get rid of her? He might still have been thinking both ways?

"No. He would have kept her on somehow. And even if he didn't our life was poisoned by her. She poisoned my life so I had to poison hers.

"I baked two tarts. One had the poison veins in it and one didn't. Of course I marked the one that didn't. I drove down to the university and got two cups of coffee and went to her office. Nobody there but her. I told her I'd had to come into town and as I was passing the university grounds I saw this nice little bakery my husband was always praising for their coffee and their baked goods, so I dropped in and bought a couple of tarts and two cups of coffee. Thinking of her all alone when the rest of them got to go on their holidays and me all alone with my husband gone to Minneapolis. She was sweet and grateful. She said it was very boring for her there and the cafeteria was closed so you had to go over to the science building for coffee and they put hydrochloric acid in it. Ha-ha. So we had our little party."

"I hate rhubarb," he said. "It wouldn't of worked with me."

"It did with her. I had to take a chance that it would work fast, before she realized what was wrong and had her stomach pumped. But not so fast she would associate it with me. I had to be out of the way and so I was. The building was deserted and so far as I know to this day nobody saw me arrive or leave. Of course I knew some back ways."

"You think you're smart. You got away scot-free."

"But so have you."

"What I done wasn't so underhanded as what you done."

"It was necessary to you."

"You bet it was."

"Mine was necessary to me. I kept my marriage. He came to see that she wouldn't have been any good anyway. She'd have got sick on him, almost certainly. She was just the type. She'd have been nothing but a burden to him. He saw that."

"You better not of put nothing in them eggs," he said. "You did you'll be sorry."

"Of course, I didn't. I wouldn't want to. It's not something you'd go around doing regularly. I don't actually know anything about poison, it was just by chance I had that one little piece of information."

He stood up so suddenly that he knocked over the chair he'd been sitting on. She noticed there was not much wine left in the bottle.

"I need the keys to the car."

She couldn't think for a moment.

"Keys to the car. Where'd you put them?"

It could happen. As soon as she gave him the keys it could happen. Would it help her to tell him she was dying of cancer? How stupid. It wouldn't help at all. Cancer death in the future would not keep her from talking today.

"Nobody knows what I've told you," she said. "You are the only person I've told."

A fat lot of good all that might do. The whole advantage she had presented to him had probably gone right over his head.

"Nobody knows yet," he said, and she thought, Thank God. He's on the right track. He does realize. Does he realize?

Thank God maybe.

"The keys are in the blue teapot."

"Where? What the fuck blue teapot?"

"At the end of the counter—the lid got broken, so we used it to just throw things in—"

"Shut up. Shut up or I'll shut you up for good." He tried to stick his fist in the blue teapot, but it would not go in. "Fuck, fuck, fuck," he cried, and he turned the teapot over, and banged it on the counter so that not only the car keys and house keys and various coins and a wad of old Canadian Tire money fell out on the floor, but pieces of blue pottery hit the boards.

"With the red string on them," she said faintly.

He kicked things about for a moment before he picked the proper keys up.

"So what are you going to say about the car?" he said. "You sold it to a stranger. Right?"

The import of this did not come to her for a moment. When it did, the room quivered. "Thank you," she said, but her mouth was so dry she was not sure any sound came out. It must have, though, for he said, "Don't thank me yet.

"I got a good memory," he said. "Good long memory. You make that stranger look nothin like me. You don't want them goin into graveyards diggin up dead bodies. You just remember, a word outta you and there'll be a word outta me."

She kept looking down. Not stirring or speaking, just looking at the mess on the floor.

Gone. The door closed. Still she didn't move. She wanted to lock the door but she couldn't move. She heard the engine starting, then die. What now? He was so jumpy, he'd do everything wrong. Then again, starting, starting, turning over. The tires on the gravel. She walked trembling to the phone and found that he had told the truth; it was dead.

Beside the phone was one of their many bookcases. This one held mostly old books, books that had not been opened for years. There was *The Proud Tower*. Albert Speer. Rich's books.

A Celebration of Familiar Fruits and Vegetables. Hearty and Elegant

Dishes and Fresh Surprises, assembled, tested, and created by Bett Underhill.

Once they had got the kitchen finished Nita had made the mistake for a while of trying to cook like Bett. For a rather short while, because it turned out that Rich did not want to be reminded of all that fuss, and she herself had not enough patience for so much chopping and simmering. But she had learned a few things that surprised her. Such as the poisonous aspects of certain familiar and generally benign plants.

She should write to Bett.

Dear Bett, Rich is dead and I have saved my life by becoming you.

What does Bett care that her life was saved? There's only one person really worth telling.

Rich. Rich. Now she knows what it is to really miss him. Like the air sucked out of the sky.

She should walk down to the village. There was a police office in the back of the Township Hall.

She should get a cell phone.

She was so shaken, so deeply tired, she could hardly stir a foot. She had first of all to rest.

SHE WAS wakened by a knocking on her still-unlocked door. It was a policeman, not the one from the village but one of the provincial traffic police. He asked if she knew where her car was.

She looked at the patch of gravel where it had been parked.

"It's gone," she said. "That's where it was."

"You didn't know it was stolen? When did you last look out and see it?"

"It must have been last night."

"The keys were left in it?"

"I suppose they must have been."

"I have to tell you it's been in a bad accident. A one-car accident just this side of Wallenstein. The driver rolled it down into the culvert and totalled it. And that's not all. He's wanted for a triple murder. That's the latest we heard, anyway. Murder in Mitchellston. You were lucky you didn't run into him."

"Was he hurt?"

"Killed. Instantly. Serves him right."

There followed a kindly stern lecture. Leaving keys in the car. Woman living alone. These days you never know.

Never know.

The Reading Guide

Starting points for your discussion

Which of the short story titles would you have perhaps chosen for the title of the collection, and why?

There is an air of melancholy and tragedy to the stories, to a greater or lesser degree. Which do you think is the most tragic? Which the least? Do you think the short story is, perhaps, by its very nature, best suited to tragedy?

Several of the stories span long periods of time, often whole lifetimes. Why do you think Munro chooses to cover such long periods of time in such a short form?

The titles of the stories in *Runaway* and *Too Much Happiness* are more abstract than those in the other two collections. In what ways are the stories more abstract?

Why do you think the final collection is called *Too Much Happiness*?

Questions for more in-depth discussion

This selection of Munro's short stories was taken from collections written between 1998 and 2009. How do you think Munro's themes develop over this period? Consider how relationships change, and the central characters. Compare Pauline in 'The Children Stay', Fiona in 'The Bear Came Over the Mountain', Juliet across the three stories in *Runaway*, the unnamed narrator in 'Hired Girl', and Nita in 'Free Radicals'.

A lot of Munro's stories have ambiguous or ambivalent endings. Does the short story form in particular allow the narrative to avoid the idea of an ending or resolution? In what way are characters able to walk in and out of the stories without consequence in a way that would not work in a novel? Consider *Runaway*: its three stories selected here cover the majority of Juliet's life, but by splitting it into vignettes, instead of in a continuous novel, how does the reader view her life and relationships? Do you still feel that there is an overarching narrative? Does she feel like the same character throughout?

The majority of the stories are populated by characters – or have one central character – who stand slightly outside of the society that they inhabit. Why do you think this is? Are there any exceptions? Perhaps take 'Family Furnishings' and 'Dimensions' as your starting point.

Characters are frequently plucked out of their natural environments. Consider how this is explored in 'Soon' and in 'The View from Castle Rock'.

Munro frequently omits to name her characters or narrators. Consider the unnamed characters in the following and why she might have chosen to do this:

My Mother's Dream

Family Furnishings

Lying Under the Apple Tree (consider the point at which Miriam McAlpin shouts 'Hey. You.' and the narrator describes it as hearing 'my name', p.340)

Hired Girl (consider the fact that Mr Hammond calls her Minnie, p.371)

Now consider 'The View from Castle Rock'. We don't know who the narrator is or how he/she is connected to the story of the Laidlaw family. Why do you think Munro chooses to distance the narrator in this way? How different would the story have been if it had been narrated by a member of the family? Which family member would you most like to have narrated it? Consider the fact that Alice Munro's maiden name was Alice Laidlaw. Why do you think she chooses to explore the history of her forebears through fiction?

In 'Lying Under the Apple Tree' the unnamed narrator talks of 'the entirely disjointed and dissimilar personalities I seemed to be made up of'. Is this true of the central characters of all of the short stories and to what extent and is this a central theme of the collection?

The stories are populated by absences – absent children and parents, dead partners. What is the purpose of these absences? Do these absent characters have as much influence over the narrative as the characters who are present? Take 'The Children Stay', 'The Bear Came Over the Mountain' and 'Silence' as starting points.

Book description

Lying Under the Apple Tree takes three stories from each of Munro's five collections over the last fifteen years. Taken as a body of work they portray a huge wealth of human experience and emotion. They are all concerned with the scope of the individual – how a person can be thrown onto a different track by a chance encounter, or how a single decision can change someone's life forever. There are moments of tenderness and human connection, and there are insights into the vast vistas of desolation caused by failed relationships, the deaths of loved ones, or merely the inability to understand someone despite the perceived closeness of a relationship. The stories cover a huge panorama of what it is to be human, and an individual. Munro takes the familiarity of ordinary life, and shows us how it can be strange and unfamiliar. Relationships are never quite what they appear, characters are constantly being uprooted and removed from their comfortable surroundings, and endings are frequently ambiguous and inconclusive.

The Love of a Good Woman is the oldest collection featured here. The stories taken from this collection look at the pressures that society places upon the relationships between men and women, and explore the tragedies, large and small, that can befall otherwise everyday relationships.

The stories from *Hateship, Friendship, Courtship, Loveship, Marriage* look at the interference of outside figures or experiences upon private relationships – either romantic, as in the title story and in 'The Bear Came Over the Mountain', or familial, as in 'Family Furnishings'.

Runaway follows a single character, Juliet, across the span of her life from being a young student to an old woman. It dwells on the vast gaps between Juliet and those she loves and shares her life with, and those who pass in and out of her life with apparent unconcern.

The stories from *The View from Castle Rock* vary greatly, from the snapshot summer of 'Hired Girl' to the generational span of 'The View from Castle Rock'. They range from nineteenth-century Scotland to small-town Canada in the not-so-distant past.

Too Much Happiness is Munro's most recently published collection in the selection. The stories taken from it are still concerned with the mysteries of daily life, but perhaps the characters are darker and stranger? Here ordinary life comes up against a disturbing evil absent from the earlier stories – there is murder and bloodshed and fear.

About the author

Alice Munro was born in 1931 in Wingham, Ontario, to Robert Laidlaw, a fox farmer, and Anne Laidlaw, a teacher. After high school she went to study journalism at the University of Western Ontario, but did not complete the course, leaving in 1951 to marry James Munro. The couple moved to Victoria, where they opened a bookshop.

Although she had written since her teens, and had had short stories published in magazines since the 1950s, Munro did not publish her first collection, *Dance of the Happy Shades*, until 1968. Since then her stories have appeared in many publications, including the *New Yorker*, *Atlantic Monthly* and *Paris Review*, and she has published twelve collections, most recently *Dear Life*, and a novel, *Lives of Girls and Women*. In 2006 her story 'The Bear Came Over the Mountain' was adapted for the screen in the film *Away From Her*.

Munro has received many awards and prizes, including three of Canada's Governor General's Literary Awards and two Giller Prizes, the Rea Award for the Short Story, the Lannan Literary Award, the WH Smith Book Award in the UK and the National Book Critics Circle Award in the US. She was shortlisted for the Booker Prize with *The Beggar Maid*, and was awarded the Man Booker International Prize 2009 for her overall contribution to fiction. In 2013 she was awarded the Nobel Prize for Literature, only the thirteenth woman to have been accorded this honour since the Prize was first awarded over a century ago.

Munro's most recent collection is *Dear Life*. When the collection was published in 2012 she announced that it would be her last.

She now lives with her husband in Clinton, Ontario near where she grew up.

Critical reception

'Munro...is an astute and lavishly confident writer, her clean, well-shaped sentences delivering a near constant supply of stinging insight, together with moments of wonderful soft-fingered grace. Her economy with words can be dazzling'

New Statesman

'Alice Munro...is sometimes called the 'Canadian Chekhov' for her mastery of the short-story form. This new selection...proves that the nickname, for all that it's become a cliché, is well deserved'

Time Out

'At 80 Munro is still one of our most fearless explorers of the human being, as she descends, time and again, headlamp on full beam, pickaxe and butter-knife at the ready'

The Times

'Munro is so good that one gropes for superlatives...[her] stories read like short novels; entire lives comprehended in a peripheral glimpse, an uncanny anticipation, a sudden intuition'

Sunday Telegraph

'[Munro's] artistry...recalls the close attention and cool detachment of a psychoanalyst'

Times Literary Supplement

Further Reading

Well-known authors of the short story include Katherine Mansfield, Anton Chekhov, James Joyce, John Galsworthy, Elizabeth Bowen and Angela Carter. Less well-known, female, writers of the form include Kate Chopin, George Egerton and Olive Schreiner. Contemporary, living, short story writers include Tessa Hadley, Helen Simpson, Julian Barnes and Rose Tremain.